Morakduum (The Reforging)

By

AR Travis

Special thanks to my family who put up with me during the writing, editing and marketing of this novel. Also, thanks to my friends who still believe in heroes.

ISBN: 978-0-6152-1510-5

Prologue

The date is the fourteenth day of Haaldemaar, in the year eight-thousand one-hundred eighty-seven of the Reckoning of Gorain. It is hard to believe that only three years separate my birth from the eight-thousandth anniversary of the liberation of our people. And yet it was those tragic three years that took Gorain from his place as High King into the depths of shameful exile and death. So I am born on the exact date eight-thousand years after his death. Such significance was lost upon me until recently and I have been forced to reconsider this fateful day, my birthday of my one-hundred eighty-fourth year.

Though I loathe the reckoning of dates, and specifically that of my questionable ancestor, yet I am forced to think of why fate has dealt me such a hand. Why would I shudder at the thought of being compared in significance to the great hero Gorain? There are obvious parallels between our lives, and to be reminded ever so keenly that my fate is not my own rebounds through my head, my heart, my soul like a cacophonous symphony of pain. Yet it was he who saved our people, liberated them from the foulest of slavery by the zarakanan, and thus cementing his name for all time as the Herald of Freedom and the one who brought on the Golden Age of the vaarakanan. Am I to see their destruction?

So desolate has my vision of the future become that I cannot bear to read the reports brought to me of another raid by our former allies, the Vaetra. Our people diminish despite all I can do to save them. What is left to me but an all-out war? The agony strikes deeply into my soul. How can war save us? Our birthrates drop, our bloodlines thin with the ages, and the gods seem not to care of our plight. Each raid leaves more kinsmen dead, lives that will never be replaced as we can barely keep up what population we have. One thing is for certain, if we do not stop the killing, darkness will claim us all.

The above entry from Dorian's journal is the only one that bears a date or a break to his present state of mind. The rest appears to be written in hindsight, so we assume that it was scribed much later than the beginning of this the third chronicle of his life.

Chapter 1

For Virak (Before the Storm)

The denizens of Morakduum were stirring and the scent of cooking meats and eggs filled the air. Using scented oils, I unbraided her beard and helped comb out the snarls. Then slowly and carefully I rebraided her beard, reciting to her my ancestry before replacing the binding ring. Morina did the same for me, a ritual we had practiced for over eighty-seven years since the day of our Binding. It was a reaffirmation of our love for one another, and I marveled again that she could love me. I never felt worthy of her, the daughter of the Patriarch of Balakarak, the stronghold of the soulsmiths. But her love pulsed through our soul-bond, I felt it as deeply as my love flowed back to her. The stones resonated around us with the Song of the Mother as if she too were singing of our love. It was an amazing oneness with our world where the natural vibrations of stones under pressure and heat so close to the molten source of the core of our world filled our senses as we finished our morning ritual.

Heading back to our dwelling, we traversed the granite arch between the flowstone pillars that held up the main chamber of our fortress of Morakduum. As far as our senses could reach in the vast chamber, we could feel the resonances of pillars, stalactites, and stalagmites that had been hollowed out for dwellings, workshops and markets. Below were many tiers of tunnels, grottoes, and openings that served as clan halls, shops, and gathering areas. Our kin went about their hurried business, all preparing for the war. The stones around us sang of their crystal content deep within the granite, over which thousands of years of limestone had built up rivers of flowing rock over their surface. Glittering in the occasional light of a stargem or from the magma vents. The rhythm and flows were a familiar song, a unity with the Mother that filled me with pride and hardened my resolve to defend it with my life.

Our home tunnel had been hollowed out by my forefathers when Morkilduum was first established over eight thousand years ago. It was a home we had not lived in since Gorain's exile until my rebuilding of our stronghold. Generations of Atharils, the Patriarchs who ruled Morkilduum after Gorain's exile, had worn the tunnels down to a level that had to be re-smoothed by the resonators and stone shapers. When I rebuilt the fortress I named it Morakduum, the reforging or tempering, as I hoped it would be a symbol of our resilience, a tempering of our metal. As Gorain's heir, it was ironic that I would be the new founder of the stronghold he had first built, the last of his direct descendants, his blood flowed through my veins in pride and in shame.

If we could win, if we would survive, Gorain's line would not end. It lived on in my daughter, Korina, my son Dorak, and the unborn child growing in Morina's womb. Lovingly I touched her extended belly and smiled at my hearth-mate before our lips met. My heart ached to know these might be the last moments we were together. We were outnumbered by our foes, but our fighting prowess far exceeded our enemies, and our technology more advanced. There was hope of victory, if ever so slight, but not to fight at all would mean certain extinction. Less and less pairings were fertile and more sons born than daughters. We were a dying race with no hope of replacing our numbers, especially with the constant threat of war and predation upon our people by our enemies. Perhaps if we were able to end the threat, we could then find a solution? It was the thin hope I held on to, the justification for my war.

The thought of another child of our line was pure joy to me. That we were blessed with a daughter as our first was a sign of the Maker's favor. Then came our son, and it was a celebrated event with our people. But the advent of Morina's pregnancy with our third was a miracle! All the elders rejoiced in the promise that our race would again thrive. There was great hope we were not headed down the road of extinction that seemed a certainty with our declining birth rates. Finally, there was a visible future! That was, until the raids began in earnest.

Donning first my under-tunic and breeks, I then put on my padded gambeson and leggings before the maille of vaarandril links. I pulled on my plate-covered boots, and over the maille I put on the harness for my legplates. Morina helped strap the articulated cuisses to my thighs, and the grieves to my calves. Ordinarily I would have then helped her, but with her gravid state, she reluctantly agreed to stay in Morakduum until our child was birthed and then weaned.

She stood there, beside the hearth in our home tunnel, the fire lighting the room in a reddish twilight from its normal pitch black. The light changed my perceptions from the sense of vibration and heat to the visual spectrum, showing the striations of stone in glittering shades of varying crystalline content. It was a beauty that did not compare to my hearth-mate. Morina's golden hair was tinged with reddish yellow highlights from the fire as I reached to caress her cheek, my gaze drowning in the pools of her jade eyes. The ping of our bonding rings in our braided beards was like music as our lips touched. Her taste was the sweetest voras-brew though it was difficult to put my arms around her in her late pregnancy. She was my life, my light, my love, and I vowed to do anything in my power to return to her side.

The scent of woodroot filled the room from the fire's glow as it crackled and spit dancing merrily and speaking of home. Morina watched my every movement as I reached for my armor on the stand beside the hearth, her love and adoration pulsing through our soul-bond, the Maker's gift to our people. The armor on the stand shone brighter than any steel forged by our kin. Its secret alloy and forging process was passed down through my family. Vaarandril was a metal only found near the molten core of our world, Vaaraduum, the Soul Forge. My name, Dorian, was given to me by my father, a forge-priest and represented the light of the fire at the precise temperature for forging that alloy. Vaarandril, the soulsteel was the most precious resource in or on our world, its hardness and flexibility greater than steel and its weight half of the heavier metal. It was a miracle of metallurgy that the Maker taught to my ancestor, Clan First Golodain Mytharia of the balakanan and he to his descendants until he was slain. Our line kept the tradition and knowledge alive, and the gods saw fit that I could pass those secrets along to my daughter and my son, as the last of the direct Mytharian line.

Morina helped slide the tabs through the buckles on my pauldrons that settled on my shoulders, and tears traced down her copper-bronze cheeks to wet her beard. When we first met, she did not have a beard. The humans had made her shave when she had been their slave, thinking that which marked her proudly as a Kinswoman of Soul made her ugly. But it had taken only five years to grow back properly once I freed her. Since that time, she was a sight to quicken the heart of any kinsman lucky enough to catch her eye. But her love and adoration was reserved for me alone once we had been Bonded. With the merging of our souls, we became more than the sum of both. It was a sacred soul-bond, the harmony, like a song whose combined notes are greater than the singular melody. Morakvaar in his wisdom gave this gift to our people so that in combining physically, our souls became one. A greater whole that could only be severed in death, and like a being torn in two, the death of one soon became the death of the other. A kinsman could not live half a life once experiencing the wholeness of the Bonding. If the kinswoman survived, though, the cure for the madness of a torn bond was to be bonded to another. A kinsman had no recourse but madness or death.

Morina's fingers traced the braid she had made after our shower, a reaffirmation of our Bonding. It was a braid that reached from my chin down to my waist. When had my beard grown so long? Was that a fleck of gray? My fingers traced the braid I had made for her down to her binding ring. Who knew when we would be able to repeat the reaffirmation of our Binding? My darker skin outlined her hand as I brought her fingers to my lips.

"I want to go with you, Dorian." She knew the request was futile, and gods but I wanted her at my side.

"You know it would not be wise to leave the stronghold in your condition. I will return as swiftly as I may." My hand rested on her tearstained cheek as I drew her lips to mine.

"But what if you do not return?" The words came out half-hoarse and choking on the intense emotion so rarely displayed.

Despite the armor that covered me like a second skin, I took her into my arms. She wept on my chest, her tears making dark stains in my red beard. Why she loved me, naught but a former slave from a disgraced clan, I would never know. I had been an unworthy marriage candidate for a Kinswoman of Soul, and rescuing her from slavery could not change that. But love me she did, and I was content in her love.

"Maker willing I will return to your side and we can raise our child in peace and hope. If we win this war, we can learn why our pairing has been so blessed while others go without. Perhaps in a generation or two we can thrive again? But we must first stop the raids and killings by the Vaetra."

Morina nodded at my words. She understood perfectly why we went to war, why we committed to the resolution of genocide against our enemies. History proved time and again why we could not trust or live with other races. Each betrayal written in the blood of our kin, lives that could never be replaced. In the final hours of our race, we had two choices, genocide of our enemies, or extinction. Hardly a choice at all.

My mate helped me buckle on my breastplate, padded coif, gorget, the maille coif, then snug on my helmet with the dragon crown hammered to the brow. It was the symbol of Gorain and his victory against Hakareth, the great dragon, the symbol of the High Kings of the Halls of the Mother, of which there had only been two, Gorain, and I. Both of us the founders of the fortress in which I marched to meet my assembled warriors. . Who would have guessed that Gorain's heir would again be High King? The irony brought a small involuntary twitch to the corners of my mouth. That fact alone was proof that our people still believed in heroes.

Our beautiful homeland had been re-inhabited by my direction from the decimation of its populace nearly a hundred years ago. Though the zarakanan of Mezosilliar did not destroy the tunnels, they did destroy the fortifications and the wards through the magma. They slaughtered and enslaved all our people within the stronghold with the help of their allies, all greedy for the wealth, technology and power of my people. It had taken me thirty years to rebuild our stronghold, with the remaining clans of the vaarakanan, the people of soul. In that time we depended on a pact with the sect of zarakanan called the Vaetra. My good friend and companion against many dangers, Liathrain was a Vaetra, and it was under her guidance and council the bargain was struck with her clan, her 'house'. I trusted her with my life, so I trusted the pact to our ultimate detriment. It was the Vaetra themselves that threatened our survival, and it was against them and their allies that we marched to war.

My glance returned to Morina's swollen belly. If all marriages were fertile we would not be in such danger. To make matters worse, the pairings that produced offspring bore mostly sons. Fewer and fewer kinswomen were born to each generation; the thought chilled me to the marrow of my bones. How much longer could we survive as a race? We had to end the raids, end the wars! Only then could we find a solution to the inexorable decline. Our once great race was doomed, sucking in its dying gasp, but we would not go quietly!

With a resigned sigh, I reached for the dark haft of the Reaver, Gorain's ancient weapon. The mere touch sent a tingling jolt coursing through my nerves. The sensation filled me with the desire for the blood of my enemies, and I could not help but wonder if Gorain's fate would be my own. Would I suffer some horrible dishonor that would banish my clan to oblivion? Would I spend eternity trapped within the confines of a weapon of destruction? Yet, I had already known dishonor. Deep shame colored my face and lowered my head, but I would not lay aside the memory for anything.

Stepping back from my hearth-mate, I slid the Reaver into its straps on my back. The haft of the vaarandril warhammer that lay upon the low wooden table in front of the hearth fit well in the palm of my hand and I smiled in gentle remembrance. Its weight was balance and beauty, a true wonder whose secrets had been passed down in my family since the beginning and taken from us with Gorain's disgrace. It had been a gift to me; a foster son, and I said a prayer of thanks to Patriarch Dorim, hoping his soul had found rest in the Underhalls of Morakvaar the Maker. With great reverence, I slid the hammer into one of the rings on my weapons' belt. I would never use the Holy Hammer of Golodain, but its symbolic presence was the soul of our people. Like Gorain before me, my weapon of choice was the axe that whispered to me of bloodshed and death. Its power and hunger far outshone the beauty of the hammer in battle. It was a mighty heirloom of death and destruction.

Far below, on the second tier of the city, the trumpets of muster sounded, and I knew that I had lingered too long. Our unborn child was almost enough to keep my lips from Morina's, but not quite. I hurried down the dark tunnels, and though I had not given my senses enough time to adjust to the heat and resonance of our normal senses, my feet knew the way. The smell of fires, breads and cooking meats spoke of the recent morning meal that had been consumed by the inhabitants of Morakduum. No warrior wanted to march on an empty stomach, a thought that made me smile.

Slowing my pace to a more dignified step, I entered the main entrance to the courtyard where my retinue awaited. My measured stride rang upon the inlaid stones as I traversed murals of past heroes and battles played out once more frozen in stone. The beauty around me reminded me of the long and arduous labors to rebuild our stronghold. The sweat and blood of our people was written in every hand-carved detail of the Hall of Heroes. The pride of the Kinsmen of the Blood sang in my veins in tune with the rhythm of my boots.

The corridor was lined with my kin, all wearing the blue and gold tabards of my livery. The symbol of clan Mytharia, the entwined runes of Blood and Vaarandril, was displayed proudly upon the breast of each one, a symbol that was once a mark of shame. They fell in behind me; taking up the measured pace I had set. At the end of the line stood a kinsman whose helmet also boasted a dragon crest and his armor gleamed in the torchlight with unnaturally bright steel. In his hands a heavy pole rested in a cup that was held to his waist by a harness, and upon the pole was a huge blue standard with gold threads embroidered upon it and fringing the edges. As he turned, the banner partly unfurled revealing the runes of Blood and Vaarandril intertwined the same symbol that adorned the breast of each of my Royal Guard.

The standard bearer bowed before I reached him, and stepped smartly out in front of me to take up the pace. Trumpets sounded as we marched through the fortified tunnel out into the courtyard where the command units awaited inspection. Though the courtyard was of tremendous size, it was not nearly large enough to accommodate the amount of warriors that had come from the other strongholds in support of our war.

Once more trumpets heralded our movement, and the gates to Morakduum were thrown open. The army marched through the streets out to the main gateway. Stepping proudly, I smiled reassuringly to those that would stay behind and guard our home. They lined the streets as they watched us march past, the kinswomen with children, the old, the injured and the garrison that would safeguard against a counter-attack. Situated between the last remnants of our strongholds and the only passage to our enemies, Morakduum had to survive against any assault led in retribution!

Looking back through the massive stone fortifications and the runic passage through the river of fire that was the Mother's Blood was held by harmonic resonance away from the street. No zarak would be able to breach Morakduum's defenses! Any who tried would perish in the flames of the magma, or be cut down by shard-shot from the cannons that manned the crenellations that reached to the ceiling of the cavern. If they somehow managed to pass the magma and the outer defenses, there were still the stone wardens, automatons made of granite and the garrison to deal with.

High atop the battlements my hearth-mate, Morina, waved farewell. Though I could not see her in the distance, I felt her presence keenly. Her lips moved in a prayer I could not hear, an acclamation for my safe return. I waved back as if in promise to return, but my soul knew I would never again enter those gates. Outnumbered by our enemy and no allies to help us, the future looked grim. But each and every kinsman and kinswoman in my army knew that not to fight was to surrender to extinction as a race. All of them would rather go down fighting than to give in to such an inevitable fate.

Chapter 2

Arshortain (Old Friends)

Songs and drums echoed through the deeps, keeping time with the rhythm of our steps, a melody as old as our race that warmed the blood in our hearts. It was a warmth that shone through the grottoes and gorges as I looked back. Their heat was like a river of stars against the cooler stones as they traversed the steep sides, doubling back to keep from too steep a descent or ascent. The sight was akin to the stars in the night sky of the surface world, only each star represented a living being, a kinsman of the blood. Fifty thousand warriors, kanan and kana alike joined in the song, weaving the harmony through the living stones that echoed our melody back to us. The sight and sound was beyond anything I had known on the surface save perhaps the sunrises and sunsets.

Our steps stirred the striations of heat layers in the air, warmed by the Mother's Blood, the magma that flowed in and around the tunnels we traversed. The currents swirled in differing shades of heat against a backdrop of the living stones that shone a dull red in our senses. Darker hues of blues, and grays colored the walls, signifying the resonance of cold waters that flowed behind and below the caverns. The ceiling was a dark mass of stalactites overhead, supported by occasional pillars of stone that still bore the marks of ancient flows of magma and water.

Ahead the shattered pillars and fortifications of the remains of Mezosilliar stood like darkened bones left discarded and forlorn. Ruined towers, broken walls, shattered stalagmites and stalactite homes were left to rot, a decay that mirrored the evil that once dwelled there. The rubble crunched beneath the vaarandril cladding of my boots that protected my feet from stray weapons. The stench of death still rose from the ruins despite that it had been more than fifty years. Was it my imagination? Surely the scavengers of the Wilds cleaned out all the bodies that had not been thrown into the magma? My hand rested on a stone and I felt the transfer of powder from the cannonshot that destroyed the wall, proof of our superior technology and might.

Behind the vanguard the rumble of the cannons shook the trail as they were pulled on heavy carts by large zorvak crawlers. Those cannons were the very same ones that laid the fortifications low those many years ago though the beasts of burden pulling them were in their third generation since then. The huge reptiles glowed an amber hue, their musculature burning white with their movement and strain. Even with the cannons, it had taken the surprise attack of our allies to finally break Mezosilliar's defenses. The Vaetra, even the thought of the treacherous zaraks was enough to churn the acids in my stomach. I spit upon the ground to take the foul taste from my mouth as if the name had passed my lips.

The memory was so clear, our betrayal at the gates of Tarazandarin. The screams of my kin dying beside me as they were mercilessly cut down. Unbidden the moisture rolled down my cheeks as I relived the deaths, the helpless rage, and the murder of my people for their treachery. My knuckles grew white on the haft of the Reaver as the weapon blazed to life sensing my rage. The unholy desire for blood and death filled me from the weapon's fury, from the soul trapped within. Through the white-blue fire, the axe blades gleamed in the shape of dragons' wings in half moons as the spike between them was an icy star issuing as flame from the mouths of the dragons. The flames cascaded down the haft to curl about my arms like a lover that whispered the promise of revenge, but the Vaetra were leagues away from where we were. The anger of Gorain welled within, seeping from the weapon and trying to gain control, but I fought it down. The calm of meditation blanketed my consciousness within its cool grasp, and quenched the rage-fire. When I opened my eyes again the eternal dark of the Halls of the Mother returned to their multi-colored hues of warmth.

An insistent nudge nearly knocked me down as the huge cave-bear, Niara came to comfort me. She had been my friend since I found her as a cub. Her mind touched mine, seeking reassurance and I sent her warmth and peace. As the bear appeared my kin backed even further from me and I was reminded again how I was estranged from them. She had always been drawn to me during our battles. Each time we marched, she joined me at some point, plowing through our enemies then feasting on their dead afterwards. She never once tasted the flesh of a vaarakanan, though many of her kin had killed enough of our kind in the past.

One nearly ended my own life on my journey of adulthood. Each young warrior, before given their title of journeyman was required to make a solo journey to the Mother's Heart. It was on that journey that the bear ambushed me, ravaged me, and though I wounded it mortally, so had it wounded me unto death. I was found by an elder kinsman and miraculously nursed back to health. On my way back from the Mother's Heart I had tried to stop by and thank the elder, but the hovel where he healed me was empty with no sign of ever having been occupied.

Niara's breath puffed out from jowls that could crush granite. It rolled over me with the stench of carrion and I nearly choked as she brought me out of my reverie. Standing three heights of a kinsman above me, her nose wiggled as she sniffed my helm. Using the ridges of my gauntlet, I scratched her chin and she chuffed in pleasure, her breath rolling across my face in a cloud of decayed flesh. Holding my breath I wondered if the bear only followed me for the carrion left on the battlefield.

In the center of the ruins of Mezosilliar, originally named Laharazduum, we found enough intact chambers to camp in. The boulders that had once been part of solid structures littered the ground leaving sad monuments to our destructive prowess. Was this all we excelled at, killing and dying? Yet our whole lives, our whole culture was built around war, its arts and crafts. What would we do if we were victorious and there was no more war? What outlet would our industry take?

As our army made camp, I wandered through the ancient city. The upheaval around me was my doing. Fifty years ago, I led the armies of my kinsmen against our oppressors in righteous fury. My blood sang vengeance for the destruction of my home, Morkilduum. We assaulted Terazandarin for their part in the war and later raids while the Vaetra aided us. As if bidden, the face of Liathrain hovered before me, dragged from my memory with great reluctance.

A nostalgic smile crossed my lips as I remembered the slender zarak when she had first vaulted up on the back of my pony. The motion had been quick and easy, as if she was born to such impossible feats. Her dark skin shone almost blue in the light of the morning sun as she regarded me with almond-shaped amber eyes. Her pointed ears poked prominently through her long mane of silver hair, unlike my own slightly pointed ears that were hidden securely beneath a thick shore of red hair and an armored cap. But that was so long ago.

Memories of our adventures filled my mind as I walked back towards my busy kin. The sad ruins filled my vision, but my mind was still focused on years past. The patrol smiled and bowed slightly as they skirted by me, and I returned a nod of acknowledgement. Naiara paced patiently beside me, not in the slightest bothered by my short-legged gait, for it suited her preferred ursine shamble. She lay down in the center of camp, making many of my kinsmen quite nervous, but Naiara never ate the flesh of a kinsman, even those that had died upon the battlefield. Was it a gesture of respect for my kin and me, or that she had a particular distaste for us? No one knew the answer but the huge bear and she had not confided her secrets.

Maps and battle plans filled my evening before retiring. Weariness overcame the anticipation of battle, and I removed my arm armor, helmet, gorget and coifs before lying down with my head propped upon the brown foreleg of the great bear. Naiara rumbled with pleasure, and I could almost feel the motherly instinct rise within her. A warning look stopped the huge sloppy tongue mere inches from my face. A disappointed whimper issued from her throat as she lay her head down next to mine. She wanted her cubs back badly, but they were gone and I did not like bathing in bear saliva.

A low growl woke me with a start, and for a moment, I remembered the bear that had attacked me as a youth. The sight of the huge jowls just above my head sent a cold shock through me. But it was only Naiara and she had scented something that was not a kinsman! The heat signatures of the watch and the many golden-yellow glows from the sleeping soldiers were easily seen, but Naiara's continued unease was a warning I could not ignore. Quickly, I shrugged back in to my armor. The tab of my belt slid into place when instinct tugged at me. Instead of reaching for my gorget, coifs and helmet, I grasped the Reaver.

The half-moon blades lit with white-blue fire, confirming my suspicions and sending bloodlust into my mind. Fighting for control of the Reaver's power, I squinted in the direction Naiara faced. Dark rocks stood out in stark relief from the dull red glow of the living stones. Nothing but the glow of outer watchmen met my gaze. When I turned to alert the captain, a blade of cold steel pressed against my throat. A slender but strong hand grasped my hair, pulling my head back and exposing my windpipe to the daggar. Inwardly, I cursed myself for not putting on my gorget first.

A familiar voice tickled my ear, sending a shiver down my spine. "Hello Dorian. It has been quite some time. I'm sure you know why I'm here."

"Liathrain. I have been expecting you. Has your clan evacuated?" The zarakanan tongue was the first language I had learned besides our own.

The blade bit deeper revealing the extent of Liathrain's anger, and I grit my teeth against the presence in the Reaver and its desire for the death of my enemy. Naiara's growls rose in intensity at the smell of my blood as it trickled down inside the front of my armor. Reaching for the cool darkness, I pushed back the rage of the Reaver, and sent calming thoughts to the great bear.

As the fire of the Reaver curled up my arms, Liathrain yanked my head back further. "Drop that hell-spawned thing!" Her snarl spat through clenched teeth as she pressed the blade deeper into my skin.

"No. You were once my friend, Liathrain. Could you now callously slay me?" The pressure of the blade lessened slightly. "We fought side-by-side for many years. Is our camaraderie to end in murder?"

The pressure returned, nearly cutting off the airflow as more blood trickled from the wound. "It is you who threaten us! You who declared war! And with your death, it will end before it starts!"

Anger welled within me, but I had to maintain control over the fury least the Reaver consume me. "It is the zarakanan that have destroyed our homes, our lands and our people! Your clan that stole our treasure, decimated our crops, and killed without mercy! You have driven us to the brink of extinction, but we have had enough!"

"My people never threatened yours, Dorian." The denial brought more anger and my control began to slip. "We helped you in your vengeance against Mezosilliar and this is how you repay us? You deserve to die, traitor!"

The power of the Reaver pulsed up my arms, filling me with the rage-fire of battle, and I barely held it in check. My control was slipping as the small cut in my throat widened.

"You may yet save your people, Liathrain." I could barely form the words through my clenched teeth as I fought for control. "Take your clan and leave the deeps. Do not make me kill you, my friend."

"Kill me?" Her laughter fell coldly on the stones and the grim faces of my kin that had been alerted by the insane snarls of the great cave bear. "Perhaps you don't realize your situation?"

"It is you who do not understand. The Reaver's power will consume you in holy retribution before my body struck the ground." The rage-fire began to curl around my shoulders, forcing Liathrain to loosen her grip, but the blade stayed steady upon my throat.

With the nobility I knew was in her, she replied, "even if I died, you would die too, and your war would be at an end. My people would be safe, and my sacrifice would not be in vain."

"Liathrain, it is our cause that unites us, not me. Another kinsman would simply take my place." That tact had no effect, so I changed the subject. "Your people do not care of your sacrifice. They have embraced the old ways of the zarakanan. Your clan broke the bargain, took more than their share of Mezosilliar's treasure. They did not release the kinsmen and kinswomen they held as slaves like they promised. When they betrayed us at Terazandarin…" The words failed in their description, but I knew I had to get through to her somehow and fast. "Since then, your people have raided our settlements, killed and enslaved hundreds of my people, destroyed our crops and food sources, poisoned our wells, and even attacked Morakduum. What were we to do, surrender meekly to slavery and oblivion?" The last words were a snarl of rage induced by the Reaver as the last of my grip was slipping away.

"You lie!" Liathrain's disbelief brought a small measure of control back to me. Could it be that she was innocent of the doings of her people?

"Kairillia has deceived you, Liathrain. Your own matriarch lies to her people, and you expect us to trust you again?" The pressure of the dagger let up once more.

A note of uncertainty crept in to her voice. "But without your leadership, the dwarven clans would no longer be united. They could not believe such outrageous lies. How could you lie to them, Dorian? I had thought you an honorable warrior."

"You know my honor, Liathrain, but do you trust Kairillia's? She is tainted with evil, and has returned to the corrupt ways of your people." I realized my mistake as the blade once more pressed home.

With more conviction she pronounced my fate, "when I kill you, your people will not risk the lives of those that are left. The clans will retreat behind their stone walls and fade from existence."

The rage flooded through me, partly because she could so callously throw away our friendship, and partly because I feared she was right. White-blue fire burst out around me, throwing Liathrain back, but not before her blade traced a deep ragged line across my throat, severing all down to the bone. The Reaver took me, engulfing me in the red pits of its hunger, caring nothing if my body was already dying. Its unholy power lifted my limbs, drove me onward, voicing the words it craved through a torn throat.

"Sarlik doria!"

With a blaze of heat and light the rage-fires burst from the blades in a torrent, blasting the zarak, curling around her, consuming her silver mane of hair as it sought to eat through her flesh. She screamed half in agony, and half in disbelief as she desperately warded her face with an armored vambrace. The blast threw her to the ground as it threatened to imbed her permanently there, melting the rock around her as if it were lead in a furnace. My lifeblood flowed down inside my armor from my ruined throat, stealing the warmth from my limbs, but the Reaver's power would not release me. Burning hunger surged through me in an all-consuming rage that would only end in the death of the zarak.

Through the haze of agony on her features, Liathrain's eyes widened as I advanced upon her. Weakly her scimitar raced the downward blow of the Reaver, barely shedding its force to the side of her head and shoulder. It shaved a slice of armor from her pauldron as neatly as if through butter. Blood splattered across her chest, and vaguely I realized it was my own, flowing like a fountain from severed arteries, as I felt colder. Scrambling to the side, Liathrain limped to her feet, the smell of her scorched flesh filled me with sadness, but the Reaver would not relent. It controlled me as thoroughly as a steam driven automaton. Was this how all friendships ended, in death and betrayal?

The Reaver turned my arms, catching the blade of the scimitar neatly between my gauntlets, and then twisting to catch the other sword between the blade and the spike. Instead of following through with the strike, I twisted the haft, locking the delicate sword-blade in an inescapable arc of destruction. Liathrain's lighter form was yanked to the left as I spun and twisted the haft. The delicate scimitar shattered from the stress, showering us in fragments of metal and sparks of released magic. I spun back to the right, but not quick enough to avoid the bite of her other sword. With ease the glowing blade passed through my warded armor, into my shoulder, and lodged itself in one of my ribs.

A gurgling howl of pain showered more blood from my ruined throat, and Liathrain stepped back, appalled at the destruction she had wrought. For a moment, her eyes filled with inner pain, knowing and acknowledging the end of our long friendship. The Reaver drove me forward though, moving my arm as if my shoulder was still in one piece. Though I could feel the pain like lava seeping through me, I could not refuse the presence that possessed me. Liathrain gasped, her burned features twisting in shocked outrage, and I knew she finally realized the true power of the artifact I bore.

Distantly, my eyes watched our match to the bitter end, but my mind was home in Morakduum. My chest ached, not only from loss of blood, but also for Morina. How she would miss me as her personal nightmare came to pass. That I should perish away from her while she was unable to aid me was her greatest fear. Our child would be born without its father, and emptiness filled me like a wasteland. I only hoped Morina would find a mate that would love her as much as she loved me. She deserved so much more.

Liathrain's next attack was weak and fumbling in her confusion, and I easily caught it in the curve of the axe blade. Another hooking twist and the glowing scimitar disintegrated in a ball of green fire and silver shards. The sweep of the blades of my axe carried me forward into the strike that would end any hope of renewing our friendship. Icy fire pierced me as I felt her cold dagger punch through the plates protecting my gut to lodge itself in my spine, but it did not halt the descent of the half-moon blades.

The Reaver quenched its rage in the blood of my friend, and was at last satisfied. I felt its power recede from me as numbness followed in its wake.

"Liathrain, why did you not listen to me?" I mouthed the words as a silent whisper through my ruined throat as my legs collapsed from beneath me.

The Reaver fell from fingers I could no longer feel, and the coldness froze my soul. I felt myself falling, but never felt the ground. My body tumbled away from me, facedown, and I could not comprehend the sight before me. Two bodies lie as if still locked in deadly combat and blood ran away from them to mix in an appallingly large pool. My kin closed in with disbelief and horror written in their faces. How could our quest end before it began?

The world faded away from me as someone yelled for the priest.

Chapter 3

Shoran (Oaths)

"It is time we talked." The voice shattered the spell of morbid fascination, and came from everywhere at once.

The scene of my death faded before me and I found myself in a vast cavern that glowed with the warmth of the Mother. Runic scripts covered the walls, but I could not read them. Even though I studied the language of the ancients, they were still a mystery to me. Was this the entrance to the Underhalls? Instinct warned me that I was not alone and that foreign eyes were upon me. Spinning on my knees I found myself face to face with an elder kinsman clad in a leather smith's apron. Even though he sat on a stone, his head was level with mine. Silver hair framed his copper features that were darkened by the soot that became a permanent part of any smith. Corded muscles rippled easily beneath thick skin. A hammer swung from his belt that defied my understanding. It appeared to be useful for both smithing and as a weapon of war, if that was indeed possible. Runes danced and shifted across its surface as if it were alive and could change its shape at will.

His deep blue gaze regarded me with paternal patience, giving me the time to take in his appearance. His lip twitched in what could have been amusement, but his aura was that of immense power, like the air before a violent storm. My mouth dropped open and a shiver of recognition passed through me. He was the same old kinsman who had saved my life as a youth when the hungry cave bear had attacked me! Unlike before though, he was filled with the aura of majesty. Not daring to rise to my feet, his name came to my lips.

"Morakvaar." I mouthed the word, but no sound came.

He laughed merrily. "Yes lad, I am Morakvaar known as the Maker."

Gathering my courage at last, I stood. "Father, please, let me finish what I have started. Our people-"

"Will do fine without you." He finished my sentence not in the manner I had intended and his blue gaze stared unwavering into my own, piercing me with its intensity.

It felt as if he had reached in through my chest and torn my heart from my breast. Was not are cause right? Was it not just? Was my life for nothing? Would our people fade and die? I fell back to my knees, my head in my hands trying to come to grips with the shattering of all my beliefs. My chest ached as if I still needed to draw breath. It took some time before my courage returned to me enough to face him again, but when I did, I found him smiling in amusement. Was he mocking me? Was the Maker cruel enough to make sport of my life? Before that thought was even finished, I realized it was a smile more of pride than amusement.

"Then my quest is over? Will my people be safe?"

"That is not why I called you my son." To me, death was hardly the beckon of a loving father. "I have need of your services, and wish you to know that it is truly my hand that forges your life. I have pride in that the heat of my forge has tempered your will into the finest Vaarandril, and you have accomplished many of the tasks I have set for you." The smile widened to include a look much like the one that had crossed my face when my eldest, Korina, completed her apprenticeship.

My mind reeled with the implications. Had all the things I had done in my life been but tests sent by the Maker? That he could compare me with the soul-steel of the gods overwhelmed me and I could but listen.

"Know that the forging is not yet complete, Gorain." I was Dorian, not Gorain. "Even now, my priest, Waradain grieves and begs for the return of your soul, and he will have his wish, but only because it is my desire. From this day forth, your destiny will be mine, but I will tell you now, in kindness, that you will never again return to your hearth." There was brightness to his eye that suggested the pronouncement brought him almost as much pain as tore through my soul.

Morina! "Maker, please! Do not do this!" My voice was lost to a howling void as Morakvaar and his cavern receded into a red haze of agony. Was it a dream? I drew in a ragged gasp as if drawing searing magma into my lungs. Electric fire ran through all of my nerves as if my entire body had gone numb and was reawakening. My lids fluttered open desperate to catch a glimpse of our god and plead with him, but my gaze rested on the faces of a ring of kinsmen. The sorrow that had creased their brows and turned down their mouths in grim lines became wide-eyed shock. The priest who knelt over me was so startled, he fell over backwards, knuckles white on the symbol of a winged hammer that he grasped. The burning fire of opening arteries and reawakening nerves consumed me in a hell of inner flame and needles as my consciousness gratefully retreated from the onslaught.

"Morina!" I wandered great dark halls filled with a cold mist. My heat sensing vision was useless, and my voice echoed back mockingly. I could hear her cry of fear and loneliness, but always it receded from me until I burst suddenly into the light. The dream turned to memory as my mind wandered the corridors of the past.

***

Beside me were my companions of old. Jaguar, the haunting beauty, the first woman who had ever shown me kindness rode on her tall war-horse and the love of her burned brightly in my breast, as did the shame of my relationship with her. Her flowing black hair was highlighted in blue as it cascaded in waves down her back, obscuring the brilliant platemaille that had been forged by my hand. She had taken off her helmet, letting her hair fall free, caressed by the breeze, and none the worse for wear beneath the feline crest of the helm. It lashed the sides of her strawberry roan, and the horse flicked its cream-colored tail in annoyance.

My heart burned with the need to possess her, and I scowled mightily at Lodath, my longtime friend, as he watched her shapely form absorb the light of the surface sun with the lust all men displayed for her. But her child had been mine, and not many others had known her touch despite her occupation in the temple of Inanna. Perhaps it was my insane jealousy that kept them away, but I preferred to think she favored my company to them. After all, it had been many years since I killed one of her unsavory suitors. Jaguar had not been angry with me for killing the vile creature, but for interfering when she could take care of herself, thank-you. Months of shunning me had taught me just how seriously she considered my offense. Had it not been for Panther, our daughter's pleading; I doubt she would have forgiven me.

Panther had turned into a fine figure of a kinswoman, if not overly tall, like her mother. She surpassed human males in her feats of strength, prowess with weapons, and adeptness with the forge. I had been mightily pleased she had chosen to learn more of my people and foster into the clan Farovar. Clan Farovar were Kinsmen of Stone and not Kinsmen of the Blood, but I had finally earned a lasting friendship among them despite our ancestral hatreds and prejudices.

Vaguely, in my subconscious mind, I recognized I was reliving the days leading up to my first meeting with Morina, but the replay of my memory did not stop. It was laid bare before me in all of its details, including the shameful association with my former human lover. It was a memory that, though damning in the eyes of my people, I would not have traded for all the gold in my kingdom.

The pony had to trot every once in a while just to keep up with the plodding horses, a fact that annoyed the little dun immensely as it rolled a jaundiced eye when I prodded its ribs. The sun shone down upon us in furious intensity that ached within my skull, and I pulled my hood further down to ease my eyes. Forty-five years of life on the surface and I still had not gotten used to the light. Flies buzzed annoyingly around both the pony's and my head no matter how many I swatted and killed. The dust rose up in a choking cloud from the horses in front, and I tied a cloth across my nose and mouth to keep the worst of it at bay. I growled again at being put in the middle, when really it would better serve everyone if I was in front, but my complaints fell on deaf ears.

Rage still simmered within me for my 'prisoner's' status and our quick departure from Thornwood Keep that had consisted of me being bound, gagged and placed under powerful spells to keep me from killing the local Count. When the old Count had died, his son took over, and the taxes that had been levied against us lightened. I had thought it was because the young Parlfrey worshipped the ground I walked on; for he had often proclaimed me the greatest hero he had ever heard tell of. When I learned that it had really been because Jaguar had made a bargain with him, including her sexual favors, I had been outraged. I had donned my armor, took up my axe and left the keep with the full intention of marching straight to Parlfrey's castle and slaying the young bastard. Jaguar had intercepted me, and cast a spell on me to hold me motionless while the others bound, gagged and kidnapped me on this 'mission of mercy'. Had it not been for the sudden change in landscape, I would have sworn our mission had all been made up on the spur of the moment simply to remove me from the source of my anger.

The trees ended; there was no other explanation. The land before us was barren, devoid of life as if the earth itself had turned rotten and festered. A mist rose from the ground as if disgorging the breath of the dead, and the wind howled with the voices of the damned. Sickly greenish-yellow light filtered down through the haze like a plague falling from the cursed open sky. The swirling clouds of shrieking mist made the head of my pony disappear, and my heat sensing vision could not penetrate the whirling tendrils. I had faced demons with less dread than I felt at that moment. At least demons and devils were living things, but what possessed that land was the antithesis of life. What dwelled in the corpse of a once living realm promised eternal awareness without life, a hell unimaginable where the soul was imprisoned in a body that was both dead yet still enslaved to some monstrous will. Facing a necromancer took on a whole new seriousness that suddenly swept away my former rage.

My pony reared and screamed in terror from the voices in the mist, and I fought to control it. Not that I blamed the poor beast, but I would not be left without quick egress should our encounter call for a regroup of our forces. My mind reached out, encompassing the panicked animal's consciousness. I surrounded it in warm green pastures and a herd of other stout mares to run with. Lodath shot me an odd look as he struggled to control his own mount. The youthful mage was just beginning to show small flecks of gray hairs at his temples, and I wondered when it had been that he began to overtake and pass my age.

Instead of the robes of a scholar, he wore a dark brown leather vest over a puffy white shirt and breeks with high leather boots. Not at all what one would expect of an archmage of his caliber. Lodath chanted a spell, trusting me to calm his horse while he did so. I touched the horse's mind as I had the pony, and watched as Lodath's brow furrowed over his yellowish orange eyes. His slotted pupils dilated as he lost himself in the trance of the arcane. Though he had also been my rival, I still owed Lodath more than a blood debt. It was his spell that had saved me from the slavers, a fate worse than eternal damnation if I was not already bound in that direction. Though he had been human at the time, the gods had since touched his life, giving him a destiny to fulfill.

When he finished, Lodath pulled out four leaves and tossed them into the air in the cardinal directions, saying a single word with each. The leaves hovered, and then began to rotate to the left. Faster and faster the little green leaves swirled until it became impossible to follow them. A ring of green fire shimmered where the leaves rotated, and gradually it grew into a green sphere that encompassed half the party. Instantly the horses within the sphere calmed and nonchalantly chewed their cud as if nothing untoward had happened. The others quickly moved their horses into Lodath's protective circle.

I slid from the stirrups of my pony so that I could see the road better. Leaving the reins of my pony with Lodath, and taking the reins of Jaguar's horse, I lead them through the gloom for what seemed endless hours. Out of the sickly mist rose a dark form, angular and large. My outstretched hand felt the damp and rotted wood that had once been a massive gate. The sad remains of the proud defenses of the mist-enshrouded keep were no longer a barrier, and I wondered if anything still dwelled within. Yet, it had been the local Baron that confessed to being blackmailed by the fiendish necromancer who supposedly lived there. He also told Lodath that the peasantry lived in fear of their very souls, and were like slaves to the vile sorcerer. Thrusting aside the rotting door in my anger, it crumbled beneath my touch as termites writhed on the ground where they fell out of the wood.

Passing through the gate was like passing out of a storm. The mist cleared instantly, and would not enter through the portal as if some magic barrier kept it at bay. Overhead, the sun beamed down on us, illuminating the courtyard in a deceptive gaiety. The flagstones were worn by centuries of booted feet and shod hooves in a neat pathway leading to the entrance of the keep. Strewn about the courtyard were massive bones, just flung around in no particular pattern. It was as if some enormous creature had spontaneously exploded, but the bones were all intact. Grimly, I picked up a bleached bone that was yellowed with age. It was nearly half my size, but by no means the largest of the lot. Curiously, there were no gnawing marks from rodents or other small creatures that subsisted on calcium from bones and antlers.

Uneasily, I glanced about, spotting each of the pieces and trying to put together the puzzle in my mind's eye. As the last horse entered, though, I was spared the riddle. My hair stood on end as I felt the gathering of energy. The horses sidled nervously until they came within Lodath's protective barrier. One by one the bones lifted into the air. Vertebrae clung to one another with the power that coursed around us like an impending storm. To the backbone stuck ribs, then shoulders and hips, a long bony tail, massive legs and forearms. Long obsidian claws tipped both forepaws and hind like swords, each nearly as tall as my shoulder and still more bones flew to the gathering monster. Never in all my many experiences, had I ever seen such a thing!

Rising from behind the keep in its hidden resting-place emerged a skull so large it blotted out the sun. Horns protruded from top and sides as if crowding each other for space. Coal pits unnaturally settled within the eye-sockets, save for an unholy white-yellow fire in the exact center. The toothy jaw attached itself to the hinge sockets, displaying a frighteningly large set of pointed rending devices.

With a triumphant roar, the dragon's bones finished mending as the icy gaze of the monster settled upon us.

"It is death to defile my keep!" Its voice was a whisper and a hurricane all at once.

Its snarl became a blast of fetid breath that struck me as I stood in front to shield Jaguar. The foul stench of long rotten air and decayed reality choked me, and I was unable to deflect the descending sword-like talons. Like a kitten's toy, its claws ravaged me, tearing great rents in armor and flesh before sending me flying against the stone wall of the courtyard. Sparks filled my vision as my head connected against the rock. For long moments, I was unaware of my companions' struggles against the beast.

Warmth filled me, the nauseous pain faded and my waking gaze settled upon Jaguar's face. Her hands moved away from my torn breastplate when her chants were finished. Her smile was a sight to fulfill my soul, but it faded as I felt the prickling touch of magic upon us. Her skin wrinkled and pulled back to the bone, her hair turned sickly gray, and she fell to the ground from the weight of her own armor. A whimper of fear and agony came from her lips as I saw past her to the finishing gestures of the spell from the undead dragon.

Fire raged within me. The creature would pay dearly for hurting Jaguar! With a roar of fury, I leaped at the monster, but with a wave of its clawed hand, the ground erupted beneath my feet. Skeletal warriors crawled forth from the earth, surrounding me in an instant and cutting off my charge. As soon as I would crush them, the cursed dragon would summon more. Lodath sent wave after wave of fire and lightning at the monster, but it laughed as if merely tickled. Hours passed and the sun soon tired of our struggles. It settled towards the western horizon as we fought for our lives. Weariness filled every stroke from my axe as it crunched through bones, scattering them into dust, and still we fought on.

Time slipped by uncounted, as more skeletons monopolized my awareness. Exhaustion had claimed everything except the need to keep moving the blades, for to stop was certain death. Fire stole through every muscle. Each stroke I made resounded through my bones, and my fingers ached to release the haft of my axe if only for a moment. My feet rested on either side of Jaguar's prostrate form, protecting her with my life as the onslaught of bony soldiers continued. I blocked blows, ducked under *others, smashed skulls, ribs, hip-bones, arms, and shoulders in an endless shower of fragments and dust until it seemed Jaguar must be buried in it. But I could not hazard a glance to see if she was still alive.*

At the end of forever, the sky began to lighten, and the flat of my blade smashed the last visible skull before me. The undead dragon itself lurched forward, its spells exhausted, and believing us to be too weary to fight. In truth, we were, for my shoulders, arms and wrists felt as if they would fall from me at any moment. My fingers were numb from repeated shocks as I blocked blows and connected with solid bone. I could no longer be certain of my grip when for the first time I saw past the dragon to the altar. The bloodstained slab of intricately carved rock had an unnatural glow in the center of it; the same unnatural light that shone from the beast's eyes as it prepared to strike us down.

Instinctively, I ran for it, sensing the great evil the stone bore. Set within the altar was a large gem that halted my desperate rush. Its facets sang of pure beauty, its unflawed center was a gleam of violet. The light purple diamond was almost as large as my skull, and spoke of a gem that might have bought a dozen kingdoms. For a moment, I wrestled with my desire to possess it. With such a diamond, I could have secured an army to utterly annihilate the zarakanan that had destroyed my home. My hesitation was a moment too long as the skeletal dragon seized and shredded Homer. The halfling's dying scream shook me from the greed that tried to overwhelm my soul and the blade of my axe descended upon the gem. In a screech of rage, the dragon turned to me and its claws dug furrows in the stone as it launched. The blades of my axe cleaved the gem, and fire rose up from it to surround me in its retribution. Bolts of searing energy clashed through me to dance upon my armor like insane demons as the magic contained for centuries was released. Enormous bones pelted me as the dragon dissembled into its constituent parts, but I was transfixed by the energy that tore through me with the vengeance of the powers of hell.

Screams of agony echoed around me, and it took me some time to realize they came from my own lips as the fires consumed my flesh. Thinking quickly, Lodath covered me with water he had summoned, ending the torment. I staggered and fell to my knees thankful for my races' high immunity to heat and magic. Had any of the others destroyed the gem, they would have been meeting their gods. Lodath came to stand beside me, but I waved him off.

"See vat you can do for Jagvar, she is hurt vit magics." I could not help but wince in the memory that my hesitation had cost the halfling his life. I deserved the pain I suffered.

Lodath's brow furrowed, but he understood my concern for Jaguar. Sagging against the haft of my axe, I shook with agony. Though my flesh felt as if all of it was scalded, it was bearable in light of my guilt. No amount of pain would bring back Homer, and though the halfling had annoyed me many times, I found myself missing his antics already.

In the distance, my keen hearing picked up a muffled yell, a cry for help from one of the towers. My feet took much coaxing to support my weight and my weary bones complained as I stumbled towards the spires. Climbing the stairs was sheer agony as my legs burned not only from the gem's retribution, but from the long abuse of fighting a full day's cycle. An iron-shod wooden door proved no obstacle to my axe, and I stepped into the necromancer's lab.

Beakers, vials, tubes, glasses, and burners decorated every inch of the table, counter and shelving space not used by books. Upon the floor in one corner was a circle inscribed in arcane symbols, which I took great pains to stay away from. To my right, suspended in the northernmost corner was a barred cage, and it was from there that the voice had come. My feet refused to budge as my eyes took in the sight of a golden-haired kinswoman. Her coppery-bronze skin was only a shade lighter than mine. She could not have been much older than I had been when I was taken from Morkilduum, perhaps fifty-four season cycles, but every line, every feature was perfect had subtle scars not marred her.

The deep green of her eyes pleaded with me in a way that words never could, and I felt as if my soul would wither and die if I let her remain in that cage a second longer. Instinct prickled my spine as I stepped forward. The step became a diving roll as a bulbous spear struck the ground next to my head. Black ichors dripped from the barbed end of the wicked spine as it withdrew to hover almost twice my height from the floor. Attached to it was a creature of nightmares. The spine became a part of its jointed insectoid tail, and one of its toothy claws shot forward towards my neck. Back on my feet, I sidestepped and brought the blades of my axe to bear. The claw skittered across the floor to rest within the arcane circle as the creature hissed in angry pain. Its tail lanced forward as the scorpion thing's ten legs whirled it about swiftly. I met the poison barb two feet above my head with sharp barakanan-forged steel.

The point of the tail spun away from me as I stared into the features of the creature. Outrage filled my soul as its face seemed roughly like a kana, but I had no time to dwell on it. The other claw screamed through the air towards me. Drawing my short sword, I jumped up and allowed my weight to drive the blade through the claw and into the stone below. Writhing in helpless agony, the creature seemed to plead with me as I swung my axe around for the final blow.

"Vorkrazak sie nea! Dorsava en Var!" My eyes went wide and my head snapped around to the cage.

To hear my native tongue spoken in that place stilled my need for violence, and I wondered why the maid would beg to spare the creature's life? Her accent had been atrocious, and I could not guess where she came from. With a grimace of disgust I stepped away from the vile thing whose profane features resembled a kinswoman.

"Such a beast deserves death in abundance. Why would you spare its life?" Her eyes widened at my formal manner, and I realized I had slipped too easily into the diplomatic training of my youth.

A great sob heaved from her breast, but her eyes were beyond tears. The scars on her face and body spoke of her long years of slavery, and I was reminded of the many similar scars I bore. My heart went out to her, and instinctively I knew she had suffered as I had, and not just from the slaver's whips. Quickly, I removed my cloak and passed it up to her through the bars. Though it was charred and torn from the battle, she gratefully took it to cover herself. My belt served to keep it around her like a robe after she cut two holes for her arms. She let out a tremulous sigh as she fought not to show the utter despair that was written in the lines of her face. Her chin showed the light haze of where her beard should have been, as it trembled then firmed into a show of fortitude.

"That creature ... was my mother." She kept her gaze firmly upon mine, hoping that I would understand.

For a moment, all I could do was stare back as my mouth dried in the wind. "Vooraduum!" The curse was a harsh croaking whisper. What else could I say to her? "One of my companions is a powerful *sorcerer. Mayhap he can cure your mother of this? In the mean time, I should get you down from there."*

The heavy chain that suspended the cage ran down the wall to a winch that was blocked. Bracing the handles on the crank with my shoulder, I knocked the block away. The force of its freedom nearly threw me to the ground, but I managed to barely hold it. My aching muscles were not up to the strain, and burned anew with weariness but I could not let her be harmed! Like a runner on a long relay, I found my head buzzing. Veins stood out on my arms and hands as I strained to let the cage down gradually. With a final effort, the iron grillwork clanged to the floor, and I sagged exhausted against the winch for several moments.

Willpower alone put my feet beneath me once more and I searched for a key. Finding none, and out of patience, I stood before the cage.

"Stand back."

The golden-haired kinswoman did as I asked, and my axe sent a shower of sparks flying through the room as the metal shrieked its doom. The small latch glowed red-hot and shattered under the blow. With a grim smile, I offered her my hand. Slowly, as if believing it all a dream, she reached out, and then leaped from the cage as if it would snap shut like a beast and devour her. She ran over to the scorpion creature where it crouched pinned to the floor. Had I the energy, I would have prevented her, but I could no longer react in any sort of timely manner. She knelt by its head and whispered as it chittered back. Were they having a real conversation? If it had been my own mother, I too would have at least made the attempt.

With a frown and a creased brow she returned to my side. Her lips barely forming the words, she spoke to me.

"She begs you to slay her, and not attempt to restore her shame." Though I understood the sentiment all too well, I had learned that life brings hope.

"If indeed that is your mother, would it not be best she returned to your side? Lodath-"

Her hand covered my lips. *"She has lost her soul, my Lord, do not make her relive her life."*

Fire filled my heart as I felt the empty hollowness inside where my own kinsman's soul should be. I knew how she felt, knew what it meant to lose my heritage. Hefting my axe, I nodded silently. With a grimness that filled me as I thought of my own future, I cleaved the beast in two as it closed its eyes expectantly. A final sigh of freedom escaped its mouth as I turned away, unable to face the contentment the creature had found in death, contentment denied to me.

In a green and gold flash, my arms were suddenly full of a grieving kinswoman. The clatter of my axe seemed far away as I put my arms around her for comfort. A lifetime of pain and sorrow passed from her, rolling down my armor in her tears as my companions entered the room.

Gratefully I saw Jaguar's weakness had been lifted, and the wrinkled withered thing she had become was again filled-out flesh. Of our entire group, she looked the most refreshed, and I smiled ruefully. Her graceful brow arched high as she saw the vaarakanan maid in my arms sobbing as if there *were nothing else in the world more important. The heat reached my ears as it colored my cheeks, but the kana was not done with her weeping.*

In typical magely curiosity, Lodath knelt by the corpse of the scorpion, a frown deepening the new lines on his face. He cocked a curious eyebrow my way and I nodded grimly, confirming his suspicion. With intense interest, he then began rummaging through the necromancer's lab.

The ragged sobs finally stopped, drawing my gaze back to hers. In a couple more moments, the kana regained her composure.

"I am Morina Tenedain of Balakarak. When I was but a lass our stronghold was besieged by zarakanan and vourdovra." She let that sink in as I stared at her in horror. The vourdovra were beasts that haunted our nightmares, the mindeaters! "With their combined might, they slew our strongest soulsmiths and overwhelmed our defenses." She seemed more at ease speaking the overlander tongue than our own language. Jaguar, Gith'r'luk, Darius, Liathrain, Kelen and I listened intently while Lodath continued rummaging through the lab. "My mother and I were taken from our hearth and sold into slavery." There were so many things the zaraks would pay for!

"Our first human master was not such an evil man, but he was old and soon sickened. He did not care what his underlings did; it was too much for him to bother. When he found out what they had... done to us, he tried to find us a safer home. The mage who came to buy us from him promised we would be well looked after, and we were sold to him. When he brought us to this keep ..."

She was unable to continue, but the corpse of the scorpion was proof enough of what had occurred. She shuddered anew, and I was reminded that she was still in my arms. With a red face, I released her and introduced myself in my native tongue. Lodath paused in his foraging to listen with interest, as I very rarely spoke my native tongue and when I did, I did not speak of my heritage.

"I am Dorian Mytharia, of the ancient Clan Mytharia in an unbroken line to Golodain. I am journeyman to the Atharil Warrior's School of Morkilduum; at least I was until I too was enslaved." Morina met my gaze in perfect understanding of what that meant. "It is my life-bound honor to be of service to you and your clan." I bowed as low as I might have to the Patriarch in honor of her noble blood.

Lodath snorted and continued his rummaging through books, papers, bottles and canisters. Morina smiled; the first I had seen upon her face. It was as if the fires of a volcano erupted within. I looked to the ground at her feet as I felt the heat in my cheeks. To cover my awkwardness, I offered my more immediate services.

"Where now will you be headed, Lady Morina Tenedain, that I might take you there in safety?"

"I have nowhere to go. I do not know where Balakarak is, nor do I know my kinsmen there. I have lived all of my life on the surface. It is only because my mother kept the ways that I know our language at all." Her voice was full of bitterness, and I chanced to meet her green gaze once more.

"Say but a word," I vowed, "and I will do my best to take you there though all the hosts of the zarakanan stood between us and your destination."

Another smile lit her features like a star descending from the heavens, and my heart skipped a beat or two. I had not realized how much her presence affected me until I stole a quick glance to Jaguar who watched our exchange with amused interest though she did not understand. Morina placed a coppery hand upon my vambrace as my heart quickened its pace.

"Thank-you kinsman. I do not wish to return as yet, but would be honored if you would allow me to accompany you." In the heat of the moment, I forgot my reservations.

"The honor would be mine." I wanted her with me.

The guess that Morina would more than likely opt to ride the stout pony with me filled me with warmth until I saw Jaguar looking at me. Her gaze was like a bucket of icy water. What was I thinking? My relationship with Jaguar ruled out ever being accepted by a kinswoman! Though Jaguar would have been more than happy to be rid of my insane jealousy, I knew I was not worthy of being a suitor to Morina. The fact I had kinship, let alone kinship with a human made me unsuitable. Not only that, but I was the third son of a dishonored clan. I had no hope of ever being considered worthy. My love for Jaguar still haunted me with the bond we had created.

Even though the slaver had abused me, there had never been a bond between Lady Alfstein and me. Was it intent that created the bond? I had willingly shared kinship with Jaguar, but not the slaver. Was it my willingness that allowed the bonding to take place? In confusion, I followed the others downstairs when Lodath finished his plundering.

Jaguar took the first watch after spending a bit of her goddess' power on me to heal the burns. I laid out my bedroll for Morina, then fell asleep as soon as I laid down by the fire. After six hours they roused me and after my two hour watch, I went and did some plundering of my own in the keep's vaults. The undead dragon had amassed a huge amount of wealth and I filled four of my dimensional sacks as well as Lodath's magical hut. The rest of the portable wealth fit in our saddle bags. Reluctantly I had to leave behind several things that were just too large to transport, but vowed to send back an expedition to retrieve them.

By mid-afternoon, we were saddled up and on the road back. The scenery was even more depressing in the full light of day, the mists having cleared during the night. Instead of the foreboding landscape it was before, daylight revealed a lifeless and blackened world with all manner of moldering rots and fungus and none of it edible! My stomach rumbled, reminding me I had spent two days with only one meal, so reached into my pack for some waybread for myself and for Morina. Gratefully she ate what I offered.

Never having rode a pony before, Morina was seated in front of me so that I could steady her with my arms. Though I was happy to have her with me, my mind and heart were in turmoil and I surely entertained thoughts no kinsman should have had. I was glad my armored cop did not betray my thoughts though it became quite uncomfortable after a time. I wished to the gods I was still a true kinsman within, but the slaver, Lady Alfstein, had already stolen my soul. If that were not enough, I raised a child with Jaguar and vowed to be by her side as long as she wished. How could I even entertain thoughts of bonding to a kinswoman? A dark cloud had settled upon my thoughts, thicker and more vexing than the veil of the necromancer.

We left the evil festering land behind just before sunset, and in the distance, were the tilled fields of a farm. The farmer was suspicious of strangers until we showed him ten gold coins, and then he graciously offered us the barn. I unfastened my bedroll and lay it out next to my pony after I had rubbed her down and gave her an apple from a barrel near the door. She whickered gratefully, and rubbed her head against me, nearly knocking me over. I scratched her ears and chin and patted her neck, feeling the contentment in her mind as I fed her some of the farmer's hay, a small amount of grain and a treat of oats. She munched happily from the nosebag as I prepared to lay on my bedroll, still exhausted and sore from the battle. Though Jaguar had healed the worst of my wounds, there were still many minor cuts I had not complained about, and there was nothing she could do for the bone-weary soreness that invaded every inch of me.

"Dorian, can I speak with you?" My heart leaped into my throat, as I shuddered within. Had she noticed my desire for her?

"What do you wish of me, my kinswoman?" I looked again into those seas of green jade, knowing I had already lost what she was seeking.

Lodath looked our way intently, his orange-yellow orbs disturbing in the low light of the barn lanterns, his slotted pupils glowing green. Instead of speaking when I faced her; Morina paced around me slowly, examining me as if I was livestock. The heat of embarrassment colored my already ruddy skin. What was she looking for? Instinct held me still as if something important was about to occur.

"You will do." She said at last.

My brow furrowed and a frown crossed my face as I struggled to understand what she meant.

As if sensing my confusion, Morina clarified, "You will be my hearth-mate."

I blinked, and I swear I could taste the stench of the barn in my mouth. Eventually my jaw worked enough to make a reply, albeit a lame one. "Y-Your hearth-mate?" As soon as I said the words, my gaze rested on Jaguar's lean form as she removed her bedroll from her saddle-pack. "I ... I can not be your hearth-mate." My voice was thick with the bitter realization that there was no return to my people.

Morina's brows shot up, and her mouth opened slightly in disbelief. "But I have chosen you, and I have no more clan elders. Would your clan elders refuse a Kinswoman of Soul?"

My refusal of the great honor of marriage was obviously beyond her expectation. Come to think of it, such a denial was beyond my experience, but I knew my impure heart could never soil that of a kinswoman. How could I tell her that I loved a human? Better yet, how could I explain that I had lost my soul? I was a profanity, a creature beyond what it was to be balakanan, I was no longer a Kinsman of the Blood, and could not consider myself a marriage candidate. Still my mouth refused to voice the terrible dishonor to her.

"I ... I just can not. I am sorry." I turned from her with my heart in turmoil and walked away.

My feet trod with more weariness than my muscles could attribute as I wandered over a green-topped hill. On the other side was an old oak, possibly as old as my father, and, had it been in my nature, I would have wept, but no tears could come to me. I was beyond sorrow, beyond despair; for I had been a slave that had wished for death time uncounted as torments were wrought upon me that even the dark gods would have been ashamed of. The memory of the slaver and her bodyguards' ministrations sent an icy shudder through me and served to harden my resolve. The soul of a kinsman could not survive such horrific things, and therefore, I was no longer a kinsman, for I still lived. My eyes fixed absently upon the spectacle of the setting sun, and thought I could not see it clearly, its last rays lit the sky with gold, silver, red and royal purple upon the scattered gray clouds. Even the sky mocked me with its gaiety.

"What is wrong, Dorian?" Lodath's voice intruded upon my dark reverie. "Why did you say that to her? You know you have hurt her deeply; she thinks you refuse her because she has been a slave." He broke off abruptly, and I knew what he was going to say.

Interrupting the tirade I knew was coming, I told him. "All of my life, I hafe dreamt of marrying." I spoke in his tongue. "It vas a dream I knew vould never be fulfilled." I met his gaze, thinking again of his odd 'blessing'. "I had never vonce considered vezer or not I vould be vorzy of such an honor." Even after forty-five years the overlander language still twisted on my tongue like a serpent, but that was not what brought the long pause. "You know my history, Lodath. You know vat I have done, vat has been done to me … Among my people, I vould be outcast for even zinking of such zings. If ever I had been known to commit zem…" I trailed off, knowing that Lodath would never understand what it meant to be dishonored officially, have your clan banished, your name stricken from the Book of Ancestors, and to be exiled from your own kin in their banishment because of your crimes.

Lodath placed a hand upon my shoulder. "You don't even know her history. I think you should let her choose. She is alone and among strange lands and people. She needs someone to take care of her."

For a moment, suspicion seized me, and I stared at him as if sizing up an enemy. Was he after Jaguar? Instantly sorry for thinking it, I shook my head. Such notions were bound to lead to trouble, and would have angered Jaguar had she known. I looked again at my 'human' friend knowing that he would never understand the intricacies of our society, our edicts and why I had to refuse.

"You do not understand." I took in a deep breath, and then let it out slowly. "It is not zat she does zie choosing, it is zat I must tell her of vat I have done, of my impurity." I looked at him earnestly, willing him to understand. "I do not know if I can face her ahnd tell her. I hahve dishonored myself ahnd must confess it to her before marriage. If I ahdmit such shame, it is to zie entirety of my people zat I ahdmit it." I met his gaze once more. "I cahn never be ah kinsman ahgain. My heart is impure, for I love ah human."

For a moment, I thought he understood, as he looked away from me into the tapestry of the sky. "I still think she should be the judge of whom she chooses." He looked back. "Dorian, I know you. This is what you want, what you have been waiting for. It is the chance of a lifetime for you to return honorably to your people. Why don't you see that?" At my snort of amusement, he got up and stomped away.

My momentary light of humor dissipated in contemplation of the dire events that had filled my life with misery. The worst of it was that it all boiled down to my series of wrong decisions. It was my choice to wander too far from Morkilduum's protecting walls that fateful day when I had been captured and sold into slavery. It had been my choice to spend an evening with Jaguar, forfeiting any chance I might have had to regain my soul. My mind steered around what the slaver, Lady Alfstein had done to me, but at least that was not entirely my fault. Even so, I could not help thinking there might have been *some way to prevent it. Perhaps if I had not removed my tunic in the hot sun, if I had not taken so long with the hunting dogs, she would not have been there to see me working in the stables? I frowned and toyed with the dirt between my feet knowing that Lord Alfstein's new wife would have found me sooner or later no matter what I did.*

The touch of a hand on my shoulder sent me spinning to the left and grabbing the haft of my axe. I took in a breath, sighting my adversary before striking. Jade green regarded me with surprise. I lowered the axe and my gaze as I felt the heat rise into my cheeks. Morina's hand reached out to mine, forcing my attention back to her face.

"Dorian, please? Why would you refuse the honor I offer you?" Her accent seemed less the more she spoke to me in our tongue.

Despite how much I wanted to leave, her firm grip on my wrist prevented me. My shoulders fell in defeat, and I supposed she would find out sooner or later.

"I ... am impure." My lips still refused to form the words.

"What do you mean? What does that matter?" Her mother must not have taught her that much of our culture.

I looked to the ground, too ashamed to meet her eyes. "I have had kinship with a human. My heart has been untrue to our people. I have known tortures that no kinsman could know and still retain their soul. I am not worthy to be your hearth-mate." The words came out in a rush, a flood of torment revealed for all time.

She stepped closer, blocking my view of the dirt and forcing me to look into the green fire. "Do you think that I care? I have lived as an outsider all of my life, been on the surface since I was a young child. I have been a slave too, Dorian. I know you are aware of what that means; only this is the first time I have known freedom. Do you think that makes me worthy? Do you think I feel as if I have the right?" She broke off, her eyes becoming bright with moisture.

I put my hand over hers to reassure her. "You are a kinswoman. Always there will be honor and acceptance for you no matter your past. Any clan would gladly take you in, Morina. But a kinsman has no recourse, no redemption."

"Dorian, there is one more thing I must tell you. It was my mother's last wish that I marry you should your clan accept me. She was a seer, Dorian, and she told me your soul is great."

"She- she spoke to you? She said that?" I looked away, my heart in turmoil.

How could my soul be 'great' if I no longer possessed it? How could I marry a kinswoman when I loved a human? Yet, her insecurity, her terrible wounds to her own soul touched me deeply, something I knew all too well.

"Yes, Dorian. She said she had never seen a finer example of a kinsman, and compared you to Darlik Hammerhand, Conqueror of the Daemon Fish." She smiled, and it was as if the sun had not left the land.

Narrowing my eyes in disbelief, I turned back. "She said that?"

"Not in that manner, no, but the comparison was there. She did tell me that if I were to marry that you would be one of the best candidates. Though she was never a true soulsmith, she did have the talent and saw within you great deeds. As my only known clan elder and student of the soulsmiths, I must listen to her words." She stared pleadingly into my eyes. "Dorian, if you had not rescued me, I would have suffered the same fate as my mother. I owe you a blood-bond, but more than that; I need someone who can understand that I have lived on the surface all my life in slavery. Someone who can understand the terrors of the dark and what it means to a slave. Who could that be but you?"

Though her logic was sound, I could not live a lie. "Morina," I said gently, "it is Jaguar with whom I am soul-bound. It is only her religion that prevents us from being hearth-mates, but not..." I lowered my eyes, "lovers."

Her jaw tightened momentarily as more determination shone in her eyes. "It is with Jaguar that I have discussed this." The impact of her words left my mind reeling, and I barely managed to catch the rest of it. "Before I came to you, she spoke to me. She told me of your involvement with her. She also said that she would be happy to see you finally achieve your dreams." The words nearly struck me down.

"Then she no longer wishes my company?" The words were a hoarse whisper, a shattering of my world. I was lost in the maelstrom and instead of struggling I let it consume me. Drowning in the fire of despair that welled up from within, I made my decision. "If you accept freely my dishonor and Jaguar has forsaken me, then I cannot refuse you."

Morina hugged me in an emotional display that made me blink twice as I felt the heat ascend into the roots of my hair. Still numb within, I followed along meekly as she tugged my arm, leading me back to the barn. Lodath stood outside, grinning like a court fool.

"She said I should be here as a witness."

I grinned ruefully. Morina knew I would be unable to deny her. She held the high ground, knowing our traditions were too strongly imbedded in my consciousness despite my willingness to try and forget them.

"Morina, I must speak with Jaguar first." A look akin to fear entered her gaze as she chewed her lower lip. Wordlessly she nodded, and I went to find Jaguar in the barn making herself comfortable on a mound of hay as far away from the smell of the animals in the stables as she could get.

"Dorian, is it time already?" She made as if to follow me to where the others were gathering in the center of the barn.

I grit my teeth, trying to fight off the tightness that threatened to steal the breath from my lungs. "Jagvar, Morina has asked zat I be her hearz-mate. I told her about us, ahnd she said zat you had told her you vould be happy for me. Does zis mean you no longer vish my company?" I could not look her in the eye for fear I would lose my careful composure.

"Dorian, our daughter has already left for her fosterage; there is no reason for you to stay with me. You need to save your people, and marriage to Morina would gain you acceptance back among them." I looked into her liquid brown eyes, losing myself again in the desire to hold her.

I never told her what kept me from returning almost as much as my fatherly duty to our child, but Jaguar was deceptively wise. "Do you no longer vant my company?"

Jaguar's gentle look became suddenly hard and cold, nearly stopping my heart from beating as I braced myself for the killing blow. "Dorian, I'm pregnant." Before a smile could cross my face, she thrust the sword home. "The father is Count Iskar Parlfrey." Searing pain gripped my heart, rending it in two, and my jaw began to ache as it kept in the howl of agony. "He has agreed to raise our child as his heir." The hardness in her voice was replaced with genuine excitement. "Do you know what that means to our temple?" Unable to open my mouth as molten lava consumed me from within, I shook my head. "The temple of Inanna will become the official religion of Harandale! Think of it! We will never have to worry about persecution from other less worthy religions!" The smile on her face was mockingly alluring as the feeling of betrayal nearly killed me.

I turned from her, my world crumbling around me. The careful façade I had kept pretending that I was the only one in Jaguar's life, crashed and burned in the fire. I wanted to put my fist through the barn wall, wanted to kill something, anything, but the only one who deserved my anger was myself. I was the one who deceived my heart into believing Jaguar loved me. I had known her nature all along, yet refused to acknowledge it.

My voice was quiet, barely above a whisper. "It is time." I walked towards the others, not looking back for fear I would break down. My knees felt like they would give out on me at any moment.

I took my place beside Morina, and nodded to Lodath. As my oldest friend on the surface, he was the chief witness to our binding. Looking at Morina's face, the pain receded from me, quenched in a cool green depth. There was nothing to keep me from giving myself to her wholly. The smell of the horses, ponies, cows and pigs was oddly comforting to me, though a far cry from the marriage chamber of Morkilduum. I looked around at the faces of my longtime companions, and though they were not my kin, they were a kind of family.

It was the hardest thing I could do to tear my eyes from Jaguar and deny my love for her. My heart nearly stopped to commit such heresy, for she knew I loved her deeply, yet she was happy for me to marry another. It was a denial that hurt more than any dishonor I could have suffered, and I realized that though she may have loved me, it was no more than her love of any corporeal pleasure.

I turned to Morina, and smiling gently, began the Ritual of Binding in the old tongue. "I, Dorian Mytharia, Journeyman Commander of the Atharil Warrior's School, do hereby proclaim my right of heritage to prove my worth for my kinswoman." I hoped Morina understood, for her expression gave nothing away. "Thorun Mytharia, Mastersmith, Clan Elder, and Lord of the Sacred Forge Bonded Geria Temchin, Masterweaver of Banarik Hall to give me birth as their third son."

I counted the crafters and nobles that had been in my direct lineage all the way back to the first and only High King, Gorain Mytharia eight thousand years ago. With the mention of his name, at the end of my recitation, Morina's eyes widened, and she chewed her lip again; a sign I later came to know meant great inner distress. Would she still accept me knowing I was the heir of such an infamous person?

My hands worked slowly to braid a long lock of her hair as I recited my ancestry. Rightfully, it should have been her golden beard, which even then looked as if it would grow out well and full, as it should have been. Her dark coppery skin offset her green eyes in such a striking manner it took my breath away. Her blonde brows arched gracefully over them, and I had no doubt I would hear the names of nobility in her ancestry as well. I was shocked to hear the name of Morina's father, Barelain Tenedain Mastersoulsmith and Patriarch of Balakarak, confirming my suspicion of her noble heritage. I let my mind complete the picture of a full beard, and felt the fire of agony turn into a new sort of warmth. Truly she was the loveliest kinswoman I had ever seen despite the minor scars she had taken from her years of slavery, and I felt keenly my unworthiness to marry a Kinswoman of Soul.

In her turn, Morina braided my beard, reciting her ancestry to me. The fiery red hair that had given me my name twisted in her hands like a live thing. My pulse raced as the realization came to me that I was, indeed, being Bonded. The highest honor I could hope for as the third son of a dishonored clan.

When Morina had finished, I went to my saddlebags and removed one of the sacks I had tied to them. Puzzled, my companions watched as I dumped out part of the contents that was more than a sack that size should have been able to hold. The sound of spilling coins, metal and gems filled the barn as Morina's eyes widened with wonder at the bright and shining hoard.

"This represents my vault, and though it does not contain the whole of my wealth, it must stand in its stead. An eighth share of this is mine."

I pulled out a wondrous amulet with fire opals, blue and black diamonds inset in vaarandril, a vaarakanan king's ransom, and about my share worth of the treasure. Soulsmithing Runes curled about it cleverly inlaid in the knotwork to conceal the protection it offered its bearer. I placed it around Morina's neck.

"This is my choice of the spoils, and my bond-gift to you, Morina Tenedain." I knelt before her. "Am I acceptable my kinswoman?"

She blinked, unable to draw her eyes away from the priceless gift I had placed about her neck. Of those present, only she and I knew its true worth to our people. Awkwardly, she drew a deep breath, overwhelmed that I should prove to be such a wealthy kinsman. The wonder on her face told me she had no real idea when she had first announced her mother's choice to me. She probably thought me a kinsman of moderate means with only enough gold to bear arms and own a mount. It would be amusing to see her reaction to the fact I was the Lord of a large keep that oversaw an enormous wealth in trade, and of the vast vaults of treasure stored within hidden locations from my many adventures.

Morina cleared her throat, and by her words I could tell this was the first binding ceremony she had ever attended. "You are acceptable kinsman." Then she remembered the proper response and grinned sheepishly. "I accept your bond-gift, and will tend your hearth and bear your children."

I stood and clasped forearms with her, our eyes locked in an exchange of disbelief that we had just been Bonded. Lodath finished interpreting the exchange of words to the others and they all stared at Morina and me expectantly. I blinked in confusion, what did they want?

"Well?" Lodath asked, and at my puzzled look he continued. "Aren't you going to kiss the bride?"

"Vat?" I frowned, and then remembered I had seen such custom at human weddings. "Among my people, such displays of affection are for private." To my surprise, Morina seized my head and drew my lips to hers, silencing my protest.

The others cheered, but I was lost in the sensation of Morina in my arms. Their voices receded into the background as I held her. After an eternity, Morina let me go and drew back, her face more red than a forge's embers. I took in a breath, regaining my sense of balance as I blinked.

"Congratulations Dorian!" Lodath clapped me on the shoulder heartily. "Better you than me!" He laughed, but there was a wistful look in his eye.

My annoyed frown made him laugh harder, and the others chuckled as they too congratulated me. I took it all in at a distance not believing I was Bonded. Looking to Morina I knew I would do anything to please her. I would make up for her lost years of slavery, show her what I could of our traditions and be more than just a hearth-mate to her, for she needed so much more.

It was three hours before dawn when we finally dispersed to our separate sleeping areas, still recovering from the battle the day before. With a wry smile I realized Morina had already planned out our impending Binding, and took the liberty of arranging my bedroll to accommodate two in the loft away from the others. What would she have said about our tradition that newly bonded couples normally spent a tanir, a tenday, apart before sharing kinship? As she looked deeply into my eyes, I decided not to bring the subject up. The need she had of comfort was a tangible thing, and I removed my armor. She needed reassurance, proof that she was a free kinswoman and that this was all not just a dream. She did not need rhetoric about our traditions, but it saddened me that the only way she knew of comfort was a physical union.

Morina finished helping me take off my armor, gambeson and under tunic. Unembarrassed, she regarded me for a moment before a slow smile spread across her face. She pulled me to her and whispered into my ear.

"You will indeed do, kinsman." She had probably never seen a kinsman unclothed before, and I could see how she would view most humans as disappointing.

It mattered not that we were in a barn; to us it could have been the Underhalls of Morakvaar the Maker. Surely he smiled upon our union and blessed us as we prematurely consummated our marriage. I slept blissfully, Morina's head resting in the crook of my shoulder as her arm draped across my chest. For the first time since being taken from Morkilduum, I was at peace with myself.

***

The dream-memory faded, and my eyes fluttered open to the abnormal light of a lantern. My vision adjusted beneath flickering lids to the harsh spectrum of light. The ruin of what was once a dwelling surrounded me in blackened fragments. Much of the rubble from the crumbled wall lay strewn across the floor, but a path had been cleared through it to the carved out bunk in which I slept. My eyes rested on a head of hair as fiery as my own, and Korina's crystal green gaze stared back at me from her bearded face.

Korina! The memory of the duel with Liathrain, our marching to war and my conversation with Morakvaar came back in startling clarity. By the ache in my bones I guessed I had not yet been freed of my torturous existence. With Korina's help, I gained my feet, though my knees felt weak and incapable of holding my weight. Fixing my daughter with what I hoped was my most discouraging look; I managed to stand on my own.

Her head turned to the cave floor, knowing what was coming. "You are not supposed to be here!" The words were more a harsh croak as it felt like I spat razors out my throat to form them. My hand worked the ragged scar that crossed my neck from right collarbone to left ear, trying to soothe the raw pain.

"Father, you cannot expect me to stay behind!" Her jaw set in a stubborn line, so much like her mother's.

"I can, and I do. You will turn back at once!" She was just as unreasonable as Morina could be at times.

"I am fit to travel. I have learned the ways of the axe and hammer! You have no right to deny me!" She did not meet my eye.

"You are also with child! It is your duty to stay behind and guard the life of one of our unborn kin! Do you not think that your mother would have been here too if it were not for her pregnancy? That is what we are fighting for, the future!" Such a long speech sent me into a fit of racking coughs that felt as if a small furnace had been lodged in my throat.

Where in the Deeps was Korina's hearth-mate, Marak? He should have prevented her from thinking about this lunacy! How could my daughter think so little of our cause?

After steadying me, she calmly replied, "Yes father, for the future. And because of the future, you need every able body that can wield a weapon to do so."

Waving a finger in her face while I strained to regain control of my voice, I finally managed to swallow. "You could have served just as well with the hearth-guard!"

Before the hacking coughs could begin again, I snatched the mug off the tray that had been brought in. Korina laughed at my sour look when the taste was of broth and not ale. At least the warm soup soothed my throat to the point where I could speak again.

"No, father. I could not serve with the hearth-guard, and well you know it! I am your heir, and my place in this battle is at your side!" She began to raise her voice, defiantly meeting my gaze for the first time.

I ground my teeth. I knew she was right, but I feared for her safety. She had not yet known the ravages of battle, being too young when we attacked Terazandarin. The wobbling of my knees seemed to spread through my system, and I took an unsteady stride before my legs refused to hold my weight any longer. Korina grabbed my arm to steady me, half concern and half mischief in her eyes.

"See? Mother was right. You do need someone to look after you."

I was silent for a moment, contemplating this new bit of information. Was it a bloody conspiracy?

"Your mother sent you?" Imagine me needing someone to hold my hand!

Korina nodded. The light of mischief danced in her eyes as it had so often when she was a child. "She said that either Dorak or I needed to go along to make sure you came back alive. And you know Dorak is too young."

The memory of Morakvaar's warning cooled my ire before it began. My chest tightened, as my heart fled to my belly.

"I will not be going back to Morakduum." I mumbled as I glanced back over my shoulder.

Instantly, the grin disappeared. "What do you mean?... Father?"

Shakily, I walked out of the ruin, not knowing what to say to her, and she watched me leave in confused silence. The pain I saw on her face equaled mine. How could I explain the maker's wishes, his bargain for my life?

Outside the ruin lay Liathrain's lifeless form in a pool of congealed blood that was half mine. Her angular features looked almost peaceful in death, a peace my soul had only dreamed of. Our long friendship ended in dark violence. Why had our paths lead us here? Weariness burned in my legs as I knelt at her side and nearly fell over her in my weakened state, but caught myself in time.

"May your gods accept you as a good and noble servant. May you someday forgive me for what I must do." I whispered, hoping her soul could hear me as I touched her forehead and closed her eyes to the world. I stood and addressed the kinsman who had walked up to me and stood in respectful silence. "Send her body back to her people with a warning. If they do not leave the Deeps, the Reaver will take them. They too have a prophecy about the ancient artifact of our people, and it is about to be fulfilled."

Chapter 4

Balakarak (Blood Stone Fortress)

The road to Balakarak wound around treacherous volcanic bubbles, glass shards, through tunnels barely wide enough for the cannons, over the Daemon Fish River on a tiny stretch of stone, and under the River of Life that was the magma flow that emptied into the Mother's Heart. It was a treacherous road and took us a month to navigate with our large army, but at last we stood before the sad remains of the legendary stronghold of the soulsmiths.

The fortress-tunnel was carved out from a huge deposit of bloodstone, the source of its name, Bloodstone Stronghold. Filigreed stonework displayed the awesome prowess of our stonesmiths, and the defensive openings at one time were invisible to the eye from the outside. But, the outer wall had been pockmarked by blasts from arcane sources and breached by gods only knew what sort of bombardment. Whatever had destroyed the effectiveness of the walls, it most certainly was not cannon fire. Small circular divots pock-marked the walls, and overlapped each other near the shutters that used to allow crossbows to fire out under heavy cover.

The blasted and enlarged holes were covered by the battered shields of our kin, riveted to the wall in a gross patchwork. A smashed wagon was fixed with iron spikes to the threshhold in an attempt to replace the proud carved stone gates. Holes in the wall further up were covered in rawhide, and as soon as I saw it my anger blazed to life. They were the skins of our fallen kin! There was no doubt in me that their desecrated corpses were used as food for the vile creatures of darkness!

Closer examination revealed the blast marks that shattered the fortifications were perfect hollowed out half-spheres, a grim reminder of the zarakanan alliance with the vourdovra, the mind-eaters. The thought of them sent a chill of fearful hatred through me. The vourdovra were abominations that fed upon the minds of the soulsmiths that had escaped the slave-lines. Worse yet, they had taught the filthy zaraks how to defeat the powers of the Kinsmen of Soul, but not their own insidious massed attacks. In my past I had faced them, but never more than three or four at a time, and in that time, a mighty talisman protected me from their assaults of my psyche. A whole city of them, Vouroussan, was to the northeast, and I shuddered at the thought of the fight to come when and if we made it to their stronghold.

The zarakanan had left Balakarak a sad ruin a mere twenty years after my enslavement. Ugarok was the descendant of the orcish high-chieftain who had led his people in the slaughter of the Kinsmen of Soul by the direction of the zaraks and with the aid of the vourdovra. It was his ugly brutish face that appeared over the battlements as the 'gates' loomed before me. Black-oil lanterns flickered on the walls illuminating his dark gray skin, which stood in stark contrast to the red bloodstone of the fortress.

From the walls, the glint of light reflected off many crossbows leveled in our direction, and behind me the engineers loaded the cannons. Must we destroy the remains of such beauty? The need to minimize our casualties outweighed the sadness. Fortifications could be rebuilt, but the lives of my kin could never be replaced, and there were still four more major fortresses to take.

"Ugarok! You have five time cycles to evacuate your tribe!" My shouts echoed through the tunnels, but were only met with laughter.

A nasty toothy grin split the ugly tusked face as Ugarok's brutish eyes narrowed and his ears turned backward like a beast's. Egged on by the derision of his fellows the chieftain made his show. "You dumb to come here, dwarflord! Ugarok tear out liver to feed his many young!"

More grunting howls of orcish laughter spread along the battlements.

"Five time cycles, or you will answer to the heir of Gorain the Slayer! Behold, I carry his mighty weapon, the Reaver!" I held up the weapon as my anger ignited the blades in blue-white fire. "Leave, or be consumed in its flames!"

The luminescent weapon reflected from his yellow eyes that widened as his nostrils flared. The beast disappeared behind the wall and arrows were loosed upon us from the concealed archers. Gurni grunted in pain as he took a bolt in his shield, the point leaking blood from the far side of his arm. The ring of missiles bouncing off my warded armor was deafening, and I felt the sting of their tips as they failed to penetrate. Thank Morakvaar for the smithing techniques that had been passed down from my ancestors!

"Boravrak en!" At my command, the Reaver sent a shower of lightning spinning outward from the flaming arc. It formed a shield of pure energy between the deadly rain of arrows and us, but how I knew to use such powers was beyond me. Once more my will fought for control against the alien presence that surged into my mind from the weapon. A deadly and dangerous presence, Gorain's tortured soul howled in fury as I kept him at bay, but the cost was always a little more of my sanity. How long before I too became a raving madman?

We backed out of range and I stood beside Korvan, commander of the artillery as the shield faded. "I guess we have our answer?" His humor broke through my morbid thoughts.

"Are the cannons ready?"

"They are."

"In five time cycles, we fire them, unless the orcs are foolish enough to attack. If they leave unarmed, let them go."

Korvan's helm dipped, but I was sure I saw disappointment in his eyes as I made my way over to Naiara. The great bear sniffed me suspiciously, as if I would be hiding wounds from her. A sloppy bear tongue lapped goo onto my helmet, not that I minded the bear's affection, but cleaning and polishing my armor was always a chore with her around.

"Kormak, have the senior watch officer report to me, and our people rest, but maintain battle readiness on a moment's notice."

Kormak had been Barelain's younger cousin and an excellent strategist. Though he was Morina's kin, his aloofness and distance assured me he did not approve of our marriage. Not only was I the third son in a dishonored clan, but I thought, acted and spoke far from the standard of my people, a stigma worse than dishonor. At least he did not know much of my past except that I was once apprentice to Dorim Atharil. Would he ever accept my kinship with his cousin, Morina? Would he forgive me those differences once I restored his clan to its rightful place? Only time would bear out the answer to those questions, but they plagued me even in my sleep.

The blaring of a trumpet sounded, dragging me from slumber to a heart-pounding awareness. A dark gray mass of howling fury flowed from the gates! Brandishing ill-kept weapons, they rushed our defenses.

"Fire the cannons!" My order thundered through the cavern as the huge cave bear stole up quietly beside me, sensing the impending carnage.

Naiara flinched as the artillery roared, but remained at my side with eyes intent on her feast of torn bodies. The cannonballs hit with an explosive shower of sparks and shards of stone, flesh and metal shredded through the front ranks of the orcs like a sword through weeds. The rear ranks stopped dead in their tracks, eyes wide and jaws working silently on their ugly gray faces. A hundred years ago, they had not faced such devastation, and the new weapons were the most fearsome magic they could imagine. Howling in terror, they began to run back into the stronghold as fast as their legs could carry them.

"Through the gates before they can close them!" I commanded the regiments forward as I sprinted after our retreating foe.

In a brown streak Naiara passed me and began to plow through the rear ranks of orcs and screams of death filled the air. Her massive paws swept one orc ten feet into the air then caught it in her huge jaws. The sickening crunch of its skull echoed through the cavern as the bottom half of his abdomen and legs dropped to the ground in a slosh of entrails and ichors. With half an orc still in her mouth, she swept her claws right and left as she pounced first on one, and then on another. It was as if she was a giant cat and this was some great game.

But though the orcs could not outrun the bear, they could outrun us and the gates slammed shut before we could reach them. Bolts and arrows rained indiscriminately down from the battlements, ringing off my armor, striking down orcs that had not been quick enough, and stinging the cave bear like biting flies. Naiara roared in fury, and continued to tear the remaining orcs to shreds of red and gray. The iron scent of blood filled the air, but I had been too close to my prey. Power seeped into my sinews from the belt around my waist; arcane energy filled every muscle as I ground my teeth. The fires of the Reaver ignited and swirled around me in a crackling arc. In rage I smote the reinforced wagon that had been bound to the gate expecting it to be a futile gesture of frustration.

The wood and iron exploded away from me in a shower of splinters as I stood and blinked for a moment to realize what had happened. "Forward my kinsmen! The day is ours!" I leapt through the still smoking remains of the wagon and in among my enemies.

The acrid smell of voided bladders filled the air around me as the orcs tore at one another to escape the burning swing of my axe. In mindless fury I pursued them, not realizing how far I outdistanced my kin. The Reaver seduced my mind with its thirst for blood and carnage. Memories of the slaughter of a once thriving culture filled me and I willingly submitted to the weapon's desire. Bodies parted before the blades, scorched and hacked in two, the blood of my enemies covered me and my boots scrabbled for purchase on their entrails. The stench of half-digested food, seared meat, offal and blood mingled in my nostrils. A part of my mind recoiled from the slaughter, knowing that the orcs never stood a chance, but the part of me that was the Reaver delighted in the smell like the perfume of a lover.

The dying scream brought me to some semblance of awareness as my gaze rested upon Ugarok. The chieftain's beady yellow eyes were wide and his nostrils flared as he panted from his open mouth. He yelled something to his two enormous bodyguards and pushed them towards me as he spun on his heels and ran for the old palace as fast as his legs could carry him. The two large orcs trembled as I approached them, and then prostrated themselves before me, howling. The Reaver cared not one whit they were helpless and I could not stop the arc of the blades as it consumed them. The raging soul within the weapon possessed me utterly.

Triumphant insane laughter echoed through the old tunnel-streets as I lighted after Ugarok. The routed warriors ran screaming from me, as the Reaver passed through their midst indiscriminately. Truly Gorain the Slayer returned through my visage, and I was horrified anew at the results. Each life was painfully etched into my memory along with the knowledge that part of me enjoyed the slaughter of the young, the old, the females and infants that fell before me.

Desperately, a band of warriors gathered in front of the palace gates, spears held in trembling hands. An amused smile crossed my face as my axe cleaved the spear points off. I stepped inside the shattered ends of my enemies' weapons intent on their deaths. In wailing voices they pleaded for their lives, but Gorain slew them all without mercy.

A crimson stream ran down the palace steps in a rivulet of forsaken life, as once it had with the blood of the Kinsmen of Soul. The thought rekindled my anger, feeding the rage of the Reaver as I spoke the command word to open the warded gates. How did I know the secrets of Balakarak? The question did not matter to the rage that possessed me. I stepped through the massive stone doors as they swung noiselessly inward, making the crude covered hole the orcs had carved out of one side laughable as a means of defense.

The frightened squeak of the guards behind the gates echoed through the hallowed chamber as they fell over each other to run from the glowing blades of the Reaver. In seconds, the vast hall rang only with a dying grunt and the sound of my iron-shod boots. The once proud carvings of vaarakanan kings had been defaced and defiled by the excrement of my enemies, their stench overpowering. All along the approach to the old throneroom of Balakarak the statues had been desecrated. The layout was so similar to Morakduum I wondered if every kanan palace was roughly the same?

The hall leading to the throneroom was lined with torches; the stargems that once gave spectral light were long gone to scavengers and thieves. Flickering fires accented the red of the stone in an eerie parody of the blood I had spilled. The stench of offal filled the air; the disgusting creatures knew nothing of sanitation. It would take many days of labor to clean the place, but my kinsmen were industrious in their labors.

The doors had long since been reduced to splintered stone, and I could still see the scorch marks of the arcane power used to break them. In my mind's eye I saw the rest of the inhabitants of Balakarak making one last desperate stand against the invaders. But the last stand became a slaughter worse than what I had visited upon the orcs moments ago. More anger rose within me if that were indeed possible. The Reaver's light grew brighter, but instead of terror, I was met with guttural laughter. The unexpected sound stopped me in my tracks and I was able to clear my mind.

The throneroom was empty of the filth of the rest of the palace, large and echoing. The columns still held carved visages of the gods, kings and heroes of our kin, unblemished. The room was twenty heights by thirty. Near the far end were steps leading up to a dais. The dais had been cleared of the thrones that normally would have sat upon it, and had been replaced by a lump of stone that was being used as an altar. Behind it was a crude carving of some unnamable abomination that the orcs worshipped. Beside the altar capered an orc dressed in a cloak made from bones fastened together. The Reaver's rage consumed me once more as I realized the bones were the remains of the former residents of Balakarak, but I forced back the red tide to see just what was happening.

The bone-clad orc was finishing some bizarre ritual, brandishing a knife above his head in one hand, and a heart that still beat in the other as he let the drops of blood fall onto his outstretched tongue. As the third drop entered the foul creature's mouth, I felt the hair on the back of my neck rise. The unmistakable sense of gathering energies filled me with unease. The shaman pointed at me and began to laugh insanely. His eyes started to glow and his body exploded into mist. It swirled into a larger and larger cloud, darkening as it grew. Ugarok backed away; more afraid of the shaman than me.

The echoing laughter deepened to something no mortal could utter, a sound so vile, it burned in my ears. Only the realization that the victim was probably a kinsman who had been their slave kept me from giving in to the overwhelming urge to flee. The blades of the Reaver, grown dull in my sudden apprehension, blazed to life with new fury, illuminating the carved pillars and walls. The fog solidified into a creature that even from the distance towered over me. It had four faces, each a skull like opening of fire, eyes empty and blazing, a hole of a nose and jagged teeth for mouths. Its torso was three sided with four arms and three goat-like legs. Its four dark horns brushed the ceiling of the hall, and its cloven hooves rang against the stone floor as it advanced towards Ugarok. The orc chieftain squawked in fear, but was not fast enough in his retreat. The daemon snatched him up like a rag doll.

"Fool creature! You hope to summon me to slay your enemies, not knowing who I am? I am your master, and I command you to fight for my amusement!" It tossed the orc, rolling him across the floor towards me like a ninepin.

Ugarok rolled to his feet, bruised, dizzy and smelling of his own excrement. He staggered a step or two before seeing how close he stood to me. Eyes wide, he backed a few more steps until he remembered the apparition behind him. Drawing a deep breath to steady his nerve, Ugarok launched himself at me, flailing with his axe as if he had never learned to fight. I backed out of his first attack, my feet instinctively carrying me to the right. His blade whistled by my head with less than two inches to spare, but experience had taught me to judge the end of his arc as surely as I knew my own kill-range.

Ugarok grew bolder when I did not intercept or strike back. With determination he stepped in throwing a more controlled flurry of blows that rang off my blades and the metal reinforcements in the haft of my axe. A quick spring to the left took me beyond his arc once more as the bewildered orc allowed his blade to slam into the floor. Its metallic clang echoed through the throneroom as it sent a shower of small bloodstone shards flying from either side of it. Stepping behind the orc, my eyes met the gaze of the daemon and for a moment the timeless hatred of eternity burned through me. Ten thousand souls had seen damnation at the hands of that creature, and they were paraded before my mind like trophies as it laughed from the gates of hell. Instinct broke the spell of the daemon in time to raise the Reaver to my defense. Ugarok's blade shattered upon the Reaver like glass against stone, but I did not escape unscathed. The metal shards burst into flame, as the arcane energies pent up within were unleashed. The hot metal fragments burned into the skin of my face as they made it past the openings in the front of my helm.

Blinded by the fire and the burning in my eyes, I swung instinctively where Ugarok had been. The power of the swing carried me to the right as I failed to connect with my target, but I had not been far off the mark. The ring of maille connecting with the floor as Ugarok dove out of the way gave me bearing for my next swing. The shock of impact carried up my arms as I felt the blades of the Reaver slice deeply into the body of my foe and catch upon his spine. The orc chief screamed in agony, and by the smell of rotten food and bodily fluids, I gathered I had taken him in the lower gut. With my boot planted in his side, I ripped the Reaver free, as it ground through bone and dragged on entrails. A weaker howl of pain told me that Ugarok would not be striking back. I stepped blindly from him, allowing the Song of the Mother to guide my feet.

A slopping slushy splat right behind me sent a chill through my gut, and I spun swinging the Reaver at whatever had snuck up on me. The impact was as if I hit water, but slightly more solid. Something slimy slid up the haft of the Reaver and seeped into the maille beneath my gauntlets. The touch of it sent a numbing chill through my bones instantly freezing my fingers, and I struggled not to drop the Reaver.

"Sarlik Doria!" The command was more a desperate plea, but immediately, the coldness disappeared as the rage-fire spewed forth.

The waves of flame roaring away from me made patterns of light across my vision, and I caught blurred images of my foes. The relief of my returning sight was short lived as my mind finally grasped the significance of what my eyes were seeing. Row upon row of slimy gray amorphous daemons slid towards me, their black sockets more disturbing than their dripping exteriors. A huge hole had been carved through their ranks by the path of the fire. The seething rage of Gorain's trapped soul entered me from the Reaver, and I surrendered my will to the hatred for our enemies that was so profound. The white-blue flames surrounded me in a warm blanket of fury as I fought the minions of hell.

The appendages of the horrors solidified into icy claws as hard as steel when they met the Reaver, and I backed to keep from being surrounded. Claws shattered in sprays of grayish dust and goo, filling the air with a stench akin to burned sewage. Icy spears penetrated my left cuisses as I spun out from the worst of the blows, but blood ran down my thigh into my boot. The wound was oddly numb from the searing cold, but I had no time to think about it. The fiends closed in, and I was forced back until I felt the hard wall of stone against my backplate. Hundreds of gray points stabbed, slashed and poked at me in an endless tide. Desperately, I wove the Reaver back and forth, smashing claws and severing gray and oozing limbs, jumping over low swipes and ducking under high ones until the wall behind me became crisscrossed with demonic scars.

A claw pierced my left shoulder, sending a shock of cold pain right through my spine and into my brain as if I had chewed on ice from the river, and another slashed my right hip. The floating plates that protected the top of my leg tore free like paper and went flying into what was left of the swarm of creatures. I went down on my knee, momentarily to recover my balance, as I fended off the triumphant attacks. The daemons loomed over me as if gloating, but they made no sound except the slop of slime when they moved.

As the wall of icy claws was about to descend upon me, I invoked the power of the Reaver once more. The rage fires consumed the press of slimy gray creatures in a ball of flame as it spun outward. The smell of burned sewage filled the air, as particles of ash floated lazily to the ground in the wake of the blast. Climbing to my feet, I prepared to sell my life dearly, and fear for my kinsmen filled me. They would never be able to withstand such a demonic horde, but as the ash cleared, only the twisted form that had once been the orc shaman stood before me. The horned daemon shrieked and gnashed its teeth before charging at me.

Fire shot through my injured hip as I pushed away from the wall, but I had no other choice. Fresh blood squished in my boot as I took a step forward leaving a bloody footprint behind. Icy fire shot through my bones, up my spine, and rang in my head like the peal of a funeral bell. If only the Reaver's special powers were not reserved for the zarakanan! Without it the greater daemon was sure to bring me down, for I could barely stand. The creature spread its four arms to keep its balance as fire streamed in traces of light from its nostrils. Its three legs scrabbled across the floor in an odd parody of an insect as its hooves scrambled for traction on the slimy surface. From its mouth came obscenities of sound that screeched in my ears like a knife across a rough plate. As it approached, one hand shot forward. A ball of energy left its palm, and though I tried to dodge it, the bolt struck true. Lightning danced along my armor and through my veins, burning as it went, heating the metal, boiling my blood, and contracting my muscles like a puppeteer.

Agony opened my eyes, and I found myself several paces back and against the wall. A grunt of heartfelt agony escaped my lips as I tried to move. The slight movement I managed brought the charging daemon directly into my line of sight. The Reaver was no longer in my grasp, and my stomach leaped to my mouth. A huge gaping maw opened in one of the creature's faces, descending towards me as if to snap me up whole! Rank upon rank of needle-like teeth filled the beast's mouth all the way back to its throat.

Its toothy jaw snapped shut where I had been, and its fetid breath sent a chill through me as I struggled to regain my feet after the roll. Five paces away, the gleam of the Reaver's blades reflected the torchlight, but the daemon followed my eyes to rest upon the weapon. A grin split its face into a line of interlocked teeth as it stepped back and scooped up the artifact. Lightning arced out from the haft of the Reaver and I closed my eyes. The rage-fires rose around the creature casting stark shadows across my lids as I could hear the irate howl of Gorain's soul in my head. The hellspawn's own screams of agony split my eardrums, sending me to the floor holding my head to keep it from exploding. The creature thrashed and desperately tried to drop the weapon, but the Reaver would not be satisfied until it had paid the price for its sacrilege.

The hideous form of the monster dissolved into mist, and fled through the gateway it had opened. The rent in our world disappeared with the daemon, and the dead shaman was left holding the Reaver as he lie on the floor a smoking corpse. It took some doing to maintain my balance while I pried the axe loose from the dead orc's hand. The howls of the daemon still rang in my ears, and for a moment, I feared it would remain so for the rest of my life. Not even the sound of my vaarandril-shod boots made it through the cacophony that still buzzed in my head. The pain of navigating the stairs was excruciating, but no more so than the agony of my soul when I viewed what lie upon the stone atop the dais.

For a moment, I had to fight the bile that threatened to surge up my throat. The vile ceremony had been as brutal as I had feared, and to make matters worse, the victim had been a kinswoman. Iron spikes had been driven through her hands and feet into the stone and it took a great effort to wrest them free. With that done, I laid her mutilated arms over the open spread of ribs that had been her chest. By the time I had pulled the blanket from my pack and laid it over her body, Kormak burst into the chamber with a handful of my royal guard. Solemnly, he approached a troubled frown beneath his amber moustache.

"Majesty, it is good to find you whole. When we heard the roaring screech, we feared the worst!" He bowed and looked questioningly at the lump beneath the blanket.

"A kinswoman. I do not recognize what is left of her face, but I believe she is of your clan." Kormak immediately reached for the cover, but I intercepted his hand. "The orcs were not kind to her, Kormak. Even I nearly retched at the sight."

His teeth ground together as he continued to reach for the blanket. There was nothing else to do, and I limped back down the dais' stairs to join the guards. Kormak's choking heaves did not stifle his wail of despair. The sound of his anguish echoed through the throneroom followed by a stream of curses to all orcs and their allies. The sobs continued when he came back down the steps, and there was murder in his eyes written in the traces of tears down his cheeks, as it was written in my heart.

"She was my mother." The simple whispered statement carried the weight of unquenchable hatred.

"We will kill every male, female and whelp." I commanded, and Kormak smiled in grim agreement as we set forth to do just that, rage giving me the strength to ignore my wounds.

Through the home-tunnels of Balakarak, we hunted the orcs as they fled from us. A company of our warriors blocked the gates against the escape of our enemies while the rest were rounded up and slain. By the end of the fourth time cycle since we reached the gates, Balakarak was purged of living orcs. Waradain and his acolytes tended to the unfortunate kinswoman and the defilement of the throneroom, re-consecrating it to the service of Morakvaar. The bodies of ten of my kinsmen were brought in to the royal chamber and laid out with honors next to the kinswoman. Waradain had tried to persuade me to allow him to see to my wounds prior to the Ritual of Mourning, but I had refused, letting the pain remind me of the aching of our lost kin.

As the throneroom filled with the clans of those who had died, I started the ritual. The name of each was spoken while a member of their clan came forward to count their deeds. Garon scribed their names in the Book of Ancestors while Waradain said a blessing for each one. Behind him, though none but I could see him, strode the Maker, gathering their souls to take them to the Underhalls. He greeted them one by one and the sight of them leaving tore at my soul. It was a crushing reminder that I would never again know the joy of sharing a hearth with my beloved Morina. When the mourning was complete, the families of the dead came to bear them off where they would rejoin the Blood of the Mother.

Waradain shook his finger in my face. "Next time, I will have your own generals hold you down when I ask to examine your injuries!"

My face flushed as I decided not to bring up my status as High King. Meekly I limped behind him into the room behind the dais for a bit more privacy as I shed my armor and gambeson. Waradain put his two fingers to his lips as his brow furrowed. His silver eyes narrowed thoughtfully as he dug in his pouch.

"Eat that." He handed me a dried mushroom whose smell told me that it was not fit for consumption.

Had I not trusted Marak's father with my life, I would never have eaten it, but the old priest knew his business well. I chewed only enough to break the fungus into chunks I could swallow for the acidic taste was foul indeed! Waradain stopped me from lifting my skin of ale to wash it down.

"Do not be a fool, Dorian. Ale will put you in the Underhalls." He handed me his skin of water, and I shrugged, wishing for something that would wipe the taste from my mouth.

The warmth of a healing spell flooded through the dull agony that began to recede into a hazy mist. The old priest looked silly as his brows worked in time with his hands. Had I any sense left, I would have realized that my good humor was not natural. At least the scrubbing of the wounds was more funny than painful. After stitching up the deep scoring of my thigh like a pair of britches, he worked on my shoulder and calf. When he was finished, Waradain left to tend others as one of his acolytes applied a salve and bandages. Realizing the effect of the mushroom was more detrimental to my state of mind than I had initially thought, I concentrated on fighting its effects. By the time the lad had finished tying the last bandage, the throbbing ache had returned. The lad then handed me a potion that would ease the pain, but warned me not to drink it for another two time cycles.

The cold blood soaked in to my gambeson and stuck to my skin, but I did not have anything else suitable to wear under my armor at the moment. The punctures and tears in my maille would be near impossible to fix without unsightly seams and rivets. Sadly I donned the tattered remains of what had taken me two years and many sacred chants to forge.

The door from the office chamber to the throneroom was a rotting skin which I ripped from the hole as I passed, speaking the command word to close the warded stone door. The Reaver hung innocently from my left hand, and I shuddered, feeling the chill run through me once more. My memories and thoughts became more and more inseparable from those of Gorain's tormented soul trapped within. The coldness crept over my scalp as I remembered it had started long before I knew the Reaver still existed, back to the time I lived on the surface of the world.

Kormak saw me close the stone door with a word and looked at me, the question plain on his face. How did I know the words? But I was not ready to answer his unspoken query so gazed upon the faces of my generals and commanders instead. Each of their eyes gleamed with the light of victory, from the darkest green to the palest silver, so different from the brown and black of our surface cousins. I smiled, allowing the heat of our triumph to fill me.

"Kormak Stoneshaper, your clan ruled here long before our enemies came. As oldest eligible kinsman of Clan Tenedain, I charge you to take up where your family's banners had fallen. I name you King and Patriarch of Balakarak, though you will owe your allegiance to Morakduum's High King. Balakarak will remain a sovereign nation in its own right, but never again will we shun the need of our kinsmen. Let it be written in the annals of Balakarak that her clans have returned home!" A great cheer went up amongst those gathered, and Kormak knelt before me.

Tears of joy ran down his cheeks as he lifted his face to mine. "To think that I have lived to see this day!" He stood up and addressed those gathered. "All hail High King Dorian, Liberator of Balakarak!"

The gathering roared approval, and I felt as if my heart would burst with pride and sorrow. There was such a long road left to travel, and ten deaths were only the beginning. Several kinsmen had located the old bloodstone throne carved with the arms, backrest and sides as winged hammers of the soulsmiths and dragged it back to the dais using the resonators to lift it in to place. I gestured for Kormak to take the throne, and his eyes darted uncertainly to it, then to me. He went slowly as if expecting to wake up at any moment. At last he sat upon it and another cheer rang through the large hall. Someone found an old cask of Balakarak's brew the orcs had not opened and the gathering instantly dissolved into a victory celebration.

In the joy and revelry, I slipped out, the heaviness of my sins too great to bear in light of the mood. My conscience ached more vexingly than my wounds as I watched the young, old and helpless hewn down by my own hand. Even though they were merely orcs, a cruel and vicious race, there were still those who were unable to fight back. When had I become such a ruthless killer? My own joy in the slaughter made me nauseous, as I looked at the Reaver. What had I become? Had Gorain the Slayer truly returned? Would I be as merciless and destructive as he had become? Who was really the enemy?

I wanted to throw the axe from me, be rid of its vile influence, but I needed it to save my people. The spirits of the dead haunted me, now that I could see them, they tormented me with cries for recognition from their dark gods, but the power of the Reaver would not let them rest in peace. The nausea became intolerable as I reflected on the vile acts I had committed that day, and my gut emptied itself of its juices. Would my end be as hideously tormented as Gorain's?

Instinct warned me I was not alone on the battlements, and when I turned, Korina was there. My gaze found other places to rest besides on her.

"When you said you would not be returning to Morakduum, what did you mean?"

Her innocent question was a spear through my chest, and I knew I could not keep such knowledge from her any longer. "Morakvaar has called me. He told me that I would never return to my hearth. I know not if this means I will die when this is done, or that I will leave and never return. Perhaps Gorain's fate will be my own? I do not think I could live without your mother." The words stopped, and no more came to my mind.

Accidentally, I met Korina's eyes that glistened in the lamplight, but she held her emotions well. "If I could take your place, I would." My ears strained to hear her choked words as her hand rested on my good shoulder.

"No, Korina." I shook my head, placing my hand over hers. "You must see to the future. You are my heir, and will soon be High Queen of Morakduum and all of the Halls of the Mother. You and Dorak are my immortality. As long as you, your brother, and your children live and thrive and bear their children, I will live on. You must keep our clan alive and keep the cause alive. Rule wisely and compassionately, and keep our people safe and free. I will pay for my sins, for they are mine alone."

Korina nodded, unable to trust her voice as I continued in a whisper. "Tell your mother that I love her more than anything."

A stubborn line appeared across her chin above her beard, but she nodded. "I will, but now you need to eat, father. I brought some food from the storeroom. You will need your strength for the next stage of our campaign."

The spell of despair broke with my snort of amusement. "Truly you are your mother's daughter. Very well then, share this meager repast with me."

Not only had Korina brought food, but also she brought a blanket that she spread out on the ramparts where we could look out over the gates. We ate in silence for a few moments, looking into the familiar darkness of the Halls of the Mother. The lanterns made it impossible to see very far, so I snuffed them, and we enjoyed the multi-hued patterns of heat and vibration for almost a cyclare. Stalagmites and stalactites broke up the patterns with their random disbursement like dark jagged teeth. The beauty of it sent warmth through me, until I remembered the pact with Morakvaar.

Korina washed down a mouthful of food with some ale. "Tell me about the surface world, father?"

Could she ask some easier question? The request brought back my anguish over having to kill Liathrain, and I wondered what had happened to the rest of my companions. Had they all made it safely back to their homes?

"There are wonders, but none compare with our homelands. The beauty of the living stones is unparalleled, and they yield up their bounty of gems and vaarandril to us." At the stubborn set of her jaw, I gave in. "On the surface, there is the sun that shines for half a day. Its heat burns in their summers, but gives no warmth in the winter. Its light is so great that it would blind you to look at it, and even being out in it burns the eyes. The other half of the day is what they call 'night'. The sun leaves the land, but it is not dark like the Shallow Lands, but more like the warm radiance of the living stones. The ceiling they call the 'sky' is vast and black at night, and is filled with tiny points of light that gleam in the darkness like stargems. They pulse with a life of their own, and guide weary travelers home, for they are constant and rotate about the world in relation to the sun."

Korina sighed, and her gaze lost focus as she chewed on a hard crust of bread and drank from her mug of ale.

"It is a wondrous time when the day turns to night, and the night turns to day. It is called 'dusk' and 'dawn'. It is at these times that the light of the sun paints the skies with many hues of reds, gold, purples, blues and black. If there are clouds, it lines them with a shimmering silver that rivals kanan worked vaarandril."

Korina looked at me sideways, her brow drawn down slightly. "What are clouds, father?"

I blinked. How could I explain clouds? "They are like wisps of vrakka wool that live in the sky, only they are full of surprises. At times, water pours from them like a small waterfall, only very slowly and spread over a vast area. On occasion, clouds make lightning and thunder, very much like the spells of the zarakanan. It is as loud and terrifying as the explosive powders our engineers make to open new tunnels and fuel our cannons."

Between munching strips of bland, dried meats, and drinking ale Korina managed to find, I continued to weave a picture of the things I had seen. A faint smile twitched at the corners of her lips as she listened, enraptured by the things she would never see. I only hoped the descriptions would be enough for her, as she would be unable to visit the surface once we had sealed the Starrift.

As I spoke of those things, I waxed nostalgic for those times I spent with my companions, righting the wrongs of their world. I thought of Lodath, the young mage who had saved me from the slavers, my dearest friend and rival. A wince of shame and longing hit me as I remembered the object of our rivalry, the tall dark-skinned priestess, Jaguar. The memory of my time with her, raising our daughter, Panther, floated before me like a dream of another life, and I lapsed into silence.

"What is it?" Korina's innocence mocked me.

"Nothing you need worry about." My voice was gruff, but the knowledge of my deep shame put me out of sorts.

With the curiosity of a child, Korina would not let the matter rest. "You are hiding something. Something that shames you, I can tell." Perhaps she was not so naive?

How could she know of such things? I clenched my jaw shut and looked away, not daring to give her any more clues. How could she understand my desire for a human? She had been raised to our values, our code of honor, and a code I had broken. The memory of the times I spent with Jaguar still affected me as if it had been yesterday, the desire still as strong. I swallowed as a chill of apprehension ran down my spine. If Korina noticed, how could I deny telling her? Her senses were uncanny.

"You knew someone on the surface, did you not? A woman who was not my mother?" My apprehension grew, and rather than confess my terrible dishonor, I got up and walked away along the battlements. Korina followed after me. "Did you know her before, or after? Was she kin?"

The heat of my anger was sudden and bright as I rounded on her. "It does not concern you! Leave me be, child!"

Her eyes blazed with her own anger. "How can you confess your love of my mother while you harbor this from us?" Her voice rose in pitch and intensity. "Does she know?"

I clenched my jaw, not realizing I had grasped the haft of the Reaver as I answered her. "She knows, and it is not your concern!"

Korina's eyes grew cold as they rested on my hand that held my weapon. "Would you slay your own? Does this surface woman mean that much to you? Is that why you will not return to Morakduum?"

The words were like a bucket of water on the fires of my anger, and I released the weapon. Had I actually begun to draw it from its straps? In a quieter voice, I replied. "No, to all of your questions. Please let me be. What has passed was gone ere I married your mother. It matters not."

"But it still matters to you! I ask again, and I wish a truthful answer. Is she why you will not return to Morakduum?" Her eyes were half accusing and half pleading.

I let out a long torturous breath, my drained anger leaving me in partial despair. "No. She was human and is probably long dead. Humans rarely live beyond fifty season cycles, and she was near twenty when we met. We were together for fifteen years, and it has been near eighty since we parted ways." I did not want to mention Jaguar's daughter to her, knowing what her reaction would be.

I had expected her derision, but instead of scorn, she asked curiously, "what was she like?"

I stared a few moments, feeling the sting of the question as much as the surprise. "Why does it matter to you?"

Warmth spread across her features as she touched my hand. "Because it mattered to you, father."

I chuckled grimly. "I kept a journal, a record of my travels, my thoughts, my heroic and even my shameful deeds upon the surface world. I still keep one, for it helps keep me sane in an insane world. I will leave you my record of the surface world when I depart our homelands."

"Your journal?"

"Yes, what you wish to know is recorded within its pages."

"And, where is this book, father?" The hungry look on her face told me that I could, under no circumstances, divulge that information.

"When it is time, it will be in your hands." Her gaze became distant, and I could almost smell the plotting. I would have to be very careful of any future use of my journal.

The weariness of the battle and my wounds weighed heavily upon me, and I excused myself from her presence. Kormak had insisted that I take the King's chamber, but I had refused. It was his right to be there, not mine. I was more than happy with one of the newly cleaned guestrooms reserved for visiting dignitaries. Within the chamber, I eased out of my armor and sticky gambeson. Taking the clothing and myself down to the bathing chamber, I clenched my teeth as the water stung in the wounds.

Black-oil torches lit the chamber, and the flaws in the red bloodstone made eerie patterns in their flickering light. The basin of water that was fed from the river was warmed by a controlled flow of magma, just close enough to give it the right temperature as I released it with the control lever. It flowed through the crystal powder and charcoal filters before coming out of the spout. The water turned red as it ran from me to the drain in the floor where it emptied back into the magma flow that had warmed it. The steam would be used to drive the pumps that refilled the reservoir. The filtered spout overhead was designed to disperse the water in a wide enough stream to wash in without too much difficulty, but I was content just to let the warm water splash over me, soothing my aching muscles. Blood rinsed out of the gambeson and I used some of the ash and oil soap for the more stubborn stains. When the soap touched the stitched up wounds, though, I could not help the tears that came to my eyes. I cursed the demons anew for their part in my misery, but in truth, I was glad to be alive.

After drying off, I used some of the antiseptic salve that Waradain had given me, drank the pain killing potion and put some fresh bandages over the wounds. Bone weary, I made my way back to the guest chamber, crawled into the bed and was almost instantly asleep. My dreams wandered through the events leading up to my rediscovery of the Reaver in Terazandarin.

***

I stood in the courtyard just inside the gates of Tarazandaran, trapped between the weapons of our enemy and the magma released too soon by the treachery of the Vaetra. The defenders were barricaded behind stalagmites, wagons, barrels, and crenellations on the inner wall, unreachable as they fired a rain of death upon us. In a hail of arrow and spells, my kinsmen were slaughtered around me. In desperation, I led them in what would be our last charge, but instead of death, we broke through their line and fought a running battle through the streets. We made the old palace gates and barricaded ourselves in. Profane runes and seals had been scribed on the walls, floors and ceilings, and we realized they had converted the ancient stronghold into a home for their blasphemous religious practices. Creatures born of shadow ambushed us, striking with claws of smoke and weapons of pain. They drove us towards the inner sanctum, believing the priestesses would delight in fresh victims. But, as soon as I entered the chamber I felt the presence of the Reaver. It called to me as a voice in the darkness.

"Blood of my blood, at last you have come to me! Call our kinsmen to arms and surely our enemies will be defeated!" The rage within the weapon was echoed in my soul as my kin were being cut down around me.

Suspended between the outstretched hands of a foul stone image of a half spider goddess the Reaver constantly spit out forks of lightning and flame at the effigy. Its rage was contained in a reddish ball of energy that seemed to feed off the power from the weapon, though the axe's fury never ceased.

The promise of revenge appealed to me more than the promise of life as the somehow familiar spirit entered me from the axe. My anger at the betrayal of our allies and the slaughter of my kin, mingled with the pent up rage of a being that had been trapped in the weapon for eight thousand years and held by the enemy all that time. Only vaguely did I wonder that the zarakanan did not destroy the Reaver, for they must have known that it would someday be their doom. The ancient weapon came to life in a blaze of blue-white fire, smote the red shield in a massive burst of power and shot across the chamber to my outstretched hand, blazing a trail through our enemies. In confused horror, the priestesses lost their sense of unity. They fought each other to escape the burning vengeance of the Reaver. So great was my desire for blood that I slaughtered them all despite their pleas of mercy. The rage never left me as we burst forth from the temple, slaying all that stood against us, for my kin were as possessed as I. It was as if Gorain's rage had spread to all that were left.

Against the odds, we triumphed, five hundred against thousands, as our remaining priests shielded us from the zarakanan spells. In our fury, we hunted them down to the last infants, sparing none, most of them slain by my own hand. When at last the Reaver sensed no more of our enemies, it released me from the madness, and I fell to my knees in grief and horror at what I had done. Even though I had saved the lives of five hundred of my kin, what price had I paid? I returned with the Reaver to Barakillanak, where the rest of the refugees from Balakarak and Morkilduum had fled.

When I learned of the extent of the Vaetra's treachery and recounted the dead to Karakdain, Liege King of Barakillanak, my heart was hardened and I swore an oath of vengeance as I handed over the Reaver. But, the weapon refused the touch of the Liege King, scorching him with its fire. Embarrassed, I placed the axe in a harness and hung it on the wall so that the priests and sages could examine it, but the Reaver never left my mind.

Dorim Atharil, former Patriarch of Morkilduum, barely registered in my mind that late sleep-cycle in which I found myself in the King's council chamber. The guards had not challenged me, as if I was invisible to them. My eyes and my mind were firmly focused on the weapon that hung upon the wall behind the Liege King. Words formed in my mouth, though I did not know where they came from, and I barely understood what they meant.

"Dozarak kilna loch krazak sion." The half-moon blades of the two handed axe began to glow with an unearthly fire.

Both sovereigns stared at me as if I had appeared from thin air. With a dreamlike quality, the weapon burned through the harness, and flew to my outstretched hand. The warmth of it spread through me, filling me with its fire, fury and desire for the blood of our zarakanan enemies. Again the words came loudly and firmly from the depths of my throat, yet from another mind.

"Dozarak kilna loch krazak sion!" The rage pumped through my veins in the fire of my blood. 'Death to all the spawn of evil!'

Such was the power of my fury and the spell of the weapon that soon all in the room chanted with me.

"Dozarak kilna loch krazak sion!"

Waradain had been there, and the high priest recognized the words of the ancient tongue. With wide eyes he whispered a name, 'Gorain'. A sad smile spread across his face as he realized what was happening. When the chant died down, he addressed the assembled nobles that had come to the war council.

"It is the prophecy, Gorain the Slayer has returned to us with his weapon. A new age has begun; an age of war, but the prophecy says that it will end in a new golden age. So it was written eight thousand years ago in the temple of Morakvaar."

That which was still a part of me was appalled. How could I be such a dangerous madman as Gorain? But that part of me was not in control, and I lapsed into sadness as the words came from the other mind.

"Yes. For eight thousand years I have waited to be returned to our people, to be reborn. Now is the time that we will purge our lands once and for all. We must unite the clans in war against our enemies and in so doing, bring about the new age." I refused to believe the words were coming from my mouth.

The presence left me and retreated back into the weapon I held, leaving me stunned and confused. I barely remembered entering the throne room, yet there I stood, in front of King Karakdain. I swallowed my stomach acids back down as every noble in the room dropped to one knee and swore fealty to me, including the Patriarch and the Liege King. I knew I had to say something, so I trusted my instincts.

"Rise my kinsmen and arm yourselves! We will be victims no longer! From this day forth, we will drive the races of darkness from our homelands! We will kill all those who are not of our blood! The Deeps will again belong to us as they did in the beginning! Let messengers be sent to all our settlements, all our kinsmen, Gorain's heir calls them to arms and prophecy will be fulfilled!"

***

Chapter 5

Torvalan (Reunion)

A curious popping sound awakened me from the deep sleep. The room about me was dark and the veins of steam from the heating ducts made warm red glowing lines along the inner walls. The sound of someone's breath was behind me, and my hand reached out slowly to where the Reaver leaned against the wall. I tensed, ready to both roll off the bed and defend myself, or spring to the attack. For several moments, I waited for the person to come within striking range as I gripped the axe tightly.

"You would kill me too?" The familiarity of the voice sent odd warmth through me, and I could not help the grin that turned up the corners of my mouth.

"Lodath?" I rolled over; the Reaver still clutched in my hands as I climbed out of the bed.

"Well, if you had some bloody light in here, you could tell!" His humor had not improved with age.

"Of course, my friend. Give me a moment, and I will light a candle." It took only a couple seconds to find my tinderbox. "What brings you to the Mother's Halls?" I struck the flint, igniting the tinder and taking a small piece to light the candle on the table in the center of my room.

"I have heard some disturbing rumors, Dorian. Rumors I would not like to believe." He sounded as aged as he looked.

His gray hair had grown long, but was carefully kept clean and combed. Bright orange eyes regarded me from behind a maze of crags and furrowed brows. Once youthful full cheeks had been sunken with the years and he looked more like a vulture than the humorous youth I had known. The signs of the short human life span brought a pang to my heart, knowing that his sorcery kept him alive. It was a bitter reminder that Jaguar was probably no more.

"What sort of rumors?" I asked, trying not to commit to any confirmation.

For a moment, we stared at each other, a match of wills as Lodath finally decided that I might give something away with more information. "They say there is trouble in these Realms. I have heard that the underground elves, er, zarakanan are massing an army of tremendous proportions. King Osric was worried that they were going to invade from below, and so he sent me to investigate."

He had not told me all he knew. "And?"

With a wan smile he continued, "I have since learned that they intend to oppose you, Dorian."

We both sat at the table, regarding each other like fencers before a match. "I suspected as much." I admitted, as I leaned the Reaver against the table close to my hand.

The gesture was not lost on Lodath and he regarded the weapon for a long moment. "Do you think I have come here to kill you?" His gaze met mine.

I clenched my teeth and said carefully, "it would not be the first time one of my friends has turned against me." There was another long moment of silence between us as Lodath considered his words.

"Then one of the rumors is true, you did kill Liathrain." He looked down at the table, a frown upon his face, and reflected in his demeanor.

I waited until he looked at me once more. "More accurately, she came to assassinate me." When I was sure I had his attention, I traced the outline of the scar across my neck for him.

Real surprise registered in his eyes as well as amazement and he whistled low. "And you survived that?"

I looked away, reminded again of the Maker's pact. "Not exactly." I confessed, but looked back, knowing he had an idea what had occurred. "Have you come here as a friend or foe?" The direct approach was always best.

"My you have gotten testy in your old age, Dorian! You know I have always been your friend, but rumor has it that you have gone mad."

The fingers of my left hand still rested upon the haft of the Reaver. "If saving my people is madness, then it is true."

"The zarakanan will oppose you, Dorian, you know that. They have gathered a great army of orcs, goblins, dark dwarves and other creatures who fear you more than the zaraks." Abruptly he chuckled. "How does it feel to be the terror of the Deeps?"

I grinned back. "Lonely."

The laughter between us was strained and insincere.

"Even the gollarans are afraid of you. You have no allies in this war, Dorian. Yet the whole of the Mother's Realms align themselves against you."

"We have no quarrel with the gollarans, but if they refuse to leave, we will force them to. We will not suffer their presence in our ancient home any longer."

Lodath shook his head. "They were right. You are mad! How can you expect to win this war?"

My people were a dying race; our last gasps were being made as our children were taken from us by the ravages of our enemies. How could I get him to understand? "We must! There is no choice for us! Either we die now in battle, or we fade from this world in a generation or two! The result is the same, but if we win, we can survive! We will win our right to continue as a race, and we will thrive again!" Lodath sat back in his chair with a distant look.

"And you think this is the only way?"

"It *IS* the only way!" My fist on the table nearly put out the candle as I emphasized my point. "Our history is written in the blood of my people, and each lesson learned cries out not to trust other races. The Vaetra have betrayed us, raided our settlements, killed and enslaved our kin, despoiled our lands and fouled our waters. Do you expect such offenses to go unanswered? Even the gollarans have been at war with us in the past. There are so few of us left, that to stand idly by is to surrender to extinction. There are fewer and fewer born to each generation, and more and more of my people die in the senseless attacks of our enemies. We are diminishing through attrition! The only way to save our people is to ensure that there will be no more war!"

Lodath's brow straightened into a stubborn line. "So, you would lead the rest of your people to their deaths in a war you cannot possibly win? You would ensure your people die sooner rather than later?"

My heart felt the sting of yet another betrayal, and my voice grew cold. "Why have you come here, Lodath?" My fingers tightened on the Reaver's haft.

Seeing my hostility, he sighed. "To warn you. The zarakanan have over two hundred thousands in their army, and they mean to see you dead, Dorian."

I looked deeply into his eyes, trying to sense deception or animosity, but found none. How could we defeat that many? In all of the Deeps there were fewer than a hundred thousand kinsmen and kinswomen, and many of them not fit to carry weapons. For the first time, I doubted our victory and my soul began to despair.

"So many?" Was I really leading our people to their doom?

Lodath slowly nodded, looking from the Reaver to where I got up to pace by the window. "I hear they have called some sort of creature, perhaps a daemon champion who knows your name. I also hear that they offer a substantial reward for proof of your death. There is no way you can win without allies, Dorian."

I turned to face the mage once more, had he come to take proof of my demise to the zarakanan? The Reaver was far enough from my grasp that Lodath could slay me with a spell before I could reach it, or even call it to my hand. The same thought was reflected in the human's gaze and for a moment I wondered if that were not his intent.

"What allies would you suggest?" If he wanted me dead, there was nothing I could do.

Instead a slow smile spread across his face, accenting the crow's feet at the corners of his orange eyes that twinkled in amusement. "King Saveyo, for one, and King Osric."

He leaned back in his chair and took out his pipe; filling it as he listened to the tirade he knew would come.

"Gollarans and humans! This is our war, Lodath, our survival! Why would they risk themselves for us when we have never been on good terms in the past?" The audacity of the suggestion amazed me.

"For the humans, it should seem obvious. The rumor of your wealth is legendary, Dorian. The few goods that have made it to the surface from your people have astounded even the best crafters among the surface dwarves. King Osric is a shrewd businessman, and would bargain with you. He is also concerned about the zarak army." Upon seeing my frown, he decided to cover the other arrangement. "King Saveyo fears you and your army. He would also bargain, aid for an oath of non-aggression and free trade."

I sighed in relief more that my old friend was not there to kill me than of any hope of aid. "And what would this aid cost us? How many troops could we expect and when?"

Lodath lit his pipe with a small wooden stick he had put into the candle's flame. He puffed for a few moments, sending swirls of gray-black smoke curling away from him before blowing out the stick. He chewed his lower lip, knowing I was not going to like the terms of the bargain.

"You know that the gollarans are not a war-like people. Their total army is only ten thousand, but they do know how to guard against the arcane arts. In return for their aid, they want an oath of non-aggression and a map drawn up concerning their boarders."

Ten thousand against two hundred thousand? The idea was as ridiculous as it sounded! Even if it were an army of wizards and powerful priests, what good would they do? I resumed my pacing, thinking carefully. There were mages amongst the zarakanan that were powerful enough to overwhelm our priests and our wards. Having a few gollaran high-mages would come in handy, but were they worth it? I looked speculatively at Lodath, wondering if there was anything I could say to persuade him to join the battle on our side. Of all the students of the arcane, Lodath was undoubtedly the most powerful I had ever known.

"The tunnels of the gollarans run parallel to ours. I see no reason why we cannot seal them as well, but I will not have it where they can make war on us in the future. What of the humans?"

Lodath winced, a sure sign I was not going to like what he had to say. "They want twenty thousand in gold weights, a hundred dwarven forged suits of vaarandril plate that will fit humans, and ten thousand vaarandril longswords." He paused when he saw the tightening of my jaw and my face flush with anger, but went on in a rush. "They will provide sixty thousand troops to attack the zaraks from the rear."

I spat the words out as if they would melt Osric with their venom. "And what guarantee do we have that they will not betray us? How do we know the troops will be there when we need them?" My voice turned to a snarl of scorn. "For what he asks, Osric should be sending an army of over three hundred thousand. Sixty is not nearly enough. I am no fool, Lodath."

His face flushed with his embarrassment. "No, Dorian, I know that. King Osric believes that most of the zarakanan army is rabble with no training. Orcs, goblins, troglodytes, and others that really do not work well together make up the bulk of their numbers. What I have seen myself confirms this. When his forces hit them from behind, it is more than likely they will break and run." His enthusiasm for his plan left out one vital detail.

"So they run towards us, splendid." I growled. "King Osric believes that a hundred and twenty thousand is enough to defeat two hundred? I am glad they recognized the fighting strength of my people, but do you not think they are overestimating us?"

Lodath's brows shot up, and he leaned back taking in a deep breath. "You only have fifty thousand? We had heard you had a greater number, near twice that."

Inwardly I cursed my loose tongue and hoped I would not have to kill another old friend. The chair at the table took my weight and my hand rested where I could easily reach the Reaver. The more I thought about our situation, the more hopeless it appeared. What could I do? If Lodath's numbers were correct, we could never defeat the zarakanan. The Reaver might protect me long enough to see the last one fall, but what happened after that? There were still the Kinsmen of Shadow and the vourdovra to deal with. One quick incursion from either of their forces and my people would be no more. If I could have retreated back to Morakduum, I would have, but against a force that size, retreat was not an option.

What if I snuck in to Fartairilzzan myself? Once I was among the zarakanan, the Reaver's power would ensure I lived to see them all die, but could I make it there alone? What would happen if I were separated from the Reaver before I made it to the stronghold? Was there some sort of magic they could use to negate the powers of the Reaver? If both the Reaver and I were lost to my people, what would happen then? Had I unwittingly led my people to their doom? What choice was there really? If I did not trust Lodath and his promise of allies, we would surely perish. Fate had sealed my options never offering me choices that were of any merit.

I put my head in my hands. Was it my fault we had come to this impasse? "If only I had not gathered the clans. If only the Reaver would have remained lost to us, perhaps we would have survived a little longer." My mournful words drew sympathy from the mage as if he understood what it meant to doom an entire race by his actions.

"I will see if King Osric can spare more men."

"We will need more than extra soldiers. It will take a tactical miracle to defeat such a force." I sighed, but already my mind was racing ahead to the possibilities.

Lodath broke into a grin. "I remember the surprise attack of the zaraks on the Farovan stronghold. You certainly pulled out a miracle then, Dorian. I have faith that you could do so again."

I returned his grin, the incident clear in my mind. "It was fortunate the zarakanan had no idea what an avalanche of snow could do. That and the diverted river won us the day, but I do not foresee such advantages here." Just in case he was not aware, I ran through our disadvantages aloud. "The zarakanan know of our cannons and have an intricate web of detection against subversives. Our sappers have been frustrated by their uncanny ability to track us. Diverting a magma flow in that area would be more dangerous to us than to them, for they will hold the high ground, and flooding the tunnels is bad for the same reasons. The only thing I can hope they are unprepared for is possible allies and a divided front." I fixed Lodath with a stare he could not escape. "Your sources seem well placed. Would they care to reveal to us the fullness of their knowledge?" He pursed his lips and nodded, but I was not finished. "How well do you know this surface king, and how trustworthy is he?"

"As trustworthy as a human can be." Lodath realized his poor choice of words at my instant snarl.

"That is of little comfort to me. I have seen how well humans keep their word." Lodath frowned and looked to the table at my harshness.

"If you pay him his price, you can trust King Osric to keep his word." He did not meet my gaze.

"I do not know who to trust any more. Lodath, you have always been a friend to me, but this is not just between us. I risk the whole of my people in this. If Osric betrays our trust, we may very well die to the last one of us. Our entire race could be wiped out in a single stroke, for our homes would be vulnerable against such a massive army. Though I have no doubt that Morakduum will frustrate their efforts for a couple of generations, but our people will never recover. Eventually, attrition will claim us all. Is your belief in Osric worth that risk? Is it worth the cost of an entire race?"

At last he met my gaze, though his face was troubled and his shoulders stooped as if from a great weight. Did I look the same? "I understand, Dorian. If there was any guarantee I could offer, I would, but what is the worth of the last remnants of an entire race?"

"Much more than the ransom of a hundred kings that Osric asks for." How could he understand how much I weighed the lives of my people over wealth? "Our very survival could depend upon his aid, but I am afraid there is nothing to guarantee his help."

For the first time, Lodath looked startled. "Are you saying you will not meet his price?"

I sighed. "I will meet his price if he meets mine. I need at least a hundred thousand troops, and I do not care where he gets them as long as they look impressive. The bulk of them can be pig farmers, and stay in the rear ranks, but they must look from a distance like regular troops. In addition to his price, I will provide him with five balakanan forged cannons and enough powder to level Fartairilzzan from the Starrift, but he will have to supply the shot." Lodath's brows shot up and his mouth formed a little 'o'.

"Cannons? What in the name of the gods is a cannon?" I think he suspected, but I indulged him anyway.

I smiled, proud of the engineering skills of my people. "The biggest fireball launcher you have ever seen, and a hundred times more devastating."

"You would give this war-machine technology to Osric?"

"It is a far cry from owning a cannon to manufacturing one. Mixing the powder for it is nothing short of volatile. Those who make the explosive powders must do so in a facility far from any home tunnels. Even the most carefully controlled situations can turn to disaster. I doubt that Osric will learn the secret too quickly."

Lodath smiled grimly. "I am sure Osric will agree to your terms. He is sending a representative to Gormarath since we must journey there to treat with King Saveyo, and the trade route the gollarans have does not pass through enemy territory." Lodath stretched, and the candlelight illuminated the dark circles under his eyes as he yawned.

When had he aged so much more than I had? "Spend the rest of the night here. I will go and roust King Kormak and the rest of my generals. There are many preparations to be made if I am to go off on this fool's mission. These trade tunnels must be sealed and the fortifications rebuilt in case the zarakanan attempt to march on us instead of waiting patiently. I believe we could have the plans in place and be ready to leave by the second time cycle."

"Time cycle?"

I remembered my own confusion over the way humans kept time. "Around eleven of the o'clock, your time."

He nodded and yawned again. "And what time is it now?"

"Nine point six five." His brow furrowed and I laughed. "Almost five o'clock in the morning on the surface at Thornwood."

The pronouncement of the time brought on another compulsive yawn. "No wonder." He murmured as he took the bed on my insistence.

The mattress that had been so large for my four foot four inch frame was ridiculously small for him. Even stooped with age, he stood over six and a half feet tall. Curled on my bed, he looked like an adult sleeping on a child's mat with his arms and legs hanging off. I chuckled quietly, for he was snoring before I had finished armoring.

Kormak's armor clanked the articulated plates together as he strode restlessly past the heavy woodroot table to the fireplace where he turned and walked back. The other armor-clad commanders moved out of the way with a rustle of metal plates and maille. The crown Kormak wore was one we had retrieved from Mezosilliar, and not the traditional winged hammer motif of Balakarak, but he did not mind. It had been that very crown that had once graced the brow of Darlik Hammerhand, one of our greatest legendary heroes besides Gorain, and at least he had not known disgrace. Darlik's crown glittered in the light of the flickering flames as its new owner displayed his agitation. My eyes idly surveyed the hastily hung tapestries that covered the bloodstone walls and insulated them against echoes as Kormak passed by, refusing to meet my gaze. The smell of the fire was of slightly moldy cloth and woodroot, serving to rid us of the last of the orcs' foul handiwork. A young clansman stuffed another moldy blanket into the fire as I watched.

Kormak's amber brows drew down over his gray eyes as he paced by me again. "This Lodath warns you that every zarak assassin in the Mother's Halls is out for your blood, and you would leave the army to go on this fool's errand? How do you know he is not a spy? How can you know to trust a human's word?"

My jaw was sore from the tightened muscles. "Because he is my friend. He has always kept his oaths to me. Besides, we have little choice." I left out the times I knew Lodath had lied to me, even though the lies were in what he thought were 'my best interests'. "This is my risk alone, and so I will go. You must understand that if I do not, our people will certainly perish. At least with this offer of allies, we have a chance."

"How do you know what he says is true? This may be a trap, and the numbers of our enemies imaginary." He paced by me in the opposite direction, and I thought it odd that he did not look at me when he spoke.

"It is verified easily enough. Find one of those disgusting Kinsmen of Shadow and question them. They should know what evil is afoot even if they are not a part of it. I want to know everything about our enemies that we can find out. I will need this information upon my return in order to finalize our battle plan." I managed to fix Kormak with an earnest stare. "I am counting on you to hold Balakarak in the event our enemies make a pre-emptive strike." Was that hostility in his gaze? I slowly pulled the Hammer of Golodain from my belt, symbol of the father of our race, and my direct ancestor. "Take this in to battle. Should our enemies attack, may Golodain Mytharia be with you."

With wide eyes, Kormak received the holy weapon and made as if to say something, but changed his mind. He idly traced the runes across the surface of the ancient hammer as Valin, commander of the shieldbreakers, spoke up.

"King Dorian, leaving the protection of the army is suicide. At least let us send an escort." Was he trying to convince me? If so, his words were completely inadequate.

"I appreciate your concern, but I can travel faster with fewer people and we are less likely to attract attention. This mission must rely on stealth and swiftness, for our enemies must not suspect a hint of it. Besides, between Naiara and the Reaver, I doubt there is an assassin left in the Halls that could best me."

"Perhaps this is true," mumbled Kormak, "but at least take my son Bailan. He is a stout warrior and will defend you to the death. You can trust him to carry your banner with honor." Valin exchanged a startled look with Kormak, and I wondered if I was missing something.

How could I have such thoughts of my kinsmen? Intrigues were for lesser races, what had I to fear from my own people? We were all under the threat of extinction. Any division in our ranks would end in our destruction, and I was sure that Kormak knew that as well as I did. I glanced to Korina, who had remained silent during my pronouncement. The exaggerated look of innocence on her face warned me that she was planning something.

"Very well, Kormak. Bailan shall carry my banner and accompany me as an emissary. We will leave in half a time cycle. You have my instructions on the fortifications?" Kormak nodded with a half-smile. "Good. Follow them well, and the entire might of the zarakanan will break themselves to pieces before setting foot in Balakarak." With my pronouncement, Korina slipped out of the council chamber before I could forbid her from accompanying me. Vooraduum, but the girl was stubborn! I would have blamed her mother, but I knew better.

When I returned to my chambers, Lodath was still sound asleep on the bed. His features took on a more youthful appearance in his slumber and I smiled in remembrance for the years I spent as his guardian and protector. Quietly I gathered my things for the journey, being careful not to disturb him until the last millicycle. I stole out of the room to collect rations from our supplies to put into my pack, and ordered that three riding spiders were to be prepared. Our need was for swiftness and endurance, for which the spiders were ideal.

For Lodath's rations, I picked through the supplies to find things that would not be upsetting to his system, or even fatal to him. The packs were strapped to the spiders before I returned to my quarters to wake the mage. Lodath met me at the door, and his smiling face put me out of sorts. Nobody had the right to be so cheerful on so little sleep.

"Are we ready to go yet?" I snapped my mouth shut and nodded as Lodath continued, "great! I am eager to see Gormorath. I have heard some interesting things about the gollaran's stonecrafting abilities."

Gollarans were too flighty to concentrate on anything worthwhile, and I could not understand why, that in the midst of one of our marvels of architecture, he would be more interested in looking at the work of a half-crazed race. "I thought you had already spoken with them." Had Lodath lied to me?

"I spoke with one of their representatives, yes, but I have not yet been to their city. I see being king has not improved your humor." With a sly look, he asked, "and, where is Morina?" As if she were the keeper of my sense of humor!

But the vision of her golden hair and jade eyes filled me with warmth. "She is back in Morakduum. The impending birth of our third child is the only thing that keeps her from my side."

Lodath slapped me on the backplate of my armor, rattling the pauldrons. "Third child! Why Dorian, I thought your people's numbers were waning! I guess you never did have much difficulty with that." His vicious jibe made it past my blissful vision of Morina's face.

Knowing he was baiting me did not make much difference in my reaction. "Such discussions have no place among us. I do not wish to hear of such things again."

His laughter rang through the room. "Well, some things haven't changed! You still are as touchy as ever." His gaze twinkled merrily despite his age as he sauntered out the door. Lodath only made it ten paces before he looked about in confusion. "Okay, Dorian, which way to the outside?"

It was my turn to bait him. "Back the way you came, mage. There is no 'outside' in the Halls of the Mother."

"Ha, ha. Very funny. Now are you going to lead the way or do I have to use the mind switch?" He fished in his pouch and pulled out a pearl, which he purposefully held at my eye-level.

"Uh, that will not be necessary." Even though I knew he would never do such a thing to me, the threat of it still made me cold inside. "This is the way to the front gate."

Lodath's age-spotted and wrinkled hand rested on my right pauldron as if I was his personal cane. "You know, I miss your surly attitude, Dorian. It has been too many years that I have dealt with people who are so indirect. It would be welcome to stand beside someone who is not afraid to speak his mind."

I led him through the maze of tunnels to the great hall and out to the front gate. All the while he spoke of his involvement with the court of King Osric, and how he despised most of the nobility. Humans were such odd creatures to plot against one another in the same kingdom, and sometimes within the same clan. It was a concept that still astounded me.

The vast courtyard was full of bustling activity as my kinsmen scrambled to repair the fortifications. Crawlers were hauling stones into place, moving them as the resonators levitated them. Once in place, they were being shaped by my kin. Upon the tops of the walls, cannons were being hoisted into position, traps were being laid and repairs to the massive stone gates were being fashioned.

Lodath stopped short in amazement at the flurry of industry. My feet too, came to an abrupt halt as I noticed five riding spiders with packs instead of three. On the last two spiders were Marak and Korina.

Boots ringing an angry tattoo, I strode up to Korina's mount. "You are not coming!" I annunciated my words carefully so there would be no misunderstandings.

Just as slowly and succinctly, Korina replied. "You cannot stop me." She grinned from ear to ear. "Besides, I would be disobeying mother if I let you leave without me. Her orders were to go where you went, and look after you."

A thousand protests died in their infancy, but I had to reason with her. "It will be dangerous. The zarakanan have offered a reward for proof of my death, and undoubtedly we will end up fighting them. Without the protection of the army, we are vulnerable targets." Seeing Korina's unconcerned look, I pleaded with her hearth-mate. "Marak, please talk some sense into her?"

"Perhaps I should talk some sense into you, Father." I could feel the slight breeze of the river on my tongue, so I shut my mouth. "You cannot expect your own kin to watch you go into great peril. It is not our way, and well you know it." Marak's chastisement made me blink repeatedly as I struggled to find something to say.

"It is a bloody conspiracy!" I mumbled before a thought struck me. "What of your mother? How will I answer to her if neither of you return?"

Korina fixed me with a cold stare; her gaze could have been a razor. "I thought you were not returning to Morakduum." Her voice was barely audible to me, and not even Marak heard her words. "How could you be made to answer for us?"

Arguing with her was futile, but I could not let her have the last word even though I knew I would regret it. "Fine, but when the fighting starts, I want you to promise to stay out of it."

The scathing look she returned brooked no interpretation, and I knew I would never receive such a promise. It was futile to argue with my kin, and I should have known better. It was a battle I could never win. Without further comment, I mounted the spider that had my pack and strapped myself in to the harness. The bright green and yellow stripes of the arachnid were plainly visible in the torch-lit courtyard. Like most of the riding spiders she was a neutered female, males were just too difficult to train, and were much less sociable. I patted the sleek chitin behind her top three eyes, and she chittered contentedly as she raised a single foreleg in friendship.

Kormak's son, Bailan entered the courtyard with his pack on his back and carrying a furled banner. When he noticed my attention, his white teeth gleamed from beneath his reddish-blonde moustache in the flickering torch-lights. His visor had been pushed back, revealing his gray eyes that shone with pride. His youthful face told me he was about thirty years younger than Korina, but he wore the full braided locks of a Master of Arms. He was so young yet had been awarded such a title, and I smiled nostalgically at the memory of my own graduation from the Warrior's Academy. The young kinsman secured his pack to the riding straps of the unfettered spider, and bowed graciously still holding the banner.

"Majesty, it is my great honor to carry this, your banner. It has only just been finished by the finest embroideries of Clan Tenedain." With that, he unfurled the banner.

I beheld not the standard that Bailan bore, but one that had passed into shame eight thousand years ago. My memory took me from Balakarak, and I stood before the walls of Sorkarak's past as the royal blue banner was burned in the courtyard. Flames licked at the embroidered enter-twined runes of blood and vaarandril, highlighting the gold thread before consuming it with eternal hunger. My hands had been symbolically bound, but instead of ridicule, there was deep sadness. I had saved them from slavery, from certain extinction, and yet, the law was the law. That their mightiest hero could commit such a crime tore at the soul of my people as my banner fell into ashes. The two kinsmen that stood to either side of me did so with bowed heads and stooped shoulders. Reluctantly, they turned me to face the outer gates and escorted me through them. One of them cut the rope that bound me and handed me the Reaver before retreating back behind the gates. The massive stone doors closed seamlessly, no way back.

"Sire?" Bailan's concern was reflected in his earnest face, drawing me from the trance.

I blinked and glanced accusingly at the Reaver that hung innocently from its straps on the spider. "It is a fine standard, Bailan. Your clan has done well. Gorain himself could not have had a finer banner, or a more honorable bearer."

He grinned again, revealing a boyish delight in the praise as he furled the banner once more and added it to the riding straps. He swung up on a red and gold striped female and settled himself in.

Lodath stood a few paces off, still staring hard at the spiders.

"Do not worry, my friend, they are well fed." I could not help the wide grin that settled upon my face.

"I will not ride one of those things."

I chuckled; enjoying his discomfort after all those times he teased me about my fear of the hellish depths of water and my dislike for boats. "Well, you could ride a crawler. Or perhaps a scorpion would be more to your tastes?"

Lodath shuddered visibly, and I laughed. "I will walk thanks."

"We do have need of swiftness."

The mage cocked a thin gray brow at me. "Then I suggest you had better keep up."

He chanted a quick charm and sprinkled some kind of powder on his boots before he turned and walked through the gates, but for every step he made, near a tenth sect passed beneath him. It had been eighty years since I had seen what he could do, and watching him brought to mind many of the more destructive things he was capable of. I only hoped our enemies had nothing to rival his skills. Would the Reaver's power protect me from the arcane arts of my enemies? It was a sobering thought and one that ended my speculation of taking on the zarakanan alone, but started me upon another more alarming course.

"Lodath, how did you find me?" The possible reason settled a chill in my bones.

With a half-grin he confirmed my fears. "Are you kidding? That weapon of yours is a sure beacon to anyone who can sense the ethers of magic. All I had to do was tune in and - oh!" His eyes widened as he caught my implication. "Good gods! I suppose I had better do something about that!"

Lodath drew the arcane figures in a circle in which he bade me to stand and hold the Reaver. A greenish light shone from the wards as Lodath chanted, and lightning arced from the axe to the figures and back. Sweat beaded upon the mage's brow as he repeated the chant twice more as the light intensified. I felt the rage of the Reaver wash through me, how dare any creature suppress its power!? I spoke calmly to the presence in my mind, reassuring it that it was not being suppressed, and merely its magical aura shrouded. I repeated the message like a mantra as the lightning began to die down. By the time Lodath had finished the third chant the Reaver was quiescent.

Lodath again headed off in the direction of Gormorath. Even though he said he had not been there, and it gave me some pause to consider if I could still trust his word. It had been eighty years since we had last spoken, and I knew how much humans could change. Jaguar certainly had changed quite a bit while raising our daughter, Panther, but not in the ways that I had hoped. Had Lodath changed, and was he merely leading me into a trap? I thought again about Liathrain. At one time I would have trusted her as much as Lodath, and yet we had fought to the death.

I shook my head. My trust for Lodath had to be sound. Our friendship was deeper than mere camaraderie. He had been like a son to me, an odd son to be sure, but I loved him like my own child all the same. Even though I had been only eighty-five years old at the time, I was still old enough to be his great grandfather. But human sons betrayed their fathers; it was a common tale among them. I halted that line of thought. Instead, I tried to lose my speculation in the scenery.

Idly, I watched the flows of calcite, like frozen waterfalls, slip past us. It was a shame that haste shadowed the beauty of the Halls of the Mother. Stalactites drooped down to merge with rising fingers of stalagmites straining to touch each other. The moist warmth of the tunnels rarely stirred except in the high-water season, which had been past for the last six tendays. The air was visibly layered in shades of heat, warmer at the top than the bottom, until we disturbed it with our passing. The riding spider had no difficulty navigating the many sudden drops, obstructive rock flows, stalagmites, and narrow channels, but Lodath was not so fortunate.

More than once, I reached out and snagged the mage's arm before he plummeted into a sudden hole in the cavern floor. Alerted by the Song of the Mother, I was aware of such dangers before he ever could be. The discordant harmony of the paper-thin rock was as blatant to me as a red sign, but to Lodath, it was invisible. He met my gaze gratefully, and the memory of his first transformation came as plainly to me as his orange eyes. It had been my fault, in a roundabout sort of way, and he had been irrevocably changed from human into something else. I remembered leaning over his lifeless body in anguish as the gollaran priestess announced that she could not touch his soul.

***

If only I had been faster or at least stood in front of my friend before the devilfish finished casting its spell. The fire-bolt burned on the retina of my memory. The black beast hovered in the air as if swimming in it. Its great dark triangular wings vibrated in some unholy rhythm that I learned was its way of casting spells. I had attacked the one on the right, trying to distract the three hell-spawned creatures when the one in the center finished its summoning. A great white-hot fire-bolt flew from the creature's tail, and struck Lodath full in the chest. I will never forget the wide eyes and twisted look of shocked pain on his face as his dying scream was cut short by the roar of thunder from the fire-bolt.

When the gollaran priestess pronounced her inability to help Lodath, I wanted to take out my angry frustrations upon her, but I remembered the ring we had found. Knowing that my words would unleash magic the like of which could destroy the world did not calm my nerves as I removed it from the mage's cold finger. It was a plain gold ring, not much thicker than a leather thong, but the air of magic about it was like the eye of a hurricane. It seemed to expand as I sought to put it around my thicker index finger. The pain in my lungs forced me to let out the breath I did not know I was holding until then. Jaguar smiled encouragement, and Gith'r'luk cocked its bug head to one side like a giant mantis waiting for prey. My mind went suddenly blank.

How did one wish for life to return to the dead? It seemed like such a simple wish, yet I had been warned that the creatures of magic that controlled such power were twisted in intent. I made a silent prayer to the Maker as I spoke the words in my own language so there would be no misinterpretation. All the hair on my body rose in a cascading tide of energy as the ring blazed to life like a descending star. It felt as if every fiber of my being suddenly became a vessel to hold power as the magic flooded outward from the ring to every part of me. It swirled around like an insane tornado of light, finally coming to rest around Lodath's lifeless form. The energy released me, and I stumbled to my knees as if I had taken a dozen fire-bolts and they had just ended. Jaguar grabbed my arm to steady me as she bent over to get a better look at what was happening to the mage.

The multi-colored spectacle seeped into his body and disappeared. For a moment, it seemed as if nothing else would happen. Jaguar bent closer and was about to touch him when his eyes snapped wide open and he sucked in an enormous breath of air. Jaguar jumped, nearly knocking me over, but her gaze never left the mage's.

"By Inanna! I have never seen such a thing!"

I looked around her shapely hip to see what the fuss was about. The light of the torch revealed orange eyes with black slits like a cat, but Lodath appeared otherwise quite normal.

"I just had the oddest dream." He frowned thoughtfully. "Why are you all staring at me?"

"Your eyes, mage." I allowed him to view his reflection in the polished surface of the blades of my axe.

His gaze did not leave his reflection as he whispered, "so, it wasn't a dream after all."

***

Those same orange eyes took a second look, not at me, but at the huge bear plodding along behind us. He put his feet on firmer ground, and I released his arm.

With a low voice he said, "it is right behind you, Dorian."

For a moment, I thought he meant we were being ambushed. Casually, I unsnapped the restraining strap on the Reaver and rested my hand upon the haft as I turned to view the threat. I was puzzled when only the huge bear and my kin registered in my sight. A grin lit my face as I realized he meant Naiara.

"Worry not, mage. The bear is my friend." As if sensing our conversation, Naiara whuffed then snorted.

He frowned in irritation. "I thought you said those bears were dangerous and could not be trained."

The accusation concerning my word of honor bothered me little. "I did not lie to you, Lodath. Naiara is dangerous, and cannot be trained. However, as my friend, she tolerates certain anomalies in my behavior as I tolerate hers. She is not my pet, nor could any cave bear ever be."

He threw up his hands. "Dwarves! Big spiders, huge bears, giant lizards, scaly dogs, what next!? How did your people get so short anyway?"

"It is your people who seem to have grown beyond your scale. I am perfectly proportioned, while you," I gestured to his lanky arms and legs, "grow out in some areas and not in others." I fixed him with a grin I knew he would interpret as I meant it.

His mouth dropped open in shocked outrage before he realized I was baiting him. Instead of the protest I knew he wanted to voice, he merely grunted. "So Jaguar told Rutger, anyway."

The comment smote home as Lodath had intended. He knew I did not like to be reminded of the circumstances of my meeting with the dark-skinned priestess. What he would have taken as a badge of honor was the pinnacle of shame to me, but one I would not have changed had I the opportunity.

"Are you sure you do not wish to ride? The journey gets more perilous as we continue. The spiders and my kin know instinctively where there is danger." Lodath looked from the huge spider to me.

As if understanding our conversation, Mira, the spider I was riding, raised a friendly foreleg as her pad hooks rested on the mage's tunic. I smiled at the spider, wishing that she were one of my prodigies. Her intelligence was quite keen, and she might really have understood. She even responded well to trained voice commands. I rubbed the joint where her head met her thorax, and she chittered in pleasure.

"I think she likes you, mage."

Uncertainly, he took the spider foot and unhooked it from his tunic.

With a large grin, I decided one more jab at my friend was in order. "If you rub the inside of her foreleg there, she just might take you for a mate."

Lodath shuddered in disgust. "Very funny, Dorian."

Bailan and Marak added their laughter to my own, but Korina gave me a sour look.

"Very well. I suppose I will have to ride, if only to keep from slowing you up." He fixed me with a feline eye. "And remember, it would not be the first time I rode one of these blasted things."

Lodath's companionship spurred the memories of many of our former travels together. I was still mulling over them when we stopped to make camp almost a full day-cycle since we had started. A calcite flow made an interesting center point for our resting-place. Bailan and I looked around for some woodroot to make a fire. Not more than a tenth league from our camp was a tributary of the Daemon Fish River, the breeze of the water tugged at my beard as I made my way around a treacherous stretch of volcanic glass.

The going was rough, and the crevasse carved out of the stone by the magma was narrow, but we managed to make it to the water's edge. Along the banks, we found plenty of woodroot, some dried and some still growing. The giant mushrooms loomed above, highlighted by the heat of the living stones. Their roots and trunks served our people as trees served the humans in the overlands. Using our hand axes, we made a good-sized bundle of wood that we piled outside of the small crevasse before climbing back through.

The hair rose on the back of my neck and the presence of watchers spurred my instincts. The heat and vibrations of the area revealed nothing to me, but the sense did not go away. Bailan and I carefully circled, making not a sound, trying to find the source of my unease, to no avail. As suddenly as it had hit me, it was gone, and I shrugged as I picked up my burden of woodroot.

"I suggest we keep a watch this sleep-cycle, sire." Bailan was clearly more shaken than I was.

I nodded as we made it back to camp with enough woodroot to cook supper and breakfast. Not far from our camp I found a fresh vrakka kill from the spiders and managed to salvage a good sized haunch. There were other corpses nearby, but they were too far gone to be edible. The fire would neutralize the venom in the haunch enough for our palate, but Lodath would be unable to consume any of it. For him, I found some bland edible mushrooms that grew around the base of the calcite formation.

Bailan took the first watch, and promptly snuffed the fire after we had eaten. He gazed out into the darkness from atop a large round rock that looked as if water had frozen in waves as it traversed the white and tan surface. I placed my bedroll so that I could lay my head upon Naiara's foreleg as the big bear settled in. The many battle scars I bore made it impossible to sleep comfortably in my armor as I had once done. The awkward joints seemed to dig in to my bones, spreading the ache through my spine and into my skull. Vooraduum but was I getting old? With a few more choice invectives muttered under my breath, I removed my helmet, gorget, arms and breastplate. For a few moments, I considered my cuisses, but the shoulder and belt harness that held them was such a hassle to remove and put on that I left my leg armor in place.

When it was my turn to watch, Bailan climbed down from the rock to rouse me. The scrape of his armor on the stone woke me instantly, and I reached instinctively for the Reaver. Looking to the sound I saw Kormak's son coming towards me, and almost relaxed until my eyes caught the glow of the Reaver's blades. Feeling my movement, the great bear also lifted a heavy lid to stare balefully at the two of us, but her nose twitched and she was instantly awake. A low rumble seemed to vibrate in my skull from the huge bear's throat. Bailan froze in his tracks, eyes scanning left and right. Two small crossbow bolts streaked in and struck me before I turned to face outward from him. The sharp sting of poison radiated out from the darts like fire.

The poison warred with my immunity I had built up during my apprenticeship. Many was the day that I had been bitten by spiders, stung by scorpions, and ravaged by crawlers while training them. It was crucial that we took small amounts of venom every tanir to keep the poisons from killing us. Korina had been through the same training regimen, only as my heir she had not been subjected to the worst of chores that I had. Bailan, Marak and Lodath had no such immunity. It was imperative that Korina and I protected them as they could not survive! Spinning the Reaver before me, I gave it the command 'boravrak en' and lightning arced into the shield. My actions served two purposes, to shed their missiles, and to draw their fire. As I had hoped, all further shots were directed my way as they recognized the weapon they feared. The Reaver kept the missiles from the front of me, but we had been surrounded. A dozen more of the small bolts found marks in my back and sides. Fortunately, they were designed to deliver their poison and let that do the work instead of for any real injury they caused. It was still pretty painful, and the amount of venom was overwhelming my resistance. I had to act quickly. Towards the far side of the flowstone, I saw a zarak that appeared to be giving hand signaled orders. Knowing my best chance was to take down their leader, I charged.

My war cry and the bear's howl of rage roused the others as they made a hasty circle with their backs together and weapons out. The vanguard of the zarakanan attacked, some with magic, and others with weapons. Their magical bolts burned into me, but fortunately my natural resistance kept the injuries from being serious. The Reaver shunted aside their weapons, shearing through them to sever the arms that wielded them. The screams of the zaraks followed in my wake as I fought my way towards their leader. Beside me, Naiara plowed through their ranks like a steam driven hammer. The next volley of envenomed darts speckled her hide like a water urchin. Naiara too, had no immunity to the venom and soon was fast asleep and at the mercy of our enemies. Korina and Marak tried desperately to save her as Bailan struggled to defend them. Lodath's form melted into that of the huge feline monster that was his 'gift' from the gods, and he promptly vanished from the range of my heat sensitive vision. But the sound of his passing was unmistakable. Zaraks screamed and died in bloody sprays of flesh where his claws tore through the darkness. That his feline form did not shed heat always amazed me, and its ability to absorb all vibration made him invisible to all of us.

The shock of another impact rattled my teeth as I continued forward. The eyes of the zarak widened with the disbelief their arrogant nature brought when a 'lesser creature' killed one of them. In a spray of entrails, I yanked the Reaver free, spinning to the left to catch the descending black blade of a scimitar on the haft between my hands. Hot metal sparks burned into my bare knuckles, for I had not put on my gauntlets. My armored boot sunk into the zarak's gut with a sickly grunt, and my greater weight bent him over double. The pommel of the Reaver easily crunched through his skull splattering bone and brain tissue across my gambeson. The ring of metal echoed through the caverns as I blocked another blade aimed for my head and dove past a wild sweep. Twisting the Reaver to tie up the lighter sword, I yanked the young female off her feet. Catching her sword arm in my right, I fended off her companion with the blades of the big axe in my left. My grip tightened on the zarak's delicate wrist bones until I heard a satisfying crack and the blade dropped from her hand. I pulled her body across me as a shield from the double set of blades that whistled in from the right. As the zarak yelped in pain, I planted my boot in the small of her back. She flew into the weapons of the two in front of her, freeing me up to continue my charge for their leader.

With unusual cooperation, four male zaraks made a line of defense between their captain and myself. Two of them worked furiously with shields and scimitars to block my axe, while the other two kept me off-balance with their blades. The Reaver came down upon the black metal rim of the zarak's shield, and sent a shower of white-blue sparks dancing across armor and weapons. The divot created by my axe ran deep, and the zarak's brow furrowed in despair as he realized the shield would not take another blow. The backswing wound around to cleave it and the dark elf in two, but a bolt of white light struck me square in the chest and transfixed me to the spot. Too late, I realized the delay had been all that the zarak leader had wanted. Her triumphant smile vanished in the haze of white that blinded me and fire blazed through me. Fried nerves screamed in protest, adding to the heat that paralyzed my mind and body. Thunder echoed around me as the energy faded, leaving a ragged burning tear from my chest through to the soles of my boots. The fire-bolt that had struck me before had burned around my armor, super-heating it as if by a forge, but this time, my body took its full fury. I sank to my knees like a rag-doll whose wire frame had been removed, but the Reaver would not let me rest. Its unholy rage filled me, driving me on despite the agony.

The bare and raw soles of my feet gave me little pause as the Reaver's rage consumed me with the need to kill. My steps were fumbling at first, the tops of feet combined with the metal from my boots as it melted into the flesh. Ashen and bloody footprints followed my course to the zarak mage next to their leader as I stepped over the dead bodies of the unfortunate defenders. They had been unable to escape the backlash of the fire-bolt, and I knew I would not survive another such blast either once the Reaver released me from its power. The mage's red-hued gaze stared at me, knowing the moment of her death. The skin of her cheek jumped, betraying her inner fear, but she did not move as the blades of the Reaver descended.

Her blood sprayed outward with more force than seemed possible and it emptied from the shorn stump of her neck all at once. Before I could pull the blades from her shoulder, I realized the red spray had not gone to the ground, but had begun to glow with an unholy light. The crimson mist ignited with the heat of a forge fire as it began to coalesce around me. The fiery fog encompassed me, burning my skin and singeing my hair. Even the retribution of the undead dragon had not been so painful! I writhed in the grip of the arcane forces, but the Reaver would lend me no rest. I could not even voice the pain, for the fire burned into my lungs as I tried to take a breath. The smell of my own burning flesh filled my nostrils as I struggled to breathe in any manner I could. I prayed to Morakvaar that I could survive such an onslaught as the Reaver drove me on to strike at the zarak leader.

In terror their leader turned to flee from me as the fiery mist began to envelop her at my proximity. The Reaver did not care if I struck her down from behind, as I was sure she would have done to any one of my kin. The rest of the zaraks fled as I bore down on them from one direction, and the unseen horror of Lodath from the other, but the rage would not let them live. I commanded the fires of the Reaver to consume them as they tried to escape. Water covered me as the last one spasmed in agony, her flesh disappearing in unnatural fire. A part of my reason knew that the source had to be Marak, for Lodath was still in his changed form. In a way, the water was worse than the retributive flames, for it seeped into my burned and cracked flesh, causing unbelievable agony, but the unnatural fire was doused. The dual pain smote my mind, submerging it in blessed oblivion as the Reaver released me from its power.

I know not when my subconscious stirred, but eventually I found the memories of my return to Morkilduum playing out in my mind.

***

My dreams wandered again through the corridor of my memories, to the times Morina and I traveled back to my homeland to raise our first child. We set out with our companions when her pregnancy became obvious, but the journey proved to be longer and more perilous than we had imagined.

Using Lodath's spells, we had managed to sneak past the orcs who had settled in Balakarak through the little used trade tunnel that led to the darklands. The perilous crossing past Laharazduum saw us confront a few cave bears, some korvas, death dog packs, and wild zovrak let alone the fields of living stone with their deadly beautiful crystal flowers. Wild spider packs hunted us, but they stayed a respectful distance from Dovira, my massive winged spider who had been my friend and companion. At last we made it to the Wilds.

Upon my winged spider sat Morina; her swollen belly was almost as large as she was, and I paced beside her through the final passage between Laharazduum, that which the zaraks called Mezosilliar and Morkilduum stronghold of my birth. I chewed my lip in concern, for it had taken us too long to fight through our enemies, but we had at last put the zarak city behind us. Liathrain strode beside me, marveling at the beauty of the crystal flowers that grew between Mezosilliar and Morkilduum. Her amber gaze followed Kelana as the elf of the deep wood knelt by one that shone in the heat spectrum as blue and gold with clear leaves.

"Are they alive?"

"Yes, zey grow only here, in zie Halls of zie Mozer. Zey are an extension of zie living stones below."

She reached out a hand to touch one, and I quickly grabbed her wrist.

"Did you not hear me? Zey are zere to lure in prey. If you touch it, it vill shock you, ahnd, ven you fall over, tubes vill inject you vit acid. Zie living stone vill absorb your minerals."

Her blue eyes went wide and she shook her long mane of platinum hair. Nervously, she fidgeted with her pointed left ear.

"But it looked so beautiful. Is it safe to be here?"

"As long as you do not touch zie flowvers, it is safe. Zie stone is qviet until avakened by zie shock of zie flowver. Gollarans have learned to avaken zie spirits of zie living stones, but ve leave zem in peace."

"Dorian, how do your people live in all of this? It just seems so dangerous." Jaguar's dulcet tones still vibrated within my soul, and I glanced at Morina to remind myself of my duty and honor.

"Ve are in harmony vit zie Mozer. She sings to us zie song of her blood. In her song is zie patterns of safety, of danger, of all living zings in zie deeps. By zie patterns of her harmony, ve know vere zie tunnel floor is veak, ven zie cave bear is stalking, how long ago zie vild sheep, the lemvar passed,

ahnd vere ve are." I moved closer to my hearth-mate, at once to reassure her, and to convince myself that I did not need to think about the time I spent with the sensuous priestess.

Morina remained silent, her gaze no longer taking in our surroundings. Instead, she stared at the back of the spider's head; her mouth slightly turned down at the corners. I placed a gauntleted hand upon her knee, trying to get her to meet my gaze. I could feel through our bond there was something wrong, and my heart ached to know she was suffering inside. Switching to our tongue, I tried to coax her into telling me what it was.

"My beautiful hearth-mate, what ails you?" A flash of green and her stare returned to the back of the spider's head. "Morina, please? Are you not well?" I felt panic stir within me at the thought that perhaps the journey had injured her or the child.

"I have no home." Her voice was muffled as she spoke to the back of the spider's head.

The anguish of a heritage denied echoed through the cavern with her mumbled words. They burned in my heart as if each were a flaming dagger. I pulled off my gauntlet and reached for her hand.

"Morina, your home is among our people, among my clan, for surely they will take us in. Does this not please you?" Her eyes finally met mine.

"Do you not understand? I know not this world, and its dangers are foreign to me. I feel I do not belong among these wonders." Her voice trailed off before too much emotion was betrayed.

I swung up behind the riding straps that held her as the spider regarded me with an annoyed set of six eyes. My arms slid around Morina's chest where it met her bulging stomach, and I allowed her to feel the closeness of our soul-bond. Her hands clutched at my arms tightly enough for me to feel the pressure within my armor. My heart grieved for her anguish, as I sought out the emotional tie in our soul-bond. Slowly our emotions merged, a gift of the Maker to our people, the singular reason we were always meant to be monogamous. When at last she began to relax, knowing how much I cared for her, I let her feel the Song of the Mother as I felt it. The rhythm of the deeps resonated in the very fibers of my being; the harmony of the pulsing of the Blood of the Mother filled her senses. Though she had been aware of it, it was still frightening to her, so I let her feel the slight differences in the song through me as we traveled a little way. With the inborn empathy of the soul-bond, she began to pick up on the meaning of the changes, how one discordance meant fissures in the rock below, and another meant the danger of the crystal flowers. Eventually, the intense feeling of isolation began to fade from her as wonder replaced fear.

"So this is how you see the Deeps?" She breathed as a faint smile crossed her lips.

"Yes." I whispered back as her lips met mine making me forget those who followed us.

"How much further is it, Dorian?" Kelana's impatient voice dragged me back to awareness, but not before I noticed a change in Morina's life energy.

Sheepishly, I let go of her and slid back off the spider. Concentrating on the particular resonance of the song, I pinpointed our location in the map of my memory.

"Ve should be zere by zie end of zies day cycle."

I looked to my hearth-mate, knowing it could not be a moment too soon. The twinge of pain from the spasm was barely visible, and had we not been bonded, I would not have known her labor had started. I only hoped there was time to reach the shelter of Morkilduum's ruins. If the smell of birth did not bring a few cave bears, there were other worse predators of the Wilds. I quickened my pace, relying almost completely on the Song of the Mother to guide our way, for there was no time to search for the right paths. Though I had known of the paths between Morkilduum and Mezosilliar, I had never traveled them. Only our merchants or emissaries had business with the city of the zarakanan, and to travel in the disputed realms alone was to invite death.

After two time cycles, the cavern opened into a sight at once familiar and horrifically foreign. The fire-field lay before the once proud gates of my home. The river of magma ran from its previously contained course slowly down the expanse of the approach to Morkilduum. Just short of the southern wall of the great cavern it seeped back into the flow that joined the River of Life into the Heart of the Mother. A small path of cooled magma ran along the southern edge up to the wall that had once borne the proud carvings of heroes and ancestral spirits invoked in knotted coils and runic wards. Only ragged lines remained of the impenetrable barrier against our enemies.

For many long moments I could but stare in disbelief until the realization smote my soul that my home, my people, my clan, had been mercilessly destroyed. My legs weakened under the blow, and I found myself on my knees in the dust and ash of the tunnel floor. An unearthly moan of a tortured soul echoed around me, and I realized it was mine as my pain wet the dusty ash. Vaguely, I had known of Morkilduum's demise, but the knowledge could not have prepared me for the emotional devastation of the sight of thousands of years of clan history wiped away. The souls of my ancestors cried out to me, through me, against such heresy, and I swore to them an oath of vengeance.

Lodath placed a hand on my pauldron in sympathy, but I felt only rage and anguish. The faces of my father and mother were reflected in every odd swirl of the fiery river that oozed over the rubble of the toppled fortifications. I could hear the dying screams of my brothers in the rush of heated air that poured from the crack the magma flowed into. I felt the crushing blows of our enemies as my uncles and cousins fell before the pitiless tide of zarakanan. I felt the dying hope of our race as I realized our fate was sealed with the fall of our last and mightiest of defenses against the incursion of extinction.

The only prayer I had left was that the tide of magma had discouraged our enemies from attempting to besiege our two remaining cities of Barakillanak and Dormakkarduum. It was in Barakillanak that I hoped to find any survivors of my clan. Our ties to them spanned not only to the fosterage of many of their smiths, but also that of my Mother's kin.

Morina's slight moan of pain drew me out of my despair and galvanized me into action. The call of my ancestors would have to wait for the birth of the next and possibly last generation. I picked our way with great caution around the river of fire. To me, the heat felt good, banishing the last vestiges of the cold that had settled into my very bones since being deported to the frigid surface world, but I could tell my companions were not dealing well with the warmth. Dorvira too, sidled nervously along the hot stones that were our only safeguard against the river of fire after Jaguar had chanted a quick prayer to her goddess to endure the heat.

The blasted remains of the Stonewardens brought me up short inside Morkilduum's massive gates. The channel where the magma used to flow in a controlled defense was crusted with cooled stone and was like a pool of hardened blood beneath the broken bodies of the once massive golems. My mind's eye saw our ancestral guardians in their proper place, watching balefully over the entrance to our home. They had seemed indestructible, and yet there their pieces lay as if blasted by explosive powders from the inside. How could any of my kin have survived such an onslaught? A hollow emptiness settled in the pit of my stomach. What sort of power could have been wielded by our enemies to destroy the magic of the Stonewardens that had been created with the soul of the father of our race?

The courtyard was strewn with cooled magma and rubble. Amazingly, the inner ward was intact as I sidled past the ruined remains of the outer gates confirming my suspicion that the outer walls had been broken not in the assault, but out of spite. The ward pillar stood in the middle of Market Road, the main tunnel that ran from the gates to the Market Square. The stones were darkened with the stains of blood, and gnawed bones lay strewn along the tunnel as numerous as pave-stones. I stared at them in morbid fascination, wondering which ones belonged to my clan. The floor of the tunnel was worn by thousands of years of foot traffic and carts that had traded peacefully within Morkilduum's Market Square. It was inconceivable that it had all come to such a sudden and violent end.

With a cold numbness that settled in my heart I traversed the length of the tunnel, leading my companions into what used to be the thriving heart of our mightiest stronghold. The octagonal cavern that had housed the huge market was bare and silent. The carved central pillar that held the mighty visage of Golodain Mytharia, father of our race and my own ancestor had been maliciously blasted to rubble. Dark stone mixed freely with white bones, as there the slaughter had been intense. Whole families fed the carrion eaters of the Deeps in that place, families that I had known and grown up with.

"By all the gods!" Jaguar's voice broke into a harsh croak.

I could not help the intense hatred that began to grow within me for all things zarakanan. With a growl, I turned accusingly to Liathrain.

"You see vat your people have done!" I felt my grip tighten on the haft of my axe as I took an involuntary step towards her before struggling with my rage.

"My people didn't do this, Dorian. We would never have been a part of it." Her voice rang with righteous indignation.

Some evil spell must have taken me, for suddenly, all I could see were enemies as I leapt forward with a snarl. The anger did not feel as if it were my own, but originated outside. It was as if I had become someone else, someone whose hatred for the zarakanan was eternal. Fire burned within my eyes, a fire that would only be quenched in blood. The zarak jumped back from my first strike, but was not quick enough for the backstroke. The blade of my axe rang soundly off Liathrain's armor and sent the lighter elf sprawling.

"Dorian! Dorian stop this!" The shocked voices seemed as far away from me as my sanity. Who was Dorian anyway?

"Jaguar, stop him, he's gone mad!"

I felt the wave of magical energy wash over me, but it did not stop me from standing over the zarak, preparing to end her life. An arrow entered my chest through the armpit as I raised my arms for the strike. In disbelief I staggered back, staring at the feathered shaft. The sight of Kelana's carefully aimed bow knocked with a second arrow brought some reason back as the fire of pain burst into my consciousness. I came to myself, weeding out the foreign presence in my mind by sheer force of will. My hand dropped the axe in favor of clutching at the shaft that threatened my life as if by holding it, I could prevent the damage that had already been done. My strength left me in a sudden rush like the blood that fountained from the wound, and I stumbled, trying to keep my balance in a swiftly tilting world.

"You shot me!" I exclaimed before I could no longer keep myself erect.

Kelana's aim never wavered as I fell to my knees and hands. The jolt of the fall sent a fresh bout of pain through me and my blood became a pool in which I knelt.

"Dorian!" Morina's cry was half desperation, half agony of her labor.

"Morina." I blinked back the pain, and snapped off the shaft of the arrow.

Pulling together all of my will, I staggered to my feet and slipped a vial from my belt-pouch. The contents slid down my throat before I stepped over to where Liathrain lay. The healing potion worked swiftly, easing the pain and sealing the wound around the shaft where it entered my lungs. My hand reached for the Vaetra.

"Don't!" Kelana warned me.

"Vorry not, elf. My senses have returned." I offered the zarak my hand.

Still gasping in air, Liathrain gave me a black look before accepting it.

"My deepest apologies, my friend. I fear the shock has been too much for me." I mumbled in her language. "I owe you for my misdeed, but first I must find shelter for Morina."

The arrow ached at the slightest movement and with every breath, but Morina was more important than my comfort. The roads wound inward as I sought out the home tunnels of my childhood, but it was slow going as I ensured each of the wards and traps were deactivated. Surprisingly few of them had been set. The zarak attack must have been sudden and ferocious to have left such little preparation. Their troops must have been stationed throughout the city before the slaughter began, and again, I wondered how such a feat was accomplished. How could so many zarakanan roam our streets unnoticed? Outside the warded entrance to our clan's tunnels was another pile of gnawed bones, and small crawlers scurried away at our approach. The door had been blasted by arcane energies, leaving scorched rubble strewn along the inside of our clan's gathering area. I knelt beside the bones of my kin momentarily offering a prayer to the ancestors for the safe passage of their souls to the Underhalls. More white monuments to greed and cruelty lie in small piles within the clan hall and each of the stone doors to the home tunnels had been shattered leaving no hope that any of my kin had escaped. Before my father's home was a huge pile of bones, torn armor and ripped cloth. I had no doubt that my father sold his life dearly before the threshold of our dwelling.

In despair I entered my empty home. The furniture had been smashed, and anything of value removed. The tapestries that my mother had woven depicting the illustrious and rich histories of my ancestors were gone, along with the items crafted by my family for generations. To see my home violated sickened me inside almost as much as the memory of what the human slavers had done to me, but I had no time for reflection. Another grunt of pain from Morina reminded me of the reason we were *there. I carried her into my father's room, and though the bed frame had been smashed and the mattress torn, it was better than the hard floor. Jaguar and Kelana followed closely on my heels and shooed me out as soon as I had set Morina down. They stretched a blanket across the threshold to replace the broken door and told me to fetch water.*

The central well in the gather area was still functional, and I managed to coax the pump into working. The grease that had kept it lubricated had long since congealed into a crusty mass, but a few drops from my water-skin broke it up nicely. I even managed to find some intact buckets that I had used as a child to carry water from the well to our home tunnel. I filled two of them and took them in to Jaguar. Lodath busied himself with practicing his arcane arts, using it to mend the furniture. By the time I had returned, he had a working table, six chairs, and the beds in my brother Koran's and my rooms repaired.

Another low moan from Morina made my stomach do flips as I paced the outer chamber. I would never forgive myself if the journey had injured her or the child. The knowledge of the few kinswomen whom had died in childbirth haunted my every thought. I prayed fervently to the Maker that she would be well and that our child would be healthy.

As I feared, the sounds of anguish brought larger crawlers hunting for food. The huge six-legged lizards circled outside the outer chamber, hesitant to take on fit adults. Liathrain drew her two scimitars and stood at my side as Rutger loosed the occasional arrow over our heads. The size of the crawlers convinced me that they were the very ones our people used for mounts and to pull carts. The many years that Morkilduum had been vacant had turned them feral. Panthro stood at my other side, his presence a comfort against the impending attack of the pack of hungry lizards. I did not want to contemplate what sort of danger we would have encountered in the Wilds.

As if on cue, Dorvira dropped from the ceiling of the gather area to land on what was evidently the pack leader. Her fangs lanced deeply into the beast's throat as she used her wings and rear legs to pull the heavy lizard back up the thread she had spun from the cavern roof. Startled and fearful, the pack bellowed and scattered. I smiled and gave the well-done sign to the spider as she began wrapping her paralyzed prize in sticky threads before consuming it.

"Ve have some time before zey vill return. Ve could use zat time to make a sturdy door at zie clan entrances. Zat vay, ve vill not have to vorry about vater."

Rutger and Liathrain helped me gather bits of broken furniture from the other tunnels and fashion a couple of crude doors to wedge into place. Heavier bits of furniture and loose rubble reinforced the makeshift door. We were just finishing the last barricade when the wail of a babe had me halfway across the gather area before I realized just what was going on. Kelana met me at the threshold, forbidding me to enter.

"You can't go in yet." Her slender hand on my chest would have been no barrier, but her tone brooked no compromise.

"Morina?" The anxiety in my voice was all too clear.

"She will be fine." Something about her tone put a cold knot into my gut.

"Vill be?" I tried to push past the slender elf, but she was quick and blocked me.

"Don't try it, Dorian. Besides, you need some care too."

Belatedly, I remembered the shaft that still hampered my arm movements. Fresh blood leaked down my side where the piece of wood stuck out. It had been quite fortunate that the head of the arrow had not ripped back through my lung. Grunting in ascent, I allowed her and Panthro to help me out of my armor. Though the vial of healing potion had sealed the worst of the wound, the arrow was still in my flesh and had to be removed. The squalls of the babe had quieted almost instantly, and I was relieved to think that Morina must be giving its first meal. I longed to be at her side, but allowed my wound to be seen to. Kelana swabbed the skin around the shaft clean of dried blood, sweat and dirt as I clenched my jaw. Panthro put a firm hand on my shoulder. Expecting the worst, I leaned against the wall, but could not help the cry of agony as the elf yanked the shaft out in one swift motion.

The blades of the arrowhead tore through my flesh once more, sending me swimming between light and darkness. The warmth of the priest's healing spells steadied the cold chills that had sent waves of nausea through my stomach. The spurting blood ceased and vanished altogether as the folds of skin closed over the wound in the warm glow of his god's power. I breathed a sigh of relief as the pain receded.

"Zank you, Panzro." The albino elf gave me a wan smile as he turned to see Jaguar emerge from behind the blanket.

Her lips twitched at the edges as she gazed upon my bare torso, dragging feelings out from where I had hidden them. Even after two years of marriage to Morina, I still loved her. For a moment, I was torn between my hearth-mate and my former human lover, but the cooing of our newborn child chased away my dilemma. I looked away from Jaguar's deep brown eyes to the barrier of the blanket.

"You can go in now, Dorian." Jaguar sighed slightly, knowing exactly what was in my heart.

Hesitantly, I passed her by to press aside the makeshift curtain. Morina sat upon the ruined mattress, and it was if fifty years of age fell from me as warmth and joy filled me. Her normally darker complexion was alarmingly pale, but contentment and pride was on her features as she gazed upon the bundle at her breast.

"Are you well, my hearth-mate?" I took one slow step into the door, my stomach still felt as if it was spinning in circles as I saw lines of sweat and pain on her face.

Her jade stare met mine as a broad smile widened her lips.

"It is a girl, Dorian." I felt the corners of my own mouth widen.

"A girl! Truly Morakvaar has smiled upon our union!" I was at her side in an instant, gazing upon the dual blessing of mother and child. "You are well then?"

"As well as can be expected, my mate. It is fortunate that we have a competent healer."

I knelt at her side; the sudden chill in my spine threatened my composure with the thought that I might have lost her. I kissed her sweaty brow assuring myself that she was still living as I put my arms around her.

"Then I owe Jaguar a great debt for your safety and the health of our child." Morina smiled sadly back, knowing how much the human had meant to me.

She changed the subject. *"What should we name her?"*

"Korina, the unchanging polish of vaarandril, and may she shine in our hearts as her mother does in mine." Morina's smile showed me the delight in both the name and the compliment.

***

The dream faded to the sensation of being on fire. For a moment, my memory refused to reveal where I was, but the dream faded into the present as Marak stood over me. He prayed to the Maker for my health as the healing warmth spread from his hand upon my chest. There was but a tiny breath of air upon my scorched skin, but it was an agony equal to any torture I had endured save that of my soul. Marak expended almost all of his energy and still he prayed for my healing. I placed a hand upon his, knowing that to continue would be pointless.

"It is all right, my son. I will manage if you will retrieve the vial from my belt-pouch." With a shameful frown, he did as I asked. "It is no slight in your honor, Marak. Power comes with age and experience. Your effort was valiant and will not be forgotten."

I drank the potion in the vial, allowing its healing magic to course through me. Though the liquid was potent, my injuries had been grave. Still my skin burned mercilessly as I donned my gambeson and armor, but it was at least bearable. The pain served as a reminder of the limitations of the Reaver. If I were mortally wounded away from zarakanan enemies, I would die like any other kinsman. The thought of Morina's disapproval at how much of my hair and beard had been singed brought a sharp pang to my heart. Would I ever see my hearth-mate again?

Another two days upon the road, and we were again ambushed. But that time, we were ready. Lodath's detection spells gave us ample warning, and we were able to crush the would-be assassins quite decisively. The rest of our journey to Gormorath was uneventful, and I wondered if we had discouraged our enemies, but my instincts began to warn me that more sinister things were on the horizon.

The approach to the gollaran city was lined with granite and flowstone that gave way to a vast deposit of marble and bloodstone. It had been remolded by the gollarans long since my ancestors had mined the area over ten thousand years ago. When the wars broke out between Sorkarak, Zarakalduum, Laharazduum and Balakarak, the mines had been abandoned as indefensible. Our people had sealed them to protect the deposits of valuable metals and gemstones in the event of our return, but sometime during our disputes with our kin and the shadow dwarves, the gollarans had moved in. We were much too occupied in our own wars to bother with them at first, but when an uneasy truce had been made, they became a center focus.

We had tried to reclaim the mines, only to find them well defended. When our troops mounted a siege, the shadow dwarves attacked our strongholds, forcing us to retreat and defend our homes. Our people became embroiled in the first zarak invasion shortly thereafter, and our numbers never recovered enough to mount another siege against the gollarans before the second and present zarak invasion.

The gollarans had wasted no time in preparing defenses, though, and the road to their stronghold was riddled with watchtowers, carefully laid stonework traps and wards of an arcane nature. Such industry towards defense seemed out of place to me, for gollarans were not known for their studious application of labor. Fortunately for us, none of the wards or traps upon the road itself had been activated, but my practiced eye picked them out readily enough. If our negotiations went badly, it could prove difficult to leave in a hurry. Was the proposed alliance an elaborate hoax designed to capture me? The jaws would close tightly if it were a trap. There would be no escape. A cold knot settled in my gut as I looked to my daughter and her hearth-mate. I prayed to Morakvaar to see them safely out of this.

Halfway down the marble causeway we were met by a unit of well-armed and armored guards. No other gollarans were visible either on the road, in the city, or even outside the defensive wall. My concern deepened and I hoped these were merely an escort instead of a restraining force. The vaarandril armor and weapons of the guards were a painful reminder of the wealth we had lost in the mines they had taken. I could tell though, that the metals has been ground into useful shapes instead of forged. That secret belonged to my family only.

"You will leave your mounts here." Their leader was a middle-aged gollaran whose nose stuck out quite far under his shiny helmet. His light gray hand gestured to a couple of younger members, and they came to take away the riding spiders. "You will follow me from here, and do not attempt to draw your weapons." My frown deepened, it was hardly a friendly reception.

The big nosed leader brought us through carved streets of marble ornamented in vaarandril and bloodstone. Even I had to admit it was quite a wonder of artistry. Lodath seemed delighted and his wide eyes could not get enough of the sight of high-arches, growling gargoyles, graceful statues and open palisades. As the first of our kind to be allowed within the great wall, I had been unaware that the gollarans had actually put some industry into the creation of the city. It was indeed a wonder to behold.

The soldiers silently paced towards a large palace that was ridiculously unimpaired by fortifications. Its high buttresses and arches stretched from the cavern floor to the ceiling in striations of different colored marble lit by stargems. The formations of the patterns and carvings were too smooth, too delicate to have been chiseled. They had to have been coaxed out with the use of the gollaran ability to draw stone. Though I had seen it in action, the efforts had been rudimentary, and I had not thought it could be such a refined skill.

The industry and effort that was needed for such displays of architecture and sculpture caused me to reassess my opinion for our diminutive cousins. Like all Kinsmen of the Blood I had been led to believe they were inherently flighty and unconcerned with long and concentrated efforts of labor or study. The city that surrounded me belied that, and spoke of many more beliefs to be shattered. The deception that had been put forth towards our people to make us believe such things was devious indeed. Suddenly, the gollarans became a much larger threat than I had ever conceived, and I hoped we did not have to test our theories of their battle prowess save as our allies.

We were escorted into the palace gates past the great stone guardians that I assumed were of similar function to our Stonewardens. The ripple of arcane forces washed over me as I passed between them, and knew that to do so alone would have been quite foolish. Lodath acknowledged my frown for both the warded gates and the massed troops within the palace courtyard. The display of force was not for my reassurance, but an obvious warning. The air was of barely repressed violence, and I was reminded all too keenly of the amount of bloodshed between our races. If I had not grown beyond the inborn greed of my people, they might have had such need of caution. The obvious wealth of the city was quite attractive to me, but I would not waste more lives in a needless quest for riches. Our purpose was to save lives, and I hoped the gollarans were of the same mind.

The leader brought us to a halt outside the main entrance of the palace, and we waited under the scrutiny of the amassed soldiers while a runner was sent inside. Hateful stares seemed riveted to me as I leaned calmly upon the haft of the Reaver to wait. Bailan stared back at the gollarans with a baleful glare as Korina stepped closer to my right with Marak on her heels.

"What do they want, father?" I hoped none of the gollarans had heard her whisper.

"To intimidate us, Korina. It seems they have not yet forgotten the Vaarandril War." I gave her a stern warning look, and she nodded almost imperceptibly.

"I thought the trade treaty had settled all that." She glared at the nearest soldier who snarled back.

"Evidently, not for them. It seems remarkable just how similar to us they really are. Fortunately for them, the clans with which they were at war have all perished save my own." I emphasized 'my' to correct a possible interpretation of Korina being in my clan. "There will be no more claims against the Mines of Gormorath."

"You think they hold a blood-grudge against your clan, Sire?" Korina made sure they heard that reference, though it was obvious the deception tasted foul.

Angry faces surrounded us in a wall of hate that met my gaze. "It is possible."

Bailan broke in to the conversation. "Well, if it is blood that they are after, then it will cost them dearly in their own."

I put my hand on his shoulder. "No. If it is blood they are after, then it is likely that mine alone will satisfy them. I will need you to return to Balakarak with word of what has occurred. Your lives are not worth the old debts. If vengeance is the reason we have been lured here, then so be it. I will face their wrath whilst my friend, Lodath, will return you to your kin."

Korina opened her mouth to protest, but realized it was her duty to continue as my heir. She clamped her teeth audibly and shook her head instead. The gollaran soldiers pressed about us in a menacing sea of light gray and vaarandril. Though half a head shorter than my kin, I had no doubt that they were a well trained force. It was evident in the easy way they held their shields and spears. If it were blood that they were after, it would be unlikely that I would be able to leave there alive. But, I could sell my life dearly buying time for Korina, Marak, Bailan and Lodath to escape. The mage frowned, knowing that our situation was a result of my trust in him, but he did not know of, nor understand the blood feuds of the clans. I could hardly blame him, but it was obvious he blamed himself.

Before I had the chance to reassure him, the runner returned, and we were escorted through the massive marble doors. My iron-shod boots rang echoingly through the long wide corridor lined with statues of gollaran leaders. They were so similar to the Hall of Heroes in Morakduum. The parody of our architecture ended at the preference for ancestor worship, however, and the opulence of the throneroom was distasteful to me. Almost every inch of wall was covered in tapestries spun with gold and silver threads. Jewelry and gemstones crusted statues and ornaments in gaudy displays of decadence. It was clear to me that there were still quite a few differences in mentality between the gollarans and my people.

Between every statue was a squad of troopers armed with crossbows and warhammers. Each crossbow was loaded and trained upon us as we were escorted down the hall. The significance of the distance between us and our escort was not lost upon me as we approached the double doors that appeared to be made of solid gold inlaid with vaarandril, gemstones and silver. It was no wonder that my ancestors had tried to regain the mines at such a cost in lives. For an instant, I entertained the thought of owning such vast wealth, marching through the streets with my kinsmen as a conqueror. I fought down the greed savagely. I would not let such things control me as I concentrated on the task at hand.

Two halberds obstructed our course as one of the palace guards addressed me. "You are expected to leave your weapons here. No vaarak is allowed to go armed in the presence of our king."

I grit my teeth at the insult meant by the abbreviation of the name of our race, but unbuckled the straps that held the Reaver. My four hand-axes took up positions beside the mighty weapon as it leaned against the wall. The gollarans gestured savagely at my dagger, and I sighed as I removed it too. The others followed suit save Lodath. One of the guards reached out to collect the weapons, nearly touching the Reaver.

"Do not touch the axe, or it will consume you in flame." My warning froze the trooper in his tracks.

Already small tendrils of lightning began to dance along the haft of the Reaver and the gollaran's eyes grew wide as he stepped back in haste. The rest of our escort left a wide berth around the weapon. Further insult was added when small gray hands padded me down for any possible hidden weapon, and the sound of my grinding teeth was not lost upon them.

"Are we guests or prisoners?" I growled, but the leader ignored my anger. Instead, he gestured with his spear for me to precede him through the door.

Bailan flanked me to the right and Korina and Marak to the left as I stepped into the vast throneroom. Lodath trailed slightly behind, and I could tell he was preparing a spell of some sort. The herald by the door gave me a sour look, but announced my presence all the same.

"His Highness, Dorian Mytharia, High King of the Vaarakanan of Morakduum."

Without further prompting, I strode towards the dais to the proper distance and nodded slightly to the gollaran who lounged on the vaarandril throne. Around me the courtiers expressed their anger and disgust that I should treat their king as less than an equal. Stargems lit the vast chamber in a dimmer semblance of surface light, illuminating their pale gray faces. The sides of the hall were packed with gollarans dressed to the hilt in gaudy finery. Spidersilk brocaded jackets and gowns were covered in gold, vaarandril and platinum threads, and red gems flashed from rings, pendants, earlobes and hats. The hall itself was decorated with tapestries of battles with my kin and zarakanan, gilded statues of grotesquely plump gollarans with big noses, and inlaid swirling runes that I could feel held some kind of arcane warding.

It surprised me that the gollarans preferred the unnatural lighting to the normal illumination of heat, for I was sure their vision in the light spectrum was even worse than our own. It was then that I realized that the decoration and wealth around them would be invisible in the spectrum of heat. It was an indication of how much appearance seemed to mean to the gollarans. The rumble of voices around me spoke repeatedly of the return of Gorain the Slayer. Unaware that I spoke their language fluently, they were free with insults and fearful speculation. Were they really that afraid of me?

King Saveyo was silent for a long period, longer than was polite as he stared at my kin and me. I returned his stare grimly wondering if he would indeed order us slain on the spot. From the periphery of my vision I could see the line of crossbowmen upon the balconies overlooking the throneroom. A single command would ensure none of us left alive, and I would not have the chance to call the Reaver. How quickly could I leap into the surrounding courtiers to shield myself? But the calculation came up short. Saveyo was shrewd, waiting for me to realize just what position we were in. As he shifted, ripples of his enormous belly shook his brocaded doublet in a very unappealing fashion.

His voice echoed from the dais through the hall designed for that specific acoustic performance. "So, you are Dorian, the reincarnation of Gorain the Slayer." The insult was plainly meant and I ground my teeth to bite back the quick reply.

Saveyo leaned his bald pate out over the expanse of his waist-line until the gem encrusted crown threatened to overbalance him. It was a gesture meant to threaten, but instead almost made me laugh at his awkwardness. How much more preferable was the simple dragon-shaped crown riveted to my own helmet? The gollaran's beady eyes regarded me from either side of his huge proboscis like a fat vainglorious vulture. He expected my anger as an excuse to order our deaths.

"I am of Gorain's blood, and I carry his weapon, nothing more, and nothing less." I admitted, hoping our mission to Gormorath was not a futile one.

Bailan, however, would not stand any more of the insulting behavior. "King Dorian is the Liberator of Balakarak, the one who defeated Terazandarin and Mezosilliar, He is High King of all Vaarakanan, and you would do better to show him more respect!"

My gauntlet on his pauldron halted any further tirade as the young warrior quivered in rage. "I believe his highness meant no disrespect. It is difficult to maintain an understanding with a people so different from our own." My words were more for Saveyo's benefit than Bailan's and the insult to our diminutive cousins did not go unnoticed by the corpulent king. "But as a visiting dignitary it is my duty to maintain an air of negotiation." The young warrior began to understand that this was a war of words as I turned from him to the gollaran. "Greetings King Saveyo. I am Dorian Mytharia; servant of the Vaarakanan and it is upon their behalf that I have come. As you know, the invasion of the zarakanan goes back many centuries and threatens the lives of not only our people, but the gollarans as well. If they were successful in eliminating us as an enemy, their eyes would swiftly turn to Gormorath. It is my intention to remove their threat to both our peoples and seal the Starrift against any return. Only then will we know peace once more."

"Are they the only ones who bear your grudge, Mytharian?" Bailan snarled at my side, and I gripped his pauldron tighter, shaking him slightly. "Will you turn your weapons this way once your enemies are defeated as your ancestors have?"

In grim realization, I began to think there was no chance of a treaty with them. The gollarans seemed as capable and eager to bear a grudge as my own kin.

"It is true that our people have had our squabbles, but it is the zarakanan that are our true enemy. Once they have been defeated, the tunnels to Gormorath can also be sealed. In that way, neither of us will have to be wary of interference."

Saveyo regarded me for a long moment, and I was finally able to read his intention. It was not revenge he sought, but to determine whether or not we were honest in our proposal. The grudge was a test of my commitment to peace between our people, but the gollaran was not through trying my patience.

"And who will draw these lines of division, the vaarak?"

My grip on my anger was severely tried as I restrained a snarling Bailan. "We will decide equally and equitably before the non-aggression pact is signed."

That answer brought a small light of satisfaction into his eye, but Saveyo had one last jab to make. "And why should we risk ourselves in your war? What would we gain by aiding you?"

"Freedom from fear and ensured survival. Is that not enough?" My patience was nearly gone, but the gollaran wanted to see how far he could push me.

"No. All we need to do is remain neutral. Once you and the zarakanan have destroyed each other, our people will have no need to fear."

My anger finally snapped and I shot an accusing stare at Lodath. Why had he even proposed the alliance with the vile barbarians?

"I see that I have wasted my time and patience!" I spun on my heels and faced the door, but a ring of crossbows backed up with spears blocked my way. "So I see that treachery is not beneath you! Well, I will show you how honorably a Vaarakanan will impart his life." I marched straight for the door, closing the gap to the threatening guards.

"King Dorian, I want you to hear my terms before you foolishly throw your life away." The note of respect in his voice got my attention, and I stopped but remained facing the door. "We will aid you in your war, but this is our price. You will not rule as High King once the enemy is defeated."

I laughed humorlessly with my back still towards him. "And who would you put upon the throne of Morakduum, a gollaran?"

Now that I was almost close enough for a good leap at them, the guards watched their king nervously from around my imposing form. I smiled inwardly. Their orders were to intimidate, and not actually kill me. The advantage was mine. The Reaver sensed my anger and the presence within the weapon seized upon my ire, but I forced myself to return to a neutral disposition. A great sigh from the throne told me that Saveyo had dropped all pretenses, and I finally turned to face him.

"That you leave it to your kin is enough for us." He made a gesture and the guards behind us dispersed to the back of the room.

The crossbows on the balcony and behind the spears were also lowered and I nodded slowly. "It was never my intention to be High King; it is an occupation I will gladly leave behind me."

The gollaran king stared at me with his mouth wide open. He blinked several times before closing it and finally a light of understanding passed between us. He knew the burdens of rulership and responsibility, but his was a position of power instead of devoted servitude. My companions showed no such understanding save Korina. She had been trained since childhood for such responsibility and was not happy at the swiftness with which it was to come to her.

"Then we will draw up the maps in the morning after our sleep cycle, but tonight, you will be welcome at my table."

"It will be my pleasure." The words came stiffly from my lips to let Saveyo know his insults to me were not so easily forgiven.

We were shown to rooms in the palace that were as gaudy as I could imagine, but for some reason I still felt ill-at-ease. My instincts warned me that all was not well, yet I could not fathom the depth of the warning. To cement my confusion, I did not feel that the threat came from the gollarans, nor the human emissary who greeted us as we were seated at the High Table with King Saveyo. Not wishing to alarm my companions, I kept my misgivings to myself until I had a better idea of what caused them.

All the next day was spent in a less hostile argument over territory. Saveyo wished to claim the mines in the neighboring regions as well as those behind the outer fortifications of Gormorath. It was a point of contention that kept us from agreement, but I had to admit, our people had not had the resources or the manpower to mine those areas for quite a few thousand years. But those had been the mines of my clan from before the time of the first zarak invasion, and giving them up would be like selling the souls of my ancestors. Exhausted mentally from haggling all day with the gollaran, I was then treated to the obstinacy of the human's demands. For the additional troops, Osric demanded another ten thousand weights of gold, a price that would have bought twice the troops in mercenaries on the surface.

Three days of arguments appeared to get me nowhere. My 'allies' had me over a barrel and they knew it. I needed their support more than they were willing to budge in their demands. All through the 'negotiations', I could not help the escalated feeling of disaster that hovered about me like a cloud. Was I really leading my people to their doom? The source of the unease continued to elude me, but leant a sense of urgency to my return. At last when pen was put to paper on both accounts, I felt as if I were spilling my life-blood upon the pages. So grievous was the cost to us, I wondered if it were indeed worth it, yet if we had no allies, we would be destroyed and my people would fade into extinction. No price was so great as to allow that eventuality.

The gollaran scribes were quick to draw up copies of the agreements, and we prepared to leave as soon as the promised gollaran troops were ready to accompany us. I felt as if I had sold the soul of my people for a pittance, but what was the price of survival? The only comfort I had was that Lodath opted to return with us to Balakarak. I had not expected him to do so, even though he was my closest friend. We had grown quite distant in the past eighty-four years, and most of it was my own fault. The argument we had upon the day of our parting was sure to have left my old friend with a feeling of not being welcome. His presence seemed to be an apology for the way his proposed allies had treated me. I tried not blaming him, for he had been truthful but his allies had not been straightforward with him.

When we were close to a time cycle from the outer gates of Gormorath Lodath turned to me. "I'm sorry, Dorian. I had thought better of King Saveyo."

I met his eyes, trying to emphasize the importance of my words. "Zese are hard times, Lodath. None of us are who ve vere. You had no vay of knowing of our ancient blood feuds, so do not blame yourself. In fact, it is I who should apologize for not telling you. Zere are ozer zings zat I regret stahnd betveen us." His eyebrows shot up, and I dropped my gaze to the cavern floor.

"Are you apologizing?" He held his hand over his heart in mocking shock. "Dorian? Saying he's sorry? Has the world ended?"

"I should know better zan to apologize to a human." I growled.

Lodath's demeanor changed almost instantly from mocking to concern. "Dorian, if you don't return to Morakduum, where will you go? What of Morina?"

My wry smile surprised him. "Zie Maker has already decreed zat I vould not return to Morakduum, so really, Saveyo did not ask of me anyzing zat I had not already been prepared to do. Vat is most grievous to me is zie loss of territory ahnd zie goods ve must pay Osric for his troops."

He went from surprise to troubled frown. "You mean you never had any intention of returning to Morakduum? What of your wife? Haven't things been going well between you?"

"I had zie intention of returning, but Morakvaar has ozer plans vich are unknown to me. As for Morina, my heart aches every time I zink of not being able to return to her side. Zie pain my absence vill cause her vounds me more zan Liathrain's dagger zrough my chest. But, Korina ahnd Dorak are strong children, more zan a fazer could vish for. If it vere not for zie impending birz of our zird child, Morina vould be at my side." I sighed wistfully, feeling my hearth-mate's absence like a mortal wound. "Morina believes zie child vill be anozer girl, a great sign for our people. For zousands of years have zere never been zie birz of two girls ahnd vun boy in a single clan." The unsteadiness of my voice made me unable to continue.

Lodath placed a hand on my pauldron, as if he were the elder of the two of us, and he certainly looked it. "I am truly sorry my old friend."

"Old?" I gave him a strained laugh, trying to throw off the pall that had surrounded me. "Who is zie old vun here? I am in zie prime of my life, but you?" Lodath shared in my laughter with a little more ease. "Vat ever happened to Rutger ahnd Kelana?"

Lodath's brows arched once more and I knew he expected an inquiry of a different person's wellbeing. "Rutger became a great Lord, a man of justice and peace. His sense of fairness was near legendary, and almost was his undoing. He became too popular with the people. The nobles conspired against him, fearful of his popularity. They tried to discredit him before King Osric, and plotted against the throne. But, with my help, Rutger was able to expose the nobles' plan. As gratitude for his loyalty, Rutger was granted a barony over the lands of those who would have betrayed Osric."

I smiled, seeing Rutger sitting in judgement in my mind's eye. "Does he still live?"

"No, he passed away sixteen years ago at the ripe old age of one hundred and one. He asked about you before his death, but none of us knew anything of your exploits since Mezosilliar." Lodath stared off into space as if seeing Rutger's last moments once more.

"Vat of Kelana?" I tried to distract him from his painful memory.

"She stayed with Liathrain, as far as I know." He shot me a pointed look as if I would know the answer.

I shrugged uncomfortably, reminded of his accusation as Liathrain's murderer. "Vat of you, Lodath? How has your life been?" He stared hard into my eyes, seeing the question I wished to avoid directly. Would he tell me if he had been involved with Jaguar?

"I served Malik, Osric's father for a time. It was handy having the backing of a king. When Malik died, I took oath to serve Osric. There isn't much to tell, really."

I stared questioningly back, knowing he was leaving out something that would possibly anger me. At his dubious silence, I refused to ask the question he was expecting. Perhaps I was better off not knowing. After all, it was the reason we had not spoken in over eighty-one years.

As we continued our journey the next day, Lodath decided it was his turn to do the asking. "Dorian, what happened at Terazandarin?" His face remained carefully neutral as I stared at him. "I have heard some disturbing rumors."

I looked away from his gold-orange stare that still seemed as innocent as it had been when he was nineteen. If only I could have remained so innocent. "Vat you have heard is probably true."

He grabbed my arm, squeezing the armor fruitlessly. "You mean to tell me you slaughtered over ten thousand of the shadow elves including children and infants!?" His eyes were full of horror for the imagined carnage.

I had to look away again as the discomforting memory filled my mind. "Not all personally, no."

He shook me, forcing me to look back. "But you were there, weren't you!?" Reluctantly I nodded as realization hit him. "You ordered it, didn't you!"

"Ah... Vell, it vas not really me."

"What do you mean it wasn't really you!? You were there. You were in command, weren't you?" His innocence mocked me.

I closed my eyes, unwilling to face what I had become, but was just as unable to escape it. The words flowed from me as if from another dispassionate observer, wishing they were not true, but how could I escape their reality?

In my native tongue I told him my tale, wishing that Lodath did not understand, but knowing he did. "We stormed the gates of Terazandarin after our engineers had loosed the magma upon it. The zarakanan managed to stop the fires with arcane magic and turned back the Mother's fury. We fought the zaraks to a standstill and besieged their fortress. Kairillia, Matriarch of the Vaetra, proposed that she could steal some of her spies into Terazandarin to open the gates to us. Our combined forces could lay waste to what remained of the Terazandarin army if we could but get inside. I agreed to this plan, as it seemed the best way, and looked to be the least costly in my kinsmen's lives." The battle was laid out in my memory as clearly as if it had been yesterday, and I lapsed into silence.

Lodath walked quietly next to my spider, knowing that his patience would compel me to continue. The gollaran commanders that were near me ceased their talking to listen, and I wondered how many of them spoke our language.

"It was the third month of the siege, and Kairillia sent her spies a message to open the gates to us. The spies had informed us of the unrest within for there was no food left. We expected an easy victory, hoping the zaraks would surrender for a good meal, as they cared nothing for their fellows. My people would lead the charge, followed tightly by the Vaetra." I paused again, clenching my teeth once more in the rage of betrayal. "My kinsmen followed me unopposed through the gates, and for a moment, I wondered why the fortifications appeared unmanned. I speculated on how widespread the starvation might have been, but I could not imagine that it could get that bad in a mere three months.

"We slowed within the gates, gazing about, and wondering why there were no zarakanan in sight. It was then that I realized the Vaetra had not accompanied our troops. Cold fear grew inside me, and I ordered a retreat for the gates, but I was too late. The magma that had been diverted with magic was loosed upon us from behind. The treacherous Vaetra had conspired with the enemy to destroy us. The ramparts that had appeared deserted a moment before shimmered and then revealed the illusion that had been cast upon them and hidden from us. It had been the job of the Vaetra to break the enemies' attempts to deceive us, and we paid dearly for our trust. Barricades appeared as the spells were released, and behind, the hot magma forced us forward into the killing zone of our enemies." My head dropped to my chest, thinking that I should have known of such treachery.

The thousands of my kinsmen that were cut down before my eyes were my fault. It was my insistence that included the Vaetra, my folly to trust them even after their odd behavior at Mezosilliar. My people had died because I failed to see the signs before me.

"What did you do?" Lodath whispered, barely able to comprehend my failure.

"The only thing I could. Our escape was cut off, and missile fire rained down upon us like the ash clouds of an eruption. Our only hope was to engage the enemy so that we could not be slaughtered like sheep. I ordered the charge, into the barricades of rock and spears. So many valiant kinsmen perished. So many, and yet we broke through their line despite the spells that lanced through us unhindered. Unable to hold our ground against such numbers, we gave way slowly, backing through the tunnels aimlessly, trying to survive as long as we could and take as many zarakanan with us as was possible.

"To our surprise, we found ourselves backed up to the former palace of Laharazduum. We slipped inside as our enemies regrouped for their final assault, and we managed to block the doors using the ancient commands." I did not tell Lodath that the words came unbidden to my lips from the depths of time, words I had never known. Perhaps a boon of my ancestors? "My kin and I fell to the ground in weariness, unable to move for some time. When at last strength returned to my limbs, I took count of those that remained and was dismayed. Of our original twenty thousand only five hundreds remained. There were at least ten enemies to every one of my kin on the other side of the doors. Already we could hear the explosions of arcane energies directed against the ancient wards in an attempt to finish the slaughter.

"Waradain, our High Priest, and his acolytes beseeched the ancestors and the gods for intervention, placing powerful anti-magic barriers against the enemy. Knowing the place of our entombment, we decided to explore the old palace against hope of some unknown escape route. To our horror, we found mutations, twisted experiments of the dark gods of the zarakanan. They retreated before our forces, but we knew such reprieve was only temporary. In every case, the creatures headed towards the old throneroom."

Again, I left out how I knew the layout of the palace. The memories that had come to me unbidden had quite unnerved me then and seemed too odd to mention. Lodath did not seem to notice my oversights and listened with rapt attention.

"When we reached the throneroom, we found that the abominations had gathered there. The dais had been converted to a profane altar where the blood of its victims stained the grand stair as it ran in a mockery of the red carpet that used to cushion the feet of petitioners to the king. A statue of their accursed goddess of darkness grinned menacingly even as she struck an alluring pose for the weak-willed. Her bare arms stretched forth, as a field of energy was contained between her delicate hands. Within the field rotated a weapon that constantly spewed lighting and arcane energy in protest to its captivity. Its defiance seemed to please the countenance of the stone goddess."

I did not tell Lodath how the statue seemed alive, and her perfect breasts seemed to heave in pleasure at the prospect of further victims. We had been entranced, all of us, and had stepped forward eagerly to please such an alluring creature even as slaves. Were it not for Waradain's deep-rooted faith, we would all have perished in her spell, and have been happy doing so. The elder priest saw the spell for what it was and prayed to the Maker to give him power to release us from its grasp. Even so, we had been reluctant to move against what we perceived as a beautiful and helpless creature. It was not until the weapon cried out to me that I was able to shake off the lethargy as enemies surrounded us.

"Held by a powerful spell, the Reaver called out to me. 'Blood of my blood,' it said, 'together we will smite our enemies. To live and to avenge our kinsmen, speak my name and call to me.' Before I knew what was happening, the words formed upon my lips. Gods curse me, but I was angry. The weapon's fury mingled with my own. The rage of betrayal and the helpless anger of the damned filled me to overflowing. I called out to the weapon, welcomed it to my hand. When its fury filled me, I went mad." My jaw clenched and again I saw the events played out before me as if it were happening as I spoke.

"I was not sure if it was my own need for revenge, or the weapon's ire that controlled me. I only knew that I cried out for blood. My kinsmen were reborn in the fury that filled me as if under the same spell. The Reaver possessed me with its might, and I struck down the zarak priestesses and their foul hellspawn as Waradain and his priests shielded me from their curses. I led my kin back to the gates of the palace, commanding them to open. Surprised, our enemies were like children before us, wailing in fear as we cut them down, a great blaze of blue white fire before us. And still my anger was not assuaged.

"I sought them out, ordered them slain where we could find them. The only vision within my mind was the slaughter of my kin as I showed no mercy for old or young. The madness drove me to kill them all no matter where they hid, no matter how much they begged for mercy." I saw again the young, the old and infants taken by my own hand. Blood flowed freely from the blades of the Reaver, covering my armor and dripping from my hands like the knell of guilt.

"When I had slain all those within the walls, my fury trained upon our former allies. The anger of their betrayal smote the reason from my mind. Those that had remained to witness our demise also fell beneath the Reaver's blades. I hunted and pursued them halfway to Fartairilzzan before the remainder outdistanced my ability to sense them. Only when the Reaver could no longer find my enemies did my reason return to me.

"I do not know to this day if I truly would have slain them all, or it was the Reaver that urged me to such carnage. If it were my own anger, I still may have shown no mercy, and therein lies my shame." I looked at my hands as if they were still covered in blood.

Lodath walked on in silence for some time before whispering, "I had hoped it was not true."

He had hoped that I had remained true to his vision of my honor, hoped I was innocent of the evil deed, and I wept inside to know I had wounded him with my capacity for injustice and murder.

Chapter 6

Bailankrazak (Betrayal/Death of Honor)

The rest of the journey back was uneventful, but all the while the sense of foreboding hovered over me like a dark cloud that grew thicker as the days went by. That the zarakanan left us in peace to rejoin the main army was alarming. I had sent out scouts, expecting at least one ambush, but there had been no sign of enemy activity. It was too quiet, and I was anxious to consult with Kormak, hoping he had found out the information I had requested.

Two days from the gates of Balakarak, so great was my unease I asked Lodath to take the risk of scrying out the enemy. Half a dozen spells failed to turn up any information, giving me the assumption that they had not just given up and left. To block such a powerful sorcerer as Lodath also told me that they were more organized than normal, and expecting us to be able to bring in powerful magics upon our side. It was an assumption that did not sit well with me. It was as if they cared not one whit that we secured allies against them, a fact that belied either foolish arrogance or overwhelming odds.

With our entire army housed within the walls of Balakarak, it still seemed empty of its former glory. There were home tunnels enough to spare and all were quartered comfortably and fed. The food worried me some, for the farm tunnels of Balakarak had been wild too long, but I did not expect to tarry. As soon as I saw to the comfort of the troops, I summoned the generals and commanders to a council of war. We had much planning to do.

When I presented the documents drawn up in Gormorath, an angry murmur rumbled through the ranks.

"My kinsmen, I know these arrangements are a grievous blow to us, yet I must remind you of the price in lives that we will save for such bargains. To ensure our children survive to live in peace is worth any price, for wealth can be rebuilt." I could still see the stubborn set of lines upon some of the faces.

"What good is a future of poverty? Would you reduce us to live like the outsiders?" Narok voiced the opinion of more than one of the officers around me.

"A full half share of the goods we must give Osric will be taken from my personal vaults. I only ask that our kinsmen match the remaining half share. Each clan will contribute a share according to their wealth, and not a fixed amount. In that way the burden will be no more than any clan can bear." The mouths of my kin were open in shock all around me.

"A full half share?" Kormak glanced at the amount on the pages and then to me. "You can absorb such a loss?"

I smiled inside, for none of them knew the amount of wealth I had gathered; though rumor had said it was great, their estimates fell way short of the mark. "Yes." Of those present, only Korina knew the secret vaults where I kept the majority of the treasures I had accumulated in my travels and adventures.

As the rumor circulated through the room, I knew my legend had grown, much to my dismay. Narok nodded his agreement, as did the others. Half the price could be met, but the full price would have left many clans destitute.

"I will leave it to the Council of Elders to assess the wealth of the clans and set a price for them. I will personally overhear protests of any clan over the rate they must pay, but this must be done quickly, for in two months time, we march to Fartairilzzan. The weapons and armor will be delivered to the humans by way of the quest tunnels before they meet us at the stronghold of our enemies. The rest of the payment will be given when we have crushed the zarakanan beneath our boots." A cheer went through the room, even though it was a little less than enthusiastic.

Kormak tapped me on the shoulder as soon as I had given instructions to a messenger to gather the required amount of wealth from Morakduum, Barakillanak and Dormakarduum. "Sire, I have news of the enemy that you may find of import."

I nodded, and turned to follow him, but the sense of unease grew exponentially. Was the news as bad as I felt it would be? I wished I had not left the Reaver in my quarters, for even though I despised the weapon; its presence brought a sense of security to me. I shrugged and followed Kormak out onto a balcony overlooking the vast cavern that opened into the market place of Balakarak. It was beautiful; the layers of warmth that eddied and swirled about the small dots of stargem light, and the blaze of kinsmen going about their business as if the war never existed in their illuminated wreaths of heat mesmerized me. I leaned onto the rail, my elbowcops ringing against the stone as I lost myself in the view.

"We captured several of the dark kin and questioned them regarding the numbers and constitution of Kairillia's army." I turned back to Kormak, something in his tone warned me he was on the verge of panic.

I stepped away from the rail so that he could speak in a whisper, sensing that it was something I did not wish the generals to hear just yet.

Kormak continued when I was close enough to hear his shaky words, "we were able to get the information you asked for through long hours of questioning. We were also able to determine the depth of planning and fortification that has gone into Karillia's expectation of our assault." He looked away, drawing in a long breath to steady his nerve, and an impending sense of danger struck me. "Your friend Lodath was optimistic. Kairillia has over two hundred fifty thousand at her command including Jubaroz of the trolls, and Hakarastor of the goblins." Something told me Kormak's unease was not the news he bore, but my mind refused to suspect my kinsman.

"It is grave news, my friend, but not insurmountable. Goblins are lousy fighters and trolls are too stupid to fight effectively."

Kormak shook his head. "That is not the worst. I have also confirmed a regiment of vourdovra have joined her."

"The mind-eaters?" I stared in shock as Kormak nodded. "But I thought they would never join with what they consider their prey." The notion filled me with dread. "I have seen lone individuals join others, but an entire regiment?" I turned from him and paced, trying to absorb the implications.

I finally faced him once more, the resolution made. "And yet, we cannot lay down and die without a fight. It is too late to retreat back to the comfort of our homes, for our enemies would surely follow. There is nothing else to be done." A strange expression crossed Kormak's face, and I began to sense the presence of others upon the terrace.

"No, we have one alternative." Ice filled my heart, knowing the moment that my own kinsman had betrayed me. "We have made a bargain."

I tried to spring to the left, but five kinsmen leapt upon me, bearing me down to the terrace stones. I struggled, but my limbs had been secured, and I wished I had learned more of unarmed combat from Morina. Kormak leaned over me, his face twisted in grief, knowing what he had done.

"I am sorry, Lord Dorian, but I believe it is for the best that you sacrifice your life to save us all. Kairillia will be satisfied with your blood and the Reaver, and she will leave us in peace."

I tried to reason with him. "Kormak, you cannot trust her! She will not keep her word!"

The rest of my argument was stifled as a cloth was forced into my mouth. I took in a breath, and knew instantly it was a stupid thing to do. An acrid tang filled my mouth and nose, and my consciousness faded from me, but not before I caught sight of the grinning zarak assassin that had come to collect me.

Chapter 7

Korvain (Eternal Agony)

My head ached abominably, but it was nothing compared to the cramps that raced through my shoulders and spine. I tried to stretch, but found myself contained in a very small area. Stuck in a crouch with my arms bound behind me, I tried to reason out where I was. Somehow, they must have smuggled me out of the stronghold. When my vision finally cleared, I could see through the bars of the small cage that held me. I was in a small square cage set in the back of a wagon pulled by crawlers. Around me were ranks of the shadow elves as they wove in and around the stalagmites that impeded our progress. Each of them were in the polished blued armor of their Matron. Over the armor they wore cloaks of shadow that gave off no heat, but their vibrations were plain enough. Nightmares of memory haunted me with visions of my former slavery. Lady Alfstein had me put into a cage remarkably similar and bound my hands and feet in the same fashion, but I had the feeling that Kairillia's treatment might be even worse than the foul slaver's.

Parched and hungry I watched my captors as they consumed their rations and drank from their skins. Forced into a fetal ball, my muscles protested endlessly against the cramped singular position. The touch of the Reaver's rage did little to help my disposition. The weapon ranted in my mind, raged and surged against the spells that held it, but needed my beckon to awaken its awesome fury. The cloth still tied in my mouth had stolen my voice and the drug within it swam in my head in nauseous tides. At an ebb in the tide, I struggled against the bonds, trying to free my hands, loosen the gag in my mouth, ease the ache in my neck and back, but all I gained was the mocking of my enemies.

"Save your strength, dwarf, for the Matriarch will have need of it." The riders surrounding the cart laughed heartily, and I had the uncomfortable feeling that my fate was well known to them.

Days uncounted I spent bound and gagged as thirst tormented me and hunger gnawed at my consciousness, but my captors had no mercy. In the delirious fever, I was no longer aware of the passage of time as the aching of my muscles subsided into their atrophy. I faded in and out of tortured delirium, as lack of food and water took its toll upon me. My bouts of fevered dreams were interrupted by momentary awareness of a few cool drops of water, but never enough. The spasms of my muscles became permanent companions as the ropes that bound me were encrusted with my blood and tore at the growing scars around my wrists and ankles. I remembered at one point we stopped, and they removed my gag long enough to force a disgusting broth down my throat. So desperate was I that I cared nothing about the taste and eagerly drank all that was offered. The pittance was not near enough to satisfy my ravening hunger, and they replaced the gag too soon. I was aware for a short time thereafter, but soon lapsed back into fevered dreams.

Once the sound of roars and screams woke me, but it made no sense to my dazed mind. I thought I saw Naiara, the great bear plowing through the ranks of my enemies as they fired spells and crossbows at her. She took a heavy toll of their numbers before they brought her down. It was a dream that merged into the nightmare of unreality that had settled around me.

A sharp pang in my chest overrode my physical torment as realization finally dawned on me. Naiara, my friend and companion was undoubtedly gone. As a cub, I had found her squalling beside her dead mother as the blood of the great bear dripped from the half-moon blades of my axe. Reports of the bear included the deaths of at least three kinsman, a kinswoman, and four children. The evidence of the predator's prowess lay in the whitening bones surrounding her lair.

Naiara's brown eyes were barely slits, not yet open to the wonders of the Deeps. My axe was prepared to rid us of one more merciless killer, but something was different about her. She seemed aware of me, and her fate as her mind reached out to me. The empathy I had shared with animals became a curse as I lowered the axe and hefted the quiescent cub. She knew I would protect her as surely as her mother, a sentience that went beyond most predators.

Naiara's memory was like a distant dream, another life away. The only thing that was real was the rage of the Reaver and the memories of Gorain that reached out to me from beyond the millennia. The Maker had been right to confine his soul to the weapon, or so the legend went, but it seemed as though I knew better. Only a part of his soul remained within the weapon, a part that fit within my consciousness too well even as I despised it. Gorain became more real to me than my own memories, and I began to question my existence. Dorian became a distant name, another dream of torment for a fractured soul.

One day, the Reaver's rage and the domination of Gorain's memories became suddenly distant and finally ceased. Bewildered, I was aware that someone had opened the cage in which I had been kept. Rough hands dragged me still curled into a tight ball though my bonds had been removed. My muscles refused to budge from that position, as unknown days had molded them into the unnatural pose. Several hands gripped my limbs and pulled them straight, tearing muscles and tendons as I groaned in pain, powerless to stop them. Cold iron replaced the burning ropes at my wrists as they continued to unmercifully tear my limbs into straight positions with a mechanical winch. My clothing had been ripped from me, as it was rank with my sweat and waste that I had been forced to live in for the gods only knew how long. I was doused with several buckets of freezing water, and I struggled to drink as much as I could. It wet my dry tongue and throat, but it was nowhere near enough to quench the fever that raged through me.

Dripping and cold they left me, my teeth chattering in the dark chamber that shed no heat. Agony flared through every torn tendon and nerve, and I cried out to the Maker to spare me the torment of my enemies to no avail. My joints swelled purple and blue from the internal wounds. I could not stand, nor lean into the chains for the pain, but shifted continuously from one sharp agony to another. Fresh blood and pus ran from my wrists and ankles as the iron bit into the festering wounds without compassion.

How could a kinsman have sentenced one of his own to such a fate? My soul felt the agony more deeply than my body, and I lost hope for my people. I prayed to the Maker to take my soul and spare my enemies the satisfaction of my pain, but every time I tried to submit to the cold darkness,

Morina's face hovered before me. How could I abandon my hearth-mate and our children? And yet the torment continued without rest, and I could neither stand nor sleep for the suffering. Dread filled me for the moments that I would be subject to Kairillia's presence, and the memory of my time as a slave loomed before me as a dark nightmare.

It seemed an eternity I hovered in fevered darkness, vacillating from freezing cold to fiery heat, and no comfort from either. Weakness filled me, and despite the pain and the tearing of flesh and bone, I sagged in the chains that held me as I could no longer hold back the darkness.

A hand gripped my hair, pulling my head back roughly and pouring some sort of cool liquid down my throat nearly choking me. Instantly, I felt its effects go to work upon my weakness, soothing my fever, bringing clarity to my mind. The darkness had been lifted from where I was chained, and I found myself staring into the vast throneroom of the ancient kings of the stronghold that was once Sorkarak. Though the liquid cleared my head of fever, it did nothing for the pain in my joints and the shackles that bit into them.

Around me I could see thousands of zarakanan, hostile stares all riveted to me. Faery glows lit their faces unnaturally, making their slanted features appear demonic as they mocked me. Feebly, and despite the pain I pulled against the chains, following their lengths to what appeared to be a dragon's mouth made of solid iron. The dragon's head was suspended upon a platform that overlooked the chamber, visible by all within. The pillars in the hall that reinforced the ceiling had once been carved in the grim visages of my ancestors, but now they bore the likenesses of zaraks lit by rings of unnatural fire. The buttressed ceiling was strikingly different, retaining the original graceful styling of my people with runes and knotwork twined within the stone. To my right was the dais and throne upon which Kairillia sat like a spider surrounded with her attendants like entangled flies.

A large zarak female ascended the stairs to stand before me. Her long silver hair flowed freely from beneath her vaarandril helmet. Silver brows arched gracefully over amber almond-shaped eyes, and I drew in a breath of amazement. Was this a ghost? Yet even as I looked, I noticed subtle differences between this formidable zarak and my old friend Liathrain. There were deeper lines of age about her eyes and mouth, and the shade of her hair was slightly off.

The zarak's gauntleted finger traced the track of the tears of agony that had taken the rest of my moisture from me. She stood about the same height, but with the weakness, I sagged below her eye-level. She gripped my red hair and pulled my head up for all to see. The motion brought fresh spurts of agony through my limbs where the tendons had been torn, and I could not help the slight whimper of pain. The zarak laughed.

"Behold the Mighty Gorain, come to slay us all!" The assembly laughed uproariously and insults fell like rain. When the furor died down, she continued. "Tell me, oh mighty one, just how was it supposed to go? Oh yes, High King Dorian with the Reaver will crush our forces with one blow! We must all run before him!" Her mocking brought much laughter. Suddenly serious, her gaze focused on mine. "Instead, we have a different fate for you. Dorian will now answer for his crimes against our people! Your trial is at hand, oh mighty Gorain! Was it not you who slaughtered ten thousand males, children, old and young in Terazandarin?"

I growled low in my throat, unable to form any sort of comprehensive reply.

"Oh come now, has the great orator lost his tongue?"

"There is nothing I have to say to you." I whispered at last, my throat refusing to allow sound, but even that effort left me coughing.

The spasms wreaked havoc on me, bringing fresh blood from the shackles and more tears of pain despite my dehydrated state. Realizing her sport would be short lived; the zarak gestured for a ladle of water to be brought. Gratefully I downed it swiftly, so she had not the chance to change her mind. Out of the corner of my vision, I saw Matriarch Kairillia shift upon the ancient throne as if bored. The zarak before me cast a nervous glance towards the dais and continued when the servant had been dismissed.

"Dorian Mytharia, you stand accused of the war crimes of treason, murder, pillage and unjust slaughter. You are guilty of attempted genocide against our race and our assembled allies. You murdered my own daughter who was your friend and comrade; killed her in cold blood! Have you anything to say in your defense?"

"There is naught that you would accept." My voice was shattered, broken and weak, as they had made my body.

"Try me. Why did you murder my daughter? She was your friend!" Her snarl was emphasized as she grabbed my beard and shook me. "Has your thirst for power and tyranny wiped every pact of decency from your blood!?"

Tendons, already torn, began to give way to the onslaught, and I could feel the bones trying to separate as they ground together unnaturally. A blinding flash of hot agony pierced my skull and my enemies delighted in my scream of pain. The zarak let me go, realizing I would be unable to reply as long as I was in the throes of such torment. My breath came in ragged trembling gasps, and I fought the urge to submit to my pain though it showed in the tears that flowed anew with my attempts to gain control. The torture I had endured as a slave had rivaled the pain I felt, but it did not make it any easier to accept.

"Answer me, vaarak dog!" She made as if to shake me once more, and gods forgive me, but I could not contemplate another bout of such torment.

"She ... came to ... kill me. I had no ... choice but to ... defend myself." Ashamed of my weakness, I prayed again for the Maker to spare me my enemies' delight.

Her backfist caught me square in the chin, slamming me against the limit of the chains, and I felt as if my wrists had been torn in half. Blood flowed freely from the shackles down my arms and sides as my head swam in waves of cold sweat and nausea. I was aware of the zarak's words only as if from a long distant tunnel.

"You lie! Liathrain was sent as a negotiator of peace and you killed her in cold blood!"

The angry roar of the zarakanan sounded like the distant sea that had brought me such terror when I was forced to board a ship in my younger days. I struggled to keep down the water I had drunk, but despite my efforts, the spasms won. Each heave was as painful as the shaking the zarak had given me, causing white flashes of hot fire to echo through my brain. It was more than my mortal soul could endure; yet some depth of stubbornness remained within me. Some spark of foolish pride in my heritage would not allow the zarakanan to win.

"The scar ... across my throat ... proclaims you the liar!"

The amber eyes narrowed to slits and she grabbed my beard once more, yanking my head back so as to expose my throat. I bit my tongue to hold back the cry that tried to leave me as blood filled my mouth. The zarak released me with a look of shocked puzzlement. Could she really not have known Liathrain's true mission? She gestured for a different servant to come forward and administer the cool liquid once more. The potion lessened the flow of blood from my wrists and tongue, and I was able to think clearly. The zarak grabbed the hair on the back of my head, drawing me to her as she whispered in my ear.

"You had better speak truly to me vaarak. Was that scar from my daughter's blade?" In her other gauntlet, she held an amulet of the moon, and its presence would know if I spoke the truth.

"Liathrain ... was sent to ... kill me." I whispered back. "I also ... perished in ... the battle, but ... Morakvaar ... had other plans ... for my soul." I realized an important piece of information had been kept from her. "It is ... Kairillia ... who has ... deceived you all."

She looked from the amulet to me and back in confusion. Liathrain's mother had been certain I was lying; yet the amulet betrayed no hint of deception. Unable to accept the truth I offered her, she made some other explanation.

"How can you fool the amulet!?" She snarled as she again shook me. "No mortal can fool the amulet of Illumia! Are you some demon in disguise!?"

The shackles ravaged my wrists and ankles once more, causing the blood to flow as they grated against bone having worn down through skin and tissue. Each of my joints flared in fiery pain, slowly tearing the tendons already ragged from their earlier mistreatment. I could no longer stem the agony from my lips as the assembled zarakanan laughed at my screams of pain. The zarak tired of shaking me, and stepped back a moment, still staring at the amulet. Eventually she turned back to me, a new certainty in her eye.

"Yet you did kill those innocents who begged for mercy at Terazandarin?"

I drew in a breath, ready to deny the accusation, but how could I? I was guilty of the slaughter and my soul knew this was justice for the deed.

"Yes." The zarak's eyes bored into my own at that forlorn admission, but instead of capitalizing on the frenzy of the crowd, her expression became more puzzled.

"We were your allies, how could you threaten us? You declared war against us without provocation. You admit to the slaughter of ten thousand citizens of Terazandarin including males, children, even infants. All this you committed without mercy even though they begged for it. Do you deny this?"

I bowed my head seeing again the faces of the innocent as they fell before the Reaver. "I do not ... deny ... the lives I took ... at Terazandarin." A great uproar of outrage filled the throneroom, but

Kairillia held up her hand for silence as I continued. "But I do … deny … that I … had no provocation … to declare … war! Your soldiers … left us … at the mercy … of our enemies. Betrayed us … at the gates … to our deaths! You stole … our property! Broke … the treaty … agreement, … attacked our people, … killed our … livestock, … burned our fields-" The zarak hit me hard in the gut, and her strength was incredible for a zarakanan.

What remained in me of the liquid was forced back out in heaves, yet she did not relent. The armored gauntlets found placement in my sides and ribs, breaking them from the strength of her fury. The pull against the chains resounded in flashes of agony that complemented each thud of her fists, merging in to one endless torment.

Sometime later, I vaguely recall being given another dose of the cool liquid and saw the throneroom had been emptied save Kairillia and Liathrain's mother. A bevy of servants hovered near the Matriarch, as a procession of dancing naked zaraks approached the platform where I was held. Uncertain of what was intended, I watched in dread as they ascended the stairs. As they drew near me, their dancing stopped, and I could see the moon amulet upon each of their breasts. Their leader had a circlet in which the moon talisman settled between her graceful brows. Her slender hand reached for me, and I flinched as I closed my eyes. What evil had they planned?

Yet instead of new torments, I felt the warmth of healing spread through me. I opened my eyes in startlement, only to have the slender priestess pull me to her and kiss my lips. Had I any strength, I would have fought it, but I had none. More healing warmth flooded through me, soothing the agony of my wrists and ankles, taking the swelling from my elbows and knees, and knitting broken ribs and internal bleeding. The sensation was accentuated by the touch of her bare skin upon mine, and despite my will I was affected.

I swallowed nervously as she ended her kiss and her hands trailed down my torso. "Illumia forgives you, Gorain, yet we may not tarry. Perhaps some other time?"

I shook my head, not able to trust my voice as the priestess smiled knowingly and left. Her entourage danced back down the stairs and out the side door of the massive throneroom as I watched. Why the sudden kindness? My vision could find no answer upon the impassive face of the Matriarch. Servants came forward with food and drink. I ate and drank until I felt near to bursting, knowing that such a meal might well be my last. When they had finished, Kairillia dismissed them and descended the stairs that ran from the dais to the platform on which I was chained.

"I have nothing but the deepest respect for you, Dorian. It is a shame we are enemies." The cold caress of magical power flowed over me with her words, and I struggled to keep my mind clear. A slender dark hand found its resting place upon my cheek. "Of course, we don't have to be enemies." The arcane energies intensified threatening my judgment as she too kissed me.

I turned my head from her lips with an effort that seemed beyond my will. "I will always be the enemy of evil and corruption."

"Oh, but your body betrays your desire, Dorian. It would please me to have such a strong male at my side."

"No, Kairillia. You wish only slaves and servants of darkness. I wish only to be returned to my hearth-mate." She frowned as she realized her spell had not subverted my will.

"If you but tell me one thing, I may return you to your hearth-mate in good time." Her grin became ferocious.

"One thing?" My will wavered slightly, but it was enough to topple my defenses.

"Yes," she said as she took my head in both her hands, ensuring I could not shrug away her kiss a second time.

Her breath passed my lips and my head grew light. I prayed silently to Morakvaar to shield me from her spell, but my will seemed to melt away. Her hands traversed my shoulders and spine, pressing me against her, as her lips never left mine. I felt my desire grow within me, felt the need to know her, as she moved against me. I would have done almost anything for her, but the face of Morina appeared before me, shaking off the spell that held me. I turned my head away from Kairillia once more, as her hands were busy elsewhere. She arched her brows in surprise, and then scowled in disgust.

"How dare you refuse me!?" Her hand brought stars to my vision, but I fancied the slap hurt her more than me.

She snarled viciously as she marched back up the dais stairs. "Get the information from him by force, then. Fetch Vairill'tar, and spare him no agony."

Liathrain's mother gestured for the torturer, and I wondered if I had done the right thing. My own people had betrayed me to the enemy; did they really deserve my protection? No it was Kormak who betrayed me; I corrected myself. Yet that a kinsman could do such a thing filled me with despair.

A slender and almost sickly looking girl approached me with a tray full of wicked looking silver instruments and I knew my grace period was over. The zarak grinned showing a disfigured mouth and a white crusted eye, as she looked me over. Her fingers stroked the tools of her trade almost lovingly as she cooed to herself before selecting one. I drew in a breath and closed my eyes, mentally preparing myself for the agony to come, and was not disappointed.

Despite my resolve, screams of pain tore from my throat as the zarak worked. They had not even asked me any questions before beginning, and I despaired that they would stop before I was dead. Needles lanced into nerves, pliers crushed tender areas and broke fingers and toes. Metal hooks tore at intestines from small lacerations. Hot irons scorched skin. No torture of the body had I endured that compared to what the zarak put me through, but I could take the physical pain. It was the torment of my soul that I felt the most. The knowledge that my kinsman thought so little of me as to betray me to the enemy was a misery that made me long for death.

When the zarak was finished, I trembled once more with weakness and agony. Nausea washed through me in cold waves threatening to evacuate what little nourishment I had gained.

"Now that we have your attention, I want the number of your troops, their constitution, and the layout of Balakarak's defenses." Kairillia crooned, enjoying the display.

"I see ... that ... your word ... is still ... worth nothing." I managed to gasp in between bouts of nausea.

Kairillia's lips curled into a cruel smile. "I was hoping you would continue to defy me. I really do admire your fortitude. Not a single male in this city could have withstood such torture and still be alive, let alone insolent. It is a shame that you are not one of us." She gestured to the sickly torturer. "He is yours until the information spills from his lips, Vairill'tar. Unfortunately, I have other matters I must attend to."

The zarak that was Liathrain's mother kept her face carefully neutral as the Matriarch descended the dais and exited the chamber. As soon as Kairillia was out of sight, she scowled darkly at the torturer.

"Don't kill him, his information is valuable. If he breaks before I return, I want a full transcript of what he says." Her amber eyes stared speculatively into my own, and an understanding passed between us.

Liathrain's mother was obviously highly placed in the military, if not Kairillia's general. She had been unaware of Kairillia's secondary agenda, and I wondered if she knew about the Matriarch's 'bargain' with Kormak. I knew the zarak would have spoken at length with me had she been able to justify it. The scar across my neck had awoken the suspicion within her, and I had a small hope that she might sow the seeds of discontent.

As the sickly zarak approached me, I realized that small hope might not be enough to help me even though it might save my people. The torturer's administrations before were merely cursory compared to her work in earnest. In no time, every nerve in my body ached and trembled, my throat no longer had the capacity to make sounds, and I pleaded to the Maker for the release of oblivion. But, the zarak knew her job well, and what frightened me, she was able to gage my limits almost exactly.

An eternity of pain was visited upon me, a lifetime of agony traced in subtle scars, bruises, burns and cuts. Just when I thought I could take no more, the zarak would relent and give me a moment's rest. If I were not aware enough, she would give me another drink of the cool liquid to clear my head so that I would feel the pain once more. At one such interval, after she had poured the liquid down my throat, she looked at me as she shook her head.

"The mistress knows you will die before you break! Why does she give me such impossible tasks?" She traced her finger along an incision with pride as I grit my teeth. "Your kind are such a pleasure to work with. You can endure so much, last so much longer." She licked her deformed lips before shaking her head again. "No, I have seen enough of your kind beneath my care to know who will break and who will not. Varalitha, the goddess of pain herself could not break you."

I felt rage building within me. Just how many kinsmen had that creature tortured!?

A fierce light came in to her good eye. "But she knows what weaknesses are contained within the soul, and she has told me yours. She delights in your torment, more than any of the others, and the mistress will know how to exploit your particular failing. You will not defeat me!" She crooned in delight as she limped out of the throneroom.

I sagged in the chains, thanking the Maker for the respite. Every nerve still shook and resounded with echoes of agony as my breaths came in ragged gasps. My soul ached with the unshakable image of Kormak's betrayal. Was that the weakness the vile creature spoke of? Weariness beyond any I had known smote my consciousness, but the pain would not allow me rest. How long had I been there? Nothing seemed real except the ministrations of the torturer and my inability to sleep. In frustration, I opened my eyes to see a set of amber ones staring back at me. The pain had dampened all of my senses, and the zarak's sudden appearance startled me.

"Kairillia told us she sent Liathrain to negotiate peace with your people." The amber gaze remained steadily on my own while her left hand clutched her pendant.

"Kai ... rillia's ... peace ... is ... murder." My words were barely a shaky whisper, as my voice had long since given out.

"So it seems." Her eyes left mine as she paced a moment before stopping before me once more. "I can't help but wonder how she managed to capture you. I cannot imagine assassins could take a creature capable of killing an entire city nearly single-handedly as she claims. There is no way I could imagine that she could vanquish Gorain the Slayer."

"I ... am not ... Gorain!" Why did they insist? Yet even as I spoke the words, her talisman glowed and I was taken aback.

The zarak raised a silver brow. "Illumia thinks otherwise, but that is beside the point. How did Kairillia capture you?"

I felt the wound freshly tear through my soul once more. "She ... made ... a ... bargain ... with Kormak. My life ... for ... my people."

"Betrayed by your own kind? How ironic." Her eyes grew distant. "It is a bargain Kairillia obviously does not mean to keep. She has ordered me to prepare our forces for departure in an assault upon Balakarak. Once through there, she means to destroy Morakduum, Dormakkarduum and Barakillanak in retribution for your 'treachery'."

"No!" Cold ice tore down my spine. "You ... cannot ... let her! It is ... she ... who ... has ... betrayed ... us all. She ... worships ... the ... Dark Queen."

"And yet it is my daughter's blood upon your hands!" She snarled. "Hers and the thousands of innocents of Terazandarin! How could I believe you?"

"Because ... I ... speak ... the truth."

"Was it not Gorain who killed our first pilgrims who searched for a safe haven? Why should I care for your people when you kill ours without mercy?" Her words struck home.

***

The memory came as clear to me as if it were mine; the blind fury of the sight of zarakanan filled me. The vision before my eyes was the mutilated body of Gelamina, my hearth-mate in that other life as she was hung over the gates of Sorkarak. The rage flowed through me as the blood of my enemies bathed my wounded soul. Morakvaar appeared before me in dismay.

"Gorain! Know you not an enemy from a friend?" I stared in confusion at the carnage I had left behind.

"Father, they were zarakanan! No zarak is my friend!"

"They were not your enemies, Gorain, but the worshippers of Illumia. They could have helped our people, but instead they will cause us pain. For this, you must be punished, and may Illumia some day forgive you."

***

An amber gaze regarded me for a long moment, as if knowing the memory that was played out before me. How could such memories be mine? I glanced again at the amulet Liathrain's mother bore. The memory must have been the Reaver's influence or its power. It had to be! My mind was desperate for an explanation and denial. I bowed my head, knowing the truth of her question.

"I ... can ... give ... no ... good reason ... save ... one. That we ... all ... strive ... to serve ... goodness."

"And yet you march against us?"

"Against ... Kairillia. I ... have ... no quarrel ... with those ... that leave."

"How do we know that you would not hunt us down as Gorain did?"

"You have ... my word."

"We will not leave our homes, and if we cannot live in peace, perhaps it is best that we destroy your kind for all time." Each word smote fear and pain in my heart as she spun on her heel and marched down the stair and out the side door.

In despair I watched the door long after she left, knowing the hour of my people's extinction. Was it my fault? Had I brought down the wrath of our enemies? I should have been able to say something; anything to prevent the horrible tragedy that shone in the zarak's face! But all I could do was to convince her of the justness of that cause. Perhaps I deserved the torture that lie ahead and behind me? My hoarse whispers cried out to the Maker to spare my people, gladly accepting my own damnation if only to save them. Yet, it was I whom had sentenced them to death.

Sharp piercing pains lanced up my side bringing me to instant wakefulness. The zarak torturer removed the needle, tasting the blood that ran freely down its length with a sickly pale tongue.

"Ah, Dorian, lovely day isn't it?" Kairillia's voice flowed from her in self-satisfaction. "I have a surprise for you." Anything that pleased the filthy zarak was sure to be a nightmare for me. I drew in a shaky breath, preparing myself for the worst.

My expectations were exceeded, when two zarak guards dragged in a kinswoman in chains. The sight of her golden hair sent cold fire through my breast. Morina! I blinked, hoping that my eyes were being deceived, but the vision never wavered. I strained against the chains in a vain hope of protecting my hearth-mate. But, my weakened muscles were no match for the iron forged by my ancestors.

"A lovely surprise, isn't it? How nice to have the family back together." Kairillia's crooning laughter made me sick inside. What was she planning for my beloved?

"Do ... not ... harm ... her." I gasped in desperation.

"That's up to you, Dorian. You tell Rhiallia what she wants to know, and your hearth-mate lives unscathed. Fail to do so, and she suffers as you suffered."

Snarling in rage, the desire for blood obscured my vision. I tore at the chains, causing them to bite deeply into my wrists and ankles, but felt no pain. The skin began to peel up my hands, starting to free me from the grasp of the shackles.

"Stop that at once, or she suffers worse!" The command was accented by a scream of agony from Morina's throat.

The sound brought my senses back with horrifying clarity as the zarak torturer stroked my mate's long golden hair. "A pretty weakness." She crooned as she selected another of her instruments.

The sound of Morina's pain tore through me in fire, burning my will, ripping my resolve into tattered rags.

"No! I ... beg you! I will ... tell you ... what ... you wish. Leave ... her be!" Maker forgive me, but my people were already doomed.

"Now then, that is much more reasonable, Dorian. You will find reward in your cooperation." Kairillia stood and gestured to the guards who held Morina. "Take her to the guest chamber. Once he has given the information we require, he can join her there." The Matriarch left and Liathrain's mother, whom I gathered fit the name Rhiallia, replaced her presence.

My will sapped from me, I answered her questions. The weakest points in our defenses left my lips in shame, but still I could not give my kinsmen to their deaths. Deception with truths that would satisfy her amulet poured out of my despair, but would not spell doom to my kin. Even though they were our weakest points towards a seige, the zarakanan would still break their army against them unless they knew the secrets I kept hidden. Thank Morakvaar that he hid those secrets from her talisman of truth, or perhaps it was Illumia herself who objected to the slaughter of my kin? Either way, I was released from my bonds, only to fall to my knees. Agony racked my body from my head to my bruised and broken toes. Muscles spasmed in pain as they strained to hold me stable, but they were unable to win against the nausea that stole my awareness and focused it on keeping the bile from my throat as I lay on the floor shaking.

In a sigh of music, the priestesses returned and tended my wounds. I was confounded trying to understand why they would heal me when I knew that Kairillia would eventually order my death. What other horrors had they in store for me? My will cringed in the dark to consider such nightmares. I pled to the Maker to spare me from their amusements. But instead of deliverance I was granted a meal as the priestesses fed me before I was led to the chamber where Morina was imprisoned.

"Dorian!" Her voice was a chorus that moved my soul as she ran to my arms.

I held her to me in the desperation of the lost. "Morina, my life, my love. Are you well?" Her golden hair smelled of home and our deep love as it covered my face, and she wept upon my shoulder.

"I thought I would die when I saw you in those chains." It was only a moment before her lips found mine, but then she drew back. "You should not have betrayed our kin for me." She said slowly.

Taking her hand was like seizing life and hope to me. "Worry not, Morina. Our people will hold out no matter the odds."

She cocked her head to one side. "You lied?"

Echoes of pain twisted the smile on my face. "You know me better than that. I did not lie. Even if I had, the zarak's amulet would have informed her."

It was obvious we were still prisoners, but at least they had given us a private room that was locked from the outside. The weariness of my torments began to overwhelm me, and I sat upon the mattress of the rope-strung bed. I drew Morina to my side by the hand that I still held. Instinct plucked at me though, and I felt something was missing, something I should recognize instantly. But my ordeal had left me beyond rational thought.

"Forgive me, Morina, but I am weary. What of our child?" Morina looked at me for a moment, and coldness settled in my gut. But before I could question the instinctive reaction, she answered.

"He was well and sleeping when they came to get me."

I mulled over the implications, my tired mind missing some vital piece of information. "Who came to get you and why?" I could only partially focus on her answers.

"Some of Kormak's kin. They said that you had been badly wounded. I made arrangements for Andira Warzeketh to care for our son and left with them. When we were outside of Morakduum, they turned on me and handed me over to the zarak assassins." She shuddered and leaned into my arms as I held her to me.

"Kormak has much to answer for." I growled, but already my eyes were closing of their own accord.

Morina snuggled against my side as I found myself lying down. How much time did we have before Kairillia would have us killed? I held her tightly to me as I drifted off to sleep. Morina's stirring woke me some time later, and my heart was filled with contentment to have her at my side.

"Hold me, my love." Morina whispered, and I took her into my arms as she kissed me.

We shared kinship for perhaps the last time, each of us knowing we would more than likely face execution soon. When she was satisfied, and I exhausted completely, we lay again in each other's arms, clinging to one another as if to life itself. It was then that I remembered our latest child was expected to be a girl. I blinked in confusion.

"Our son?" Morina regarded me for a long moment.

"My task is finished, I may as well drop the pretense." To my horror, I held not my hearth-mate, but Kairillia. "Our daughter will be the strongest leader our people have ever known." She rubbed her belly with an evil smile.

My rage snapped within me, blinding me with fury. I seized her by the throat snarling like a wild beast. With a gesture and a word of power, I was immobilized as arcane energies surged through my system overriding my resistance. Calmly, Kairillia removed my hands from her throat finger by finger.

Too late I realized that the wrongness I had felt was the absence of our soul-bond! If only I had listened to my instincts!

"You will pay for that, vaarak. Only because the goddess has decreed I acquire your seed do you live at all. With that necessity done, I have no further need of you save as an amusing toy. But, you will be punished." She removed herself from the bed with a half-smile at my immobile form. "It was enjoyable, Dorian." As if reading my unspoken question, she laughed heartily. "All an illusion you gullible vaarak. Your hearth-mate is still in Morakduum, my sources tell me." She laughed again, and moved as if feeling my embrace once more as I watched in helpless fury. "You should be honored that your child will be the chosen of the Dark Queen." She turned to the door and called the guard. "Take him back to the chains and make him sorry he was born, but don't kill him yet. I fear he has not told us all that he knows, but he will learn obedience. When he has known the price of his folly, throw him in to the pit to contemplate his crimes."

They placed me back in the chains, but instead of calling the torturer, a zarak female took out a multi-stranded whip that had bits of iron and bone laced within the ends. The other zarak wrapped her knuckles before sliding her gauntlets back on. When the one with the gauntlets tired of inflicting internal injuries upon me, the other lacerated my skin. They traded off their punishments; until I was sure I had no untorn patch of skin save my forehead and no unbroken bone save my legs. The pair of them seemed tireless, but I was not. Weariness and agony had already claimed my senses, and I barely knew that I was still being beaten

Again, the zaraks judged my tolerance too well, and before my consciousness fell into darkness, they unchained me. The two of them dragged me from the throneroom to the courtyard of the palace. To one side was a grate from which the stench of offal, decay and death wafted upwards, a smell I had known too well in my past. It was the odor of a prison for unwanted or disabled slaves. Without ceremony, they threw me down into the hole. About ten feet down, I landed hard on my left shoulder. Fresh fire lanced through me as the joint gave. Fighting off the nausea that threatened my consciousness, I sensed something moving in the dark, and I forced my knees beneath me. My right hand found the shinbone of some unfortunate victim, bits and pieces of rotting flesh fell from it ripe with parasites that squirmed beneath my hand, but it was my only weapon, and I prepared to sell my life dearly.

"Dorian?" The voice came from far away, but it was vaguely familiar. "By the gods, is that you Dorian?"

Dazed, I was sure the figure coming towards me was a hallucination. Old callused hands reached for me, and I snarled a warning.

"No more ... illusions! I ... will not ... fall for it!"

"Dorian?" The uncertainty in the voice was laced with hurt. "Please, my son let me help you."

Despite my warning, the gnarled hands reached for me. The festering bone drooped from my hand. Illusion or no, I could not strike the image of my mother. With my free hand, I attempted to hold back the aged hands to no avail. My strength was abandoning me as was my will to fight.

"No more! Kairillia ... I will not ... be taken in ... again!" It was more a desperate plea to retain my sanity than any real attempt to dissolve any deception.

"Do you not know your own mother, child? Please, for the Maker's sake, allow me to tend your wounds!" The gray haired kinswoman who resembled my mother so strikingly pleaded with me.

I blinked, wishing it were true that my mother had survived the devastation of Morkilduum. "I do know ... my mother. She died ... when the zaraks ... invaded our home. This ... illusion ... holds no faith ... with me." I said wearily, willing to allow the fallacy to continue if only I could rest a while.

"And this, my son, died in the crawler pits nearly a hundred and thirty years ago, but there he lay before me like a dream unbeckoned. It is an illusion I welcome." The old kinswoman was in tears half of joy, half of sorrowful disbelief.

My pain-fogged mind reasoned that Kairillia would not have known so much of my past. Was the kinswoman who leaned over me indeed my mother? Instincts spoke of warmth, the hearth of my childhood, the loving touch of a parent. No weariness or agony could take away the joy as this time I listened to the whisperings of my heart, even as my mind tried to disbelieve. To her left side, I thought I recognized my father's sister, and by her, my cousin.

"By Morakvaar! How? I was ... sure you all ... had perished ... in Morkilduum." The wonder and joy that filled me was beyond any greatness, beyond any treasure I had known.

"And we were sure you perished in the crawler pit!" Strong yet weary arms embraced me and despite the grinding of my broken bones I felt elation fill the emptiness left by Kormak's betrayal.

The questioning look in my mother's eyes begged an explanation, and despite the agony that shuddered through my bones, I had to tell her what had happened so long ago. "I ran across ... a zarak raid. Saw them take ... a slave-line of ... our kinswomen. I turned back ... to report ... this to the ... patriarch ... but the zaraks ... found me." The memory of how the kinswomen died filled me with shame, so I skipped that part of the tale. "They sold me ... to the humans ... on the surface. By the time ... I ... returned... Morkilduum ... had been ... destroyed." My kinsfolk listened patiently to my tale before my mother told me hers.

She tore her shawl into strips to bind my wounds as she spoke. "When they brought us your things, Thorun was devastated. Rightfully, he could not understand how you could be so careless as to be caught by crawlers. Even so, he mourned your loss for nearly five years, not once tending the forge. The great destiny foretold for you he swore was an illusion. The one thing that brought him out of his sorrow was our fourth child. Belara was a beautiful girl, and her hair was the same color as yours. Raising her brought life back to him, that was until the night before her thirteenth birthday." My mother broke off, as her face became a picture of the horror she saw within.

"It was then that the zaraks attacked. No one knew how they got in to the city, disabled the wards, and opened the gates. Without warning they were among us with spells and weapons. Their soldiers were everywhere, giving no time for alarms or defense. They struck swiftly towards the temples, cutting down our priests before they could ward against their magical assault. With their priests and their mages unhindered, they razed the city, slaughtering soldier and citizen with abandon." I groaned, part in my own pain, and part for my kin whom my mind's eye saw cut down without mercy.

Lira Warzeketh appeared beside me, and the healing spells she cast eased the worst of my pain. I smiled in thanks, but I do not think my features were very cooperative. Lira had been only ten when I last saw her, but she was now over a hundred and forty. When she finished chanting her spells, my mother continued.

"They underestimated our inner defenses, though. Your father rallied the clans, and led the countercharge. As a forge-priest, they did not understand his powers. He drove them back, and would have defeated them if it were not for the vourdovra." She shuddered involuntarily, and I could not imagine what she was seeing in her mind's eye. "One stalked him from behind, shooting a long tentacle from its hideous body. When it connected itself to the back of his neck, the creature sapped his ability to call upon the Maker's power, but he was not yet defeated. He sliced off the creature's tentacle, and attacked it head on.

"So many of our kin perished, and the zarakanan rallied around the vourdovra and concentrated their efforts against your father. It was then that he told the Patriarch to gather the survivors and flee Morkilduum while he remained to delay the enemy with the Patriarch's sons. Barok and Koran also stood at his side as the zaraks pushed them back to our home tunnels. Belara and I had been cut off from the escape route. We took up weapons and waited in our home for the end. Your father fought his way back to where we were and stood outside our home tunnel, fighting off the enemy as if he were Gorain incarnate." I flinched at the reference, but fortunately my mother was watching the inner scene.

"The vourdovra came again, this time lancing out with its mind. Your brothers fell instantly, and without their protection of his flanks, the zarakanan dragged Thorun down." With a gasp of anguish, her tears fell upon my face as she held me. "The zaraks came into our home, and Maker forgive me, but I did not get a chance to attack our enemies. They cast a spell upon your sister and I, placing us in a deep sleep. When we awoke, we were chained and the zaraks led us away as slaves over the mounds of our dead kin. Belara remained at Mezosilliar and I was given to Kairillia for her assistance in the assault."

"What!?" I stared in shocked disbelief, momentarily forgetting about the massive amount of internal injuries I had suffered. "That blasphemous witch!" The violent snarl left me coughing in spasms of agony and a small amount of bloody froth trickled from the right corner of my mouth.

Lira hurriedly chanted another charm of healing; trying desperately to stem the injury that would kill me if left untended.

Incredible sadness entered my mother's eyes as tears continued to splash upon my face. "Golodain's line is no more." She wailed in despair. "How could the Maker favor us?"

I touched her hand, my own shaking like a babe's first movements. "No ... mother. Do not despair... Golodain's line ... continues. I ... have married ... and my hearth-mate ... has born me ... a fine daughter ... and a strong son. Even now ... she tends our third ... child, another ... lass." Her tears stopped with the magnitude of my announcement.

"Two daughters?" Her gray eyes fluttered in disbelief.

I managed a slight smile. "Yes. Two ... Morakvaar favors us." The effort to speak brought more spasms to my lungs, and the strain of my system to rid them of the offending fluid that filled them expended my strength.

***

My father's face haunted my dreams, and I remembered his red flame-like hair that wreathed his ash-stained features. Eyes so much like my own smiled upon me as I stood at his knee adoringly. His callused hand ruffled my hair that was only the tiniest shade more gold. The smoke curled from the wood-root pipe at his mouth, smelling like the incenses in the temple. If ever there were an incarnation of Dormakkaar, surely he looked like my father, Forge Priest and keeper of the Sacred Flames. Though Thorun served Morakvaar, truly he held all the secrets of our people's success with the forming of metal.

At my frown, he laughed joyously, and strong arms snatched me from my place at his feet. He hugged me tightly to his massive chest, and I could smell the sulfur of the forge-fires all about him. Contentment filled my small heart, as I reveled in the love of my father. After a short time, he released me, but kept me upon his knee. His smile of pride struck deeply within, filling me with self-indulgence. The fire within the hearth crackled merrily as my mother turned the haunch of the vrakka, preparing for my older brothers' visit. The smell of the cooking meat filled our tunnel with the fragrance of home. I smiled secretly, and leaned back to my father, trying to reach around his barrel chest with the arms of a ten-year-old.

Thorun placed a hand upon my shoulder to get my attention, and I looked up into his crystal blue eyes. "Remember, son, the duty of every kinsman is to pay homage to the ancestors and your elders. Part of that homage is choosing the path of your apprenticeship. Barok is nearing his mastership as a smith of fine axes, hammers, spears and swords, a proud addition to Golodain's line. It is his betrothal to Lorianna that we celebrate this week's end. Such a high honor deserves admiration, for Barok will continue Golodain's blood."

He shot my mother a warm smile that she returned as she refilled my father's mug of ale. With a grin, he consented to my request for some of it. The frothy brew tickled my nose and left a premature cream-colored moustache upon my lip that made both of my parents laugh uproariously.

"Our little kinsman growing up already!" My mother laughed as she turned back to the hearth. Her gown rustled, as if it were a part of the harmony of the Deeps that resounded through me.

Treasures and trinkets framed her golden hair from above the fireplace, treasures made by our family for generations. Beautiful works of inlaid weapons, jewelry that defied the eye to delve its intricacies, carved and bejeweled mugs that could have served kings, and all manner of small clockwork wonders that I wanted so bad to see the inside of. Upon the walls, were the works of my mother's labors, adding to our family treasures. Tapestries played out our histories of heroes and battles, grand ages of times past. Her weavers' talent was unparalleled, and even the Kings of Barakillanak and Dormakkarduum came to buy her work as they did my fathers' weapons and armor.

My father gazed absently at the form of my mother as she worked, a content smile upon his face. "Koran," he said quite suddenly and I caught my balance before falling from his knee, "is a craftsman of fine armor, and is nearing the end of his apprenticeship. In fifteen years, Dorian, you too will enter into your apprenticeship. I have three Mastersmiths, including myself that have requested you as an apprentice. The other two are Favoran and Larok. You must choose wisely, my son. Who do you wish to apprentice to?"

Perhaps the brew was strong, lending to my self-indulgence, but with childish enthusiasm, I broke my father's heart. "Dorim Atharil!" He blinked, the expression on his face was of hurt disbelief, but I did not notice. "I want to be a warrior! I want to ride the crawlers into battle, hunt with a spider at my side, and fight alongside the watch-spiders as they repel intruders. I want to work with the war-hounds, be their friend and master!" My mother blinked several times with her mouth open as she spun around to regard me.

"Dorian!" Her chastisement puzzled me, but by her tone I knew I had said something terribly wrong.

With an anguished expression my father waived her off. "No, Geria. He is being honest. The truth must never be punished no matter how painful it is." He looked at me, and I could almost swear I saw a tear. "Dorian is different; we have known this since his birth. Morakvaar has other plans for him; the priests told us so at his Naming. Though what the Maker's plans are will remain unknown, I can only assume he has put this desire within our son's heart. Dorian's talent with the animals only confirms this part of the Maker's plan."

The dream turned for the worse at that point, and I saw the masses of zarakanan overwhelming my forces at Terazandarin, only the scenery changed. Terazandarin became the fortress-tunnels of Morkilduum, and the battle included my friends and relatives that I had grown up with. Chains held me as the zaraks laughed at the slaughter of my kin. They pointed out my family as they were killed, and the torturer loomed at my side. Her deformed mouth twisted in delight as she inflicted new pains upon me with each death. The zarakanan surround my father and brothers, and I knew that if I were free, I could save them. But I was chained, and those chains were more than physical.

A vourdovra hove into view as I watched in helpless horror. Its four legs paced through the carnage as if it were never under threat. Its tentacles lashed out, piercing the helmets and skulls of my kin, draining their life from inside, and lazily feeding itself to bloating. The creature turned almost casually, and the harmony of the Deeps changed to a discordance that smote like a hammer. My brothers dropped instantly as the shock rendered them unconscious. The zarakanan leapt upon my father from all sides, dragging him down and ending his life. The vourdovra lashed a tentacle to each of my brother's helmets and continued its feast. Its brain-like body rippled in delight at the carnage and death it wrought upon my people.

***

Fevered sweat covered me as I awoke, and my heart felt the despair of captivity that was the feeling that had haunted me every day as a slave. The darkness and stench of the pit surrounded me in festering putridity, a testament to the zaraks' treatment of my kin. Pain wracked every nerve, and I wanted to surrender to the beckoning eternal darkness, but the feel of warm arms around me pulled me from the paths of death. My awareness slowly returned, and I found myself cradled in my mother's lap as if I was still only a ten-year-old. Lines of age were almost enough to disguise her face from me, and the scars of slavery marred her cheeks and neck. The ache of my own scars echoed her agony. The sight of my mother's puffy lids tore my heart to know her sorrow. When she saw me stirring, she gestured to Lira once more. The exhausted kinswoman tried one more time to heal me, but I was past her ability.

"Save your ... spells, Lira. I ... go to a fate ... where healing ... will not help." The warm glow of my kinsfolk around me gave me one last comfort as I prepared myself for the journey to the Underhalls.

But the zaraks had other plans. Pushing my kin aside, the zarakanan guards came.

"Tell me, vaarak dog, where is your master, King Dorian!" The large female commander grabbed one of my kin and shook her.

My mother stared from the zaraks to me and whispered, "King?"

My wan smile barely hid my agony as I could feel the cold numbness of death stiffening my limbs, "That slipped ... my mind."

Light shone down from the grate as if through a long tunnel, and I could see soldiers pushing their way to me. In the midst of the armored zaraks was a high priestess in the robes of their moon goddess, and I prayed to Morakvaar that he would let me pass from this life before they reached me. But before the darkness closed over me, the cleric placed her hand upon my chest, chanting a litany to her goddess a melody that was both haunting and powerful. When she had finished, the warmth of life chased away the numb cold, filling me with renewed vigor. If only she had let me die, for all I could see was the face of the torturer looming largely in my mind. A cold fist seized my gut, as my nerves felt the raw stimulation from the dullest of memories, but it was still enough to make me wish they had let me finish my journey to eternal peace. The soldiers hauled me to my feet and dragged me limping back up the ladder they had lowered into the pit. Keeping her relationship to me secret, my mother's anguished gaze haunted me long past the time I could see her.

Chapter 8

Khazadana Korina (High Queen Korina)

The familiar sight of the throneroom awaited me as did the deformed zarak torturer. Weakness stole through my limbs and clenched at my gut as I was chained again and prepared for her ministrations.

For endless time she did not tire of inflicting torment upon me, never expecting that I would answer any of her questions. Needles dipped in caustic substances slid beneath the surface of my skin, burning the tender flesh within. Small cuts lacerated the areas behind joints and between limbs, before the same liquid was poured on them. Incisions allowed larger instruments dipped in the same fluids to find tender nerve centers, bruise and burn internal organs, but never enough to kill. Red-hot irons crisped flesh that was not sensitive enough for the cuts, followed by the burning substance that left me with no voice left to my agony. Just when I believed the twisted creature had run out of ideas, she would surprise me with new ways to experience pain. Never in my wildest dreams would I have imagined how much agony could be experienced in one lifetime before death.

The pain was a type of madness, stealing my sanity an instant at a time until all moments were the same. Eternity writhed alongside my tortured frame, an eternity in which my mind wandered in search of meaning other than agony. And always the memories of Gorain stared back at me from the abyss as if more real than my own.

At some point I was aware that I had been left alone, and awake. Vairill'tar was there as soon as my eyes were opened. Another vial of the liquid brought back my consciousness from the fever of agony, but it did not heal the damage done, or ease the pain. Cognizance faded in and out, and I thought I heard the zarak torturer complain that she could not continue her work because there was no place left that had not already been over-stimulated. In disgust Vairill'tar stomped away. The darkness stared back at me as I tried to focus on anything besides the torment that wracked my senses.

My body shook with echoes of agony through all of my nerves, and I was exhausted enough to sag into the chains. My legs were too weak to stand, and the ache of my shoulders could barely be felt over the continuous hum of pain through the rest of my system. The emptiness of my gut was probably another echo, as was my thirst. I drifted between awareness of pain and oblivion for time without end until I had a very odd dream.

"Dorian!" The whisper was urgent and came from my left.

Was I hallucinating or hearing voices?

"Dorian, it's me!" Sanity was a far concept, as I could swear it sounded like Lodath.

"Lodath? What ... are you doing ... in my dream?" My voice sounded like some pitiable dying creature, and my head swam in nausea.

"I think I can help you escape, but it will take time."

My choking laughter rang through the hall like a mad thing. "Time? I am ... sure to have ... as much time ... as Kairillia ... wishes to... see me...in torment." Spasms brought flaring pains through me, but there was nothing in my gut to vacate, and I regretted laughing.

"I am sorry, Dorian." Lodath's sincerity touched off what little remained of my rational thoughts.

"My life ... is forfeit, ... Lodath. What ... matters is that ... Kairillia means ... to march upon ... Balakarak. You must ... warn them." I tried to hold on to awareness, but it was quickly evading me.

"If only I could transport you out of here! But the hall is warded, as are your chains! I have tried to undo their enchantment, but my power rebounds off them like a child flailing at a warrior." I could hear him pacing, but I could not see him. "But, there is one thing I need to tell you. Korina has rallied the army and is marching this way in secrecy. She hopes to catch Kairillia off-guard. I think Korina will make it, and she is only two days away as we speak. I do not know if you can survive that much longer, but you have to try."

If only the dream were real! "If ... what you say ... is true, then ... Kairillia may ... try to use me ... as a hostage." More spasms threatened me, but I repressed them with a great effort. "You must ... not allow that ... to happen." I looked to where I could hear his feet pause in their restlessness. "If... you cannot... free me,... you must ... slay me now."

"No. I won't. There must be some other way!" The quaver in his voice betrayed his deep friendship, a love between comrades, but I had to make him understand. Even if it was a dream, it was important, for I had heard that if you died in your dreams it would become reality.

The nausea within me would not be repressed any longer though, and for a few moments I could do nothing but retch and cough. Blood ran down my chin and beard, and I stared at the bright red drops and pink froth collecting on the stones by my feet. Even if he could loose me from the chains, I was too weak to even crawl. There was nothing but death ahead of me. The thought gave me an idea.

"Lodath, ... if you could ... bring the Reaver... I might ... be able to ... use its power ... to escape." It was only a dream, and the false hope it gave me would only end in a deeper despair.

"I will try, Dorian." His robe rustled as he paused a moment as if looking back. "I'm honored to have known you, Dorian. You have been my best friend and a father when I had none." His steps quickly faded from my hearing, and I lapsed back into darkness.

***

My dreams were of Barakillanak after the birth of Morina's child. The gates of the fortress had been sealed permanently for the first time since their construction, and only a small arched door allowed access to the inner city. An aura of doom hung over the stronghold like a tangible presence and I was saddened that my kinsmen had been reduced to such a life. What was once an open and friendly city was a brooding keep full of suspicion and foreboding. At one time, I would have been accepted in with warm greetings and eager buyers for the skins I brought from hunting, but only grim faces and spears welcomed me to the home of my mother's kin.

Morina sighed tiredly from her place on Dorvira, the spider that had been my companion for over fifteen years. The once beautiful luster of the arachnid's chitin was worn and grayed with age, and it grieved me to know this was probably her last journey. Morina too looked pale and ill, and she struggled not to show it. She held Korina tightly to her breast as the babe fed, but her arms shook with weariness. Jaguar had done her best to supplement her health, but her healing supplies had long since been exhausted in our fight against the zaraks. Worry filled me, and I prayed to the Maker to keep my mate and child well as I approached the unfriendly guards.

The points of their spears never wavered, but I could tell the kinsmen of Barakillanak were unused to wearing armor or carrying weapons. The vaarakanan on the left wore the full braided beard of one bonded as it's blondish-gray weave hung down near to his thighs, and I touched my own braid that barely fell halfway down my chest in recognition of his honor. A slight softening of the eye told me that part of the suspicion melted with my gesture of respect.

"Who are you that seeks entrance to Barakillanak?" He asked almost rhetorically, but I knew I would not be allowed in until I satisfied custom.

"I am Dorian Mytharia, Journeyman Warrior and Huntsman of Morkilduum. I bring my hearth-mate, Morina Tenedain of Balakarak. I have come to find my kin, to know if they still live, and to seek shelter for our infant daughter." The blonde kinsman smiled in disbelief.

"You have a daughter!? As your first!?" He lowered his spear and stepped forward to get a look at the babe.

Obligingly, Morina interrupted Korina's meal to allow him to see her. Reverently, the elder kinsman took the fussing babe, as a smile lit his features.

"Morakvaar be praised! She is a lovely child, kinsman!" He handed her back to Morina and without threatening, gestured at my companions. "And who are they?"

Glad that Liathrain and Kelana had stepped behind Lodath and Rutger, I explained that they were my friends and had helped me fight my way past the forces of Mezosilliar. Despite my words, though, the guards hardened their features.

"You and your mate may pass the walls, Dorian, but they must remain outside." His tone told me that there would be no argument.

"Then I will be forced to seek shelter elsewhere though Morina is ill. These are evil times when a kinsman cannot look to his clan for aid." I said bitterly. "At least tell me this, does Thorun Mytharia, my father, still live?" The two kinsmen exchanged anguished looks.

"There are some Mytharians that have survived to seek shelter here, but Thorun was not among them. Some say he stayed behind with Dorim's own sons to delay the enemy long enough for many to escape." The younger kinsman said as if dreaming of the heroic death that could have been his.

I leaned heavily upon the haft of my two-handed axe as the confirmation of my father's demise smote me a mighty blow. But, I realized the two had given me the pass I needed for my companions to enter Barakillanak's walls.

"You say the Patriarch's sons, yet he himself did not stay behind?"

"No. He led the refugees here, guarding them against our enemies' hunters."

A weary smile crossed my lips. "Then tell him that his foster son has returned to his side, and be quick, for I am the last of Golodain's line and my patience is worn thin."

The elder kinsman flinched, and then gaped in surprise. He elbowed the younger guard. "You heard him. Go and tell Patriarch Dorim that Dorian Mytharia is at our gates and wishes entrance for himself and his allies."

As the younger kinsman disappeared, the elder leaned against the stone wall. "I thought that all Mytharians were smiths. How is it that you are a huntsman-warrior?"

"My father arranged for me to be fostered to the Atharil clan." Though he looked at me quizzically, I did not explain.

"An outsider?"

"An old tradition that should be re-examined."

He nodded, realizing that I would not discuss it. "For your hearth-mate's sake, I hope the Patriarch confirms your tale. It will not go well for you should he not." His tone was thick with prejudice against a kinsman that did not follow his clan's craft.

"Spare me your threats, for I have faced dangers that would wither your soul to dream of. That I should be here at all is a testament to the truth of my words." The thought that he could question my honor only brought a weariness of heart to me instead of the righteous anger that should have been there.

The elder kinsmen looked at me puzzled, expecting a much more violent reaction. Instead of confronting him, I went back to speak with the others.

"Ve must vait until zie runner confirms my identity vit zie Patriarch. It vill not be much longer."

I placed a hand upon Morina's knee, as she met my concerned gaze and nodded weakly. Jaguar understood my unspoken request instantly when I looked to her and she moved up beside Morina. Softly she chanted a spell to temporarily help Morina, but my mate badly needed rest in a safe place. The birth had been very strenuous, and our journey from the ruins of Morkilduum had been hounded constantly by the forces of Mezosilliar.

With the ripple of magic, the elder kinsman snapped to the alert, menacing Jaguar with his spear. I stepped between them, snatching the spear from his hands with ease.

"She only aids my mate in her illness. You would be wise not to tempt my anger further." I growled barely above a whisper.

The elder kinsman swallowed nervously as my double bitted axe rested on his throat in a steady one-handed grip. It was not until that moment that he realized how competent a fighter I was. Such underestimation was clearly a sign of an amateur warrior. His green eyes stared into mine, pleading for me to be a friend and not the villain he suspected. After a long moment, when I was sure he realized how easily his life could have been ended; I lowered the axe and handed him back his spear. He breathed a sigh of relief and great respect entered his eyes for the first time.

"You must be of Gorain's line to be so great a warrior." He realized his error as I narrowed my eyes. "No offense kinsman. Gorain was the greatest warrior our people have ever known. I did not mean to confer his dishonor upon you."

Through clenched teeth, I admitted his accusation. "Gorain was my direct ancestor. As I have said, I am the last of Golodain's lineage, but with Morakvaar's grace, Korina, my daughter, will continue that line."

At that moment, the other guard came rushing up. "Bavoran, ... the Patriarch was beside himself...! He wants to see Dorian right ... away!" He managed to gasp in enough breath to say. "King Karakdain also expressed great ... interest in seeing him. He is to be afforded every courtesy of any noble."

Bavoran bowed deeply to me. "My apologies kinsman. May you someday forgive me and return honor to my family. I will personally escort you to the palace to atone for my dishonorable conduct."

I placed a hand on his shoulder and smiled. "No insult is taken. These are hard times indeed, and our enemies threaten our existence. Had I not seen the devastation of Morkilduum with my own eyes, I would not have believed it possible. Under those circumstances, your suspicion is well placed, and I hope it will keep your clan safe." I gestured to the others. "Bavoran vill lead us to zie palace. Zere ve can at last rest in safety." Jaguar arched a graceful brow over her dark eyes at my pronouncement, but said not a word.

The streets of Barakillanak were crowded with natives and refugees alike, struggling to go about their lives, but every head was bowed and shoulders stooped. Furtive glances met my eyes as I followed Bavoran, but every kinsman or kinswoman that caught sight of the two elves recoiled in terror. It was as if they were already beaten and enslaved, and anger grew within me. My people were never meant to live in fear!

The palace was a close duplicate of the one in Morkilduum. So similar was it that I could have led our party to the throneroom with my eyes closed. But, the splendor of the halls was overshadowed by a darkness of the spirit. It was as if the will to live had been drained from the people. In silent contemplation, I followed Bavoran to the courtiers' hall. The noble kinswomen of the hall were there to greet us and begged to care for Morina and our child. She did not want to go with them, but I would not allow her to strain herself further. It was one of the very few times she actually listened to me.

With my hearth-mate in good hands, I followed Bavoran to the king's council chamber with my companions close behind.

"Your Grace, may I present Lord Dorian Mytharia?" Bavoran bowed to both King Karakdain and Patriarch Dorim as he introduced me.

For a long moment, Dorim stared at me as if seeing a ghost. "By the gods, lad! I had not thought this possible!" A tear formed at the corner of his left eye and rolled down a cheek more wrinkled than I remembered. "I thought it a cruel joke, but to see you -"

He took three strides to cross the room and encompassed me in a huge bear hug. With great elation I returned his affection. "Father, it brings joy to my heart to know that you live!" Ever since I had saved his son's life, he had insisted I call him father as well.

He pushed me out at arm's length to examine me. "Lad! The Maker has smiled upon us that I live to see you! I had thought you dead those many years past! You have filled out quite well, a fine kinsman, and you have the look of a fierce warrior!" His eyes drew distant, and written in them was the vision of the death of his sons.

Smitten with the despair of Morkilduum's demise, I dropped to my knees. "Father, forgive me that I did not return quick enough with my warning. I should have been able to escape capture and warn our people of the zaraks' treachery." I bowed my head in shame, remembering that day all too well.

Tenderness entered his old eyes as he pulled my chin up with a gnarled hand. "Do not blame yourself, Dorian. Rather it is I who should apologize for not recognizing you sooner. If I had given you your Mastership the day I had planned, you might not have been so eager to prove yourself by wandering so far. It is a decision I shall regret to the end of my days. What happened to you, my son?"

I smiled inwardly at the confirmation of his love and pride in me; it was a moment I would savor for the rest of my days. "I happened upon a war-party that had raided the Delvaarin settlement. They had taken several of our kinswomen as slaves, but there were too many zarakanan soldiers for me to rescue them. I identified the zaraks as coming from Mezosilliar and tried to return to report their crime. But, their outriders had seen me, and I was quickly surrounded. Matriarch Lillan'itza had me sold to human slavers to avoid discovery and make a quick profit. I spent thirty years with a slave collar about my neck in service to the surface dwelling humans. It was these companions who helped me evade my pursuers once I managed to escape."

He placed a slightly trembling hand upon my shoulder. "Rest easy my son, for it was a mere seventeen years after your disappearance that the zaraks attacked. There was nothing you could have done, and had you been there, I think it likely that you would have perished. Indeed Morakvaar has saved you for greater things as the priests foretold at your Naming." He sighed, and then grinned slyly as he touched my braided beard. "Now tell me of this? You are all the family I have left to me, and I wish to know how much of a family I have."

I blinked several times, considering the implications of his words. Had he just proclaimed me his heir?

"Her name is Morina Tenedain."

His eyes widened, "Tenedain?"

I smiled and nodded. "The same. Her father was Patriarch Beralain of Balakarak." He frowned sadly at the past tense. "Her mother and she were taken when she was but a child. They too were sold to the humans as slaves until I found them. Her mother had been turned into a horrible beast by an undead dragon that my companions and I slew." An odd light entered the Patriarch's eyes and he gave a quick glance to King Karakdain who nodded. Puzzled, I continued even as I tried to understand what was happening. "In return for their freedom, Morina's mother begged two boons of me, one that I marry her daughter and two that I free her spirit from its monstrous prison. Morina would not listen to my profession of unworthiness though I begged her to marry a kinsman of higher standing with no mark of dishonor upon their ancestry. But she insisted that we honor her mother's last request. I could not reasonably refuse. The Ritual of Bonding was witnessed by these, my friends," I gestured to my companions, "and Morakvaar smiled upon our union, blessing us with a child." I paused to let the significance of my next words carry the weight of joy I felt within. "Her name is Korina, and we vowed to raise her amongst our kin."

"A girl! As your first!?" The huge grin that spread across Dorim's face seemed to wipe out years of grief and pain as he gave me another bear hug. "My son, I could not wish for happier news! Your family is my family! Though you were born a Mytharia and carry that name, I consider you one of my own. Tomorrow I wish to see my granddaughter, but tonight I wish you present as the future Patriarch. There is a war to be won, and I will need your aid for my arm and wits are not as strong as they used to be."

I was overwhelmed and filled with sad pride. That Dorim cared so much about me returned a sense of belonging, the sense of soul I had been missing for over forty-five years. I smiled and hugged him back as if I was his son instead of a dishonored fosterling. A feeling of elation erased so many years of confusion and anguish as it flooded through me.

"Your pardon for a moment as I see to my friends' needs?" I bowed to both the Patriarch and the King and they nodded their ascent.

As I left the room with my companions, Jaguar elbowed me. "So you really are a prince, eh?"

How could she have doubted me? "Not a prince, but a noble of zie oldest line of my people. But, as I have said, my ancestors vere disgraced. Zat Dorim has made me his heir is nozing short of astonishing. Perhaps zie Maker has had his plans in my life after all?" I smiled wanly, wishing once more that the sensuous priestess had granted my request of marriage, but the thought of my lovely bride Morina made me glad that she had not. "According to zie Patriarch, ve vill be marching to var. I assume it vill be against Mezosilliar. You are velcome to stay here as long as you vish, but I vill understand if you do not vant to."

"What, and let you have all the fun?" Lodath burst in. "You've got to be kidding."

***

Another bout of fevered pain interrupted my dreams, and I knew I must have been hallucinating again when Kelana appeared before me. The swirling green tattoos that would have helped hide her in the forest, shone out against her pale skin in the faery glows that lit the throneroom of Fartairillzan. She pressed a damp cloth to my head, bringing blessed coolness to my fever. To my lips she held a cup of water which I drank quickly, feeling it course down my throat to my gut. I never would have thought the taste of water could be so sweet.   Another cup followed the first, and then another until my shrunken belly was full.

A small measure of life returned to me with the replenishing of moisture.

"Zank you." I breathed hoarsely as she continued to mop dirt, sweat and blood from my face.

"They say you murdered Liathrain." She said at last, and paused to look me in the eye.

I frowned sadly. "Kairillia ... sent her to kill me. I had no ... choice but to defend ... myself ahnd my kin." She clenched her jaw and narrowed her eyes. "I vould not ... lie to you, Kelana. She vas my friend ... too."

"Kairillia says you are mad, and that you kill without thought or mercy when free. I would not have believed her save both Liathrain and I were at Terazandarin when you slaughtered all those innocent people."

"If you vere zere ... vy did you let Kairillia ... betray us!?" I snarled, feeling a deep wound opening in my love and trust that I once held for my companions.

"Kairillia said you had become ambitious and dangerous. She told us that the dwarven kings had made a bargain with her to not allow you to return from Terazandarin because they were afraid of you."

"My people ... vere mercilessly slaughtered! How could ... you have called ... yourself my friend!? How could you have ... believed zat my people ... vould betray me?" As I said the words, I realized how hollow they sounded in light of my current situation. Kelana merely raised a brow as I sighed in anguish. "Zere vas no such ... bargain. Vy do you zink ... zey made me High King? If zey did ... not trust me, I vould ... have been exiled."

"But that still does not explain Terazandarin. Dorian, how could you have done what we saw you do? All those helpless people you killed, how can I believe that you are not mad?"

"Ven I first picked up zie Reaver, ... it possessed me. I vas unprepared ... for its fury. Zie veapon fed upon my ... anger, my rage at my ... kinsmen's deazs. I could not stop it, ... ahnd did not vant to." I confessed before looking her in the eye. "If you vish ... to place madness upon ... me, so be it, but ... first, you must know ... zat Kairillia no longer serves ... Illumia. She has been tvisted by greed ... ahnd desire for powver. She has been meddling vit ... artifacts empowvered by Lillain, ... zie Dark Qveen... Zie mistress of evil ... has turned her mind."

"Kairillia has told us that you had intended to betray and murder her at Terazandarin once her forces had been weakened in the battle, and that she had the information from Moravrak of Dormakkarduum. That, the bargain, and the divination of your soul were the reasons for her holding back at Terazandarin." At my puzzled expression, Kelana continued. "She showed us that you were actually the reincarnation of some insane murderer and that you were starting to show signs of his madness."

I grunted humorlessly. "Ahnd you believe ... such nonsense? No kinsman has ever been reincarnated ... in all of our recorded history. Zough many ... souls of zie ancestors have ... returned to assist zie living, ... reincarnation is unheard of. It is Kairillia who is mad. If you ... vish proof of vat ... I say, zen go ... to her inner chamber ... ahnd find zie artifacts ... she stole." The weariness of the conversation sapped my remaining strength, and I could feel the fever returning.

"I will do as you ask, Dorian, and tell Liathrain what I find."

Liathrain? It must have been the fevered dreams that returned to me with a vengeance.

The chains rattled as they were being unlocked, and my delirious mind tried to make sense of what was happening. Another draught of the cool liquid was forced down my throat, clearing my head. Kairillia stood before me shaking her long mane of silver hair. Beside her were soldiers bearing the weapons of war. Nervous tension rolled out from them like a tangible aura. Something unexpected had happened, and I hoped vainly that it was for the good of my people.

"It seems as though I have gone through all this trouble for naught. Your daughter has rallied your army and is only half a cycle's journey to our walls! You have caused me no end of troubles, Dorian, but you have been a worthy adversary." Her slender hand ran down through the red hair that was left on my chest, making me flinch as she touched the open sores. "I could almost wish that you were one of us."

"Even were I ... one of your perverted kind, ... you would be the last ... female I would touch." I snarled, but she seemed to find it amusing.

"What a pitiful thing to say to the mother of your child." She knew how to strike hard and deeply against our traditions. "Aren't you supposed to protect me and take me in to your clan?"

"Never! What you have was stolen! ... The worst kind of ... betrayal!" I snarled, but I knew she was correct in her assumption.

Our traditions were very strict regarding such things, though the assumptions made were those of our own race. By law, I would have to protect her as the mother of my child, but there was no guarantee that she had conceived.

"Regardless, I think Korina will do almost anything to get her father back, don't you think?" She gave me a sly look. "Even if he is a rogue and a lascivious pervert who sleeps with the enemy?"

The weak growl was all that I could manage.

Kairillia laughed, but I could tell she was uncertain. Her voice was vaguely hopeful when she proclaimed. "Yes, Korina will bargain for your life."

"She... will not." I hoped what I said was true.

Rough, gauntleted hands dragged me from the chamber. Their grip was painful on the lacerations and burns that covered me and fresh blood flowed from my wounds. Nausea shook me, bringing chills of cold sweat to my brow as they took me to the outer wall. In a grotesque parody of my ancestor's hearth-mate, Gelamina, I was tied to a crucifix and suspended above the wall where my kin could plainly see. Red dripping streams ran down the woodroot supports to splash wetly on the platform above the gates of Fartairilzzan.

The dark cavernous Wilds greeted my vision as I looked out over the tunnels before the gates. Like a river of light, I could see the heat of my kinsmen approaching and my heart sank. The familiar cold chill of death lurked on the periphery of my senses, and I prayed to the Maker to take my soul before my daughter could attempt a bargain. The haze of pain kept taking my vision from the scene before me, and I kept seeing the visages of my ancestors watching with anxious faces. Would my death bring righteous anger as it had to Gorain's army eight thousand years before? Vaguely my mind hoped that Lodath had not been a dream, and that he would bring me the Reaver. But I knew how foolish a hope that was. 'Morakvaar, please have Korina attack and not be concerned for my safety!' Had he even heard my prayer?

As the parley group approached the walls, I was heartened. Korina wore my armor and the dragon crown upon her helm. It was a powerful symbol to both my people and to our enemy. I was dead to them, and they mourned my loss as a martyr to our cause. There would be no bargains and no mercy. I smiled proudly as my daughter caught my eye, but it was the most I could do before the weakness overcame me. My head sagged, but at least I could see what took place in front of the entrance. Despite my need to concentrate, my vision blurred from time to time and my mind wandered down dark corridors.

Korina nodded grimly in acknowledgement of my unspoken command. It was uncanny how she always seemed to know my mind, and the sorrow on her face was overlaid with determination. Shrewd in politics, Kairillia recognized the gesture in both our visual exchange and the instantaneous transition of power to the new High Queen. She snarled in my direction, and I could see the desire to end my life burning within her. I drew in a ragged breath, hoping that the Maker would accept my soul as the zarak drew her dagger.

When the deathblow did not come, I opened my eyes in puzzlement. Kairillia's breath on my face startled me as she stood on the platform where I was.

"By Lillain, I should kill you now, but if I do, your kin will be enraged." She snarled. "But, I think it will please me more in the long run that you watch your people be slaughtered and contemplate this as I sacrifice your heart and soul to the Dark Queen." Her whisper was barely audible to my ears. "The first one you watch die will be your heir." The soul of evil possessed her features as she gestured casually over the ramparts.

To my horror, the cavern walls appeared to come alive as Korina was cut off from the main army by the cowardly ambush. "No! You fiendish... git of a spider!" I began, and would have cursed more, but coughing spasms wracked my lungs and drew blood from within and without.

Kairillia's hand sparked with arcane power that arced and danced through my nerves from where her fingers touched my chest. The agony reawakened the hurts done to me by the torturer, making them fresh again in an instant. The entirety of the pain I suffered over long days came to me at once, tearing a cry from my already hoarse throat. Laughing, she descended the stair of the platform to join her retainers and watch the 'show'.

My awareness left me for a time, though I could hear the thunderous boom of artillery and eldritch counter attacks. Despair filled my soul that my daughter had probably perished, and I longed for death to finish its course as it crept through me in slow stages. But rage began to build within me, an all-consuming fire that was around me as well as within. I wanted to rend the zaraks with my bare hands, as my blood seemed to catch fire within my veins, chasing away the chill of death.

The words left my lips before I began to realize the source of the rage. "Dozarak kilna loch krazak sion!"

The stones beneath and behind me shattered upward, but the shards did not penetrate the white-blue flames that surrounded me. A light as bright as the sun leapt into my hands no longer fettered by the charred ropes as I dropped to the platform. Righteous wrath filled my limbs with power as the Reaver filled my mind with the craving for zarak blood. The platform crumbled beneath me from the Reaver's flames, and I climbed to my feet from the ash and rubble, facing towards my nemesis.

Dimly I recognized that Lodath had really been in the throneroom and had managed to accomplish a feat I thought impossible! Had he survived the Reaver's wrath? Was he trapped somewhere within the palace? I had to find him and return to him the favor of my rescue! It all happened in a fraction of a second as time came to a standstill.

In slow motion, Kairillia turned to face me with real terror in her eyes. She touched an amulet and spoke a command word as I drew back the Reaver. Too far out of my reach, I hurled the weapon at her like a blazing comet. A gateway of black fire appeared before her and I feared she would escape my wrath. Instead of passing in to the gate, a horrendous creature emerged from it as the Reaver clipped its leg and slammed into Kairillia's form.

The demon creature's greenish-black limb spouted gray ichor over part of Kairillia's guard, melting them like acid. Horrible screams of agony rippled through the pulsing of the Mother's Song in my veins. The others leapt away from the demon in terror and ran towards me with swords bared. Weaponless, I awaited my doom. To my astonishment, they did not stop to finish me off, rather ran pell-mell away from the hideous being emerging from the opened gateway.

Four sets of greenish-black limbs covered in horny spines erupted from the portal dragging behind them a bulbous dripping body that was half spider, half humanoid. A screeching roar echoed through the stones as it voiced its displeasure at being wounded. The sound smote my ears and echoed through all of my nerves as if it were an evil parody of the Song of the Mother. My head swam in agony and I was unable to move, the discordance paralyzing me on the spot.

Kairillia's hand tried to staunch the blood and viscera from the massive wound my axe had made in her gut, staring at it in disbelief. The blades of the weapon still burned with blue-white fire from where they came to rest caught up in some of her entrails. Her eyes snapped back to where I stood immobilized by the demon's screech, and a slight agonized smile passed her lips. She chanted healing spells to stop the blood that flowed from her, but I doubted if she could cure herself quickly enough to survive. The spider-like monstrosity leapt upon me, piercing my shoulder and thigh with sharp pincer claws. The pain was no more than already ravaged through my system, but the shock made me cry out, and the Reaver's rage beckoned me to call it.

The weapon arced back to my free hand as the demon sunk its venomous fangs deeply into my gut and its pincers stretched my body to near separation. Hungrily it began to suck the meager juices left within me as I commanded the rage-fire.

"Sarlik Doria!" The cry preceded the half-moon blades as they descended upon the beast in a white-blue blaze.

A screech of rage and pain followed the separation and burning of its spider head, leaving only its humanoid half on wobbling legs. The rage-fire protected me from the gray fluid that ate at the very granite of the walls. I pulled out the fangs, feeling the illness of the venom, but the Reaver possessed me utterly. The claws swept the stones where my head had been and raked furrows in the granite fortifications. Rolling under the bulbous mass I struck with the axe.

The roar of agony surged through my nerves, the vibration immobilizing me in the crucial moment of recovering my feet. A pincer struck me a glancing blow, throwing me out of range of its next attack, and I silently thanked the Maker. The demon leapt again, but I was ready. The blades of the Reaver passed through the swollen body and up into the humanoid one, burning as it went. The creature screamed as it dissolved into a lump of gray ichors that swirled around like mist and was sucked back into the portal. The dark luminescence of the gateway snapped shut and disappeared as I staggered forward, stumbling over Kairillia.

Black ichors and blood oozed from the massive rents in my abdomen where the creature's fangs had pierced me. My eyes traveled from the mortal wounds to that of my adversary. She had managed the impossible, the tear in her gut was closing fast.

"You wouldn't kill the mother of your child, would you?" She said quietly, and I could feel the stirring of arcane energies.

The Reaver passed through her skull, and parted her down the middle before I thought of a response. "Yes." I said belatedly.

Bolts and darts whistled in, but none made it through the rage fires that burned around me with hellish heat and brightness. This is was its purpose! The utter annihilation of the zaraks! The zarakanan upon the ramparts began to throw themselves from the wall rather than face me as I approached them with the Reaver. But the rage within did not care, and drove me onward, slaying my enemies with reckless abandon. When the ramparts above the gates were clear, the thirst of vengeance drove me on. My feet found paths within the walls of the keep and down into the city-tunnels where the families dwelled. My reason, my will fought against the rage, tried to stay my hand from its course of destruction. But like the rising river, the tide of anger was unstoppable. As if reliving the horror of Terazandarin, I was unable to keep the Reaver from tasting the blood of the helpless. The old, the young, the wounded and the healthy were not spared. The eyes of the doomed stared back at me, pleading for mercy from a madness that had none.

Through the streets of the city I ran like the avenging angel of death, and Gorain laughed insanely at the carnage. The zaraks fled from me, their weapons turning molten if they were foolish enough to defy the Reaver's rage. Arrows and bolts were shrugged aside with ease and consumed in the rage fires that surrounded me. My will cried out in anguish to see the innocent slaughtered, but I too, was powerless to stop it, or was I? Did I really wish to end the carnage? What little was left of my life waned in the face of the Reaver's vengeance.

When Gorain tired of the slaughter, finding fewer and fewer victims, the weapon's fury led me back to the soldiers manning the fortifications. The spark that was my will was fanned into flame as I realized the fortifications were still intact. Our cannons had not yet breached their defenses, and I had to find out why! Being outflanked beyond the walls the only hope for my kin was to break through and take shelter against the superior numbers of the enemy outside. If I did not help them, they would all be slaughtered!

'Just as you slaughtered the zaraks?' My conscience smote me, telling me that if I could halt the Reaver to help my kin, I could have stopped the slaughter. I was guilty, a mindless killer without mercy or conscience as Kelana had accused. What had I become?

The Reaver glowed innocently from my grasp, its rage quiescent in my need to help my kin, and furthering my guilt. But time was of the essence. How many of my people died while I was engaged in the slaughter of innocents? How many lives could I have saved had I not allowed the thirst of vengeance to overthrow my reason? Contemplating my crimes, I stalked through the narrow tunnels that ran behind the outer wall slaying any zarak I came across. Arrow slits and ballista emplacements became my targets, but the walls continued to hold against our artillery barrage! The resonance came to me as I paused, the thrumming of powerful magics, the fortifications were being warded! Following the waves of arcane forces led me to a round chamber within the sheltered wall.

Into the corridor came the sounds of chanting barely heard over the roar of combat that resounded through the stronghold. Cautiously, I inched forward resisting the need to rush in and destroy. The room was roughly round, half natural and half chiseled out of the stalagmite that was its foundation. In the center stood an enormous anvil from when my ancestors had used the room as a temple-forge. The zarakanan had tried to disguise it with a cloth covered in symbols of Illumia, the crescent moon, the rising star and the tome of truth, but the current occupants had nothing to do with the goddess of enlightenment. Near the entrance on my side of the chamber, a unit of soldiers stood guard over a ring of female zaraks dressed only in diaphanous threads of black that resembled the weave of spider webs. Their lithe forms writhed in the throes of ritual ecstasy as waves of arcane energy radiated outward in cacophonic discordance with the Song of the Mother. It was a mighty spell of disruption for the power of the artillery and affected my kin's ability to fight. The vile rupture in the order of the universe cut off our ability to sense the Song. For my kin, the shock would render them helpless, but I had lived for many years on the surface where the Mother's Song could not reach me. My first few days away from the Halls of the Mother, however, had been a horror beyond reckoning.

The spell had to be broken, but instinct warned me to be still for a few moments, and I knew better than to ignore the premonition. Without warning, a fire-bolt flashed into the room from the entrance on the other side. The soldiers rushed to intercept the threat only to be consumed in a massive ball of flame. Before the smoke had cleared, I stormed into the room, intent on catching the priestesses by surprise. But not all of the soldiers perished in the flames and they rushed to intercept me.

They need not have bothered, for within two steps from the circle of priestesses the chants changed pitch. Energy surged around me, and I was snatched from my feet by an invisible force. The air was crushed from my lungs as the unseen hand closed inward. From the other side of the room, another fire-bolt transfixed the priestesses whom had cast the spell as the soldiers bore down on me. The energy released me, and I dropped to the floor gasping for breath. The Reaver forced me to my feet in time to intercept the soldiers' weapons with a clumsy block. A tall figure entered the opposite door, his hands forming the pattern of some new conjuration. My concentration wholly on the warriors trying to take my life, I barely had time to recognize my old friend. It hadn't been a dream! The confirmation warmed my blood and gave renewed energy to my attacks. Lodath had come to help me! Nothing would stand in our way!

Their circle broken, the four remaining priestesses focused their efforts on eliminating us. Two of them faced me, one speaking a word that solidified the substance of the air and slammed into me like a charging ram. The blow sent me flying back from the line of soldiers, and into the stone wall. White sparks filled my vision as I connected with enough force to flatten my lungs and fracture my skull. Dazed and unable to breathe, I fell flat on the floor, trying vainly to suck in air. My lungs burned with effort, but refused to open. Booted feet rushed towards me, and I realized that the Reaver was not in my hands. Desperately, I tried to call the weapon, but for endless ages I could not draw a breath.

With the certainty of the damned, I watched as my enemies descended upon me. A light-headed euphoria filled me from the lack of air as my chest heaved. When there were but a pace between the zarak soldiers and me, air at last rushed in, galvanizing me into action. I scrambled to the left as the zarakanan cut me off from the Reaver to my right. Gasping in desperation I finally managed the words.

"Dozarak ... kilna ... loch krazak ... sion!" For each of the words that left my lips I dove between sword blows.

Spears and daggers ricocheted from the wall where I had been, ringing out their impotency. The scrape of weapons and the sting of crossbow bolts added more scars joining those of the torturer before the Reaver burned through the ranks of the zarakanan and into my hand. Not missing a beat of the dance of death, I whirled the blades around as white-blue fire consumed my enemies. But the priestesses were not finished casting their spells of destruction. One spoke a different word that became a vibration, then a scream that tore through the Song of the Mother, twisting it to resonate through my nerves and over-stimulate them. It was like activating all possible combinations of sensation at once, a chaos that smote my brain like a hammer. Instantly dazed the overload cut off my contact with the Reaver. It overwhelmed my senses allowing neither thought nor action. There was no difference from the venom creeping through my system and the impact of my enemies' weapons. It seemed forever that I was immersed into Vooraduum itself. Nothing but the living hell existed in that time.

The sensation abruptly stopped, but my nerves still resonated painfully. The ceiling above was slightly out of focus and I wondered why I was staring at it until I realized I was flat on my back. A zarak blade was buried in my shoulder, and another descending towards my neck. In fascination I watched the sword as it clove through the air, but I could not move. In expectation of the blow I closed my eyes, but instead of death the sound of thunder opened them again. Charred dust flitted across my vision as I tried to see where the zaraks had gone. My muscles refused to move as if the commands were still blocked by the cacophony of noise traveling through my nerves.

An old and wrinkled hand appeared before my face, and I followed the extended arm to the face of my former companion. "Well, hurry up! There are more soldiers coming and laying down on the job is a bad way to end your life!"

Agony shuddered through my bones, and more fighting just did not seem worth the effort. I was so tired, a weariness that took away the pain my body suffered. Sleep beckoned me with loving dark arms, and for a moment, I considered accepting her charms. Lodath's eyes were wide and his brows arched in a line of frantic concern. Was someone dying? A tear rolled down his wrinkled cheek to splash on the floor in front of my face. Slowly, the rage of the Reaver crept back in to my nerves that had been shattered by the spell. The power of the weapon drove back the weariness, but not the pain. I wanted it to leave me alone! I would much rather have gone to sleep than to feel the torture that was my existence.

"Dorian, your daughter needs your help! Please! For the gods' sake, get up!" His hand hovered near my bloody shoulder as if he wanted to shake me but was afraid to hurt me.

I let out a long breath of agony. Goaded on by the Reaver's power, I grabbed his hand. "Zen, let us not tarry here." Through sheer force of will I hauled myself upright, allowing the rage-fire to possess me as I pulled the sword from the sheath of my flesh. Metal grated on bone, tearing a growl from within, but I was past feeling individual wounds.

The chamber rocked suddenly and violently, throwing us from our feet as a shower of debris rained down. "I zink zie cannons are vorking now."

Lodath shot me a dirty look as he brushed off the dust that covered him, but we had no time to discuss it as more troops stormed down the corridor towards us. I called the Reaver to my hands, and charged into their midst. Four of them went down instantly by the blades and fire that raged around me, and the rest panicked. With a shout, the two of us lit off in hot pursuit.

"You don't look so good." Lodath told me as he caught up with me.

"Neizer do you." The blood of several wounds leaked through the jerkin and breeks he wore, and he smiled wanly in agreement before turning his attention towards our retreating foes.

We followed the soldiers into the courtyard before the gates. The walls trembled from the blasts of artillery and began to crumble as the cannons began to make headway against them. Soldiers were mustering in the courtyard to repel my kin as they attempted to breech the walls. At least fifty zaraks stood before us, startled as we appeared behind them. The surprise did not last long as shouts reformed the units facing us before we had the chance to reach them.

"Just like old times, eh Dorian?"

"Hmm. Hopelessly outnumbered? Yes, it is like old times." I agreed as Lodath began his familiar incantation of fire. "I only vish I had my armor."

The blood had noticeably drained from my features and my hands looked deathly pale. Idly I wondered what scolding words I would hear from Morakvaar when the Reaver's power left me dead. The same thought seemed to occur to Lodath as he glanced at me after releasing his spell.

"Doesn't that hurt?" There were so many wounds upon me; he failed to single any of them out.

I grunted ascent as the first wave of soldiers charged us. With a roar Lodath's features elongated into a giant cat and he instantly vanished from my sight. But shredded disembodied limbs and the screams of the dying marked his passage well.

"Sarlik Doria!" I invoked the last charge of white-hot fire, incinerating the first group of troops that tried to surround me. It would be several days before the Reaver could gather enough energy to do it again.

The doorway served as a filter, allowing only a few through at a time, and I used it well. The Reaver delighted in the zarakanan that fell before me, as the pile of their bodies began to hinder their fellows' attempts to get at me. In their awkward attempts to cross the corpses of their comrades, they exposed themselves more readily to my strokes. The fight was rather one-sided until I felt a spear pierce me through the back. The zarak had been too eager to thrust her weapon home that her aim had been low. The point of the spearhead came through the front of my gut, and I backhanded the wielder with the Reaver. A satisfactory crunch told me my aim was much better. A quick glance back down the corridor showed me several more zaraks with spears rushing towards me. If only I had someone to cover my back!

Lodath was nowhere to be seen over the pile of bodies in front of me, and I cursed that the bloody zarakanan were agile enough to leap over it and still get to me. Not wishing to face the spears, I fought my way up the pile and down the other side. With relief I found not many of the zarakanan left in the courtyard, and the wall had been breached. My kin poured through the gap, sweeping our enemies before them.

The courtyard was filled with blood and bodies, as I fought my way to the female commander that gave orders. Recognition stopped the killing blow mid-swing. The Reaver raged and screamed within my head to slay her, but I could not kill Liathrain's mother.

I fought hard against the hate, gritting my teeth to control the weapon. "Take your people and go. Kairillia is dead and so is her evil!"

For a moment, she considered trying to kill me, but her eyes traced the amount of wounds that should have already done so. "It seems the prophecy spoke truth. Gorain the Slayer has returned to destroy us and nothing can kill him." She murmured sadly. "Very well, Gorain. Kill me if you will, but I will not go without a fight!"

I growled, trying not to let the frustration feed my anger. "Did you not hear me!? Please go, for controlling this weapon takes all I have! You are outnumbered and surrounded!" The lie sounded convincing as the roar of the cannons that I had given the humans reached my ears from the far side of Fartairilzzan. "Even now our allies attack you from the rear! Your cause is hopeless here, but part of my bargain with Osric was to allow you to live in his kingdom should you decide to leave peaceably."

The dual sounds of artillery and the sound of our troops inside the wall startled her. She had been sure we would never have gotten within the stronghold. Her confidence was instantly shattered, but she clutched at the glimmer of hope I had given her. Inwardly, I was glad that zaraks were so easily shaken, for truly they still outnumbered us badly.

"You will not hunt us if we leave?" It was a question she did not expect me to agree to.

"Upon my ancestors' graves I swear I will not follow any zarakanan who leaves through the Starrift." The Reaver ranted within, blazing its anger through me and my control nearly slipped in my weakness. "Go quickly, though, for I do not know how long I can control this weapon! Know this; I could not follow you if you are out of range of the Reaver's detection, for your assessment is true; once its power releases me, so too will my life be forfeit."

She blinked, finally understanding what my offer entailed. Not only was it her people's freedom from the war, but freedom from their fear of me. Grimly she nodded knowing that for me to let her leave meant my own death.

"Kairillia was a fool to underestimate you, but her foolishness was not nearly as deep as my own. I forgive you for my daughter's death and place the blame in its rightful place. We have longed to return to the surface, and thought that Kairillia would lead us there, but it is you who have set us free. Call off your troops and your allies, and we will leave."

I nodded, hanging on to control of the Reaver by a thread. "You may not believe this, but I lost a piece of my soul the day I killed my good friend." Gorain raged in my head against the zarakanan that stood before me. "Now please go, for I can scarce control this weapon; it takes all that I have. Hurry and send your intent to Korina and we will part in peace." Close to us the fighting halted as the zaraks laid down their weapons with their general's surrender. A cascade of silence began to reach outward in waves as the litany of peace spread throughout the stronghold and to the tunnels beyond.

The world faded from me as I used deep meditation to control the Reaver. Sometime later I was aware that I had fallen to my knees, but the only thing I could focus on was my endless struggle to control Gorain's rage. The comings and goings of those around me were but echoes in the darkness, and it was a shock to suddenly hear my daughter's voice.

"Father!?" The fearful alarm tore my attention from the weapon to focus on her as a stab of cold lanced through me to think she was in danger.

When I realized her terror was in my shattered appearance, it was almost too late to regain control of the Reaver. The warming touch of a healer flowed through me as they tried desperately to return my life-force that was almost non-existent. Blood returned to my veins, bringing fiery needles, but the agony barely lessened.

"Can you drop the weapon, father?"

I shook my head, not daring to think about anything other than control, but I had to know. "Are they leaving?" With the slight distraction, Gorain seized the upper hand.

My grip tightened on the axe as I prepared to give the zaraks a good sendoff to remember. Someone was calling my name, but Dorian was a stranger.

"They are leaving, and their allies have fled, Dorian! Your army hunts the ones that went back in to the deeps and Osric's forces have allowed the zarakanan to pass through them. Osric says that they can stay in his lands as long as they agree to pay homage to the throne and fight in his wars." A strange old human spoke to me, and Dorian's memories named him Lodath.

The Reaver blazed in my grasp as I saw only the torn visage of my mate, Gelamina, upon the battlements like a profane sign. There was only the fleeting mind of Dorian that battered helplessly upon the periphery of my cognizance. The vision and memory of Gorain completely overrode what was left of my consciousness. "Dozarak kilna loch krazak sion." I growled as I spun on my heels towards the nearest concentration of zaraks I could sense through the weapon of the soulsmiths.

The fiery haired kinswoman that Dorian knew was my daughter snatched up the haft of the spear that trailed behind me. Tears stained her cheeks as the agony brought me up short. My legs collapsed back to my knees as blood streamed anew from the entrance and exit wounds. She came around in front of me and reached for the Reaver. Lightning arced along the haft of the weapon and up and down her arms as she cried out in pain but did not let go.

"No!" Both Gorain and I cried out not to hurt a kinswoman who was also my heir.

She wrested the weapon from my hands. Despite the rage that still echoed through me, I could not hurt a kinswoman! With great effort, my fingers unbound from the axe. The Reaver's control receded in the background leaving cold darkness in its wake. I could not hurt my kin! As the power left me, so did my consciousness.

Chapter 9

Sorkarak (Singing Stones)

My eyes focused on the gossamer cloth that rippled above my head revealing gross perverted scenes like the murals I had seen in a vulgar inn. The coverlets that shielded me from the chill air were of a fine silk-like weave and I tried to feel them with my left hand without success. In a moment of panic, I pulled my right hand to my face. It was whole and unfettered, but my left arm had been tied to my ribs by bandages. It was only then that I remembered a zarak blade had skewered my shoulder. Pulling back the covers, I was reassured that the rest of my arm was still attached. In relief, my eyes traveled to a nightstand where a wash bowl had been set and the familiarity of the item sent another cold shock of panic through me.

The room was the same one in which I had been put with the illusory 'Morina'. It had been in that very bed that the vile spider's git had deceived me in to breaking my vow to my mate and took a piece of my soul. Quickly I scanned the room for a weapon, anything I could use against the zarak, but the small effort I had made to ensure I was still whole exacted a weary toll upon me. My stomach clenched at the thought of being at Kairillia's mercy. Nausea filled me, and I begged the Maker for forgiveness wondering what I would tell Morina if I ever got the chance to see her again.

My heart leaped into my throat when the carved stone door swung noiselessly inward. For a long moment I was not sure if I beheld my daughter's face or if it were another illusion. The memory of the battle seemed surreal to me, as if I watched it through another's eyes. Like a dream it unfolded in my memory, much less real than the days of my torment.

"Father?" Korina's voice was full of concern as she crossed the woven rugs to sit at my side. "By Morakvaar, it is good to see you awake! Waradain was unsure if you would make it." She kissed my forehead as if afraid of touching me anywhere else.

By the way I felt, I was glad that was all the contact she made. As my adrenaline leaked away, I began to feel every mark the torturer had given me, and every wound I had suffered in battle. My body shook with pain and weariness, and I wondered why the priests had not healed me. Shame for the unworthy thought colored my face, how many of my kinsmen might have perished if Waradain had spent most of his power on me? The old priest could save many more lives by healing each a small amount rather than fully healing a select few.

My daughter took my hand and held it to her chest as relief flooded through me. "My heart leaps with joy to see that you live!" My whisper was hoarse and I cleared my throat. "I had despaired when the zaraks and orcs cut you off from our army!" My voice was tremulous like a shy child's, and I was unsure if it was from weariness or the memory of the walls that came alive.

The ache stabbed through my chest; I might have lost my child! Korina's expression softened as she squeezed my hand, and I was struck anew at how she always seemed to know my mind. Then a sly smile lit her face.

"I brought you a gift, father." Unfortunately, the empathy seemed all too one-sided.

"Dorian?" The voice was music as my gaze beheld my hearth-mate.

For a moment, I took in her golden hair framing her face, her golden beard braided with three beads, two vaarandril and one gold, the binding ring that held it and my heart quickened. The sight of her sang through my soul as sweetly as the song of creation, but a dark cloud lurked within. My memory of Kairillia's deception filled me with dread, and I felt a pang grow in my chest to know that I was unworthy of her. The memory of Kairillia accented the new wound upon my soul, though she was an evil creature, I had slain one that claimed to conceive of my child! For some small mercy at least there was no soul-bond. I was not sure why, but at least I did not violate a sacred bond and felt no new tear in my soul. What had I become! How could the heart of a kinsman beat within me? The knowledge of my violation of the sacred bond to my mate smote me deeply and I looked away from Morina's eyes.

My hearth-mate took our daughter's place at my side, and I felt that I would rather tear out my heart than to confess the hurtful deeds to her. But, there could be nothing but honesty between us, she would know through our soul-bond if I kept anything from her. But had I not committed another crime against our honesty long ago?

Morina's callused hands rested on either side of my head, forcing me to meet her eyes. "Dorian, what is wrong? Waradain said that once you awakened, there would be no more danger of losing you, but you seem so far away." A world of anguish trailed lines across her face that had not been there before.

"I-..." I looked at Korina, then back and our daughter nodded as she left the room. "There is something I must tell you." I let the words out in a rush, hoping for some sort of absolution from the responsibility. "Kairillia deceived me into thinking she had captured you. She used an illusion to..." As fast as I tried to spit out the words, they still faltered.

Morina looked puzzled for a moment, and then understanding dawned on her. "You mean you had kinship with her!?" The full emotional implication had not yet struck her, but I could sense it building through our soul-bond. "Did you not sense that there was no soul-bond!?"

"I-... I was weary..." The excuse was feeble in my own ears, and I dropped my eyes to the bed. "No, and I should have known."

The joy I had sensed in Morina became a deep wound. She turned from me so that I did not see her distress, and she trembled trying to suppress it as it leaked through our bond. My soul bled with her heart, as she could not help the tears. So intense was the pain that flooded through me from her that I gasped in air as if I was drowning.

"Perhaps it would have been better if Morakvaar had allowed me to die, for you do not deserve this torment, and I do not deserve to be your mate." My voice did not sound nearly as miserable as I felt both inside and out. I could not even begin to contemplate confessing to my earlier indiscretion, though the memory came quite plainly to me. Morina did not respond and her shoulders stooped as if from a great weight. That I could wound her so drove my will into the dust. What sort of creature was I to be so careless!? How could I ever make up for such a heresy!?

For long moments we sat each in our private anguish before Morina finally turned to me. "I think perhaps it would have wounded me more to know that you had died, my love." She sighed deeply as I could feel her forgiveness through our bond.

My anguish intensified as she put her arms around me. "I truly do not deserve your love, Morina. I was never worthy of your honor, and prove my unworthiness time and again. It would be better for you if I had died and that you could marry a more model kinsman than I."

"Dorian, if you do not stop that, I will have to injure you some more!" She smothered any further protest with her lips, and gods but it felt good to have her at my side!

I let the guilt slip from me, for holding on to it would only injure Morina more. My good arm wrapped around her, and I reveled in the sensation of love and warmth as the joy of her presence filled me. An alarming wail startled me enough to reawaken the ache of my injuries, and I cursed myself for not observing the bassinet before. Morina was over the crib instantly, retrieving our newest child. Proudly, she brought the fussing bundle over to the bed to show me. Dark golden wisps of hair framed the tiny round face of a healthy lass, and I smiled in pride. Morakvaar must at least have favored Morina, for he could hardly have love for a rogue such as me! To bless us with two daughters was a boon that had not graced any clan since the first zarak invasion!

"She is beautiful, my mate. What have you named her?" I smiled at the healthy grip that was applied to my finger by a small pudgy hand.

"Geria, after your mother. And may she bring laughter and joy to those around her." Our lips met before a thought belatedly came to my mind and I pulled away, much to Morina's annoyance.

"My mother!" Excited, I called for Korina and her mother stared at me as if I had lost my mind. "Korina, quick! Where are the freed slaves being kept?"

She popped into the room too quickly, and I wondered how much she had heard through the crack in the door? "They are in the temple being tended by the healers, why?" Catching on to my excitement, but not sure of the source, she stared at me intensely.

"My mother is among them!" Both Morina's and Korina's eyes widened as a huge grin split my daughter's face.

"I will go fetch her!" Korina dashed out the door like the ten-year-old she once was.

Our babe's fussing drew us back from the spectacle, and Morina was quick to suckle her. Contentment filled me as Morina leaned into my good arm as she fed our child. It was a moment in eternity, one I would always cherish within my heart and soul. If only we could live out our lives in peace, but Morakvaar's pact intruded on my euphoria even as my old friend entered the door.

"Awake at last, I see." Lodath's eyes had black puffy circles beneath them, and new wrinkles creased over old. He smiled impishly to my mate. "It is good to see you again, Morina! Now I can rest knowing that you are here to watch over this ungrateful lout!" His eyes twinkled in mischief though anguish had written novels upon his features.

"Again, wizard, I am in your debt. How can I repay you?" My sincerity had no effect upon the levity in his features.

He tossed a heavy tome that I recognized on the space by my feet. "Well, you can finish your book. I rather like my role in it. Korina said I should give this to you while she tracked down your mother."

I gave him a wry smile. "No doubt the pages are already well-worn. Between the two of you, I doubt I have any secrets left." The trespass against my privacy was strangely distant in my weariness and I found myself opening my eyes with a start, never realizing I had closed them.

"That is enough for you, my mate!" Morina scolded me before rounding on Lodath. "And you, you scallywag, can go get some sleep yourself!" I could imagine her gentle smile to belie her words. "It is good to see you again, Lodath. Dorian always reminisces about your adventures together; perhaps this will finally shut him up?"

"Ah, so I am to be the pacifier? I see how heartfelt your gladness is!" Lodath quipped as he slipped through the door before Morina could catch him in it.

When Geria had finally fallen asleep at her breast, Morina deftly placed her in the bassinet without waking her. Her robe fell to the floor before she curled up against my right side, and I realized how much I missed her being there! I think I fell asleep as she kissed me, but my transition to the land of dreams was seamless. Guilt haunted my slumber and I dreamt of the painful memory of my first betrayal of Morina's trust.

***

The charred ruins of Mezosilliar surrounded us as we discussed with Kairillia the division of plunder retrieved from the vaults. Patriarch Dorim smiled and nodded to Morina where she stood at my side, a look of grim satisfaction on her face as she stared at the bloody hammer in her hands. A troubled frown crossed King Karakdain's features at Kairillia's eagerness to have her priestesses 're-consecrate' the temple of Lillain. Our thoughts must have been the same as my mind's eye viewed the mutilated corpses that had lined the walls bringing nausea to my gut. Why would anyone be eager to revisit the site whose very air spoke of vile corruption and whispered with the voices of the damned? A chill ran down my spine as we agreed to allow her people to clean out that den of wickedness. The discordance in the Song of the Mother had made our priests violently ill and they had been loathe to return.

The negotiations over Mezosilliar's spoils were long and heated, but eventually we agreed to a lesser share in return for our kin that had been sold to Fartairilzzan as slaves. Kairillia promised that those she held had been treated well and would be released as soon as she returned. Her flowery words insisted that they had been bought out of pity for their treatment. Why didn't she let them go before? I was about to ask, but Dorim silenced me with a glance of his stern gray eyes and a shake of his head.

Already he and King Karakdain knew there was trouble ahead of us, but need kept us as allies to the Vaetra. Mezosilliar itself retained a few slaves of our kin, and we were glad to reunite them with their clans.

All the zarak prisoners we had taken were given to Kairillia who assured us that they would be well treated and given the chance to convert their worship to Illumia. Dorim wanted to keep some of them as slaves to help rebuild Morkilduum, and was surprised at my vehement denial. At least he allowed me to have my way in that regard. How could we be any better than they were if we had kept slaves?

The bodies of our kin lined the rubble-strewn passageways we traversed, my friends trailing behind as we paid our respects in the Ritual of Mourning. Of the forty thousand warriors who followed us from Barakillanak, five thousands would never return to their hearths. Victory was extremely costly to us, but even more so to the Vaetra. Near ten thousand of their number paved the streets in their blood. But, Mezosilliar, the largest stronghold of the zaraks, would trouble us no more. Almost a hundred thousand zarakanan had dwelled there and kept almost twice that number in slaves of several other races including our own.

As I looked upon the faces of my kin who lie in honor, my heart ached to know that they could never be replaced. Their lives, their accomplishments were at an end, and the loss of their numbers could not be recovered.

Each name written in the book of ancestors was like a wound upon my soul, one that would not heal. The recounting of their deeds echoed from the ruins as if the very stones honored the dead. After the first twelve hours, my companions sought their rest, but I stayed with Dorim and Karakdain through all three days of the Mourning. My mind dwelled heavily upon the blood-toll of Mezosilliar, upon the settlements that they had decimated, the destruction of Morkilduum, and countless other hapless hunters and traders that fell prey to them. Our retribution did not equal the havoc and death they had caused. A hundred forty thousand dead zarakanan hardly compared to over two hundred thousand Kinsmen of the Blood who had been victimized by Mezosilliar.

At the end of three days, the long procession to the River of Life began. Outside the southern gate of Mezosilliar, we gave the bodies of our kinsmen back to the Mother. The Vaetra made no such mourning for their dead, but quietly burned them on the northern side of the ruins. With a weary mind and soul, I surveyed the utter destruction wrought by our cannons and the arcane arts of our allies. It seemed not a single building carved from stalactite or stalagmite survived intact. The stronghold that had once been Laharazduum was no more, and all record of the clans that had lived there had been wiped away.

The dead of Mezosilliar were gathered and thrown into the magma tributary that joined the River of Life, a better fate than they deserved, but it was the simplest thing to do with them. Dorim, Karakdain and I then went to our rest as Kairillia retrieved her 'share' of the spoils. It was determined that all things made by zarak hands would be hers and all things kanan would be returned to us. It was an arrangement that displeased Kairillia, but she finally agreed. While we rested, her people packed their wagons and returned to Fartairilzzan. It was when we awoke from our slumber that we learned that she had taken the things from Lillain's temple instead of destroying them as we had agreed. She had also taken more than her share of the treasures we agreed upon. It was a deed that left me with uneasy thoughts about our future.

After a long conference with Dorim and Karakdain, Morina and I met with the rest of our companions at the midday meal. I could tell by the furtive glances and reluctance to speak that they had decided to leave. Lodath finally looked to me as I smiled and nodded in understanding.

"It is not such an easy zing to see so much carnage, but I zank you for staying ahnd aiding our cause. Our people vill not forget your role in zies matters." I wanted to say more, but it dawned on me that the people I had thought of as my family, my kin, were leaving. It was unlikely that I would ever see them again.

Liathrain broke the uneasy silence. "Kairillia has asked me to become a member of her personal guard, and I have accepted."

The news gave me hope. With Liathrain close to the Matriarch, it was unlikely that the trouble I foresaw would come to fruition. At the very least, Liathrain would be able to give me warning of Kairillia's acitivities. My smile was broad as I grasped her forearms.

"It does me good to know zat you vill be zere. Kairillia gains a formidable varrior to guard her. I know zat you vill fare vell in zies endeavor. I hope zat you vill remain in touch vit us." Liathrain eyed me as if she suspected the true reason that I was glad for her appointment, but I looked to Kelana before she could divine it from my soul. "Ahnd you? Vill you stay vit Liathrain?"

The wood elf laughed. "Why not? The wonders of these caverns have yet to be revealed to me, and I am eager to start learning of them."

I nodded and looked to Rutger. "It is high time I felt the sun on my face and the wind in my hair. I wish you well, Dorian, but you can keep this infernal darkness." I smiled; knowing Rutger tried to dismiss his feelings, but did not do an adequate job.

"What will you do now, Dorian?" Lodath's eyes were on Jaguar not me, and I felt the heat of jealousy rise within.

"Patriarch Dorim vishes for me to rebuild our home of Morkilduum. It vill be a long ahnd hard road for us, but I zink it can be done." He looked away from Jaguar as his face reddened when he noticed me staring hard at him. He had always been jealous of my relationship with her and the thought of him with her burned within me.

Lodath cleared his throat. "Patriarch Dorian, eh? Who would have thought?"

I kept my eyes on him as I replied "I am still qvite young for my people, ahnd Dorim is not yet ready for Krazakvarein." What was the humor in his statement? The others laughed uproariously.

Irritated by the humor at my expense and my growing unease with Lodath's attention to Jaguar, I merely grunted in response. This sent them into more laughter.

"Well, I think it is time to say farewell to this stale darkness and smell the fresh winds of the wild forests." I frowned, the insult to my home added to my anger, but Lodath did not seem to notice.

Rutger and Jaguar sighed wistfully, and it was as if I had been betrayed when Morina nodded rigorously to the sentiment. Though there were some things of the surface that I had come to appreciate, their world could not compare to the wonders of the Halls of the Mother. I could feel her song vibrating through my soul, filling me with her secrets. It was a sense of oneness, a belonging to the earth that no experience in the surface realms could compare with, but I realized my companions were not Kinsmen of the Blood. They were not the Mother's children, and I pitied them for their shallow solitary existence. But when Morina expressed misgivings about remaining in the Deeps, it smote me hard, and I got up from the table and took a short walk.

I could feel the eyes upon my back as I headed for the Glowfish River on the north side of the city.

"What's the matter with him?" Jaguar asked as I stormed off.

"I think he is upset that we are leaving, but doesn't want to admit it." Lodath answered smugly before his words were lost to me.

Since my marriage to Morina, he had incessantly tried to win over Jaguar, even going so far as to bring her gifts in my presence. I tried very hard to leave behind my love for her, but I might as well have torn out my lungs for all the good it did me. The more I thought of Lodath with Jaguar, the angrier I became. The last straw was a vision of my daughter, Panther, returning from her apprenticeship and calling Lodath 'father'. The vision near drove me mad, and I pounded my fist on the rock of the outer wall.

"Dorian, aren't you going to say goodbye?" Lodath's voice fueled my anger.

I rounded on him. "Goodbye ahnd good riddance! You vanted Jagvar, now you have her! I do not vant to see you or her again!"

"I know you don't mean that." Lodath said, backing up a step at the look on my face. "Dorian, I'm not after Jaguar-"

I snarled menacingly. "You vould lie to me? I see zie vay you look at her, see zie zings you have done to make her yours. I should part your head from your shoulders! It is only because you vere my friend zat I do not kill you." The guilty look on his face was all the fuel I needed. Against all reason, I could not let her go.

"Dorian, you are married to Morina. You have no claim on Jaguar and never did." Lodath warmed up to his own anger. "The only thing you have succeeded in is alienating her with your incessant jealous behavior. She never wanted you except as a toy to be used when she saw fit anyway!" The truth struck more deeply than any wound, slapping the pride of my being soundly upon the cheek.

The axe came swiftly to my hand as I leapt at him with a snarl. "It is you zat is jealous! You zat vhispers zings to her to alienate her against me!" My first swing tore his robe, but missed his body. Madness, insane jealousy, dark rage and possession took my reason far from me. What a fool I had been!

Lodath finished a chant that transfixed me with a fire-bolt. "It is you who are mad, insanely jealous. Jaguar never loved you, and never will!" Again more truths burned the hatred deeply into me.

Lightning arced along my armor, dancing upon it like tiny daemons. When the power released me, I sank to my knees before the return strike slammed into me from behind. Before I recovered from that, he sent a storm of magical darts into my chest, throwing me back to the ground. I growled in pain, and rolled to my feet for another go, but my blades passed through empty air. With a slight popping sound, Lodath appeared behind me, a blade pressed to my throat.

"Don't make me kill you, Dorian. This is not a fitting end to our friendship." He whispered in my ear. "Jaguar was never yours, and she will choose whom she sees fit to choose." With that, he disappeared again.

"Mark my vords, mage. I vill kill you if I see you again!" As soon as the words left my mouth, so did my anger. What was I doing? Lodath was right, Morina was my mate and I had neither right nor claim to Jaguar. "No, I am a fool, Lodath. I cannot forsake my oldest and truest friend, not for such a foolish vim." I turned back towards the gathering to apologize before my companions left for good.

They were already gone by the time I made it back, and I sorrowed that I had parted in anger with Lodath. Morina was troubled by my display, realizing where it stemmed from, and I took the time to make it up to her before she left for Barakillanak to rejoin Korina. But, I had to stay in Mezosilliar while there was still work to be done. Weary of heart and body, I returned back in the evening to where I occupied one of the hollowed out stalagmites. One room remained intact, and it was in that hovel that I had set up my 'office' and placed a bed that had survived the bombardment.

I walked over to the desk and put down the long lists of items that had been sorted and packed that day. My helmet joined the pile of accumulated papers on my desk as I used my dagger to strike the flint into the tinder so I could light the candle. My instincts suddenly warned me that I was not alone, and I spun on my heels drawing my axe. Jaguar stood in the room next to the bed, her dark skin barely concealed by a robe of silk. I swallowed, trying to suppress the desire that raged within me. My bonding vow to Morina repeated itself in my memory, but the mantra failed to exorcise the feelings that welled within.

I stumbled backward against the table, hoping that I had the fortitude to walk away. Jaguar stepped lightly over to where I stood, and I turned to the door before her dark hand rested on the skin of my neck.

"Aren't you going to say goodbye to me, Dorian?" Her voice low and alluring as ever halted me in my tracks.

"I zought you vere eager to leave." Losing the battle with my desire, I turned to her. In a last desperate effort I said, "I am happy to be married to Morina."

She let the robe slip from her shoulders as she pressed my head against her firm stomach and her breasts brushed my forehead. "But you know I can't leave without saying good-bye." Her breath stirred the hair on my head igniting the fires I had tried to keep at bay for over a year.

"I can not do zies to Morina-" Jaguar's full lips silenced me as she leaned over and undid the buckles that held my pauldrons in place.

Gods forgive me, but I could not refuse her anything. I still loved her, and knew it might very well be the last time I saw her. We shared a night of passion that rivaled any we had ever known. It was the desperation of two lovers that knew there would be no more memories. Though the thought of my marriage weighed heavily upon me, I still did not wish it to end. When at last she left my side, I was full of guilt for the last precious memories of my former human lover. The bittersweet parting of my first love filled me with pain and regret. The dishonor of breaking my vows to Morina haunted my conscience, and I wrestled many nights with my indiscretion, wondering if I could ever look my mate in the eye again.

***

Shame smote me anew as Morina stirred quietly in her sleep. I did not deserve her love. She should have been married to a devout kinsman, one who kept our traditions and not a confused debased creature that could not control their emotions. Twice, I had broken my vows and proven that I was not worthy of the title of kinsman. Yet, what was I? Voices and memories not my own warred in my head with my experiences, leaving me confused as to who and what I was. Had it started the day I had made my journey, my quest for adulthood, or perhaps before? But, speculations had to wait, and business took precedence.

There were so many things to accomplish, pay the humans, sort through what remained of Fartairilzzan, repair the fortifications, ensure the farms were still workable, and resettle the clans along with those who survived the war! These were just a few of the pressing matters before me. Dozens of other items filled my head not the least of which would be arranging new pairings for the widows of the dead kinsmen. Morina would be a great help at least. It had angered many of the clans that I arranged pairs outside clan boundaries, but to their chagrin, every pairing had produced offspring. Morina informed me of the kinswomen's interests, as they would not speak to me of their feelings. Morakvaar favored Morina's council, and the amount of children that had been born in Morakduum bode well for our people's future. These things, though not physically taxing took a heavy mental toll upon me as I recovered. Endless mounds of paper occupied every waking moment and I longed for the days where I could thrust it all aside and pick up an axe instead of a pen.

It was several weeks before my wounds were healed and I was healthy enough to retrain. Korina had seen to the Mourning for our dead and the initial preparations of Fartairilzzan for our habitation including returning its old vaarakanan name, Sorkarak. After the second day of re-strengthening, my daughter came to talk with me.

"Father, I know your plans were to go on to complete the quest of evicting our enemies, but which way do we turn our attention?" She sat on the bench by the training grounds as I wiped the sweat from my brow.

"That is a matter that has been heavily upon my mind. I think that we should clear all the smaller strongholds of our enemies while we repair Sorkarak. The trolls and goblins will be easily rousted after the defeat of Kairillia." I stopped talking as I saw a sly, smug smile on my daughter's face.

"Already done. While you were languishing away, I sent out an expeditionary force to Karaznak and foisted Jubaroz and his cronies out. Vokazan was deserted by the time we got there, and we suspect the goblins fled through Zarakalduum to the Shallows." She smiled at my astonishment and asked her question again a little more succinctly. "Should we assault Vouroussan, or Zarakalduum next?"

I merely stared for a time before a slow smile spread across my lips. "You make a formidable Queen, Korina, for your wisdom seems at least as great as mine, probably even more so. You tell me which you would tackle first."

"Zarakalduum. The Kinsmen of Shadow will be difficult, but more easily overcome than the vourdovra." She smiled, certain she had made the right choice until I shook my head.

"That is precisely why they should be last. Vouroussan will be the most difficult and costly in lives. If we attack Zarakalduum first, we may not have the numbers to overcome the vourdovra." I put the cloth down and sat next to her on the bench as she contemplated my answer. "Korina, we understand the shadow kin. They are, after all, vaarakanan, even though they have lost their way. Worst of it, we could barter an uneasy peace with them. Who knows, perhaps even Morakvaar will someday forgive them?"

"I see there are a few things that I still need to learn of warfare, father." She looked at the dust of the practice arena as two combatants stirred it to life.

I put a hand on her shoulder as I smiled my encouragement. "Korina, it is my hope that such lessons can be left behind our people once our quest is complete. Gods willing, there will be no more need of combat or warfare once we have settled Zarakalduum. Then we can turn our attention to the important matters of preserving our race."

She looked from the two struggling warriors back to me. "How can we defeat the vourdovra?"

It was my turn to idly stare at the combatants as they parried and dodged, struck and wrestled. "When I traveled with my companions, we found an amulet that blocked their mental powers. Lodath's spells seemed to attract them in droves, so I gave the amulet to him to protect him from them. Perhaps he has found a way to reproduce it? I will have to speak with him about it."

Korina nodded absently and followed me back to the bathing chamber. "Do you think that we can overcome them?"

I stripped off my sweaty breeks and stepped under a filtered spout before releasing the water. "When we fought a city full of demon fish and vourdovra before, we found that they had a centralized mind. This 'overmind' controlled all of them in the city, and once we killed it, there was enough chaos that we were able to destroy them one by one. Without direction, they are helpless." I said between using the borax and oil soap and rinsing in the filtered water.

Korina leaned against the wall, staring thoughtfully off into the warm radiance of the tunnels. "Father, I do not want to be High Queen." She whispered almost plaintively.

I stepped from the water and began to dry myself with a bathing cloth. "Neither did I want rulership when the clans swore fealty to me. It is a great burden, my daughter, but I know you will bear it proudly."

She sighed deeply. "I wish that Dorak would have been the oldest."

I laughed as I put a hand on her shoulder and we walked to the changing room. "Now Korina, you know that Dorak's personality is not suited to be king. So if he were older, it would only mean that you were a younger more inexperienced queen." She grinned back.

"Morakvaar preserve us from my youth!"

We both shared a laugh, knowing what a terror she had been.

"I am truly sorry for being so headstrong, father."

I put on the clean clothes I had left there before going to the practice grounds. "It is a sign of inner strength, Korina, but gods know we could have used a little less of it." I grinned to soften my words. "At least you did what you thought best, even though your decisions were a little misguided." She knew I was speaking about her clandestine Bonding to Marek.

Korina flushed, looking away from me. "It was what we wanted."

I finished dressing and gathered up the two dirty cloths and my sweaty clothes as we headed for the palace. "I am the last to blame you, Korina. I never told you that I was in a similar situation as a youth, but I was too caught up in my ambitions to see the truth of the matter. Had I taken our cause before Dorim, it is possible that he may have relented, but I was not so willing to put my honor on the line."

Korina stopped dead, astonishment written on her features. "You!? You had a love interest as a youth?"

"Well, to be quite honest, she was my best friend, but she thought of me as more than that. As an outsider to clan Atharil and the third son of a dishonored clan, I never even thought I had a chance at marriage. The best I could have hoped for was to attain my Mastership and be accepted into the Atharil clan. Kavria thought differently, and when she was betrothed to another... Well, that is in the past."

"She loved you and you did not love her?" I looked away from her piercing green-gold eyes.

"I was young and foolish and in love with my profession and honor." I turned back to her. "I had assumed that we would have been Bonded, for everyone knew of our close friendship. It was unthinkable that Kavria would be betrothed to another. When the council of elders announced it, I was shaken to the core." The painful memory of having my belief in our authorities torn to shreds was still a sharp wound. "It served to remind me of my lowly status. I was an outsider to my clan for not taking up my father's profession and an outsider to clan Atharil by birth. Added to that my oldest brother had been Bonded, and as the younger brother I was not even a candidate. The dishonor of our ancestor, Gorain was brought up numerous times thereafter, and I was too ashamed to protest. I did not dare go against the wishes of the council for fear our clan would be banished. I thought that it would be enough that Kavria and I remain friends, but after her marriage I was forbidden to see her again." I could not believe how much that disgrace still hurt.

"So that is why you ranged further than the others, to prove yourself to Dorim?" I nodded as Korina shook her head. "Why did Kavria not plead her case?"

I smiled at my daughter. "I think she did, but her consort held much power and wealth. He was also of eldest son of one of the clans of Atharil and it was his voice that reminded the council of Gorain's dishonor. You must know that a rebellious kinswoman's desires were the last things considered when the council chose mates. I had tried to do things differently, and had swayed the council to some extent, but it is still difficult to unravel millennia of tradition."

Korina merely grunted an ascent as we continued into the palace gates. The two kinsmen that stood watch snapped to attention as we passed, and I wondered if I would ever get used to the gesture of honor. The wide courtyard was full of activity as Stoneshapers carved huge blocks of stone to fit into the holes in the walls that had been blasted by the cannons. Scaffolds and tackle guided the stones lifted by the resonators into place as they were shaped and smoothed into the gaps. The sounds of the forges could plainly be heard as fasteners, hinges, doors and shutters were repaired or replaced. All seemed as it should excepting the amount of humans still within the city walls. But that was a concern for the High Queen. The burden of High King was no longer upon my shoulders leaving me strangely lighthearted and unfettered even though I assisted her heavily with the tedious affairs of running the kingdoms.

My proud gaze followed my daughter as she made her way to her offices, and after leaving the soiled clothes to be laundered, I sought out my friend Lodath. The Garden of Stones still struck me with their beauty, but the gravity of my errand sobered me before I found the mage. Lodath stood by a bench overlooking the Daemon Fish River that danced hellishly below. To us it was a reminder of damnation, but to the mage it was a sight to enrapture the soul. The winds that rushed through the Garden of Stones caught on thin wafers of calcite and silicate causing them to vibrate. The harmony produced by the wind and the condensation dripping on other thin stones was something beyond a choir. It was an audible echo of the Mother's Song, a beauty of the Deeps that had been lost to us for seven thousand years.

It was the first time I had heard the singing stones, and was momentarily immobilized by the awe of them. The melody stirred memories within me, memories that were not my own, and I found myself standing next to an auburn haired kinswoman whose golden eyes smiled into mine.

***

"Gorain, at last we are bonded! I thought it a lifetime that the council debated what was to be done!" She leaned into my shoulder as I put my arms around her protectively. "When you slew Hakareth and saved us from his lair, I thought it a certainty that the elders would allow our bonding."

I lifted her chin to look into her eyes, my heart filling with warmth. "I am glad they did not deny us this bonding, my mate." The song of the stones echoed around us as we stood in the far corner of the garden.

"We have waited long enough! I do not care if we are not in the marriage chamber, be with me now." She whispered conspiratorially as she pulled my lips to hers.

"Gelamina! What a shameful thing! It has not yet been a full ten-day!" I whispered, and we both snickered silently as we sank to our knees in the soft bed of moss to consummate our marriage.

***

"It is the most beautiful natural wonder I have ever witnessed." Lodath's words startled me and brought a flush of warmth to my cheeks as if he could hear my thoughts.

I walked up beside him, looking out onto the hellish river. "Twenty five thousand years ago my ancestors found this place." I answered in my own language, not wishing to twist my tongue around the surface speech. "They named it Sorkarak, Fortress of the Singing Stones. Eight and a half thousands of years ago, the zarakanan came here begging shelter from their wars. The king of Sorkarak at the time was Valkardain Mytharia, a distant ancestor, and many proclaimed him as Valkardain the Kind. He took in the vagabonds, compassionate and eager to learn of their origins. We had not known other races besides our own estranged kin, and the appearance of the zarakanan was a mystery and a wonder."

"You had not known other races?" Lodath looked at me with raised brows.

"No. My people came here from the Sundering after wandering for many thousands of years through the Deeps. Other races came from above, whereas ours originated from deep underground where a portal led to Morakvaar's forge within the heart of Dolamakduum. The only other race we had known was the dark kin, the children of Atlazar who betrayed and murdered most of our Clan Firsts. It was they who instigated the Great War and because of the war, Morakvaar caused the Sundering." I paused realizing that Lodath was probably the first human to be privy to such deep history.

Lodath confirmed my summation. "No book of dwarven history has ever mentioned anything about what caused the Sundering, only what happened afterward."

I nodded. "It is forbidden to speak of such things outside our race, and I trust this knowledge will die with you?"

With a look of disappointment, Lodath finally agreed. "As you wish, Dorian, but you know it is a great temptation."

"One I know you are not young enough to fall for." The mage laughed bitterly at my statement, knowing the truth of it. "It was those zarakanan that Valkardain took in were actually the vanguard of an invasion force." I continued the tale as Lodath listened with rapt attention. "Once they spied out our numbers and fortifications, some of them returned to their generals with the information while others remained behind to open the gates from within. They told Valkardain that they were going to retrieve the remainder of their meager survivors of their 'Great Calamity'. They claimed that the Great Calamity was a widespread die out of their crops, a phenomenon we ourselves had witnessed in the Deeps when an area has been farmed too long without replenishing the soil. Though we pitied them, we also thought them foolish, but it was really our own folly to believe them.

"The zarak scouts that stayed behind murdered the watchmen and left the city open to the vast army that descended upon Sorkarak while they slept. Gorain, my direct ancestor and sister-son to Valkardain, was taken as a slave along with his family. Valkardain and his immediate clan were tortured, humiliated, and then executed." Lodath shifted uncomfortably as if viewing the scene in his mind's eye.

"For a hundred years, Gorain worked the mines of our clan for our enemies, not knowing if his mate or children still lived. One day, they said he went mad and slew his masters with his pickaxe, tearing the slave collar from about his neck, his madness allowing him to thwart its control. His fury was unstoppable and he freed our kin. They swore fealty and followed him from the mine. They fought their way to Balakarak and begged safety within the walls. Reluctantly, they were allowed in as beggars and servants, for at the time, we did not value our kinsmen outside of our own clans. It was a dark time in our history." I shook my head as Gorain's memories showed me the scenes all too clearly.

"Your people made servants of their own?"

I nodded, "sometimes even enslaved other clans. Those were bad times, and why the slave collars were invented. Atlazar must have been mightily pleased with us, but Morakvaar was determined to teach us a lesson. So he allowed the invasion to take its course. Though Gorain begged for the soulsmiths to create him a mighty weapon to drive back our enemies, Morakvaar forbade them to give it to him. The axe was forged of a piece of Gorain's soul and quenched in the blood of his enemies, but with Morakvaar's edict, Gorain left empty handed with his soul rent in two."

The wind changed slightly in intensity and so too did the pitch of the harmony around us. "Truly there are wonders here in the Deeps," sighed Lodath. His eyes scanned the surrounding flowstones as if picking out the individual sounds in the chorus. "If Gorain did not get the Reaver, what happened?"

"He went to Laharazduum, Tharakarak, Barakillanak and to Dormakkarduum, trying to raise support amongst the clans." It was as if I relived those days, seeing again the wandering, the starvation, and the despair, feeling the horrible rent of a torn soul. "And though I garnered enough followers to make an army, it was not nearly enough to defeat our enemies." Lodath raised a brow and cocked his head to the side, but I continued on, heedless of my change of view. "I led them back to the most defensible site in all of the Deeps, what was known as Morkillarak, silver-steel pass, and there we went to work. From the surrounding deposits of granite, we constructed mighty defenses, a drawn line against the incursion of the zarakanan. Morkilduum was born, and the zarakanan broke themselves upon the fortifications we had built." I paused, finally realizing that I had gone from third to first person narration.

My gaze rested accusingly on the Reaver held carelessly in one hand. "Sometimes, Gorain's memories try to control me." The excuse sounded lame to my ears, but I knew those memories were more truthful than reciting what was in the history books.

Lodath stared intently at the weapon and then quizzically at me, but I could not tell what he was thinking. A distant look glazed over his eyes as he nodded his head and mumbled something under his breath. The hair along my neck and arms stood on end as I felt the gathering energy around him. I waited out whatever spell he had cast, until his attention returned fully to me, expecting an explanation, but none was forthcoming.

"Was there some point to that exercise?" Lodath blinked rapidly, a gesture I knew meant he was thinking of some excuse that would satisfy me.

In a startling display of candidness, he told me the truth. "I was trying to determine if your memories were induced by the weapon or not."

When he did not continue, I prompted him. "And?"

It was a moment before Lodath spoke to change the subject. "What happened after the zarakanan attacked Morkilduum?"

Would he tell me what he had seen? But I knew the stubborn set of his brow and chin. "The zaraks laid siege for several tendays, long enough for their army to begin to starve, for they could not break Morkilduum's defenses. On the sixth month of the siege, Gorain sallied forth with his army, taking the enemy by surprise. The zarakanan were thrown into confusion and were defeated by a force less than half their number because of their poor preparation. The zaraks were routed and fled in different directions. Those who fled past Tharakarak met their end on vaarakanan weapons, for King Malakar had finally realized the depth of the zarakanan threat to us and threw in his lot with Gorain. With the reinforcements, Gorain pursued the zaraks back to Sorkarak, but they rallied and met his initial assault.

"Seeing the folly of attacking a force nearly twice his size, Gorain ordered his army to fall back to Tharakarak to regroup. It was his hope that he could enlist the aid of Balakarak and Laharazduum as they were the closest to the threat. While he petitioned Laharazduum's king, the zarakanan laid siege to Balakarak. This motivated the remaining kings, and they all swore fealty to Gorain and made him their High King as the last of the direct line of Golodain. They promised him their armies if he would lead them against the zaraks. With a mighty army of our kinsmen, Gorain marched forth once more to break the siege of the stronghold of the soulsmiths. Morakvaar saw the uniting of our people and smiled. He allowed Gorain to receive his weapon in hopes that a new age of cooperation and respect would settle upon our people once the zarakanan were defeated." I broke off as Gorain's memories again seized control of my mind.

***

The vast army was camped out upon the approach to Sorkarak. I had personally led the forays to the seven mines, freeing all of our kin whom had been held as slaves. Gelamina had been interned in one of them, and she stood again at my side as my heart soared in gladness. Two of our sons had survived, but I learned that our youngest had suffered a lingering death at the hands of our enemies. He had been taken to serve in one of their houses as a slave and eventually as entertainment. The knowledge had driven home the hatred, set it afire within me like a living entity.

***

A large hand on my shoulder startled me, and I whirled defensively placing the Reaver's blades between the threat and me. "Dorian?" Lodath's look was not one of surprise, rather of concern.

"Yes?" Even though I was unsure who Dorian was, I knew the human meant me.

"You were telling me about Gorain's siege of Sorkarak?" He prodded my memory, and I wondered why he referred to me in the third person.

I nodded and continued. "We had freed the slaves, and my mate, Gelamina stood with me. It was a joyous time for us, for we had not seen each other for over a hundred years. Two of our sons had also survived, and we held a feast for those we had freed before moving on. That night, ..." Terror, pain, horror stopped my words, but eventually I felt compelled to continue. "After we had gone to sleep in each other's arms, I thought I had heard a noise. I could have sworn I had awakened, but did not remember anything until morning. I was outside my cavor," at the mage's confused look, I clarified, "a kind of tent. I was unclothed and facedown in the dirt. My head ached, and I remembered a zarak had been inside. Immediately, I threw aside the cloth, nothing but blood and empty bedding met my gaze. The groan of my eldest son drew my attention, and I ran to his side. He had been placed upon my chair, nails through his wrists and ankles. The zaraks had stripped him of his manhood, and he was only then coming to. My next eldest had been made to witness the deed, a spell of silence cast about him, and when our priests had removed it, we learned of what became of my hearth-mate." The pain and rage filled me anew, igniting the Reaver in my hands. I shook with fury and anguish, not knowing which to fulfill.

"Relvea nest falall." Lodath's words echoed through the garden, striking me within and without in their strength.

As the echoes of the spell released my nerves, I stared at him puzzled. "What was that about?"

His mouth smiled, but his eyes remained worried. "I think you need a rest, Dorian. This campaign has done more to you than you realize."

"What do you mean?" For me, the past few minutes had not occurred.

"I think perhaps you need to do quite a bit of soul-searching. You do not seem sure of who you are any more." His gaze never wavered from mine as the memory of my speech returned.

I looked at the Reaver accusingly, but knew it was not just the weapon. "I am sorry, Lodath, but I do not know how to stop what is happening to me." Dismay stole the strength of my legs and I sat on the bench, purposefully leaving the Reaver leaning against the wall and out of my reach. "You are right in that my memories are not my own any more. Ever since I acquired that cursed weapon, I have not had a moment's peace with my own mind." His raised brows told me that he knew it was much more than that, but I did not want to contemplate anything else. "I know what had happened to Gorain is happening to me. The Reaver swallowed the rest of his soul as it is doing to mine."

Lodath's mouth opened in surprise, and he looked as if he were going to tell me otherwise, but let me continue in my belief. Instead he asked me about Gorain. "What happened to make you believe the Reaver swallowed his soul?" His robe seemed to reflect the bluish-gray hue of coolness even though he glowed with the warmth of his blood and I wondered what enchantment was laid upon it.

"When Gorain had driven his enemies from Sorkarak, it was not enough to quench his rage. He hunted them down as they cowered and fled. Neither male nor female nor infant was spared his ire. So obsessive was his anger that his kingdom faltered and our people were left without direction in their hour of need. And so it was that the Clan First of the Orudin came to him, the only known surviving Clan First of the original seven clans. She begged him as a friend to put aside his vengeance for the good of his people, but he refused. Then, hoping to end his madness, she confessed her love of him since his childhood..." I stopped, the memory of the shame that had come upon our clan from that moment left me speechless.

Five thousand years of our clan begging for scraps from others, living as little better than slaves in disgrace and three thousand more where we slowly climbed back into society weighed upon my shoulders as if it were my own fault. The torment I had suffered as a lad, knowing that the scorn of Gorain was scorn of my clan, tore at my soul. By Lodath's interest, he thought it an endearing tale, one that human legends were made of, so little did he know of our culture.

"So what did Gorain do?" He said dreamily.

"He confessed his desire of her, and they shared kinship outside the bonding." It was easier telling him this than it had been for me to recite it in front of a classroom full of my peers, but it still bit deeply within me to know I too had committed such a base act. "For a tenday they spent time together, but Gorain's rage soon took hold once more. He left her arms to continue his quest for vengeance, and in confused desperation; the orudin went to the Council of Elders for guidance. When the council learned of what Gorain had done, they were outraged that he would dare defile a Clan First. They sent a party to retrieve him from his hunt, tried him and banished him. It was only by the orudin's insistence that they spared our entire clan from his fate. We were stripped of titles and holdings and set adrift in the Deeps as beggars and vagabonds. Gorain himself felt nothing but ire as he continued his quest for vengeance.

"He tried to find out where the zarakanan came from and encountered a group of them. The orudin, realizing her error sought him out, but when she arrived, he had slain all of the zarakanan even though they had been unarmed and begged for mercy. Morakvaar appeared to him then, chastising him for killing the zaraks. He told Gorain that they were servants of good and could have helped his people, but instead would bring us misery. Kairillia certainly proved the prophecy, having done more to devastate our people than any other zarak in our history. As a punishment for his deed, Morakvaar was said to have confined the other half of Gorain's soul within the Reaver until the end of time. His was a tortured captive soul to know nothing but the rage of battle for all eternity." I sighed heavily even though Lodath was my friend, it was as if confessing to the worst crime myself.

"How sad. Do all of your love stories turn out so tragically?" I stared in open-mouthed shock, forgetting for a moment the huge difference in our cultures.

"What?"

"Well, you and Jaguar seemed to have a tragic ending, Gorain and the orudin, Gorain and Gelamina, Darlik Hammerhand and Veronia. I'm depressed just thinking about it! Don't your people know how to tell happy tales?" He lapsed back into his own tongue in his rant.

"Tales!? Is that all you think of? I speak of our tragic history and you want entertainment! Typical human! How could you possibly understand? What I have told you took eight thousand years to undo the shame! When I was born, my father was a forge priest, and yet he could not openly claim such like lesser clans. He had to take scraps of payment for articles that would have bought a kingdom, but since our clan was in disgrace, we had nothing save what we made. I was the first of our clan to be accepted back into the palace of Morkilduum since Gorain's exile and only because Dorim took pity upon my father even as he coveted my father's work. It was not until I saved his oldest son's life that a true friendship grew between us. Before then, I lived in his house as little more than a servant." I paused as I remembered those painful days as a youth.

My feet paced the stones of the garden not even looking at the crystal flowers, nor the elegant sheets of multihued flowstone, but upon the memory of the early days of my apprenticeship. Though it was expected for new apprentices to get the lowliest of jobs, for me it was even worse. From the first day, it had been my duty to clean the stables of the riding spiders, though they were unused to my presence. Several bites had to be cauterized to stay the spread of poison, leaving hideous scars, but I was determined not to bring more disgrace upon my family. Each new obstacle made me more desperate to prove myself. A fierce desire had settled in my heart to see my clan revered again. I learned from the masters with a will, and executed my tasks quickly and thoroughly. It was during those years when Kavria first befriended me. She was an outrageous rebel of her clan, and I represented the opportunity for mischief.

When the other lads were allowed time on their own, I spent mine studying, or hunting to improve my skills. Kavria would go out with me, finding in me the champion of her rebellious nature. Though I tried to dissuade the notion, she thought that since I did not follow my clan's heritage, that I must be rebellious too. I had to admit, though, I enjoyed her company immensely. I was lonely, and she was the only one who had accepted and looked upon me as an equal. I kept her out of mischief and she gave me incentive to work hard enough to be accepted into clan Atharil. There was hardly a day where we were not together.

It was almost a punishment to visit my parents, but my father loved me even in my prodigal career. Though my mother did not approve, she lent me her moral support anyway. When I was in the twenty-fifth year of my apprenticeship, my eldest brother Barok was named a Mastersmith, and it smote home to me that I would always be an outsider. But, it was a great day for us as a clan. To be openly proclaimed a Mastersmith in the Second Naming Ceremony was an honor forgotten by my family. It was as if eight thousand years of being little more than beggars had finally been vindicated. The attitudes of the other clans were instantly changed. My father began to earn the respect and profits he should have had all along.

In retrospect, though, I had to wonder what had happened in the background. It had been four months earlier that I had saved Vergadain's life. Was it a thanks to our clan that Barok was openly proclaimed? Certainly from that moment on, I was treated more like a foster son than an unwanted apprentice.

My boots came to rest before those of the old mage, reminiscence ceased as did my pacing. "Lodath, do you ever wonder what might have happened had you done things differently?"

Lodath threw back his head and laughed long and hard. "Why Dorian! We will make a human of you yet! That, my dear friend," he said as he wiped a tear of mirth from his orange eye, "is one of the most common of human failings! Of all the dwarves I have ever met, you are the first to ever ask me that."

A sharp pang entered my chest. How different was I from my fellows? I decided that it was better to continue our former conversation than to go where that chain of thought led me.

"A hundred years after Gorain's death, a large deposit of vaarandril was discovered in the wilds between Sorkarak, Balakarak, Tharakarak, Zarakalduum and Laharazduum." Lodath snickered, realizing I was avoiding his accusation. "Greed strangled the alliances and without the High King to arbitrate, war broke out between the clans. Morakvaar was displeased, as once again we killed and enslaved our own kind. In the midst of our wars, the zarakanan returned in greater numbers. They fell upon our undefended strongholds, taking Sorkarak and Laharazduum in the span of two ten-days. The clan war was instantly dissolved as our people scrambled back to the protection of our fortresses. During the later part of that war was when the gollarans snuck in and occupied the further reaches of the mines, the most indefensible ones that had been abandoned because of the war." I leaned upon the stone wall as I looked down into the bluish-black depths of the cold water far below.

Lodath sat upon the rail, it being about the height of a bench to him. "I find this history lesson fascinating Dorian, but I know you have some other reason you came to speak with me. What is it that you wish?"

I smiled humorlessly. "I suppose such short lives make humans impatient." Lodath snickered and nodded as I continued, "the zarakanan had brought many slaves with them, slaves that bred quickly, and more races that we had not seen. The new abundant availability of prey also caused a boom in the population of the formerly reclusive vourdovra. The rebellious slaves the zaraks brought with them were freed in hopes that their numbers would soon overwhelm us, for the goblinoid races were hereditary enemies. It took a couple hundred years for the goblinoids and the vourdovra to make an impact, but our people became separated as the travel between strongholds lessened because of the danger.

"Trade dwindled, accusations of interference were rampant, and all the while our numbers began to decline. The zaraks sat back to watch the chaos they created, and we indulged them with wars over real or imagined wrongs. We hunted down the camps of orcs, trolls, goblins, troglodytes, and other nasty sub-races, and as soon as we destroyed them, another group bred a whole vermin-tide worth of the creatures. All the while, those who died in war could not be replaced in numbers, and a new frightening realization descended upon us. Each generation saw fewer kinswomen born among us. At first it was not noticeable, but as time progressed, our decline took on alarming proportions."

"Did you ever find out why?"

"It is what we are fighting for."

"If you do not know what caused the decline, how can you be sure that winning this war will save you?" Lodath knew I was terrible at subterfuge.

"It was during the arrival of the zarakanan when our numbers began to fail. Once we are rid of them and all other threats of war, we can concentrate on finding a solution to the problem. With no more enemies to fear, my people can find the cause and rectify it."

"I hope you are right, Dorian. I would hate to think you caused all this bloodshed for nothing." Lodath's face remained carefully neutral as he avoided my shocked stare.

A cold uncertainty churned my gut to think that my friend could demean my cause. "It will not be."

The chill spread through me. What if I was wrong? Would I lose my soul to the Reaver as Gorain had? I snorted in dry amusement at the thought of Gorain and I trapped for all eternity within the confines of the weapon, driven mad by our own bloodlust.

"Lodath, do you remember the amulet that protected the wearer from the mind powers of the vourdovra?" He nodded, finally meeting my gaze. "Do you still have it?"

"Ah, at last you get to the point. Yes, I do." I could tell his mind had already leaped ahead to where my questions were leading, and the purpose of our conversation. "I have attempted many different variations of duplication of the device to no avail, Dorian. I have studied it long and hard, yet its mysteries still escape me. If only your soulsmiths were still alive. I firmly believe it is their work."

I dropped my eyes to the path, trying to keep hope alive within me. "Do you think there is any other defense against them?"

He shook his head. "There are a few spells, but not enough strength to break linked psionic power. I doubt if you could bluff your way through these as you did in the other vourdovra city."

The sounds of the stones eddied and flowed around us, but I found no comfort in their harmony. My mind could not conceive of failure, but it loomed before me like a dark cloud. We had to defeat the vourdovra, there was no question of that, but every time I thought of assaulting their city, the coldness grew within. How could we fight what we could not see or feel? How could we win against an enemy that could control our fears and emotions, an enemy who fed upon them as much as the physical essence of the mind? I shuddered in the memory of their feeding habits.

"If Sorkarak means singing stones, what does Morakduum mean?" Lodath tried to distract me, and for a time I humored him.

"Morkilduum was the 'the eternity of the silver-steel forge'. Morakduum means to reforge or temper. When Dorim bid me to rebuild our home, it did not seem fitting that it should be as if the zarakanan had not destroyed our lives. As a rally point and a testament to our people's spirit and unity, it was decided to name the rebuilt stronghold Morakduum. My kinsmen needed a symbol of hope, something to inspire them into the belief that we were strong again, and that we would survive. Against all odds, we weathered lean food supplies, raids from Terazandarin, and even an attack by migrant kardovra."

"The rebuilding of Morkilduum must have been quite costly."

"More in blood than in money, but yes. In time, though, more and more kinsmen came to aid in the reconstruction. Morakduum became the symbol I had hoped for. Thirty years into the rebuilding, it became clear that we could not continue and defend ourselves from the raids perpetrated by the zaraks from Terazandarin. We beseeched Kairillia for aid once more in an effort to overwhelm our foes to the point where a battle could be won quickly and decisively. It was our hope that we would take them by surprise and it would be over with minimal cost in lives, but when we arrived, we found the zarakanan fully entrenched as if they had warning. I later learned that Kairillia had sent messengers ahead, warning the Terazandarin zaraks of our impending attack.

"Her treachery nearly was our undoing, but that we succeeded became a huge draw and a rally point to Morakduum. Kinsmen and kinswomen from the remaining strongholds, settlements and outsiders alike came to bolster our ranks. Soon after, the priests and historians identified the weapon we brought back as the Reaver, but none of them could touch it. The day it chose to reveal its powers to our people by my hand, the Patriarch, Dorim Atharil, and the liege king of Barakillanak, Karakdain Hammerhand, proclaimed me High King. The rest of the nobles followed suit and swore fealty to me despite my protests."

Lodath nodded as if it were the news he expected. "I had heard you pressed your people into service, but I did not believe it of you. Trouble is, Osric does."

The mention of the human king reminded me of the other reason I had sought out Lodath. "Speaking of Osric, why have his troops remained in the city? They have been compensated with the amount agreed upon. The armor and weapons were delivered before the assault. Their continued presence is a burden our food supplies will not bear long, and they are spreading unease among my people."

Lodath flushed and turned from me with his head down and I wondered how long he had known what he was about to tell me. "Osric's general does not believe they have been compensated properly." He mumbled low enough that another human would not have heard him.

I felt the cold shock turn into burning anger. "What do you mean!? I have paid them enough to finance three kingdoms for a millennium!"

"They want a share of the spoils. I have tried to reason with them, but they insist that it is their right."

I could feel the warmth in my ears as the anger was reflected in my voice. "They have no right to the treasure stolen from my people! The blood of my kinsmen is in each and every item! They shall not see one coin of it, or they risk war! Tell them that it is better for them to leave with what they have than to never see the surface again!"

"I have already told them that in so many words."

I could feel the burn in the muscles of my jaw as I spoke between clenched teeth. "Then why are they still here?"

"The general has convinced his troops that what happened between your people and the zarakanan is in the past, and that it was treasure you did not have before they helped regain it." Lodath bowed his head as if ashamed that he was of human origin. "They are sick with greed."

The Reaver ignited in my hands as the rage filled me. "Then it is time to cure their illness!" I growled as I moved past him.

The old mage put a hand on my shoulder that would hardly have restrained me even in his youth. "Dorian, you cannot afford to fight Osric's men and still win against the vourdovra!"

"Try me!" The words were more the snapping of a beast, and I paused to wonder at my own anger.

"Is that you or Gorain speaking, Dorian?" My ire cooled instantly as the words sunk in.

Were they my words? I paced along the garden wall and back, pondering the situation and allowing myself time to think reasonably. Would the humans listen to me, or would this lead to war? I let my frustrations out.

"What do you propose? If we share the treasure, we will not have the resources to rebuild. If we fight for it, we will lose too many to fight the vourdovra. The humans place us in a precarious position for their treachery!"

Lodath winced at my words even though they were not directed towards him. "I have sent back word to Osric. With luck, he will order the troops to withdraw. On the other hand, he may decide that dwarven gold is worth fighting for. I am uncertain what to expect, so we need to make contingency plans."

I blinked several times to cover the second cold shock to my system. "You mean that you do not trust him? I staked my peoples' lives on my trust of your judgment, and it might have cost us everything? How could I have believed in you?" A dagger through my gut could not have made me more nauseous or caused as much pain.

I sat on the bench; unable to contemplate the risk I had taken with my people's survival.

"Greed is a funny thing among humans, Dorian. You have as much as admitted that your own people suffer from the affliction also. Unfortunately, General Wolfgang has seen the vaults, and his heart is set on possessing all that is within them."

"I will give no vaarakanan gold to humans, neither will my kin. What is left is only a fraction of what was taken from Morkilduum and Balakarak. It is as precious to us as the blood of our kin who died for it, and we will not share it with anyone while we still live."

"I fear that this will lead to bloodshed." Lodath shook his head as he left me with my troubled thoughts.

Chapter 10

Arhoran Tashor (Oath of the Coward)

Councils and conferences went by in an endless parade, some over the humans, some over the supplies. As the newly appointed Chamberlain, I had more duties than I had as High King! Was this some revenge of Korina's for turning over the duties of rulership to her?

My greatest concerns and meetings involved the humans. Osric's soldiers were not only becoming a burden, but were beginning to make a real nuisance of themselves by starting fights and harassing my kinsmen. I had to settle a large brawl that broke out when a human made overtures towards a kinswoman. The repercussions of which were still boiling in the minds of her clan. It would not take much to push my people over the edge, and trying to keep the peace was like sitting on a barrel of cannon powder.

To add to my growing frustration, Korina had sent for Kormak and his kin who were his accomplices. They were to be tried for treason within the week. How could I judge Kormak for doing what he thought was best for our people? Was I not guilty of the same thing? Even though the thought of betraying a kinsman to our enemies sickened me, I could understand and forgive him his reasons. How could I sentence him to death? With a heavy heart I refused to sit on the tribunal.

Korina had nodded at my refusal as if she expected it. Pride filled me as I watched her grow into her position. A father could not have asked for anything more, and I thought of the future as I walked into the Great Hall of Sorkarak with my kinsmen.

A shudder filled me with ice as the iron dragon's head caught my eye from the right-hand side of the dais. The agony of my internment flared anew as if the zarak torturer were again at my side. Paralyzed, I could not tear my eyes away from the memories of my wrists in the shackles that hung from the dragon's mouth. The carved pillars took on a sinister appearance even though our stonemasons had begun to reshape them. The low roar of voices became the howling taunts of the zarakanan as they mocked me, and the visages of my kin became the demonic features of my enemies. The sound of chains from behind filled my veins with ice. I spun on my heels, ready to fight for my life, but instead of the zarakanan, my eyes locked with Kormak's.

The change in him stabbed guilt into my soul even though he betrayed me to the eternity of agony I suffered. The proud line of his shoulders was stooped; his hair and beard were an unkempt mass of graying orange. Lines of despair wrote of his failure upon his face, and shame haunted his eyes with visions of death. A small glimmer of hope appeared as he saw my pity, and he fell to his knees before me.

"Lord Dorian! I am ashamed that I did not believe in you! End my dishonor, my Lord, and slay me!" His shackled hands gripped my breeks in desperation as he shook with emotion.

"I can not. Kormak, the blood of my kinsmen is more precious to me than my own life. To kill you would go against everything I have fought for, everything I believe in."

"No! Please!? I cannot live with the shame I have brought upon myself! Worse yet, the disgrace I have brought upon my hearth and clan! Only you can forgive them by slaying me and releasing them from my humiliation! Let the shame die with me, I beg you!"

I took in a ragged breath as I realized the injustice I had served him. "I am sorry, my kinsman, but I have given up the right to judge you."

His eyes widened in shocked horror as he realized what I had done. How could he obtain forgiveness for his clan if I did not give it to them? My chest tightened as I remembered Bailan's valor in defending Korina and Marak. I had made the wrong decision once more, and felt my failure keenly. I only hoped Korina had more wisdom than I. Kormak smote his breast in despair, seeing the only hope for his clan disappear. The kinsmen guarding him looked almost as miserable, and I wondered if they were members of the Tenedain clan. Slowly, they took him up the stairs that led to the dragon's head. To my relief, they did not place him in the shackles, but let him and his kinsmen stand in their chains upon the platform.

Silence spread like water through the room as Korina marched into the hall at the head of a file of elders. The long gray beards of some were braided back into the mass to keep from dragging the floor, and I looked to the streaks of gray that had developed in mine. Their robes were grayish-white, signifying the dignity of their age as each bore a badge from their clan upon their left breast. The dragon crown of Gorain sparkled on Korina's brow sending a gasp of wonder through our people. Her boots rang a steady beat upon the stones and up the stairs until she came to a halt in front of the throne. Her black clothing was highlighted in vaarandril threads in depictions of Gorain's epic battle with the dragon Hakareth. The gilded collar sparkled in the light of the stargems promising jeweled origins. She looked every inch the High Queen, and I wondered if I had ever looked so imposing. Instead of taking the throne, she waited until the council was seated in their places on the tier just below before striding over to stand before the prisoners.

"Kormak, you stand accused of treason and conspiracy against your former High King, Lord Dorian Mytharia. You have betrayed our people and nearly caused the extinction of our entire race. You are accused of collaboration with the enemy in a conspiracy of genocide and murder against your own kinsmen." Her voice rang through the hall, a trick of its design. "Do you deny these accusations?"

For a moment, Kormak merely shook, rattling the chains loudly. His eyes closed to the stares of his kinsmen as he struggled to find his voice, knowing that his next words would condemn him to death and his clan to exile.

"No." The hoarse word, though barely a whisper carried through the hall with ease as my kinsmen held their breath.

Those that stood with Kormak fell to their knees, knowing they were doomed, and their kin who were standing in an anxious knot to my right wailed in despair. Korina met my troubled gaze as she cleared her throat. The crowd became silent as she passed judgment.

"Your fate, and the fate of your clan have been deliberated upon by the council. We can not justify the execution of our own kin." A surprised murmur ran through the crowd and Kormak stole a glance to where Korina was looking. "But!" She silenced the assembly once more. "Neither can we forget such trespass against us. We can only consider the reasons behind your choices. The decision has been made and a new law is to be passed. This new law shall be our highest law and it will be that no kinsman shall slay another even in retribution." A collective gasp echoed through the chamber, and all around solemn nods accompanied the pronouncement.

Confusion over the fate of the prisoners was reflected in every gaze including my own as we held our breath waiting for the sentence. "In light of this new law, punishment of such a heinous act must fit the nature of the crime itself." Korina's eyes almost danced with the flames of mischief as she turned from the assembly to lock gazes with Kormak. "You are to be sentenced to the oath of Tashor!" I blinked several times as a roar of surprise then approval rocked the chamber.

Tashor? Surely Korina did not mean to have me take them in! Yet as I contemplated the implications, she continued to confirm my fears.

"You will be bound to serve the one you sought to destroy. You will give your lives, if necessary, to defend his. Should you fail in this duty, you will be exiled and your clan will suffer the fate of those who have broken Tashor." Each member of Kormak's group shuddered as they contemplated what that meant to their clan. Korina paused to let it sink in before throwing them a lifeline. "If, on the other hand, you perform your duties with honor, your clans will be restored with no stain upon their history. The memory of your crimes will be stricken from the records and from the hearts of our people. This is the judgment of the Council of Elders."

From the look on some of the elders' faces, it was not the judgment of the majority, but the wisdom displayed by its execution could not be denied. Each and every one of them nodded in agreement before rising and leaving their places on the dais. For a moment, there was not even a breath in the great hall, then an explosion of sound as the sentence was discussed. Only as the crowd began to disperse did Korina show any sign of nervousness. She shifted impatiently from foot to foot peering at me as if expecting a tirade of disapproval. Instead, I met her gaze, smiled proudly, and bowed to her wisdom. A large grin of childish delight danced in her eyes as she took her place at the end of the line of elders as they marched from the dais out the side entrance.

After she was out of sight, I scowled, wondering what I would do with ten kinsmen sworn to defend my honor with their lives? Korina wanted to be sure there was someone to 'look after' me when I left the Deeps, and I watched her depart with some trepidation.

As the 'benefactor' of the punishment, it was my duty to stay behind and witness the sentence. When the crowd cleared, I wandered over to a pillar and leaned against it to wait. Kormak's hearth-mate, Liria stood anxiously to one side as first dread, and then relief warred for possession of her features. My heart went out to her as the uncertainty of her mate's future loomed between them. As Tashor, he would never again reside at their hearth. Grief gained final control as Kormak's hair and beard came off in curling lumps under the shaver as Liria realized she was now considered a widow. As the gaoler applied the viscous salve to shaved skin she wept, and I wished to the Maker that I could comfort her anguish. But, the edicts of our people were quite plain. A new mate would be chosen for her, a punishment in itself, for I could see the love she bore for Kormak.

Why had he chosen to betray me? Was he still angry that I, a Mytharian, had married the daughter of Beralain? I shook my head; no betrayal to the enemy was worth a clan grudge, so how could he have believed Kairillia when he knew of her former treachery? I wished that I could talk to him of it, but that would be a breach of protocol. His former life was over, and his deeds wiped clean. To bring it up would be an insult to his family.

Lodath appeared at my side as the gaoler moved on to the next prisoner. "What are they doing, Dorian?" He whispered.

"Tashor is the oath of a coward who has caused death in battle." I was surprised at the sorrow in my own voice. "The clan of those who were killed is served by the Tashor as a means to reinstate their family's honor. Those who are sentenced to Tashor are no longer considered kinsmen, so are shaved to prove they do not exist. It is a mark of shame that the salve makes permanent."

"So you are saying that these dwarves are now your slaves?" Lodath's face twisted in surprised disgust.

"No, more like an honor guard without honor." He relaxed slightly, but his face was still troubled at my clarification.

"Who is that?" His eyes rested on Liria as she shook with great heaving sobs.

"Kormak's widow." Lodath blinked several times, not quite understanding. "The Tashor are considered to be legally dead." I clarified again.

"That is monstrous!"

"That is better than bearing the brunt of his dishonor!" I snarled back.

"There are times when I do not want to understand your culture!"

"No one asked you to! Personally, I find humans incomprehensible at times, and at others, I wish I did not understand." The memory of my meeting with Jaguar stood out in my mind as a sore example of my misunderstanding of humans.

But Lodath was not done finding fault with our ways. "How could you be so cruel to your own kind and still profess you care so much about them? This is just so much hypocrisy to your own beliefs, Dorian."

"It is a confirmation of them, Lodath. Ordinarily, Kormak would have been executed and his clan banished in shame. Believe me, I know what it means to live with the mark of dishonor. At least now his clan does not have to live with his shame." Lodath looked at me in surprise at my fervent tone.

He stared at Liria's weeping form, and it was plain he wished to comfort her as much as I. Placing a hand on his arm, I waited until he acknowledged my intent before whispering. "I do not zink anyvun vill gainsay your consoling her. I am forbidden to do so. It is vun time zat being human is not such a bad zing." I spoke in his language to be sure no one overheard me.

Lodath's brows rose in surprise as a sad smile pulled at his lips. He nodded acknowledging that I wished to do what he was allowed because of his humanity. Even kneeling, Liria's head still only reached the tall mage's shoulder. His whispered words gave her a start, and she paused in her grief to glance my way. Transfixed by her gaze, I could do nothing but feel her pain. What if I had lost Morina? Worse yet, what if I knew she were alive, but was forbidden to see or speak with her? I forced down the rising panic at such thoughts. It was better than living in disgrace for generation after generation for a crime committed long before half the clans had names. But, the realization of the edict made me determined to do something about it.

Liria stared at me, boring in to me, tearing at my soul like the claws of a kardovra as Lodath continued to whisper to her. Sometime during his one-sided conversation, her expression softened and she nodded as she looked away, and I wish I knew what the mage said. I let out my breath, realizing only then that I was holding it. The gaoler was finishing the last salve as I turned back to him. Out of the corner of my eye, I saw Liria turn away, unable to face the terrible humiliation of the punishment of Tashor. As one, the prisoners knelt before me and intoned the words of their sentence.

"We are shamed in the eyes of Morakvaar having caused the deaths of our kinsmen. We are shamed in the eyes of our people having broken faith with them. We are shamed before our kin having dishonored our clans. We are shamed before you owing a great price. We beg your acceptance of our vow as Tashor to right the injustice of our deed. We beg forgiveness of our clan by your mercy. Strike our names from the Book of Ancestors to erase our dishonor. We beg you to accept our lives as payment for our crime so that by our service our clans know not our disgrace." Their stares pleaded with me, for by our law I could still demand their clans be banished by not accepting their vow.

Lodath was right; we could be cruel. "Though your crime is grievous, there is no greater honor than forgiveness of innocence." With my first words, much of the tension eased from them. I continued the ritual words of acceptance. "May your clans be absolved by your deeds, and may your heroism someday regain your name. I name you Tashor to clan Mytharia." Wide eyes met my inclusion of the clause to regain their names, and I could tell it was more than they hoped for.

Kormak almost smiled as the gaoler removed his chains, but the others still seemed in a state of shock as they numbly followed Lodath and I from the Great Hall. Morina was not going to be happy with ten shaven kanan following us around.

"I assume that the sentencing pleased most of your people?" I nodded to Lodath. "Your daughter seems to have a depth of wisdom to her as well as a great amount of intelligence." Something about his tone told me he was considering some puzzle.

"She has made me proud. I could not ask for a greater legacy than the deeds of my children." I broke off wondering if Lodath had any inclination as to how it felt to be a father.

"I assume Korina gets it from her mother." I knew Lodath's banter was friendly, and at one time I might have indulged him. Seeing my reluctance to comment back, he sighed. "What exactly does Tashor mean? I am not familiar with the word."

"In the ancient tongue of Dolamakduum it means 'owned by fear', or 'coward'."

The tunnel opened up to the large central hallway as we made our way back to my quarters. Our boots echoed softly, as the tapestries that lined the walls absorbed the sound. The stone floor had been worn down in the center from the years the zarakanan had lived there and not smoothed it back out. At the far end of the hall, some of our stonemasons were hard at work equalizing the level of the granite. Their chants rang through half the palace as the stone carried the sound as it softened and molded back to an even surface. The smell of fresh shaped rock filled the air with its heavy scent and mingled with the scent of the salves from the Tashor. The smell and activity soothed some of the tension as the pride in my people's accomplishments filled me. The sight of a human soldier, however, ruined the moment for me.

Reminded of one of my chief worries I turned to Lodath. "What news of Osric?"

Lodath's jaw tightened and his brows drew down like dark clouds. "Osric supports Wolfgang's claim. He says that the spoils should be divided into three equal parts, a share for them, a share for your people, and a share for the gollarans. His response was well received by King Saveyo who supports Wolfgang's claim and has turned his troops back towards us to receive their share."

"I will kill that meddlesome human with my bare hands!" The Reaver echoed my sentiment from the harness on my back, and I struggled with my rage.

"That would surely lead to war, Dorian."

"I am loath to risk the lives of my kinsmen in battle, but what choice do we have? The only other recourse is to kill them in their sleep, and we are not so dishonorable. We will not share the blood-price of our kinsmen with them. Why do the humans not understand this?" I snarled in frustration.

Lodath sighed again. "No, they do not understand, and therein lies the problem. I believe I may be able to give them what they want, and still not touch the vaults, but I fear for you, Dorian. If I create the illusion of wealth and they take it with them, when the spell ends, their anger will be great. I would not be surprised if a price was put on your head."

I laughed at the irony. "It would not be the first time. I would gladly take the risk on my own to save the lives of my people."

"But unlike the first time, Osric will know who you are and where to find you."

"Well then, I will just have to be whom he does not know and be where he does not suspect."

"Morina was right." He exclaimed as we turned down the narrower tunnel with the parade of Tashor behind us. "You are suicidal." His expression turned distant. "So, does this death-wish have anything to do with Jaguar?"

The words stopped me cold as I stared at him in disbelief. How could he be so callous? The memory of that fateful day when I had done all I thought was necessary to preclude asking Jaguar to be my mate came back to me in startling clarity. Even the clothes I wore were brand new from the tailor's. The bright red tunic was highlighted in gold at the sleeves and collar, accenting my flame-red hair and coppery skin.

***

I had secured the governor's suite at the inn, and commissioned a fine dinner as Lodath had instructed me. The tavern wench, Jillian, was aware of my plans, and had insisted that I wear sweet smelling oil she claimed would top off the bath and the outfit. I had felt ridiculous, but Lodath had insisted it was important to have everything perfect, even as he warned me that I was headed for disappointment.

As usual, I ignored his demeaning attitude towards Jaguar, for my heart knew nothing but goodness of her. The gifts of a finely crafted vaarakanan pendant, and a jeweled ring held their places in my pouch. All that remained was Jaguar's presence. With no little trepidation, I walked down the hallway to her room to knock on her door.

Before I had the chance, the echoing sounds of two people came to me from inside. I paused before the meaning of the sounds sunk in to my consciousness. Rage shook my hands as I threw open the door. In a single bound, I was across the room, never wondering how I could have leapt so far. My hands closed about the throat of the interloper as I threw him to the floor. Only when he grasped my wrists in desperation did I bother to look at his face. I let go in surprised pain as I recognized my good friend, Gerald. My heart was torn from my chest and spit upon the two edged blade of betrayal by my friend, and betrayal by Jaguar. For a moment, I drowned in the hellspawned river of confusion as my breath refused to enter me and my heart stopped beating.

"Dorian! Stop this at once!" Jaguar's angry scream barely registered in my mind.

"I'm sorry, Dorian, were you two involved?" I blinked, trying to force air into my lungs.

"Yes!" My word was barely a hissing squeak.

More vehemently Jaguar responded. "No!"

The invisible fist tightened, squeezing what little breath I had managed out of me, crushing my lungs and heart in one fatal blow. "Jaguar ... I -" I had no more air, and the sight of her naked anger smote me into hell.

Unable to do anything else, I walked out the door and downstairs to the tavern. Not even a full barrel of vaarakanan brew could ease the pain in my chest, or quiet the torment in my mind. I found myself out on the bridge, without the courage to throw myself into the raging torrent of the river. So I sat until Morakvaar granted me enough bravery to face my worst fear and condemn myself to the hell of cold water.

***

The feelings I had buried for nearly a hundred years threatened to swallow me once more. The torment of my heart, being nothing more than Jaguar's occasional lover nearly smote me down. I drew in a deep breath trying to steady a picture of Morina firmly in my mind.

"I am sorry, Dorian. It was a moment of indiscretion." Lodath looked at me as he had when he thought I was dying.

For a few moments, I thought I was, but managed to regain control of the hell that raged within. "No, it is I who should beg forgiveness. I vas wrong to ever seek comfort outside my race. Perhaps you are correct in assuming I have not felt zie desire to survive as strongly since Jagvar's refusal to be my hearz-mate." My eyes scanned the patterns of the polished floor, avoiding Lodath's gaze. "I suppose now is a good time to know. Vat became of Jagvar?"

Lodath's large hand descended upon my shoulder with a sympathetic squeeze. "She really did love you, Dorian, but you are right in assuming her love was nothing more than her love of any pleasure. Perhaps it was something more, for she often spoke of you. Certainly, she thought highly of your abilities and you became the basis of much of her comparisons. In fact, I think you have become something of a legend, though I doubt you would take much pleasure in it."

I felt the heat of my embarrassment all the way in the tips of my ears. I could just imagine which comparisons she was making, and what sort of legacy I had left behind.

"I'm not sure what happened after Jaguar became Matriarch and High Priestess of her order, for I hardly saw her after I took a position in Malik's court."

I finally met his eyes, barely whispering the question and dreading the answer. "Did she ever marry?"

Lodath shook his head. "Not to my knowledge."

I let out a sigh of relief, strangely gratified by the news. "Zen I sorrow for vat her clan might have been."

Lodath gave me a sideways glance. "Surely you knew she had children."

I nodded, seeing Panther's determined face, and the more painful news of her pregnancy by Count Parlfrey. "How is Panzer?"

Lodath's eyes never left mine. "She's fine, and so is your son, though they miss their father."

"Vat!?" I was not sure I had heard him correctly. My mind raced ahead, thinking that Lady Alfstein's son had survived despite them telling me of his still birth and had finally sought me out, but that was not the implication.

Lodath nodded as I finally grasped the situation and fresh pain smote my soul. It was bad enough to know I had betrayed my vows and Morina's trust, but there had been even further reaching consequences than I imagined.

"Vat is his name?" I whispered, hoping that none of the Tashor had ever learned the surface tongue.

"He looked so much like you, Jaguar named him Dorian junior. He went to live with the Farovar clan at the age of fifteen. Snagger took him in as his own son." At my pale look, Lodath stopped.

I had never told Morina about that night, and knowing where my indiscretion led, I doubted I could ever face my hearth-mate with the truth. In a daze my feet led me to the door of my quarters, but icy guilt stopped me upon the threshold. How could I face Morina, knowing what I had done? My crime was worse for the fact that I was a kinsman, and Jaguar was human. Gorain's crime paled against what I had done.

"She doesn't have to know." Lodath tried to be helpful as I wished that I had perished in the battle and never learned of Jaguar's son.

"If I can not be truzful to my mate, who can I be truzful to?" Yet still the doorway yawned before me like the gateway to the Abyss.

The door opened before I could reach for it. The fire from the hearth framed Morina's golden hair and gave a halo that ringed her beauty. How could I ever have done anything to hurt her?

"Dorian, why are you standing in the tunnel?" The unseen hand gripped my lungs, and I could not answer her. "What is going on?" She turned puzzled eyes to the Tashor.

Taking the easy out, I responded to her second question. "Korina has sentenced them to the oath of Tashor."

She raised a brow, but opened the door all the way to allow us entry. Little Geria nestled in her arm as she took her supper, and my mother was busy laying out the table with our dinner. Mother frowned at the amount of people who filed in and she stared outright at Kormak's shaven head. Morina caught my reluctance to meet her gaze as I struggled with my indiscretion, but she said nothing. My guilt pulsed through our soul-bond despite all the discipline I could muster. Thinking to avoid the conversation, I headed for the cellar and brought up a barrel of ale for me and a small cask of zarak wine for Lodath. The smell of roasted sheep in voras sauce permeated the dwelling, reminding me I had not eaten since the morning meal. Lodath sat awkwardly in the short chair, but managed to get his long legs under the low table only to have his feet stick out the other side.

A shy tap on the door revealed the kin of the Tashor had brought their meals, and I remembered the burden of the daily ritual. The Tashor bowed their heads and accepted the bundles, forbidden to meet the gazes of their families. I had known that kind of disgrace knew what it felt like to be an outcast and probably deserved it more than they did. My supper was bland to my taste despite its enticing aroma. Instead I took solace in the ale as Morina gazed at me worriedly, reminding me that my emotions could not hide from our bond.

Half the cask could not soothe my guilt and I found other things to talk about. Our conversation turned to the many adventures I shared with Lodath, carefully avoiding reference to Jaguar, but there was no life to the tales. When at last Lodath nodded off in the middle of a sentence, I knew I had no more excuse to avoid Morina. A cold knot settled in my gut as I sat on our bed and removed my tunic.

"What is wrong, my mate?" Morina put a tentative hand upon my shoulder.

My heart felt as if it would burst as the coldness crept through every vein. "I- ... Morina, you know that I love you..."

The muscles on her jaw made her golden beard jump slightly before she nodded.

"And you know that I would not hurt you..." I broke off, as I knew how hollow the words sounded.

Morina simply stared. If I had not known her, I would not have seen the utter confusion in her gaze. I drew in a deep breath, still unprepared to confess my terrible sin to her. I looked away from the green fire that consumed me.

"When we met, I told you that my heart had not been true to our people." The words fell like stones in water, resting heavily in the room.

I stole a glance to her eyes as they began to widen in revelation then deep anguish. Her pain smote me through the soul-bond as it did through my heart. I loved her deeply, and knowing I had caused her such agony was a mortal blow. Why she loved me so completely defied my understanding but the wound I had made in her heart I felt as keenly as a dagger in my breast.

"I know..." She whispered hoarsely. "I knew the night you were with her. The soul-bond..." She could not continue, and the pain in her eyes smote my heart.

"I am sorry." I whispered as the warm tears tickled my cheek before wetting my beard.

A thousand torments I endured as a slave and a captive. Horrors beyond imagining still dwelled in my memory, yet they had not brought me to tears so easily as the pain in Morina's eyes. Her tears were coals heaped upon my already burning soul.

"And now you have learned that she bore a child." Her voice was on the verge of breaking.

"Yes." I whispered unable to trust my voice.

We both sat in silent tears feeling keenly the break of trust between us. Deep shame filled me for keeping such a thing from her, and even more shame that she knew of it and said nothing. How could I have broken my vows so easily? Morina did not deserve to be wounded so.

"I do not deserve your love, Morina, and you do not deserve to be treated this way." I repeated the confession out loud.

She met my gaze with red and puffy lids. "I knew your flaws when we were bonded. I accepted them even though you begged me not to. I am as much to blame knowing where your heart lay. It is why I said nothing, why I kept my pain to myself." She looked down again. "I suppose we should visit your children, for they should have a father."

I reached for her hand, but it was too soon for her and she snatched it away. The rejection smote me and I put my tunic back on. The Reaver sat snugly between my shoulders as I left our temporary home tunnel in a daze. When I came to my senses, I found myself on my knees in the Garden of the Singing Stones, begging the wind for guidance and trying to find meaning in the harmony around me. But, the Mother refused to reveal to me her secrets, and I was left with my shame. I sat on a bench as my agony left me with nothing but emptiness. Gorain's memory nagged me, as I sat upon that very bench with Gelamina at my side. The vision mocked me, showing me the depth of my crime. Gorain's mate had been dead when he shared kinship with the orudin, but I had committed a far worse error. Morina was alive and well when I spent my last evening with Jaguar.

The Tashor stood at a respectful distance, leaving me to my despair. Their presence was a keen edged sword, a reminder of what I should have been. The dulcet tones of the rock formations filled the air around me, but the guilt gave me no peace. How could Morina have believed in me for all those years even though she knew I betrayed her trust? Would she still wish to accompany me on my journey for Morakvaar? Though I could hardly bear the thought of being without her, it would be for the best. Perhaps when I was gone, she would find a more worthy mate than I could ever be.

"Why is mother so upset?" I was too deep in despair to be startled by Korina's voice.

I could not muster the inner will to look at her, so kept my back turned to her in silence.

"It is about that surface woman, is it not?" I drew in a sharp breath as I snapped around to look at her.

How could she know so much? "Lodath and I believe we can do something about Osric's men." I deemed a quick change in subject was in order. "We can give them what they want, and protect our interests."

Korina narrowed her eyes, but humored me. "How?"

"We need a bit more privacy for that discussion. This is not the place."

She looked around the garden and nodded, but her harshness returned. "Fine, but when we have finished discussing your plan, you will explain to me why mother is so upset."

"As you command." My voice was stiffly formal in response to her demand.

Her goldish red brows drew down. "I am still your daughter. You do not have to speak to me that way."

I curbed my inner turmoil to realize my love for my oldest. "No, but as High Queen of Morakduum, I should be more respectful. I apologize for the reason, though. Forgive me if you will."

Korina walked at my side, but the only sound she made was the echo of her booted feet. Once in the royal office, she ordered the Tashor to keep watch outside as we entered. From the carved woodroot desk, she pulled out a large ingot covered in runic wards. Her hand passed over it twice and she spoke the words of invocation as the runes glowed softly. Ornate tapestries hung from the four walls as the glow of a magma vent provided illumination for the rest of the room. A waist high table in the center of the room held several maps and the desk in the corner was covered with charts and lists. Empty shelves lined the walls, carved from the stone in flowing lines of knotwork animals and geometric shapes.

"We can talk now, and no one will be able to listen. What do you propose, father?" Korina lifted an anxious brow.

"Lodath can create the illusion of wealth on wagons laden with stones. For a time, they will see the treasure they desire and believe we have given them a share of the vaults. He assures me that the illusion can be made to last until they try to test its validity upon the surface. In this way, the humans will leave and trouble us no more." I hoped she would not catch on to what would happen afterwards, but it was a false hope.

Korina paced a few moments. "If the humans make it to the surface before testing the validity of the treasure, they will be enraged once they find out it is fake. If they find you when you leave the Deeps, it will not go well with you. If, on the other hand, they learn of the deception before they reach the surface, it will lead to war. Either way, it is too risky."

I had thought it was a good plan, but she did have a point. "What do you propose then?"

With a sly smile she smashed the plan to pieces. "A compromise, of course. I will give them a third of the treasure in the vaults if, and only if, they help us defeat the vourdovra. In that way, we can save the lives of many of our kin, and that to me is more precious than any treasure."

I smiled slowly as I shook my head. "Truly you are a wiser ruler than I. I do not like the idea of our treasure going to humans, but you are right. The lives of our kin are worth more than the whole of the money in the vaults. However, if the humans refuse to help us fight the vourdovra, and still demand a share of what is ours, then please consider our proposal."

Korina nodded thoughtfully before her expression became hard. "Now, tell me why mother is crying."

The heat of shame colored my face as I looked at the empty shelves. The books that had been there were removed by the zarakanan, leaving only a couple of moldy tomes from the time before their invasion.

"I told you of the woman I knew before your mother." I spoke to the books, not daring to turn around for the nod I knew Korina made. "Before we parted company, and after your mother returned to Balakarak, she came to me." I could hear the gasp of repressed outrage. "My heart was weak, and I could not help but fall into her embrace. Today, I learned that she bore me a son I have never seen." The storm gathered behind me, and I knew at that moment, I had betrayed the trust of my child.

"How could you!? How could my own father be without honor!?" The exclamation was a mixture of horror, anger and disgust. "How could you profess the values of our people to me!? All those years you taught me of duty and honor, all the while knowing your unworthiness to even voice them!"

Her words smote me like a hammer, driving home the bitter shame of my existence, but she deserved at least an explanation. "Korina, you must understand even if you cannot forgive. It is important to me that you know the circumstance. The heart knows nothing of honor. I still loved her, and if she were still alive..."

"If this were known, all of our clan would be banished! No dishonor of Gorain can compare to what you have done! I am sick with shame, knowing that you are my father! Your shame is the shame of us all, and were it not for the fact that our people think so highly of your heroism, I would sentence you myself! But, I must hide this knowledge, this disgrace, for it would break our people's spirit to know of it!" She had believed in me, but I had let her down.

"Even Morakvaar had his moments." As soon as the words left my lips, I knew it was the wrong thing to say.

"How dare you compare yourself to the Maker!?"

"Well, he did spend three nights with Valkaria." The excuse sounded weak. Why could I not keep my mouth shut!?

"That has nothing to do with this!"

Perhaps I had been among humans too long, for her anger began to grate on me. But really it was a need not to admit that I could be anything so vile. In my mind I justified it was none of her business, and was far in the past. The matter was between Morina and I.

"Why not? If the Maker could make his mistake, then why am I not allowed?"

"You are *not* the Maker! To insist on an excuse for this shame is beyond reason!"

She was right, and I had no excuse, but my pride could not let it go. "I know you are upset, but the matter is long past!" The deep breath calmed my ire as shame replaced the warmth of anger. "I do owe you an explanation, though it will not pardon my action. Jaguar was the first woman I ever... shared willing kinship with. At the time we met, I was confused and alone. The things I experienced as a slave had taken my soul..." For a moment, I could not continue. The nightmare threatened my sanity, but I managed to beat back the darkness. "I knew that surviving such heinous treatment was a sign that I was no longer a kinsman."

My hoarse words stopped again, and at Korina's confused stare, I realized I would have to relate the terrors that haunted me still. "The surface world was frightening in its vast emptiness and oppressive to my wits especially after thirty years of a hell you could not imagine. The Song of the Mother could not reach me, and I knew not where I was, nor how to return. I had resigned myself to living in the human world, for seeking refuge with the Kinsmen of Stone would have been suicide, and I had already tasted their hospitality more than I wished."

Korina's snarl lessened as she sensed the intense emotion within me, but her anger was almost as great as her shame. Though my explanation would never heal the wound I had just caused between us, she did have the right to know it all.

"I was an outsider, Korina, taken from everything I had ever known. I had died within. The fire of the kinsman's soul had gone out, and I merely existed because my body lived on. Though my reasons for being with Jaguar were probably wrong, it was her presence that finally drew in a new spark, a new hope. I began to believe that I had a reason to live, someone to live for. Perhaps a human was a poor choice for my affections, but my heart did not know how to choose. I had been lost to our people, and no longer considered myself a son of the Maker."

She paused in her pacing as morbid curiosity replaced her ire. "What could have happened to you to think of yourself that way?"

I shook my head seeing Lady Alfstein and her perverse bodyguards entering the kennel where I was chained. "I do not think you are ready to learn of such things. The ways of the humans can sometimes rival the worst stories of demon spawn. Suffice to say, they drove from me every ounce of pride in my heritage, until their deeds made me wish that I had never been born a kinsman, let alone been born at all. I prayed each night as I writhed in pain that I would not wake to another day. The soul of the vaarakanan had been driven from me as surely as any hope or desire to live, yet with the slave collar around my neck, I could only wish for the release of death. When I escaped, only the terror of becoming a slave once more drove me, not any desire to live on. Aimlessly, I ran from the slavers until they nearly caught me. Were it not for the two humans that helped me, I would have perished even if I had to strike the blow myself to keep from being captured. I swore an oath of blood-debt, to repay my rescuers with my life."

Korina had stopped pacing and was staring at me in shock. "Did they...violate you? How did you live through that?" Her mind had grasped the concept I had hoped to spare her from, but I should have known better.

"Many nights, I hoped and prayed that I would not live another moment. The slave collar's magic kept me from allowing myself to die, though many days I was too weak from agony and loss of blood that I could not move to feed myself or drink water. I dreaded the days that Lord Alfstein was away, for it was those days that their torments were the worst. Lady Alfstein knew she would be found out if I was too weak to perform my duties while the slaver lord was home. Unfortunately, he was gone often." Even the memory of the horror and agony left my soul in tatters and I silently questioned the Maker for the billionth time why he had allowed me to suffer so.

"Suffice to say, I was dead as a kinsman because of my experiences. I had not thought seriously of returning to our people, or hoped to retrieve my soul until after I met your mother. If it were not for my oath to my rescuers, I would have allowed myself to die. I still do not know if I possess a soul, or that I must earn it back. But I have tried to live as a vaarakanan for our family's sake, though I doubt if it matters in the end. Perhaps when I have left the Deeps and you have a chance to read my journal, you will understand. And though I can not ask for, nor expect your forgiveness, at least you may know my reasons for my shortcomings."

Korina frowned, her bottom lip puffing out as if she were a young child. Her golden tinged red hair reflected the light of the stargems, making it appear as if she were wreathed in fire. I wanted to hug her and comfort her to drive away the dark visions I saw in her expression, but knew she would be offended for treating her like a small lass. Deep in my despair, I was not prepared as she stepped suddenly towards me, threw her arms around my chest, and sobbed into my beard. Her sobs shook through me, and I wondered if she cried for her mother or me.

"I am sorry if I am not the father I have led you to believe I am. I have tried to do my best by you, your siblings and your mother, but I know I am far from a model kinsman. You, though, have made me very proud. I have never met a finer kinswoman, or a wiser ruler. Our people are blessed by Morakvaar to have you. You are strong of mind and spirit, and not many could match you in battle."

Korina silenced me. "I do not want you to go, father." She sobbed at last. "I do not care about your shortcomings. There is not a finer kinsman that has lived among us since the gods left us to our own. We will be less when you leave. It is not fair that the Maker will take you from us. If I could take your place, I would." Did she really believe in me?

I kissed her hair as I had so many times when she was young. The pride I felt within swelled in my breast like a living thing. Whatever the Maker's plans for my future, I could face them with alacrity knowing that my children far surpassed me.

"No, Korina, my destiny is my own. But I will go in pride and honor to know that you rule in wisdom greater than Dormakkaar himself. Dorak will be there to support you, his power is great, or so Waradain tells me. He may even be the next High Priest to the Maker. And then there is little Geria who will also be there to support you, and my mother, Geria Temchin, will be your counsel. I face my fate with gladness if only for our people. You are a great leader, Korina, greater than I could ever be."

She sniffed away the last of the tears as she nodded and I let her go. With heavy steps, she paced the room once more. It was nearing the eighth cycle and neither of us had slept. Korina finally stopped in front of me, her expression unreadable.

"I think that you should go back to mother." She whispered before turning and leaving me alone in the chamber.

For a time I wrestled with my conscience. I did not want to face Morina knowing the shame in my heart. Yet, I knew I had to make amends somehow. How could she still love me? In a way, I almost wished that she would reject me, sentencing me to the oblivion I so badly deserved. But, I knew better, even as I thought it would be better for her if I were banished without a name. The Tashor picked up my pace as they fell in behind me, and I wished to the Maker that Korina had not given me this constant reminder of my unworthiness.

Morina's pillow was stained with her tears and she breathed softly in her sleep. I wanted to hold her, yet my shame stayed my hand from awakening her. Instead, I found places for the Tashor to rest and rotate watches, as they felt necessary. Kormak's presence still made me nervous as my memory saw the events that led up to my internment by the zarakanan, but I did my best to ignore the fear within.

The covers stirred slightly as Morina took in a deep breath, drawing my attention to her beauty once more. Her golden hair fell about her head like a gilded tiara fit for the finest queen. Her reddish-bronze face was set within the wreath like a beryl; her beard was the final setting as it flowed down her breast in the braid of her bond to me. Though her beard was not as long as it should have been, it made her seem younger and even more beautiful. The braid ended in the binding ring, and I took in a ragged breath as I was reminded of the vows I had broken. Absently, my fingers traced the braid in my beard down to the binding ring as it hung close to thigh-length. The proud symbol of my age and of the honor of marriage meant so little to me as I thought of how I had wounded Morina's soul. I almost wished that she would have me cut it off as Nailyth had done to Morakvaar when she learned of his indiscretion. It would be less than I deserved. My eyes returned to her face only to find her jade green gaze regarding me. Not able to bear the pain within them, I looked away.

"I am sorry. A sorry excuse for a kinsman." I whispered, not knowing what else to say.

"I knew you loved her, but I had hoped to replace her in your heart."

There was naught but honesty within my words as I turned back. "You have, my love, so many years ago. I should have told you when it happened, and for that I was wrong, as wrong as the deed itself. For that, there is no excuse."

Her fingers silenced my lips and traced down the braid in my graying beard until they rested on the jeweled binding ring. Her gaze returned to mine in pools of green fire. My mind flooded with apologies, pleas of unworthiness, and entreaties that were long overdue. How could I have caused her so much pain? She never deserved the anguish of her life, or the shame I put her through. How could I have been so foolish as to throw away Morina's trust for a mere night's pleasure?

But despite my misgivings, her hand closed firmly around the binding ring as Morina pulled my lips to hers. My arms pressed her against me and I felt her tears as they rolled down her cheeks.

"I told you then that I accepted you." She whispered in my ear. "I knew you loved her, and I think I can forgive you for following your heart. But, she is long dead, and you are still mine."

"Heart and soul, my love." I kissed her fingers then held them to my breast as my blood pumped within.

She pulled her hands from mine and placed them on the back of my neck as she lay back down tugging me with her. "Prove it." She whispered in my ear as mischief danced in her eyes once more.

I grinned widely as I removed my boots, breeks and tunic. It was a wonder that she could love me, but rather than question the validity of the phenomena, I deemed she had better receive what she asked for. Though I did not get any sleep that night, I was content. There were no more secrets between us, and Morina had forgiven me.

Chapter 11

Savaan (The Bargain)

The two human guards watched me pace the room; their attention focused on the Reaver that glowed softly in my hands. They stood stiffly next to the left side of the door to the council chamber where muffled voices could be heard within. The other side of the door was flanked by two of the royal guard in full vaarandril platemaille that put the shoddy human armor to shame. The stone walls of the small antechamber reflected the sound of my boots echoingly as their attention remained nervously riveted on my movements. Their black and silver ring-maille, perfectly matched at one time, had missing bits in different places, a testament to their participation in the battle. Though their presence spurred my ire, I tempered my annoyance with the knowledge that they helped us rid our stronghold of the zarakanan. The Tashor had tired of trying to remain between the humans and me, so they stood at the ends of the stone benches carved from the walls. Shifting from foot to foot with anxiety, the ring of the plates of their armor added to the tromp of my boots.

Behind the carved woodroot door, I could hear Korina speaking with Wolfgang. Her negotiations sounded as if they were going badly, and I feared for her safety. My anxiety pulsed through the Reaver, as it threw its unearthly light upon my face from below when I passed the humans again. That I had been left out of the conference grated on my nerves as I ground the woven cloth beneath my iron-shod boots as I crossed it in front of the door. My armor clanked and rattled, echoing hollowly against the unfettered granite walls as I paced. The stone benches along the walls of the room were empty of the normal petitioners in light of the impending violence that all our people felt coming.

When the door opened, Wolfgang came through it, his face red with anger. The two guards snapped to attention as their general looked at me. His fury quieted for a moment and he sized me up as if expecting to face me in battle. I recognized the challenge in his stare, and tightened my grip on the Reaver as the double blades ignited. The white-blue flames curled up my arms, sending eerie flickering shadows upon the walls. Wolfgang's hand strayed to his sword. The Tashor were instantly at my side as the tension mounted in the room.

"You had better reign in your women, dwarf!" He snarled at me.

In fury, I took a step towards him. "Ahnd you should learn respect, human!" The royal guard, the Gorvaruum Vrakkar, closed in on Wolfgang from behind ensuring the human did not try to retreat into the royal office. "Zies is our vorld. You are zie vuns zat do not belong here. You should leave before zie darkness svallows you whole. I svear if you insult our High Qveen vun more time, I vill personally spit you upon zie Reaver!" The white-blue flame danced maniacally in my gaze as I showed the human my extra set of canines and carnivorous dentition.

In contempt, the human glanced at my kinsmen. "You need others to fight your battles?"

"Not vit a covard zat needs to insult our kinsvomen!" I stepped past the Tashor to face him. To my kinsmen I said, "keep your distance, but be wary of treachery. I will deal with this creature myself."

As the others stepped back a pace, Wolfgang knew I had called his bluff. "Vell human? Is zies a good day to die?"

Towering over my slightly less than four and a half feet of height, he began to draw his sword when Lodath came through the door.

"Dorian, if you kill him, it will mean war." The mage thought quickly.

Not taking his eyes from me, Wolfgang laughed. "Him? Kill me? You've got to be joking!"

"No, Wolfgang. If you engage Dorian in battle, it will be you that perishes. I have seen him kill immortal daemons, you would not even be a challenge." That finally got the general's attention. "The demon on the battlements was killed by Dorian, and so was Kairillia and her entire elite guard. He destroyed the ward on the walls that kept the cannons from being effective. An entire city of demon fish fell beneath his blades, even before he gained the artifact he now carries. He has saved my life dozens of times over, and I have never seen his equal." Even as he sneered in disbelief, uncertainty came into Wolfgang's countenance. "Yes, he is the same Dorian that is sung about in some of the ballads at Osric's court."

I lifted a brow at Lodath and wanted to know just who had taken liberties with my name, but I knew intimidation was in order. Wolfgang met my gaze unwaveringly.

"Are you really all he says?" His tone implied it was not true.

Silently, I let my confidence relay my answer. The tension was interrupted, though as one of his men came into the room to deliver a message. Seeing the standoff, he paused at the confrontation. His dark eyes widened as he recognized me, and shaken to the core, he edged next to his general.

"My lord," he whispered, unaware that I could not only hear but also understand, "do not challenge that one. They say he is a legend reborn. He destroyed an entire city of over fifty thousand of the dark ones practically by himself. And, I hear he is the same as the Legend of Harondale!" I frowned as I was reminded of the madness that took me at Terazandarin.

With confirmation of my skills by his man, Wolfgang rethought his actions. "Very well, dwarf. I will save our duel for the end of the week I have given your High Queen to give us our share of the spoils."

"My suggestion ist zat you be gone by zie end of zie veek, before your army is added to my 'legend'." I stepped back to allow the humans to leave as Lodath shook his head.

"Korina offered them twice their fee, but Wolfgang refused. He wants a full third of what is in the vaults." He sighed as he leaned against the wall, and fatigue shook his once proud form.

"There is more than one way to sway a man." I let the satisfaction of my latest thoughts show through my smile. "If Greed works well on humans, will it be enough to sway the soldiers away from their commander? I think the troops would rather profit than die for Wolfgang's greed."

"Dorian, you are a sneaky bastard! I am proud to be your friend." Lodath's grin equaled my own.

"Wolfgang's lieutenant is a bright one, I believe his name is Ahnton. He is young enough to maintain ideals, and may just be persuaded to help us in return for huge profits despite his general's desires." To one of the Vrakkar, I said, "tell Korina, I will find a way to get us the help we need and save the treasures of the vaults, but she needs to have faith in my decision. I will return in two time cycles."

Lodath and I made our way to the human encampment through the maze of tunnels on the eastern side of Sorkarak. Two chainmaille armored humans blocked our entry with drawn swords and menacing frowns. Behind them, the more open areas of the farm tunnels showed their preference for the oppressive open spaces common to the surface world. Another point of contention had been attempting to get them to abandon the farm tunnels so that they could be put to their intended use to help feed our army and supplement the human's rations, but Wolfgang would have none of it.

It took some doing, but I managed to arrange a meeting with Anton after a generous bribe to the guards. From the smell, I could tell the humans had not quite figured out our easy waste disposal, or the filtered shower system. I made a mental note to instruct them in their use should the opportunity arise, more to ease our work of cleaning up after them than for any concern over their hygiene.

We were led to an old granary that the humans had converted to serve as their headquarters. The hastily constructed furniture displayed their favor towards items that were as temporary as their short lives. The rough-hewn legs of the table were an eyesore as they struggled to support the heavy wooden door that served as the tabletop. Behind the table was a chair whose legs had been extended to serve the human's more lanky structure, and I sighed to see the workmanship ruined.

Anton was young for an officer. His blonde hair stood him out among his darker haired countrymen. Blue eyes almost as light as those of my kin gave him a striking appearance as he sat in the chair on the other side of the makeshift table. The bargain was explained in great detail to him, and I stressed the amount of riches to be gained once vouroussan was defeated. But the young lad was at a loss on how to deal with Wolfgang.

"How you deal vit your general is your problem, but rest assured zat if he defies our edict, all of you vill die. You can eizer join us ahnd earn riches beyond your dreams, or perish for Volfgang's foolishness." Anton leaned back in his chair, his blue gaze coolly calculating.

"A war with us would be costly, Lord Dorian." He tried to play the game, but even though he was cunning, he lacked experience.

"Vit sheep farmers? Do not insult me, Captain. It vas I who bargained for zie main body of your army. I know very vell vat troops you employ." The impact of my words was visible in the frown beneath his cream-colored and barely formed moustache.

"You know the composition of our army, and you still ask for our aid?" He was a bright one.

"Ve need numbers, not expertise, Captain Anton. Our enemies, zie vourdovra, can not be defeated by force, but by sheer veight of numbers." He considered for a few more moments.

"And what am I to tell these farmers? Throw your lives away, for our dwarven friends need you to die for them?" He fixed me with an angry stare. "It is one thing to die for your home, country and king, but another to throw your life away for strangers."

"Ve vill train zem to fight vell, ahnd it vill not be for nozing. Zie gold ve have in Sorkarak's vaults is a pittance compared to vat is in Vouroussan. Should ve fail in our qvest, ve vill guarantee zie survivors a full zird of vat is in Sorkarak's vaults. So even if zey perish, at least zeir families vill live vitout poverty. Vill you put zies to zem?" His distant look dissolved into a grudging smile as he leaned over the pile of scrolls on the woodroot table.

"You do have a way with words, Lord Dorian. I could almost swear you were human."

I took his proffered hand with a smile of mischief on my lips. "Is zat an insult?"

The Captain chuckled. "Who would have guessed? A dwarf with a sense of humor! Very well, sir, I will spread the word and let the troops decide. But, if General Wolfgang gets word of it, I will deny all knowledge and blame it on rumors in the taverns."

"Good, zen I vill avait vord from you vizin zree days. After zat, it vill be too late to bargain." Anton's mirth disappeared immediately, but he did not protest as he saw us to the door.

"Three days. You don't ask for much, do you?" At least I understood sarcasm, unlike most of my kin.

"Ve have no choice. It is a deadline given by Volfgang zat ve must beat. After zree days, ve vill be prepared for var against you to defend our homes, country ahnd qveen." A golden brow arched appreciatively at my reuse of his words.

"If you do not see me at the war council in three days, it will mean that the people have refused your offer." My nod was all Anton needed, and we left the makeshift office.

"I zink zat you should talk to Ahnton alone ahnd assure him zat you vill back him before Osric. I believe zat is his vorst fear." Lodath's raised brows and pursed lips told me what he thought of having to run interference.

"You are playing a dangerous game, Dorian. Suppose Anton gets rid of Wolfgang, but Osric has him banished or executed for mutiny?" He watched me carefully and frowned when I shrugged.

"I vill have to count on you to prevent zat situation. Besides, I ahm sure zat Ahnton knows zie risks. If he does not meet us at zie council chamber, zen he has decided against it. I ahm sure zat Osric vill not object to larger profits."

"If you succeed." It was my turn to regard him with a furrowed brow.

"Vy are you so pessimistic? Are you not supposed to be zie optimist? Alvays on our travels, it vas you who zought ve vould triumph." Lodath's frown turned up at the corners of his mouth.

"That's because you were always the grumpy one. Someone had to lighten the mood."

The smile came unbidden, warming me with pleasant memories. "So now zie roles are reversed. You are grumpy, ahnd I ahm optimistic."

Lodath laughed so hard, he had tears running down his cheeks as he leaned heavily on my shoulder. When he was finally able to draw a breath without giggling, he slapped my shoulder. "You've a long way to go towards being optimistic, Dorian."

"I ahm optimistic!" Something about my insistence made the mage dissolve into a boneless mass that weighed heavily across both my shoulders as he fought to remain upright and breathe between fits of laughter. Was he mocking me?

"Oh, Dorian! Now I've got to pee!" He gasped, between snorts and howls of mirth.

He ran off in the direction I pointed out, moving deceptively quickly for a human of his age. When he returned to where I leaned against the tunnel wall, he was still wiping the tears from his face on the long sleeves of the puffy shirt he wore beneath the leather jack.

He giggled again and said in broken phrases, "I suppose… for a dwarf … you're optimistic." He dissembled into more laughter as I waited patiently for him to recover.

"Zis is vat I get for having human friends!" I growled good-naturedly.

We reminisced about our journeys together on the surface and in the Darklands, from fighting orcs to banishing demonic manifestations of evil gods. So involved was our conversation, that the journey ended quite suddenly outside the audience chamber, the office that Korina used to administer her duties as High Queen. The seriousness of our situation returned in full force as the guards scowled darkly at Lodath, merely because he was human.

"Tell Korina that I have planted the seeds of an arrangement with Osric's forces. With the luck of the gods and a little reliance on human greed, all will be well." The guard nodded, his dark blonde beard obscuring the royal crest on his blue tunic before he slipped in the door.

Korina sat with her back to the door, and I wondered why. A heavy cloud permeated the room; an almost tangible manifestation of whatever mood possessed her. The door closed quietly behind us, and a quick glance revealed we were alone. Not even Lodath would risk her mood.

"How dare you make a bargain behind my back!?" Her words were barely above a whisper, but crackled with anger.

Her cold fury stunned me for a few minutes, and she turned towards me with eyes blazing behind a reddened face. When my reply lacked in immediacy, she prompted me. "Well!?"

"I thought that you wanted an end to this idiocy. I did what I thought was in our people's best interest." Her brow lowered further.

"It is no longer your responsibility! You are not High King anymore!" Her voice rose in pitch and intensity. "You make a bargain with deception and treachery in the name of our people! How dare you abuse our honor so!"

Despite my love and respect for her, I felt the heat of anger rise within. Who did she think she was talking to, some lad not even into adolescence? How did she dare to speak to me that way!? For a long moment, I was tempted to turn her over my knee as my teeth ground audibly. If that was the way she felt, then she could handle it all on her own!

With a flourish that was more mocking than sincere, I bowed. "My apologies, Majesty, I must not have been thinking. Far be it from me to wish to help our people!" Before she could react, I spun on my heel and left the room.

My anger carried me aimlessly through the city, leaving Lodath behind and the Tashor hard pressed to keep up. What right had she to be angry with me? I had done my best to try to keep our people from a needless battle and secure allies in the upcoming assault on Vouroussan. How dare she question my efforts!? Did she have any idea that time was of the essence? The vourdovra could not have been prepared in the event we defeated Fartairilzzan; delay could allow them to build their defenses. We had to move quickly, or we would lose our window of opportunity to take our enemy with minimal casualties. Why could she not see that!?

Chapter 12

Vourazak (Confusion)

The sound of weapons ahead brought me out of my angry thoughts. Why had my subconscious led me to the practice field? The grunts of my kinsmen were mingled with the echoing clash of wooden axes or swords on shields. An angry voice rose over the din for a few moments as the Weapons' Master chastised the combatants, bringing back memories of my apprenticeship at the Warrior's School of Morkilduum. A bit of exercise was just what I needed as my feet turned in to the changing room.

Taking out a padded training uniform, I selected a wooden two-handed axe from the weapons' rack, changed and proceeded out on to the field. Dust swirled around two young lads as they struck and parried in the dance of battle. To one side, three Weapons' Masters looked on shaking their heads. Grinning foolishly, I snugged the metal helmet over my face and tucked my beard inside the padded armor before I could be recognized and joined the line of youngsters waiting their turn. The Tashor stayed behind at my signal.

One of the Weapons' Masters gestured for the next two in line and took them over to the right hand side of the field, and the other pointed to me and the lad who ran up behind me to take the left. At my practiced salute, our 'teacher's' eyes narrowed thoughtfully. A slight nod from him accompanied the easy way I settled in to my guard, but my opponent was not so graceful. The Weapons' Master frowned behind the helmet and stepped between us, eyes on the gray streaks in my beard that were visible. Gesturing for the lad to return to his place, the trainer faced me. Silently, the helmet dipped forward, acknowledging my skill and signaling the start of our match. Why did he not speak?

The Weapons' Master's eyes widened in disbelief as the feigned blow to his right leg became a clear strike to the left of his head as I passed behind him. Determination lit in the narrowed slits behind the helmet as he signaled the ready once more. The clack of wood on wood resounded through the practice ground, and he was not so quick to misjudge me a second time. Dust rose in a cloud around us as we circled, seeking breaks in each other's defenses. The breeze from the Daemon Fish River whisked away the choking flume as the staccato beat of his flurry stopped all other activity as the clack of the weapons echoed through the arena. The ring of eager spectators around us grew with each pass.

Frustrated, the Weapons' Master backed out of my reach and circled, the symbol of Dormakkarduum clearly marked on his tabard that covered his padded armor. His light brown beard was tucked in to his belt, and I could see neither hints of gray, nor signs of wrinkles at the corners of his eyes. How could he have such a long beard and still look so young?

The surge of adrenaline through my veins erased my anger with Korina as I began to enjoy the game of strategy with my unknown adversary. With a quick jump forward, I snapped my hands up and the blades down straight behind his guard to ring solidly on his helmet. He growled and dropped the two handed axe in favor of two wooden battle-axes from his belt. One of the young lads quickly snatched up the weapon as his smile suggested I was about to get it. My opponent settled into a defensive stance once more.

In an explosion of fury, the Weapons' Master launched blow after blow, and I was forced to retreat as the shock of repeated impacts rang as much in my grips as in the air around us. When I thought he would surely tire, the blows came even faster. Hard pressed to catch them all, I sidestepped left, then right, trying to avoid the 'fatal' blow. Just as my left foot lifted from the dirt for another retreat, my opponent dropped to the ground. I was so astonished that I did not swing at the open helmet, and the leg sweep slammed me on my back as the air whooshed out of my lungs. The wooden blade of a battle-axe loomed in my vision as it pressed against my throat. The cheering of the lads was deafening, and I grinned despite my short wind. Nodding in acknowledgment, I climbed back to my feet. When I was able to breathe freely again, I signaled my readiness.

We sparred a total of twelve matches while the crowd grew and loud cheering filled the practice arena. Never had I met such a match for my fighting prowess, and though I wanted to break the tie, we were both too exhausted to continue.

"Good kinsman," I panted as my axe trailed on the ground, "never have I met one as skilled as you." I managed a tired salute. "Tell me your name, and I will toast your expertise in the tavern."

The Weapons' Master clasped my proffered forearm. "Likewise, kinsman." I stared in astonishment at the feminine voice as light brown locks fell free from her helmet as she removed it. "I am Harrakuli, Weapons' Master of Dormakkarduum." No wonder she had not spoken before, as she delighted in the unbiased match as much as I had.

Returning her grip, I could not help the huge grin that split my face as I removed my helmet. A cry of approval ran through the crowd as I was recognized. "Well met, kinswoman! I would gladly share a tankard with such a skillful warrior."

"It will be my honor, kinsman. I must say that I had been eager to pit my skills against yours, and my expectations have fallen short of the reality. You are truly the best I have ever crossed weapons with, Lord Dorian."

We laughed on our way back to the showers, explaining some of our best tricks that we used on each other. Even though it was a public shower, the sight of her nakedness brought me up short as I turned back from the weapons' rack. All soldiers were considered equal, but for some reason, I could not get past the sight. Something about her was alarmingly familiar, and I could not help wondering where I had heard the name 'Harrakuli' before. But, my wits were too befuddled to pull the memory out of its cobwebs. She turned a questioning brow my way and I could feel the heat all the way in the tips of my ears as I spun on my heels.

"I am sorry." My murmured apology was muffled by my attempts to pull the sweaty padded tunic over my head as the other trainees entered the showers.

The warm water ran down my neck, soothing the tired muscles as I sighed in relief. The soap scented with mirkroot served to rid me of the dirt, stench and sweat of the arena. The excited chatter of the lads echoed through the room as they ranted about the match between Harrakuli and I. The crowds eventually thinned out to reconvene in the tavern next door when I decided that I had stood under the soothing water long enough. Flipping the lever, I jumped when a pair of fingers lightly traced one of the scars on my back.

"Such pain you must have suffered." Her breath was warm on the back of my neck and sent chills down my spine.

Ducking out of her reach, I kept my eyes fixed on the towels as I took one. She followed me back to where my things hung in the changing room, and the grace of her movements sent my thoughts down paths they should not have traveled. Why was she watching me? Surely she knew I was Bonded? Morakvaar, but I hoped she did not notice how her presence affected me.

"I meant no disrespect kinsman. I am sorry if I offended you." Relief flooded through me. Is that all she wanted, to apologize?

But, she had made no move to dress as I pulled on my breeks and tunic, as if she wanted me to think of her. Her braided beard did nothing to hide her breasts even though it hung nearly to the ground, and for a moment, I missed the binding ring. "No offense is taken." Using the excuse of buckling on my weapons' belt and harness, I turned from her and tried to get the vision out of my head. By the length of her beard she must have had at least another hundred years on me, yet she looked as young as Korina.

As if turning around was a signal, she sighed and picked up her things. By the binding ring in her beard, she was bonded too, so what did she want from me? I had the odd sensation that I should know what she was after, that I should know who she was, but it was just out of my reach. The sounds of her dressing took much of the tension from me. At least I would not be distracted by her lithe form, a temptation that ordinarily would not have bothered me.

The Reaver slid into the sheath on my back as the handle slipped into the strap by my shoulder; its weight was a comfort as I turned once more to face Harrakuli. Instead of a gown, she wore breeks and a tunic that was belted at the waist. Two vaarandril battle-axes flanked either side of her hips, and the air of power around them nearly equaled that of the Reaver. Of course a Weapons' Master would prefer clothing that would not hinder her movements, and I wondered why I had expected otherwise. She regarded me for a long moment, as if she were on the verge of confessing some deep secret. Instead, she shook her head, smiled and led the way to the tavern.

The large open chamber was full of excited vaarakanan and humans. They crowded around the tables carved from the bottom of the pillars that were once joined stalactites and stalagmites. The crowd strove to consume the stores of ale that were being shipped from Barakillanak, Morakduum and Dormakkarduum. The smell of sweat and brew was near overpowering, but soon faded from recognition as the young kinswoman working the bar asked us our pleasure. She smiled heartily as I announced a round for all within the walls as I pulled a handful of platinum coins from my pouch, and cheers accompanied her scurry back to the line of tapped barrels behind the carved stone bar. Tales of our match echoed from near a hundred throats as I threw back the first mug without stopping for air.

The stew was made from dried meats, and though it was doctored with fresh mushrooms, roots and lichens, it was still below standard fare. But, it was a welcome change from the rations all the same. The smell of baking bread accompanied the opening door to the kitchens as all conversation ceased to appreciate the aroma. Fresh loaves were passed around to all the tables, making up for the lousy stew.

More ale washed down the last bit of bread and soup as I leaned back from the table to do some serious drinking.

The hum of conversation around me continued as others finished their meals, and I casually listened in on tales of fighting prowess and war stories. The flash of Harrakuli's gold eyes, the color of an Orudin's yet in a vaarakanan was odd. Was she a half-breed? The continuous flash of gold told me that she had kept watching me most of the time.

"Is your mate still in Dormakkarduum?" She stared blankly at my question for a few moments, and then shook her head.

"My mate is dead. I have not been bonded to another, and do not want to be." She frowned at my raised brows. "I wear the braid to honor his passing. I will not remarry unless his soul returns." It was my turn to stare blankly.

"You expect your mate to be reborn?" My incredulous words finally broke her gaze. "Has there ever been such a thing among us?"

"I do not know the Maker's plans, and could not pretend to." She looked as if she was going to continue, but instead fell silent as she found an indiscriminate spot on the stone floor to look at.

"Even were he reborn, would you still be alive when he was old enough?" A sad smile touched her lips as she shook her head and did not answer. How old was she, anyway?

Her devotion to her deceased mate stirred me, and I wondered if Morina felt the same way. I knew I would not have the strength to continue if my hearth-mate preceded me to the Underhalls of the Maker even if Morakvaar himself promised she would return to my side. My hand rested on her shoulder, expressing my appreciation of her persistence.

"I surely would not be able to bear the passing of my mate. Such strength of soul is rare indeed." When her gold gaze returned to mine, it was full of moisture. Her lips moved silently and I could feel the need she had to confess whatever secret she held, but it was not forthcoming.

For a moment, I had the overwhelming urge to hold her until her tears quieted. The need was nearly as strong as the pull of a soul-bond and only the shock of such a notion held me still. Deep within her golden orbs was an image of a kinsman, not unlike me. My empathic talent rarely stirred for people, only animals. I wondered why it worked at that moment. Did she think that I was her mate reborn? My ragged intake of breath broke the spell, and I blinked into my empty mug. I flagged the barmaid for another round, trying desperately to avoid thinking of Harrakuli. My love for Morina was as deep as my soul, and I would not endanger it for anything or anyone.

For a few moments I was unaware that the noise in the tavern had quieted. One of the other Weapons' Masters appeared before me as I put my tankard down with an empty thunk. I stared at his white-gray eyes wondering what he wanted before he spoke up slowly and loudly enough to carry through the chamber.

"Lord Dorian, many of us are curious what happened when you were betrayed. How did you escape? And, tell us of your battle with the demon upon the ramparts. All of us saw its hideous form emerge from the portal before we were embroiled in combat from the treacherous and cowardly attack of the zarakanan."

"Yes!" A chorus of voices responded. "Tell us your tale!"

At my frown, the shouts grew more insistent. Harrakuli's hand rested on my forearm. "Your people need to believe in heroes, and such tales make stronger hearts, Gorain."

An electric shock ran through me with her use of the name, but she was looking elsewhere when I turned to her.

"Please, Lord Dorian? We have need of such inspiration if we are to fight the vourdovra." The Weapons' Master pleaded once more.

Resigned to my fate, I told them of my internment by the zarakanan as one of the humans interpreted for the others. I spoke of the journey deprived of food and water and of the pain upon my arrival. When I spoke of the 'trial', my kinsmen growled in the injustice. They stared in sympathetic pain as I told them of the torture I endured, the illusion of Morina and the confession of Balakarak's 'weaknesses'. But, I did not tell them of Kairillia's deception later, or what came of it. They smiled as I spoke of meeting my mother, and the gladness in my heart that she still lived. But again, I left out the strange dream of Kelana and her words. A knowing smile touched the lips of my kin as I spoke of the 'dream' of Lodath.

A loud cheer echoed through the tavern from both vaarakanan and human throats as I relayed the sense of the Reaver and my escape from bondage. They gasped in awed terror as I told them of the demon and murmured with satisfied vengeance when Kairillia perished in the tale. Nods of acknowledgement coursed through the room when I spoke of destroying the covey of priestesses that warded the walls against our cannons.

"So that is what happened!" The same exclamation rang from many throats as I concluded with meeting the zarak general and the subsequent surrender of our enemies.

Long moments of silence followed as the crowd still pondered my words. Like the rising of the tides of the ocean above, the cheering started and arced like a wave in a crescendo of epic proportions.

"You have missed your calling, Lord Dorian. You should have been a storysmith!" Cheers followed the comment.

"I think that would have been easier by far!" Laughter echoed around me as I found my mug had been refilled.

The tales of other warriors rang through the night as I could swear we drank every last drop of brew in the tavern. It was near the ninth time cycle when I stumbled out with the last stragglers, one of the Tashor gripped me under the shoulders on either side. My insistence of my own stability got me a face full of dirt as they allowed me to test my balance. Harrakuli helped me to my feet and offered to assist, but Kormak waved her off. Somewhat disappointed, I let the Tashor drag me to our temporary quarters.

My head throbbed in waves as I sat up on the divan. The rubbing of my temples did little to soothe the dizzy nausea that threatened to vacate my gut. The fireplace to my left was cold and empty, and I could hear little Geria squalling in the room I normally shared with Morina. Half in guilt and all in pain, I stumbled towards my daughter's cries. A sharper pain registered in my hazy mind as my shins caught the tea table and sent me sprawling. How did the table get there?

"Vooraduum arak en vaar!" My cussing evoked a response from my mother as she emerged from the kitchen tunnel.

"Your soul will rest in hell, Dorian, if you keep overindulging yourself!" She skirted my prone form with a tray of food, and the normally enticing smell made my stomach churn urgently.

The smell of brimstone from the magma at the other end of the waste tunnel did not help ease the heaving of my gut. Why had I drunk so much? Vague flashes of memory bespoke of the contest of capacity between the Weapons' Masters and I as bets were laid out. Though I had survived longer than two of them, Harrakuli slugged down her mug as I remembered gazing up at her from the floor and wondering how I had gotten there. With a vow of non-indulgence, I held my head as I left the privy. Even the cold water from the well did little to revive my well being, and I slunk back in to the common area to lie on the divan once more. Thinking I would feel better after a few more hours of rest, my eyes closed to the room.

No sooner had I shut out the dark ceiling overhead, than I found myself being shaken. "You had better sober up quick, father. Your presence is needed in the war council." Korina's face hovered over mine, as the room seemed to rotate slowly around her.

My groan brought only laughter, but it hit me that Korina no longer seemed angry. "War council? I thought that was in three days?"

Korina flushed and her eyes left mine to gaze at the floor. "I am sorry, father. You were right to offer the humans a bargain. I guess I still have much to learn. Captain Anton has accepted in lieu of General Wolfgang who seems to have taken ill quite suddenly from a wound received in the battle. Anton wants you to train his troops as we prepare to leave for Vouroussan." Her eyes danced as they returned to mine.

My wan smile was probably not as enthusiastic as she wished, but I could hardly manage more as my head throbbed with the motion of sitting up. "I still have things to learn myself." My mutter was not lost on her as she snorted and stood up straight.

"We convene in half a time cycle, and I expect to see you there." Korina spun on her heels and lighted out of the door.

The grim faces of my kin were arrayed around the large woodroot table as I spread the tunnel maps across it. Only the human captain bore no signs of gray that the rest of the room's occupants displayed. His two feet of height over our people made him stand out even more. The click and clank of platemaille filled the background with noise as Korina's generals shifted for the best view. The smell of oil and leather preservatives permeated the air with their pungent odors, masking even the rank of a long night of drinking from at least four others that I recognized in the room. The stone walls amplified the rattle of my armor, and echoed it back to me a hundred fold despite the tapestries that tried to muffle it. The sound rang through my head like the striking of an anvil, and I tried to make my movements more deliberate to avoid the noise.

Lodath stood by my side, towering over the human captain. His orange-gold eyes reflected the light of the stargems and glowed softly, intimidating even my stout kin. His long gray hair hung almost down to his waist, but he kept himself clean-shaven. Instead of the robes most mages wore, though, he wore a puffy blue shirt under a black leather jerkin and slim black breeks more like a rogue's. He cleared his throat noisily and prepared to translate and I winced at the noise once more.

"As you all know, save perhaps Anton, the vourdovra represent the greatest threat our people face." The sound of my own voice echoed painfully through my skull, but I continued. "Their powers of the mind cannot be thwarted by our priests, or by arcane lore. Only the soulsmiths had the power and ability to block them, and there is our most grievous wound. Since the zarakanan destroyed Balakarak and murdered or enslaved the soulsmiths, we are vulnerable to attacks by the vourdovra. There are a few among us that retain mental talents, but not in enough numbers or strength to fend off the amassed might of our enemies." A young lad brought me a mug of cold water, and I took a long draught before continuing.

"Since we cannot rely upon a frontal attack to be successful, it is vital that we breech their defenses in some other fashion. I have met with our engineers' guild and discussed plans to remove the foundations beneath their city and collapse their tunnels inward." A murmur of surprise rumbled through the generals.

"Lord Dorian, will that not be a great risk to our homes? If Vouroussan becomes unstable and the Mother shakes the earth in her slumber, all of our cities may be destroyed!" Bavorn's features had paled slightly from within his vaarandril helmet that was decorated with the snarling visage of a cave bear.

I nodded. "That was one of the possibilities we had to consider. Unfortunately, you are too correct, Bavorn. There is a solid pillar of granite that ascends the northeast of Vouroussan. This foundation serves to stabilize much of the northern tunnels that would otherwise have collapsed long ago. So, we had to go back to ancient surveys of the area and discovered a large hollow under their central chamber." I pulled out the map of the tunnels under Vouroussan and pointed out the area in question as all present struggled to get a good glimpse.

"We plan to breech this hollow and climb up under the central city. A few well-placed explosive blasts should be sufficient without destroying the surrounding tunnels. Once inside their defenses, we can assault them with numbers in hopes that there will be too many of us for them to overwhelm with their mental powers." I took another drink, but my head still felt like an anvil as the furor rose in the room while the generals discussed the improbability of such an assault.

"That is suicide!" Though Anton did not quite understand just what the vourdovra were capable of, he had grasped the concept of danger.

"There is more to it than that." The noise died down as all attention turned back to me. "We know that the vourdovra are ruled by an 'overmind'. Just who or what it is remains uncertain, but from Lodath's scrying, we have found that this section surrounding the chamber has been sealed off as some sort of sanctum. They have managed to ward this area against his power. It is my belief that this 'overmind' now dwells there. The object of the foray will be to kill or destroy this force that unites them. In the ensuing chaos, the vourdovra will be easier to deal with. The problem is we will have to make the vourdovra believe we are still attempting a frontal assault." I turned to Anton and allowed Lodath time to finish interpreting for him before continuing.

"That is where your expanded numbers of non-military personnel will come in handy. I will need them to fill in the numbers of our reserve force while the veteran soldiers help us in the assault from the inner city." Anton's face turned grim at the last part of the interpretation.

"What happens if you don't find this 'overmind', or are not successful in destroying it?" Silence pervaded through the room as I finished interpreting his question for my kin.

I ran a hand through my red hair, stalling for a better answer than the one that came immediately to mind. "We will have to fall back and regroup." That was of course, if there were any survivors, and the grim looks on my kin reflected the same thoughts.

But, Anton seemed satisfied with the answer and nodded agreement. The assembled generals kept their gazes on me wondering if I would tell the human the full truth. When it was apparent that I would not, many frowns were turned my way. Deceit, though known to my people, was as dishonorable as lying, and I could tell that their opinion of me dropped dramatically. At least they recognized the need for it, though, as they kept their misgivings to themselves.

"Who will lead the assault on the overmind?" Anton's voice held a note of hysteria and my kin frowned at what they perceived as human cowardice.

"I will lead the initial foray while the bulk of our forces invade the city. My team's mission will be to seek out and destroy the overmind and regroup with the main army as soon as possible." The other generals did not seem surprised at my announcement, but Korina stared at me with disbelief for a moment.

"Father, you cannot do this!"

"Your Majesty, I alone have the best chance of success in this mission. My bonding to the Reaver and my meager mental talents allow a greater chance at resisting the vourdovra's control. The team I will assemble will consist of the strongest talents to give us more than a hope of winning through. If we strike swiftly enough, I believe we will succeed."

Korina kept frowning as if she did not believe a word of what I was saying. Lodath's grim face confirmed her assumption that I had put myself on a suicide mission, and perhaps they were right? But, I could not ask anyone else to take the risk that I was unwilling to face myself. The pain I had caused Morina loomed large before me, squeezing the breath from my lungs. She deserved so much more than I could give her. Perhaps with my death, she could finally marry someone more worthy of her?

With the initial plans laid out, we discussed the particulars long into the night regarding who would lead what force and what their objectives were. Overall, an air of doom prevailed, but I had no doubts that my kin would fight to the utmost of their abilities. I only wished that there were some way we could have replicated the amulet that Lodath carried. The zarakanan had taken more from us than could ever be replaced when they destroyed the stronghold of the soulsmiths.

It was the middle of the ninth time cycle when we finalized our plans and left the council chamber. On the stone bench outside, I found Morina fast asleep. The lone tapestry that adorned the wall was one that my mother had made many years ago depicting the final battle of Gorain against the zarakanan that controlled Sorkarak. To either side of the bench grew a cultivated farosvarum, a type of fluorescent fungus. The mushroom shed yellowish green light over Morina's recumbent form, illuminating her like a slumbering goddess. That she had waited all that time for me warmed my heart as much as the concern for her health churned the acids in my gut. She woke as the sound of conversation filled the outer chamber when the generals and commanders left. She blinked in sleepy confusion as if she did not know where she was. She sat up and rubbed her eyes as I made my way to her side. When she looked up her smile was like the sun.

"Dorian. What time is it?"

"Near the first time cycle, my love. You should be in bed." I took her hands as she stood and we began to walk back to our quarters.

"I am going with you to Vouroussan." Her sidelong glance awaited my reaction.

I stopped in my tracks, pulling on her arm to make her face me. "No. I will not have you risking your life in this assault while our daughter is still so young. Morina, she needs you to take care of her."

"Dorian, I cannot stay behind again! You have no idea what it does to me to know that you could die and I would not be there. Every day it makes me ill to think that it could be the day that I learned you had been killed. I cannot make it through another campaign without knowing on a daily basis whether or not you would be coming home. I will not be left behind again!" The desperation in her voice smote me in the chest, but she would be better off without me.

Despite the odd looks of our kin, I took her into my arms. "Morina, I love you, but I cannot let you do this. Geria needs one of us to care for her and raise her. If we both die, where will that leave our child?"

The stubborn line appeared above her brow. "Then you stay and I will go, but I will not stay behind again to die a little bit every day. You cannot imagine what it is like to be left behind!"

I held her tighter as the tears rolled down her cheeks and my vision blurred. "Morina, I am expendable, you are not. As a kinswoman, your life is precious and your death would be a tragedy beyond consideration. I am a kinsman; my death would be no more than a sorrow. If I died, you would be allowed to remarry and be accepted into any clan. I have no recourse; our people tolerate my presence solely because of this war. When it is over, there will be nothing for me without you by my side. Gorain's heir will never be welcome among his own people. My risk is the more logical choice."

"Not to me! I could never marry another! You are the only one I will ever love!" She clutched at my tunic with the desperation of the lost. Why did she love me so much when I was nothing but a poor excuse for a kinsman? Her tears wet my beard and slowly seeped into my red tunic. "I will go with you even if I have to sneak into the back ranks!" The words made it through her sobs.

I raised her chin so that she would meet my gaze as I kissed her, trying to ease her fears. "I will not leave you, Morina, but do you not understand how terrible I would feel if something were to happen to you? If you went with me, and met with some horrid fate, I could never forgive myself. Geria needs you, and your stability. If I lost you, I would be unfit to care for her."

The stubborn line appeared above her brow and I knew I was going to lose the argument. "I am going with you, and you cannot stop me!"

A thousand arguments died on my tongue as I considered their affect upon Morina's stubbornness. "Very well, my love. It will be good to have you at my side, but first I must speak with you in private." Her golden brow furrowed in curiosity, and she followed me back in to the council chamber.

The wooden door echoed hollowly in the empty hall as I closed it behind me. Intent on my actions, Morina watched as I pulled out the amulet I had borrowed from Lodath and placed it around her neck.

"No one must know of this, keep it hidden at all times."

"What does it do?" She held the amulet out to the end of the chain so that she could examine the contents of the locket. For a few moments, she seemed mesmerized by the violet gem that sparkled from inside the glass that covered it.

"It will shield you from the vourdovra's power. If you will not be dissuaded, I will at least ensure that you are protected. If any of our kinsmen turn on you, even me, you must slay them. It is one of the things they can do." My voice brought some awareness back to her, but she still stared at the amulet.

"Dorian, is this the only one you have?"

"We have not been able to replicate their making. Lodath confirmed to me it is of the making of the soulsmiths, and there are no master craftsmen left." A worried frown settled on her features. She knew the dangers of the vourdovra, but I was not sure if she understood the implications. "Promise me that you will protect yourself no matter who it is against?"

"How could I kill you?" It was as if I had asked her to cut off her own head, and her tone implied the task was just as impossible.

"If the vourdovra take control of my mind, it will not be me, and slaying me is a kinder fate than the one they would give me. Promise me, or I will have Korina put you in the dungeons until we are quite thoroughly engaged with the enemy."

She looked at me defiantly for a time, then sighed and nodded. "I promise you, Dorian, though this is the hardest thing you have asked of me save staying behind. Your mother has already asked to look after her namesake. Little Geria is near past wanting to nurse, and already is preferring ground food."

I smiled at her and held her hands. "Come, we have less than a time cycle to be ready to leave."

Morina pulled me to her, and kissed me passionately. "We had better get started then," she murmured around my lips as her voice danced with mischief.

Chapter 13

Vouroussan (City of the Mind Eaters)

Despite my urgings for speed, it took us twenty days to maneuver our army through the tunnels to the outlying caverns of Vouroussan's lower level. Korina appointed me Supreme Commander and Warlord of her armies, relieving my duties as Lord Chamberlain. It was an apology of sorts, but there was still tension in her manner towards me. I put it down to the insecurity of youth and hoped someday that wisdom would bridge the gap that was growing between us. In my soul, though, I knew better. Her beliefs had been shattered, and I was no longer the hero she worshipped. I had betrayed her trust, the very foundation of her ethics and honor, and she was only just learning what that meant.

In a roughly ovular cavern we made camp as thousands of small shelters dotted every piece of level ground including the ledges and flattened stalagmite tops. Lodath bade me to leave a large open area in the center and as my kinsmen watched, he displayed the awesome powers at his command. Taking a pinch of powdered granite into his fingers, he spread it on the ground before him. The prints of his boots made a clockwise circle roughly forty feet in diameter as his voice rang through the cavern in an arcane rhythmic chant. At select intervals, he inscribed a symbol of power in the dirt as the increasing energy began to make my hair stand on end. Waves of wild energies coalesced inward as he finished the circle and continued his chant. Sparks of eerie light lifted the granules of rock into the air as they began to grow in size and form together.

Massive buttresses with crenellated fortifications rose before our eyes. They formed into an impregnable granite fortress that filled the open area from the cave floor to the roof high overhead, but Lodath was not finished. Dipping his finger into what looked like a small vial of blood, he invoked the arcane energies once more. As his chanting reached a crescendo, his finger began to glow an unearthly green as he inscribed some symbols along the outer walls. The symbols glowed for a few moments then faded into nothingness. Lodath's satisfied smile turned my way, and I shook my head at his extravagance.

"Using so much energy, you might as well have walked up to the gates of Vouroussan and introduced yourself." My growl took him aback for a few moments.

"Don't worry you grumpy old codger! I used a shielding spell before we left." The insult still disgruntled me even though it was spoken in his language.

"You ought to look in zie mirror sometime, mage. Vat you see might surprise you." Lodath ignored me as he opened the gate and strode in as if he were the High King.

"Are you coming, Dorian?" With a sigh, I followed him into the fortress, Morina tight on my heels. She refused to let me out of her sight for even a moment.

As we approached the stronghold of our enemies, the very air was thick with oppression and she became more insistent upon being with me at all times. Morina refused to stay with the camp when I went out with the scouting party to survey the site where we were to breech the inner chamber. How could I refuse when her mental talents were stronger than mine? She was the daughter of a soulsmith and a Kinswoman of Soul. If she had trained as a child, she too would have been a soulsmith. The unfortunate thing was that there were no more Master Soulsmiths to train her, so her talents were still largely untapped.

The courtyard of the impromptu keep was terribly familiar if smaller than the original version at Thornwood Keep. A nostalgic smile crossed my lips as I ran my fingers along the stone top of the well that sat in the exact center. To my left were the old stables where I kept my forge before moving it underground, but in Lodath's version they were barracks. To my right was the old storeroom again converted to barracks. Straight ahead were the doors of the old keep that opened into the corridor that led to the Great Hall. The only thing missing was the wondrous smell of Frieda's cooking that constantly wafted through the keep making everyone's mouths water. Morina smiled at me with the same nostalgia for our home on the surface.

No, not the only thing missing, I amended as in my mind I remembered my daughter Panther's smiling face as she greeted me upon my return from one of our forays to Tethyr. Only three years old, she stood more than half my height. Behind her stood Jaguar, her mother with a sad smile as she whispered in Panther's ear. The child squealed in glee and ran as awkward as a three-year-old might across the courtyard to throw her arms around my neck as I knelt in the dirt. I tried to keep the pinching joints of my armor from hurting her as I lifted her to my shoulder to sit on the wide pauldron. Already she weighed twice that of a normal human child, but there was not an ounce of fat on her as she displayed the broad features of my race. My heart leaped with joy and pride as she proclaimed loudly, "This is my daddy!" The vision faded as I noticed Lodath and Morina staring hard at me. I let the smile fade from my lips immediately as we entered the Great Hall.

Like a thick blanket of fog, the oppressive air of doom settled over our army. With Vouroussan so close, death could strike at any moment. Even knowing the threat, there was something sinister about the despair that seemed to be reflected in everyone's manner. It was as if the very stones radiated fear and loathing, an aura so strong it affected my stouthearted kin. As bad as it was for my kinsmen, it was by far worse for the humans, they were a wreck. When we had gathered around the old wooden table before the hearth, I beseeched Lodath for aid.

"I do not know how much more the humans can take. Is there some way you can help them resist the aura of Vouroussan?"

Lodath thought about it for a while as his white brows drew low. "I can make a barrier around the camp, but the minute the troops leave the enclosure, they will be vulnerable again. The problem is that this type of fear is created within the minds of the individual, a 'beast of id' if you will. The only way I could think of to counter-act this would be drugs or a mind-altering spell, and then the troops would be useless."

"The barrier will have to do for now, then." I turned to Korina who had followed us in. "We will have to move quickly to keep the troops from panic. My team should be ready to accompany the engineers within a time cycle. With your permission I will go prepare." She nodded as I went to spread the word.

We crept through the smaller tunnels that approached the hollow beneath Vouroussan as the aura intensified. Every scurry of an unseen creature made us jump uncharacteristically. The fear and feelings of inadequacy grew like the chill in my bones and the furtive gazes of my kin reflected the same internal terrors. Though I knew it was ridiculous to be as flighty as a superstitious child, never-the-less, I could not repress the feeling that doom crept upon my heels. The kanan of the Tashor that surrounded me seemed to edge closer as time went on. The only one who was unaffected was Morina. The amulet must have been working against even the thick oppression in the air.

So intense was the dark cloud of emotion that emanated from Vouroussan's proximity that at first I did not notice the increasing amount of humidity or the rapid drop in temperature. But when I passed an outcrop that nearly cut off our path, I noticed it was laden with beads of moisture. Instead of the reddish hues I was used to, the heat patterns changed to colder greens and blues. Calling our party to a halt, I pulled out a stargem and the map of the area. There was no doubt we were in the right tunnel, but according to the old survey, the Deamon Fish River was still leagues away. Had the denizens of Vouroussan diverted the water? Tovar, one of our Master Engineers swiped his hand down the wet stone as his brows drew down. He exchanged a look of misgiving with me, and I nodded grimly as we neared the area we were to set our explosives.

At the foundation point we had determined to be the weakest, a small stream dripped out from a minute crack in the wall. The crystal and granite mixture barely resonated in its frigidness, and the chill of the place settled into my psyche. The odor of brine filled the air in the small round cave, something I had not smelled since my trip to the coastal surface town Waynesport. Tovar stuck an experimental finger in the water and smelled it as the others gathered in close.

Salt, but there is no saline vein nearby. His hand signals relayed what I already knew. *We will have to fall back and regroup. Opening this chamber will drown our army where it sits.*

Agreed. We will move to the upper chambers first. As I turned to give the order to withdraw, pain lanced through my head like a spear. It felt as if I was being struck repeatedly between the eyes with an axe that split my brain again and again. My psionic defenses rose automatically, but such was the power of the assault that they overwhelmed my meager amount of talent as if it did not exist at all. Around me my kinsmen fell clutching at their skulls as blood rushed from their noses and ears. Their bodies spasmed in agony as screams of pain echoed down the tunnels. Fighting down the pain, I looked to the fissure at the rear of the chamber we occupied.

The four vourdovra there barely gave off any heat making them near invisible, and the only sense I had of them was vibration. The tentacled monstrosities advanced on my helpless kin, intent on slaying them. Their appendages lashed out and attached to the skulls of four of our party, but I would not allow the slaughter to continue. With a howl of rage that was half agony, I stumbled to my feet and charged. Seeing my desperate action, Morina was quickly at my side, her mind unaffected by the psychic attacks. The four turned towards me, massing all of their power to strike me down, and the blow sent me to my knees as my mind reeled between blackness and the desperate need to protect my people.

My brain felt as if it was slowly cooking inside my head, but I forced my feet beneath me by sheer effort of will. My staggered steps towards the vourdovra seemed to surprise and intimidate them for a moment as all four backed a pace or two. Desperately I held the Reaver before me as if it alone could save me from their assault, but I could feel my will crumbling before their combined might, my sight becoming dimmer by the moment. As suddenly as it started the power vanished and I drew in a breath of relief as the pain still echoed through my head. The tickle in my moustache smeared the back of my gauntlet with blood as I wiped it away. My feet managed a few more steps towards them, as Morina engaged the first in line, her axe flashing through the darkness to ring solidly against stone as the vourdovra vanished.

The beast reappeared behind her and lashed out with a tentacle, but the vaarandril helmet I had forged for her held strong and repelled its vile attack. Two of the fiends pounced on her and held her down trying vainly to disarm her as I staggered towards them. The other two faced me, changing their attack against my unprotected mind. Instead of raw mental power, they attacked my already fragile view of myself as a kinsman. They brought forward the memories of my kinsmen, how they looked at me like an alien or an outsider. Whispered conversations murmured 'Gorain reborn' in horrified or disgusted tones as the words smote my soul. Corian again reviled my ancestry to the Council of Elders denying my right to be recognized as a foster member to the Atharil clan, forever damning me to outsider's status.

The shame of my youth became the prayers for death as Lady Alfstein allowed her guards to do what they would when she herself had tired of torturing me. The magic of the collar ensured that I did what they asked without complaint, feigning whatever emotion they ordered of me. The agony of my soul recognized its own loss as I lived through what no kinsman should have. The mere knowledge that such things had been done to me not just once but many times over the course of three years made me wretch in shameful horror as I fell to my knees beseeching Morakvaar for my death. The Reaver fell noisily to the cavern floor as I smote my breast with my gauntlets as if I could tear out my own heart and end the torment of guilt that I had survived the slavers' treatment. Mournful cries of a damned soul rang through the darkness like the knell of Vooraduum's messengers crying out the names of the evil souls bound forever in hell. My will retreated from the onslaught, hiding from my shame as the other presence entered my mind to take up where I had vacated.

A passenger in my own body, I felt my hands grip the Reaver once more as my feet steadied beneath me. The fighting in the gap intensified as Morina threw off the two predators, hacking the forelimb clean from the shoulder of the beast, as it's mental howl screamed through my numb mind. In helpless horror I watched as I stealthily approached her, drawing the Reaver back for a quick downward stroke. My will rebelled. I would not! Could not kill Morina! The presence lashed me down with more visions of Alfstein's ministrations. The whips, the degrading acts, they were too strong a fear for me to overcome as my body took the final step, swinging the great-axe in an arc of destruction.

As if on instinct, Morina whirled at the last second, shunting the blade with one of hers, shattering it in a shower of silver sparks even as it knocked her down with the force of all my strength. The magical blades sunk halfway into the rock between her feet as she scrambled on all fours away from me. *No! Strike me down!* I prayed she would hear me, but her eyes merely stared in horror as my feet stepped forward for the next killing blow. Powerless to stop it, the Reaver swept through the darkness towards my mate. *Morakvaar, please do not let me kill her!* I pleaded with the Maker and Morina dove out of the way to my left as I nearly wept in relief.

"Dorian! Dorian it is me!" Her voice echoed through my mind as it tore my soul in two.

Another step brought the backswing as deadly with power as the one she had dodged. Her eyes searched mine for a hint of recognition, but only death reflected her gaze as the Reaver clove through the air. The Reaver! My will sought out the soul of Gorain that dwelled within the weapon. Surely his will was greater than mine was, and together we had a chance to defeat the singular mind that invaded my head!

Rage! Death! Kill! Hot fire surrounded me, burning with fury restrained for eight thousand years, yet it fit so well into the empty space of my soul. A bellow full of bloodlust echoed through the chamber like a trumpet as our souls blended inseparably. There was no more Dorian, only Gorain, a being made whole once again. Almost belatedly I remembered the stroke as it parted the air towards the golden-haired kinswoman. Too late to pull the blow, I allowed a change in the angle of my wrists, barely missing the top of her head and burying the metal deep into the stone as it screeched and sparked.

Sagging for a moment in relief, I breathed as the foreign presence fled from my new awareness and power. The kinswoman blinked as I smiled sheepishly before the rage took me once more. How dare they try to make me kill one of my people!? With the snarl more like a beast than a kinsman, I leapt at them, the Reaver describing an arc of blue-white fire. The echoes of their fear reverberated through my mind as the great-axe split the first directly down the center of its brain-like body. Its tentacles twitched in the ichors of its blood and fluids, spasming like worms drying in the heat of magma.

The second lost the front half of its body as I followed its desperate leap to escape. The third that had already been wounded was put out of its misery by a casual backstroke. The forth had fled as if the minions of hell were after it. Bracing my feet wide, I hurled the Reaver through the fissure. The blades flashed in white fire as it flipped end over end before embedding in the vourdovra's central brain tissue, splattering it like the yokes of smashed eggs. But the rage did not leave me. When I retrieved the axe, memory returned to me. They made me try to kill my hearth-mate!

"Dorian!" The name finally registered as a part of me I barely remembered as the kinswoman screamed it again.

Who I was returned to me completely in a moment as the rage receded leaving me dazed and disoriented. Blood and bits of bodily tissue dripped from my armor as my eyes trailed down my arms to the Reaver. The greataxe was covered in gore and some unnamable internal organ slid from the half-moon blades to splat noisily on the stone. Beneath my feet was an unrecognizable pool of blood and guts that had been hacked up enough that only feet and claws were identifiable as belonging to a once living creature. What had I done? What had happened to me? How could I have lost myself so completely to the rage?

Morina took a hesitant step towards me, and the memory of wielding the Reaver with the intent to slay her smote my chest. Fiery agony spread from my heart through my veins at the thought, and my knees turned to jelly. How easily I might have snuffed out the life of my love! The vourdovra had thrust aside my will as if I were naught but a child. If I had not been able to regain control, I might have killed all of my kinsmen who began to groan and regain consciousness. Morina's wide eyes spoke of her terror that lanced through me, and I dared not to breathe, not to move for fear of losing control once more. We had been helpless against their mental assault and there had been only four of the vile beasts! We were not ready to fight them!

Seeing the pain in my eyes, Morina finally approached, but the mistrust of my control was plain in her demeanor. Each furtive glance at the Reaver was another dagger thrust in my chest as hot tears cleaned some of the gore from my cheeks.

"I can not think of any apology that comes close to the crime I nearly committed." The words echoed the horror that I felt within me as my chest heaved with the effort to divest myself of the vision of swinging the Reaver at Morina.

The hesitation left her as she rushed to my side, throwing her arms around me despite the grime that still dripped from my armor. "Oh Dorian! I was so afraid! I could not kill you, even though I knew it was not you who-" Her voice broke as she sobbed into my blood-soaked beard.

The Reaver slipped to the stone floor of the cave with a loud clang as I strove to hold her. My life, my love, and I had nearly killed her! The moans of pain from our kin separated us and focused our attention away from the agonizing memory. Of the fourteen members of our scouting party, seven survived besides Morina and I, and none of them seemed aware of their surroundings. I prayed to the Maker that their minds had not been damaged beyond repair as Morina herded them back towards our camp. Using the packed canvas that would have been my tent, I wrapped the five bodies together. Though I did not like treating our dead kin like cargo, neither did I wish to leave them for the vourdovra's disgusting feeding habits.

Dripping with sweat as every muscle in my body burned with exertion, I finally made it back to camp dragging my heavy burden. The weight of the dead was nothing compared to the weight of guilt that plagued my heart. It was as if I had slain them all with my own hand, for it had been my orders that had sent them to their deaths. The growing number of somber faces watched as I pulled the grisly canvas into the center of camp. Two stout kin joined my efforts by the outer watch, making the progress much swifter. Nearly every soul in our army was gathered around the gates of the impromptu keep as their murmurs rose like the ocean tides. It was obvious to all our initial foray was a horrible failure, and it drove morale into the dust that 'Gorain Reborn' could be so easily overcome.

Waradain came swiftly, as our kin parted to admit him. The old priest paled as he saw the vacant expressions of the living and the bundle of canvas that contained our dead. "Morakvaar save our souls!" His hoarse whisper invoked protection against the dread that was upon every brow. His gray eyes traced over the gore that was slowly drying on my armor with a horrified questioning look.

With an agonized frown, I unwrapped the bundle revealing the bodies of our dead kin. Waradain almost sighed in relief when he realized I had not killed them, but he did not know how close his assumption had come to be.

"What happened, Dorian?" His gaze lifted from the task of arranging the dead to meet mine as I paused while I helped him.

"They ambushed us." It was all I could manage as the crushing weight of guilt smote my chest and my vision blurred as I tried to choke down the grief that welled within.

"How many?"

I shook my head, unable to form words as I fought to control the emotions that broiled and churned in my mind.

Morina's whisper was like a bolt of thunder striking down the priest as she told him. "Four. Only four."

A growing tide of voices spiraled outward echoing back from the stony walls of the cavern. How could we possibly triumph over an entire city when four of the enemy could lay low a troop of fourteen? The answer was that we could not. Our campaign was at an end and though we had defeated the zarakanan, our future was far from secure. How much longer could we survive against the dark threat of extinction?

Despair settled deeply upon me as I realized there was no way to victory. The attack of the vourdovra on my psyche reopened the wounds of my past, exposing my shame like an infected sore upon my conscience. I had failed! Failed in my duty to follow my father's trade, failed my apprenticeship by allowing myself to be captured by zarakanan, failed my vaarakanan heritage by surviving the nightmare no kinsman could, failed Morina by betraying her trust, and failed my people by not leading them to victory. Worst of all, I had failed to prevent the inevitable future of extinction that loomed like the angel of death over our race. I was worse than a failure, for I had led my people to hope only to dash them into the pits of despair in the end. Perhaps I deserved the damnation I was sure would come to claim me.

Chapter 14

Forkarzak Tava Nae (A Change in Plans)

The wavy patterns of wood grain in the table were as good an excuse as any not to meet the gazes of my kin. The fire in the stone hearth behind me gave no cheer to the room as the grim faces were riveted to mine. The crusted blood on my gauntlets cracked and flaked off as I flexed my fingers experimentally, and I wished I had been given time to wash the grime of the battle off my armor. At least the burning woodroot masked the smell of blood and death that covered me. Hard-soled boots scraped and shifted across the stone floor of the Great Hall as the unease and fear were like a tangible presence in the air.

"What happened, father!?" Korina's sharp tone made me jump, but the lethargy of despair crept back almost as quickly.

The commanders and generals leaned forward to hear my despondent mumble. "I already explained we were ambushed. It was as if the vourdovra knew where we were and why. I would bet that they are mustering a force to finish us off as we speak. I could not help what they had done to me. There is no defense our people have against them without the soulsmiths."

"What did they do?" Her morbid fascination was salt on the wounds of my soul, and my shame turned me from her. But she would not be denied an explanation, and seized me by the shoulders as she spun me around. "Father! We must know what they did! How can we fight something without information!?" With each word, she shook me as if she could force victory out of me.

With a low growl in my throat, I firmly removed her hands. "Do you not understand!? We cannot fight them! Do not make me relive the experience again!" For a moment we locked gazes as our wills battled for supremacy, but I had already been defeated and the shame turned me from her once more. "You want to know, then I will tell you the hopelessness of it all." I murmured to the fire before turning back to her. "They used raw power at first, burning into our minds and overriding our defenses as if we were children wielding toy axes against veteran warriors. Our kinsmen fell then, clutching at their heads as blood flowed from the ruptured veins within. But I knew I had to stop them. Fighting back the pain, I stumbled forward, Morina at my side." The vision haunted me as I lost focus on the room around me. I saw the whole thing again, laid out in its full terror as my lips described the horror to all.

"When they saw I still defied them, they sent another wave of energy, stopping me in my tracks as Morina attacked. I was nearly driven into darkness, but seeing Morina fight alone tore open a reserve of desperation within me. I forced myself to shunt aside the agony, pushing forward to help my mate as two of the beasts bore her down." I shuddered again as the vourdovra in my mind pounced on Morina and slammed her to the ground as one tried to take her axes and the other tried to remove her impregnable vaarandril helmet. "The other two turned to me, seeing that I was still a threat. With my defenses gone, they changed the form of their attack, dragging before me every nightmare I had suffered in my lifetime, every fear I held within. They exploited my terrors, made them insurmountable until my will retreated before the onslaught. Once they had control of my will, they took control of my mind."

When I did not continue, Korina paced before me. "What did they do!?" She demanded, and was met with silence. "Damn it father!? We have to know!"

My shoulders drooped as the shame smote me. "They made me attack your mother." My whisper could barely be heard. "I can not go back." My tone was as lifeless as I felt inside.

First horror then pity crossed her features. Her eyes went to the floor as she shuddered and turned away for a few moments. Taking a deep breath, she turned back.

"What of the mission? Did you find the chamber, and can we still breech it?" I could not believe she was asking this of me.

Korina was deadly serious, and with a sigh I answered her question. "We found the hollow was filled with salty water. If we breech it, our army will drown unless we move to the upper tunnels until it is drained."

She paced again, her fiery hair barely keeping pace as she whirled first one direction then another. In a kinder voice she continued her interrogation. "Did you notice any limitation on their power? Anything we can use against them?"

I stood aghast, had she not been listening to me? "Korina, there is nothing we can do! We have no soulsmiths, and those few we have with talents are like flailing children against their power!"

Her voice became cold and hard once more. "Father! You know as well as I we cannot turn back! Defeat is not an option! You once told me there was no situation that was hopeless, are you saying now that you are a liar?"

I blinked, the eyes of my kin stared and I could see their knowledge of my former deceit of the humans plainly in their demeanor. I swallowed uncomfortably, wanting to confirm the hopelessness if only to assuage my guilt. Were we really without hope, or was I trying to cover for my inadequacy? I drew in a shaky breath and finally nodded to Korina.

"You are right. We can not turn back and so must once again accomplish the impossible." My mind focused carefully on the vourdovra's attack, critically analyzing their tactics even through the agony of my soul. "I believe their power is limited to what they can see. The first attacks were strongest, as the fiends looked directly at us one by one. For their second attack, they had to wait until all of my defenses had been drained, and they were in close proximity. Both vourdovra had their eyes riveted to me as they used their powers. I would guess that they must be fairly close to use their abilities, and their tactics suggest they prefer ambush over a frontal attack."

Korina smiled encouragingly, and in her eyes was the look of admiration that she had always displayed since childhood. It was the unshakable belief that her father was indomitable, immortal and capable of anything. It was a smile that warmed my soul, giving me hope and faith again. I hoped I could live up to her expectations.

"If we attacked from two directions, we may just have a chance. I suspect the vourdovra believe we are too frightened of them to try a frontal assault. I propose we change our strategy to match that arrogance. Our secondary objective should be the overmind and our primary should now be full assault. The cannons should be able to level their defenses from outside their range of power, however, we will have to be extremely cautious about our crews being ambushed. The vourdovra have exhibited the limited ability to teleport using their mental energies. I do not know the extent of their range for this ability, but that means that there is no safe ground." The lure of the puzzle served to bring me out of the lethargy of despair. My mind raced through the possibilities, evaluating each for validity.

"Once we move our camp, I believe we may be able to reassess our strategy and come up with a feasible plan, but it is vital that all of our troops be schooled on the vourdovra's means of attack. No one should be allowed to wander alone, not even to relieve themselves, for that will open the door for our enemies' control and infiltration. We will reconvene our war council one time cycle after we have moved to this area." I pointed out a large open chamber three levels above where we were.

The vigor that had returned to me seemed to give hope back to our generals, and that we had a plan of action served as a distraction against the despair. They left the Great Hall with a sense of purpose instead of doom, and seeing their ability to cope filled me with pride.

I was about to leave to go to my room where I could wash up when Anton stepped in front of me. His features grim he stared accusingly down on me. His hand rested firmly on the hilt of his sword, and I was grimly reminded the Reaver could not be drawn so quickly from the straps on my back. His gaze darted quickly between the haft of the weapon and where my hands were in anticipation of violence.

"You should have told me how dangerous this assault would be! How could you be so deceitful? I thought dwarves were honorable people!" His words smote my sense of guilt and he watched me wince with every pronouncement. Satisfied he was right, he continued. "We are leaving, and we will take reparation for our trouble from Sorkarak's vaults! If you attempt to stop us, you will have more than the mind-eaters to worry about!"

"You ahre right, Ahnton. I did deceive you in order to gain your support. If zere is ahny fault, it is my own, not my people." He gaped in astonishment at my admission. "You may go if you vish."

His surprise turned instantly into suspicion, as I knew it would. "You'd let us leave just like that? You'd advocate the funds of Sorkarak's vaults without consulting your High Queen?"

"Vat vould be zie point? You vould never make it back to Sorkarak vitout us. So, really I am not endangering any of our people's funds. Vy vould I try to stop you ven our enemies vill do zie job for us ahnd zie distraction might prove to be valuable?" His jaw clenched as the fire of anger lit his countenance.

"You knew this all along didn't you!? You knew we couldn't leave once we got here! You'd planned this from the start!" The sword came halfway out of the sheath as I snatched his wrist to prevent the draw.

"Do not zrow your life avay, Ahnton. Zie only vay out of here is to cooperate vit us or in deaz. I apologize for using you, but know zat zies failing is my own ahnd not zat of my people." I held him still as easily as he might have a child, and he realized just how close he had come to losing his life.

Understanding crept slowly into Anton's gaze as a slow ironic smile spread upon his features. "You really are more human than any dwarf I've ever met. I never thought I'd be deceived and used by one of your race, something I'll never forget. Very well, Dorian, you win this round, and if we live through this, you'll have to buy me a drink when you visit Lodath sometime."

A large smile found its way to my lips. "Vy vait zat long? You should enjoy life vile you cahn lad. I vill share a drink vit you before zie next var council." I let the smile fade instantly as I glanced furtively around. "Oh, ahnd do not tell my kin how human I have become, vill you? It vas hard enough to convince zem zat I vas not a stranger zie first time."

Anton's laughter followed him out the door. "Fear not, my friend. Your secret is safe with me."

Though I had made light of the situation, the comment still bothered me deeply. Had I allowed myself to become too human? My eyes traced the wood grain of the table once more. The torment I had suffered as a slave haunted my thoughts mercilessly. Was I truly a kinsman? Did I have any right to proclaim myself vaarakanan? The answer was too painful to consider, so I lost myself to thoughts of strategy and the impossible task of conquest.

Morina met me at the door to our room, tears streaking her cheeks. "You were right, Dorian. I should not have come." She searched for a confirmation of her pronouncement in my features. Her eyes went to the floor as she held out the amulet. "I put us all in jeopardy because I had the amulet and you did not. I am sure you could have prevented our kinsmen's deaths if you had been protected. I do not think I am as dangerous under control of the enemy as you would be." I silenced the rest of her protests with my lips, and she sagged into my arms as if all the life had drained out of her.

The encounter had hurt us both more deeply than I had imagined. "Hush, my love," I murmured into her ear. "We must both put this behind us if we are to go forward. There is no way that we could have foreseen what was to happen. It was more my fault than yours. I was the one who insisted that you be protected." She looked grateful and nodded. "Morina I am glad that you came. It is good to have you at my side. I do not think I could remain steady without your presence. Just being there for me gives me hope and security in who I am. If it were not for you, I would have lost myself to the darkness long ago."

"None of us knew what was to happen." She repeated, as the haunted look returned almost instantly to her. "What would have happened if you had killed me?"

I drew in a sharp breath. "I really do not wish to think about it. Morina, we are alive, and together still, that is all that matters. What has happened was a lesson we should not forget, but a lesson that has passed. We learn, and we move on. To do otherwise is to let them win."

"Just hold me, my husband, and do not let me go," she breathed into my ear as she drew me tighter to her wiping some of the gore onto her clean clothes.

From the moment I rescued her from the necromancer's tower, Morina had loved me. For eighty-four years she had been steadfast, a constant that had never changed while I brooded over my relationship with Jaguar. How many years had the distant look on my face caused her pain? She knew I had loved the human, yet had accepted me anyway, an honor I scarce deserved. Could I have done the same? I remembered the agony I suffered every time I suspected Jaguar had been with someone else. And though it brought the fires of rage to my soul, I suffered in silence for her, the same way Morina suffered for me. It took by far too many years for her to replace Jaguar in my heart, but it had happened. Even so, I still could not help the memories and the longings that still visited me. Too many times I wondered what it would have been like had Jaguar accepted my proposal.

***

Before I had the chance to blot the thought from my mind, another memory paraded before my mind's eye. We had delivered the malfunctioning elemental control ring to the Eelhold, but the finishing of the deed did not fill me with satisfaction. Instead, the thwarted rage simmered deeply within. Less than three days ago, Jaguar had 'questioned' Iskar, Count Parlfrey's son on the whereabouts of Thornwood Keep. The others mocked my naiveté in believing she merely talked to him as we waited in the hall. My irate refusal to acknowledge her status as a priestess of Inanna was burned into my soul when I found myself outside Iskar's door.

From several paces down the hallway I could hear them; my sensitive ears used to picking up faint vibration differences in underground tunnels had no difficulty hearing their expressions of passion.

"Hey Dorian, you thinking about making it a threesome?" Homer quipped from his place closer to the door.

The halfling realized his mistake a moment too late as he slammed into the stone wall, my fist full of the collar of his shirt. Beside me, Rutger strained to hold my arm with the battle-axe clutched in my left hand.

"Lodath! For pity sake! Put him to sleep before he kills the stupid halfling!" The Ranger yelled through teeth grinding in strain.

We had left for Eelhold shortly thereafter, my companions not waiting for me to regain consciousness. And though we had saved the inhabitants from an unruly water efreet, the knowledge of Jaguar's actions burned within me, stealing any satisfaction I might have held. So great was my inner pain and rage that I wandered into the hills near the hold alone, seeking some solace from the wretched knowledge that I could never be anything more to Jaguar than an occasional lover. Not even the faint resonance of ore-filled mountains could soothe the fire that raged within.

The rotting remains of a forest marked the destructive path of the efreet, and I stopped by a tree stump twice my height. The coppery desert stretched out below, reflecting the emptiness within as I beheld the vastness of the surface realms. Not even the oppressive openness of their world could quench the anguish, and I punched the half-rotted trunk of the tree. Why!? Why was I so foolish to believe Jaguar could be mine? My other knuckles indented themselves into the bark with a crunch that revealed termites had been hard at work. Why had I allowed myself to share kinship with a woman of questionable morals? The knuckles of my right hand connected once more with the force of my frustration.

I knew what she was like! I had no one but myself to blame for the delusion that I could change her. But as a vaarakanan, it could not make a difference in the way I felt. We were a monogamous people by design, and willingly sharing kinship was the bond that melded two souls forever among us, a spiritual as well as chemical bonding process. The universe itself would crumble and fade before a soul-bond would, and I had willingly committed myself to Jaguar. Maybe I was as naive as the others claimed?

Each thought was another blow as my knuckles smeared the deepening indentations in the splintering trunk of the dead tree with my blood. I had trapped myself in a pit that I could not climb out of. Drawn to the flame of Jaguar's candle like a blind moth bent on its own destruction, I could do nothing to change my heart. But, neither could I stop the hurt, the anger that consumed me when I was reminded of her duties as priestess of a goddess of pleasure. Would the pain ever go away? Would my obsession turn to unfulfilled madness? How much better would it have been if I had perished in Mezosilliar when the dark elves first took me captive? Better yet, if they had killed me when they discovered I was spying on their raiding party, I might never have known the despair that I could not warn my kin. But why stop there? I should never have been born! My parents would have been spared the pain of my difference. They would never have been shamed by my need to follow another craft.

The pounding of my fists kept time with the groans of torment that escaped my lips until I was too tired and too full of physical pain to raise my fists again. The sun had climbed high above like a merciless yellow eye spying out secrets in the vast openness. The weariness of traveling all night finally caught up with me, and I sat dejectedly at the base of the rotten stump. I tried to open my pack and get out some rations, but my fingers refused to cooperate as they scabbed over and shook with pain. Fresh blood welled down my arms as I did my best to wrap the damage in my torn spare shirt. Too exhausted to make my way back to the hold, I let my eyes close for a short nap.

The pounding in my head awakened me, and the clank of chains sent a chill of fear through my gut. I would not be a slave again! Despite my resolve, my worst nightmares came in to focus as my vision cleared. Thirty red and black liveried warriors rode on horses or in the wagon next to me. Their hard faces told me of their experience in battle, and the lines that left their marks of cruelty could only belong to mercenaries or sell-swords. Cold unreasoning terror spread through my bones as I felt the heavy iron collar around my neck and followed the thick rings down to shackles on my wrists and ankles. The chain that ran from the collar was fastened with a heavy lock to the base support of the wagon, as I realized there was no escape. The pounding in my head centered on a ticklish crawling sensation that I knew was blood running down the side of my face. 'No! Morakvaar save me!' The words refused to make their way out of my tight throat. How could this happen!? Why!? The questions in my mind were replaced by the visions of torment from my past.

The wagon stopped by a field of tall grasses touched golden by the summer sun. The mercenaries in red and black tabards dragged me down from the wagon, not bothering to allow me to catch my fall. A grunt of pain escaped as my hip took the brunt of the four-foot drop to the hard-packed road. Dust rose all around as the two caravans met.

"By all zie gods, do not give me to zat evil voman!?" I pleaded with the mercenaries as my eyes caught sight of the soldiers in red and gold livery. "I can pay you tvice vat she has offered you!"

"You make a mistake, dwarf. We're not mercenaries, we're bounty hunters, and you're an escaped slave wanted for murder. It's our civic duty to return you to your proper place. What Alfstein does with you after that is none of our business."

"If you are an honorable man, zen slay me now. I vould razer die zan go back. No vun should suffer zie tortures I vill endure if you return me." My hope faded as the human smiled evilly.

"Who said anything about us being 'honorable'?" The others laughed heartily as the dark-haired leader handed over the chain in exchange for three large heavy sacks.

The sun began to sink behind the flat horizon, and another cold chill traveled up my spine and clenched my gut. Where were the hills!? The soldiers must have traveled quite a ways to leave them behind, for even looking back the way we came I could barely make out some irregularity to the south. An icy fist gripped my heart as I realized my companions would not know where to find me. My only hope of rescue from this deepening nightmare began to fade. The options that were left to me were to find a way to escape or die before Lady Alfstein could put the magical collar back around my neck. I struggled with the chains, testing their might against mine as the links began to groan. Light flashed through my skull as one of the guards stilled my efforts with a club matching the lump on the other side of my skull.

The ache in my head deepened the terror that clenched my gut as my eyes focused on the inside of a covered wagon. The chains that ran from my wrists were secured to opposite sides of the buckboard supports, and my ankles to the back. Plush furs cushioned my bare back from the wooden floor as a black-painted fingernail made its way down the side of my face, trailing along my neck before tracing the length of my torso. Terror and loathing warred for control in my mind as nightmares threatened my sanity, and the priestess of the Mistress of Pain laughed in delight. Her dark hair fell freely down her shoulders to partially hide her bare breasts as she leaned over me.

"I've missed you, Dorian. You see, human males just simply have no stamina. They're so boring compared to the long evenings of fun we used to have! In fact, I missed you so much, I had to come all the way out here to meet you." Her voice was full of her unhealthy desires as she seized my head in both of her hands and whispered huskily, "in the name of the mistress I greet you in celebration of your return home."

I wanted to scream, to cry, to lose myself in insanity, but her black painted lips covered mine before the familiar power of evil coursed through me. Like a thunderbolt it resonated through all of my nerves dragging a moan of pain from my throat as the vile demoness drew in my exhalation of agony as if it were ambrosia. She shivered as if in the throes of passion before straddling my hips.

"By the goddess, I missed you!"

I prayed to every deity I had ever heard tell of, human, dwarf, gnomish, elven, even those that were evil I swore undying loyalty if they would but deliver me from this nightmare, but no answer came as the runic collar was locked around my neck once more. Hot tears stained my cheeks as I tried to distance myself from what was being done to my body. The physical agony was nothing compared to the torment of my soul as the mistress of pain whispered of my shame. With the collar to control my will, I was powerless to resist the command to enjoy the priestess' debased rituals to her hell-spawned goddess. The nightmare deepened as her two bodyguard assistants climbed into the wagon at her bidding.

Agony reverberated in every nerve I possessed, dragging me back from the darkness of unconsciousness. The bars of the small cage bit in to my back, shoulders, knees and arms as they tried to find room enough to exist. So great was the pain and the terror that my gut heaved in desperation to vacate the evil that had been wrought upon both mind and body, but there was no solace. Cold sweat beaded upon my brow and ran down my cheeks and nose to darken my beard with moisture. 'Morakvaar how could you let me suffer so!?' My soul cried out to the Maker, pleading release and an end to my tortured existence.

When my gaze cleared of the dark haze, I could see the slaver where she sat upon the bench-board next to where I was imprisoned. Her black eyes traced the outline of my form crushed into the cage that was too small for a hunting hound. My blood stained the furs that still lined the bottom of the wagon and a small pool of it congealed beneath the cage I had been stuffed into. By the deepening shadows dancing across the canvas as the wagon swayed with movement, I could tell I had been unconscious for most of the day. Agony and weariness stole the chill of fear from my gut as I regarded the slaver.

I had two months of freedom, only to be recaptured and sent back to hell. How could the gods be so cruel? My mind froze in despair as I prayed for death again and again, but with the collar I could not take my own life. When night came and the wagon stopped, the slaver had me chained once more as she worshipped her goddess of pain to the tone of my screams. Shuddering in agony, they dragged me from the wagon and chained me to a tree when she had finished.

"Though I am happy that you can return home, Dorian, you must be punished for leaving." Lady Alfstein nodded as her bodyguards began to lash me with glowing whips that struck me down to my soul.

When they tired of that game, they merely pummeled me with their fists until I lost consciousness.

"Dorian." The soft voice finally registered as something beyond my despair, beyond the blackness that had become my mind.

I was a toy again, a plaything for a mistress of pain and my mind shut down to avoid contemplation of my future. A hand touched me and I shuddered as icy fingers gripped my gut. Was it time again already? I could hardly feel the pain of being crammed into a tiny cage so great was the agony that tore through every nerve. I tried to shy away, to avoid the creature that sought my flesh, but I could not even flinch in the tiny box made of bars.

"By the gods! What have they done to you!?" The voice was not that of the slaver and my mind struggled to comprehend that it was not a wishful dream that would lead to more pain.

"Jagvar?" The pitiful voice was hoarse with self-loathing and despair. How could I believe my friends had come for me? I was a slave again and could not allow such hopes.

"Take it easy, Dorian. We'll get you out of there." No, it was just a fanciful dream that ached in my breast.

But warmth flooded through me as I was released from the cage. Gentle hands held me as a mother cradled a fearful child and the healing power began to take the shaking agony from my nerves. Full lips pressed against my brow that was covered in cold sweat as I was gently rocked to soothe my tortured mind.

"Leave him with me and get the rest of the bastards." It was Jaguar's voice, and I prayed I would not awaken from this madness.

The shackles were removed from my wrists and ankles and I wondered what depraved thing would be asked of me. The full lips were pressed to mine as more healing warmth flooded through my system bringing with it a greater measure of awareness. Jaguar's eyes were closed as she kissed me, holding me to her.

"Morakvaar, dorsava sie nie tolak." Her dark brow furrowed, as she looked at me puzzled.

"In the common trader's tongue, Dorian. I don't understand you."

"You... you are real? I am not dreaming?" Though she had healed quite a bit, I still shook in fever and pain.

In answer, she held me to her breast and let me feel the beat of her heart as she kissed my forehead once more. "I can't believe anyone could be so cruel as to do those things." She murmured as she removed the instruments of torture that had been left still attached to me.

"Zank you." Was all I could manage for some time. "Please, zies collar... take it off." I lapsed back into fevered dreams for a few more moments as more healing warmth passed over me.

When my awareness returned, Jaguar's brow was beaded with perspiration, and she held me to her beneath the furs. I managed a weak smile before I faded into exhaustion. I awoke cradled in Jaguar's arms, and my head upon her chest. I would have wept in relief if it had been in my nature. She felt me stir, and kissed my forehead as she caressed my back and sides. Her dark skin upon my reddish-bronze was medicine for my soul, and I smiled gratefully up at her. No longer feeling the collar upon my neck, I breathed deeply the breath of freedom.

"I knew you vult come for me. I ahm in your debt."

"I cannot believe that a woman could be so cruel as to do the things to you that I had seen. Was she the one who misused you as a slave?"

I clenched my jaw and nodded, "yes, she is zie vun. I vult rahzer hahve died zahn hahve gone zrew zaht ahgain." I turned from her, shuddering with the memory.

She drew herself up behind me, melding her long and sinuous form against mine. The contact of her skin was a stimulation I was not sure I was ready for. Her breasts pressed into my spine in an awareness of her sexuality that aroused me as she kissed my shoulder. She knew I needed something to *block out the memory of what had been done to me, and I could but comply to fulfill the longing in my heart. She made passionate love to me for most of the rest of the night, and by morning; the time I had spent with the Slaver was but a distant nightmare.*

Before I drifted off in her arms, I had to ask, "Jahgvar, I zink you know zaht I love you. I vhant to ahsk your clahn if it vult be okay for you to be my hearz mate, but I zink I vult vahnt to know if you vult vahnt zies first?"

She looked at me and smiled as she kissed me. "That's the sweetest thing I've heard, Dorian, but, I'm not ready to settle down just yet."

I looked at her somewhat sleepily and asked, "zen you vill let me know ven you ahre?"

Her melodic laughter was not mocking, but amused, and I fell asleep in her arms once more. When Jaguar stirred near mid-morning I woke sleepily.

"Rest more, Dorian, you will need your strength." She said as she kissed me.

Sighing in contentment, I did her bidding, but the mid-afternoon heat woke me in the baking insides of the covered wagon. My clothes had been torn beyond repair as I picked up the pieces that had been scattered in the corners of the wagon. I looked at their tattered remains and wondered what I was going to do. While I pondered my predicament, Liathrain climbed into the back of the wagon and I pulled the fur back up.

"I think this might work." She regarded me from beneath silver brows as she spoke her native tongue.

She dumped off a uniform from one of the Slaver's guards, and sat down on one of the bench-boards. Modesty was unknown amongst her people and mine, but I had lived among humans too long.

"It took us quite a while to figure out what had happened to you." I wanted to tell her to leave while I dressed, but would she think I was ungrateful? "You should have told someone where you were going." Liathrain's rebuke irritated me even as I realized it expressed her concern. How ironic that a dark one would care what happened to me.

I pulled the large tunic over my head, as Liathrain watched, making me a little nervous. It just fit around my neck and shoulders, and I folded the sleeves back at wrist-length. Pulling the tunic back off, I used Liathrain's dagger to cut the sleeves.

"I needed to be alone for a while." I told her in the language of the zarakanan.

The tunic hung about knee length to me, and I could at least stand up with some modesty intact. Turning from her, I pulled on the trousers and measured them to mid-calf level.

"Jaguar?" Liathrain's question was intrusive, and I resented it.

Practically everyone knew about my personal life! It was not so bad that they knew, but it was a source of constant amusement to them. I cut the trouser legs and pulled on my boots over the tattered edges.

"Of course, Jaguar." I looked at Liathrain, and for some strange reason, I thought maybe she could help me with my dilemma. "What do you think she meant by she was not ready? And, why would she laugh at me when I asked her to tell me when she was?"

Liathrain gave me a blank stare. "What are you talking about?"

Did I really want the zarak to know? "Never mind. It is not important." I sighed, and slipped on my chain shirt over the tunic.

Buckling on my weapon's belt with the short sword, I gathered my axe, shield and helmet. Liathrain climbed down out of the wagon first, and I followed shortly after. I was pondering the idea of asking Lodath about what Jaguar had said when my eyes rested on the Slaver where she was chained to the tree. Rage flared within me, and I tightened my grip on the axe. Seeing nothing but red, I strode directly to her with the intention of burying my axe in her skull. I was vaguely aware of Jaguar's voice, but the meaning of the words did not reach me until later.

"No, Lodath, he needs to do this. I saw what she did to him."

I drew back my axe, ready to strike her head from her body as Lady Alfstein wailed in fear. Muscles tensed for the blow, and I began the step forward that would carry the momentum through the weapon.

"Dorian! Please! This child is yours!" She screamed as the blade clove through the air to shave a few hairs from her head before embedding itself in the tree trunk.

She had begun to show her pregnancy already, but I had assumed it was from some other source. Why would Morakvaar punish me so? Why did the child have to be mine? I left the axe embedded in the tree and walked away in stunned horror. The Lady Slaver's uncontrollable sobs faded behind me. It was not bad enough that the depraved woman had tortured me for years, but for her to bear my child was more than I could take! I drew out my short sword, feeling its beautifully balanced weight in my hands as I crested the hill. Halfway down the other side, a tree lie where it had fallen many years ago. I sat upon its rotted corpse; a fitting place for what I knew must be done.

Jaguar's rejection was a fresh wound to my soul, and the knowledge of my kinship to a Slaver had pushed me over the edge. With slow and deliberate movements, I removed my chain shirt and placed it on the ground at my feet. I looked at the glittering blade of the sword for a few moments, marveling again at the vaarandril, and thought of my father. He would have been devastated to know what I had become. I was an outsider, a bastard child that would live without a clan. All I could see was the horrified face of Thorun when I told him what had become of me and of my half-human child. It would have been my duty, my honor to be the hearth-mate of the one who bore my children, but I could never marry the slaver woman. I would rather die. I turned the point of the vaarandril sword to my chest and tensed my arms in preparation for the final strike. But a tingling sensation washed over me, bringing darkness in its wake.

When I awoke, I was bound once more, and cursed Lodath for his arcane arts. My soul was already dead; there was no reason for the body to continue. Why could Lodath not see that?

"Release me at once!" I demanded of him in my native tongue, knowing he understood me.

"You know I will not do that. I cannot let you kill yourself, Dorian. Did you not once tell me that your people needed help? Who is to help them if you die this senseless death?"

"I am dead already. Dead to my people, dead to my soul. The only thing that remains is the shell that lives on long after it should be gone." Suicide really was not one of the things that Morakvaar would accept. If I was not already, I would be doomed if I continued with the course I set. *"But, you are right. It is shameful that I would seek death at my own hands, but what do I have left to me?"*

"Give me your word that you will not attempt to kill yourself, and I will let you go."

I nodded, after all, the world was a dangerous place, and it need not be my own hand that struck the deathblow. *"You have my word that I will not strike my own death."*

***

The memory of those days was a turning point in my life, one in which I no longer cared whether I lived or died. At every opportune moment I sought a reckless death in battle only to be thwarted time and again. But Jaguar had also conceived and the birth of our child, Panther brought me hope again as I strove to be the type of father Jaguar wanted me to be. It was a blissful time in my life when I forgot that I was a kinsman and lived as the father of a half-human child. Jaguar and I spent many long days together with Panther, an illusion of family that I had craved for so long.

"Dorian?" Morina's green eyes were full of concern as I realized my face was skewed with my inner agony.

"I am fine, my love. We need to get moving and I think we both need another trip to the showers." The blood had soaked into her clothes and had smeared into her hair and on her face as she sniffed and nodded.

Though my past plagued me anew with the fresh reminder the vourdovra had dragged from my memories, I allowed Morina's love to comfort my pain. Her presence was a balm upon the wounds, healing them and making me whole. She was the reason I lived, my hope, and my love. For her I would do or be anything.

Chapter 15

Voorahaarin Geradain (Waterborne Terrors)

With the camp resettled in the upper tunnels, I stalked the passage that led back to the hollow. The heavy pack full of explosive powders weighed down my steps, but we still tried for stealth. At the sweaty outcrop of rock, I halted the team.

'I will scout ahead. Wait here for a tenth time cycle then complete the mission.' Tovar's second, Haalan looked at me as if I had grown three heads when I gave the hand signals.

"Are you insane!?" He whispered despite our need for silence.

"No, I stand the best chance of surviving an attack from our enemies. If we send scouts, they could fall prey to the vourdovra's mind control. I want you to set up a buddy watch, so that each kinsman not only watches for enemies, but for his buddy." I whispered back in irritation.

"But what about you? What is to stop them from taking control of your mind?" The prospect clearly daunted Haalan, but then the light of understanding crept into his eyes. "You are not coming back, are you?"

"Someone has to draw them off. Good luck, Haalan." He stared back with a look of half sorrow and half admiration.

"Good luck, Lord Dorian."

Keeping to the sides of the tunnel, I crept as quietly as my platemaille would allow. Vourdovra had lousy hearing, but their heat sensing vision was infinitely sharper than ours. If Morina knew my true intention to lead away the enemy to give the engineers a chance to blow a hole in the chamber, she never would have let me out of her sight. The absence of the Tashor was at once a relief and a feeling of being exposed, but it was questionable whether the six that survived would ever recover their minds. Their blank stares filled me with rage at our enemies, another grudge the vourdovra would answer for.

Righteous fury filled me as I caught sight of the chamber where we had been ambushed. How dare they make me attack my mate!? Removing my pack, I set it beside the dripping crack in the wall for Haalan to recover once I had distracted our enemies. My fingers tightened on the Reaver as I clenched my jaw. The floor of the chamber was dark with the blood of my kin and the vourdovra as the blades of my great-axe began to glow white-blue. For a minute, I was puzzled. Was the Reaver reacting to the presence of my enemies? Were there zarakanan about? As soon as I concentrated on something other than my anger, the blades darkened once more. I was missing some clue, but instead of tracing back, I became suddenly aware of other presences nearby.

The amulet that hung securely in my armor began to burn with heat as the hair on my arms rose in the aftermath of the power that washed over me. "Alright you brain-sucking bastards, come get some of this!" I whispered as the Reaver lit up the chamber once more. Feigning injury, I dropped the axe and clutched my helmet as if in the throes of agony. Making sure my gauntlets clutched the haft as I twitched, I fell heavily on the weapon. Cautiously three of the four-legged monstrosities slipped through the crevasse in the back of the chamber. Their tentacles darted through the air as if tasting it for the presence of other enemies. Their brain-like bodies quivered in uncertainty as the eyes set in their shoulders watched me intently.

The first one shot a bone-tipped tentacle ringing off my helmet as it approached. A hiss of frustration echoed through the cave as I tensed for action. A clawed prehensile paw scraped my ear as it snatched at my chinstrap. Rolling over onto my back, I brought the blades of the Reaver around. Bright fire made the creature close its eyes in reflex just before the blades burned through its body leaving a smell reminiscent of fried eggs. Gore showered me as the creature's entrails and brain-matter splashed out of the gash like the innards of a ripe melon. Continuing the roll put my feet beneath me as I used the momentum to charge the remaining two. The smell of my burning flesh wafted out of my armor as the amulet warded off their attacks, but adrenaline consumed the pain as rage flowed through my swing.

Both the vourdovra leapt back, but only one of them made it through the small gap. The other rebounded off its fellow and the wall, falling back onto the blades of my axe as the creature was torn in half with a messy splat and the cracking sound of its spine. The two pieces of the beast landed on either side of me as more bloody tissue covered my armor. Before the last one could disappear, I was through the fissure, hot on its heels. Its claws scrabbled on the rock ahead and it fled down the tunnel as if chased by the Destroyer himself. It barreled through a gathering of six more of the vile beasts, scattering them like a flock of sheep as the panic spread.

With growing glee, I realized that although the vourdovra appeared agile, they had absolutely no stamina. After the first few minutes of the chase where they outdistanced me, it was obvious I was gaining ground. In seconds I was on them, swinging as I rushed forward. With every swipe of bluish fire, a vourdovra screamed in agony as it went down, its tentacles writhing in death like some beached ocean creature. Too quickly, it was over, and I stood among the bodies of my enemies, drinking in my victory with elated satisfaction.

Searching their pouches and packs revealed nothing useful besides some gold and silver coins. Disappointed, I turned to rejoin the demolition team when instinct warned me of danger. From the north I picked up the small sparks that signified the firing of muscles in a cold-blooded creature, and I squinted to get a better look. Hundreds of the sparks lit the darkness, and I began to back out the way I came. Turning, I saw the same coming towards me from the south. They had surrounded me, but they did not look like vourdovra. Straight ahead and to the left of me I saw another opening, and I sprinted for it as I finally identified my new assailants as human. But why were they cold, and why would they help the vourdovra?

Twisting through the smaller tunnel, I kept looking for ways to further impede my pursuit. The humans were gaining ground with their longer legs, as the tunnel was not small enough to slow them. Were they under mind control, or had something more sinister happened to them? The memory of the daemon fish slaves came clearly to my mind. They were covered in the slime of the fish that served to subvert their will and change them into water-dwelling creatures. Did the vourdovra do something similar? I shuddered at the thought. Deep water held enough terror for me without the prospect of having to spend the rest of my days enslaved and worse yet, forced to live in water!

My footsteps echoed down the tunnels as I strove to outdistance the humans, but I might as well have not even tried. Their longer strides quickly closed the gap between us, and I was forced to turn and fight or be struck down from behind. The throng surged forward like a pack of hungry dogs, snapping with jaws of steel blades. The ring of my axe and armor as they shed blows reverberated in my bones as I backed slowly away. At least the narrow tunnels kept them from surrounding me as I let the Song of the Mother guide my feet backwards. For every three blades I caught on the sweep, four more slid beneath my guard to spark against my armor. Though none of them scored a fatal blow, I soon felt the weight of pain slowing my reactions. A hundred minor wounds added my blood to the gore that dripped down my armor as I parried and struck and parried again.

Even my stubborn nature soon realized I was doomed against such an overwhelming force. Jumping back, I gripped the Reaver in both hands.

"Sarlik Doria!" The fire leaped from the blades, burning a hole through the ranks of the cold humans in a raging inferno.

The stench of burned flesh was more like rotted corpses thrown on a fire than that of living beings that had been cut down, and I felt a chill shiver down my spine as I fled. The humans faltered in their eerie silence and the amulet around my neck burned hotter as if they were part vourdovra. By some inaudible singular command they all chased after me once more.

It was a futile race as my sense of the Mother's Song told me that I was rapidly approaching the center of Vouroussan. The ring of a sword against my backplate spun me on my heels as I backpedaled once more. Ducking, dodging, and parrying I made my way steadily backwards, steadily towards my doom. 'Morakvaar, lead my people to victory.' I prayed as I sensed the tunnel opening behind me. If the humans surrounded me, I was done for.

In a hellish blue-white fireball I sent the Reaver's power through them once more, gaining a few precious seconds to assess my path into Vouroussan. As I spun and ran into the open cavern, I was nearly struck motionless by the sight before me. Thousands of vourdovra went about their business, in the city, some standing on their hind legs to use their prehensile forepaws, and some wandering around on all fours. Pillars of stone housed the gods only knew what kind of businesses the vourdovra thrived on. Hundreds of arched openings dotted the stone, but all of it was dead and cold to my sight. What had happened to the living stones? How had they managed to divert the magma flows far enough away to make this a cold slice of hell?

A troop of vourdovra 'soldiers' moved ahead to intercept me. Their bodies were encased in hardened leather, leaving their front shoulders bare enough to allow them vision. Their tentacles protruded from the slotted open sides and their forepaws held weapons of all makes and descriptions that I assumed they had stolen from their victims. They looked for all the world like headless turtles, but ones with deadly purpose. The revelation that they even had soldiers was a frightening one, and one that I had been totally unprepared for.

With a final burst of speed, I commanded the last of the rage-fire into the group of soldiers before smashing through their line. Even armed and armored their fighting prowess was little better than a lad into his first whiskers. Two strokes and a quick thrust had me through the unit and out the other side as I sprinted for the large stone building ahead of me. A part of my mind whispered to give up, and that there was no escape, but I would not give up! If I could do enough damage to help my kin towards victory, then by the gods, that was what I would do! I hewed down soldier and civilian alike as I passed, leaving a trail of screaming and dying vourdovra behind me.

Ahead of me were two armed guards, and behind me, the humans' weapons scraped on my armor. A quick feint and a downstroke removed the guard on my right as a solid kick to the armored body took down the other. But as I spun to face the humans, a longsword pierced through the chainmaille in my armpit, stabbing partially through my chest and embedding itself in my shoulder blade. My right arm went instantly numb as I wielded the Reaver in my left. The strain of the weapon's weight was beginning to tell on me even through my magically enhanced strength. The human backed a pace to avoid the blades as I kicked open the door behind me and backed over the threshold to throttle the amount of enemies I faced. Instead of following up on my retreat, the humans snatched the door shut and locked it from the outside. The slam of the stone bolt was like the knell of doom as the flash of pain from my wound finally smote my brain.

In a daze I looked around quickly, but could detect no movement or enemies. Had the vourdovra intentionally driven me to this spot? Was I to be entombed in this chamber forever? Trying to take a deep breath, I was instantly reminded of the near fatal wound. A moan of agony escaped my lips as my legs sagged beneath me. Dropping the Reaver with a loud clatter, I grabbed at the wall to support my weight as my head swam in nausea. Slowly I levered my back to the wall and slid down to sit on the cold floor. A few minutes of fumbling and I found the vial in my pouch.

The disgusting taste barely registered as I swallowed half of the contents and waited for its healing power to restore me enough to be able to remove the sword. The hilt still dangled from the crease in my armor as blood flowed down both the inside and out of my cuirass. A thick trail of red followed me from the door to where I sat as it cooled slowly from red to purple to blue. The wound closed over the sword, making me wish I did not have to pull it out again, but I could feel the blade pushing against my lungs as I breathed. Trying to be careful, I braced myself and gripped the blade as close to my skin as I could reach. The blade screamed out across my rib bones, tearing another howl of agony from my lips as I struggled not to black out.

My hand shook with pain so badly; I barely managed to get the lip of the vial to my mouth as I swallowed the rest of the potion. A convulsion of pain flung the small glass container from my fingers to smash into a thousand fragments on the ground next to me as wracking coughs seized my chest in an iron fist. Bloody froth dribbled from my lips into my beard and I wondered which would win, the healing potion or the puncture I had just made in my lung tissue while pulling the sword out? Darkness spared me the debate as another spasm took my awareness from me.

A thick stench of rotting flesh permeated my nostrils, making my throat close to avoid breathing it. Coughing spasms gripped me to expel the vile atmosphere, and tears leaked from my eyes in the strain, blurring my vision. Cold chills filled my gut as I realized the movement I sensed was less than a pace away. In the fit of hacking, I snatched up the Reaver and spun away from a large fist that slammed into the ground where I had lain. The scrape and rattle of my armor as I scrambled away was accompanied by a squishy splat, then another.

Instinct prickled my spine, and I dove away once more as another impossibly huge fist glanced across my back, giving me an extra shove. Sticky slime dripped from my shoulders where the thing had touched me, and the stench was incredible. It was worse than the smell of the slaughterhouses I had passed in the surface cities, viler than the rotting pits of the necromancer. So intense was the odor that it soon made me dizzy as I scrambled to avoid the thing that attacked me. Even the fishmongers could not compare to the decayed sickness that emanated from the creature.

With my feet beneath me once more, I managed to avoid the clumsy rush and face my enemy. The sight of the monster was even worse than the smell. It stood nearly three times my height, filling the chamber from floor to ceiling as its glowing red eyes seemed riveted to me in single minded purpose. Vaguely humanoid, its form seemed made entirely of rotting vourdovra brain tissue that constantly leaked pussy fluids and slime. Fighting the bile that threatened my throat, I dodged another resounding blow that shook the stone beneath my feet.

Before the monster could withdraw its sickly arm, I swung the Reaver. The blades sizzled through its flesh as if it was butter, and the lack of resistance surprised me enough to prevent a speedy recovery. Rancid gasses spewed from the wound and greenish-gray fluid spurted onto my armor, the smell of which made me retch. The other fist slammed into my chest armor, pinning me to the wall for a hundredth time cycle. The cuirass buckled under the onslaught, but managed to keep me from being instantly pulverized. The snapping of my ribs filled my ears before the fist receded and I fell to my knees. The dented breastplate restricted my lungs, but at least it held my fractured ribs in place as I struggled to catch my breath.

Pushing off with hands and feet, I rolled away from another blow as the next swing impacted inches from my head. My great-axe bit deeply into the creature's shoulder, nearly parting the arm as another gout of gas and slime fountained outward. Though the monster made no sound, in the distance I could hear the thrashing of some great beast as it splashed around in a pool of water. Was I that near the inner chamber? Was this the sanctum we had planned on breeching? Hacking and choking, I felt the dizzy nausea begin to overwhelm my resistance. Before I could recover, two slimy hands snatched me up, pinning my arms to my sides. The strength of the creature was astounding, overwhelming my magically enhanced power as if I were naught but an infant.

The giant lifted me from my feet, and carried me in front of it like a prize towards the thrashing in the water. The putrescent odor surrounded me, choked the air from my lungs and nearly drove me into unconsciousness, but I struggled hard to maintain my awareness. In the tunnel ahead, tentacles writhed forth from the water like a nest of snakes as the beast that held me adjusted its grip to my upper arms. The stress of my own weight and that of my armor on my shoulders was painful on my partially healed wound, and I felt the weak tissue tearing along my side. My jaw ached as I struggled not to voice the agony I felt as the slimy tentacles reached out to touch me. Like the fingers of a blind man, they ran up and down my armor, across my face and shoulders leaving the foul sticky stench all over me.

One of them poked painfully into my reopened sore as if wanting to worm into my chest, and panic seized me. I kicked at the writhing mass, but the monster held me firm as it continued forward and the tentacle seemed to lick hungrily at my wound.

Other tentacles wrapped around both arms and legs, helping propel the vile giant forward and nearly pulling me from its grasp. Ahead the tunnel opened into a vast cavern lit by a putrid greenish light that emanated from the depths of the brine lake. Moving beneath the surface, I saw an enormous shadow that pushed aside the glowing waters as it shot more tentacles to encompass the creature that held me. Several vourdovra in what appeared to be ceremonial decorations lined the edge of the water as they worshipped the leviathan within the depths. One of the cursed mind-eaters approached me, its height almost half again that of the others as it stood on its hind legs. An extra set of tentacles writhed along its sides, and the chill in my blood settled in my bones as I wondered what they were for.

The appendages from the water that already wound tightly around my arms and legs gripped harder as the giant was absorbed back into the tangled mass. The odd vourdovra with the extra tentacles approached me. Kicking and struggling harder I made my bid for freedom as I tried to use the Reaver in my trapped left hand. The tentacle that licked at my wound shifted downward as I could feel the hot fire of some unnamable organ that shot out from the tip and wrapped around my intestines. My scream of agony echoed along the walls of the open chamber, as the vourdovra's tentacles seemed to shiver in delight. The slightest movement brought raging fire to my gut as my struggles weakened and ceased altogether.

The large mind-eater removed my weapons' belt before searching me with tentacles and paws. The language of the Deep Realms traders came from the creature, echoing down its feeding tentacle in a gross parody of speech. "So at last Dorian Mytharia falls before us. How is it that we could sense you before but cannot now?"

The beast made the mistake of coming too close to my left hand in its search, and I flipped the blade around to dig into its shoulder. The creature's eye burst out of the crushed socket and hung from a bloody thread halfway down its torso. A howling scream echoed through its appendage as it jumped back.

"Monster! Two legged fiend!" It paused in its curses and I could feel the buildup of mental energy like static in the air as it healed itself. "I should kill you myself!" Its feeder tentacle slid up under the back of my helm resting uncomfortably on the base of my neck.

"Morakvaar arak en vaar!" I breathed as cold sweat ran down the side of my face and I swallowed the lump that tried to choke me.

"Ah!" The vourdovra's expressed its satisfaction as the tentacle withdrew slightly to wrap around the chain of the amulet. "So this is your secret!" Its clawed hands snapped the chain loose, leaving a red indentation on my neck where it had been.

Instantly, the mental energies of the vourdovra around me invaded my mind in a hellish cacophony of thoughts and images. "Much better."

The tentacle returned to the base of my neck as I grit my teeth for the end. The bone tip pierced the skin and began to burrow slowly through my skull. The echoes of my pain seemed to please the vile creature as my arms and legs twitched involuntarily. Knowing the creature could have ended the agony in an instant did not help, as it preferred the slow torture it put me through.

A massive wave of energy vibrated through the water to wash over everything in the chamber and the vourdovra withdrew its tentacle before it had finished burrowing through my skull. Though the painful drill through my cranium had not been finished, my head pounded with the agony. The mind-eater turned from me to face the pool, carrying out some inaudible conversation with the unspeakable abomination that I was sure was their overmind. Three vourdovra approached and one of them reached for the Reaver. The creature exploded outward in a shower of lightning as the axe repelled its vile touch. The other two jumped back with questioning looks towards their leader.

Another silent conversation ensued before one of the remaining vourdovra removed its ceremonial robe and secreted some sort of slime on it. With the cloth wrapped protectively around its hands it took hold of the weapon as the tentacle that held my arm clamped down hard enough to bend my armor. Stubbornly, I kept hold of the haft, fighting against their efforts to disarm me. A spark of energy ran through my mind, stunning my nerves for the instant it took to wrest the Reaver from my grasp. Without the reassuring presence of the weapon, I felt exposed in a way I could not have imagined.

The 'leader' approached me once more, speaking through its tentacle. "Though I would savor tasting your mind, you have been reserved for a higher fate." Did the monster sound jealous? "The Elder will consume you itself, a fate you do not deserve."

"Believe me, I would much rather it was you." The thought of being dragged down into the hellish water only to be consumed by some amorphous horror appealed even less than having my brain sucked out a hole in the back of my skull. My comment seemed to anger the vourdovra, though I doubt I could have imagined why.

The tentacles lifted me again, and began to drag me into the water. If only Lodath could see this he would understand my unreasoning fear of the depths! As I approached the water, I could not help the surge of panic that flooded through me. Though it pained me to know I was giving the vourdovra their enjoyment of my terror, I was beyond reason. The instinctive fear of deep water that my people shared lived within me. I struggled and thrashed in my desperation. Near mad with panic, I lashed out however I could, kicking and biting to no avail. The depths of the water loomed below like a hellish nightmare. Beneath the surface I could see the form of a huge mass of brain tissue, and the tentacles that held me came from it. My panic-fogged mind barely registered that at last I beheld the vourdovra's overmind.

My boots had barely touched the water when an explosion rocked the chamber's foundation. Several secondary explosions convinced me that my kinsmen had finished their job, and somehow without the knowledge of the overmind. Tremors ran through the stone, and I felt the imminent quake that would follow. The water began to drain out of the lake, as I was dragged below the surface. Struggling frantically, I tried to break free but the tentacles of the underwater horror gripped me like ropes of iron. I fought without thinking, without knowledge, without reason. My terror had blinded me to all else but the sensation of being dragged under the water to my death. It seemed forever before the darkness took my panic from me, and I felt another tentacle wrap tightly around my neck before blacking out.

Chapter 16

Orudin (Blessed Ones)

When I came to it was in the spasms of choking. Saltwater and bile vacated both my gut and my lungs, but each wracking cough brought fire through my chest and shoulder. It sparked up my spine to explode in my brain as if the pounding headache were not enough. Cold stone pressed against my face made colder by the disgusting slime that covered both the floor and me. Was I still alive? The aching fire that raced through my nerves convinced me I had not yet returned to the Underhalls or gone to Vooraduum.

Trying to escape the bile and slime, I barely managed to lift my head a fraction of an inch before being stopped by the ring of stone against my helm. The vibration of the metal penetrated into my head like a spear thrust, setting my teeth on edge as I groaned in pain. A dizzy haze of nausea radiated outward from the back of my helmet, and my consciousness faded for a while.

When I awoke, I was determined to discover the extent of my injuries. It seemed like time cycles had passed before I managed to worm my right arm free. The movement tore against the scab before I was able to confirm my fear. The back of my helmet had been crushed inward and my hand was covered in blood as I brought it back before my eyes. The heavy stone that lay across my left shoulder did not shift as I strained against it.

Exhaustion stole over me both mentally and physically. It would be so easy to give in, to sleep forever. I longed for the peace of the Underhalls, but the vision of Morina's face held me steady. How could I think of leaving her behind? For her sake I reassessed my situation.

The chamber I was in looked to be the one we had originally planned to place the charges, but it was full of debris and fallen stones. Worm-like eel creatures writhed in their death throes all around me, one less than a hand's breadth from my face, and I wondered what they were. Two large slabs of rock pinned me even as they served to ward off much of the other fallen debris. One of them was angled off my pauldrons and the other across my back above the top of my hips. The coldness of the slime and water made it hard to see any more details of my surroundings, and my weary mind found it difficult to care.

Something still restricted my breathing, though, and I remembered the tentacle that had wrapped around my neck just prior to blacking out. Tearing the vile thing from my throat, I contemplated calling to the Reaver. Immediately I suppressed the thought. If I invoked the weapon and it was still held by the vourdovra, it would lead them right to me. Would my kin think to search for me? They probably thought I was dead, but at least I was on the trail for the secondary assault team. If our people had not already passed, I might be able to get their attention.

Time dragged on as the ache in my head and shoulder worsened, but the absence of feeling in my spine or legs began to worry me greatly. Had the rock snapped my back? If my kinsmen found me and removed the stone, would I die? Though Waradain's healing power was great, I doubted if he could repair an injured spine. Would I be crippled?

Voices! My eyes opened, but I could scarce remember closing them. Bare blue-gray feet the color of shale surrounded me, and ice gripped my gut. Had the Kinsmen of Shadow come for me? Attached to the feet was plated armor made of stone that seemed as flexible as a second skin. Above the armor was a bluish-gray face with white hair and beard. Unnerving silver eyes stared back at me. They were the color of quicksilver and reflected my gaze like a mirror. A shiver of recognition passed through me as I realized I gazed upon legend come to life. Orudin! Memories of childhood stories paraded through my mind as well as the reminder of why they had passed from history to legend. Shame burned on my cheeks as I remembered it was Gorain's folly that had alienated us from their race.

One of the bluish-gray skinned dwarves reached right through the stone that settled on my back as if it were not there. When he touched me, I felt the healing warmth flood through me before the stone seemed to lighten. Several hands gripped me, pulling me through the rock as if through air. Laying me on a pallet, they carried me through the solid stone like it was little more than a thick mist. Even though they had healed me, I still felt nothing from my legs or feet. The power had not touched the wound on my left shoulder, and I began to suspect they had no intention of returning me to my kin.

If I could convince them somehow to join us, we would have a much better chance at defeating the vourdovra! Orudin had soulsmiths among their number! My hope died in its infancy. The orudin carried me into a small round stone chamber devoid of everything save a ledge that they set me upon. Several of them regarded me silently before one by one they disappeared through the wall. The agony returned to me tenfold, stealing my strength and sapping my will. How could Morakvaar's chosen be so cruel as to let me suffer alone? Why had they brought me to this place? On the verge of shock from trauma and cold, I shivered endlessly, igniting the fires of pain in my wounds.

Unable to sleep, my weariness grew with the raging tide of agony. Why would they just leave me? It made no sense to rescue me from the cave-in only to let me die alone in a small empty stone chamber unless they meant it to be my tomb. I thought of Morina as sorrow squeezed my chest. Would I ever get to see her again? The picture of her weeping inconsolably tore at my heart. To know I was lost, but not to know if I was dead would be a terrible burden for her. Would she be able to move on? She would be better off without me, but would she ever see that? The aching of my soul kept time with the throbbing of my wounds as I waited for time uncounted on my captors' return.

Exhaustion had nearly claimed victory over my pain as my eyes fluttered open at a faint sound. One of the Orudin stepped out of the wall and into the chamber. With a gesture of his hand, the floor rose up to form a stool upon which he sat and regarded me silently.

After a few moments, I felt I needed to say something. "Greetings, cousin." The hoarse words reflected how badly I felt, but I tried to be friendly against all hope.

"We are no kin of yours." The flat tone betrayed neither anger nor disdain, and I wondered whether he was simply stating a fact or he was being hostile.

As if my words had been some cue, his hands moved over my armor before he slid it through my body without undoing the straps. I gaped in astonishment for a few moments, reminded anew of their legendary powers. The cuirass clattered to the floor where he dropped it as he examined my shoulder with a slight frown.

"There is much damage here, but I think we can ease your pain for a time." Putting words to action, his hands passed over my wound as the warmth of the spell penetrated to my bones, stilling the shivers as I sighed in relief. For the first time a faint smile touched his lips as he bent close with a conspiratorial whisper. "Personally I think our people should join you in ridding this place of the vourdovra. But, unfortunately, the damage you have done to the gem fields is irreparable. I am afraid there will be no mercy for you." He leaned back as if he had not meant to be kind.

"You are orudin?" He could see that I already knew.

"I am surprised your people remember, but you are a Kinsman of the Blood, the keepers of history. I suppose I should not be surprised even though we had been careful not to have any contact for close to eight thousand years." He clicked his tongue and shook his head, "I am afraid there is nothing I can do for your back injury until after the trial. I have heard it said that you are Gorain returned, is this so?" He passed a hand over my helmet before removing it as well.

This was not the time I wanted to be thought of as Gorain.

"So they tell me, but I know who I am. I am Dorian, son of Thorun, nothing more. I found Gorain's weapon, the Reaver, and that is all."

He looked at me with raised brows, "You mean you do not believe in prophecy?" His surprise turned to an instant frown as he examined the back of my head. "The gods themselves must have saved you from such a close call with a vourdovra. It is fortunate that neither wound is fatal. How can you not believe there is a divine hand in your fate?"

"I cannot deny that Morakvaar has some interest in my fate." The reminder of my pact with the Maker was all too plain. "Though I am unsure about prophecy, I must admit the parallel of my life to Gorain's is too close to be coincidence." Since he made me think of it, my life was uncannily like Gorain's.

"You were held in slavery then?" The warmth of his healing spells took away the worst of my headache as the shaking began to recede.

"Not as long as Gorain, nor by the zaraks, but I had been enslaved," I grudgingly admitted.

"And you lost your soul?"

I narrowed my eyes, wondering what the orudin was getting at. "In a manner of speaking, I suppose that could be true." It frightened me to think that I was nothing more than an extension of Gorain's madness.

"Morakvaar gave you back your soul, and you led your people against the zarakanan and the enemies of our gods?"

"What do you want from me!? To admit that I am Gorain? What difference would that make?" His questions made me doubt myself, and I became angry.

"If you stand before our people, they will know you. No matter that you call yourself. Dorian, or Gorain, they will know you."

The chills kept creeping up and down my spine as he spoke and I started to wish he had not come to heal me. "We were never at war with your people. You were honored among my kinsmen, why would it make a difference?"

He smiled widely as if I was the brunt of some unknown joke. "You misunderstand. We too have a prophecy that the return of Gorain will usher in a new golden age for our people. It has just been so long since we stopped hoping Gorain would return."

My mouth dried out as I stared at him in shock. It was as if my mind had gone completely numb, and I could think of nothing to say.

"My kin have witnessed our conversation and have heard Harrakuli's testimony. But the damage your kinsmen have done to our food source has left us with little future prospects. We must find another field that has been blessed by Dormakkaar." The sorrow was a heavy weight on his words, and as he finished speaking, a ring of orudin entered from the walls.

"Harrakuli believes beyond a shadow of a doubt that he is Gorain." My eyes found the orudin Elder; his white beard meticulously combed and braided was looped back upon itself and still brushed the floor.

"Gorain he may be, but his people are still responsible for the disaster. Their reckless demolition has destroyed our crops and doomed us to starvation! I say he and all his kind should pay for what they have done!" The angry one was a bit younger than the Elder, his braided beard not quite as long as mine.

The Elder shook his head before fixing the impetuous one with a grim stare. "And have two races become extinct in a generation? No, the price is too high." The ancient turned his gaze to me. "But perhaps a bargain can be struck? We will help you in your war, Gorain, but in return, we will need your people's help to feed us."

"Honored one, I am no longer the leader of our people, but I may have some influence upon my heir. If it is within my power to persuade Korina to agree, then it will be done." The Elder nodded as if he was aware of the passage of power.

"Your word will have to do for now." He turned to the first orudin that had healed me. "You may repair all of his injuries. I am satisfied with the conclusion of our conversation." His silver eyes bore into mine once more. "The anger between our races has long passed, Gorain and we realize we are less now without our cousins. You are welcome among us and we will share a meal together even though our rations are meager." His expression softened somewhat and he smiled ever so slightly. "Harrakuli has anguished enough over your return. It is time we satisfied the Clan First."

Harrakuli! No wonder I had thought the name familiar! That she had appeared as a Kinswoman of the Blood disguised her completely! As my mind raced through the history of Gorain and Harrakuli, the priest healed my spine and the numbness receded from my legs. The orudin helped me to stand as my feet were still a bit unsteady, and two younger lads came to escort me to a bathing chamber after the cleric removed the rest of my armor. The maille sat in a dejected pile of dented and abused metal, and for a moment I grieved for its loss. Since she had become High Queen, Korina had claim to my vaarandril suit that I had forged by my own hand, but I could not begrudge her the armor and hoped it would serve her well. The twisted steel that had been forged by me in the lands above was my only set for twenty years before completing my masterwork and it was a loss I would regret for some time.

The warm water felt good as it washed the grime and blood from me. I let the memory of sparring with Harrakulit play through my mind. An ironic smile tugged at my lips. No wonder she had matched my skill! As an immortal, she had all the time in the world to study the art of fighting. She had probably not even fought to her full potential either, sparing me embarrassment in front of my people. Her intent curiosity finally made sense to me, and the scars she had traced on my back must have served to confirm my identity to her. I wanted to blame my memories on the Reaver, but I knew that was no longer true.

Coldness gripped my gut as I wondered what would happen between us. The reason for the alienation of the orudin had been Gorain's affair with the Clan First. Even though I tried to suppress the foreign memories, they came as plainly as any others revealing a blue-gray-skinned Harrakuli in my arms. Her fingers traced the thick hair of my chest as her gold eyes invited my lips to hers. The desire raged through me as if I had shared kinship with her, and I was shocked at my own ability to shunt aside my feelings for Morina. It was as if we had already shared a soul-bond, and I had to wonder just how much of Gorain's essence I had inherited. What would happen if Harrakuli came to me? Would I have the strength to refuse her?

Swallowing uncomfortably, I finished washing out my gambeson and smallclothes before being escorted to another small cave. Laid out on the stone bed was a set of deep blue clothes embroidered in gold and vaarandril, clothes worthy of my ancestor, Gorain. Axe wielding warriors chased stylized dragons around the cuffs, up the ridge of the arm, around the neck, down the front and around the bottom edge of the tunic. Across the back was a dragon rising from a nest of gems. It was a poetic piece of artwork, one I was loath to soil by wearing, but there were no other clothes besides my wet ones.

The round table in the center of the room held a stargem that lit the chamber with a comfortable glow, accenting the flickering light of the magma vent opposite the bed. The warmth soothed the last of the aches from me, but did nothing to still my troubled mind. As I sat in the woodroot chair, the only non-stone furnishing, I thought carefully over the events that led up to my meeting with the orudin. The cold returned to my bones when I realized that since uniting my will with the soul in the Reaver, it had been strangely quiescent. The fact that it responded to my anger instead of zarakanan enemies sent a shiver down my spine. Gorian's soul must have melded with mine! Yet, I felt no different. My heart and mind were still that of Dorian, or were they? More memories came clearly to me from that other life. What had I done? Had that feeling of his presence filling a hole in my soul been mere coincidence?

The epiphany shook through my bones, reverberating through every nerve and vein. I *was* Gorain! My reason could no longer deny the facts, much as I wished to. My failing all along was not because I was Gorain's heir, but because I was Gorain himself. His tormented soul was my own! Would

I suffer the same fate, or would I be able to redeem myself in the Maker's eyes? At least I had spared the remainder of the zarakanan, but was that enough difference to save me from damnation? It had been my friendship with Liathrain that had allowed me to overcome my experiences and my instinctual hatred of her race. My heart grieved to know I owed her so much and yet that friendship had ended in a fight to the death.

"Lord Gorain, it is time we left." One of the young orudin brought me out of my reverie.

The two lads took me through a series of tunnels connected only by their ability to move through solid stone. Even if I had wanted to leave their company, there was no way I could retrace my path on my own. The hall they led me to was half full of orudin as they sat around a series of long tables whose ends faced a singular table that ran the width of the large cavern. Behind the 'High Table' sat the orudin Elder, and he gestured for me to take up the seat on his right hand. All conversation ceased like a wave as word of my presence spread and all attention turned my way.

With the uncomfortable memory of Gorain's indiscretion coloring my cheeks, I made my way over to the Elder. My discomfort was made complete when Harrakuli herself came to sit at my right side. She stared long at me, seeking out the soul-bond she had shared with Gorain, and finding a faint echo within me. No wonder she had attracted me back in Sorkarak! Thinking desperately of Morina, I swallowed back the longing that filled me. I would not dishonor my hearth-mate a second time!

As if reading my thoughts, anguish twisted her features. "Welcome back to the land of the living, Gorain. We... I have waited eight thousand years for your return." The sad longing struck deeply into my soul, whispering of ages of devotion only to be rejected in the end. She drew in a deep breath to steady her voice before continuing. "I must apologize for the former deception, but you must understand we had to be certain you were the one."

Torn between my former life and the one I now led, I could not allow myself to waver in my resolution. "I can not imagine your pain or your devotion, Harrakuli, but I must remind you that I am not the Gorain you knew. I have lived this life as Dorian, and though I may have Gorain's memories and perhaps his soul, I am not he."

Her eyes left mine to wander over the crowd that listened intently. "No, I suppose you are not the same, but you will someday be forced to acknowledge who you are. No amount of lifetimes will change that, but even one experience can change a kinsman." Her eyes returned to mine. "Very well, Dorian, your name makes little difference to the soul within." Again I felt the urgent pull of the soul-bond that Gorain had shared with her, and I fought the need to take her into my arms.

How could I refuse her? Sweat beaded on my brow as I forced my thoughts to focus on Morina. A group of orudin entered the chamber carrying bowls full of red and blue gems. They placed one of the large bowls at intervals along the table, reminding me of the orudin's culinary requirements. A lass of about twelve years brought in a tray of roast crawler and voras stuffed with fenrai. The aroma set my mouth to watering as my stomach growled longingly. I popped one of the stuffed mushrooms in my mouth immediately, savoring its spicy flavor. It surprised me how good the cooking was, considering the orudin ate neither meat nor vegetable that we knew of. Perhaps we were wrong? Yet there was no meat on the other tables. The blue-gray kinsmen around me took portions of the gemstones, and their noisy mastication echoed through the hall. With a heavy conscience I remembered the accusation that we had destroyed their fields and I hoped they would be able to find another cavern where the living stones bore the fruit of gems.

The same young lass refilled my mug with rich dark ale as the meal drew to a close. The main body of the orudin begged their leave to go about their business as the elders drew closer around the table. In their mugs was a thick red liquid that looked like distilled rubies or a watery wine paste. Was that the blood of the living stones?

The Elder to my left began the council by having me relate my encounters with the vourdovra and our intentions in the assault.

"Unfortunately, Gorain... Dorian, the creature you describe as the overmind did not die in the explosion. It was able to survive outside its watery environs, but we do not know for how long." The Elder took another sip of his mug before continuing. "Your assault team was faced by its fury, overwhelming a large number of your people and some humans. It turned them back on your main force, and your High Queen ordered a retreat rather than fight her own." The corners of my lips turned down as I listened grimly to his tale. How could we fight them? "The good news, if you can call it that, is that the vourdovra are busy trying to repair their underground lake rather than mustering to attack your kin."

With a sense of urgency I seized upon the plan that formed in my head. "We must destroy the overmind before they can return it to the pool. It must take a tremendous amount of its power to sustain itself in the air. That and the control it exerts over its people must pretty well consume all of its concentration and much of its energy." Horror stopped my words as I realized what I was saying. "By the gods we must act quickly if we are to save those who have been taken over!"

The council members around me nodded in agreement, but no ideas were forthcoming. "Even we are susceptible to the mental abilities of the vourdovra, Dorian. How can we attack them without losing the majority of our forces?"

In frustration I spoke my thoughts aloud. "Without protection there is no way we can face them." The loss of my amulet was a grievous blow to our ability to fight, let alone the absence of the Reaver.

"Protection?"

Realizing I had spoken aloud, I explained about the talisman. "Yes. In my travels, I found an amulet that protected the wearer from the powers of the mind. My companions and I never found anyone who could duplicate it. The one I had was taken from me by the vourdovra with six tentacles. They also took the Reaver. Would it be vain to hope that you had found anything similar?"

The elders conversed amongst themselves for a time, their murmurs filling the hall.

"No," eventually the Elder spoke, "but we have found a type of stone that confuses them. Its song is deadly if you hold it for too long. It is the mineral that opened the Starrift. A large chunk of it lies at the bottom of the Rift. We have found that its song cannot penetrate through heavy metals like gold and lead, but carrying it into battle would be suicide."

Another discussion ensued as to whether or not the stone would actually turn the vourdovra's powers, but my mind had already seized upon the idea. "Can you mount this stone to a shield faced with lead?"

All eyes turned to me as if I had suddenly started foaming at the mouth. "It would kill you." The Elder finally spoke their misgivings.

"Then it is a death I will gladly seek if it saves the lives of our kin. How long will I have once I take up the device?"

The Elder looked to Harrakuli who had paled almost to the point of fainting. Seeing the Elder's distraction, the priest answered my question.

"No more than a full day cycle. It is possible that you may be healed of its destructive song, but Harrakuli is the only one among us who possesses such power."

"So even if I put down the shield in that time, you are telling me I will die anyway unless Harrakuli heals me?" He nodded as both our eyes turned to the Clan First.

"Though the minions of hell stand between us, Dorian, I will find and heal you." Her hoarse whisper was full of emotion that whispered through the faint soul-bond and I longed to hold her to me as Gorain once had.

"Regardless of your ability to find me, I must insist that I take on this task. If it ends in my death, so be it, but remember me in song."

"Very well, Dorian. You will have your shield on the morrow and we will join your army." With the Elder's pronouncement, our meeting became a discussion of tactics until I could barely keep my eyes open.

The strain of my injuries and the healing sapped all of my energy too quickly for my liking, but there was nothing I could do. Another yawn split my face as I struggled to stay focused.

"Enough, Dorian. I will show you to your room." Harrakuli interrupted, and by the look in her eye, I wished I could have seen myself there. Instead I nodded sleepily and allowed her to drag me stumbling through the walls.

The room was like the one in which I had dressed save there were tapestries lining the walls. The stone bed bore a thick sheepskin with the wool still on it, and a nightstand formed from the wall held a stargem. In a corner to one side of the central table stood my armor arrayed upon a stand as if I were wearing it. The metal was smooth and the dents and scrapes completely gone. It looked as if it had been newly forged, and I gaped in astonishment as I ran my finger along its cool surface.

"Stone is not the only thing we can shape." Harrakuli's explanation accented the fact that she wore a second skin of vaarandril rather than stone.

Her hand was still upon my arm as if it were the most natural place for it to be, and the vision of her sharing kinship with Gorain filled my senses. Ruthlessly I suppressed the thoughts, focusing on my love for Morina. Nothing would come between my hearth-mate and I again! Seeing my eyes upon her hand, Harrakuli released me with a deep painful sigh. She sat down at the table, staring with remorse into the stargem.

"I could wish that you remembered me as Gorain. It has been a long and lonely life since Ungir died." Her eyes turned to me as a crystal tear rolled down her cheek. "You were the only light in those long years of darkness, and I have waited all this time for your return only to find you taken by another. How can Morakvaar be so cruel?"

For a thousand reasons I echoed her question, but within me I knew the Maker had a plan. Another yawn stole my chain of thought as the sheepskin bed called to me. Would it have been impolite to ask the Clan First to leave? The next yawn overbalanced me as the weariness stole my ability to remain stable. A worried frown crossed Harrakuli's face for a moment, before realization dawned on her.

"I am sorry, Dorian. I presumed too much. Take my bed, and I will return in the first time cycle." This was her home?

Embarrassed, I stammered an apology. "I could not put you out of your home. Please, if you lend me a bedroll I will sleep on the floor.

She stood and came over to where I waited. Sorrow filled her countenance as she looked at me.

"I could not trust myself if I stayed here with you. I loved Gorain with all my soul, and I know that you are a part of him, the same, yet different. You look so much like him." She tried to stop her hand from reaching out to me, and I tried to hold back Gorain's memories.

We were both unsuccessful, and I found myself in her arms, kissing her passionately as Gorain would have. This was not right! I was Dorian, not Gorain. I loved Morina, and would not hurt her! Harrakuli saw my dilemma as I pulled away from her.

"I think I will go now." She said bitterly as she disappeared through the stone wall.

Sighing in relief, I also felt a touch of disappointment. Gorain's memories taunted me, but I was Dorian and comforted myself with that fact. Taking off the elaborate tunic and breeches, I crawled onto the bed. A light skin from a couple of crawlers sufficed for a blanket, and I was soon sound asleep.

***

The tentacles wrapped more tightly around me, squeezing the breath from my lungs before dragging me under the surface of the roiling ocean. Out of the depths came terrifying nightmarish shapes. Daemons with the bodies of eels and bodiless brains with glowing eyes paraded before me. I opened my mouth to scream for help, but inhaled salt-water instead. Tentacles lashed me like the slaver's whip, and unnamable horrors brushed against my skin. I kept thinking I would drown, but instead the terror went on. One of the shapeless horrors loomed before me and as it turned towards me it bore the face of the Lady Slaver as it wrapped its tentacles around me. It grinned in glee at its torment of me. My heart leaped into my throat as I saw a smaller horror approach with a cross between my features and the slaver's.

"Hello, father." It said.

***

"NO!!!" Trying to get my bearings, I sat up as my heart raced in my chest like a stampeding bull. Putting my head in my hands, I tried to erase the vision of the half-breed child. At least the real one had been stillborn. Its half vaarakanan half-human face had sickened me to the core knowing of its conception with Lady Alfstein. I do not think I could have lived if the child survived. Lodath and Rutger had convinced me that it was not worth killing the woman after the child had been born dead, though she deserved far worse than death for what she had done to me and quite possibly others since. But killing her might have led to war and the deaths of thousands of innocents. It was a price I had grudgingly paid. Setting her free and unharmed was the hardest task that had ever been set before me save trying to deny my love for Jaguar.

I found myself pondering what had happened those many years ago. The more I thought about it, the more I realized that it could have been a trick. Neither Rutger, nor Lodath had really been enthused about my desire to kill the woman, though they certainly understood my reasons. The petitions that were sent to the local Count for her return were just shy of threatening as apparently she had ingratiated herself with Duke Heinrick. If the child had truly died, would they have been so adamant about me not killing the slaver? Would my friends have tricked me into believing the child was stillborn when it truly was not? Why else would they protect the mother against me? Was there really that much fear of Duke Heinrick's retribution?

When I returned to our army, I was determined to ask Lodath the truth. Knowing that Jaguar had borne a child that he knew about and had not told me was bad enough. The thought gave me pause to consider just what sort of debased individual I was. No vaarakanan, in or out of our history had known more than two kinswomen, and even they were thought of in unkind terms. What sort of tales would mothers tell their children about me? Would the tale of my meeting with the orudin be truthful? At least I had not fallen to temptation with Harrakuli!

That thought brought back to me Gorain's memories, and I felt almost as guilty as if I had done those things myself. How could I ever face Morina again? I tried to sleep, but Gorain's memories, and the freshness of my nightmare lent me no rest. When Harrakuli returned in the first cycle, I was sitting at the table.

Our eyes met, and I had to turn away. The longing I had to be with her filled me with as much guilt as if I had been already.

"You look like you have not slept."

"I dreamt of being dragged under the water by the overmind again. After that, I could not sleep." It was only half the truth.

"We are ready to journey to where your army is camped as soon as you are."

I nodded and got up from the table. Harrakuli handed me my clothes and gambeson. The look in her eyes spoke volumes, and I shook my head. Dressing in front of her, I felt awkward, but managed without too much embarrassment. She helped me buckle on my armor, and took my arm to lead me back to where her people waited.

Chapter 17

Krazak Vaar (Death of the Soul)

Two warriors paced the route of their watch in front of where we emerged from the stone wall and for a moment, I thought they were going to faint as their features drained of all color. If they had not recognized me in front of the large war party of blue-gray dwarves they may have thought the Kinsmen of Shadow had joined our enemies' side. As recognition returned some color to their faces, they looked more closely at the increasing number of kinsmen that crossed into the cavern.

"Tell her Majesty Korina that I have returned with allies" With a quick nod, one of the sentries scurried off as if he had seen a ghost.

Following his trail, we caught the attention of my kinsmen. They lined the approach and stared in wonder at the orudin that followed behind me. The despair that had settled in lines upon their faces lifted into hopeful determination. With a rather unqueenly hug, Korina met me halfway through the camp as she ran into my arms.

"I should never listen to anyone telling me you are dead until they show me your lifeless and mutilated body!" Her voice held an hysterical pitch displaying both elation and great worry.

"It is good to see you too!" The orudin laughed with me.

Her gaze rested on the blue-gray dwarves behind me as she gaped in astonishment, "are they orudin?"

"Yes, they have come to aid us in the war." If I had told her that Morakvaar himself had come to join our ranks I do not think she would have been less surprised.

"I do not know how you manage it, father. Every time we think you are dead, you come back with more hope for our people."

I looked through the crowd of troops, but there was one face I did not see. "Where is your mother?"

Instantly, Korina's expression went from wonder to dark despair, and I felt an icy hand grip my heart. "She went mad when she heard you had not returned with the demolition team. They told her that you drew off the ambush, and left the way clear for them to complete their task. She would not be consoled, and went to find you." The coldness spread through my veins the more I listened. "We caught up with her at the gates of Vouroussan, but it was too late. The vourdovra had taken possession of her mind, and brought her inside the gates before we could rescue her. Their defenses drove us back while our main force attacked them from below." A tear ran from Korina's eye as she struggled to relay the events to me. "Our forces met with a hideous creature whose powers were unimaginable, a creature made of pure mental tissue and energy. Its power overwhelmed our army, and turned our people against each other. I ordered the remaining warriors to retreat so that we did not have to fight our own." Her breath came in ragged gasps as she fought to maintain her composure.

"It is all right, Korina. You did the best you could." I felt colder than the winter snow on the mountains in the overlands.

With my arm around Korina's shoulders we went back to the conjured fortress, and I allowed Harrakuli to go over the battle plan with her and our generals while I thought about what to do. The ache in my soul left no doubt that I would have to find Morina. I knew exactly where she would be, but could I make it there before she met with some horrible fate? My mind refused to contemplate the possibility that she was dead to me. She had to be alive, I could feel her soul-bond! To save her I knew I would have to do battle with the vourdovra with six tentacles. Even if I had to slay the overmind alone, I would win her back! But without the amulet or the Reaver, I could not be certain of making it that far. The only thing left to me was the shield with the death-stone.

A sense of urgency filled me with icy blood as I left the gathering and sought out the orudin who bore the lead-lined chest. Beseeching him for the contents, I might have gained the item, but Harrakuli had guessed my intent and met me there.

"You will have to wait until our plans are complete. If you leave with the shield, not only will you die, but your people will be slaughtered by the vourdovra." She tried to make me see reason, but I ignored her and asked for it anyway. The orudin refused to give it to me at Harrakuli's insistence.

"By the time our army is ready, it will be too late for Morina! I cannot wait here any longer for you or for anyone if I am to save her! You know what they will do to her!" I could not help the break in my voice as agony filled my soul. My beautiful hearth-mate, my life, my love, how could I wait a moment longer?

"And then we will lose you both!" Harrakuli grabbed me by the shoulders and shook me. "Dorian! She is dead already!"

"No! You only say that so there will be no reason for me to refuse you!" She looked at me in shock, and then turned away in shame. "There is still a chance! There has to be! I will find her, with or without the shield! I must, do you not understand!? I love *her* with all of my soul!" Tears streamed down my face. I could no longer focus on Harrakuli, but I knew she had turned away from me.

"You will never know how much I understand. When Gorain's soul was taken by the Reaver..." she could not continue, but I had no sympathy for her.

Was she right about Morina? No! My mind froze at the concept. Morina was NOT dead! I could still feel her life though it was faint. She could not be dead! She could not leave me alone; I would not let her! Turning from Harrakuli as if in capitulation, I went back to the fortress and in to my room to gather my spare axe. Though it was nothing like the Reaver, it still hummed with power as the runes beaten in to its surface glowed with an angry red light. It was there that Kormak met me, his head drooped in shame for succumbing to the vourdovra's power, but at least he had survived. With more than a little apprehension he watched as I hefted the axe that had served me for decades before I found the Reaver.

"Going after her is suicide." His voice held no emotion.

I looked him coldly in the eye. "And this matters to me? Without Morina, I have nothing to live for."

He picked up his axe and shield, as he smiled grimly. "Well, to death then?" Kormak had reason enough to save Morina and I could not deny him the chance to save his cousin even though the thought of his loss grieved me.

We left Lodath's conjured keep only to find a troop of soldiers led by Korina outside the gate. Their grim faces held a touch of sorrow as they surrounded us with weapons bared.

"Father, do not do this! I need you to lead the assault on Vouroussan." Her pleas fell on deaf ears.

"Korina, your mother will die if I do not rescue her! Do you not care for your own mother?"

"She is dead already! If you go, you will only join her!" She turned to her guard. "Restrain him!"

"If you delay me now, your mother will surely die! Do not make me fight my own kin!" I readied my axe. Nothing could keep me from Morina's side, not even the blood of my own kinsmen. "Korina, I can still feel her soul. There is still hope!"

The guards hesitated as Korina cried out in grief. "Father, please! You know that they will kill her rather than let you recover her. She is already lost to us and you expect me to let you go to your death as well? Father, I want revenge as badly as you do, but if you go now, all that will be lost!"

"Morina is alive! She may even now be suffering horrible tortures of the mind! I have to save her, Korina even if it is through the bodies of my kin! She is my life, and I can not bear the thought of living if she is gone!" Hefting the great-axe, I advanced upon the guard as they backed uncertainly.

With determination, I strode slowly through their midst as they reluctantly parted, but not a one dared reach for me. Kormak followed in my wake as Korina shed bitter tears of frustration and fear for my safety. Believing she was seeing the last of me, she fell to her knees and smote her breast in grief. Perhaps she was right, for if I found Morina dead, I would not return.

Stalking towards the chamber where I had been trapped beneath the stones, I detected movement ahead of us. Holding up my hand for Kormak to halt, I snuck forward only to find Harrakuli waiting for us. In her hands she held the chest that contained the shield, and behind her was the bulk of the orudin forces.

"If you must go now, then we are ready. We will travel in the rock, and come upon them from below. There are things we can do in that way to help. Korina's army is also readying for battle, and will follow as soon as they can be mobilized. Take the shield, Dorian, and may Duumakarzon guide your way." She used the ancient word for the Lord of Sacred Knowledge.

Looking into my eyes, she opened the chest as her pain smote my heart. Before my hand touched the shield, I could feel the stone's discordant song. It was like a searing agony to my nerves, but if it would lead me to victory, I would gladly endure its song of death. So great was the stone's power that it warped the Mother's Song around me, changing it into a horrible parody of life. It sang of decay and warped mutation, and I had never known fear of an object more than I felt for that stone. But my need was greater than my fear as I settled the straps upon my right arm and prepared to leave.

Kormak stared at the shield in horror as he knelt before me, and I could tell he feared it even more than I did. "My Lord, let me take the shield. It is my duty to protect and die before you. If you must take this evil thing, then let me bear the brunt of its death."

His bare features reminded me of his oath, and though I did not want his blood on my hands, I really had no choice. With a heavy conscience I handed him the shield. "Very well, Kormak. But stay close. If the stone is death, then it will take us both. May the orudin witness your bravery and bring word back to our people to absolve your family." Several of the orudin warriors nodded and Kormak smiled sadly.

Harrakuli looked as if she were going to say something to me, but thought better of it as she gave the signal to her people. To our astonishment, Kormak and I watched as the orudin descended into the stone beneath their feet and disappeared from sight. When Kormak's wide eyes regarded me; I shrugged and motioned for him to precede me along the tunnel. Long before we reached the ruined chamber, the stench of death wafted up the winding cave. Cautiously, we peered around the bend. Choking back the bile that rose in my throat, I turned away from the bloody scene. Kormak was not so hardened, and his shoulders heaved as he vacated his gut. Placing a gauntlet upon his backplate in sympathy, I looked back towards the tunnel leading to the chamber to determine if our enemies were near.

The cavern floor was littered with the bodies of both our kin and the human soldiers. Congealed blood covered the walls, the floor and the other bodies, as they lay askew in the poses of death. Kinsman fought kinsman and human as weapons were embedded in flesh and bone. My soul ached to know their sorrow, and fire grew within my breast. The open eyes of a kinsman stared in horror as death took him, another kinsman's axe buried to the haft in his chestplate. Bending over him, I closed his eyes before I noticed the pool of blood beneath his helm.

The cursed vourdovra had come through the tunnel after the massacre. Not even sparing the dignity of the dead they had feasted upon their brains. Congealed blood dripped sloppily from the hole burrowed in the back of his helmet through his skull. Kormak stared at the hole after he recovered his composure, and retched once more. Gently, I set the kinsman's head back down as the rage built within me. Every last one of the dead bled from a similar hole. It was as if the massacre was not enough for them, but they had to defile our dead with their vile feeding habits just for spite!

Cold chills ran up and down my spine as I thought of Morina. Through the soul-bond I could feel her fear and loathing increase a hundred fold. What were they doing to her!? With a greater sense of urgency I gripped Kormak's arm.

"We must get moving!" My harsh whisper helped bring some measure of control back to his features as he stood.

As we moved towards the chamber I began to feel the effects of the song of death that hummed around us. It was akin to the time I had spent too long working in the summer sun without my tunic, for my skin felt as if it were burning. Was the stone the same power as the sun? It had, after all, fallen from the heavens to create the Starrift. Could our kin ever harness such energy for their own use? Shaking my head, I concentrated on the task at hand. Was the stone able to make the mind wander or was I passing into delirium because of its effects?

The sounds of stonework echoed through the tunnel from up ahead, and we slowed even further to mask our movements. The ringing of hammers, chisels and the scrape of stone spoke of the work being done to repair the chamber we had destroyed. Kormak nodded in agreement as I exchanged a glance with him. There was no doubt that our enemies lie just around the next bend.

In the ruined chamber was a group of close to a hundred of our kin. Their blank stares spoke of the vourdovra's mind control as they went about rebuilding the wall with stone and mortar lined with bitumen. Their gaunt features and the dark circles around their eyes spoke of the vourdovra's abuse of them. They were past exhaustion and looked as if they had not slept or ate since the assault four days ago. Nearer to us was a small group of four of our despised enemies as they supervised the repairs. On the other side of the chamber near the fissure where they had first attacked, stood several more vourdovra that appeared to be concentrating on maintaining control.

Unreasoning red rage filled me, something I had previously associated only with the Reaver, but I knew it was now a part of me. Gorain's anger filled me with righteous wrath at the abuse of my kin. With a howl of fury I charged from our vantagepoint directly into the group of four vourdovra. Kormak followed tight on my heels as I split one of the vile beasts in half with my great-axe before it recovered from its surprise. The other three attempted to focus their power on us, but as Kormak turned the shield towards them, they howled in pain. Their bodies shook with agony and I stepped forward putting them out of their misery.

The kinsmen in the room stopped their labors instantly and turned towards us with deadly purpose.

"Kormak, we must get through them without doing them any harm!" But I was at a loss as to how to accomplish this as our kin began to surround us and we fended off their blows, and then an idea struck me. "Duck behind your shield, and I will put my shoulder to your back. I think I can push us through without doing too much damage."

Clenching his jaw, he did as I asked, and I fended off a couple more blows as I put my magically enhanced strength behind him. Like a ploughshare through an unbroken field, we went through the mass of our own kin, tossing them aside with little more than bruises to show. Though I strained in the press, the magical strength lent to me by the belt around my waist kept us moving. The ring of several blows deflected off my armor, and I blocked several more from hitting the both of us as Kormak concentrated on keeping his feet. As soon as we passed between our kin and the controlling vourdovra, they blinked as if awakening in the first cycle of the day and stared around themselves in confusion. The shield had broken their mind control!

Digging in to my reserves, I pushed harder, trying to get to our enemies more swiftly. As the last kinsman was pushed aside, I snarled at the vourdovra that stared at us in shock. A couple of them kept their wits and attempted to use their mental energies towards us only to be foiled by the death-stone. As we reached them, the front ranks of the beasts began to writhe in agony from the horrendous song of the stone. The rear ranks panicked as we began to slaughter them like sheep, and they ran from us in stark terror. Watching their retreat I saw the occasional vourdovra be sucked into the stone below as the orudin attacked. Our kin surrounded us in relief, gratefully cheering our victory and their freedom though they were exhausted.

"Lord Dorian, we will gladly take up arms and follow you!" A kinsman of clan Gordain offered and was echoed by many others.

"No, my kin. Your enslavement to the vourdovra has left you weak and in need of rest. Please see to your needs, for I am sure there will be plenty of time to rejoin our troops before our campaigns are finished. The army will follow soon enough." Though disappointed, I could see that many of them were struggling just to keep standing.

Kormak and I climbed over the rubble to the edge of the opening that once held the lake of salt-water, leaving our weary kin behind.

"What happened to the humans?" Kormak voiced the question that puzzled me as well.

"I do not know, but I fear it may be connected with the second ambush I faced." A chill ran down my spine as I remembered the ranks of silent cold humans that attacked me.

Kormak shuddered, not wanting to ask. Instead, he slung the shield on his back and searched for hand and footholds to climb the repaired section of the wall. The bowl-like edifice was cloaked in darkness, as the greenish glow from before had somehow been connected with the slimy water. Only a small pool of it remained at the bottom of the basin, but it was obvious it was beginning to fill up again. Above us the sides of the basin were smooth, running almost vertically to the lip. The rhythmic sounds of some vile ritual echoed through the vast cavern from the dry platform of the inner sanctum, and I shuddered to think what sort of worship the vourdovra indulged in.

Setting my axe down, I pondered the question of how we were to scale the wall. Even with my gauntlets off, my fingers could find no purchase. Taking off my pack, I rummaged around for my pitons and hammer. Just as I pulled the first piton out, a rope dropped down from a hand's breadth under the ledge. With a wry smile, I remembered the orudin as I put my pack back on and slung my axe through its straps. Sweat poured down inside my armor as I climbed up to the ledge just below the line of the inner sanctum. Kormak scrabbled over the edge as the sounds from the vourdovra were joined with screams of agony and death.

Our eyes could not believe the bloody orgy that met us as we swung up into the inner sanctum. Twenty vourdovra moved about in the synchronous patterns of some blasphemous dance of death. Within this outer circle of crazed worshippers, ten more of the abominations stood on their hind legs as their tentacles wrapped securely around the bodies of their victims. Their clawed hand-like paws held the heads of seven of our kin and three humans as their feeding tentacles pulsed in rhythm with the movements. The screams of horror and pain came from our kin, filling me with blinding rage. In the center of the gathering was the overmind, sagging without the support of its watery home, and in desperate need of sustenance as it sunk four of its tentacles into the brain-bodies of four vourdovra that writhed in what appeared to be ecstasy. The hums of the four that were being consumed by their overmind were those of longing fulfilled as they died.

The flash of my axe and the sickening thud of its passing made me aware that I had crossed the chamber and attacked. Another glance at my dying kin stole the small amount of rationality I had left. The runes inscribed on my blades left fiery trails of red light behind as it burned through limbs and tissue. On the periphery of my consciousness I saw some of the vourdovra be sucked down into the stones below them signifying the orudin's attack. Claws rebounded off the blades of my axe, some breaking on impact, and some impaling themselves on the half-moon edges. Shorn limbs bounced off my armor as the crunch of bones severed them from joints or smashed through the long centers. Gore rained in a red tide of blood as Kormak and I hacked our way towards the overmind.

Out of the corner of my eye I saw a troop of vourdovra soldiers bearing down on us from the tunnel I had been carried through by the slimy golem.

"Kormak! Enemies to the right! Back to back!" As the soldiers approached, he moved to fight at my back.

The brunt of the charge met the fury of my great-axe as it passed through the body of their leader. Sparks rang from the iron bars that reinforced the haft between my hands as the sword struck it. The soldiers swarmed around us like a wave breaking upon a lone stony island. Swords and spears angled in like a forest of steel each leaf a messenger of death. It was impossible to stop them all, and the ring of blades on my armor filled my ears even as they added my blood to the gore that covered me from head to toe. My two-handed axe wove back and forth, hooking weapons, punching forward through the leather armor of the vourdovra, cleaving through flesh and bone, and parrying the impossible storm of weapons.

Like all storms, though, the rain of steel lessened and finally broke as the bodies piled beneath my feet. At my back, Kormak parried a spear with his shield, cleaving its owner through the center of its brain-like tissue in a messy shower of grayish-red tissue. A sword sliced in to my left while a spear flashed on my right before homing in. The blades of my axe met the sword one-handed as I sidestepped the spear and grabbed the haft. The look of surprise was permanently frozen in the wide eyes of the beast as my axe parted its shoulders down the middle, the vertebrae barely slowing its progress through its chest cavity and its brain-matter. Not waiting for the vourdovra to fall, I followed the swing back around, showering blood and entrails through the air. The vourdovra with the sword was so busy watching the axe that he did not notice the spear in my right hand aimed for his chest.

The point punched through the leather armor on both sides as blood fountained out the two wounds. The vourdovra doubled over and fell at my feet as the storm ended. A heap of dead and dying monsters surrounded us as Kormak and I exchanged triumphant smiles even as weariness crept into my bones. His armor was a little less scored, the shield having kept more of our enemies' weapons at bay, but he still bore the marks of battle.

The overmind was nowhere to be seen as we climbed over our fallen foes to the ring of our kin. Bile rose in my throat as I saw a kinsman staring blankly into space. Blood and fluid streamed down his bare back from the hole in the base of his skull. Grayish-yellow tissue trailed for a short way down his neck to his shoulders as if it had been pulled out hastily.

"Morakvaar arak do vaar." The benediction seemed lame, but I would not let him suffer.

With a heavy heart, I used my dagger to end his life as Kormak choked back his need to retch. Another kinsman was on his knees screaming in pain as he held the back of his head. Blood and fluids leaked through his fingers, and he struggled to push the bloody tissue back in, his voice hoarse with his continuing agony. His eyes focused on me for but a moment.

"Please help me!" Were the last words he spoke as he collapsed onto the stone floor his face frozen in pain for all eternity.

The others had already perished, their faces twisted with the horror of their deaths, and the urgency to find my hearth-mate pressed upon my soul. The sense of Morina's presence had intensified and I knew I was close to finding her. Noise and movement from the lip of the former lake spun us on our heels as we prepared to meet more of our enemies. The familiar crest of the dragon-helm sent a wave of relief through me as Korina swung up onto the ledge followed by dozens of our kin.

"Our army is behind me, Father. Lead on." She was red-faced and out of breath with her effort to catch up, but her eyes spoke of determination.

The pride and love in my heart must have shone in my gaze as I nodded for she smiled back before turning to give orders. When her back was turned, I steeled myself against the burning nausea I felt growing within me. The death-song of the stone ate at my insides as if cooking them slowly and its destructive harmonies resonated in my bones. Kormak looked nearly as ill as I felt, but he turned and led the way out the tunnel towards the central square of Vouroussan. We both knew that death crept through our bodies and that even if we triumphed, there was no escape.

"Korina, just make sure you stay away from the song of death in the shield Kormak bears." She turned back to me, eyes full of rebellion. "For once, child, do as I say!" The stern rebuke made her blink.

Reluctantly she nodded and allowed us to get a head start away from the gathering of our troops. A trail of greenish putrid smelling slime clearly marked the path of our enemies as they struggled to carry their overmind to some safer location. The door to the inner sanctum was secured against our exit, but the lock was no match for my magically enhanced strength. Two swift kicks shattered the latch as I stumbled through the door to keep from falling over. Several vourdovra broke off from the main group ahead of us to intercept as we ran after them.

"Do not engage them, Kormak, let the army take care of them! We need to break through and destroy that thing!" As I spoke, several of the vanguard disappeared into the stone floor and I wondered how the orudin heard me.

Kormak and I smashed through the rest of the intervening beasts as if they were naught but children in a game of 'Capture', their bodies flying back in dismembered pieces. They turned to chase after us, but paused in uncertainty when the war-horn was sounded. The cries of revenge echoed through the caverns of the city as our kin crashed into the ranks of the vanguard. Kormak and I raced ahead as the sounds of battle filled the air like a roaring tide.

The vourdovra hurriedly squeezed the overmind through a huge set of golden doors and tried to swing them shut before we arrived. Seeing the gap closing quickly, Kormak slammed the shield sideways in the opening. Bracing my feet against the closed door, I pulled open the other, flinging several of the vourdovra from their paws as they fell over each other. The heavy door smashed against the stone wall with a satisfying crunch as blood pooled from underneath it. A single tentacle twitched dejectedly and my boot squished it as I passed.

Inside the structure was a huge hall like an amphitheater with an altar for a stage. Another temple? Behind the altar was a golden statue depicting a creature like the golem only with close to a dozen tentacles arcing from its profane sides. Each one was buried in the skull of some unfortunate victim carved in stone. Not even repeated polishing could cleanse the bloodstains from the surface of the golden altar as the flickering light of torches reflected from the ruddy discoloration.

The stench of the overmind filled the temple as the vourdovra set it down and turned to face us. The one with six tentacles darted out the side of the structure with more than a dozen of its vile kin, and I would have followed it except I knew the overmind was more important. But deep in my gut I felt certain the beast was on its way to kill my hearth-mate. The choice was set before me in agonizing clarity, Morina's life, or the lives of thousands of my kin as they stormed through the city. I knew that if I left with the death-stone, the overmind would be able to use its power freely once more. Our army would be decimated in one fell blow! Praying to the Maker as tears threatened my vision, I attacked the vourdovra that stood between their master and me.

In desperation the vourdovra fought back with a ferocity they had never displayed before. With claws and tentacles, they lashed out against us, bearing us down with sheer weight of numbers. Pinned beneath at least half a dozen of the monstrosities, I struck with fists, feet, even biting a tentacle that tried to remove my chinstrap. The foul slime filled my mouth with a bitter taste as its putrid stench gagged me. The snarling scream of the creature accompanied the scrabbling of its claws as they raked down my helm before scoring a long line down my forehead, across my cheek, along my chin and catching in my chain coif. Its white eyes glared from its shoulders as it struggled to get its feeding tentacle up under the back of my helm only to be frustrated again by the vaarandril links of my coif. The close call shuddered through my nerves as I felt the pressure of its bony tip barely touch the skin of the scar on the back of my skull through the opening of one of the rings.

Planting my feet firmly into the underbelly of the vourdovra, it flew from me as I kicked outward. My hand found the haft of my axe as I rolled to my feet and ended the creature's attempts on my life. Spinning outward with my axe, I managed to clear a small space around me. A flailing leg beneath another mound of vourdovra let me know where Kormak was as I laid into them from behind. Three of them went down before Kormak was able to kick free. Blood trailed from beneath the back of his helm, but he appeared to be still cognizant. He seemed only partially disappointed that death had not found him yet as he rejoined my charge towards the overmind.

With our combined effort we were able to fight our way to the abomination as its flailing tentacles smashed through the bodies of its own people in its efforts to thwart us. One of them wrapped around Kormak like a steel rope and squeezed hard enough to begin crushing his armor as easily as crumpling parchment. The runes flashed red as my axe struck the tentacle and magical sparks flew outward in a shower of red fire. For an instant frozen in time I struggled against the ward, sinews burning in both arms with the strain. Another tentacle snaked around my neck, but not before the ward gave way. A roar of agony shook the temple as my axe sheared through the creature's appendage.

In its spasm of pain, it dragged me across the chamber, slamming me against the wall as sparks flitted before my eyes. Dazed, my hands went to my throat and I realized I was unarmed. The tentacle tightened, crushing the vanes of my helmet and the rings of my coif into my neck. My lungs burned for air as the thing lifted me from my feet, hanging me like a living noose. From the vantagepoint I saw Korina at the head of our army as she charged into the temple. Her eyes widened in horror as she saw me struggling to breathe far above the reach of any help. The world blurred around me as the beast slammed me into the wall again. My lungs were on fire and my head pounded in the fury of the blows I had taken. My vision receded down a dark tunnel, but I felt strangely euphoric.

The pressure around my neck ceased suddenly, and I was surreptitiously dropped fifteen feet to the hard stone floor. With a loud crash, my armor rang in protest as it buckled from the impact. The sweet air that had rushed into my lungs for an instant was slammed back out as I gasped in desperation. It seemed like forever before I was able to take a breath, but at last more air made its way into my chest. My blood pounded in my ears as I tried to roll over only to find myself beneath another pile of vourdovra. I flailed ineffectively with my right arm as two of the beasts held on for dear life to my left. One of them succeeded in clawing through my chinstrap, leaving deep furrows down the side of my face as my own blood blinded me. With glee the vourdovra flung my helmet aside. Its prehensile paws gripped the chain coif, yanking it and no little amount of my red hair from my head.

I caught the first feeding tentacle in my right hand, but the second slammed into the base of my skull tearing a cry of agony from my lips. The feeling of the beast's internal teeth grinding the edges of the hole in my skull sent cold spasms of horror through my gut. Before it could extend its feeding organ the beast sagged onto me as blood and ichor showered down from the blow it had taken.

Tears of relief replaced the ones of terror and pain as Kormak held out my axe to me. Snatching the vile tentacle from the base of my skull, I rolled to my feet and took my axe from Kormak. Around us the battle was coming to a close as my kinsmen hacked the vourdovra down. The death that crawled through my body from the stone he bore stole the strength from my arms and ached through every bone. It was hard to think straight and I could feel my reason treading on shaky ground. My internal organs burned as the song of destruction wrote its harmony over the stanzas of health and life. I staggered under the onslaught, wanting nothing more than to surrender to the darkness that called to me.

Terror! Agony! For a moment, I thought I was reliving the vourdovra's attack, but realization slammed through my senses.

"Morina!" It was a howl of pain, of desperation.

The temple was far behind me before I realized I was running. The cold unreasoning terror pulsed through the soul-bond as strong as if it was in my head. 'Morakvaar protect her!' But I knew in my heart that she was dying, I could feel her life force receding from my soul, tearing it asunder as it rent through our bond like a thunderbolt! Blinding agony pulsed through my veins as fire consumed my heart and mind. Without reason or knowledge, my feet continued to bear me towards her as darkness consumed my soul in a conflagration of hell-fire.

The chamber was lit with stargems, revealing the opulence enjoyed by the vourdovra's leader. It lay on a raised platform; its legs tucked beneath it like a lounging dog on a bed of cushions. Morina's lifeless jade eyes stared back at me widened with pure horror and pain from where she sat propped against the platform. The vourdovra's clawed hands released her, letting her fall unresistingly forward as agony pulsed through my soul like the Mother's Blood through the Deeps.

A scream of rage echoed all around me and I wondered vaguely where it came from. The world seemed unreal as my mind felt the presence of the Reaver.

"Dozarak kilna loch krazak sion!" Blue-white fire burned through the dim light of the stargems, but it seemed as if it were far away, like it was happening to someone else.

Bellows of rage echoed through the chamber as vourdovra bodies shattered away from the blades of the Reaver. From somewhere in the distance of reason, I saw Kormak pick up the axe I dropped in favor of the Reaver as he laid into the enemy with a vengeance. The vourdovra with the six tentacles jumped over my strike and fled through the tunnels. It was too far ahead and I doubted I could catch the beast as my legs stumbled in weariness. The haze of pain clouded over my senses and I could feel the ending lines of the song of death approaching. It killed Morina! That one thought gave my feet wings as I struggled to catch the fiend. Not even death could deny my vengeance.

In a small opening in the tunnel I caught the vourdovra as it rounded on me. Shaking with exhaustion we faced off.

"I guess you will be joining the overmind after all, in death!" But it seemed unafraid.

"As you will join your mate soon." It replied to me, and I narrowed my eyes.

"You foul beast!" My snarl lacked impetus as agony shook my hands. It was all I could do to keep hold of the Reaver.

"I found her taste exquisite. Her mind was full of interesting memories. Did you know what her master had done to her? He was an amusing human, to be sure. I often wondered why lesser species had two separate genders. Who would have guessed it would make a convenient means of torture?" The voice seemed full of perverse enjoyment.

The growl of a mad beast filled the chamber. Was that sound from me? The white-blue fires of the Reaver burned through the air, but even my hazy mind could tell it was clumsy. The vourdovra easily sidestepped the blow as its feeding tentacle shot towards me. Unsure of my reflexes, I threw my arm up to fend it off as I turned. The bony point bounced off my vambrace with a sharp ping. For an instant, my back was to the beast. My mind registered the long dagger it had held a moment too late as the point erupted from the front of my breastplate with a hiss like a serpent. But the vourdovra's aim was fatal only to itself. What may have instantly killed one of its own kind was a mere annoyance to my dying body. The Reaver left a fiery arc of doom as it lit the chamber. With a look of bewildered surprise the vourdovra's two halves fell away from me.

Not three paces behind me Kormak lie on the floor. Sweat ran down the sides of his bare face, tracing over the lines of agony written there. His gray eyes were glazed over with the same pain that echoed through mine. Distraught, his gauntlet reached towards the point of the dagger that protruded from the vicinity of the bottom of my ribcage.

"I... failed." His voice bore more agony from his soul than from his flesh.

"No, Kormak. You... saved my life from the overmind, and you... acquitted yourself well in battle. Your family is absolved of your shame. Rest... in peace, my friend." The anguish vanished from his face as a peaceful smile touched his lips.

"Tell Liria... that I love her."

"I will." His eyes lost focus as the death song came to a close for him.

Stumbling in agony, I wondered if I would live to tell his family anything. The ragged hole that tore through my very being wept for Morina. Death crawled through my veins and through my bones. My body ached from more than the wounds it had taken. The stone on the shield was nearly finished with its fatal work. All that remained was to join my hearth-mate in death. Barely aware of my surroundings I stumbled back to the vourdovra's quarters. A tight fist squeezed the breath from my lungs and the blood from my heart as I saw Morina's crumpled form. The blow smote from my breast to vibrate every nerve in fire. Morina! My life, my hope, my love! The howl of a lost soul echoed through the darkness that clouded all but the sight of her golden hair splattered with blood.

The Reaver fell from fingers no longer able to grasp. It clattered on the floor like the knell of doom that crept through my body. My legs faltered as I stumbled forward then crawled on all fours to Morina's side when they failed altogether. Holding back the darkness for a few moments longer, I struggled to reach out to her. Her cold cheek smote me like the hammer of a giant as I held it next to mine. Tears splashed wetly upon her pauldrons, running down the back of her armor as the mournful cries of a damned soul echoed around me. But life would not return to her jade green eyes.

"Morakvaar, why!? Why her!? I was the one who made the bargain!" My arms shook in agonizing weakness that could no longer hold Morina's weight. Pressing my lips to her cold forehead, I lay down beside her. "You gave me life and hope, and with your death it is gone." The breath hardly stirred the strands of gold upon her face.

Stretching out next to her, I placed my arms around her. I would hold her one last time, for all eternity, and I surrendered to the darkness.

Morakvaar stood before me, separating me from Morina. I moved to join my mate in her journey to the Underhalls, but his strong arm blocked my way.

"It is not your time, yet. I will call you when it is."

"I cannot live without her! Please, if I must go back let me bring her with me? Do not make me leave without Morina, I beg you!"

"Her task is done, yours is still ahead of you."

"No! Great Father, do not be so cruel!" Did he not understand? Sending me back without her was worse than damning my soul to Vooraduum!

His expression softened. "The rest of who you are calls to you, my son. It is time you fulfilled your oath to another from long ago."

Chapter 18

Krazakdain, Morakdain (Bane of Death, Bane of Life)

A tear trailed down my cheek, and as it trickled into my beard it brought the darkness of my mind to some awareness. Morina was gone! Her life extinguished because of me! Emptiness howled through the barren desert of my soul as her absence stabbed through me like a sword. The torn soul-bond burned like fire within my heart and mind, leaving only the desire for death. Why had Morakvaar denied me that right!?

Warm strong arms held my head against something hard, but I cared little for my surroundings. Darkness was my world and pain was my life. My eyes could not bear the sight of anything else, so I kept them closed tightly. Pitiful sobs echoed from the walls to fill the room with the agony that was my soul. Morina was gone! How could I live on!? It was unfair that I had been denied death! How could Morakvaar be so cruel as to make me live while my beloved journeyed to the Underhalls!? The arms rocked me like a small child, but there was nothing that could quench the raging fire left by the ragged tear in my soul.

The arms tightened about me pressing my head against what felt like living stone as it rippled with movement. Lips pressed to my forehead. The power of a healer coursed through me, chasing away the echo of the stone's death song, but not the memories. My eyes saw nothing but Morina's lifeless body in my arms, and my ears heard nothing but the Maker refusing to allow me to die. I screamed, I raged, I howled at the unfairness of it all. I wanted to die, to be with Morina, yet even that was denied me!

Exhaustion finally took me in my madness while I was held by someone. Who it was mattered very little. All I wanted, all I knew was death. Darkness overtook me once more, but this time there were dreams.

***

Dim light filtered down from above as I stood at the bottom of the Starrift. The ragged walls of the crater had long since succumbed to the ministrations of earthquakes, water and temperature. The hole in our world had nearly been closed over by the Mother's Blood, but it still bore the ragged scars of the star that fell from the heavens thirty-five thousand years ago when our race was still settling this region.

Stonemasons and orudin were hard at work sealing up the opening that led to the trade road I stood upon. The light from the rift was slowly closed off leaving a hole only large enough for a kinsman to pass through. With a heavy heart, I turned back to see a long line of warriors, their armor scored by the battles we had faced. Every face was turned to me expectantly as if reading the last chapter of a new legend. Korina stood at my right, the knotwork dragons biting each other's tails as they cavorted across the surface of her new armor. It was the last masterpiece I would create in the forges of my father.

The warmth of the living stones swirled in the air, the reddish background of my world. Would I ever see it again? My kinsmen glowed as multihued spectrums of heat, lights in the darkness of forever. The flowstone backdrop was a frozen waterfall of solid rock as it cascaded down the walls of the ancient trade route to the surface. Further down the cavern I could see the battlements of Sorkarak. Carved stone dragons guarded the gates and the grim visages of the ancestors frowned on invaders with eyes of granite. Would my people be safe?

The Reaver passed from my hands to my daughter's. The weapon was strangely quiescent, allowing her to grasp the haft without retribution.

"Where I am going, I will not need this. A part of me will always be within it, and it will guard against our enemies, as will I. Someday, I will return again, when our people need me most. Keep the Reaver, I will need it then."

With one last look at my kin and my world, I turned towards the diminished opening. At my back was everything I had ever known or cared about. Ahead of me were exile and the pain of living. My feet were reluctant to leave the place of my birth, but what choice did I have? The light of the Starrift surrounded me as I stepped through the opening, a cold dim light of an unforgiving vast world of emptiness. It was a world without Morina, without my children, without my people, but my heart was already a barren wasteland.

The orudin sealed the opening behind me as I watched my world disappear with a finality that could never be changed. Morakvaar stood next to me, his silver-gray hair obscuring part of my view before he turned to me.

"The time for our war is not yet upon us, Gorain. Use these years wisely as you prepare. There are many that need your help, and my other children suffer. Help them, and you may yet redeem your soul."

"I would rather join Morina, but you have already denied me death." My bitter words echoed back along the canyon walls.

"If you had died, you would not have joined Morina." The coldness of his gaze reflected the winter within me.

"How many lifetimes must I live before I am absolved?" Frustrated anger tainted my respect for the Maker.

"As many as it takes for you to learn what it is to be a kinsman." His sigh was the wind as it howled eerily through the passage to the surface.

"It was your hand that forged my soul, bound in that which should never have been. The fragments will never make a whole and I will be divided forever. How could I be a kinsman?" Suspicion burned in my mind. "Or is it that which you count upon? Someone to control, to be your servant among mortals because I can never gain my place in the Underhalls?"

His eyes blazed with anger. "Know your place, Gorain! Even a servant knows who is master!"
As quickly as it came, the ire cooled. "No, I made you as my child. And as my child, I feel pride in your
accomplishments and shame in your failures. My goals are the same as any father, to see a son grow
into a fine example to others, and perchance one day to exceed him." He placed a reassuring hand upon
my shoulder. "Do not grieve, Gorain, for there are others who need and love you."

My soul howled in frustration, in anguish. "There is no one for me but Morina."

Morakvaar smiled at me like an indulgent father with a naive son. "Are you so sure?" With that,
he disappeared from my view.

Through the stone wall came Harrakuli, and I cursed Morakvaar for putting us together, but only
passingly. I did not want to be Gorain to her, but I could not deny the attraction she held for me. She
walked up to me, put her arms around me and kissed me passionately.

"Where do we go now, my love?"

"To the surface. Morakvaar tells me there are those who need my help there."

***

Warm skin conformed to my right side as I awoke. Was it all a dream? Was Morina's passing
merely a nightmare? My hand moved to caress her hair, to comfort myself in the knowledge that the
nightmare was over. The long locks of hair slipped through my fingers in a cascade of silver, stunning my
mind and freezing my heart. What had happened to her hair? Gold eyes gazed into mine as a blue-gray
hand caressed my cheek. What had she done!? How dare she lie with me!? My hand grasped a fist full
of the silvery locks as I ground my teeth in rage.

"What are you doing!? Why are you in my bed!?" My hand quivered with the need to vent my
anguished ire upon the kinswoman at my side.

Harrakuli's brow creased in sorrow as she looked away from me. "You do not remember? It
was my arms that comforted you in your grief, my healing spells that cured the death that crept through
your body, my hands that nurtured you through the long darkness you wept for Morina. When your
body had given out and your soul cried for an end, I was the one who brought you back by Morakvaar's
will. When you wept, I comforted you. When you hungered, I fed you. When you begged for release, I
loved you." She turned from me as her silver hair slid freely through my hand.

The soul-bond I had shared with her as Gorain was stronger than ever as I felt her deep need for
me. My anger drained away to shame. "I- I am sorry."

What could I say to her? What had I put her through as I wept for my beloved? Harrakuli
turned back to me, her face full of pain. But, instead of words, she placed a gray hand on either side of
my face and pulled my lips to hers. Her body against mine filled me with Gorain's memories of her, and
for once, I did not suppress them. I let myself return her kiss, let myself embrace those memories of
another lifetime, let myself believe in hope once more.

When I awoke in the first cycle, Harrakuli was in my arms, and I could not help the terrible
feeling in the pit of my gut that I had betrayed Morina again. How many days had it been since she died,
and I was already in the arms of another kinswoman? The nagging ache followed me from the bedroll

and out of the small cave we were in. How could I have done such a thing? What kind of perverse creature had I become? Was I no better than a fickle human was? Each question smote my conscience like a herald proclaiming my shame.

It took me some time to find my way back to Vouroussan. The tunnels I traversed were worn smooth by years of erosion from the Daemon Fish River when it used to pass through there. The harmonies of the Mother's Song guided me back, but not without having to retrace my steps more than a few times.

Each stride spoke to me of how I had soiled Morina's memory. Every breath was a reminder of the hurt I had caused her while she lived. The beating of my heart spoke of every moment I spent without her, knowing that I lived while she had been taken from me. What right had I to grieve when I broke faith only days after her death? The only right I had was to seek death in Krazakvarein, but Morakvaar had made it clear that I would be denied even that. I had never been worthy of Morina's love and only proved it with my actions after she had passed on.

Through my blurry vision I could see two kinsmen on watch up ahead. They stood alert, their shields bearing the crest of clan Farovar, the winged mug of the brewers. The plates of their armor bore the scars of our recent battles, but they had kept it well. Fresh oil glistened from its surface and from their axes, a reminder of the pride I had no right to. Behind them loomed the gates of Vouroussan. Demonic icons carved upon their surfaces stared out at me as if in delight of my wickedness. Of all the cities in the Deep Realms, Vouroussan and Gormorath were the only ones that had not been formed by the hands of my ancestors.

The eyes of the guards widened as they recognized me. "Lord Dorian! The orudin said that you were in their care!"

My eyes turned from them as the shame smote me. "I was." My hoarse whisper puzzled them. "Where can I find Korina?"

"She is in the vourdovra temple. She asked that you go there as soon as anyone saw you." Nodding absently, I entered the city.

Outside the temple the streets were empty, a reflection of the growing darkness within me. The golden doors stood partially open and I slid between them. On the altar far below a blood red cloth had been spread. Upon it lie Morina encased in her armor save her helmet and holding her battle-axe and shield upon her breast. Her yellow hair cascaded gently down her shoulders, resting like a cloud of purest gold around her head. Her braided beard lie straight down her chest to her waist where the binding ring, symbol of our marriage, held it. Next to her head was the vaarandril helmet I had forged for her, the winged hammer motif arching proudly from the brow-line to fold back around the helm in hammered gold.

The temple tiers were full of my kinsmen who came to gaze one last time at Morina's beauty, to honor her memory and hear of her deeds. Korina knelt at her side, holding her mother's hand as if whispering a bedtime prayer. It was so like how Morina had put her to sleep as a child, and the memory smote me like a hammer. They were honoring her, and I, the one who should have been at her side, had been dallying with Harrakuli as if Morina had never been the most important thing in my life! My chest tightened, squeezing the breath from my lungs and tearing at my heart like a spear as I turned away. I was not worthy to honor her! The truth burned through my being as I stepped back out the doors and crouched beside the temple.

My soul ached in pain and guilt as well as the horrible agonizing loss. Why had Morina loved me? All I had ever brought to her was pain, heartache and eventually death. If she had not married me, she would not have died, of that I was almost certain. Even though I had rescued her from the undead dragon, I was never a worthy candidate for a Bonding. Why had she left to find me when she would have been better off with me dead? It was my fault that she had been murdered, and that thought tore at my conscience again and again.

Sobs wracked my shoulders as tears flowed through my fingers and down my beard. I was no kinsman, and even the humans knew that. I was unworthy to honor Morina's memory, and as guilty as her murderers. The shame hurt almost as bad as the loss. For time uncounted I crouched outside the temple, an outcast, a former slave, and a dishonorable perversion of a kinsman who dared not interrupt a true ceremony of passing. My soul bled rivers of agony in red tides as my tears pooled mournfully on the stones below. A hand rested on my shoulder, and a tall figure joined me outside the temple gates. When at last I looked up, I saw Lodath gazing at me with concern.

"Why aren't you inside?" He asked me.

How could I tell him? "I am not worthy of her remembrance. You know I was never worthy of her."

Lodath sighed, and I could tell he remembered the day of our marriage. "As then, it's what she would want that matters, not your perceived worthiness."

Though I knew he was right, my mind rebelled against the sacrilege. How could I defile Morina's Rite of Mourning? But I could almost feel her presence, her will that whispered to me. She would want me there, even though I was unworthy.

"Come with me, then, Lodath. Help me face what I must. I fear this is one battle I have not the strength for."

We entered the temple, and approached the altar. Near halfway there, the loss struck me hard as I saw Morina's face. I stifled the howl of pain that threatened to escape me, and felt as if my knees would give out on me. Lodath steadied me with a grip on my arm. Standing still, I wrestled with my grief. The emptiness seemed to spread through me like a dark wave of despair. The darkness filled me, taking my pain to the depths beyond my feeling. In a daze, the scene before me took on a surrealistic air. At last I knelt at the altar, staring unbelievingly into the face of my beloved mate, a hearth-mate I had betrayed once in life and once in death. Hanging my head in shame, I could not form the words, could not recount her ancestry as she had told it to me on the day of our marriage. The pain stole the breath from my lungs.

Korina had been about to recite her mother's lineage for the book of ancestors, but had stopped when I entered the temple. She stared at me, expectantly, but I found no voice within me. Shakily, I took Morina's cold hand from around the battle-axe, and pressed it to my lips. My heart felt as if it were burning, spreading icy fire through me. I tried to speak, but only sobs escaped my lips. With a look of understanding, Korina finished the Ritual of Mourning for me.

Days might have passed as I knelt before the altar, for I was aware of nothing save when they came to take Morina's body. They placed her in a stone cask and Korina gave the order that she was to be entombed below Morakduum. She was the first of the High Queens to be buried there. Long after they left, I sat at the foot of the altar, with my head in my hands, unable to face going on. My kinsmen left me there, hoping that time would heal my wounds, but they knew better. No kinsman ever survived the severing of a soul-bond. Lodath sat on one of the stone benches in the temple, watching me to make sure I did not attempt to take my own life. If ever there was a time that I was tempted to break my word, that was it, but would I have learned what it meant to be a kinsman? Even if I had not given Lodath my vow, Morakvaar had already refused me passage to the afterlife. How could I argue with that? Darkness filled my chest where my heart had once been, a cold emptiness that seeped through every vein.

A blue-gray hand lifted my chin, and I looked into Harrakuli's face. I wanted to be angry; to blame her for my guilt, but I could not. It was my fault, a fault I had since before I met Morina, before even Jaguar. Was it the slaver that broke me? Could I lay all my sins at the feet of that cruel and evil woman, or were they truly my sins? Was it some problem of my character since birth? The memory of the dream spoke of my tainted soul, but was it my fault?

As Harrakuli stared into my eyes, I could not help but remember her as Gorain did. The concern pulsed through Gorain's soul-bond, a horrible parody of the ragged scar left of my bond to Morina, but just as compelling. The memories of Gorain's time with her flashed before me as if they had happened to me yesterday.

A youth with reddish-blonde hair smiled up at a silver-haired orudin who held a bright blue gem out to him. With delight, he took it, not only because it was beautiful, but also because Harrakuli had given it to him. He stared into her gold eyes wondering what it would be like to be orudin. The sapphire glittered in the light of the stargems like a beacon in the dark. Slowly, he handed it back.

"I could not take your food, honored one." Her smile was like the harmony of the Mother as it sang in his veins.

"Gorain, if only all of your people were as you, perhaps you would know peace."

"With inspiration such as you, how could they not be?" Her laughter was the sound of crystal chimes.

"Dear boy, you are like vaarandril ore surrounded by shale. It is a pity that you are betrothed to another." It was the only time Harrakuli had ever expressed her feelings until the day when she stopped his bloodthirsty hunt of the zarakanan.

As if reading my mind, Harrakuli pleaded with me. "Let me help you, Dorian." But I was beyond her reach.

"No, those days are over. Though I may remember Gorain's life, I am not the same as he was then. I loved Morina with all my heart and soul." I did not know how to deal with the deep connection that Harrakuli had made with me. "It is too soon for me to contemplate our past. Give me time to remember Morina and what she meant to me."

Harrakuli reluctantly nodded and left, an expression close to agony on her features. Why was she so interested in me? What was Gorain to her? What could an immortal possibly want with a tainted soul?

The hoard of Vouroussan was as vast as I had imagined. Thousands of years of predation upon my people and the zarakanan had filled their tunnels with the bounty of their kills. The pile of gold, silver, platinum and vaarandril glittered like the sun descended to the Deeps as it was heaped in the center of the vourdovra temple. Gems sparkled like stars amidst the splendor in a rainbow of different colors from the pile where they had been placed. Jewelry and decorative works of art of all descriptions and make sat to the other side as our people took careful inventory.

The wealth contained in the vaults of Sorkarak might have made up less than half of what was gathered from Vouroussan. The warriors under my supervision were more than happy to help load the wagons of Osric's remaining troops. Even though the carts were overflowing with their bounty, they could carry less than a third of the wealth. My kinsmen thought it was a small price to pay to be rid of the humans for good. A good portion of the treasure was given back to the clans to repay them for the monies gathered to hire Osric's soldiers.

Korina called a meeting of the Council of Elders to determine the disposition of the remainder of the wealth, and she required all her generals and nobles to attend. The gathering filled less than half of the vourdovra temple, leaving a large gap between where I stood at the door and the nearest kinsman. My daughter's eyes were rimmed with dark rings and new lines of worry traced outward from her lids as she listened to the council.

As Warlord, I was offered a significant proportion of the spoils, and there was quite a bit of surprise when I turned it down. Gold had no more meaning to me; nothing had meaning. Morina was gone, and with her all things that I cared about vanished from my reckoning. The only things that were real to me were the lives of my kin and my people nothing else mattered. With that said, I left the gathering, not interested in how they squabbled over the treasure.

Outside the temple, the humans were preparing to leave. Despite the coldness that I had wrapped my emotions in, the sight of Lodath joining them stabbed through the indifference. My feet found their way next to the cart Lodath had climbed in to. Anton stood beside it, as he marked in a ledger.

"You were right about the wealth in this city. Would that we could take it all, but I know we've more than enough to fill each man's coffers and the king's vault. We paid dearly for it, though." The lieutenant's face had gained almost as many lines as I had before the battle, though I knew I outdistanced him by far after. "I know your people suffered greater than ours, so what remains should be yours."

His supposed generosity made no impression on my despair. It would hardly pay for the lives we had lost. Of the fifty thousand warriors that had left Morakduum, only twenty-two thousands were left. The line of our dead stretched the length of Vouroussan twice over and the Ritual of Mourning would take nearly a month to complete. Our clerics were hard at work preserving the bodies so that they would not rot before the ceremony was finished. So many had died, and I had led them to their fate. Their blood was on my conscience as much as our enemies'. Was it really worth it? Would our people ever recover from the devastation to our numbers? Would we be able to defeat the Kinsmen of Shadow with so few warriors left?

Of all the unanswered questions, the last one worried me the most. Zarakalduum was a powerful city in its own right. The Kinsmen of Shadow were nearly as adept warriors as we were, and their armaments were of similar caliber. It would take more than great tactics to defeat them; it would take incredible luck and the blessings of the gods.

Directing my thoughts away from the future, I thought about the past as I watched Lodath settle himself on the benchboard. "I had zought you might stay, but I understand. I vill miss your company my old friend."

"I need to report back to Osric and help the lieutenant explain what happened to the general. I don't think there'll be a problem, what with all the gold and precious stones we're bringing back." He paused and looked at me with a long and searching expression. "You won't forget your promise, will you, Dorian?"

As much as I wanted death, it had already been denied me. With a rueful grin I replied, "I have no choice in zat matter."

Lodath's expression was sympathetic. "When you've finished your mission, you can find me in the capitol. Any of Osric's men should be able to lead you to me."

I clasped his outstretched arm. "I vill be zere if I am able. Farevell, my friend, ahnd may fate be kinder to you."

He smiled grimly and nodded. The wagon pulled out in front of the remainder of the army. Of their eighty thousand soldiers, twenty thousands would never return to the surface world. Vouroussan had exacted a terrible price from both our peoples. They set out on the trader's road back towards the Starrift and to the winding upward trail that lead to the surface. My eyes followed their progress until the last wagon rounded the bend.

Chapter 19

Kovas Karzakaran (The Price of Victory)

The cleanup of Vouroussan continued as I consulted with the commanders to set up watch rotations. With the amount of wealth gathered in the temple, I knew it would only be a matter of time before we would face the greed of one of the dragons of the Wilds. They had plagued us since their first appearance in the Deeps two thousand years before Gorain was born. Inevitably whenever we were caught outside of our strongholds with a significant amount of wealth, the dragons came. They had some peculiar sense of the resonance of gold and precious gems.

Anton was fortunate that his road to the Starrift passed under the watchful eye of Sorkarak. With him leaving first, he had a better chance at avoiding attention, especially since we still kept the bulk of the wealth in Vouroussan. Navoran volunteered to oversee the watch rotations and to assign troops to garrison the city, leaving me to find Korina and prepare for the Ritual of Mourning. When I failed to find her in the temple, one of the royal guards was able to point me in the direction she was last seen.

The inner sanctum that was the saltwater pool was cold and dark, the warmth of the living stones had been banished long ago by the vourdovra. The heat of Korina's form was like a ray of sunlight, so bright was her outline against the chill of that evil place. Her tunic bulged slightly around the waistline, betraying her pregnancy to all eyes, and I wondered why she was not in armor. Was it getting too tight despite the fact it was made for my larger form? Perhaps it was time for her to step back from the fighting?

The sense of sorrow emanated from her like a dark cloud as I moved to stand on her left. Her furrowed brow covered her stare at the remainder of the pool as she frowned into the darkness. Her pain tore at me when she turned, and her puffy lids spoke of long hours weeping. Where was her mate?

She fell into my arms, collapsing as if all her strength had been sucked dry. "Marak is badly wounded!" Her wail tore at my heart. "Waradain does not know if he will make it."

Was my daughter to be torn as I was? Her tears wet my beard as I held her tightly and kissed her forehead like I had so many times when she was young. "Waradain is the finest priest I know. He will not let his son die, Morina. Marak will be well in no time."

"He could not bring mother back!" The ragged scar that was left of my soul ached in fire, but I had to comfort my daughter.

"Morakvaar came for your mother and took her to the Underhalls. He has not come for Marak, so take heart Korina. He will recover before you know it, you will see." Her sobs stopped, but she made no move to back away.

Holding my daughter almost soothed the constant pain of my soul. The memories of her childhood paraded before me in loving joy. Even her mischief was a balm to my inner wounds. Her first spider protégé brightened her smile to a radiance undreamed of as I remembered giving it to her to train. Though it had never been a pleasant task to change her swaddling cloth, I still looked back on it with heady nostalgia.

Reliving Korina's infant days brought my mind sharply around to my new daughter Geria. Would I be a fit parent to raise her on my own? The question burned into my chest, the answer a resounding negative. How could I expect to take care of her when I was doomed to a life of exile? What was I to do? If I took her with me, it would be unlikely that she would learn to be a proper kinswoman.

Without moving away or lifting her head, Korina spoke to me. "Father, I have been thinking. What will happen to Geria when you leave?" She had to be able to read my mind! It was too uncanny how she always knew what I was thinking.

Was Korina a latent soulsmith or did she have an intensified version of my empathy with animals? "I do not know. When I leave, I intend on searching out the rest of our people who were enslaved by the zarakanan and sold upon the surface. It is scarcely the sort of life conducive to childrearing. Besides, I am hardly a model kinsman for her to pattern her life. As an outsider with no clan, how could I expect her to lead my sort of life?"

Her green eyes stared earnestly into mine. "We are your clan, father, Marak, I, Dorak, your mother, Marak's clan, you even belong to the Atharil clan and the rest of Mytharia."

Korina knew better, but her protest warmed me anyway. "What clan would accept Gorain the Slayer as one of their own?" Her face turned away from me as she stepped back out of my embrace.

Slowly she admitted, "none." Her hoarse whisper barely reached my ears.

Was she too refusing to accept me? Feeling the tear in my soul ache even more I turned my eyes to the ruined chamber. Without Morina, my own children would not claim me. Truly everything I cared about had been stripped by her death, even my offspring. The despair darkened around me, nearly choking the breath from my lungs. Why would Morakvaar make me live? Yet in my soul I knew why, the answer was in the dream. If I died, I would be damned forever unless I found some way to redeem myself in the Maker's eyes. In bitter frustration I realized that winning our campaigns would not be enough. What could I do that would satisfy him?

Korina turned back with an earnest expression. "I want to raise her, father. When our child, Dara is born, I will be able to care for them both." How did she know her unborn child was a girl?

"Though it is against our traditions, it would probably be the best solution." Korina cut me off abruptly.

"Tradition be damned! If we are to survive as a people, a few traditions will have to change!" Her vehement attitude surprised me. Was she not the one who tried to follow traditions by the letter?

"If we deny our traditions, will we survive as a people, or will we be lost in the flow of time?" A people not following the roots of their civilization lost so many things.

Korina nodded slowly. "Yes we will, and we will be stronger for it."

Korina's wisdom brought fatherly pride to me despite the fact that I felt estranged from her. It was a small light in the darkness that had become my life.

Concern flooded her features as she gazed at me. "You look worse than I feel, father. You should get some rest."

"I have tried, but sleep escapes me." It had been two full day cycles since I had been with Harrakuli. Every time I closed my eyes, I saw nothing but Morina's features warped with pain and self-loathing as she stared at me with dead eyes. The vourdovra had violated her mind before she died, dragging out horrible nightmares of her past.

"Did you know what her master did to her? An amusing human to be sure." The words echoed through my mind again and again as I ground my teeth in rage and anguish for what Morina had been through. That the vile beast had found amusement in her dishonor and abuse drove me near mad with the desire to kill. Suddenly, with crystal clarity, I realized why Morina loved me.

"We were the same." My whisper betrayed the sobs that welled within once more. "She loved me because she felt unworthy because of her shame. She loved me because I knew the terror, the horrible dishonor that we both had to live with because of our enslavement."

"Mother told me of those days she was a slave. She told me you had suffered in a similar way." Fresh tears were falling from her eyes as we shared our grief. "She said she loved you because you were always so gentle with her, so careful, and in a way, she liked your shyness too." She stepped back to me and I held her once more.

We embraced each other, and I was unsure who was comforting whom, until at last, we were both exhausted of tears for our loss. Unsure if I was able to sleep, I agreed to try and rest first before accompanying Korina in the Ritual of Mourning.

Though I did fall asleep, nightmares plagued my rest. In one of them, the vourdovra leader took control of my mind once more. It slipped one of the eel-like creatures into the base of my skull, and I could feel it burrowing into my head. It changed me, slowly, painfully, until I was one of them. In the dream, I was the one who killed Morina. The shock was horrible and I woke with my heart racing and fresh tears wetting my cheeks. My guilt pressed down on my chest as I cried out for absolution.

The echoes of my pain came back to me from the walls of the empty quarters. No more would my rooms be filled with warmth or love. My pacing could not relieve the terrible aching loneliness, the ragged edges of my torn soul cried out for release, but there was no solace. The pain of Morina's loss would not let me rest. Every time I began to doze off, another nightmare woke me with new guilt, new agony. Why had Morakvaar denied me? There was not much else my people needed me for. With the exception of Zarakalduum, our campaign was near an end. It was torment to be left behind and alone. In anger, I pulled the binding ring from my beard and threw it against the wall. What good was the binding if we could not be together for all eternity? What good were vows if they could not be kept? Why had he taken her from me? Morina had so much more to live for; it seemed a horrible injustice. She could have remarried anyone she chose, could have had a life with our people, where I had none! Yet, I was the one who lived on while she had been taken!

The anger passed once more into despair, and I sat upon the edge of the bed in anguish. Slowly, I unbraided my beard, remembering a moment in our time together for each twist, and knowing she was gone forever. That simple ritual affected me more than anything ever could. Tears soaked my cheeks and my beard as I submitted to this final act of farewell, a finality that had no return. Morina would never again renew the binding as she had every day for the last eighty-four years. Never again would I braid her golden beard, place on the binding ring and restate my vows. It had been our ritual, our affirmation of love and permanency. How fleeting it all was in reality.

Korina knocked on my door as I finished the last twist. Pulling on my trews, I poured some water into the washbowl before telling her to enter. The water helped clear my head from the lack of sleep as I splashed it over my face. When I turned to Korina, she looked almost as haggard as I felt. Shock lit her features as she registered the missing braid. A flurry of emotions crossed her face until she suppressed them.

"It is time for the Mourning, father." She wanted to say something else, but I was glad she did not.

We left my quarters after I had buckled on my armor. Our dead had been laid out in the central square, the only place in the city large enough to accommodate the amount of bodies. To see so many shook me. Was I really doing the right thing? Was what we were fighting for worth those lives lost? I prayed to Morakvaar that it was so, that our children for generations would be free from fear, but doubt nagged at me. What if our enemies were able to unseal the Starrift and invade our homelands once more? What then? Was all this death worth it if the peace did not last?

Those questions plagued me as I stared into the haunted faces of the relatives of those who were dead. In an odd sharing, they seemed to take heart in the recognition of my loss of Morina. In all fairness, it probably was right that I, who had started this war, suffered loss and pain as even the lowest soldier. At that moment, I felt closer to my people than I had for the last eighty-one years I had lived among them. I shared their grief, their horror, their loss, and was at last partially accepted for it.

The names of the dead, their deeds and their ancestry rang through the cavern like the keening of a brass bell, rolling along the walls, arching across the roof of the cave to escape at last through cracks and fissures to hide forever in the unforgiving darkness. Each name was like a piece of my soul that floated beyond, torn off in excruciating agony to be tossed to the flames of eternity. For cycle upon cycle, day upon day it lasted until the final name had been recited, and the last predecessor honored. Twenty thousand names joined the book of ancestors, the history of our bloody war.

At the end of the ritual, I parted ways with Korina, but instead of making my way back to my quarters, I wandered aimlessly through the tunnels of Vouroussan. I wandered far and for a long time. Past exhaustion, everything was unreal to me. The sound of running water drew me and I followed its echoes far from the city. When Harrakuli found me in the chamber where the springs came cascading down the side of the cave wall in an immense waterfall, I did not know if I was awake or dreaming. She knew my pain, knew my need not to be alone with my fears, and knew I needed comfort and shelter from the dreams.

As before, she held me in my pain, only this time I was aware of more than just her comfort. My need was more than shelter from the storm of death that raged around me, it was a base need. That part of me that had shared souls with Harrakuli would not be denied. I reached out to that part of me that dwelled within her, and merged as one being. When I woke with Harrakuli in my arms, almost a full day had passed. We lay on the soft powdered rock upon my cloak. Harrakuli, almost shyly, kissed my lips, as if she expected me to send her away again. I smiled gently at her.

"Thank-you, Harrakuli. I had need of your comfort, but more than that. I do not think I could love you as Gorain, but I am glad of your company."

She smiled, snuggled into my arms once more, and I fell back asleep. I had no nightmares, only pleasant dreams and memories of Morina and our children. When I awoke once more, Harrakuli sat upon a rock next to the pool at the foot of the falls. The outline of her figure against the warm water was a beauty I would never forget. She was perfect as only an immortal could be, the first of her race, the only living ancestor goddess out of all the seven clans. Not daring to question why she wanted me, I walked around to face her. When I kissed her lips, she sighed deeply as she put her arms around me. Her vaarandril clothing that served as her armor melted from her like water to congeal in a pool like it was fresh from the smelters. She stood with her skin pressed against mine, igniting my desire for her.

"Can you purify this water?"

With a puzzled expression she asked, "why?"

"I feel like a bath." She stared at me as if I had lost my wits. "Please?"

Shaking her head in disbelief, she did as I asked, and I gently pulled her into the water. I had to stifle my shudders at the memory of the overmind, but this was shallow water and I could see the bottom. After some trepidation, Harrakuli relaxed and began to enjoy the sensation of my hands as I washed her. The heart of the Mother warmed most springs in the deeps, and this was no exception. It was quite pleasant, and reminded me of some of the warm baths I had taken while on the surface. It had been over eighty-three years since I had taken a bath instead of our standard filtered showers. For Harrakuli, I was sure it was the first time. After we had washed the dirt and grime from the battle and the days after from us, she held me to her and kissed me once more. We made love again in the shallows of the pool, a sensation I had not felt since Jaguar and I bathed together. It was ironic that deep water would bring me great fear, but I could find such pleasure from the shallows.

When we were both dry, we dressed and I returned to Vouroussan while Harrakuli went to take care of some business with her own people. The watchmen seemed startled to see me as they waved me through the gates, and I wondered how I had gotten out of the city without their notice. My usually perfect memory was still hazy over what had happened from the Ritual of Mourning until I had awakened in Harrakuli's arms.

"Lord Dorian, Queen Korina has been looking for you."

"Thank-you kinsman. I will meet with her forthwith. Any news of import in the last couple days?" My mind made the quick calculation of the time I had spent away.

"Our outer scouts have returned with news that Hakareth is on the move. We have readied our defenses." The kinsman seemed alarmed at the news he relayed to me.

Hakareth was the sixth of his line, his ancestor having been slain by my own hand as Gorain. Thinking about the dragon, I wondered if he sought treasure or vengeance.

"Thank-you again. Keep well."

"And you, Lord Dorian." It bothered me that he called me Lord instead of kinsman. It was another separation, a small gesture of non-acceptance. Was I getting paranoid? Perhaps he only meant it as a gesture of respect?

In the center of the city, a young kinsman met me. His dark red hair was almost brown and sweat beaded on his brow. The blue and gold tabard he wore over his armor marked him as a runner for the court, but I could not remember seeing his face before. He took in a few gasps of air as if he had been running more than a normal messenger should.

"Lord Dorian! Her majesty requests your presence at the Eastern Gate." He panted a couple more times as he turned expectantly.

Dutifully, I caught up and walked beside him. "Tell me, kinsman, what do people say about me?"

He kept his eyes straight ahead as he responded. "That you are Gorain returned."

It was a neutral answer that was not very reassuring. "Is that good or bad in your view?"

His gold eyes betrayed a distant orudin ancestor as they turned my way. "I believe in the prophecy, but some believe that Gorain's dishonor returns with him."

"What do you believe?" Was it really that important? Yet I craved the acceptance of my people above all but the return of Morina.

"Lord Dorian, I know what my eyes behold, and never have you acted dishonorably towards our people. Though some rumors state disturbing things, I am glad to have lived in your time. This is the age of new legends, new prophecies." His enthusiasm and almost boyish awe made me smile.

"Thank-you kinsman, you have restored my faith. What is your name?"

"Zarakdain son of Gordain Bailanvaar, my Lord." He flushed as if embarrassed.

My smile only made him redder in the face. "Did you live up to your name?" But in the pits of my memory the names of several members of clan Bailanvaar including Gordain were spoken in the Rite of Mourning.

The lad smiled back and proudly proclaimed. "Yes, my Lord! I slew three of the zarakanan in the battle of Sorkarak!"

"As many as that?" That such a young warrior had been able to claim three kills was quite a feat considering the martial skill of the zarakanan.

His eyes drifted down as he confessed that he had help. "I was the wielder of the great-axe in our team."

My gauntlet rang on his pauldron as I gave him a friendly slap. "Still, three kills for your first battle is outstanding, lad. I did not do so well in my first skirmish with the zarakanan."

If I had told him the overmind was standing behind him, I do not think the lad would have been more astonished. "You!? But, Lord Dorian, you must have slain over a thousand in the battle! We saw you! And we saw the demon..." He shuddered. "What happened in your first skirmish?"

"I was captured and sold as a slave barely wounding one of them, but let us not dwell on the past." It was my turn to feel the cold fingers run down my spine. "I would rather you address me as Dorian, or kinsman. Humans have need of such titles as 'Lord', but we do not. We are all Morakvaar's children."

His face lit up as if I had given him a great gift. "Were you scared when you faced the demon, kinsman?"

"No, I felt only rage at the thought of the zaraks ambushing Korina under a flag of truce. The only thing that frightens me is the damnation of my soul, for it is the one thing that will keep me from Morina's side when I die." When I thought about it, though, I realized there was another thing that frightened me. "Well, maybe not the only thing."

"You are afraid of something?" The disbelief in his voice made me smile.

"Yes, lad, even Gorain Reborn has his fears. I must confess that the overmind frightened the wits out of me. When it dragged me into the pool of water and I began to drown..." My armor rattled with the force of the shudder that shook me at the memory.

The young clansman stopped and stared at me open-mouthed, his face twisted in a mix of sympathy and horror. "It dragged you into the water?" The thought obviously terrorized him almost as much as when it happened to me.

"Yes. I had never felt so close to damnation in Vooraduum as that moment. The cold watery hell that surrounded me was terrifying beyond words. But, fortunately, it is over. The blast that emptied the chamber came just in time. The orudin found me before my injuries had killed me and nursed me back to health." He turned and walked with me again as we approached the Eastern Gates.

"Truly Morakvaar favors you, kinsman. To see so many close calls is a certain indication of your destiny." His voice was wistful, as if he wished he were destined for great things.

"Lad, having a destiny is a curse, not a blessing. Those who are called upon to do great things are also cursed to suffer horrendously. They must endure hardship after hardship and sacrifice after sacrifice. Believe me lad, being an ordinary kinsman would have been my greatest wish." Zarakdain looked thoughtfully at the construction going on at the gates.

"It must have been painful to be betrayed to the zarakanan." His whisper was barely audible.

"Kormak's treachery was more than a physical duress placed upon me. It burned in my soul that a kinsman could betray another to his enemies. Through all of our history I had never heard of any of Morakvaar's worshippers committing such a terrible crime against his kin. It was a deed worthy of Atlazar's followers. But even so, his reasons were noble if misguided. At the end, though, he acquitted himself well. He died an honorable and heroic death." Kormak's dying features appeared in my mind and I felt the pain of his passing. More blood was on my hands, and I wondered if that was what the Maker meant.

Chapter 20

Hakareth (Great Wyrm)

The gates loomed before us with its carved gargoyle-like vourdovra peering outwards and away from us. Hopefully it would not be long before our people replaced the hideous beasts with something more appropriate. When Korina saw me, her expression turned grim and I prepared myself for her ordering me to do something I did not want to hear. A massive iron bar was levered into place as the stone gates were shut with a resounding boom that echoed through the city. The workers struggled to mount iron shutters upon the ramparts in an attempt to keep missiles and dragon fire at bay. Four hastily mounted ballistae lined the wall facing the tunnel, and I could see the tackle and a resonator being moved to hoist a cannon into place.

My daughter moved to stand at my side as I watched the preparations. "I take it you have heard the news."

"Yes. The watchmen at the Southern Gate informed me of Hakareth's approach. He may not be here for treasure." Korina's green eyes fixed on me and I steeled myself for her orders.

"I want you to promise me you will not leave the city."

"Korina, if Hakareth is on his way here for revenge, do you not think I am endangering the lives of our people?" She shifted uncomfortably.

"I am not going to have this argument with you. You know we are stronger as a whole than as individuals. We will stand together against the dragon."

"If Hakareth is after me, then if I leave, he will not come here." An anguished look passed over her features.

"I know you want to die, father, but we need you! It has been your tactics and strategy that have gained us victory time and again, your fighting prowess that has pulled us through the impossible."

"You forget that it was you who led our people into battle since Balakarak." The reminder made no impression as her face hardened.

"Regardless, I have ordered the gates sealed in all directions. The point is moot, no one may leave or enter until this business is finished."

"I promise I will not leave this city until I am sure the dragon is only after me." Korina frowned, her fingers running down her reddish-gold beard. "But if I do find out that the beast is out for vengeance, then I will do what I think necessary to protect our people."

She opened her mouth to protest, but thought better of it. Not believing I had actually won an argument with my daughter, I beat a hasty retreat to the ramparts before she could change the outcome. The warriors manning one of the iron shutters were more than happy to give me space to look out.

The tunnel stretched straight for a considerable distance before bending upward, and I wondered if it were another route to the surface. At the very least, I was sure it led to the Darklands and more hunting grounds for the vourdovra. Such a vast city of the beasts would require an enormous supply of prey. A large ballista was still being assembled on my left, the engineer grumbling about the incompetence of his workers and the amount of time they were taking. Some things would never change. To my right, a unit of warriors manned the shutters, four to an opening. Each of them wore a suit of plates over chainmaille and carried a crossbow. Strapped to their waists were a variety of weapons, axes, hammers, and even a sword or two. All around me was an air of confident expectation, and I shook my head at the arrogance.

Upon the surface world, and in places I traveled, I had met several of the beasts. Each one was a terror in its own right. The scarcity of the dragons that dwelled in the Halls of the Mother had instilled a false sense of superiority, the same that I had seen upon our enemies. Gorain had slain Hakareth more than eight thousand years ago, and my people expected me to be able to handle this one as well. What they did not know was that I already carried the scars from the half dozen dragons I had faced in the past. At the time I fought them, though, I had a group of companions whose special skills were inimical to my success. Even then, we had barely escaped with our lives.

The empty tunnel refused to show sign of the intruder for time cycles on end, so I occupied my mind thinking of Harrakuli. What was I to do? My heart and soul ached in mourning for Morina, yet I could not deny the bond that Gorain had with her. What I could not understand was why she would choose me. As a mortal, I would grow old and die in what was merely a moment of her lifetime. But had I not shared a bond with Jaguar and loved her even though I would have outlived her? Somehow, the thought that I would survive long after her death had never occurred to me until that moment. Perhaps Harrakuli was not so different. Did she think beyond the span of my life?

"There!" The lookout pointed up the road where I could barely see a spot of heat moving towards us.

"That is no dragon." The shape was of a zarak, and my knuckles whitened on the Reaver as I considered what it meant to have a lone zarak approach us.

"It could be a deception, Lord Dorian." Nodding in agreement, I watched patiently as the figure approached.

The outline of her angular face was quite plain as she reached the gates. Her silver hair flowed down her shoulders near to her waist, parted only by her pointed ears.

"Halt, zarak! What is your business here!?" The sentries trained their crossbows on her slender form, ready to loose a rain of death at a moment's notice.

"I seek Dorian, the one they claim is Gorain Reborn." Her clear voice rang through the tunnels and echoed in my frozen blood.

It had to be a ghost, or some foul trick as I gazed into Liathrain's amber eyes! Keeping out of her line of sight, I crept over to the sentry.

"Ask her name."

He looked at me with raised brows, but then turned back to the zarak as I kept away from the openings in the crenellations. "What is your name, zarak? And why do you seek Lord Dorian?"

"I am Liathrain Vaetra one time companion and friend, and I wish to speak with my killer." Icy fire passed through my soul as the wound was reopened.

"You are too late. Lord Dorian perished in the battle and the time to honor him has passed. Your kind is unwelcome among us, so get ye hence from here and return no more!" The kinsman whispered to me and I was surprised the lie came so easily to him. "It is a trick, my Lord, or I am a fool."

"My sources tell me that Dorian lives, and I am sure he would accept an audience with me. Tell him that I am here." The zarak leaned casually up against the wall as if preparing for a long wait.

"Most likely, but there is one way to be sure. Ask her what Kelana found." The dragon might have heard my whispers if it was impersonating Liathrain, but the dark elf would never have heard me on her own.

The sentry nodded as I cursed inwardly, such an acknowledgement would surely alert Hakareth. "If you speak truly, then tell us what Kelana found."

When the zarak bowed her head, instinct sparked within me. "Have all kinsmen use the wet-cloths now!" Along the battlements warriors scrambled to heed my order.

Whether the beast used fire or corrosive gas, the cloths would offer a little better protection than just the shutters. The ballista crews cranked their machines into firing position as the freshly mounted cannon stood primed and ready to loose massive destruction in the form of millions of tiny rock shards. Crossbows pointed down as every finger tightened on the trigger ready to fire. At any second, I expected the transformation from zarak to reptilian menace.

My jaw dropped in astonishment as instead of transforming, the zarak replied. "Kairillia had deceived me and my mother. She sent me to kill Dorian on false pretenses. I am here to make peace between us." Was she a ghost, or had Liathrain been restored to life?

The gatewarden frowned at my request to be let out, but complied with my wishes. A note of uncertainty in Liathrain's gaze put me immediately on my guard as instinct sent an icy shiver up my spine. My knuckles whitened on the Reaver that shed no light so close to its intended purpose. My signal ensured the gates were secured behind me as I faced the creature I was sure was not my old friend. With a sickening feeling in the pit of my stomach I wondered how the dragon had learned of Kelana's secret. Had the elf perished at the claws of the wyrm?

"Dorian?" The questioning note was immediate confirmation of my suspicions.

"I am his pledged kinsman. What you wished to say to him can be said to me." When had I learned to lie so easily?

"I wish to apologize to him personally and to soothe over relations between your people and my house." The resemblance was uncanny, even the voice was perfect. How could Hakareth have known Liathrain so well?

"I will tell him you have come." Not daring to turn my eyes from the beast, I backed towards the door in the massive gate.

Either my gesture of distrust, or its inner instinct warned that I did not believe the ruse. In an instant, a massive gray claw descended upon me, pinning me to the floor of the cave. The swiftness of the attack was a blur to my eye, and though I tried to dive out of the way, the beast caught me as easily as a pouncing feline catches a mouse.

"You are Dorian! Your weapon betraysss you!" The hissing screech of the wyrm resounded through the cavern from its long sinuous throat.

In answer, I buried the Reaver into its muscled foreleg, splitting the scales with an audible crunch. Snarling in pain, it pressed down on me, and my armor buckled under the creature's weight. Barely able to draw a breath, I commanded the rage fires into the blades still buried in the dragon's leg.

"Sarlik Doria!" The flash of light blinded me for an instant as the talons of the dragon tightened convulsively.

A roar of rage and pain shook the tunnel, dislodging stones that rained down as my armor began to crumple inward. The metal plates that would normally protect me became my death trap. The grinding of metal against my bones echoed through my skull as the pain erupted in waves of fire. In desperation I swung the Reaver, hoping the dragon would release me before my ribs succumbed to the pressure. The crack of the metal blades against burned bone and tissue brought more loose rock tumbling from the darkness above. Already strained by the previous wound and compounded by the fire, the leg shattered from the impact of my panic enhanced swing. The smell of burned flesh filled the air, no longer contained within the beast's iron hide.

The dragon's unearthly scream rang in my ears, deafening all for leagues around, but the release of pressure did not help me. My ribs struggled for space against the collapsed plates of my armor, finding no room for my starved lungs. The howl of agony from Hakareth turned into a barely intelligible curse before it drew in a mighty breath.

"You and all your foul kind will pay for this insult Gorain!" The words were formed as the gust of foul gases burst from the dragon's mouth.

The greenish-yellow cloud engulfed me as with my fading cognizance I pulled out the wet cloth from my pouch and threw it over my face. To my relief, the corrosive gas ate through the straps that held my armor in place allowing a breath of foul air that was barely filtered by the wet cloth to pass into my lungs. With my armor hanging off me by threads of leather that survived, I rolled to my feet with new vigor. From the corner of my eye I saw the signal to fire as the crossbow bolts rained down from the ramparts. The angle of my escape had put me in their direct path!

"Baravrak en!" The first few bolts ricocheted from my armor as I invoked the magical shield, but one of them had found purchase in my right calf.

Blood welled from the puncture as I grit my teeth, but I had no time to tend the wound. The rush of air was all the warning I had before the beast's massive jaws scooped me up. Rolling between teeth yellowed with age, I swung the Reaver as I turned, burying the blades deeply in the roof of the dragon's mouth. The snapping of its jaws served to slam the blade deeper into its skull as the teeth punctured through my tattered armor. Incisors sheered through my right leg at the knee, as my attempt to invoke the rage fires became the venue of my pain. The sound of my scream was strangely dead inside Hakareth's mouth as if the dragon stifled the smallest indication of my survival. At least I did not have to worry about the bolt wound, but that was little consolation to the white flash of fire that raged in my head.

Swallowing down the acidic bile that filled my throat, I managed to invoke the rage fire in ragged gasps. At the same moment the white-blue fire burst forth, the dragon shifted its tongue slightly, shoving me directly into the line of its yellowed teeth and bit down once more. My mind froze as the sensation of two sharp canines piercing me from above and below burst onto my consciousness. My gut was on fire as my sundered kidneys shut down all sense of reality. Overloaded, it was as if my nerves refused to acknowledge any more pain. In slow motion it seemed the dragon opened its mouth to howl its dying gasp. Would Morakvaar let me die? Impaled on its lower canine, I could do nothing as the dragon thrashed around in its death throes.

As suddenly as the attack had been, I found myself lying on the ground. Confused, I stared into the darkness, but could not see the dragon. Cursing, I realized I had fallen prey to an illusion, nothing more than a spell conjured to test my abilities. As soon as I recognized what had happened, my wounds disappeared. Feeling rather foolish, I got to my feet. Only the best of Lodath's spells could have rivaled the perfection of the illusion even down to the smell of burnt flesh. The wyrm's deftness with the spell bespoke of its power and age. A chill crept down my spine as I realized it was no mere dragon we faced, but an ancient evil beast that had spent close to a thousand years brooding on destruction.

"Alright, Hakareth. You have had your fun, now reveal yourself!" My voice echoed back emptily from the distance, the only answer I received.

Warily I moved towards the door in the gate. Where was the blasted creature? The small stone door in the right wing of the gates stood open, and a light blonde haired kinsman urged me to hurry back through. With one last glance down the tunnel, I sprinted for the door.

Barely ten paces from safety, a thick dark-gray coil dropped over my shoulders from above. The vile beast must have been invisible! In rapid succession four more coils slipped down to cover me from my hips to my shoulders, pinning my arms tightly to my sides, but not tight enough. Thinking quickly, I slipped my left arm partially out through the coils and passed the Reaver back to my free hand with a flick of my trapped wrist. Unable to get a full swing, I still managed to bring the weapon to bear on my enemy. At least this was no illusion!

The kinsman in the door's eyes grew wide as he yelled over his shoulder. The coils tightened around me, spoiling my blow as my arms were crushed to my sides. Barely keeping hold of the Reaver, I rested the blades against the coils. The dragon had tricked me into using all but the last reserve of the weapon's rage-fire, and I invoked the final blaze before it could crush the breath from my lungs. The flames heated the body of the creature, but I could see it did little damage.

A snake-like head full of needle teeth hissed in anger as the dark gray coils tightened. My armor was no match for the beast's strength, and slowly gave way beneath the onslaught. A squad of warriors rushed from the door, shields locked in an impenetrable barrier of defense. Seeing their attempt to help me, Hakareth tightened his grip on me as wings formed from its thick body. The additional pressure crushed my chestplate inward, popping my shoulders out of joint with a painful crack. With a down-swoop of air all that was left behind was the clash of the Reaver as it fell from my numb fingers to the stony floor of the cavern.

Crossbow bolts pinged off its iron hide like the ineffective sting of insects, but the ballista slammed through its scales as it roared in pain. The coils around me disappeared, and I was dropped surreptitiously. Though I was thankful that my kinsmen had better aim than in the illusion, I knew I could not miss the ground. The crash of my armor on stone rang nearly as loud as my howl of agony as I felt the tearing of my ligaments in my left shoulder. My arm lie at an unnatural angle as I tried to move, only to give up as nausea washed over me in waves of cold sweat. Mustering all of my will, I pushed my knees beneath me as the sound of running boots approached. The dragon got to me first, and though it missed me with its snake-jaws as I rolled onto my back, its tail did not miss as it swooped by. A flash of light burned through my skull. Fighting back the darkness, I focused on the booted feet that surrounded me, forming a ring of shields to protect me.

As Hakareth wheeled for another pass, the other ballista fired almost point-blank into the dragon's side. The bolt penetrated below its right wing and the roar of the wyrm's agony shook loose several stalactites. A shower of rocks pelted downward, but all I could do was turn my head. It hurt too much to do anything else. Stones bounced off my helmet, some leaving permanent dents and ringing in my ears.

Out of the corner of my eye, I saw the long sinuous form expand to fill the cavern as Hakareth revealed its true form. Forepaws the size of an adult crawler arced outward stretching talons longer than I as if clawing the air. Massive hindquarters used to launching tons of weight into the air curled behind the beast in its flight like a lizard swimming in water. The span of the dragon's wings brushed either side of the great tunnel as it prepared to dive back towards us. The huge gaping maw of its teeth gleamed like spears in the dark as it opened to swallow the entire group of us whole. With the speed of a stooping hawk, it swept downward, its size growing larger by the second until nothing else could be seen. The air whistled through its wings, shrieking like a banshee out to gather souls.

Expecting to feel the bite of those incredibly large teeth, I closed my eyes to the inevitable as the muscles of my jaw ached almost as much as my shoulders. The sensation of falling popped open my eyes in surprise. It was as if the stone itself had disappeared beneath me. Harrakuli's smiling face bent over mine.

The orudin had come up through the stone and pulled us below it to escape the dragon's jaws! They brought us inside the gates of Vouroussan before ascending back through the stone to deposit us in the courtyard.

The dragon's howls of rage echoed from the other side of the gates as its tail slammed into the fortifications again and again. The cavern shook with the wyrm's fury and large cracks appeared in the stone gates. Showers of rocks and dust rained down with the impacts as they reverberated along the walls and ceiling. The screams of a couple unfortunate kinsmen told me that not all the stones that fell were small ones.

While I was focused on the widening crack in the gates, Harrakuli gripped my left arm and snapped it into position with a firm yank. Fiery pain speared through my system radiating outward from the abused tendons. My yell of pain was more a yelp of surprise as I spun angrily on her.

"Warn me before you do that!" Throbbing stabs continued to lance up and down my arm and spine, but Harrakuli soothed them with her healing powers.

With another crack, the top of the gates splintered inward and the fore-portion of a gray muzzle tried to lever its way into the stronghold. The iron scales ground against the stone as the beast tried to shatter the remains by sheer muscle to no avail. Taking in a sharp breath, I spun to watch in awe at the ferocity of the dragon's attack. Harrakuli took the opportunity to snap my other shoulder back in place, sending another bout of dizzy nausea through me.

"Vooraduum! Do you delight in torturing me!? Did I not just ask you to warn me!?" My growl barely made it past my grit teeth.

"If I had, you would have tensed up and made the job impossible." Her healing power flowed through my right shoulder, mending the rent tendons and torn muscles. "You dropped this." She handed me the Reaver, and for a moment, all I could do was stare.

How was it that she was able to handle the weapon? Even Korina had suffered the anger of the Reaver, yet Harrakuli had handled the axe with alacrity. The reminder of her divine power made me uneasy. Why would she choose me? The axe felt good in my hands, though and I shrugged my shoulders testing the healing she had done. My arms felt like new, but my armor had taken a beating. The straps had all but disintegrated from the corrosive breath, so I shrugged out of it and left it in a pile.

The roars and pounding of stone vanished moments before I finished removing my armor. Instinctive dread filled me and I wondered what the beast was planning. As if in answer to my unspoken question, the gate simply vanished into non-existence. The dragon's aura of fear rolled through the empty space like a thick fog, paralyzing my kin.

Like an iron-gray juggernaught, the wyrm steamed into the city its teeth and claws bringing death in rending waves of armor and blood. Nothing stayed its deadly rush, not even the blast of the cannon that stood in the courtyard as it discharged its load in the dragon's face.

The ripped scales hung from its bloody muzzle as bits of armor hung out from between its teeth where they had been lodged by the power of Hakareth's jaws. Black talons shredded the cannon and crew in one fell swoop, crushing them between razor sharp claws and solid stone. Red welled from under the beast's forepaw as it snapped at Harrakuli a moment too late. The orudin vanished down into the rock beneath her feet as the threat to her life galvanized me into action.

With my own bellow of rage, I ran between its forelegs as it turned to the unit of crossbows to my right. Hakareth crouched, intending to crush me beneath its weight, but I used its downward momentum to sink the Reaver deep into its belly. Sticky ichors fountained over me from the wound as the stench of the beast's innards made me choke on my own bile. With its entrails hanging from the wound, Hakareth screeched an unearthly noise, but did not stop its deadly progress as it plowed through the crossbowmen. Sword-like teeth rent metal plates like paper as the screams of the dying filled the air. Blood welled into the air from a dozen mortal fountains and the stench of bowels and half-digested food filled the air.

Wrapping my arm in the guts of the dragon, I swung myself upward into its belly. Struggling against the slimy bodily fluids that leaked around me, I found purchase and braced myself against the dragon's ribs. The Reaver cut through organs and tissue as the beast's stench threatened to render me unconscious. Howling like a mad thing, Hakareth stopped its advance. Reaching into the wound with a taloned forepaw, it snatched me out, piercing me through the abdomen with an obsidian claw. Its form melted again into that of the snake, and its wound began to disappear. Not when we were so close! Victory was turned around as the snake's coils slid over me and it took to wing once more.

In a red tide, my life-blood poured out the wound like a fruit's juices as the coils tightened. The triangular head of the snake dipped down to drink it from the gaping rent in my gut as I felt my strength drain from me. Feebly I swung the Reaver with what little room I had to move my forearms, but the beast was quick. Its triangular head darted out of my side and towards my head as I could but react dully. Its jaws closed around my helmet, the only remaining piece of my armor, and it showered me in my own blood.

The dragon's breath was full of the stench of rotting carrion, but an odor I would have gladly endured had I been allowed to breathe. The coils continued to tighten around me, bearing splintering force to my ribs as they began to crack. My vision became blurry as my awareness was strangely detached from my predicament. With barely any strength left I swung the great-axe towards the top of my helmet. Though I felt the impact of the weapon on the neck of the wyrm, it did not release my head, rather slid its jaws down to my shoulders in the grotesque manner of a snake. Its needle-teeth dug in to my flesh as I swung again, putting all the reserves of my energy into my last bid for life and freedom.

With a loud crack that resounded through the beast's body its neck bone snapped on impact. The body convulsed in agony popping my ribs as blood soaked my leg and pooled in my boot from the wound in my gut. The dragon's black ichors filled my mouth and nose as I struggled to breathe. Vaguely I had the sensation of falling, but my consciousness fled from me long before I hit the ground.

Chapter 21

Garan Kraz (The Living Dead)

Soft lips brushed my brow as arms encircled my head, holding me to a warm breast. Harrakuli's gold eyes met mine as I was finally able to focus. Her smile brought more warmth from within.

"Taking care of you is beginning to be a full-time job! I wonder if this is Morakvaar's punishment for my participation in the war?" As puzzlement crept into my expression, she quickly changed the subject. "You know, killing a dragon when it has you high in the air is really not a very smart thing to do, Dorian."

"How was I to know, the beast had its damned mouth over my head!?" My smile told Harrakuli that I was not really angry at her insult. "How did I survive the fall?"

Her anguished frown told me of her helpless fear of the moment. "Lucky for you, you had other friends that followed Hakareth here. I had no time to channel a manifestation that would save you."

Behind her head I could see the stone gargoyle-vourdovra that stood on either side of the gates and I realized we were still in the courtyard. Two paces away was the severed head of Hakareth in its original form. A black pool leaked from the ragged tear where the Reaver had slammed through both flesh and bone. The iron scales along its brow gleamed coldly in the torchlight, but the feral yellow eyes stared in lifeless agony in the widened slotted pupils. The arcing horns propped the head up at an odd angle as its long forked tongue sprawled outward between large rending teeth so much like our own. Were we of the same creation as the dragon? The gaping maw could have held an entire squad of warriors and I shuddered anew at my narrow escape from death.

Dizzy nausea wet my brow as it threatened my vision when I tried to move. Harrakuli gripped me tighter. "Shhh, rest a while. The priests are on their way with a stretcher. Even though most of your wounds are healed, it will be many days before you will have your full strength back."

With a sigh I relaxed back into her arms, my shoulders propped up against her thigh. "Who was it that halted my fall and how did they do it?"

The dark-skinned face of a zarak hove into view and for a moment, all I could see was an enemy. Gorain seethed within me as rage filled my blood with fire. But as I looked closer, the anger turned to astonishment. Liathrain's brows drew down at my momentary lapse, but cleared when she saw my grin of recognition. To either side of her stood a grim-faced kinsman with an axe held ready to deal death.

"By the gods, I never thought I would see you again, especially not among the living!" She clasped my forearms in greeting despite the attempts of my kin to prevent her, but even that small movement ached in my bones.

"We have both been through the hells, Dorian, and it looks like neither of us is welcome there." The irony in her voice brought a broader smile to my lips.

"I am glad to see you alive. My heart has been in torment since the moment we fought." Thank the Maker that her blood was no longer on my hands!

"Were is your better half?" Liathrain stared pointedly at Harrakuli as she spoke to me.

A stab of fire ran through me, filling me with shame for enjoying Harrakuli's embrace. "Morina is dead." The words whispered past my lips barely formed.

Liathrain's bowed head told of her respect for my mate. "I am sorry, Dorian. She was a good friend, and more than a saint to put up with you." Was that an insult?

"She was my life. I never deserved her love and now she is gone forever." A hot tear renewed the agony within my soul as it ran down my cheek to wet my beard in helpless pain. "She is gone, and the Maker has forbidden me to follow. I do not know if I should even try, for she is probably better off without me."

"Was no one able to bring her back?"

"No." My voice broke as I admitted my failure. "Morakvaar would not permit it. It was my fault she perished and not even Waradain could bring back her soul."

"You can't blame yourself, Dorian." Liathrain switched to her native tongue. "If she was destined to die, there's nothing you could've done."

"My absence caused her death. Her greatest fear was that I would disappear or be killed when she was not there. When she learned that I did not return with the demolition team, she went to find me on her own." The torn soul-bond welled pain through me, choking off my words.

Grief filled Harrakuli's eyes as she spoke. "No, Dorian. If you must blame someone, then blame me. If I had not taken you from the cavern where you were trapped beneath the boulder, you would have been found. Perhaps the tragedy could have been avoided." She looked as if she wanted to say more, to confess a terrible secret, but instead she fell silent.

Did she know that Morina would perish? Her people already knew I was Gorain, so why had they taken me? Was Harrakuli so obsessed with Gorain that she would allow Morina's death simply to clear the way for her affections?

"Did you know?" My voice failed me, but Harrakuli understood the question too well.

Her face turned from me, her gaze finding anywhere to rest except on me. "What happened was Morakvaar's will." She avoided the question, but her words gave me the answer as surely as if she had confessed to murdering Morina herself.

The hot knife of betrayal seared through my soul once more. Even Kormak's actions seemed a mere pittance compared to Harrakuli's willing participation in Morina's death. How could she!? Kormak at least had betrayed me for what he thought was best for our race, yet Harrakuli had allowed Morina to die for nothing more than selfish gratification! The injustice howled through the barren wasteland of my heart like a damned spirit in need of sanctuary. How could I ever trust her? How could I have fallen so easily into the trap she had woven for me? If only there were a soulsmith alive that could rend the soul-bond she had forged with Gorain, I would gladly have dealt with the pain! Even then, our bond pulled at me, whispering of her affection for me. If I could have mustered the energy to tear my heart out of my chest, I would have, but all I could manage was an inner howl of torment as I wrestled for some sort of equilibrium.

"How did Hakareth know about you and Kelana?" I would have said anything to distract me from the horrible wound that was killing me from the inside out.

Liathrain raised a silver brow at my flat tone, but humored my request. "We were hunting in the Darklands when we happened upon another shadow elf hunter. To our amazement, she bore the sigil of the Goddess of Knowledge. Her house seemed uncannily aware of what was happening in the Deep Realms and she spoke at length about her angst over Gorain's return. I assumed she was of the house whose pilgrims were slaughtered by Gorain, so did not suspect her, as I should have. Her words had a mesmerizing effect, and soon Kelana and I found ourselves under her spell." She faltered at the admission of weakness, but my grim nod confirmed the awesome powers of the beast.

"I too fell prey to Hakareth's spells. The wyrm had extraordinary power. There is no shame in succumbing to an enemies' superior force." Liathrain smiled wryly.

"I had thought our kind immune to such spells, for nothing of the sort had ever worked in the past. Despite my normal caution I found myself confessing secrets that I would not have told my truest friends let alone a stranger. Kelana too found her questions irresistible. When we awoke in the morning, the other hunter had vanished along with the spell. Knowing we had been ensorcelled, but not knowing to what end, we tracked her back to you. Unfortunately, we were not in time to warn you, for your battle with the beast was nearly over by the time we arrived."

"Hakareth must have intentionally tracked you down to learn what it could of us." The foresight of the dragon amazed me let alone the fact that it had to know that Liathrain was alive.

"But why you in particular, Dorian? She seemed overwhelmingly interested in everything about you and your exploits."

"Hakareth is the eldest surviving dragon of the Deeps and the sixth descendant of its predecessor who bore the same title. It was that Hakareth that I slew over eight thousand years ago. The beast was out for vengeance."

Liathrain narrowed her eyes thoughtfully. "So you are Gorian! I had hoped Kairillia had deceived us about that too." Her frown deepened as uncertainty crept into her gaze.

I was unable to look at her as I sought for what to say. "Liathrain, I may have Gorain's soul, but I am my own person."

"Are you? What did you feel when you first saw me? Rage? You can't hide from what you are." My cheeks heated with shame.

How could I deny the truth? "I am still Dorian, and even though there has been blood shed between us, I consider you my friend. It was that friendship I honored when I bargained a truce with your mother. And perhaps it will be that friendship that saves me from Gorain's damnation. To see you alive again has given me some hope for my salvation."

Her face broke into a huge grin as her eyes danced with mischief. "You always did take things a little too seriously."

The old argument between us seemed so fulfilling, so full of life. "What else am I to do, brush off everything like you flighty elves?" It was not quite enough to distract me from Harrakuli's part in Morina's death, but it was a start.

The priests struggled to get me on the stretcher and Harrakuli followed along with the Reaver in her hands. As the only one who could carry the weapon besides me, I could not make her stay behind. But within me resentment and anger burned brightly. My gaze found Kelana as they lifted me from the ground, and I bid the two elves to accompany me to the infirmary, much to my kinsmen's dismay. Though many hostile stares followed their progress, not a word was spoken.

Two days passed as my friends came to visit every day, not finding any welcome elsewhere among my kin. The strength seemed loath to return to me, so many injuries in so short a time. I felt stretched thin by the healing, as if the substance of my being had been rolled flat like dough and made to go over a mold too big for its entirety. But I was determined not to languish, and forced myself to move, and I stood panting, clinging to the bedpost with the effort of walking across the room as I spoke to my old friends.

My fingers ran along the lighter colored scars from the dragon's teeth as I sighed. Another set of marks to join the chorus that adorned my skin both front and back. Amusingly enough, the scars were roughly triangular running from my shoulders halfway down my chest, looking for all the world like a permanent necklace of pain. Liathrain raised a brow as she studied the assortment of scars including the one across my neck made by her dagger.

"I can see that you've kept up your tradition of staying in harm's way." Liathrain glanced at Harrakuli who refused to leave me alone with the two elves before looking back. "Dorian, I may have need of your assistance. In exchange for my life, I was given a quest to fulfill. The goddess told me that the means to fulfill this quest involved you and your need to absolve yourself to her. In light of your confession to being Gorain, I can see why you would need absolution from Illumia."

The memory of Gorain's rage directed against the pilgrims returned to me as if it had just happened, and I looked at my hands as if expecting they were still stained with blood. "I know not how to atone for my crimes, but if you hold the answer, then I will gladly accompany you when the time comes."

As if a heavy weight had been lifted from her shoulders, Liathrain straightened and smiled. "I had my doubts after all that has passed between us, but you give me hope of our former friendship. It is a friendship I will gladly renew." She held out her hands to me and with a smile of my own I grasped her forearms firmly.

A young blondish-white haired kinsman knocked on the open door and I beckoned him to enter. "Lord Dorian, I am glad to see you up. Queen Korina has held off the Feast of the Living as long as she dared so that you may attend. But our people are restless to continue with our traditions and will be delayed no longer. She has consented to hold the feast this evening cycle. I was told to bring you word of this in case you have recovered enough to attend."

With an even larger grin I turned back to Liathrain. "I see your timing has improved slightly. Not only do you miss the better part of my battles, but arrive just in time for the celebrations!"

Not missing a beat she responded well. "What are friends for?"

"Tell Korina that I will be there. I could use a few mugs of ale to bolster my strength. And tell her I will have guests." Both the young kinsman and Harrakuli frowned at the elves, but neither commented.

Liathrain met Harrakuli's somber gaze with curiosity. "I have never seen a dwarf like you. You are a dwarf I take it?"

A scowl turned her mouth down as Harrakuli's eyes narrowed. Without saying a word she left.

"She is orudin, blessed of Dormakkaar." I answered for her, but never would I confide her status as Clan First despite the anger over her part in Morina's death.

A troubled frown passed Liathrain's features. "Even though I heard your confession to be Gorain, I had hoped it wasn't true. The old legends have come to pass and the 'ghosts of the rocks' have returned."

"There are many interpretations to prophesy, Liathrain. Have you considered the fall of the zarakkanan to mean only the fall of the worshippers of Lillain?" When I held out the Reaver, Liathrain jumped back with her weapons half drawn. "It no longer controls me, I control it wholly. You need not fear it, nor me. You see? The blades do not glow in rage until I command them. The curse of Gorain is broken, though I do not know if I will ever be able to redeem myself in the eyes of my people." Taking a deep breath, I let it out slowly, thinking of all the things I had done in this life that damned me still.

She stared at the Reaver and me with suspicion. Her hands never strayed from her weapons even after I had strapped the axe into the harness on my back. "One thing I will ask is that you leave that thing behind when you assist me with my quest."

"You do not ask me anything I was not already prepared to do. The Reaver belongs to my people, and I will not be the instrument of its loss. The weapon will remain with my daughter."

At last her hands left her weapons. "Perhaps you have broken the curse. I had my doubts when the priestess prophesied I needed you to fulfill my quest."

"There has been much time lost between us, Liathrain. When we have eaten and had a chance to refresh ourselves, perhaps you will tell me of your adventures since Mezosilliar? It would please me to know what you two have been doing since then."

Both elves grinned wryly. "Not nearly as much as you have, Dorian, but we will tell you what we may. On the morrow, we'll discuss my quest."

We exited the infirmary with enough time to spare that I could wash up and change into some fresh clothes. The hostile stares of my kin towards the elves were getting worrisome, and I hoped that none would attempt to assault them while in my company.

"I think it would be wise if you accompanied me to my quarters. My kinsmen will take many years to cool their ire over the wars between us." Liathrain gave me a sly look and I knew what was coming.

"So you've finally invited me to your quarters. It took you long enough." Playfully, she took up my arm as if I were her escort. "Dorian, dear, do you think there's a future for us?"

My deep sigh and rolled eyes made her laugh and let go. "I was about to say I missed your company, but now I think I was better off without it."

Both elves laughed merrily as we reached the tunnel that had been assigned to me. The apartments were cut into a massive stalagmite that spiraled upward. The spacious arcing rooms were almost oppressive being designed for the vourdovra's tastes. Chest high pallets were carved from the stone in strategic locations about the dwelling. Two of them were next to a stone table that had one hinged side and a hole in the center. A cold shudder passed down my spine as I imagined what it was used for, the bloodstains still apparent on its scrubbed surface. In one corner was a small pool full of saltwater, but nowhere was there a fireplace or a vent to the lava flow. The coldness of the place was horrible, but at least I had a blanket with my bedroll.

Forgetting the difference between my culture and the surface elves for a few moments, I undressed and washed up. My mistake was quite plain when Kelana stared open mouthed at me when I was drying my face.

"Forgive me, I keep forgetting that you have different standards of modesty. Among my people, there is no need for such things. We are a close-knit society where privacy is an unknown concept." My stammering words only made Liathrain smile as she stepped next to me.

"It's okay, Dorian." Her fingers traced up my side as I tried to step back. "I rather enjoyed the show. Perhaps I will find out what kept Jaguar's attention for so long?"

In embarrassment, I backed into my private room with the facecloth held protectively before me. Shutting the door on Liathrain, I leaned against it wondering what had possessed me to conveniently forget about the different societal view. Though it was good to see my old companions, and I had completely forgotten about Liathrain's disturbing interest in me. In the past, I had my relationship with Jaguar to hide behind, and after that, I had my marriage to Morina. Neither shield was available to me any more, nor a way I could shed her advances without offense. The matter was made even more difficult because to a zarakanan, sex between trusted friends was expected. To them it was no more of a deal than a warm greeting. In retrospect, it seemed a very bad idea to offer my quarters as sanctuary to my former companions.

The brocaded jacket fit snugly over the spider-silk shirt, perhaps a little too snugly. Had I gained weight? Shrugging, I pulled on the matching red breeks, noting that the drawstring had shortened. How could I have gained weight during our campaign? The many nights I had spent in taverns or at the ale tent offered a clue, but drinking had never effected me before. Was I getting old? The gray hairs in my beard stood out like beacons in the near darkness, and the death of my mate weighed heavily on my shoulders. The only thing that made my life bearable was the alcohol brewed by clan Farovar.

With the intention of drowning my pain in ale, I led the elves to the central chamber of

Vouroussan, the only place large enough to accommodate the feast. It seemed a journey that was far too long and I was weary and shaking by the time we reached the old sanctum. Roasting on several spits near the back of the chamber were large chunks of the meat from the dragon. Makeshift tables spread along the length of the cavern low enough that no chairs were necessary. The low roar of many voices echoed through the cracks and fissures, rebounded back and magnified by the stone walls.

Many of those voices stilled as the two elves stepped in behind me. Not wishing to cause trouble, I sat at the empty end of a table near the door instead of making my way to the High Table. Conversation was slow in returning, and many hostile glances were shot our way until the food was served. The dragon meat was supplemented with stuffed voras, boiled spider legs in lemvar butter and bread. Several casks of voras ale were tapped and served in generous portions, much to the disgust of the elves. With a laugh at their distaste, I told Liathrain where to find a couple small casks of wine I had saved from Sorkarak for Lodath's use. Since the mage had left for the surface, I saw no reason why they could not have it. The dark one returned a few minutes later with the goods gratefully clutched one under each arm.

A storysmith named Farzak entertained us as we ate. His baritone voice filled the chamber with ease, almost as if the room had been designed to carry such sounds to every ear. The Ballad of Gorain nearly put me off my appetite as the final strains sung mockingly by my younger peers told of my clan's shame. Three more mugs of ale in rapid succession allowed me to ignore the words enough to focus on the food. Halfway through the dragon steak, I realized the stanzas being sung were none that I had heard before. Glances from my kin kept switching from me to Farzak as the words began to register. He was singing about our campaign! I found Korina's proud look as I stared at her accusingly. Shrugging innocently from across the room, she could not fool me. What on earth had possessed her to have the storysmith add my life to the Ballad of Gorain?

Liathrain and Kelana on the other hand listened in rapt delight to Farzak. The verses fit well into the ancient ballad, and I had to admit the storysmith had outdone himself even though I thought he overstressed my 'heroics'. The tempo and melody changed abruptly, but the transition was eerily smooth as Farzak relayed the verses to the battle of Vouroussan. Reaching for my mug, I tried to drown out what I knew was coming. Even though I tried not to hear, when the pitch of the storysmith's voice changed to a haunting note I could not help but listen. He sang of my quest to find Morina, and the heroic charge into danger for the sake of love that ended in tragedy. Such was his mastery in the skill of weaving his tale, that even my sturdy kin bowed their heads in grief. I stared into my mug to hide my pain, and my thoughts were in turmoil. Farzak had managed to bring back to me all of my despair at being left behind in the land of the living.

Would I ever earn absolution for my crimes? Would I ever see Morina again? A stab of fire ran through my heart. Morina would be lost to me forever. That thought alone was enough torment to see my soul through eternity in Vooraduum. It was Vooraduum. All the ale brought in to Vouroussan would not be enough to soothe the ache that burned in my chest as the vision of Morina's mutilated skull floated within my mind again and again.

Liathrain's sharp elbow brought a growl to my lips before I realized that there was silence and all around, my kinsmen stared expectantly at me. What did they want? My mind raced to the conclusion of where I was and what would normally be expected at the end of the feast we attended. Taking a deep breath while a lad refilled my mug, I got to my feet to address the crowd.

"We have all passed down a great road." I looked to the clans I knew had lost members. "Soon our quest for freedom from fear for our children will be at an end. The Halls of the Mother will be clear of our enemies, and will be sheltered from their return." Bowing my head, I found the words difficult to utter, but I knew my people needed the closing. "But the price of freedom has been great, and written in the blood of our kin. Let us never forget that. As we honor our dead, we celebrate the life that has been granted those who remain. As long as our people live, those who died will be remembered and honored for their part in bringing about a new golden age for our kin." The mug seemed unusually heavy as I lifted it. "To those that have passed before us, and may we meet them again in the Underhalls of the Maker!"

As one, all drank deeply, remembering the names and faces of those dear to them. With my mug emptied, I sat down, seeing Morina's face reflected in the damp foam. Forlornly it settled, left behind from what had given it life, so much like my soul. The lad with the pitcher filled it anew, and the foam danced again but it was only a parody of its former life. New foam quickly banished its existence, and I wondered what sort of parallel my life would take.

The storysmith interrupted my morbid thoughts, raising his mug to toast life as much as I toasted death. "To Dorian, Gorain returned. The one who has led us to victory and delivered us from our enemies!" A great shout went up among my people as they drank my health. When it died down again, Farzak again lifted a newly charged mug. "To Korina Mytharia, High Queen of Morakduum, may she continue to reign with wisdom and honor!"

The toast to Korina was fit enough for me to drink with pride, but I wished in vain that Farzak would give more credit to my daughter's leadership than my fumbling abilities. Liathrain and Kelana watched me closely, and I found it difficult to decipher exactly what the elves were thinking. Trying to put my pain aside, I needed any distraction to keep from spoiling the celebration of life, a thing which I did not wish to celebrate at all.

"Now that you know what I have been up to, perhaps you will tell me what you two have done since Mezosilliar?" What I really wanted to know was why Liathrain had not informed me of Kairillia's raids on my people, but asking such a direct question would have undoubtedly offended the zarak.

To my surprise, it was Kelana who took up that gauntlet. "When we left Mezosilliar, Liathrain and I went to Fartairillzan. She renewed acquaintances with her family and the few friends she had. It was chilling, at first; being viewed with such hatred and in some cases, open hostility. It was only because I was afforded the protection of House Vaetra that I did not find a knife in the back, or poison in my drink. In time, the dark ones became near accustomed to my presence, but I still felt ill at ease, and Liathrain was also growing restless. The intrigue and politics of their court was not the type of adventure we preferred, and so we set out. Liathrain promised to show me all the sights of beauty in the Deep Realms, and teach me of its dangers as well."

Kelana paused to take another appreciative sip of some elven wine. "After seeing the Garden of the Singing Stones, I was eager to see what other wonders there were to behold. We decided to go to the Firefalls first, as Liathrain told me the wonders of the sight of the lava cascading down hundreds of feet to splash and churn in a deep pool of glowing whiteness. It was a sight not to be missed." Kelana paused as her hand hovered over the sweet breads.

Nostalgia filled me as I remembered my journey to the Mother's Heart. To the zarakanan, it was naught but a sight, but to a Kinsman of the Blood, it was a sacred quest. The transition from childhood to adult was measured in the change wrought by the Heart of the Mother. The two elves did not hear the Mother singing to them in her Halls for they were not her children, so most of the beauty was lost upon them. At the Mother's Heart her voice became a harmonious chorus, a beauty to strike even the loudest dumb with awe. As a child I had gone there and wept for the beauty, but I left a kinsman, not to shed a tear again until I returned from the surface to find Morkilduum in ruins.

The light-skinned elf devoured a roll and sipped for a moment on the wine before continuing. "In the first day of our journey, we ran into an orcish raiding party. They were attacking a settlement of gollarans. The guards had all fallen but one and some of the orcs were having their sport with him. Others busied themselves dragging the citizens out of their homes and pillaging. Some of the older and stronger children were shackled to a slave line; others were being killed. Liathrain and I waded into their midst, and the orcs knew nothing but the flash of our blades as they died. We slew near a hundred of them before the rest ran in terror. The gollarans were grateful, and we helped them rebuild their village. We waited for reinforcements from their stronghold before traveling on."

The elf's eyes rested on a point just over my left shoulder, and I turned to find Farzak listening intently. With a grin I offered him a chair opposite me, grateful that I was not at the High Table. Returning my smile, the storysmith nodded his thanks. With over half our number in the hall, it was full of noise, and a few kinsmen and kinswomen had brought instruments. They struck up some rowdy tunes as the revel went in to full swing. Some danced and some sang to the music, and the elves stared for a few moments in amazement.

"I never thought I would see the day when dwarves partied!" Liathrain shook her head as she spoke, as if trying to banish a sight that should never be.

The last few drops in my mug were replaced once more. "You have only seen the side we show to others. Such celebrations are a private matter within our society. It is one of the few times when emotions are freely expressed and never remembered after." Half the tankard slid down my throat before I expounded on the meaning. "You see we strive for perfection in everything we do, including the few celebrations we have."

Liathrain narrowed her eyes thoughtfully as I downed the rest of my mug. The ale made me light-headed and forgetful of my troubles as more memories of our past adventures paraded before my mind's eye. I smiled back at Liathrain as I refilled my tankard.

"Well, Kelana, what happened after you helped the gollarans?" Taking another swig, I leaned back in the chair.

Kelana finished her wine and refilled her mug. "The day after we left, Liathrain took me hunting for wild lemvar. It was as majestic as seeing a great stag stride out of a tree line in the morning mist to bellow a challenge to all other stags. To see the lemvar bucks guard the whispery retreat of the does was nearly as moving as that. Their nimble silent feet left almost no tracks, and their curled fur dampened their heat."

Remembering the times I had hunted lemvar training my spiders made me smile longingly. Before the zarakkanan captured me, I had the reputation as one of the best hunters in Morkilduum. I wished fervently for those times, and the innocence of spirit that was my youth.

A tray of baked zarkalez was brought to us, and I devoured the spicy mushrooms with relish. Liathrain too dug into the still steaming hot delicacies. Kelana reached for one in curiosity, but I caught her hand before she had the chance.

"I do not think you should try these. They may be hazardous to your health."

She gave me a disdainful look, and popped one into her mouth anyway. Fully expecting her to go into convulsions from the potency of the enzymes in the mushroom, I watched her closely. Most surface dwellers would have died eating one. To my surprise, she took another one and soon half a dozen of them were gone. Liathrain laughed, and I shrugged off her amusement at my expense.

"I see you have built up an immunity for our cuisine." Finding my mug empty again, I poured more into it. "To your health then?" The two elves raised their glasses, and I drank my tankard dry once more. "These mugs do not seem to hold as much as they used to." My grumble seemed to amuse both elves immensely.

It took a few minutes for the elf to recover her breath, but before she could go on with her tale, I felt the urgent need to rid myself of some of the ale. "Forgive me for a moment, but I need to visit the privy." For some reason, though, my feet did not catch up with the rest of me, and I found myself sprawled on the ground. Laughing, the two elves helped haul me to my feet as my coordination lagged my thought. "Maybe I did drink more than I thought?"

Not daring to trust her voice, Liathrain merely nodded as she barely held her mirth in check.

The ale must have taken all of my senses, for the next thing I knew, I leaned closer to Liathrain and whispered. "You know, if I had not been with Jaguar, I might have considered your offer. You are kind of cute, for an elf." She almost let me fall again, but I caught myself and realized just what I had said. "I mean, well, I meant..." I broke off flustered and staggered away from the two elves to relieve myself.

Standing next to the outbuilding for a time, I cursed my loose tongue. At least Harrakuli had sat with Korina at the High Table instead of with us. How could I explain that slip of the tongue to her? Harrakuli, gods but what was I to do? If she had not detained me, I may have been able to save Morina, but since she had, I had found a way to save my people from sure defeat. I loved Morina, but Harrakuli was a part of my soul, and I both loved and hated her for it.

I paused the thought. Loved? By the Maker, but I was becoming a confused individual! The merging of my memories with Gorain's must have been threatening my sanity. I, Dorian, loved Morina, and never would I betray that love. Sitting down with my head in my hands, I realized I had already done just that. The memory of the time I spent with Harrakuli at the waterfall filled me with guilt. I loved her then, with all of Gorain's soul. When I did not return to the gathering, Liathrain came to see what was taking me so long.

"I loved Morina." I insisted to no one in particular.

"I know, Dorian. Perhaps you should retire for the evening?"

I thought about that for a minute. "No. I have not heard the rest of your adventures yet." I did not feel like hearing a story, but I could not face going back to my quarters when Morina was not there.

Liathrain gave me an odd look as she helped me back to my feet. We were halfway to my quarters when I realized we were going in the opposite direction.

"Wait! The feast is the other way."

"You have had more than enough to drink, Dorian."

"I have not even passed out once!" Kelana's laughter joined Liathrain's as they both dragged me semi-resisting back to my quarters.

I grumbled in protest as they rudely shoved me into my room. Irritated, I sat on the bed and took off my boots. Exhaustion crept over me, and I did not even bother undressing or with the blankets. It seemed no sooner had I merely stretched out on the bed than I was asleep.

Chapter 22

Tava Nae (No Choices)

The next day, I awoke with the vague recollection of being lost in a vast dream-maze. How I got undressed and in the covers was a mystery that my mind refused to contemplate. Memories of the evening before were limited to pulling my boots off and falling asleep. In the outer chamber, I could hear voices. The cold water in the water basin was sufficient for a quick wash until I could make it to the showers. My head was still fuzzy from the ale I had consumed. The slightly dizzy nausea reminded me of another pressing need. Pulling on my breeks, I went to find the privy without so much as a greeting to the two elves.

To make up for my rude manners, I stopped by the soldier's mess for some black mushroom tea and biscuits for Liathrain and Kelana. By their expressions, I was forgiven when the last of the biscuits were devoured and we sipped our tea.

"Did you pass the night well?" Both light and dark elf gave me a very strange look that baffled my understanding.

"As well as could be expected," Liathrain finally answered. "I do admit your people leave a lot to be desired in the hospitality department."

"For that, I apologize. They see only an enemy in the face of an elf. There will never be trust between our people, but at least as individuals we can change." No sooner were the words out of my mouth than Harrakuli walked in with an expression of open hostility towards the two elves.

While still looking at them, she spoke to me. "What are they doing here?"

"They are here at my invitation. I was just going to ask Kelana to finish telling me of their adventures since Mezosilliar."

Liathrain stared at Harrakuli as the orudin sat next to me. The shadow elf's gaze was distant with some contemplation that I could not imagine. Harrakuli's face was flushed a darker gray, and her eyes narrowed with barely suppressed violence as she returned the zarak's stare. The temperature in the room felt as if it dropped below freezing. Trying to cheer things up slightly, Kelana attempted to finish her tale.

"We left off while hunting lemvar." Remembering Kelana's description of the lemvar hunt, I nodded in affirmation as she continued. "We took a good sized buck, and continued on our journey to the Firefalls."

"Did you finally learn to clean your own kills?" I smiled wickedly as I reminded Kelana of her formerly incompetent attempts.

"I always could, Dorian dear, but I just found it more convenient that you clean them."

Harrakuli's expression darkened at Kelana's words, but she ignored the orudin.

"How typical." I muttered good-naturedly, smiling until I caught Harrakuli's ire.

She was livid, and my humor left me immediately. "I think you and I should have a talk, Dorian."

There were many questions I needed answers to, so I stood up in response to Harrakuli's request. "Ladies, if you will excuse me?" My expression of respect only seemed to anger her more, but Kelana and Liathrain merely nodded in amusement.

The orudin not only led me outside the dwelling, but through the nearby rock wall and into a hidden chamber. It was as if a smooth bubble had formed in the earth long ago and remained intact through the centuries. There was neither fissure nor opening of any kind and I wondered how the air had gotten in. For a few moments, it seemed if Harrakuli meant to leave me there. Could I really prevent her from doing just that? Did I want to try?

"You spent the night with those two creatures!?" It was more accusation than question.

"Hold on a tenth cycle!" My surprise began to mutate into anger. "I have done nothing of the sort! I slept alone!" A nagging doubt made me even angrier. I had no memory of how I got from sleeping in my clothes to not.

"Yet they stayed in your dwelling the entire time you slept?" Harrakuli paced the small bubble, hands firmly planted on her hips in whitened fists as if to keep them from lashing out at me.

"Well, yes, but-"

"How could you dishonor yourself so?" She would not give me a chance to explain, but I would make her listen anyway.

"Where else could they go? None of my kinsmen would give them shelter nor hospitality. They are my friends and should be welcome in my home."

"And in your bed?" She kept her back to me, and I could not tell if she was angry or hurt.

"You have no right to accuse me! You who knew Morina was going to her death and did nothing! You who prevented me from saving the life of the woman I loved! And why? So you could steal my memories and replace them with Gorain's!? So you had no opposition for my affections!? You let Morina die for your selfishness!" How dare she judge me!?

Harrakuli spun to face me, opened her mouth, and quickly clamped it shut again. The anger seemed to drain from her leaving a sickly pale expression behind. "I am sorry." She whispered hoarsely.

My mouth hung open in horrified shock with the confirmation of my suspicions. My hands burned with the need to kill her, to bring justice to the one who took part in Morina's death, but a part of me could not. Instead I turned from her and pounded my fists on the rock wall in a helpless, painful rage. She reached out to me, and for a moment it was all I could do to keep from hitting her, but I held it in check.

"Leave me! It will be too soon ere I see your face again!" I growled in barely controlled rage.

Tears rolled down her face, and somewhere within me it hurt to see her in pain, but my anger was too great to acknowledge that part of me. She had betrayed Morina to death, and that burned within me with an unquenchable fire. Harrakuli left along with my only way out, but I did not care. If I were to be entombed there for all eternity it would not be enough to ease the agony of my soul. At least it would be a quicker and more merciful fate than to live with so much pain.

My fists pounded out my frustrations on the walls of the cave, turning my hands into bloody pulp, but I could not stop. The rage, the pain was too great. I cursed Morakvaar for his complicity in Morina's death, for surely he had conspired with his chosen in this. Raving like a madman, I cursed and raged against everything I suspected might have conspired to tear my soul asunder until I was hoarse and exhausted. A river of grief flowed from my eyes until they were no longer capable of moisture. My heart cried out against the crime I had committed. Sharing kinship with the woman who was instrumental in the death of my hearth-mate or at the very least was knowledgeable of her fate. It was the worst sin I could imagine. Feeling the lack of air as a descending blanket of peace for my tortured soul, I finally collapsed.

"Why do you curse my name?" Was this a dream or was the Maker standing over me? "Do you wish to face the damnation of your soul?"

My anger was still fresh. "What difference would that make? You have damned me in life, why not in death as well?"

Morakvaar's tone bore great anger as his gray eyes danced with white-blue flame. "Fool! Wretch! It was I who gave you a semblance of life, and gave you hope in the form of Morina. I brought you to her, sheltered you while you fought the necromancer. It was I who ensured you eighty-four years of happiness with her before I called her home. If you had not pleased me, and her plight moved me so, she would have died the day you killed the undead dragon. That was her fate! And this is how you repay my kindness, by cursing me?" His rebuke shriveled my anger and left me with the foolish apprehension of a naughty child as I considered his words.

"I am ashamed, Father, forgive me my fool's nature. Truly, I thank you for the time we had together, and for the beautiful children you have given us. I am sorry your gifts were wasted on such an ungrateful wretch as myself." I could not help but wonder why the Maker spoke with me given my idiotic behavior.

Morakvaar laughed. "You amuse me greatly, Gorain. It is because you entertain me that I have given you another gift, one that you have scorned. You will have to make amends if you wish to keep her."

"Forgive me, but I cannot just yet. I thank you, but Morina was too precious to me to leave behind so easily."

Morakvaar looked thoughtful. "Think what you wish, but you may not have a choice in this for long. Harrakuli has waited eight thousand years for your return, and I doubt she will be patient for much longer."

He took my hand and led me out of the chamber, back to the vourdovra city. When Morakvaar left me, I remembered my bloodied hands, but when I looked, there was not a mark upon them. Why would the Maker care what happened to me? Was it a good thing to amuse him?

My quarters were empty when I got there, and I wondered what had happened to the two elves. A passing kinswoman answered my question with disgust.

"The orudin have taken them and good riddance! Why would you care about those heathens?"

"They were my friends, and saved my life as many times as I have theirs. We have been long time comrades in arms. It is they who accompanied me upon my return from the overlands and helped in the taking of Mezosilliar."

A small light of understanding and pity lit her eyes. "Well then, you had better hurry. The orudin elders are to execute them in the seventh cycle."

I clenched my jaw in anger. Was there no end to Harrakuli's treachery? She would stop at nothing to ensure there were no obstacles in her path. My mind faltered over the possibility of the two elves actually being obstacles, but who knew what the orudin thought?

"Where?"

"At the temple."

"Thank-you, kinswoman." The words echoed over my shoulder as I ran off towards the temple.

It was nearing the end of the sixth cycle, and I had but moments to reach my friends. Bursting through the temple doors, I saw Liathrain and Kelana locked in cages of stone that were slowly shrinking as the orudin elders looked on in silence.

"Stop this at once!" I yelled, and all of the orudin turned to face me.

As they did so their faces paled, and each bent a knee and bowed their heads. I stared at them in puzzlement for a moment until I realized there was a presence next to me. The Maker stood crowned in a wreath of fire, his thick muscular arms crossed over his chest. His aura of majesty flowed out from him in a wave as even the two elves stared in awe. Without so much as a word, he vanished as he winked at me. Would I ever understand the mind of our god? Better yet, would I ever understand myself?

Striding quickly down the central aisle, I came level with the impromptu court. "Release them at once! What right have you to hold my friends and threaten their lives?"

"The right of kinship." Harrakuli said at last, her voice a hoarse whisper.

I stared at her in open-mouthed shock. "Kinship? You are?"

She nodded, but defiance was in her eyes. "They deceived you, seduced you, and as your first mate, I claim kinship. They must die and you will be mine." What was she saying!? She was admitting to all the sins we had committed, but I still did not understand what that had to do with the elves.

"You are mad! Nothing ever transpired between the elves and I!"

"There are plenty who saw the zarak enter your quarters with you and not exit." Why was she insisting on this fallacy?

"That means nothing! It is my honor at stake, and I will lay my honor on the line. Nothing happened between us!" Even as I spoke the words, I could not help the doubt. What had happened while I slept? "There is no soul-bond!" The finality was a relief to me as I realized I could not have shared kinship with either of them.

"Elven souls are not compatible with ours. There could never be a bond in kinship." She blew a hole in my confidence. "Your honor is already broken. I confessed I seduced you, and the child I carry is yours." Did she not understand that she had just doomed herself to exile with me?

"How can you do this? Why?" Three times she had betrayed me.

She came closer to me and whispered, "because the Maker promised you to me. I will not let them stand in my way, and I will use what means necessary to keep Morakvaar's gift."

"Let them go, Harrakuli, you win. If you release my friends, I will marry you." What else could I do?

She thought for a few minutes, and then nodded. Loudly she announced, "I believe you, Dorian. I will trust your word that nothing occurred between you and the heathens. They can go, but you are still bound by the laws of kinship."

I clenched my jaw and nodded. "It is as you say." Why had she taken this course of action? She had to know that eventually I would accept her. With Gorain's soul within me, I could do no less.

The anger of the past leaked out from the depths of my borrowed memories. Gorain had been banished for the very same crimes, yet because Harrakuli had allowed herself to conceive, the law provided for her protection and the protection of her chosen mate. Why had she not done this before? Why had she waited a lifetime? The questions rising from Gorain's memories nearly drove me insane. How could a kinsman live being at war with himself? How could the Maker allow such a fragmented soul to survive?

The orudin elders insisted that we be bonded without delay, and word spread through the city like wildfire. The bewildered faces of thousands of my kin came to witness my repetitive disgrace. Gorain's sins were now my own. The same thought was reflected in my people's eyes as they watched the Binding Ceremony. But there was no rejoicing in our pairing, only shocked disbelief and bitter disappointment.

When the ceremony was over, Korina passed me with an accusing gaze. The unspoken question brought pain to my soul. I wanted to tell her I had no choice, that the Maker had decreed these things even before my birth, but what meaning did that carry? The need to be with Harrakuli haunted those times we were together. My kinsmen left, some shaking their heads and others still in shock. At my bidding, the orudin grudgingly released Liathrain and Kelana to my custody.

"You had better come with me." They nodded and fell in behind me.

With a few hostile stares of their own, Liathrain and Kelana followed me to the gates of Vouroussan.

"I will hear the rest of your tale when I leave this place. Tell me where I might find you when at last my quest is at an end?"

"We will find you."

I smiled and clasped Liathrain's arm. "I am sorry you were caught in this," I shot a hostile glance at Harrakuli, "display of our darker nature. I look forward to our next meeting."

Liathrain looked past me to the orudin. "I think you have your hands full. Good luck, Dorian."

I chuckled ruefully, "I think I shall need it."

When the gates were sealed behind the two elves, Harrakuli took me firmly by the arm and led me back to my quarters. A part of me wanted to be with her as she helped me undress, but the other cried out against the blasphemy to Morina's place in my heart. The orudin's blue-gray fingers traced the braid of my beard with satisfaction as her left hand closed firmly around the binding ring. With her right, she drew my lips to hers. What choice did I really have? Was I naught but a slave to fate? Gods, but all I wanted was to live out an ordinary life with Morina when we returned to the Halls of the Mother!

Morakvaar's words chastised me once more. He had given me eighty-four years that Morina would not have had otherwise. She had given me three wonderful children, more than any kinsman could wish for. And, she had given me back my sense of soul, a reason to live not just to exist. Her beauty was something I would cherish to the end of my days; the Maker's greatest treasure and he had given her to me for a time.

Perhaps it was too soon for another kinsman, but I was never afforded the luxury of time. Even though I knew her complicity in Morina's death, I could hardly blame Harrakuli for following her own fate. Allowing Gorain's memories and feelings to fill me, I surrendered to my fate. But still Morina's face haunted me well into the night cycles. When I was sure Harrakuli was sound asleep, I left her to settle my mind.

Without knowing why, I found myself back at the waterfall. Without Harrakuli's divine power, I dared not enter the pool, but sat on the stone beside the water instead. Despite my angst for the deep water, I found the noise of the falls to be oddly soothing as I grieved for Morina. Would she ever forgive me? Would I ever see her again in the Underhalls?

"Father?" Korina's voice startled me, and I wanted desperately to disappear beneath the surface of the pool.

"Korina, what brings you here?" My back was to her and I dared not look at her face.

"Why did you do it?" The bitter anguish was so clear as it pierced my soul like a hot dagger.

The question was so simple, yet so complex. "Fate? Korina, know that I loved your mother more than anything, but I cannot escape who and what I am. Gorain loved Harrakuli those thousands of years ago. When your mother died, I could not face the dark alone. You cannot imagine the howling void brought on by a torn soul-bond, the despair, the madness. The wound in my soul could only be healed by my bond with Harrakuli, both she and I knew it. I had only known her on two occasions, but she is the oldest of her race. It was her choice to conceive or not, but my choice to let Gorain's memories live in me. The soul-bond we shared when I was Gorain drew me to her, but I know it was no excuse. I wanted to be with her, and therein lies my shame. Gorain's dishonor is mine as well."

"I cannot pretend to understand what is happening, father. I could only hope that you would have respected mother's memory." Her calm disdain hurt more than if she had cursed me.

At last I faced her. "I can only tell you that I had no choice in the matter. I spoke with Morakvaar."

Her eyes narrowed, "meaning?"

What could I tell her except the truth? "He told me that I should rejoice for the time Morina and I had together."

"What else did he say? The orudin told me they had seen him appear with you in the vourdovra temple."

"That Gorain had been promised to Harrakuli. I tried, Korina, and when I resisted his will, I was forced to comply. I had no choice, but I must confess, it is not totally against my will, and that is my shame."

She turned from me. "The orudin think as you, that there was no choice in this. It was the Maker's decree, but from this day, you are no father of mine."

I stopped myself from reaching out to her. What could I possibly say? She was right to reject kinship to me. Everything I taught her of our people's ways cried out against my behavior. It was for the best that I leave our people with my shame when our mission was complete. Korina left, and the last part of me that was Dorian left with her. What was I without Morina and my family but Gorain reborn, Gorain the Slayer, the exile in dishonor? Even my family was to be taken from me not by the Maker, but by my shameful actions.

Vouroussan had exacted a heavy toll not only in lives but also in faith. An aura of despair settled upon my kinsmen as the word of my dishonor spread throughout the ranks. Over and over the same questions were asked. How could a great leader and hero fall so far from grace? What good was Gorain's return if his shame returned with him? Not a soul from my clan would speak to me, not even my daughter except in council for our campaign. Already, I was an exile among my own people. All that remained was that I leave, but Harrakuli persuaded me to stay until we had finished the siege of Zarakalduum.

The remaining treasures of Vouroussan were carted back to Sorkarak as our army prepared to depart. Though my presence was unwelcome at the council meetings, there was the matter of a garrison and supplies that needed to be ironed out. When we met to discuss strategy, all conversation was unusually formal. It was a great stroke of agony to me to be addressed as 'General Dorian' by my own daughter, but it was less than what I deserved. If I felt ostracized by my people before, it was nothing to how they treated me after my marriage to Harrakuli. None of them would speak to me unless directly addressed, and even then in as few words as possible. The only one who accepted me was Harrakuli, and I was unsure if I wanted her acceptance.

The road back to Sorkarak was excruciatingly long. With Lodath gone and no one speaking to me, I found too much time to think. Morina's death and my disgrace haunted my every footstep. How could the Maker expect me to live in isolation? It went against our very nature to be alone. Everything we did as a people was done as a group save a few private moments within one family, but I found myself solitary in all my activities save sleeping when Harrakuli would join me in my tent. When I sat to eat, none of my kin sat near me, when we marched, none but Harrakuli walked beside me. My heart grew wearier by the day until I wanted nothing more than an end to the pain.

Chapter 23

Zar Narakar (Dark Messenger)

Sorkarak welcomed us back as heroes, but I found no comfort in the cheers. The festivity only served to wound me deeper. To think that I fought for a way of life I could not live by made me sick inside. Would they greet me with open arms if they knew? Guilt and shame kept me from responding as my feet became heavier with each step. When the palace gates were closed behind us, I sighed in relief. The Steward informed us that a feast had been planned in the sixth cycle as well as telling Korina a message had arrived from King Rokarzan of Zarakalduum.

There was much work to be done in preparation for the final stage of our campaign, but it still brought a pang of agony to my chest when Korina seemed relieved I did not want to attend the celebration. Instead, I ordered a copy of all surveys, ancient and modern concerning Zarakalduum's surroundings. Poised on the edge of the Heart of the Mother and the basin of the Daemon Fish River, any engineering project had to be carefully planned. Of all the battles we had faced, I knew that Zarakalduum would prove to be the longest. The Kinsmen of Shadow were adept warriors, but they suffered from the same plight we faced. The decline had hit them hard as well, perhaps even harder since they were the only colony of their race in the Halls of the Mother.

The best way for us to defeat King Rokarzan would be a prolonged blockade of supplies. It would be easier on our numbers and probably force surrender without too much bloodshed between us. The problems lie in cutting off all access to the city. Many tunnels crisscrossed through Zarakalduum carved by both the river and the Blood of the Mother. The distraction of the puzzle served to take my mind off being ostracized by my people as I examined the maps thoroughly. There were serious anomalies between the ancient surveys and the more modern ones, and by cross-referencing, I discovered an amazing secret. The Heart of the Mother used to be at the center of Zarakalduum! While my kinsmen celebrated, I pondered the revelation. What had happened? How did the flow of the Mother's Blood change?

A knock at the door disturbed my contemplation, and I left the maps only to find Korina's determined face. "General Dorian. I am to meet the messenger from King Rokarzan in a cycle. I want all of my commanders present." For only a moment, her eyes, so much like Morina's met mine. A spasm akin to pain washed over her face, but like the breeze from the river, it was gone just as quickly. "We will meet in the council chamber."

Bowing low as the anguish near stilled the beating of my heart. "It will be as you say, Majesty." It was all I could do to force the words past my lips.

A fire dancing in the hearth lit most of the chamber. Torches lined the walls reflecting off the polished armor of a dozen kinsmen. Grim copper-bronze faces regarded the lone Kinsman of Shadow, his dark gray skin outlined plainly against his black scale armor. His pale yellow eyes were like those of feral rats, and not anything like the few kinsmen of my people whose eyes were golden. His black hair was almost indistinguishable from his armor had it not curled thickly down his shoulders. In the manner of all dwarves, his beard and moustache were well trimmed and hung down to his waist, betraying his age. Thick black brows furrowed beneath his lifted visor as his gaze fixed on me.

Keeping his gaze on mine, he handed a canister to Korina. "Unto Korina Mytharia, High Queen of Morakduum does his Highness, King Rokarzan, King of Zarakalduum send his most humble greetings." I snorted at that and earned an annoyed look from both Korina and the messenger, but he continued, "it has come to our attention that the Kinsmen of Blood do declare war against all those not of their race. We, the Kinsmen of Iron, propose an alliance to finish our enemies and drive them from our homes."

The heat of anger rose within me, but before it passed the boiling point, Korina spoke out. "How dare you profane the name Kinsmen of Iron? Your people betrayed the old ways! You are Kinsmen to the Shadow now, and will be until you make restitution! You are the enemy! How dare Rokarzan even believe that he is kin to us? You tell that sniveling coward that there can never be peace between us!" My pride in my daughter was tempered not only by the situation, but by her disavowal of family.

The messenger acted as if he expected her tirade, and calmly rolled the scroll he was reading from and pointed to the sealed scroll case he had handed to Korina. "In that case, I have been instructed to give this to you. It is a declaration of terms for your surrender. When His Majesty, King Rokarzan, brings forth his army to do battle, you will see why."

My senses prickled with danger, and I put my hand over Korina's before she had the chance to open the case. "Your Majesty, in light of these hostilities, I would advise caution in this matter. Let me open the case elsewhere. I will bring you whatever document it contains when I am sure it is harmless."

The messenger's eyes seemed to almost gleam in hungry anticipation, as if he had expected this turn of events as well. "No, General, we will have this messenger open the case under distant supervision." Korina smiled in grim satisfaction as the shadow dwarf paled.

Taking the case from her hand, I grinned maliciously at the messenger.

"Krozarak!" He yelled and ducked under the table as all hell broke loose in the room.

The scroll case vanished, leaving behind the dark shimmering essence of an open portal as air rushed into its darkness. The vortex pulled me in, and it trapped me in a dimensional no-man's land. In the hazy blackness stood a daemon whose horned skull opened into a grimace of death. Its four arms were poised to do battle with sword, axe, whip and claw. In its sockets were the black fires of the Abyss, and its skin burned with its cold rage. The daemon advanced, its expression that of a starving beast. My people would suffer terribly if the abomination managed to get past me! The creature the Matriarch had called up was a mere imp compared to the greater daemon that faced me.

"Gorain!" Its base rumble sent fire through my nerves as it spoke, as if the true name of my soul invoked agony by the powers of the Abyss.

Pulling the Reaver free from its harness, I held it before me. "Be gone demon! You will find no slaughter here!"

Its laughter sent more pain through me, and I had to fight to keep hold of the Reaver. "It is you I have come for, Gorain. Lillain has decreed your death and a reward for your soul. When I have taken it to her, I will consume the lives of your people. One by one I will devour their souls."

I fended off its clawed hand with a shower of sparks from the mighty axe only to feel the lash of its whip pass right through my armor. It tore a line of fire across the skin and muscle of my back, and I felt blood rush down my spine to baptize my gambeson in the unholy rite of the Abyss. A grunt of agony escaped me, as the wound burned continuously with black heat. Dodging left took me past its sword, but its four arms worked to keep me off-balance. The haft of its axe wedged within the blades of the Reaver, and I twisted, pinning the weapon in the crease of the half-moon blades. With all of my weight and strength, I bore down on the weaker support. The haft of the demon's axe shattered under the strain, giving me a breath of triumph before the onslaught continued.

The overbalance of the maneuver caused me to take too long to recover, and the demon's claws raked through my armor, tearing it and the flesh beneath as easily as slicing bread. Bloody fragments of tissue followed the claws into the air as black fire filled the wound, burning to ash what little was left of my shoulder. The force of the blow sent me sprawling to the ground ten feet away from the daemon's clawed feet. The scream of agony that escaped me echoed through the hazy darkness of the portal, but the abomination merely laughed.

Fending off the sword one-handed, I could not stop the soul-sting of the lash. Pain snaked across my chest in a deep swath of fire. Dropping the broken haft of the axe, the daemon attacked with both of its clawed hands. As the first one darted towards me, I rolled right and the claws raked furrows in the stone where I had been. The bloodstone melted as if exposed to unimaginable heat in the wake of those obsidian daggers of death. Rolling to my knees, I swung the Reaver at the daemon's exposed arm. Black and white fire warred for dominance as the Reaver bit deeply within the bone.

"Sarlik doria!" The fires raged against each other, the black against white-blue.

The flames rose as my will locked with the daemon's. Its other claws slashed down my right leg, tearing the metal armor like paper, and shredding my flesh with impunity. Dark fire raged in the wound bringing unbelievable agony, but I could not let it win! Staggering to my feet despite the incredible pain, I tore my axe free in time to fend off the sword. As I invoked the power of the Reaver, it lent strength to my shattered shoulder. The demon's claws met with the blades, and the ring of metal echoed into infinity. The impact nearly took the weapon from my hands, but I was rewarded with a scream that felt as if it tore the heavens. The shock of the blow traveled from my shoulder to my brain and sent sparks swimming in my eyes, but the Reaver's power held me steady.

Not knowing how I did it, a piece of my soul entered the weapon, igniting it with the desperate rage I felt at the threat to my kinsmen. Power flowed through me, lighting the air with white-blue flame. The daemon's whip lashed out, and I stepped forward to cut through as it curled around me. Snarling in rage, the demon threw away the useless whip as it attacked with its three sets of claws and its last weapon. Catching the sword between the blades of the Reaver, I used the power flowing through me to snap it in half. Fire burst around me in raving sheets, and the icy heat burned my skin beneath my armor. The smell of singed hair and crisping flesh filled my nostrils, but my mind refused to acknowledge the pain. Two of the daemon's clawed hands struck my shoulders from either side, pinning me in its grasp as its claws pierced through my armor. It held me before it, and its sinew moved beneath red flesh in preparation to tear me in half. I swung the Reaver over my head and straight down between its shoulders. Bisecting its horns the axe imbedded itself deep into the demon's chest. Its skull flopped to either shoulder messily splashing the half-fluid contents everywhere in motes of dark fire.

With a hideous shriek the daemon fell, slamming me into the ground as it toppled forward. Black flames shot from its gaping wound all around me, setting me on fire with its icy heat. But something parted the flames. Someone sheltered me, bathing me in cool radiance as I was lifted from the daemon's claws. I was healed while sparks still dwelled in the embers of my life. Lips breathed on those sparks, fanning the embers back to a small flame.

"I will not let you go so easily. You are mine now."

The last thing I remembered for a long while was Harrakuli's desperate tears on my burned face.

A whispered breeze stirred the air around me bringing unbelievable agony. It was as if I was on fire once more. The small wind was nothing to the touch of the creamy salve that was applied to my burns, and a moan of pain followed instantly. Hands quickly grabbed my arms and held them down.

"Easy, Lord Dorian. Another day, and we will be able to heal you fully." It was Waradain, but I could not open my eyes to see for sure. "It has taken all our power to bring you and Harrakuli back from the brink. This salve will let you sleep until then."

The pain of the salve was fading as I rejoiced in my soul. He had called me by my name, spoken to me with respect. That small gesture made all the agony of the universe bearable.

Warmth bathed me, but not fire, soothing warmth that lapped away the burning, leaving blessed coolness behind. It filled me, surrounded me, nurtured me, and left me tired, but blissfully free of pain. The bandages were removed, and I blinked in the light of the stargem. Waradain's lined face betrayed his own exhaustion as he smiled in satisfaction. I fought to stay awake long enough to thank him again for saving me, but all I managed was a whispered 'thanks' before I slept again.

The feel of a soft caress across my cheek woke me. My eyes seemed leaden, but I managed to open them. Harrakuli smiled as I focused on her face. She kissed me with an odd desperation, which belied her worry.

"Never do that to me again." She whispered in my ear as she threw her arms around me.

"It was not my choice." My voice sounded as bad as it felt coming through my throat.

She drew back, and I could see the tears before she quickly wiped them away. She brought over a tray with a bowl of broth and some bread. Dried strips of meat completed the small meal, and half a mug of ale had me feeling normal, but very tired. By the time she took the tray away and joined me in the bed, I was almost asleep. Her arms slid around me as she held me tightly to her.

"I will not let you leave me so soon." She said fiercely as I fell asleep.

My dreams were of Morina, and the many times she held me so. Each time I dreamt of her holding me, sorrow echoed through my soul. In the final dream before waking, I stood in a mist-filled land. Morina stood before me, and I reached out to her. She turned from me and walked away saying 'you are not mine any more.' I woke up calling her name.

Grief filled me again for what I had lost. Harrakuli held me to her, and I was torn between my anger and Gorain's love. The two conflicting emotions warred for control of my soul. Perhaps it was some inherent weakness in my character that I gave in to Harrakuli's desire? I was never good at opposing the will of the women in my life. That did not mean I never tried, it only meant I never won.

The stubble of new growth on my chin was distressing. I felt naked without my beard. The short tips of hair peeking out from the top of my head were bearable, but never in my adult life, had I gone without a beard and mustache. No vaarakanan would willingly lose either, and for once, I was no exception. It was as if I had been sentenced to Tashor, and I felt ashamed to show my naked face. Though the healers had been able to heal me without scars, they could not make my hair grow back. Only time would heal that grievous wound. I sighed into the looking glass. Except for the lines about my face, I looked like a pre-pubescent child. Even the hair on my chest and arms was missing, not to mention the rest of me. The price I paid for the safety of my kinsmen!

Harrakuli tapped her foot in exasperation. "You are like a primping human! Hurry up, everyone is waiting for you."

I touched my chin again and grinned at her mischievously, "Without my beard, you have no way to prove you can tell me what to do."

She narrowed her eyes for a moment, and then returned my mischievous smile as she convinced me she did have the right. I would rather have spent time with her than what faced me, but we had no time for such activities and Harrakuli knew it.

"All right, I will be ready in a few moments." I dressed and put on my armor, but my helmet did not sit right on my head without my hair. In addition to my padded coif and chainmaille, I ended up putting a face towel over my reddish-gold stubble to snug the helmet on correctly.

The throneroom of Sorkarak was full of my kinsman, some of whom smiled in greeting and some turned their backs. The sight of the dark dwarf chained to the dragon's head on the dais brought me up short. A chill ran through me to grip my gut as my mind's eye saw me chained there. Surely Korina could not mean to kill him! Had she not been the one who proclaimed the law that no kinsman shall slay another? The shudders that ran down my spine to curl in my stomach would not relent as visions of the zarak torturer flashed through my mind.

Staring at Rokarzan's messenger I barely registered the five shaved dwarves that quietly took up their places by my side. Tovar and Balaran Stoneshaper, Jorak Karastan, Venzar Golodain and Larazak Zarathain were all that were left of the Tashor. Their recovery had been painfully slow, but Waradain had been able to save them from their injuries inflicted by the vourdovra. Though they were silent, I could not help but notice their stares at my bare face. Walking unclothed amongst them could not have caused me as much embarrassment, and I wanted nothing more than to hide my face behind the Reaver's blades. But the spectacle of the shadow dwarf held me riveted.

A kinsman that was almost as tall as I climbed the stairs of the dais. Black cloth held tight to every curve and a black hood obscured his face. "For treachery under a flag of truce, and attempted assassination of our Queen and her generals, you are sentenced to death by fireworm. May the Maker have mercy on your soul." The executioner read the sentence, and the Kinsman of Shadow shuddered.

"No!" All eyes turned to me at my protest. "How can we proclaim moral superiority if we commit crimes against our own laws!? It is our highest law that no kinsman shall slay another!"

Korina narrowed her eyes as she stood up from Sorkarak's throne. Resplendent in her black embroidered robes, she was every inch the regal monarch. "General Dorian. This assassin is the enemy, not a kinsman. He tried to kill you and all of us here. May I remind you that we do not intend to parley peace with Zarakalduum? They forfeited all claims to the rights of kinsmen when their ancestors killed our Clan Firsts. This execution is no more than lessening the amount of enemies we face by one." She turned to the executioner. "You may proceed."

The burly kinsman nodded as a clay jar was brought to him. With long metal tongs, he removed the stopper and reached inside. Worms the size of my thumb glowed brighter than stargems with their heat as he removed them one by one and placed them on the hands and feet of the dark dwarf. The captive screamed in agony and kept screaming as the worms ate their way slowly through his flesh towards his heart. The stench of burnt meat and hair filled the room, and I turned my head away in my inner torment. How could we claim to be better than them?

"You disapprove?" Harrakuli asked me.

"Are we any better than they are? Are not all kanan children of the Maker?" Could I make her see reason?

"No, Dorian, the shadow dwarves are not the Maker's children. They have given their souls to the dark powers. They have no place in the Underhalls."

"So because they were born of the Kinsmen of Shadow, they have no chance to redeem themselves? Surely the Maker had to allow for the damned to salvage their souls, or what would be the point in my existence?" If there was no hope for them, what hope did I have?

Harrakuli looked at me in disbelief. "Dorian! That creature tried to kill you, and all your kinsmen and kinswomen. If you had not managed to kill the daemon, it would have slain everyone in Sorkarak."

"Except your people."

She looked at me as if trying to get across a simple concept to a very dense child. "The dark dwarves are evil, they should all die."

I sighed, "Every death diminishes us all." Harrakuli just shook her head and ignored me the rest of the time we stood in the throneroom.

The storysmith, Farzak stole up beside me. "Lord Dorian," he whispered so low that I could barely hear him, "what really happened?"

"I wish everyone would just call me Dorian, or kinsman, or even Gorain," I did not mean to be grumpy, but the reminder of my torture and the display of dark violence put me out of sorts.

"My apologies, Dorian, so what happened when you left the feast up until now?"

With a backward glance at the still suffering shadow kin, I motioned for him to follow and I left. "You want to know the truth?"

He nodded. "I cannot believe the things I have been told. I would prefer to hear them from you," he said as we exited the throneroom to the tunnel outside.

"What you have heard is probably true."

"You, uh, had an affair with the orudin First, Harrakuli?"

"Yes."

"Did you have kinship with those elves?"

I narrowed my eyes. "What do you think?"

"I do not believe it."

"And so you should not. Harrakuli was there to save me from the darkness following Morina's death. If not for her, I would have destroyed myself. Between her and the Maker, I will find no peace in death for some time. Do you know what it is like to be denied the right to accompany your mate to the Underhalls?"

His jaw clenched trying to imagine my pain. "No. I could not imagine a life after your hearth-mate died." He fingered his unbraided beard, and I realized he could only imagine a life with a hearth-mate.

"Take heart, kinsman. There is the chance that those who live through this war will find happiness."

He looked thoughtful for a time, and I found myself grateful if only for the chance to talk with a kinsman who did not scorn me. "So Harrakuli never left the memory of Gorain behind? I am glad to know that at least there is a sort of continuity. It only stands to reason that once you had returned that you would be hers, but to take your hearth-mate to make room for the past?" He shook his head in imagined grief. "Truly I pity you, kinsman. Who can understand the ways of the Maker?"

"If it is some comfort, Morakvaar told me that it was because I pleased him that he spared Morina's life by sending me to her. He gave us eighty-four years that she would not have had otherwise. I told him that I was grateful for those years and for our children. In truth, kinsman, the matter of the orudin vexes me. I find within me the anger that Harrakuli conspired with Morakvaar to take Morina from me. Yet at the same time, I cannot deny the oneness of our souls, nor can I deny the Maker's words regarding Morina's borrowed life. If you can see any clarity to this tale, please enlighten me?"

Farzak stared at the tunnel floor for a long time. "In truth, I see no clarity. Indeed it is a very convoluted matter made all the more complex that you are Gorain reborn. You do remember the time you spent with Harrakuli from before?" I nodded and he continued, "Then she does have the right of kinship to you even if there was no child."

"But therein lies the difficulty. Gorain was refused the right to see or marry her. He, ... I was exiled because of it. Harrakuli allowed it to happen."

"I did it to save you from yourself, Gorain." I had not heard her steal up behind me, and started when Harrakuli spoke. "You had gone mad with your blood-lust, your thirst for revenge. I had hoped that the exile would have cooled your ire, calmed your madness. When I realized my error, and my need, I left to find you. But, when I caught up it was too late. I blame myself for your fate. If I had taken you as my hearth-mate it would have ended there. You might have stayed with me until you died old and happy." Her voice was full of pain.

"I might have, and been there for the return of the zarakanan, or at least the Reaver would have been there. They might not have conquered our lands. Our people would still be strong." Was the matter that complex?

"No Dorian, your people had already begun to war amongst themselves again, and well you know it. It was the zarakanan that taught your people to value life."

I drew in a breath to argue, but knew she was right. "Possibly, but how do you explain the decline?"

"I cannot, at least not yet. I can say that a large factor has been the continuous wars among the clans. Since your people have learned to value life, you have but to rid yourselves of your external enemies. Perhaps once the clans have a chance to mix bloodlines once more, your people will recover? But such a chance could only come after peace."

I nodded grimly, no wonder Morakvaar had set me on that path.

"I would like to record your history in our teaching ballads." Farzak surprised me utterly with the request.

I grimaced, "as a good or bad example?"

With a wry grin he replied, "both. Gorain's life is already a part of our history; it is only logical that his reincarnation also is recorded in our history. Dorian, you are as big a legend as Gorain ever was, but you live among us now."

"When I leave here, I promised I would leave the chronicle of my life as I have written it with Korina. I know not if she still wishes it." The hurt of her disavowal of kinship to me echoed freshly through my soul.

"What do you mean? Why would she not?"

Trying to find words for such a hard subject, I closed my eyes. "She no longer considers herself my child."

Farzak looked down at his feet. "That must truly be a hard thing to bear. What of your son, Dorak?"

"I have not seen him since we left Morakduum. He is only in the third year of his apprenticeship, but it is high time that I wrote to him. I must also visit with Geria and my mother. It is a visit I know will be painful. I know not how to explain my disgrace to my mother, nor how to say good-bye to my daughter."

"I do not envy you, Dorian. I could only imagine what it would be like to have a family, but to lose them? I could not even begin to know your pain."

"We will have our own family, Dorian." Harrakuli annoyance was plain in her voice.

"But we will have no home, no hearth to live by. There will be no clan, no stronghold, and no fellowship with our people. We will be alone in a harsh world, exiled from our kin." Had she ever lived outside the bounds of her people?

"None of my kin would gainsay you. You could live among my people if I wish it so." As Clan First, it would most likely be so. How could her people refuse her request?

"To live among the orudin without acceptance would be the same as exile. Morakvaar has already told me that I will not be allowed to remain in the Halls of the Mother, so the argument is pointless." Did I really want to leave?

She sighed and took hold of my arm, trying to comfort me. "At least we will be together."

I was not sure if that was a comfort, but I had no choice in the matter. While I thought about the bleak future ahead, my kinsmen began to exit the throneroom. Waiting until they were all gone but a few stragglers, I entered the throneroom again. Harrakuli and Farzak tagged along just in front of the five shaved dwarves. Morbid curiosity gripped me, and I stole a glance towards where the messenger had been chained. The sight of his still smoking corpse made me shudder. How could we be so cruel?

"General Dorian, we will meet in the second cycle to begin discussing our strategy against Rokarzan. I have sent out scouts to capture and interrogate any of our enemies they find as well as spy out their defenses and strength. We have received some information back that may be useful." Korina's tone bore a little less formality than it had before, and I wondered just how much the fight with the daemon had affected her.

"Very well, your Majesty. Is there anything else you wish of me?"

"I wanted to thank you, General, for saving our people, and for saving my life."

"It is my duty to defend my kinsmen and my Queen."

She looked almost as if she wanted to say more, but dismissed me instead. I bowed and left, wishing in vain there were some way to bridge the void between us. All the things she had made me proud of now brought me nothing but pain and sorrow, another lash in the torture of my soul. How much easier would it have been to seek death, an end to the suffering? Instead, I sought the tavern, a temporary reprieve from pain.

It was odd remembering that the tavern was the first place I spoke with Harrakuli. She too had a nostalgic grin on her face as we sat at the same table that we had a lifetime ago. It had been Morina's lifetime, Gorain's lifetime ago, when I was still only Dorian, a confused, but content kinsman. Only a few months passed since I had been a father and not an outcast whose purpose was fulfilled and discarded.

Why did I not realize how much I had until it was lost to me?

I tried to drown the question and the pain it brought in several mugs of ale, but it only seemed to get worse. No attempts to cheer me succeeded, and all attempts at speech fell short. There was nothing that could be said, nothing I would say that could change anything. After about the twentieth mug, I lost track. Sometime later, I was aware of being woken up and dragged out of the tavern.

All too soon, Harrakuli was shaking me awake. "Dorian, you have just enough time to clean up before your meeting."

"What time is it?" I could not help the grouchy tone, and I felt vaguely ill.

"One eight five. I tried to tell you not to drink so much."

"What else is there left to me that is my choice?" The sight of my beardless chin in the looking glass only served to darken my already foul mood.

Chapter 24

Zarak Garan (Shadow Rising)

Korina's face reddened all the way to her ears when I arrived. "You are still drunk!" The alcohol must have been heavy on my breath.

"You can blame yourself for that, Majesty!" I snapped back, and instantly regretted it. "I... I am sorry, Korina, forgive me for being a fool."

Her face reddened in anger. "Perhaps I should find a new general that can attend meetings sober?"

A collective gasp went through the advisors and commanders present. "Perhaps you should." Her words had wounded me beyond repair.

For a few minutes, I thought she would do just that, and I contemplated leaving the deep realms a little earlier than planned. "If I could find a replacement, I would," she said at last. "Take your place, General." Her tone could have frozen the entire realm.

I bowed and stood next to the table where maps were being unfurled. The adrenaline flowing through my system served to remove the effects of the alcohol, but not my temper. The room was like a thin sheet of glass over the raging sea, and everyone stepped as lightly as possible upon it, all the while knowing it would break.

The scout was a young white-blonde haired kinsman whose gold eyes never ceased roaming the room as if he would discover something new every time he looked. Was I ever that hyperactive? At Korina's nod he approached the table and bowed low enough that his scruff of a beard brushed his knees.

"Majesty, I bear grave news. The forces that had allied themselves with Kairillia have not all fled the Halls of the Mother. Rather, they have sought shelter and pledged their swords to King Rokarzan. He has also gained allies of the zardakkan." A chill of angry fear coursed up my spine, and by the looks of the others, they had the same reaction.

"Zardakkan! The Destroyer's people!? What would they possibly gain by serving Rokarzan?" Why would those pledged to destroy our race ally with the Kinsmen of Shadow? As I voiced the question the answer became obvious. "They are using him to devastate both our peoples! I had thought the greater daemon beyond the powers of the Kinsmen of Shadow, now we know how they managed it." Coldness swept over my features as I could feel the blood draining away from them. "That means Katzuk himself has vested an interest in our war." My voice was barely a whisper, but every kinsman in the room paled.

Korina stared at me for a long time, her eyes intense enough to bore through my soul. "Maybe it is not just the war that draws the Destroyer." She said slowly as all turned sharply to regard her, but her gaze remained fixed on mine.

Another chill coursed up my spine as I considered the implication. Was the Destroyer's war already upon us? If that was so, then that would mean… The lump in my throat refused to back down no matter how many times I tried to swallow it.

"You cannot mean he is making a preemptive strike." Korina's brow furrowed and she looked away at last.

"It is possible, and it fits in with the prophecy." All turned from her to me slowly as the realization dawned upon my kin.

"You know what I am, it is unlikely that I am the one. Morakvaar would never choose such a tainted soul for his champion." There was no way that I could fit the role, but I had to admit the description fit all too well. Breaking the chain of conversation, I turned back to the scout. "Lad, how many enemies do we face and where are they situated?" My gesture brought him to the map on the table, inviting him to explain all the information they had gathered.

Still in shocked awe he stared at me as he stepped up to the table. Remembering his purpose as his hip touched the table, he turned to the maps and cleared his throat.

"Barek estimates that there are five thousand zardakkan garrisoned in the western lower section of Zarakalduum." He gestured to the second tier of the map by the lower gate to the Daemon Sea. "Haran has reported that the combined might of the orcs, trolls and other refugees is another twenty thousand and garrisoned to the east upper section. Urek says the total of Rokarzan's army of shadow dwarves number another twenty-five thousand, and they still man the main battlements and the central city."

Studying the maps and mulling over the information I came to the same conclusion I had earlier. "It will have to be a siege." Voices rose in protest, but I held up my hand. "We do not have the numbers for an assault, but I have considered an alternative. Because the Blood of the Mother used to run its course into the heart of Zarakalduum, I believe we could alter its present flow to do so again. But this only if the siege proves a failure. If at all possible, I want to avoid more deaths than are absolutely necessary. The biggest challenge we face is cutting them off from all supply lines, but I believe with the orudin, we can meet that challenge."

Pulling out the traced overlay I had made when I first studied the maps, I put it over the one on the table. "When we returned from Vouroussan, I took the liberty of studying all of the former surveys of Zarakalduum. The marked areas are where we need to block off tunnels, and the axes mark where we should have barricades and cannons. The tunnels marked in red are the ones that will convey the magma into the heart of Zarakalduum should it become necessary to do so. I want everyone to memorize those so that no one will be caught in them." My forefinger found the fissure marks where the lava was diverted from its old course.

"Here is the blockage that forced the re-route of the Mother's Blood. Our engineers estimate it will take two hundred pounds of explosive powder to remove the blockage and return the lava flow back to its original tunnels." Troubled eyes turned my way.

"But that would destroy the Heart of the Mother!" The others nodded, the very thought of that sacrilege was distasteful.

"That is one reason why this course of action should be our last resort. Though the magma may be channeled back into the diverted path, our engineers could not guarantee that a new blockage would be successful. Such an undertaking also involves great risk, for if the fissure is not correctly widened, an opening could be made into the Daemon Sea." More troubled stares met my gaze as their thoughts turned to the Daemon Fish invasion fought off by Darlik Hammerhand.

"Your pardon, my Lord, but Urek also says that there are at least a hundred clerics among their assets. What if they have the ability to use their divine spells to feed their people as ours can?" The young scout brought up a very good point.

"I doubt their power is great enough to feed an army of fifty thousand for any length of time, but it is a valid question. It is the one aspect of the siege that has given me doubts. Even though they may not be able to extend the food supplies for any length of time, it might be enough to stifle our ability to hold them. Like as not, we will end up resorting to unleashing the lava upon Zarakalduum. Our fortifications will have to be rigged so that the tunnels can be collapsed behind us. Since our numbers will be spread so thin, we cannot afford to face a full assault of Rokarzan's amassed army. Our tactics will need to involve separation and elimination." Grim nods accompanied my assessment.

The only unforeseen item was the role of the zardakkan. Their presence made me uneasy as I pondered our practiced guerrilla tactics we had used for thousands of years against the dark ones.

"Releasing the magma flow upon Zarakalduum is not very reassuring, General Dorian. I am sure you remember what a disaster Terazandarin was." Korina's face was full of concern and for a moment, all I could see was her mother.

Clearing my throat, I pushed the vision of Morina aside. "Terazandarin was a failure because we entrusted our safety to the Vaetra and they betrayed us. There will be no such betrayal at Zarakalduum."

"What if Rokarzan attacks before we have our defenses in place?" Bailan flushed with embarrassment at his outburst, but I smiled in acknowledging his question.

"That will be a risk we must take. If that happens, we will be forced to fall back to a more defendable location." Kormak's son was a strong thinker and I had no difficulty with his appointment as king of Balakarak and leader of their clans in my army.

"Where would you suggest? These tunnels do not provide a very good position." Bavorn started a discussion that went on for much of the day and into the night cycles.

Generals and kings alike discussed the tactics and plans until it had been well over a full day's cycle. Weariness fought for control over my eyelids as the morning cycles slipped by. The strategy and placement of our troops was finalized by the end of the third cycle though, and to my relief, the council was adjourned. But something nagged at my subconscious, and instead of seeking rest; I remained to stare at the maps.

"General Dorian." I stiffened at Korina's harsh tone.

"Yes, Majesty?" Keeping my back to her, I continued to stare at the maps even though they no longer held my attention.

"Your insubordination was intolerable. I will not have it happen again."

At that moment, I wanted desperately to spank the living warmth out of her. How dare she speak to me that way? Outwardly, I kept my anger in check.

"It will not." When I had suppressed my anger I turned to face her. The tears on her face were something I was unprepared for, and I forgot the rage that was building within me.

Korina glanced over her shoulder as if to ensure we were alone. "I tried to hate you, despise you for betraying my mother, but I could not. The night before last, mother came to me in a dream. She told me that she was not angry with you for doing the Maker's bidding, and somehow I knew it was more than just a dream. She said that she was glad that you had the chance at happiness once more. She told me how badly it hurt you not to be allowed to follow her into death. I did not realize until then how much I loved you, and what it would mean if you had died. Finally, I tried to imagine what it will be like when you are gone and could not."

"Korina, I only wish there was an excuse for my behavior."

"I am not finished," she cut me off. "When Marak was wounded, it hurt me deeply to see him so, but I began to imagine what it would be like if I lost him after mother told me these things. I tried to imagine what I would feel if the Maker denied me the right to follow him, and could not. It tore my soul apart to realize what you have been through, and then to realize what I had done to you by denying kinship. I have since repented my sins before Morakvaar, and now I repent before you. I am sorry, father."

She hugged me as she had so many times as a small child, and buried her face in my shoulder as she wept. "You need not apologize to me. You did what you felt was right, something I have always been proud of you for."

"But something I should never hurt you with, something which you taught me, gave me such a shining example for most of my life. I should be much more tolerant and charitable as many errors as I have made as a child. To learn of two of yours should have made me glad to know you were mortal."

I kissed her hair, once again feeling a father's pride in a daughter. "To have you call me father again is enough for me."

"But it is not enough for me. Would that I could give you back the crown of Morakduum, for it sits heavily upon me, and is rightfully yours."

"What? You would curse me so soon after apologizing?"

She looked into my eyes with a sharp burst of laughter. I grinned widely, and she punched me in the shoulder.

"I think you could use a drink." She frowned heavily before she considered my suggestion. "You do not relax near enough. If you take life too seriously, you will find that all the fun has left you behind. After that, you can do nothing but cry for the sadness that is left."

"I suppose you are the expert on that account. Very well, father, lead on."

"I think the tavern is not open yet. How about you join me there in the fifth cycle?"

She nodded, and we went our separate ways. When I returned to my quarters. Harrakuli was waiting for me. My mood was considerably improved, and I took her into my arms and kissed her passionately.

"I ought to let you attend strategy meetings without me more often." She grinned.

"Korina is my daughter again, that is all that matters. Though she does not approve of our relationship, at least she will accept it."

"And what do I get if she finally approves of our relationship?" She teased.

Letting Gorain's memories take me, I led her to the bedroom. After a few time cycles of reacquaintance and then rest, Harrakuli and I showered in the bathhouse before heading to the tavern to meet Korina. The meal of roasted zorvak and mushrooms went down well as Harrakuli ate some of the zorvak and then consumed a small bowl of gems and drank her wine-like liquid. Korina and I talked over several mugs of ale. Most of our conversation consisted of memories of Morina and the good times we shared together. Musicians gathered in the hall, and struck up a few merry tunes. Marak danced with Korina and I with Harrakuli. It was good to see my daughter enjoy herself for once in her adult life, and our reconciliation brought a small amount of peace to my soul.

When most of the dancers were busy drinking, the storysmiths came. Ballads of past heroes and heroic deeds were sung. Songs of treasure hoards and vile enemies vanquished filled the night cycles. For some reason I did not feel like drinking as much as I would have. Something still nagged at me about the strategies we were planning, and instead of drowning the thoughts; I wanted to examine them thoroughly. Korina, on the other hand, went a little overboard, and was snoring with her head down on the table. Marak was not much better off, and was singing softly to himself on the verge of joining his mate. Harrakuli begged her leave to visit the privy.

An overwhelming sense of danger prickled my nerves suddenly, and I thought I caught a bare glimpse of movement from the corner of my eye. My hand reached behind my chair to grip the Reaver only to find it not there! Adrenaline surged through me until I remembered I left the weapon back in my quarters, but the sense of warning intensified. My eyes rested on the Hammer of Golodain that hung from Korina's belt as she continued to snore. Debating whether or not to wake her, I reached for the lanyard that secured the hammer in place.

In a flash the zardakkan assassin exploded from the shadows, his spear aimed for my daughter's unprotected back. In a desperate leap from my chair, I put myself between the weapon and his target. The icy blade slid into my side, piercing upward as I tried to twist away. The point scraped off my ribs, running between the bones and skin as it lodged in my armpit. My left fist caught the assassin in the jaw; knocking him back and giving him the momentum to yank loose the spear.

The bladed edges of his weapon ripped through my side as blood showered the stone floor. In my right hand, the hammer came free from Korina's belt and she mumbled something in her sleep. The five Tashor leaped from their places to join the fray, but they were not in time to stop the zardakkan from thrusting his spear home once more. Dodging right, I grasped the haft of his weapon in my left hand, but something was terribly wrong. Not only was I bleeding profusely, but fire seemed to race through my system, and cramping the muscles in my left shoulder. The blades had been poisoned!

The hammer went wide as a sudden spasm threw off my aim. The assassin pulled out a sword as he yanked the spear free from my arm that refused to respond to my commands. Instinct was all that threw the hammer into the way of the spear as it thrust towards my head, but it did not save my right arm. The short sword thrust into my right bicep as I turned to keep it from entering my chest. The tip lodged momentarily in the bone before being snatched back like the recoil of a striking serpent. Though pain shot through me, the wound would not have been crippling if it were not for the fire of poison that spread like a plague from where the sword entered my flesh.

Immediately my arm spasmed in pain, dropping the hammer from my convulsing fingers as toxin began to work on my whole body. Shaking in feverish pain, my mind barely registered the assassin's final attempt to take my daughter's life. Having no other recourse, I threw myself between him and Korina as his sword passed through my lower ribs, shredding lungs and organs with equal abandon. Frustrated rage filled the zardakkan's sickly greenish-yellow eyes as my weight tore the sword from his hand. Behind him I saw the flash of an axe blade as Venzar parted the assassin's head from his shoulders.

The spasms shook my whole body with agony as my muscles tore against one another in the throes of the poison's final phases, but the wound in my chest would beat the toxin in the race of death. My breath came in ragged gasps as blood filled my lungs. Before my gaze faded, I fixed my eyes on Korina's confused and groggy face. Would I get to see Morina now? Had I redeemed myself in the Maker's eyes? Darkness gathered around me, and I knew my answers would quickly follow.

Instead of Morakvaar, though, Harrakuli's face hovered before me once I became aware. She held me tight to her chest as her divine power coursed through me. She cursed the zardakkan and their entire breed as she had my kinsmen hold me down while she removed the sword. When she looked to see if the assassin was dead, he could not be found. A full search of the surrounding area turned up nothing more than his weapons. Greatly disturbed, Harrakuli half carried me back to our quarters, as Korina and Marak tagged along. The dwarves of the Tashor did not stray more than half an arm's length from us the entire way, ashamed at their repeated failure to protect me.

Harrakuli helped me to the bed, but despite my weariness, I could not sleep. The voices from the outer room filtered in to where I lie on the bed. Still feeling a little feverish from the residual effects of the poison, I wanted to sleep, but found the conversation was too compelling to ignore.

"How can we prevent this from occurring again?" Korina asked, and I could tell she was still slurring her words slightly.

"We can set wards against the evil of the zardakkan, at least that will give us warning if they approach us." Harrakuli suggested.

"The smiths can forge talismans that will also bear this protection upon them." Marak's voice too bore the taint of alcohol, but at least they were thinking straight.

"Very well, I will give the orders for the talismans, and if you will do the honors, Harrakuli, and place the wards?" I could only imagine Harrakuli's nod, but the long silence baffled me.

At last Korina's hesitant voice could be heard. "I owe you an apology. I had thought you an evil person for what you did to my father. It was not until my mother spoke to me in a dream that I realized you loved him instead of just wanted him for your own selfish reasons. I still do not condone your actions, but realize the matter is too complex for any of us to understand. I will never forgive you for your part in my mother's death, and I pray to Morakvaar that my father someday comes to his senses. I fear that my prayer will be unanswered, but as I love my father, I will not come between you."

"I understand your anger, but there was nothing I could have done to prevent your mother's death. The Maker had decreed her time over long before, but because Dorian pleased him, he gave them time together. Morakvaar knew that there were hard times before your father, and gave him a reason to face them with hope instead of desperation. It was always his intention that Gorain return to my side, a promise he had made to me eight thousand years ago. Morakvaar was kind to your father and mother to let them share so much time together, and in a way I admit I was jealous. I suppose I should have learned patience, and for that I am truly sorry. It was poor of me to be so impatient, for I knew in my heart that Gorain could not refuse me for long." Harrakuli stopped abruptly, not wanting to continue.

"So you did know my mother was going to die!"

"It is a hard thing to be immortal. To watch those you care about grow old and die, to know when others will leave before their time, to know so much but not be allowed to act on any of it. If your mother's time had not already been extended beyond her calling, I would not have interfered.

"Do you know what it is like to wait thousands of years for the one you love to return? To live on and on, day after day, year after year, alone and never knowing when he would come again? Such was my punishment for allowing Gorain's exile. You cannot even imagine what it is like to pass through millennia knowing that someday the kinsman you love will return to you, and never daring to love another in case he should come in that time. Imagine being alone among your kin because of your fate, then to finally know your mate is alive and in love with another and that their children should have been yours. It is a pain almost too great to bear. You will do almost anything to get him back, to save your loved one from himself. Perhaps I brooded on my loneliness too long?"

"Do you have any idea what it is like to be taught what it is to be a kinswoman by someone you admire? To know the love and warmth from that parent as they demonstrate those values on a daily basis? Do you know what it feels like to lose your mother, and watch your father compromise the principles he upheld so high? To see his spirit and pride crushed by an unkind fate lain upon him from a time before his birth? To watch helplessly as the creature who caused all his suffering seduces his soul?"

"No, and more is the pity. I was never birthed, never knew parents, but was a parent myself. I have had many children, but never knew what it was like to be young and innocent. When the Maker breathed life into me, I was an adult, and Ungir, my mate, was an adult. We were never children. We knew our principles, our goals, and our skills. We never had to be taught, but had to teach. When Ungir died, I was devastated. He had been my companion for five hundred thousand years. I mourned his passing for another thousand years until I met Gorain. His soul was so much like Ungir, strong and passionate. Even as a boy, I recognized his spirit, and a part of him seemed to know me.

"But, Gorain was a Kinsman of the Blood, and I was orudin, so I did not allow myself to think of him as other than a friend. Even then, I could not deny that I began to love him as I had Ungir. When the zarakanan came, Morakvaar refused to allow me to interfere. He told me that the Kinsmen of the Blood had to learn a valuable lesson. He was displeased they had begun to war amongst themselves, and so allowed them to have a true enemy to fight. I had to watch as Gorain was taken as a slave, abused and tortured until his spirit was broken. No harder thing had I ever witnessed. I wanted to destroy all of the zarakanan, but the Maker told me that Gorain must learn that lesson, that the Kinsmen of the Blood had to learn the value of their own people. They had to learn that kinship was more important than who had more gold or silver or precious stones.

"Gorain learned, but in turn he forgot the most important lesson, compassion. When they killed Gelamina, his wife, and mutilated his children, he went mad. He swore vengeance upon all of their kind, not just those who had done the deed. He hunted them, the sick, the wounded, the old and the young, showing no mercy, sparing none. I tried to stop him, despite the edict between our people. I loved him, and showed him that love. To my surprise, I found that he loved me too, though could never before admit it to himself or his people. I tried to convince him to leave behind his quest for vengeance, to ensure his people's safety instead. I bid him lay down his arms and rebuild, but in the end he refused. He took up the Reaver to continue his thirst for the blood of his enemies. I went to the elders to seek their advice, but when they learned what I had done, they were furious. I could not stop them.

"They demanded that he be exiled, and Morakvaar forgive me, I let them do it. I had hoped that his exile would cool his blood. But, it did not. The rest you know."

Their voices mesmerized me; the words so long unspoken held me captivated as I struggled to understand their views. Korina's anger became clearer, but Harrakuli's obsession still mystified me. Did she believe I was Ungir? Sometime along this contemplation, their voices faded from my reckoning and my thoughts became vague dreams of a great city whose architecture was of marble and alabaster gilded with vaarandril. A city where our people lived in peace with the other clans and traded goods and skills freely.

Sometime later, I was aware of a presence in the room with me, dragging me from the dream. A single eye registered Harrakuli's profile as she shut the door behind her, and the pleasant dream of the great city called out to me as I closed my lids once more. But instead of dreaming, instinct prickled along my spine. There was something wrong with the way Harrakuli had moved! Both of my eyes rested on her as she turned back my way, but my soul knew what was missing. In a flurry of blankets, I rolled off the bed just as the spear struck where I had lain.

The tearing of the bedsheets made no sound in the darkness, and chills ran up my spine. The fiend used a silence spell to prevent anyone from hearing my plight! The form of Harrakuli melted away from the zardakkan like heated wax as the lithe form leapt onto the bed, stabbing at me with its spear. Its slim form barely made indentations in the woven padding as its yellow pits glowered at me in the darkness. The point of the double-ended spear homed in on the bridge of my nose and the reedy arms of the zardakkan drew it back for the final thrust.

The room spun in my eyes long after my roll was completed, and the unmistakable taste of bile filled my throat as my arm wrapped around the scrawny neck. Nausea clouded my vision with spots of darkness as the remains of the previous poison fought for control of my consciousness. The spindly zardakkan slid straight down, dragging me forward slightly with its weight. The stone floor slammed into my back and shoulders before I registered what was happening. The talon-like nails of the assassin drew blood along my jaw where it had assisted my downward fall only to take a more secure grip around my neck. Its sinews bunched as my neck muscles burned with the effort to prevent the twist. Helplessly I flailed at my enemy, but my blows were like those of a child by the time they reached the zardakkan, and it shrugged them off as it adjusted its grip again. Pain lanced through my chest as my lungs struggled to fill with air. The dark spots in my vision whirled insanely around the room as they grew larger, but my feet managed to find purchase on the wall.

Heaving with all of my might, the crack of my skull against its jaw resounded in my head if not in my ears. My hand closed around the shaft of its spear and I yanked it free as the zardakkan reeled from the blow. Filling my chest with sweet air, I swung the spearhead around. The assassin scrambled away, but I followed, rage boiling the nausea out of my blood as eerie silence swallowed our struggle in a blanket of obscurity. The sparks flew from where the spearhead struck the wall, but the zardakkan was long gone as I spun on my heel once more. Surprised cold fear gripped my gut as my next thrust was shrugged aside with ease by its open palm. The assassin was perfectly trained and more than my equal with the residuals of the poison in my system. Stars blackened my vision as the knuckles of its right hand connected solidly with my jaw.

Staggering backward and half blind, I instinctively fended off the next blow with the spear haft. My eyes focused a moment too late as the foot of the zardakkan flew through the air, connecting solidly with the side of my head. The impact brought darkness as I felt my jaw snap shut before I hit the wall with the other side of my head. Barely aware of my surroundings, I felt the spear tugged out of my weak grasp. Some instinct of self-preservation ignited within me as I mouthed the words that invoked the Reaver's power.

"Dozarak kilna loch krazak sion!" Though no sounds traveled through the enchanted silence, the Reaver blazed to life brighter than it ever had.

The white-blue fire was like a storm beacon as the axe sailed through the air to my outstretched hand. Like a whirlwind of doom, it spun in my hand, catching the head of the spear between the opposed half-moon blades. The haft of the lighter weapon snapped in two, but the zardakkan adjusted its grip. With blurring speed it spun the two ends as separate weapons, striking twice as fast as before. The blades of the spear rebounded off both haft and metal as I struggled to deflect the assassin's attacks.

The zardakkan paused as its foot slid on one of the bedsheets, and I struck back at him. With contempt, the assassin shrugged aside my blow and almost casually thrust the spearhead in his left hand into my side. The one in his right described an arc towards my head, but instead of ducking from it, I stepped in, driving the spear deeper into the wound, but denying my enemy its target. Surprised, the assassin met my shoulder already off-balance. Its smaller form rebounded and fell away as I followed its neck down with the Reaver's blades. Though I could not hear the impact or the shatter of its bones, I felt them travel up my arm to resound in my soul.

Fiery spasms spread outward from the wound in my side, as I struggled to the door. Fumbling with the latch, I barely managed to lift it from its mooring before collapsing on the threshold. Instantly, the Tashor were at my side, but their voices were distant as the poison worked upon me for the second time that evening. It was then that I realized the assassin's true target had been me all along. First the messenger, and then the assassins, did the enemy really believe I was the key to their victory? How stupid they were to think so, but I was unlikely to get the chance to tell them.

Chapter 25

Tarzak (Ambush)

The chime of the midday meal woke me as it vibrated through the walls of my bedchamber. Was it the third cycle already? The heaviness of my lids tried to drag them back down over my eyes, but the sight of movement sent a cold shock of adrenaline through me. My heart slowed as I realized it was only Balaran of the Tashor. His shaved head turned from me as he flushed in shame. Never in our history had a Tashor failed to protect his charge twice, and that they both had happened on the same night was a brutal stroke to their hope of redemption.

Trying to sit up, cold nausea knotted my gut, putting sweat on my brow. But I would not be bested by illness or poison! Battling the swimming dizziness in my head, I reached for my tunic. A firm hand intercepted mine as I stared into Balaran's stern features.

"Harrakuli says you are not to get out of bed for another day." Balaran's brow was creased with new lines as they crept from his eyes and the corners of his mouth as well.

"Another day? How many days has it been?"

"Yes, my Lord. It has been two days since the attack. Though Lady Harrakuli was able to neutralize the poison, it had already damaged much of your nerves and organs. The vile git used gavros venom! It took this long for both her and Waradain to heal you." Undiluted awe colored his voice.

Gavros? No one had ever survived such venom to my knowledge. "Balaran, surely you realize I cannot remain confined forever." My words were more confident than I felt as the room spun and rocked around me as if I was aboard a ship.

"I know only that we have failed you twice and to allow you to injure yourself would be beyond Queen Korina's tolerance." The image of my irate daughter scolding the Tashor was plainly written in his demeanor.

"Then give me a shoulder to lean on." The room refused to stop spinning even after I had dressed and leaned heavily on Balaran's shoulder.

Swallowing down the bile that burned in my throat, we stepped through the door. Balaran eased my controlled fall onto the couch as I struggled to stay reasonably upright. The sting of sweat in my eyes blurred Harrakuli's shocked expression, but the flush of anger was plain enough.

"I knew we should have tied you down!" She stared angrily at Balaran who swallowed uncomfortably under the heat of her gaze.

"You would have to do just that if you expect to keep me a prisoner." My voice was weaker than I had anticipated, carrying much less humor than I had tried for.

"Next time, I will." She snarled, but the worry on her face belied her harsh words as she sat next to me and slipped an amulet about my neck.

The light of the torch flickered off from the finely worked vaarandril pendant, revealing exquisitely carved feather wings arcing gracefully over a runic hammer. Every vein of the minute feathers was lovingly carved into its surface, and as I held it before my eyes, I could feel the warmth of the holy power within it. The runes upon the surface of the hammer glowed softly with inner strength, a rune of warding and a rune of watching. It was a beautiful work of art, but more than that, a powerful talisman.

"What is this?" Harrakuli stared at me, her expression full of anguish.

"It will warn you if our enemies approach. I will not allow you to come so close to death again." Though the love of her ran deeply within me, I could not help the pang that stabbed through my chest.

"You need not worry over such things. Morakvaar has already denied me that path." The echo of my voice was as forlorn as the howling of a lone wolf upon the dales that I had heard on the surface when I lived there.

Harrakuli's jaw tightened. "Just because Morakvaar has denied you the path to the Underhalls does not mean he will deny you death. He may let you rot in purgatory until he decides he needs you once more. Believe me, you do not wish to wait there, and what is more, I... I would lose you again." It was not my deathwish that bothered her, but my refusal to let go of Morina.

The thought built the anger within me to a bonfire. "Do you think that matters to me!? Do you think it is easy for me to forget who I am only because I have no choices in my life? How do you think it feels to wake up one day as someone different? To have memories of two lives, one that belongs to a stranger? To be always divided in opinion, to not know whose eyes to view things with? It feels as though you are being possessed, forced into a way of life that is not your own, forced to leave behind you all that you have ever known or loved. I feel as if the chaos of hell has taken my soul. There is no order, no clarity, I do not know who I am any more!" The dark tunnel swallowed my soul, whispering of other lifetimes, words, pictures, insanity.

No kinsman was ever divided in thought or soul, and every kinsman knew who they were. How could I consider myself a vaarakanan when I did not even know my own mind? Why had the Maker done this to me? Why could I not have remained an ordinary kinsman, content in my youth to know the world and myself? Chaos reigned in my soul since the day the Reaver claimed me. Why did Morakvaar torture me so?

The inner reflection sought answers in the faces of those around me, but all that I saw was disbelief and shock. Harrakuli recovered first.

"I am sorry, Dorian. No one but Morakvaar could know what effect being reborn has upon the soul." She placed a blue-gray hand upon my cheek. "If I could help you, I would."

"I cannot blame you, but it is pure torment to live in such confusion. Would that I could speak with a soulsmith, but that will have to wait until I can find one. I can only hope that some still survive upon the surface." The reminder of my future put a thoughtful frown upon Harrakuli's face.

The sitting room was silent save for the spit and crackle of the fire upon the hearth. The soft glow of the flames lit the tapestries that covered the stone walls; tapestries that I recognized were my mother's work. Their depictions of the great battles and heroes of old took me back to my childhood, where many such works of wonder hung in our home tunnel. How had my father, a disgraced descendant of Gorain, managed to win the hand of the envy of Banarik Hall?

"What will you do once our wars are over?" Waradain's curiosity interrupted my reflection.

The old priest scratched his beard as if his question was merely a passing interest, but the light of adventure shone in his eyes. "The Maker has told me that I must find our kin still enslaved on the surface. After that, I had not given it much thought, but I have always believed that we could find the others beyond the Starrift. There must be other realms where our people can be found, and beyond those, Dolamakduum. I will spend my last breath trying to find the sacred city, even if I am not allowed to enter." The wry chuckle startled the others in the room. "That is, of course, if the Maker allows me any choice in the matter."

Waradain nodded while Harrakuli stared at me for a long moment. "That journey is perilous, but perhaps you are the one to take it."

What in the Underhalls was she talking about? Did she know the way? Her golden gaze reflected my puzzled features back at me, but I could not gain the slightest hint of what she was thinking. The throbbing in my head erased any wish to try, as I closed my eyes to shut out the spinning room for a few moments.

A hand shook me back awake as I blinked in confusion. Where was I? What happened? My eyes had only closed for a moment, yet the hand that shook me did so in the dark, the fire having long since burned out.

"Dorian, your mother is here." Harrakuli brushed the side of my face as if I were a young child.

"My mother?" Rubbing the sleep from my eyes, I sat up as the room tilted alarmingly.

At my groan, Harrakuli supported my shoulders and I leaned in to her gratefully. "Yes, and she has brought your daughter. She is in the kitchen preparing tea for us." Once she was sure I was upright on my own and steady, she handed me a struggling bundle of legs and arms.

The gurgle of my child brought light to my soul as I gazed upon her round face. Her golden hair was already thickening into a glorious mane of yellow fire, and her green eyes were the exact shade of Morina's. My breath caught in my throat as I saw her, she was growing so much to resemble her mother. The tear splashed wetly onto the blanket before I could catch it as I held her tightly against my chest. The pain of Morina's absence tore at my wounded soul, welling within me like a tide of murky waters.

Ignoring Harrakuli, my mother placed the tray on the low table before the divan. Her wrinkled face looked even more drawn since I had seen her last, but at least she had filled back out since the slave pits. Lines of worry had deepened on her face, and her gray hair held barely a hint of its original golden color. With a slight grunt, she sat in the chair opposite me, her gown a rustle of brownish gray around her knees.

"Korina tells me that you are leaving us after the war." Though she did not look directly at me, I knew her attention was fully focused on my answer.

"Yes. The Maker has told me that I would never return to my hearth. In truth, I could not, for the memories that remain there would tear me asunder. There is no place for me amongst our people, not since the incidents at Vouroussan, and perhaps there never really was before either." She met my gaze for only a moment before looking away again. Was that shame or pity? "I trust you have heard of these things?"

She nodded, still refusing to look at me as if I was some unclean beast. "My son, I cannot even imagine what you are going through, but you are my son. I only want you to know that even though I cannot understand, I still love you. But I have to know if everything I have heard is true."

"That all depends on what you have heard." My stalling did nothing to make the confession easier. "Can you condemn me for a sin committed before I was born?" She focused on me once more with a gaze of cold iron. How could I keep from telling her? "It is true."

She looked away again as if she had just been told I was dead for the second time. In a hoarse whisper she asked, "All of it?"

A spark of anger lit within me as I realized what she meant. "Of course not! There was no impropriety between the elves and myself! How could you think that of me?"

"There were many things I thought beyond you, Dorian. Things I was proven wrong over." Each word was a rasping pain echoed both in my mother's voice and in the beating of my heart.

"And it makes no difference if my bonding to Harrakuli was decreed over eight thousand years ago?" Why was I bothering to justify an act I knew was wrong?

"So soon after Morina's death!?" Her snarl put the finger to the heart of the issue, and I hung my head in shame. "I am glad that your father did not live to see this day. At least he perished thinking his son had died with his honor intact."

The fist tightened around my chest, squeezing the breath from my lungs. "And now you know why I must leave. It is neither right nor proper for me to live amongst our people. I wish the Maker had allowed me to die with Morina." A large tear rolled down my mother's cheek to splash wetly on the floor, and my soul ached to know the pain I caused her.

"Two sons and my hearth-mate slaughtered by zarakanan, a daughter lost to them who might also be dead and a son who has lost his soul. Is the Maker angry with me?" Her voice echoed with hollow despair.

Little Geria wriggled insistently in my arms, dragging my attention back from the darkness. At least there were my children, and their accomplishments had made me proud of them, even if I was an unworthy role model. Picking up a biscuit from the table, I quieted her fussing while Harrakuli changed her swaddling cloth. It had been twenty-three years since Dorak was that young. My mother watched with tears running down her cheeks, and I wondered if she remembered me at that age. Was she wishing she had that time over so that she could change what had happened?

My daughter's face kept echoing Morina's in my memory, filling me with grief once more. Why had the Maker left me behind? Why did I have to atone for Gorain's sins as well as my own?

"When I am gone, will you care for your granddaughter?" Without looking at me, mother nodded.

It was a bitter joy to care for my daughter for the day, but when mother took her in the evening, I had the uncanny feeling that I would not see her again. Little Geria would never know her father, and that pain smote deeply. The next few days were filled with preparations to march, and finally we were upon the roads leading to Zarakalduum.

The tunnels leading south from Sorkarak were in disarray. A rock fall had blocked one of the main routes, and a stream of magma flowed freely across another. None of our kin had engaged in trade with the Kinsmen of Shadow for over three thousand years, and the old roads were incredibly difficult to navigate with an army. More than once, we lost a day's travel having to backtrack and take another route. Fortunately, our far-ranging scouts kept us from having to lose too much time.

Beside me at the head of the column strode Bailan, the Mytharian standard held proudly in his hand. His helm bore the crown of Balakarak, but he insisted on personally carrying the banner. To his right marched King Karakdain of Barakillanak, and I wondered that he would lead his army at his age. But there was not a sign of weakness or age in his bearing even after a month's worth of marching. Darlik Stonehammer had been crowned king of Sorkarak less than a month before we left, yet he stood to Karakdain's right. To my left, Marak wore the crown of Morakduum with great uncertainty. Korina's gravid state was to the point of being a great hindrance, and I was grateful that my mother had convinced her to stay behind. King Gemlan of Dormakkarduum was on his left, and beside him was King Jolak of the orudin. The kings had joined many of the generals as we neared the final battle in our campaign.

My eyes traced back along the line of warriors from the six strongholds. Twenty thousand of them, and we faced an army again over twice our number. But this time, we faced an army that knew our tactics and used them themselves, an army that was of like mind even though they had given their souls to darkness. By the grim faces around me, the others knew this as much as I. Would King Rokarzon expect a siege, or was he expecting a frontal assault? The question troubled me greatly as I contemplated our strategy again and again.

Less than four days march from Zarakalduum, we set up camp to finalize our plans. Our forward scouts had gained enough knowledge of the area surrounding the fortress of the shadow dwarves that we could make final allocations for deployment. For many hours I discussed with the kings the updates to our maps and what affect it had on our siege. Many more tunnels had opened, and several had been closed off. With the changes, it looked as if a siege would be impractical, and we decided to set our perimeter and use the diversion of the magma flow into the city first. With barricades and defenses in place, we could withstand the enemy advance outside of their stronghold.

When the meeting adjourned, I stretched my legs by walking around the camp. orudin and stonemasons were hard at work setting up defensive battlements in the event we were forced back. This very cavern would be our rally point should things go wrong. It was a shame to have to work the stone along the natural cavern walls, for the flowstone and mineral deposits were exceptionally beautiful there. The gentle patterns of mixed calcium and shale were mesmerizing, and I stared at them for a long time before Harrakuli came for me.

"Dorian, you need your rest." By the tone of her voice, I was sure that sleeping was not what she had in mind.

She led me back to our tent, and despite the presence of the Tashor, she reacquainted me with more of Gorain's memories. Her exotic beauty captivated me utterly, but more than that, I felt oneness with her that was more intense than the soul bond I had shared with Morina. It was as if we were two halves of the same soul, becoming a whole in our shared moments of passion. But always the guilt would follow. My heart wept for Morina, and cried in anguish that I could so easily cast aside what we shared together.

Sometime in the night, my anguish turned to dreams. Morina came to me, her visage that of a corpse too long in the grave, but fresh blood still leaked from the hole the cursed vourdovra had put in her skull. She stood just out of my reach as I could but stare in helpless horror. The need to hold her welled within my breast, but my fear immobilized me. Tears leaked from her sunken shriveled sockets as sweat rolled down my brow. Her mouth opened, but instead of some horrible noise, her tone was as clear and melodic as it had been in life.

"You have been promised to another." Before she turned away, she was as I had first found her in the cage in the necromancer's tower. Her golden hair flowed behind her movement with the grace of an avatar's wings. Her green eyes were jade firebrands as they burned into my soul as she left me.

"No! Morina, come back! Morina!" My voice echoed into the darkness as I reached for her, but she faded like mist in the twilight.

When I awoke in the morning, a heavy cloud of guilt choked my breath. Harrakuli stirred slightly in my arms as another wave of anguish shook me. The growing love I felt for the orudin struck home the enormity of my betrayal of Morina's memories. As I had so many times before, I begged Morakvaar to choose someone else to torment.

The anguish hung over me as we mustered the troops and headed onward, leaving a small detachment behind to finish the fortifications. Over and over, I went through the events at Vouroussan, wondering if things would have turned out different had I done something other than I had. Would Morina have lived if I did not lead off the ambush? Would I have been able to save her if the orudin had not detained me? The questions kept plaguing me, but there were no answers. All I could hear was Morakvaar telling me that Morina had lived beyond her time.

So complete was my misery that my surroundings passed by without the slightest acknowledgement of their wonders. Without warning, two crossbow bolts pinged off my armor. As if coming out of a dream, I looked around dazed as I felt the sting of one that found the opening in my right elbow joint. Icy fires lanced up my arm, as I was galvanized into action. Spinning the Reaver in front of me, I invoked the lightning shield.

"Boravrak en!" More bolts streaked in, rebounding off the shield, and falling harmlessly to the tunnel floor.

Warriors with shields moved up to deal with the crossbowmen, but the ground suddenly erupted beneath our feet. Twenty zardakkan warriors materialized as if out of nowhere while twice that number of shadow dwarves crawled out of hidden pits in the stone floor. The amulet around my neck was as quiescent as it had been when Harrakuli handed it to me, and I wondered how they had shielded their presence from it.

"Sarlik Doria!" The white-blue flames rose around me instantly, but there were too many of them.

The shadow dwarves surrounded me quickly, cutting me off from the army and beating back the others. Six of them leaped on my arms, sacrificing themselves to immobilize the Reaver. Ten more bore me to the ground, intent on separating me from the weapon regardless of the cost in their own lives. Zardakkan spears pierced through my open joints, pinning my arms, shoulders and legs to the ground. With dread, I felt the poison of their weapons seeping through my system. In seconds the scene was fading from my vision as twisted zardakkan faces surrounded me.

Chapter 26

Vooraduum Sion (Hell's Son)

The rattle of chains woke me. The sound rang in my soul like the bells of doom, sending icy shivers to coil around my gut. Reflected in the ringing of iron links was the sound of captivity, the sound of pain and agony not yet realized, the sound of losing my soul. I began to wonder if there would ever be a time when I would not have to hear it again. Was I already sentenced to Vooraduum?

Around me was a gray-walled temple to the profane god of destruction. Twisted guardians of stone leered from the alcoves like demons that delighted in torture. Sickly yellow-green light oozed up from a hole in the exact center of the round room as if it were alive with malice. Tendrils of the gangrenous light wrapped around my calves, accenting the fact that my armor and clothing had been taken from me. The slimy tendrils slid along the edge of the altar I was chained to, filling me with cold revulsion.

Looming over me was an obsidian effigy of the Destroyer, its surface shimmering with a life of its own. The depths of the stone twisted and whirled as if in eternal agony. A zardakkan guard stood at either end of the altar, their gray armor dull and lifeless as volcanic pools of acid. One of them met my gaze and its smile revealed many pointed teeth as it turned on its heel and exited the chamber. The other turned to face me, its hungry expression poised as if ready to start its feasting on my pain without its companion. Six more figures ringed the room, but they were immobile enough to be silent gray statues. The small hairs on my neck rose as I realized what they must be. Vachtralian! The ancient evil champions of destruction were but frightening children's stories, but I had no doubt that they stood there in that vile chamber awaiting their god's bidding.

The armor of the vach was mottled in shifting patterns that wove in forms of tormented souls. They each stood twice the height of a human man, each of them carrying a two-handed sword the size of an old crawler. The more I watched them, the more the anxiety grew within me. Was the Destroyer's war already upon us? Was this the war Morakvaar had spoken of?

A flicker caught the corner of my eye, and I looked quickly back at the statue of Katzuk, the Lord of Destruction. Ice froze the blood in my veins as the effigy began to move, its shimmering black surface becoming living gray skin. The zardakkan that had been leaning over me yelped and prostrated itself before its god, shivering in uncontrolled terror.

"So, you are the champion that Morakvaar would send against me? How pitifully vulnerable you are." His voice made the air scream in vile fear as loathing filled me. "He has woefully left you only half trained. It will be my pleasure to complete your knowledge. You will become my champion as I almost had you when you were known as Gorain. This time, Morakvaar will not be able to interfere."

Perhaps it would have been better if I had been dead? If I had thought myself damned before, I knew with utter certainty that there would be no redemption after Katzuk the Destroyer was through with me! A stab of anguish cut through the icy chill of fear. Morina was lost to me forever, and I would never see the Underhalls of the Maker! How could I resist the power of a god? The hood of its robe shadowed the avatar's gray face, but feral yellow points of light glowed within the features of the deformed creature that rose from the depths of the shadows. Would I ever see Harrakuli again, or was this monstrous being going to intern me in Vooraduum forever?

With the ease of unknown strength, the clawed hands of the avatar snapped the chains that held me to the altar, picking me up by the shackles on my wrists. The iron rings dug into my skin, grating against the bone and sending rivulets of blood down my arms. My grunt of pain amused Katzuk as he gestured for the zardakkan to lower a hook on the end of a chain. The rattling of chains sent another chill through my blood with the certainty of my captivity. Gods, but I hated that sound! The dark avatar chuckled fiendishly as he slid a link from each of the two chains over the hook, leaving me suspended above the grayish-green pool. My own weight pulled on my shoulders without mercy, straining both muscle and tendon to the tearing point.

Below me, the slimy water bubbled and churned as if in anticipation of tasting my flesh. The crawling sense of panic ate its way up my spine, settling in my throat. Each bubble was a face in torment, crying out its eternal damnation, and each wave was a grasping desiccated claw reaching for me. The tide of unreasoning terror began to drown my thoughts in cold unending torment. Struggling in vain, my tendons popped and tore, but my mind was beyond recognition of the damage or the pain. The icy reign of fear over my mind was unbreakable, controlling me, telling me to struggle against the sentence to the Abyss.

"Welcome to Vooraduum, Gorain. The hell of your people calls your soul to damnation." With that pronouncement, the avatar motioned for the zardakkan to begin lowering me into the pit of water.

"Morakvaar arak en vaar!" I pleaded with the Maker to save my soul, but met only the laughter of the Destroyer as I struggled to keep my feet from touching the gray ooze.

My heart pounded, each accelerated contraction a greater fiery pain as it tried to burst from its place in my chest. I had to move, had to get free, but the gray pool drew nearer. I could not let it touch me, could not be submerged in the water! Katzuk's laughter only served to fuel the adrenaline that pumped through me. My soul was about to be swallowed by the Abyss, the watery hell sucked at my feet, touching them in an unholy slimy caress. My panic-fogged mind only fleetingly wished for my boots.

The glowing gray liquid greedily claimed me bit by bit, as nameless faces appeared and screamed silently echoing my own terror. Slimy hands reached from the pit to help drag me down into the chaos. As the liquid closed about my head, I realized the Shadow Lord was taking my soul. In my panic, I swallowed the liquid. It burned as it slid down my throat, but as soon as it hit my stomach, it became cold as the icy mountain winds of the overlands. The chill crept through my veins, spreading numbness like a plague. Gray icy fire raged through my brain, stilling my thoughts. Though I was aware, I was completely unable to think of anything on my own. But at least the fear had left me.

Memories and visions cavorted through my mind as if being tweaked by external hands. Every thing I had done that was shameful, deceitful or evil was reviewed; every thing that had been done to me was paraded before my mind's eye as the demonic avatar materialized before me in the gray hellish liquid world. Over and over, it reviewed the times I spent in slavery, the words I had spoken to the zarakanan Matriarch that had sentenced my kinswomen to their deaths. The two worst things that had ever occurred in my life were examined in vile and disgusting detail.

"The deaths of your kinswomen are a worse wound to you than your treatment at the hands of the slaver woman? Amusing, to be sure." Katzuk pawed through my memories, dragging everything wrong out once more. "You are already evil, Gorain, why do you fight your nature? See there? You caused your father great pain, wrongly choosing a different profession than what had been in your family for generations. It was a great sin and shame to your clan, making you an outsider." The gray hands moved through me like insubstantial ghosts, invoking the sorrow and guilt I felt almost as if they were the strings of a harp to be plucked for his pleasure.

The anguished face of my father gazed down at me with a troubled expression as once again I broke his heart. "I want to be a Warrior! I want to train the spiders, be with them when they make their first kill!" The pain on his face was agony to my soul.

The cold smile of the zarakanan Matriarch chilled my spine as she announced. "Sell them to the humans, but kill the male. He is too old to train."

"No! I beg you, let my kinswomen go! Kill me if you wish, but do not sentence them to such vile futures!" Her stony gaze stopped me cold.

That breech of protocol brought a flush of rage to her. "How dare that male vaarak address me! He shall suffer torment for the rest of his days! Kill the females before his eyes so that he knows what he has done! And, when the torturers have made him scream until he has no more voice, I want him to live to remember his sins! Sell him to the humans, and place a slave collar upon his throat!"

In horror I watched as they slowly tortured the kinswomen to death for my error, my sin in which I knew better. Each scream was another rent in my soul, another guilt heaped upon my conscience. My heart grieved anew for the loss of their lives and I burned with the shame of knowing it was because I had angered the Matriarch. My soul wept anew with my responsibility for one of the most heinous crimes of my race, the death of not just one, but fourteen kinswomen!

The next scene Katzuk showed to me was the day I had finished cleaning the stables only to find the slaver's wife watching me with hungry eyes. With agonized shame I saw the torments, the reactions I could not control when her and her minions violated me.

"See, you are evil for taking pleasure in such vile rituals." Katzuk drove home the worst of my agonized fears.

How could I deny the evidence of my own body? How could I claim I hated what had been done to me? The knowledge sickened me to the core, showing me how rotted my soul had already been. But the voice within me asked if any male would not have done the same. The question was a mockery. Was I an animal unable to control my reactions?

The soldiers that came to Milborne and tormented the villagers to get at me were next. The way they treated the mayor and his family for sheltering my presence from them was horrible, and all because I was an escaped slave and wanted for murder in another kingdom. It was my fault that the mayor lost his life, and my fault that his wife and daughter were tortured and abused while I prepared for the soldiers' assault on Thornwood Keep which never came.

The torment of my memories continued until I could take it no more. My will was broken in my shame and self-loathing as Katzuk remade my memories in its image.

"Now that you are prepared Gorain, you will be my champion, and I will begin your training. Remember your youth?" He paused as images of my father's home appeared in my mind. "Ah yes, I see that you do. There, your brother, Koran? He is jealous of you. Your mind is sharper, your hand surer and swifter than his. This is what really happened those many years ago." The scene played out before me as clearly as any of my memories.

With a wave of my hand as I passed his forge, I bid my father good day as I set out to train my new prodigy. The black and gold spider kept pace on my right, drawing the envious eyes of many with her striking patterns. Thorun nodded and waved from his forge as I left for the side-gate of Morkilduum and passed out of the scene.

Koran appeared before my father with a helmet of his own crafting shortly after I left. My father grimaced with distaste, and showed him the minute flaws in the metal. It was a finer helmet than ever crafted by humans, but it was not good enough for a vaarakanan mastercraftsman. Koran's face fell.

"Why is it that nothing I do pleases you, father? I try my best, but you delight more in Dorian's reputation than my armoring. He is not even a vaarandril smith! How could you love him more?"

The scene did not ring true to me. Koran had never been jealous, and had been a fine craftsman, but the gray liquid that pumped through me as surely as my own blood stifled my thoughts again. The scene was played over for me, as if it were a true memory and not a fabrication by an evil god.

"Dorian has made me proud, and even though he does not follow our family tradition, he has proven his own worth. The Patriarch himself has said he never had a finer apprentice, or a warrior with as much promise with the axe. Go, Koran, and perfect your art so that we may also have pride in you."

Instead of returning to his forge, Koran left for the market where some zarak traders were selling goods from the overlands. He spoke with one of them, and they handed him some gold coins. Koran glanced guiltily around him before returning to his forge. The zarak smiled evilly and spoke to his fellows.

"A bonus for the Matriarch. One of their Animal Masters routinely strays beyond Morkilduum's boundaries. We will take him as a gift to her."

My mind refused to accept the fabrication; I knew what had happened was my own fault. My memory was quite clear, running into the raiding party. I had been detected and captured by their scouts. There was no betrayal! Koran was a fine kinsman, he would never have been jealous, nor sold me to the enemy!

The gray fluid stilled my outrage once more, and replayed the memory. I fought it, railed against such a violation of truth, but my anger was stilled and the scene played on. Over and over it filled my vision and my memories, the gray liquid overriding my sense of reality and justice until I was unsure what the truth was.

The gray lips smiled at my apparent progress. The Destroyer delighted in the lies he fed me as he began to work on the next item I was fully aware of, Kormak's betrayal. He showed me the deal with the Matriarch while I was negotiating with King Saveyo, and the money Kormak was paid to hand me over to the zarakkanan. Only in Katzuk's version, greed and hatred rather than the intention of saving our race motivated Kormak. My mind refused to consider such heresy, and I tried hard to remember Kormak's final moments as he laid his life down to protect me. But my memories were torn from me and rebuilt in Katzuk's twisted ways. And so it went on forever, the Destroyer's perversion of my memories.

The orudin became responsible for Morina's death. My kinsmen became hateful and spite-filled people who tried to rid themselves of me by causing Morina to go off to her death. My daughter had stolen the throne that was rightfully mine. Every memory of those that had been my kinsmen, my family and my friends was mutilated and twisted into evil motivations to hurt and deny me my right to live with Morina. Every small slight was replayed with exaggerated detail. All these things became a part of my memories, my rage, my new desire for blood. As his final words of training, Katzuk promised me that if I righted the injustices of my life, he would bring back Morina. With blind determination, I would succeed no matter the cost! Morina would be at my side again even if the world burned into dust.

When he was finished, Katzuk pulled me out of the gray fluid world, but the foul liquid still pumped through my heart and soul. His zardakkan priests clad me in armor similar to his silent gray warriors; armor that kept me linked to the gray world and the twisted memories implanted in my mind. A shadow dwarf then handed me an axe of the same disturbing gray metal as the armor.

"Go my champion, destroy our enemies and earn the right to rule your world with your beloved Morina. Kill those who have done you great evil and you will set all to right again." Katzuk's voice reverberated through the chamber. "The tharilkanan will be your instrument of revenge. Khazarik, my High Priest will see that your orders are carried out."

With a wave of his hand, the temple disappeared from my sight to be replaced by a stone dais. Around me were throngs of Kinsmen of Shadow going about their daily business. Their dark gray skin drew my eyes to the armor that covered me. Was that what happened to them? A sea of black hair and sickly yellow eyes turned my way, re-igniting the fuels of my rage as the gray fluid pumped through my veins.

The city tunnels of Zarakalduum were of onyx, a fitting home for the shadow dwarves. Carvings of demons and blasphemous creatures stared from columns and stalagmites. Scenes of violent conquest and slavery adorned the walls. Tiled mosaics of evil symbols covered the area around the dais where I stood.

With an unsteady step, I walked towards the vile creatures, but the shadow dwarf priest put his hand on my arm. "Not yet, Gorain. We must wait for King Rokarzan."

At my snarl, he removed his hand quickly, but my oddly formed legs did not seem to move right. The click and scrape of claws bothered me immensely until I managed to lift my right leg without falling over. Did I always have clawed feet? Why did I feel as unsteady as a newborn? The talons on my hands convulsed around the axe with my irritation, but I felt the need to wait as if it were burned into my brain.

The crowd before us grew as shadow dwarves stopped and stared in fearful wonder. Their continued attention began to irritate me greatly, and my lips pulled back from long teeth as the crowd backed a pace or two.

"Be at ease, Champion of Katzuk. These are not your enemies, but your servants." The priest made sure his words were heard by the majority of those present as he continued to hold me by force of will.

"They will serve or die! I have no patience for this!" The growling voice that issued from my throat belonged more to a demon than a kinsman, but my struggle against the mental energies of the priest kept me from questioning its origin.

If these pathetic creatures were to be my servants, then I would tolerate them until my quest was finished. But when Morina was by my side once more, they would all perish under the blades of my axe, starting with the priest that held me! As if sensing my animosity, the cleric pointed out the approach of some sort of retinue.

The guards surrounding their king slammed their shields into laggards that were not fast enough to get out of the way. They approached the dais as a round shadow dwarf stepped up to the top. His ample gut slopped over his belt, and it was obvious that his meaty arm had never wielded the axe that hung at his side in earnest. His haughty tone set my teeth on edge immediately.

"I, King Rokarzon, greet you, Champion of Katzuk. For many centuries, we have awaited your arrival. With you beneath my command, our age of greatness is about to begin." He lifted his head so that he could stare down the bridge of his bulbous nose at me.

"I cannot say the same of you, worm! You are unfit to shine the boots of your lowest soldier! No kinsman would allow themselves to succumb to such weakness as is reflected in your pathetic build!" The crowd gasped as I snarled out the insults to their king. "You have not the eye, nor the skills of a warrior. Get thee hence from my sight, and never return to your betters!."

Rokarzon's yellow eyes went wide as his gray cheeks darkened in fury. His mouth worked silently trying to voice his rage as his hand reached for the axe at his belt, pulling it halfway out of the straps before he realized what he was doing. His ire vanished as his cheeks went near white when I stepped forward to meet his challenge. He let go of the axe, and it flipped upside-down, sliding out of the ring on his belt to clatter on the stones. The wide sickly-pale gaze rested on my clawed foot as I stepped on the haft of his weapon. Sweat began to bead his brow and he dropped to his knees when he realized I had not stopped menacing him.

"You cannot kill me! I am the king!" The flabby cheeks shook with his terror as my axe whistled through the air.

With a satisfying thunk, the blades of my weapon chopped through his spine, sending his fat head spinning back down the stairs of the dais. The crowd parted before the splattering gore and the head of their king that rolled to a halt ten feet from the bottom step. His body toppled as if just realizing it was dead, and rolled down the stairs to join its head. A tingling sensation coursed through me, and I could feel the power of the soul of Rokarzon being absorbed and added to mine. Khazarik merely stared open mouthed as the blood began to pool beneath his former king. The guards made as if to attack me, but gray flames rose around the axe, covering me with a shield of unnatural fire. Hunger filled my eyes with the need to devour more of their life-forces. Immediately they backed off as if recognizing my divine right to rule and the unnatural craving for their souls.

"I will tolerate no weaklings in my presence! Nor will I tolerate command by incompetence! You will follow my reign now, and together we will vanquish the Vaarakanan once and for all!" My voice carried over the crowd as if borne on the breeze of thought to each mind. "We march on Morakduum's army in one time cycle. All those able to fight will be ready. We will crush the Kinsmen of the Blood beneath our feet, and I will have my vengeance!"

The high priest shook his head, as if clearing it from a bad dream. His face troubled as he stared at me wondering if his god had sentenced his people to death. Whatever he saw hardened his resolve as he turned to address the crowd.

"Katzuk's Champion, your new king has spoken! We will prepare for battle immediately! His is the mouth of our god and his blade is Katzuk's hand. Sound the trumpets for muster!" Quietly the old priest whispered. "You sure know how to make an entrance, Gorain." Scattered shouts of enthusiasm slowly became the roar of approval, revealing Rokarzon's disfavor with his own people.

The army took slightly more than one and a half time cycles to be ready for the preemptive strike, and the growing number of headless bodies in the courtyard was the measure of my impatience. Among those leaders who had their units ready within the time cycle allotted, I chose my generals from them and led them to the primary deployment zone that was to be manned by the siege troops of Morakduum, but all was quiet.

Scents wafted down the tunnels to me, the smell of Kinsmen of the Blood, but not many of them. "Set up to ambush the vaarakanan and await my return."

The newfound speed and growing agility filled my veins with fierce joy as I stalked down the tunnels that were to be blockaded only to find no trace of my kin. Had they returned to Sorkarak without me to lead them? For a moment I was plagued with doubts. Why would a people who hated and despised me have me for a leader? The gray fluid surged through my mind replacing my confusion with dark visions of betrayal and hatred. It whispered the promise to return Morina to my side, setting the fire of battle alight within my eyes. All the minions of hell would not keep me from bringing her back!

Chapter 27

Tevoor (The Soul of Evil)

Dark tunnels passed in blurs of striated stone, and still the faint scents led me on. The crisscross paths of ancient flows of lava left pits under thin shells of volcanic glass, shards of razor-stone and false tunnels ending in blank walls. But none of these frustrations would thwart my quest for vengeance whose fulfillment would bring back my beloved.

Crazed visions of tortured anguish filled my mind from Katzuk's gray fluid, driving me mad with bloodlust. The desire to slay and destroy was all that was left of my mind. Like a beast from Vooraduum, I stalked my kin, sniffing them out in the maze. With the unnatural grace and speed of a demon, I was but a flitting shadow in the darkness, a whisper of death in the ear of my prey.

Vaguely a part of me recognized the intersection, and knew with a certainty that I would find my quarry in the tunnel that was meant to redirect the flow of the Mother's Blood into Zarakalduum. Had the vaarakanan abandoned the siege?

Ahead the faint sounds of tapping drew my ear. The smell of warm blood and sweat filled my nostrils and the desire for the tingling sensation of absorbing another life-force stilled all other thoughts. Whisper quiet I moved among the stones, hiding my heat in their shadows as I neared their location. The shapes of seven warriors were outlined in shades of reds and yellows and they watched the tunnel diligently. Their whispering voices echoed clearly in my ears, and for a moment my mind was drawn from the haze of bloodlust.

"Do you think Lord Dorian is still alive?" The tone was that of one who did not want to give up hope.

Was that my name? Why did the kinsman have concern for me? My memory conjured a vision of a thousand faces turned in unison to cry out the name.

"Hail King Dorian, the Liberator of Balakarak!" Were these the people who had betrayed me? Were these the ones that took my beloved from my side? Their adoration belied the fury in my mind. How could those people have such love and respect, yet still be capable of the atrocities Katzuk had put into my memories? I faltered, stumbling to a halt as the confusion settled upon me. Who was I? Who were those people?

Searing icy pain ripped through my senses as the dark voice smote through my mind. "Kill them, Gorain! Slay those who betrayed you and took away Morina! Kill them all and your beloved will stand again at your side!" The bass resonance echoed through me, vibrating in every bone and nerve as the gray stillness crept from the helmet securely clamped to my head overriding all of my thoughts. The scenes of violence and hatred were replayed once again in a moment's time, refueling my rage.

One of the younger warriors swung his crossbow quickly in my direction. "By the gods! What in Vooraduum is that!?" The heat receded from their faces, as weapons were made ready.

"Truly that beast comes from the pits of the Abyss lad, fire or we are finished!" The veteran put words to action as a bolt ricocheted off my gray armor to ring loudly against the stone behind me.

An unearthly howl of tormented rage echoed through the tunnels, but there was nothing for me but the lust for the souls ahead. The smell of their blood pumped in my veins as my jaws longed to feel the heat of their necks. The sound of shattering metal filled the air as my axe sliced clean through two of theirs and another two bolts pinged off my armor to collapse in spent twisted shapes.

The thud of the axe against flesh sent fresh ecstasy up my arms as the warrior's life-force filled me. Hunger, ravening desire and so many sources nearby! Through the red haze, I saw their weapons descend, but they were so slow! I easily stepped past the strokes as they flashed their deadly song a heartbeat behind my own. The screeching ring of torn metal was followed by the dying scream of the second warrior, as he was held in place by my axe. The gurgle of blood cut the noise short as his essence left him to dwell in my increasing fire. The weight of his body was as slight as a shield when I stepped behind him, the weapons of his comrades sinking in to his flesh.

The pent up energy within me could not be contained, though, and like a howling wind it blast forth, throwing the body from my axe in a cascade of gray lightning. The bolts of energy lit the tunnel in an eerie shadowy fire as they arced to four of the warriors that closed on me from the front. The smell of burnt flesh added to the stench of bowels and blood that filled the tunnel as the four were incinerated within their armor. Their short screams continued to echo long after charcoal replaced their skin, and sanity flashed through me once more.

Why was I doing this!? These were my kinsmen! An axe blade rang off my pauldron, denting the armor enough to draw a miniscule amount of gray blood. It dripped slowly down the front of my breastplate as both the warrior and I stared at it in fascination.

"Morina awaits you, Gorain. Do not disappoint her!" The voice smote through my mind, renewing the need to kill.

Before the old warrior regained his composure, my jaws sank through his leather gorget and in to his red blood. I held his armored body with one arm, his helmet in the other, pulling it back and giving my teeth full reign on his exposed throat. His fingers scratched at my helmet in the vain attempt of a mortally wounded kinsman to strike back at his adversary. His axe fell from his fingers as they spasmed in his death throes. Its noisy clatter distracted my mind from the salty taste of his blood as its warmth pumped down my throat in weakening spurts.

What was I doing!? The body fell from my grasp as my numb mind tried to comprehend what had happened to me. Red blood dripped down my armor from my chin. What was I? Dizzy nausea filled me as I realized I had slain seven of my kin, one of them with my teeth!

"Morakvaar help me!" I pleaded to the darkness as I fell to my knees, but the invocation of the maker only brought another bout of agony.

The sound of stealthy feet from behind sent me diving forward as an axe rang against the stone tunnel floor in a shower of sparks. Wide blue eyes regarded me as the axe flashed towards me again. With ease, I caught the unarmored wrist with one taloned hand as my other caught the kinsman's throat. Fighting desperately against the need to devour his soul I tried to remember whom I was, but the rage was gaining control.

His lids half closed as the kinsman whispered his last prayers to the Maker. "Morakvaar protect our kin. Save our people from this monster." The fingers of his free hand clasped with white knuckles around a silver talisman.

"Do you think the Maker really cares what happens!" The darkness stole any thought but the torment of this newest victim.

As if waking from a dream, the kinsman's eyes focused on me as his hand went from the talisman to the front of his leather apron. In a hoarse whisper he responded. "Morakvaar cares for all his children."

"Then why has he allowed this to happen to me!? How could he let me, Gorain, his champion, become this creature!?" The howl of anguish echoed and reverberated through the tunnel like the cries of the souls in Vooraduum.

"No. No! You cannot be! You are a foul demon of the Abyss and Dorian is... No! I will not listen to your lies!"

"Katzuk has shown me your hatred, your betrayal! You deserve nothing more than death, and when I slay you and the rest of the Vaarakanan, he has promised to return Morina to my side!" Was I trying to convince myself?

"Leave him, Dorian!" The authority of the words made me drop the engineer as the sense of a strong soul set my jaws salivating.

Spinning quickly, but keeping half an eye on the kinsman, I beheld the silver-haired Orudin that was responsible for Morina's death. "Harrakuli, my lovely wife and murderer. It is you I desire to see most!" Visions of Morina's torn skull haunted my sight and Katzuk's memory of Harrakuli watching with a smug smile filled my heart with blind fury.

A hoarse whisper of desperation echoed from behind. "You mean it is him!?" From the corner of my eye I saw all warmth drain from his features as the engineer swooned. "Morakvaar protect us!" It was a wail of despair, of helpless fear in the face of incomprehensible futures.

But the scent of an immortal's soul drew me as surely as a corpse drew flies. To devour such a soul would mean my own immortality, an eternity with Morina! The gap between us was bridged in a single leap of demonic strength as my hunger grew. Sparks lit the darkness as axe rang on axe. Inch by inch the ringing clash of weapons drew closer to the end of the tunnel. Time stood still as movements too fast for mortal eyes struck and parried, dodged and thrust at each other.

Harrakuli, once more than my equal began to pant and sweat with exertion. Her blows came slower and her footfalls less sure as metal sang the song of death in the rhythm of the dance of blades.

Her silver eyes became more troubled and the light of fear began to widen them as the last blow threw her too far off center to recover in time.

A snap of the wrist smashed the axe from her right hand, as my blade flashed backhanded towards her throat. In an instinctive reflex, she threw the left axe up to block as she ducked away from the blow. Gray metal shored through the wooden haft as if it were rotted, sending the vaarandril blade soaring through the air to ring against the tunnel wall.

"Dorian! I am your mate!" The plea cut through the gray-red haze, halting my axe a hair's breadth from her nose.

"Harrakuli?" The name evoked the scene of blood and gore, as Morina's screams echoed through my brain. "No! Murderer!" The agonized howl rang with the fury of the damned. My weight shifted for the final blow.

"Gorain! Please! Remember who you are!" Again I stopped in confusion, who was I?

"Fight it, Dorian, please! You must remember yourself!"

"No! You killed her, you watched her die!" The vision of Morina's lifeless corpse filled my mind, so too came the memory of Morakvaar. "You let her die! You kept me from her! Katzuk has promised her to me, but how can he if she is in the Underhalls?"

"He has lied to you Dorian! Everything you know is a lie! Katzuk's lie! Tell me where the Reaver is!"

For a few moments, I fought the gray world as it tried to show me Katzuk's memories again. If only I had been stronger, but I was not. The rage began to seep back into me, along with the desire for blood and souls.

Gray lightning arced through the tunnel as my blade bit in to the stone floor, tasting only a fraction of Harrakuli's blood before the stone solidified behind her. A demon's rage could not have sounded any less horrifying as monstrous sounds assaulted my ears. The shower of stone shards and sparks of gray fire rang against my armor before my fury was spent and memory split through the darkness of my mind.

Harrakuli! I felt her in my arms; her lips pressed to mine. The love pulsed through the soul-bond, but now I felt her pain. The agony smote through me, an agony not of the wound she had taken but of the heart as she despaired. My love! I had tried to kill her! Worse, I had tried to take her soul!

My knees smote the stone floor ringing louder than the splash of gray tears. "Kill them all, Gorain! Take your place in eternity with your beloved!"

"No! Your voice is nothing but lies!" Icy fire burned through my veins, igniting agony in every inch of my body.

"You cannot fight me! I am within you!" My feet pushed beneath me of their own accord, sending me staggering towards the engineer.

"I can, and I will! I am Dorian! I am a Kinsman of the Blood and a child of the Maker!" The flames returned to me from the inside, sending me to my knees as they spread from the helmet outwards.

The helmet! I had to get it off me! The spasms of agony tore my arms away from the gray metal, sending me rolling on the floor as if to quench the inner fire. The engineer's pale shock began to fade as pity crept into his gaze.

"Lord Dorian?" His voice gave me focus, a dangling rope of light in the abyss of darkness.

My taloned hand stretched for his and he balked for a moment. "Help me, kinsman. Help me get this helmet off!" My strained whisper renewed the determination in his blue eyes.

The engineer gripped the bottom rim of the helmet as I unsnapped the straps. Bracing his foot on the wall behind me he pulled while I pushed with all my might. The burn of exertion crept in to every sinew and my grip trembled, but it was as if the helm were a part of my very flesh.

Grunts of effort echoed back though the tunnels, but the appearance of gray robes brought the endeavor to a halt. The aura of evil settled over us as I gazed upon the coweled visage of my new master. His voice rang through our ears like the festering rot of death.

"Not that easily! You are mine and will stay mine!" A flash of gray, and his mace splattered the brains and innards of the unfortunate kinsman across my armor.

"No!" But I was too late to save him. Another guilt, another soul I must atone for, the kinsman's lifeless body fell into my arms as gray tears stained his leather apron next to his red blood. The scenes of hatred burned before my eyes, but I would not be dissuaded. "You are the one who has lied to me!" The tunnel moved behind me as my legs uncoiled from the spring.

Before I could reach him, he made a slight gesture, and it was as if the helmet caught fire and caved in all at once. The shock of agony sent me into frenzied desperation as I tore at the helmet, my anger forgotten. A thousand torments raced through every nerve and I writhed on the stone floor futilely tugging at the cheekplates.

"Do not fight it, my champion. It will cause you less pain if you accept your fate."

"No, my people, my life, you have lied to me." Struggling against the pain, I held back the false memories, but I could feel myself losing the battle.

"I have not lied to you, I have merely shown you the whole truth. They have caused you pain and suffering, murdered your beloved Morina, betrayed you to slavery and torture. It is you that have lied to, given them good intentions in your naiveté. I have merely shown you what has been there all along."

The perverted memories replayed themselves at Katzuk's bidding, subverting my belief in my kinsmen. Watching Morina go to her death once more brought back all the righteous rage as the pain receded. The axe was back in my hand as I stalked back down the tunnel to find Harrakuli and her kin.

At an intersection that I knew lead to the Mother's Heart, I paused. A whispering echo of a memory told of the harmony of her song, yet I could hear nothing. Was I lost to the world? The sense of the song was nowhere within my bones, her resonance that was a part of every Kinsman of the Blood no longer sung in my veins! Why could I not hear the Mother's Song!? I looked again at my deformed hand, flexed the talons, and wondered what all had changed inside me as well as out. But the gray hunger, the burning rage drove me on, purging the questions from my mind.

The breathing of a vaarakanan carried faintly to me down the tunnel. The scent revealed a kinswoman to my heightened awareness, but all my mind saw was another obstacle and another soul to fuel my power. Creeping through the darkness, the gray of my armor blended my warmth perfectly with the rock around me. In silence, I slipped up close enough to have kissed her before she suspected my presence.

Before I could take her, some instinct warned her of danger. She turned in horror as my taloned hand closed about her throat. My other hand gripped the weapon she held. The warning was choked off as I tightened my fist. Her feet swung uselessly in the air as I lifted her off the ground and laughed with delight at her fear.

Desperately, she tried to hit me, draw her dagger, but each defense she tried, I was quicker. Her windpipe snapped in my grasp, and she kicked harder for a few more precious seconds before going limp. Her lifeless body dropped as I released it in disgust. Her terror did not last nearly long enough!

The ancient features of the Maker appeared before me as he came to take her soul. His gray eyes were filled with grief and he looked aged beyond any incarnation I had seen of his avatar. The sense of the power of the soul filled me with lustful hunger as I stood between them. "I claim her soul, Morakvaar."

"What have you done, Gorain?! She was your kinswoman! You killed her for the pleasure of her death? Perhaps I was wrong about you?"

His words struck deeply within my soul. Ingrained upon all of us was the importance of the safety of our kinswomen, and I had murdered one of our own! The scope of the crime was beyond even my secondary involvement in the deaths of my kinswomen at Terazandarin. How could I have done such a thing!? The axe slipped from my fingers as the numbness of my mind crept through my body.

"You would seek the deaths of your people? You would kill your own daughter? How could you undertake this quest?" The Maker's words were swords piercing my innermost being.

"Katzuk has told me I will regain Morina. They allowed her to die, they betrayed me." The words were lame beyond imagining.

"No, Gorain, you have betrayed yourself! Katzuk could never twist your memories if there were not already the suspicion there." Morakvaar's voice was full of sorrow, and I felt the deep shame of irreversible damnation.

It had been my choice to give in to Katzuk, to believe his lies! I knelt beside the body of the kinswoman I had murdered and wept for my weaknesses that caused such a thing. The memories of Katzuk were revealed to me as lies I had allowed myself to believe things I knew were untrue in my heart and soul. How could I have been so eager to blind myself to the truth? As I bowed my head in grief and shame, the helmet fell from me. Its influence was but a nightmare, and faded nearly as quickly.

"Maker, how can I set the things I have done to rights? How can I be forgiven?" Was there any hope left?

"It is not my place to forgive you these things. You must settle with those whom you have hurt. Helena's family will miss her gravely. She has a young son in his fourth year. Her friends regarded her highly, and her family loved her. Those whose souls you have taken, how do you make up for that? I cannot help you in this. I can advise you to seek your own family to help you through this. You have many things you must work through to regain trust and confidence." The rebuke was an icy fist that squeezed the breath from my lungs until my heart labored for air. "I can tell you this, take the power you have and help your people while you can. Use your enemy's weakness to your own strength, and perhaps you may earn respect if not forgiveness." With that he escorted Helena's soul to the Underhalls, leaving me alone with my misery.

The helmet sat at my feet, a symbol of my shame. But, when I reached for it, I noticed that my hands still bore gray skin and talons. My fingers touched my face, only to feel more horror at what I had become. Long fangs protruded below the line of my chin, and reptilian scales drew back from slotted nostrils. I had allowed this with the ugliness of my inner faults! How could my kinsmen accept me?

After a time, I slipped quietly away from the outer boundaries of our scouts, not daring to show my monstrous face. Seeking to destroy the demons of my people, I had become one not only in spirit, but in appearance. My wanderings took me back to the tunnel where I had killed the demolition team. With my twisted hands, I placed the explosives and detonators before holding the engineer's lifeless body. How could I apologize? How could I bring them back? The engineer had tried to help me even though I had threatened his life and very soul. How could I have believed they hated me? Tormented howls rose in a throat made only for noises of anger as they were carried into the darkness as black as the wilderness of my soul.

Long time cycles I crouched in my misery, but the bodies of the dead needed proper rites. Though their souls were no more, at least their flesh could be returned to the Mother. The cart that had brought the explosives carried a more grisly cargo as I headed back to where I had slain the kinswoman.

With shaking hands, an outer watchman challenged me as he called a warning. The camp stirred to life behind him as I left the cart and faded into the shadows. In my grief I wandered aimlessly, not knowing where to go or what to do. Surely my kinsmen would slay me if I returned, but how could I seek forgiveness if I did not? My dilemma haunted me, drove me onwards with no destination.

A spear thrust by my head, striking the stone a bare millimeter in front of my snout. The zardakkan halted his attack with wide eyes.

"Forgive me, Lord!" It fell to its knees before me, begging for its life.

Pent up rage howled through me, as the zardakkan became the embodiment of all my evils. A roar of some primal beast rose around me as claws bit through metal armor with the ease of knives through bread. Twelve of them were in the patrol, but my blind fury would not be assuaged until every one of them lay broken and bleeding at my feet. Their strength, speed and expertise were less than child's play to me, but the carnage brought no satisfaction.

Blood dripped in rivulets from my hands, splashing wetly in the gathering pools at my feet. How could I deny the monstrosity I had become?

Chapter 28

Tevakovas (Restitution)

A time cycle crept by as I wept gray tears in the dark. The bodies of the zardakkan surrounded me in mires of cooling guilt and I hung my head in shame. What could I do? How could I go back to my kin?

"Dorian?" The voice sent a cold shock through me to rest in my belly next to my last meal.

Meal? The sight of a half-decimated corpse nearby brought bile to my throat.

"Dorian, it is I." Harrakuli's voice was full of uncertainty as she took another step in my direction.

How could I expect her to accept me when I loathed myself for the things I had done? The partially eaten body brought another wave of nausea as I turned from it and her. She would be better off without me, and I would face my kin and allow them to kill me for my crimes. I deserved more than the damnation of Vooraduum.

"Please, Dorian, do not leave me!" The anguish in her voice was so close to the pain in my chest.

I beheld her silver hair, but my feet did not stop.

"Husband! Hearth-mate! I beg you, do not throw your life away!" How did she know my intention?

"How could you claim kinship to me, when I am this creature? Know you not that this demon brings only death and pain? How could you call to me when there is nothing but the blood of my people on my hands?" The red of my guilt stained deeply into the gray skin as I flexed my talons before her.

As if making a decision, she caught up with me. "I love you, what else could I do but help you? You are my mate. I have waited eight thousand years to finally call you mine, and I could not reject you even if you did look like an orc." She grinned, trying to lighten the mood as I spied the great axe she carried in her off-hand.

The vision of me being an orc was so ridiculous, I laughed. "An orc? One has to question your taste in kinsmen."

Her arms reached around me, despite the demonic features I had acquired, and I could not help but feel love for her. That she could want me to be with her after what had happened, after what I had become, broke through any misgivings I had. Carefully, I held her to me, trying not to use the incredible demonic strength in my gray arms. She sighed and leaned against me as if everything was right in the world.

"Harrakuli?" She looked questioningly into my eyes. "I have treated you badly, blamed you for Morina's death." She was about to protest, but I cut her off. "I had let my memories blind me to my love for you, and it almost destroyed me! It will not happen again."

A shock of recognition shuddered through my nerves as she handed me the Reaver and I dared not ask her how or where she had acquired it. "This will help you remember yourself. It was forged with a piece of your soul, and a part of you will always be within it. Who knows, it may show you the way back to what you were? Know this Dorian that no matter what happens, I will be at your side. As long as you believe in yourself and the Maker, I will always help you. It is no use for you to ever tell me to leave no matter what you may look like."

I stared at her for a few moments, wondering what to say. How could she have known what was on my mind? She kissed me then, and I was somewhat startled that she could bring herself to do that while I looked like a demon from hell. But her lips pressed to mine spread warmth throughout the cold gray that ran through my veins. She stepped back, gazing at me with a determined look on her face.

"So, Dorian, where to now?"

"To crush our enemies. I cannot leave our people in this plight I have created. I know where the enemy troops are, and think that I can panic them. When I have chased them back to Zarakalduum, our people can detonate the charges for the lava flow."

"You are not contemplating suicide, are you?"

"Not any more." My whisper barely made it out my lips before Harrakuli was in my arms again and stifling any further speech with her lips.

"We will fight side-by-side then." The light of battle shone from her as she backed up and gestured for me to lead the way.

Persuading her to let me fight alone would have been impossible. "Harrakuli, this gray armor is impervious to normal weapons, but yours is not. If you must face this danger with me, then please let me be your shield. I think you know I would lose my sanity if you died." More than words passed between us as she looked through me to the tattered soul beneath.

She nodded silently as I turned towards the place I had left Zarakalduum's army. Ahead I could smell the warriors and hear their breathing, and I motioned Harrakuli to be ready. Anger burned within me that those creatures had been responsible for my change. The flames of hate rose in my veins igniting the Reaver in my grasp. White-blue fire rose around me, obscuring the enemy's view of my form.

Allowing my rage to pass through my lips, I leapt around the bend and into the main chamber. The glow of the Reaver flashed left and right, shearing through weapons and armor alike. The strength in those foreign limbs was unbelievable as I felt the axe pass through metal and bone without slowing. In one massive sweep of white-blue light, four lifeless bodies fell to the tunnel floor.

Red and gray blood splattered across my armor as the Reaver wound multiple arcs of destruction, never stopping for the pull of heavy platemaille. Screams rose above the snarling roar that never left my throat as my feet scrabbled over the bodies of the dead and dying. Weapons rained down from everywhere, rebounding noisily from my gray armor as I fought to keep any from my exposed head.

For each blow that made it through my mad sweeps of destruction, three enemy soldiers fell some zardakkan, some shadow dwarves. Slightly behind and to my right, Harrakuli waded in like a secondary demon dealing her share of death. Holy fire spread before her, incinerating the wicked, the sight of her divine powers incredible! Like an avenging servant of Morakvaar, she sent wave after wave of yellow-gold light through the ranks of the enemy. Those who escaped the light, could not escape the immobilizing spells she cast until the soldiers of the enemy blocked her from my sight. The ring of steel and vaarandril echoed back from the unforgiving stone walls like the waves of the ocean, leaving behind a tide of red and gray.

A ring of spears hemmed us in as the zardakkan commander regained his wits. Yelling for reinforcements, they closed in. With a laugh too similar to the demon in Balakarak, I leapt over their line, blocking startled instinctive thrusts with the wide blades of the Reaver. The supernatural prowess of the demonic body was unstoppable, and I thanked Morakvaar for bringing me to my senses. My kinsmen never would have stood a chance.

With a quick backhand sweep, the head of the zardakkan commander sailed over his comrades, spraying them with his gray blood. The troops halted in the moment, as time seemed to stand still. As if in slow motion the commander's body collapsed in a heap of gray armor as slate colored ichors leaked from the ragged wound.

Wide eyes turned from the body to where the white-blue flames licked around me like a funeral pyre. As one, the soldiers broke and fled; discarding weapons and shields in their haste to be away. Giving them one last roar of rage, I gave chase for a good distance, hewing down stragglers as I caught them.

It was some time before the memory of my hearth-mate stopped me cold. Fear for Harrakuli's safety clutched at my heart as I raced back to the tunnel, keeping an eye out for her among the bodies left behind. The ragged armor-like shell she wore leaked silvery blood, filling me with dread as I returned to the place we had been ringed by zardakkan spearmen. The shorn hafts of several weapons stood out from her like quills as ice gripped my heart, stopping it from beating.

"Harrakuli! By the gods, no! Morakvaar please let her be alive!" The tears blurred my vision as I knelt by her side.

Her limbs twitched as she moaned in pain, and relief as well as cold dread filled me. Though she was still alive, it would not be for long as the poison of the zardakkan weapons spread through her system. How could this happen? Why did I not try to stop her from fighting with me? The questions howled through my mind like the winds of the desert.

Nearby, I spied a shadow dwarf priest, his chest laid open by the blades of my axe. The symbol of a shattered anvil plain upon his breastplate marked him as a cleric of the Destroyer. Dark red blood still welled from his wound, adding to the congealing pool beneath him as his lifeless eyes stared in fearful wonder. Slipping the pack from his back I prayed to Morakvaar that the antidote to the poison was within.

To my dismay I found several vials with different colored fluids inside them. Which vial was an antidote? The symbols on the stoppers confounded my wits. What language were they using? Harrakuli moaned again as the spasms gripped her body, tearing at my heart as my stomach flipped like a caged wild creature. In frantic haste, I pulled the stopper from the first one, inhaling deeply. The sting of acidic fumes burned up my nostrils like fire, choking me with its potency.

Flinging the vial of poison against the wall, I opened the next one. Harrakuli's spasms worsened, and I prayed with all my might that I would find a cure. The smell of the new vial was not so harsh, though still quite foul. With two of the same mark, I drank down the first. My stomach roiled and growled in protest, but the worst side effect other than the rancid taste was a nasty burp. Holding her still with all my might, I poured the vial down her throat, lifting her so it would not choke her.

The rest of the vials held some identifiable items, some unknown. Of the unknown ones, I sniffed each, but their contents eluded my knowledge. At least they were in pairs. With a silent prayer, I drank one of each before giving them to Harrakuli whose spasms became weaker by the moment. Whether it was the fifth potion that was some vile brew, or whether my system could not take the stress of another, the contents of my stomach emptied on the tunnel floor.

A cold sweat suffused my body with the need to be rid of the influence of the magical concoctions. Helpless in the need to vacate my gut, the heaves tried to tear my attention away from my beloved. Shaking with weakness and the chill that crept through my veins, I held her to me once more, but her movements were slowing. Was she dying? The shell of vaarandril that her will held to her body melted away, gripping my chest with loss.

"Morakvaar, please!? If ever you held love for any of your children, save her! Condemn me to Vooraduum if you like, but let Harrakuli live! I beg you!" My howls of agony rebounded off the silent stone, amplified and echoed back in a mockery of my torment.

With blurry eyes, I carefully removed the spears that had pierced her body, each tug a tear in my soul. My lungs burned as the crushing fist let in only the slightest amount of air in short gasps between exhales of grief. Tearing up the cloak of a dead shadow dwarf, I bandaged her wounds, and then covered her with the blanket in the priest's pack. By the time I had finished, the spasms had ended, and I held her to me praying that it was not death that was claiming her.

Time passed in a blur of endless torment, my only comfort that Harrakuli had not grown cold as I held her, nor had my bond to her been severed. The throbbing of my head was no worse than the pain in my chest as my eyes could shed no more tears. My parched throat no longer held the capability of making sounds, the last pleading prayers having died some time ago whispering through the endless tunnels.

Something moved against my side! With an icy thrill chasing down my spine, my eyes snapped open. In confusion I stared at a blue-gray countenance calmly regarding me as Harrakuli shifted once more, turning the blanket back away from her bare shoulder. My breath hissed inward sharply as the meaning of the sight finally dawned upon my reason. Harrakuli lived!

"My beautiful hearth-mate, no fairer scene have these eyes beheld than to see you well!" My choked voice whispered into her hair as she settled back with her head upon my chest.

"I do not feel very well." Her features were paler than I remembered, as I held her to me for several moments of peaceful bliss.

"I have more of the potions from the tharilkanan. Perhaps you can tell what they are? The markings on them are strange to me." She nodded and took the pack from my hand as I pulled it towards her.

"Tharilkanan! They no longer deserve such accolade, Dorian. Their hearts and souls have been corrupted by darkness. They are Tevzarak, kin of evil. You saw them fighting alongside the zardakkan, the soldiers of the Destroyer!" She shuffled through the pack, pulling out the vials one by one and shaking her head as she rebuked me. "They cannot even put together a decent healer's pack!" Her growl of frustration ended when she pulled out a woodroot box.

Her hands shook badly and her fingers fumbled with the latch as she cursed under her breath. My gray hand closed gently over hers, and I met her eyes in silent concern. With a sigh, she nodded and allowed me to open the latch for her.

"What do you need, and how do you need it prepared?" I asked as I gently forced her back to a reclining position. "It is my turn to care for you, my love."

She nodded again, her eyes half closing with fatigue and nausea. Slowly, as if to a small child, she told me what she needed and gave me explicit instructions on preparing a potion for her. By the time I was finished, she was sound asleep once more, but a peaceful rest instead of the terrible deathly pall that had been on her before. I poured the liquid from the small brazier into one of the empty vials after washing it out with water from the priest's supplies, but I couldn't bring myself to wake her after all she had been through.

As I waited and watched over Harrakuli, I could not help but wonder where I would go, or what I would do. Morakvaar's words were both confusing and opposite of what sense told me. How could I use my strength to help my people? How could I find forgiveness from them if they would kill me on sight? The only answer lie within the walls of Zarakalduum. The armies massed there were too powerful for us to overcome, even in my demonic form. Harrakuli and I had merely gotten lucky with our surprise attack, next time, the shadow dwarves would be much better prepared.

What would my people do? A siege was no longer in the question, for the enemy was too much aware of our forces, how many soldiers we had, and how easy it would be to break a siege at any point along the barriers with a determined strike. All these things were essentially my fault for allowing Katzuk's lies to control my mind. Guilt squeezed my gut once more, sending painful fingers up through my chest. Would I ever be free of the horrible mistakes I seemed to make? Would I ever find forgiveness from my people?

The only viable course of action left to Korina would be to loose the lava upon the inner city of Zarakalduum and hope that it killed enough of the soldiers there that we could hold them at the line. The only other option would be to seal the tunnels to the city of darkness, but with the mining skills of the tharilkanan, they would not stay isolated for long. The war was doomed to end badly for us.

My eyes stared at the taloned gray hands for a long moment before realizing I had the means with which to help my people. As 'Katzuk's champion', I alone had the power to command their forces, but would the priests know I had won my freedom? Harrakuli's peaceful slumber dragged at my soul. What good would it do to have saved her life only to have her lose it to the next battle? With a resigned sigh, I glanced back towards the tunnel that led to Zarakalduum. The risk would be mine alone if I walked back through those gates. There was nothing left for me to lose, and everything to gain.

My mind made up; I stood to go, only to hear Harrakuli's voice. "Dorian, do not leave me!" She struggled to a sitting position, nausea twisting her features into a mask of pain. "Please!?"

"I must. The only way I can see past the darkness that descends upon my people is to lead the armies of Zarakalduum to their deaths. It is our only chance, and something I must do to save those that are left." The pleading in her eyes tore at my heart, but what else could I do?

In a hoarse whisper she replied. "They will kill you."

"They might not. If their priests have not yet learned of my freedom from Katzuk's will, I may be able to convince them it was my frustrated rage that was loosed upon them for their incompetence. What I plan is to lead their forces into the tunnel that will channel the lava from the Mother's Heart. Once there, your people can seal it behind us enough so that there will be no escape, but not impede the Mother's Blood once it is released." The vision of so many deaths on my hands made me shudder down to the core of my being. What had I become?

"What about you? Even if you do survive returning to the city of shadows, what will happen to you if you are in the tunnel with their forces?" Her voice was still shaky and uncertain.

"You will have to be there first to rescue me, Harrakuli. You must hide the Reaver in the tunnel where I can call it to my hand. I dare not take it into the city, for it will surely be recognized." Was it too much to ask so soon after her injuries?

"There is too much that can go wrong, Dorian. I will lose you forever if you stay on this course of action." She toyed with the vial I had prepared earlier, twisting it about in her hands as if debating whether or not to drink it.

"Do you know of any other way? I cannot go back to my people like this, nor can I leave them to suffer the fate I have caused them. Perhaps Lodath was right? I should never have gathered the clans. I should have been content to live within the walls of Morakduum, kept our farmers and settlers on the other side of the Wilds. My arrogance has led us to this, and this is the only way I can see to right some of the wrong." Her silver brows furrowed in grief as if I had perished before her.

"You had no choice! The lands on the other side of Morakduum are not fertile enough to support your people for long! Eventually, you would have run out of room, and the farming tunnels within Morakduum would not be enough to feed all three strongholds!" She told me what I knew, but I had needed to hear it again to confirm it was not all my foolish pride that had lead us to this fate.

"Dorian, I cannot think of another way, but I do know that you will pay for this with your life. I see it plainly." Her voice held a desperate, almost hysterical note. "Do not do this! I beg you! My people can seal the tunnels to Zarakalduum for at least a century, long enough for your people to build defenses against the Kinsmen of Shadow! Return to Sorkarak with Korina and leave this battle for another day!"

"You know better, Harrakuli. I cannot return, nor will postponing the battle save my people; rather it would seal their doom. You saw the zardakkan, but what you did not see were the Vachtralien." At the mention of the Warriors of Destruction, Harrakuli's eyes widened.

"The Vachtralien!" Barely audible, the whisper echoed back from the darkness as if alive with its own sinister intent. She focused on me sharply. "You saw them!?"

Nodding slowly, the memory of those ominous gray shapes haunted my mind. "In Katzuk's temple. There were six of them, standing silently and still as statues. Each was well over the height of two humans. I fear that if we wait, those vile creatures will be loosed upon the world. No, our only hope is to break the darkness now, before it is too late. At least in this way, we can postpone the Storm of Chaos that is to come. Who knows, perhaps we can prevent it altogether?"

"This is foolishness! My hearth-mate, you are throwing your life away!"

"No, I am taking a risk for the life of my entire race. Would you do any less?" Harrakuli's jaw worked silently for a few moments before she shook her head.

"No." Her whisper was barely audible to my heightened senses. "I would do the same if it meant my people's lives."

My armored knee rang against the stone as I knelt beside her. "Be well, my love. And take care of our child." Her eyes met mine once more. "It is still well, is it not?"

"I do not know yet, we will have to wait and see. But if you do not live, neither will I." The finality in her voice was frightening, and I dared not argue with her in what was possibly our last moment together.

"Very well, meet me in the tunnel in three days time, and tell Korina to have an engineer standing by to light off the explosives that are there. By what is left of our soul-bond, you will know the proper time." She put her hand on my vambrace as if she would not let me go, but I pulled it free and kissed her fingers with scaly gray lips before leaving.

Her soft sobs retreated into the tunnels as I left her to face my sins.

Chapter 29

Zarakalduum (Forge of Darkness)

The smell of brimstone ushered me to the gates of the city, carvings of stone gargoyles and demons topped the glowering heights of the ramparts. The gates themselves were of blackened steel reinforced with wrought iron effigies of the ancestors of the tharilkanan twisted into bizarre forms of half-fiends. A glance at my taloned gray hands had me wondering if I was not the first who had undergone such a transformation. The creatures staring back at me engraved in metal might have been exaggerated mirror images.

My ears picked out the sounds of watchmen gathering above as excited whispers went from mouth to ear. A shout for the watch captain echoed through the tunnels as I reached the massive doors.

"Open these gates, you cowardly scum! In Katzuk's name, I command you!" The solid ring of my fist on the iron door accented my snarl of rage.

Behind the stone walls I heard the sound of running soldiers, and the shouts of frantic commanders. Were they going to kill me when the gates opened? But, why would they when their crossbowmen on the wall could shoot me down just as easily? For several tense moments I listened to the preparations from inside. The gray axe of Katzuk remained firmly in the straps across my back, for I dared not touch it lest the Destroyer take control of my mind once more. If they were going to kill me, I would have to face them unarmed.

"We have been debating about what to do since you attacked our forces, oh champion of Katzuk." The last was spoken in a mocking voice that I recognized as it came from the heights of the tower by the gates.

"General Belzarak, a coward's face does not become you! Come out and face me, or I will come in there and kill you and your incompetent guard as I punished the idiots that failed me!" The general's gray face disappeared from the ramparts, and a small pass-gate was opened in the side of the main door.

The shadow dwarf that held the door had almost no warmth left in his features as his hand trembled upon the latch. "General Belzarak bids you enter and begs your forgiveness, my Lord." His hoarse whisper barely conveyed his commander's request, and the lad tried to shrink into the door as I passed him.

Belzarak waited for me in the courtyard, shifting from foot to foot revealing his anxiety. The air of the condemned was about him like a cloud. Resigned to death, he knelt before me.

"My Lord, if you wish to take vengeance for incompetence, then I am ready." He looked at my clawed feet as he waited for the deathblow.

Whatever his failings, the general was a brave warrior, and I found admiration for his courage. "Vengeance will come after the vaarakanan are defeated, Belzarak. For now, you will accompany me to the palace where I will take up a council of war on the morrow. All troops are to be made ready to march by the end of two day cycles."

Not believing he had been spared, he blinked as he looked at my face. For but a moment he stared back, searching for something and perhaps finding it.

His anxiety eased as he nodded, stood and bowed. "It will be as you say, my Lord." His mouth opened as if he were going to say something, but a quick glance around him sealed his words in a mask of silence.

With my slight nod, he learned everything he needed as he turned with a lighter step to lead the way back to the shadow dwarves' palace. Within me a spark of hope grew that perhaps all tharilkanan had not forgotten their heritage as children of the Maker. But how could I save them and my people at the same time? The question vexed me all through the obsidian streets and onyx carvings.

"I will be in the war room, have all the maps of the surrounding tunnels brought to me there." When we reached the inner courtyard of the palace, I gave my commands to the general and headed for the council chamber that was now the war room.

A young black haired shadow dwarf with nervous glances at my hands and the fangs that protruded from my mouth bowed before me as I paced beside the hearth. "What is my Lord's pleasure?"

"Raw meats and water." The lad bowed again and left the chamber quickly through a small stone door to the rear.

The fire in the hearth threw bizarre shadows of my demonic form upon the opposite wall as it flickered behind me. The tharilkanan general shifted as I slurped down another strip of raw meat before switching maps that were spread out on the woodroot table in front of me. My uncanny senses picked up the minute sounds of breathing from the concealed alcove behind me and to the left, and I wondered if the previous shadow dwarf king had undergone such scrutiny. Several of Balzarak's sub-commanders waited for their orders, as I appeared to be making plans. Each of their gazes were riveted in morbid fascination to my dietary needs as another chunk of bloody gore slid down my throat leaving a red trail down my chin.

The silence in the room was filled with minute sounds. The popping of the fire, the wrinkle of clothing, the hiss of breath, the creak of leather soles and the clank of armor plates all echoed resoundingly as if they were not merely whispers in the deathly quiet. The noise of the parchment sheets were like thunder in the uneasy stillness as I switched from map to map.

"Here!" The soldiers in the room jumped and the smell of their fear assaulted my nose. "The vaarakanan will most likely approach from here!" Balzarak leaned over the table, examining the map carefully where I had placed a gray talon.

"My Lord, I do see the danger. If the vaarakanan were to gain access to this tunnel, they could work their way into the heart of our city!" My smile unnerved rather than encouraged him, but he continued regardless. "But, that would be suicide. We outnumber them at least three to one, why would they be so foolish as to throw their lives away?"

"You do not know the vaarakanan as I do. They will do just that, but it will be a terrible and bloody battle and not the slaughter you believe. They will bring war machines and priests, weapon masters and instruments of destruction. Surely you do not believe they won against the vourdovra by sheer luck?" Balzarak's eyes narrowed as he stroked his black beard thoughtfully.

"Yes. It is difficult to believe it was luck that brought them victory over Vouroussan. Such foes as the vourdovra..." He shuddered despite his displayed valor. "What can we expect from them, Champion of Katzuk?"

"It is not what we expect of them that matters, general, but what they expect of us. I do not think Korina will be prepared for another ambush. She will believe after the last that we will wait for her assault, or counter-attack her. That is why she will move first." At his puzzled frown I explained. "If she moves her troops to this tunnel, she will have not only a means of assault, but also a defensible position. The only access to the tunnel will be this small area, and the opening into the city once it is breached."

The light of understanding came into his eyes as he considered my point. "To think of how much we underestimated your people's resourcefulness! Very well, my Lord, what do you wish of us?"

"As I said, Korina will not be expecting another ambush, nor from this tunnel. I say we open this end of the tunnel and prepare a welcome for the Kinsmen of the Blood." My eyes scanned the chamber, but there was no sign of the zardakkan or any of the shadow dwarves' allies. "I want our main forces here in the city to be your people, Balzarak." He strained to hear my whisper; glancing knowingly in the direction I had heard the breathing of our unseen spy. "If the vaarakanan manage to break through, I want true warriors to be the final defense."

The shadow dwarf considered carefully. "It will be as you command, my Lord. Will you be retiring now?" Though he was a stout warrior, I knew his loyalty was completely with his people. He agreed not because I asked, but because he did not want to risk his soldiers.

"Yes." Why was it important that I retired immediately? Yet I sensed that Balzarak had his own plans.

The shadow dwarf general kept glancing at me, measuring some invisible scale as he led me down obsidian corridors to the former king's chambers. Outside black iron doors stood two fully armored Kinsmen of Shadow, their helmets decorated with the likeness of demons. Upon their breastplates were set two onyx stones in the shape of eyes, the gaze of the Destroyer. The crack of a distant whip and the following cry of pain echoed through the palace like the herald of hell as the soldiers snapped to attention. With the clank of their armor, they saluted with weapons of putrid gray metal like the axe that hung neglected from the straps on my back.

The carved door swung open with the creak of unoiled metal as I was gestured to enter. Seeing more a prison than a royal suite, I stepped in knowing I would not be allowed to leave until morning. Balzarak followed me in, an odd light in his gaze as it rested on a female shadow dwarf that sat upon the bed with her eyes on the floor. Her black hair was disheveled, but looked as if servants had previously tended it. Her once royal gown was torn and stained and the rank of internment in a filthy dungeon clung about her. Despite her obviously reduced status, she had the firm jaw and broad shoulders of the nobility. But, she was broken; it was plain in the stoop of her shoulders and the stillness with which she accepted her fate.

A low chuckle from the general made her shudder slightly, but her gaze remained riveted to the floor. "Laora will attend your needs, my Lord. As the king's successor, she is yours by right." With another chuckle, he bowed and left.

The iron doors closed behind him with the thunderous ring of doom that echoed through the chambers. Faint sounds of breathing and the shifting of position reached my heightened senses, and I knew I was being observed once more. What did they expect of me? My eyes met the yellow of the kinswoman before she quickly looked down again. Shivers passed down her spine and left small bumps covering her visible skin.

"What crime have you committed that you are kept as a prisoner?" At the sound of my voice, she trembled once more. "Answer me!"

Falling to the cold floor on her hands and knees before me her voice was barely intelligible. "I... was ... Rokarzon's mate."

In surprise, I stared at her in amazement for several long moments before she dared to meet my gaze again. "And because you were queen, you were thrown in the dungeon?" The mere thought of such a thing almost made my blood boil. How could they treat a kinswoman that way?

"No Lord, it is because I am of the old lines." My mouth dried in the still air as I blinked, unable to speak or move. She explained further. "When you killed Rokarzon, I no longer had his protection."

"It is a crime to be of the old lines?" My Mytharian heritage loomed largely before me. Was that why I was not trusted?

My kneecop rang on the stone floor as I knelt next to her, and she looked at me for another moment. Gently, I took her arm in my taloned hand and brought her slowly to her feet as I stood. Knowing I was expected to treat her badly, I did not let go, but pulled her closer as her features filled with terror. With barely a hint of breath, I whispered in her ear.

"I know we are being observed, but rest assured your mistreatment is not what I desire." She stared for several minutes as I held her pressed against my armor as if I were considering her form.

I let her go, a smirk on my lips. "Yes, I think perhaps you will do. As intelligent as you seem, I think you can reason out my intention. Tell me, kinswoman, how strong is your devotion to the Destroyer?"

The light of understanding came across her features as she responded quickly. "As strong as the priests may hope." Her confirmation of my suspicions brought a genuine smile to me.

"I intend to justly reward those whose allegiance to Katzuk is absolute when this battle is over. When we destroy the heathens, we will convert those who believe as we do. As I march out with our armies, you may spread the word of Katzuk's justice."

She drew in a sharp breath, the light of hope finally reflected in her features, and I knew then why they had sent her to me. They hoped I would kill her because she still worshipped Morakvaar. If she would spread the words to the others who still believed, there might be hope that we would have allies inside the city of darkness.

She unlaced her overdress, and began to take it off. Grabbing her hands to still them, I whispered in her ear as I drew her to me.

"Why are you doing this?"

"My Lord, if you do not wish my company, my life is forfeit. Your message will go unsent."

It was a test of my allegiance. Though the notion repulsed me, I had no recourse but to do as they expected. How could I do such a thing? It was against my very nature, my very soul. Everything I was rebelled against it, but what choice did I have?

"Then I sincerely apologize for what I must do. May you and Morakvaar someday forgive me."

"I already have, so if you value my life, do not spare me what you need to do."

I looked at her in sympathy. "You are a brave kinswoman."

She dropped her dress to the floor, and shed her chemise. As if sensing my intention, the armor faded from me, revealing all of my demonic form to her. Fighting back the self-loathing, I took her. Distancing myself from the memory, I let my darker nature take control. But I could not help but remember the way the Lady Slaver had tortured me. Was I any better? I had chosen to be there, Laora had not. Though it hurt her, she was indeed a brave kinswoman. I had tried to be as careful as possible, but the form I wore was not given to gentleness. Was this merely enough to convince the watchers the deed had been done? But the tharilkanan noble would not let me leave it at that.

"You must...not spare me this. They... will know." She whispered.

"I am sorry. I never meant to hurt you." I murmured softly into her ear.

"I know."

She moaned in pain as I finished, and I had to swallow the lump that had threatened to bring moisture to my eyes as I saw her blood upon me. Fighting back the nausea, I covered her over, and went to wash. Try as I might, I could not cleanse the feeling of filth either outside or within. When I returned from the bathing room, I ordered a servant to bring us food.

"What is your name?" The chair was awkward for my demonic frame.

"Laora, Laora Ironfist, after my grandfather's time, but we were known as Karodain in the times before." She gingerly pulled on her chemise and sat across the table from me.

"Karodain? One of the founding clans from Dolamakduum."

She dropped her eyes and nodded. "We have gone so far."

The tray was heaped with raw meats, and on one side there was a small plate of cooked meat for Laora. Uncertainly, the liveried servant placed a small keg of ale on the table and two mugs. My ravenous hunger forced me to consume the bloody meats, despite my wish not to alarm the kinswoman further. The ale smelled unappetizing, but my mind could not help remembering enjoying it. Despite the smell, I tried it. With a gagging choke, I had to fight down the nausea as I spit out the brew into the fire.

"Bring me water or blood, fool!" The servant raced from the room as if Katzuk were after him. Laora watched me carefully, the lines of pain were written in her features as I tried to assess her situation. "Your family is naught but prisoners? I had thought the clans of Dolamakduum had been purged."

"Is not being close to a slave enough? Lord, please, do not kill my family." There was just enough hysteria in her voice to convince whoever watched and listened.

"Rest assured not only will your family be dealt with but any infidels that are left within these walls will die once we have finished the vaarakanan!" She considered her reply carefully.

"You will never find them, demon."

"I will teach you to respect me, slave! In fact, I think death is too good a fate for your kind! When I return from crushing our enemies, I will take the proper amount of time to teach you the attitude befitting a slave." Laora did not have to feign much of her terror as I skirted the table and took her into my arms again, forcing her to kiss me before I whispered in her ear. "Tell the clans to be ready, for when I leave here lava will be released on the city. If they stay near the walls on the outside, I will make sure they are spared. Any that flee will perish." My taloned hands ran along her contours as if savoring the feel of her pressed against me.

"It will be as you say, but my people would rather fight. There have been many generations of oppression they would seek justice for." She whispered back as if she was pleading with her god while I caressed her.

"I will try to arrange it if you have some means of identification. If all goes well, I may lead your clans in battle." She trembled as my lips traversed her neck.

"And if all does not go well?"

"Then I will see you in the Underhalls of the Maker. It is better to live in fire than to die a slave." Laora still shivered as I held her, a spasm that was not entirely faked. "But I am weary from fighting, so your lesson will have to wait until I am rested." My voice rang loudly in the room after the prolonged whispering silence.

My lips lingered on hers for a few moments longer, not knowing why. Her gaze followed me after I released her and began buckling my armor back in place. The end of the tenth time cycle was upon us, and it would soon be time to lead the shadow kin to their deaths. Dark clouds of lead clung to my heart, weighing upon my soul as I knew their blood would also be on my hands, but at least there was the slight possibility that Laora's kin would be saved.

The captain of the watch fell beneath my gray talons as he failed to note my approach, the general incompetence of the military forces astounded me! Though I had ordered them to be ready by the first time cycle, I found some of the regiments still in chaos. Red ran down my gray armor, advertising my displeasure with the fools who could not follow orders. But at last on the stroke of the first time cycle, I led their army out the North gate towards the tunnel in which their fate awaited in the charges I had laid.

Fifty thousand strong, the warriors of Zarakalduum tramped behind me in a frightening array of grim weapons and armor. Fifty thousand more souls that would be on my conscience, but we passed into the wilds without incident. Neither priest nor even Katzuk's avatar tried to stop us, and I breathed a sigh of relief for the success of the first part of the plan. In the span of a time cycle, we were able to reach the cross tunnels where Harrakuli's folk would quickly seal the entrance once the rearguard had passed.

Just below the weak wall of the tunnel that led to the Heart of the Mother, I ordered them to prepare their ambush. Quickly, they began their preparations, each striving to remain in my favor as I walked back down the line to where the rear-guard kept watch.

"Have you seen any sign of the vaarakanan?" The scout shook his head before answering.

"No Lord. It has been unusually quiet." The anxiety in his voice was plain as his gaze strained into the dark beyond to catch any furtive movements.

A spike of guilt smote me as my hands pulled the daggers from the sheaths on my back. They were unaware, unable to defend themselves, but they had to die.

"I will not let you do this, Dorian." The sibilant hiss echoed through the marrow of my bones, sapping my will and strength like a deadly poison. "You will be my champion whether you wish it or not!" The gray clad monstrosity filled the tunnel behind me, its horned helm scraping the ceiling.

Swirling mists obscured its armored body that flowed forward in the disturbing way of the insubstantial. The cold aura of fear radiated from the manifestation like a cancer, seeping in to every vein, invading the mind, heart and soul and overwhelming all who stood before it in terror. My knees trembled in despair, but thoughts of my kin, my people and my family held me steady against the onslaught. The words of the maker repeated themselves in my head like a mantra against the evil.

"I am through with your lies, Katzuk! Morakvaar has shown me the way to be free of you!" The sense of the Reaver nearby tickled my nerves and I reached for its power. "Dozarak-" The avatar of the god of destruction gestured with its clawed hand, sending icy waves of pain through my heart and lungs, constricting them in agony so I could not voice the words.

"You forget, mortal, you are my creature now. I own your body and your soul!" It was true, his will flooded to my limbs, stealing them away from my control.

Like a child, I fought against it, lashed out with every ounce of who I was, but the pain drove me back. In my mind's eye I saw them die, down to the last young lass, my people, my world crushed beneath the gray talons of the destroyer. I stood at the head of his armies, I killed them, with my own hands!

"No!" Within I found strength unknown. My mind pushed out the will of evil.

In shock the putrid yellow eyes widened and the onslaught was renewed in desperation. The breath was stolen from my lungs as agony seared through every nerve, every vein. Fire rushed through every fiber of my being and screams of torment were torn from my lips. Not even the zarakanan torturer could have caused such pain! My arms and legs jerked in spasms, out of control as I hit the stony floor and I could but watch as the avatar chuckled and glided over to me. The mist solidified into Katzuk's hand in the form of the helmet which he slipped onto my head. Helpless I could do nothing, not even duck out of the way. The strap fastened with magical impetus, and instantly the pain was gone. Whispers, lies, deceptions filled my mind and memory once more, but I knew them for what they were.

My hand reached for the Reaver. "Dozarak kilna loch krazak sion!" In a blaze of light the weapon burst from its hiding place and leapt into my palm. The avatar backed as the light of fear appeared in its eyes. "Morakvaar has shown me the way to defeat you, and you cannot take that away from me! You are the father of lies! You have no power over my mind or the truth!"

In a growl of rage the avatar of destruction gestured again. "But I do have power over your form!" Again the searing agony filled me, resonating through every part of me, holding me weak and powerless as Katzuk swung his mighty gray hammer over his head.

My fingers fought to keep their grip on the Reaver as agony vied for control of my nerves. Movement was impossible as my muscles contracted from the pain. The avatar stepped forward, transitioning into the strike that would end my life and any hope of saving my immortal soul. Once I was out of the way, Katzuk would be free to destroy the rest of the Kinsmen of the Blood. His minions would overrun the world with no one to stop them! Harrakuli would die! The realization brought helpless rage, a rage that touched deeply into the power of the Reaver. Its power, its purpose to feed upon rage returned a hundred fold, igniting the blades like the blaze of the sun.

The ancient powers of blood and rage gave me the strength to act despite the agony that still ravaged my system, a power that Katzuk could not control. Katzuk's hammer smote the ground with the sound of thunder, but I was no longer there. Rolling back to my feet, the Reaver's blue-white fire met the second swing. The cataclysmic impact shook the tunnel as arcs of lightning cascaded into the walls, throwing shards of stones in their wake. The Lord of Destruction paused, hatred, rage and fear fighting for control of his mind. The question was almost tangible. How could I fight him!?

Despite the agony I stepped forward for the counter-strike. The blades of the Reaver whistled through the air a song of death. Instinct alone saved the avatar as the hammer moved to parry the blow at the last possible second. But the impact threw off his guard. Like a beast of fury I leaped to the attack, the blue-white fire tracing arc upon arc of blazing hell against his weapon. Storms of lightning blasted through the tunnel, tearing at the ceiling and walls as they began to shudder from weakness.

In fear of his life, the avatar opened a gate to the Abyss, summoning forth demons to combat me, but as they appeared, I struck them down with the Reaver's flames and sealed the rift. My gaze returned to his from the task, seeing his fear and smelling it upon the misty winds that surrounded him. His will broke and he turned to flee, but I caught him in two strides, the blue-white blades of the Reaver parting his armor and flesh with ease from his helm to his waist as a vortex of gray howled from the wound. The whirling storm of mist engulfed his form, and encompassed me, igniting the gray fluids that had replaced my blood. Screams of agony echoed down the tunnel, uncontained from my lips as the power that sustained me ebbed back into the Reaver leaving me at the mercy of the pain. I saw down the tunnel the explosions as the charges were set off to let the magma flow. Darkness stole my consciousness as the torment reached its crescendo.

Chapter 30

Morakkanan (Reforging the Clans)

The white hair of the elder was more the color of finely worked vaarandril as his moustache lifted with his wide smile. Muscles rippled beneath coppery-bronze skin as he placed his hands on his hips. His crystal blue eyes regarded me, twinkling with mischief.

"I knew my faith in you was not misplaced. You have earned your forgiveness from me, you only have to earn it from your people, and then you will truly know yourself." His voice stilled the roaring of the molten rock flowing around us as if we were in a bubble.

The breath caught in my throat as I watched the magma pass less than a foot from where I stood. Had Morakvaar come to take my soul? Harrakuli was obviously late to our prearranged meeting. The Father of Souls seemed amused to watch the blood of the mother flow around us on its way to cleanse Zarakalduum.

"You have come a long way, Dorian. You have brought about the reckoning between the Kinsmen of Iron and the Kinsmen of Blood, you have united them with the orudin, it only remains that you gather the Kinsmen of Stone and the Kinsmen of Wood. You have already smoothed the way for the Kinsmen of Stone. Your quest here is almost finished, and when you are done, you will have sheltered the Kinsmen of Blood and the Kinsmen of Iron from the storm to come. They at least, will be safe from the darkness."

"What of the Orudin? What of the other kinsmen?"

He smiled patiently, "I can not tell you the whole of the future, now, can I? All will depend upon you and your actions. I will tell you this; you may accomplish much if you follow your heart."

"You mean I should go and free my sister from slavery?"

"Among your other quests, yes. Find your sister, and then seek your future. We will speak again, my son." The stone was past me and beyond before I realized we had moved.

Upon the granite floor knelt a blue-gray skinned figure with long silver hair. Her shoulders shook with grief as crystal tears wet the stones. Hands clenched in fists smote her breast as howls of grief echoed into the darkness.

"Daughter, weep not, for I have brought him from the fire back to you." Morakvaar wagged an admonishing finger at her astonished features that gazed in wonder at the two figures before her. "Do not lose him again!" With that, he disappeared, leaving me facing her and the orudin elders alone.

Harrakuli simply stared for long moments. For a time I thought perhaps there was something wrong. Self-consciously I glanced over my hands, feet, and beard. A moment later it dawned on me that I had been returned to my normal form! I was left with only my natural gifts and the Reaver which fell from my uncaring fingers as my arms were suddenly full of the love of my soul. Tears of joy mingled together from both my cheeks and hers as our lips met. How could I ever have doubted my feelings for her? It was a moment of triumph, of joy and reunion that was burned into my memory forever.

Around us, the orudin elders shifted uncomfortably as they witnessed the passionate renewal of our love for one another. If they had been reluctant to acknowledge our binding before, there was no doubt left as to the rightness of it. At last they smiled in embarrassed acceptance before beginning their barrage of questions. Holding up both of my hands after Haarakuli backed from me, I managed to silence them.

"I will tell my tale to all, for our people should know what has happened. I have much to answer for and it is only fitting that I be judged by all at the same time." The memory of the things I had done as the servant of Katzuk weighed heavily on my soul. "Take me now to the gates of Zarakalduum, for I must intercede on the behalf of the Kinsmen of Iron who are still Morakvaar's children."

For a moment, the ring of blue-gray skinned orudin simply stared in shock, but they had already acknowledged I was Gorain and had pledged their allegiance. Had it been otherwise, I was sure they would have left me where I was, or even killed me for such heresy. Harrakuli thrust a cloak at me as she nodded at my lack of clothing for emphasis. The coppery-bronze tone of my face darkened as I realized I had been left without raiment, and quickly wrapped the cloak around my midriff.

"We must make haste to Zarakalduum, and meet with the representatives of Clan Karodain." The orudin did as I bade them, taking me straight through the intervening rocky walls and grottoes.

The clash of weapons and the cries of bloodlust and the wounded smote our ears as we arrived at the main blockade. Thousands of the dark dwarves assaulted our defensive positions as they sought to escape the fiery doom that roared through their city. Behind them the vast cavern was lit by an inferno of molten rock as it poured in from the Heart of the Mother straight into the center of the once great settlement. Stalagmites that encased towers and homes of grandeur disintegrated in the onslaught as the screams of those caught in the conflagration echoed through the tunnels. The stench of sulfur and brimstone barely covered the scent of crisped flesh as the magma spread outward, destroying everything in its path more surely than if Katzuk himself had done the deed.

The dichotomy struck me, as I shuddered down to the core of my being. Was I truly any better than they? That I could wish such utter destruction upon the children of Morakvaar was a terrible revelation of what I had become. But there was no time for weeping. The blades of the Reaver ignited to the sounds of battle, stealing the desolation of my soul and filling it with the rage and lust for battle. Commanding the last of the assault, I found my daughter, Korina at their head, fighting desperately against the masses trying to escape the flames of purging.

Blue-white fire cut a swath of red to her, but I could not stop there. The Reaver hungered and there were still enemies before me. By fury alone I drove them back as a column of my kin rallied behind me, chanting my name as they recognized my presence. In a blaze of light, the enemy fell back from our advance, fear and confusion dividing their ranks. Behind them another force of tharilkanan had mustered, but instead of advancing on us, they fought their own kin! Laora! She had managed to rally her clan and those loyal to the Maker!

With the fires of the Reaver on one side and the assault of their own kin on the other, the shadow dwarves that worshipped Katzuk were quickly disheartened and surrendered. Laying down their weapons they begged for mercy as Korina ordered her forces to take them captive. Cautiously Laora approached me, eyes on my nearly naked form.

To cover the awkward moment, I addressed them; certain Laora had not yet recognized me. "Kinsmen of Iron you once were, I name you such again. Let the onus of shadow be left behind. Today is the day of reckoning between us."

Korina made her way through the crowd to where I stood, and stared at me in astonishment. The love of her and the pain of her mother's passing smote me at once, but I resisted the temptation to draw her into my arms.

"Korina, High Queen of Morakduum, do you accept the presence of the Kinsmen of Iron whom have sworn allegiance to the Maker?"

She was so shocked, she just nodded, and I smiled.

"Laora, your people are welcome among us as in the days of Dolamakduum."

It was then that the tharilkanan kinswoman recognized me. "We are in your debt, Dorian Mytharia. Thank you for delivering us from the prison of our own devising. May Morakduum become as great a legend as Dolamakduum." She bowed to Korina. "Majesty, my people are at your service, command us as you will."

Admiration for my daughter warmed my heart as she quickly recovered her composure. Straightening her shoulders, she became the High Queen in an instant. "I welcome the children of the Maker." Releasing her held breath, Laora clasped her outstretched forearms.

The tunnels echoed with the shout of relief from the freed tharilkanan, but my kin were less than enthusiastic. Korina's worried frown echoed my fear that it would take many generations to heal the distrust and hatred between our clans, but at least it was a start. Holding my arms out to the nearest shadow dwarf, I started the greeting, the beginning of the healing. Reluctantly the vaarakanan slowly joined in, then a little more amicably as I backed away from the furor. It was good to see the clans attempting to get along after thousands of years of war.

The stone was warm against my back, easing the tension from my shoulders as I leaned in to it until I saw that Laora had quietly followed me to the edge of the crowd. "That form suits you much better." The intensity of her gaze brought the blood to my cheeks. "Thank you for what you have done for my people."

The returned smile must have shown more of my angst than I wished. "If it had not been me, it would have been another. I did nothing but the Maker's bidding."

"How many would have had the courage to do what you have done? You risked everything to save my people from the hell we created." The hem of her tunic brushed against my calf, and I adjusted my stance so that she was not so close.

"You are attributing motives that I did not have. My thoughts were to save my own people, and to make restitution for my acts while under Katzuk's control. My meeting you was pure chance." She stepped up to me once more, her left hand idly tracing down my arm, reminding me of what I had done to her.

"Nothing is done by chance. Our meeting was an answer to my prayers to the Maker to save our people. Your bravery in allowing it to happen will not be forgotten by us." Her eyes traced up and down my normal form hungrily. "Yes, that shape suits you much better than our last meeting." I felt the heat of her breath on my chest, as I tried to swallow the knot in my throat. "I could claim kinship to you." Her voice was deep, and full of intent.

"Laora, nothing would please me more if I were not already Bonded. But my love for my hearth-mate is absolute. Please do not do this to me or her." My eyes scanned the crowd frantically for Harrakuli to no avail.

Undaunted by my proclamation, she moved up against me, reminding me of her shape beneath the tunic. "Then meet with me in four days time, and we will discuss my claim." Her breath stirred the small hairs of my neck and warmed my ear, sending a wave of wanting through me before she stepped back, taking my forearms in her hands in the traditional greeting of my people.

Her smile filled me with need and self-loathing as she left to greet more of my kin. Harrakuli would not be pleased if she knew of our former meeting, or of our projected rendezvous. "Morakvaar, if you value our Bonding, please do not let there be a child in her womb." The prayer was one of fervent desperation.

How had I become such a depraved kinsman? Since my enslavement by the zarakanan, I had not only endured such base acts unwillingly, but I had also committed crimes against our people and our code of honor of my own free will. I did not deserve the accolade of the hero, but more of the remorseless criminal and worst of perverted diviants. In all of our history, even our mythology, no kinsman had ever had more than two mates, and yet in the span of my years I had been with no less than five. Would history be kind to my memory, or would my people learn of my disreputable acts and sully my clan's name for eternity? How could I leave such a legacy behind for my daughter and son? What would happen to them if my indiscretions were known?

It was the first moment I recognized emotionally that I would be leaving the Halls of the Mother. I had to. My secrets gave me no choice but to conceal my nature in the obscurity of absence. My gaze followed Laora through the crowd, her stare occasionally meeting mine, and I knew she wanted more from me than I was willing to give. But what choice did I have? What choices did I ever have?

The feast was the beginning of the long Rite of Mourning starting at the end of the last course. Of my people, two thousand would never see hearth and home again, two thousand more wounds in my soul, two thousand more drops of blood on my hands. But for the tharilkanan, it had been a disaster. Between the lava and the conflict, fifteen thousands of their numbers were dead and twice that wounded many more to join the dead in the next few days. Not even our priests would be enough to save them.

Each of their names were recorded in the Book of Ancestors before their bodies were offered back to the Mother, freeing their spirits in the conflagration at her Heart. When we were finished mourning our dead, I helped the tharilkanan with theirs, standing beside Laora in her grief.

So many of the Maker's children had perished, and then so few were born among our people, my heart was bleak considering our future. Was this the last gasp of a dying race? Would our peoples finally be able to reverse the trends of death and infertility? For a moment, I considered it would be a good thing if Laora had conceived; anything to stem the tide of extinction that threatened our race and anything that had a chance of binding the clans together as one. What did it matter I lose my own name and honor? Shame again smote my soul. The thought was unworthy of my clan, for it would not only be my honor at stake, but Korina's, Dorak's and Geria's as well as that of my mother, our ancestors and descendants.

Two days I stood with Laora, helping recount the names of the dead and those who had found death in the infirmary. But at the end of that time, she at last spoke to me. "I have no family left to carry on my name or heritage. I wish a child of my own, and I can think of no more honorable a father than you."

The worst of my fears were in her words. How could I refuse her, and yet comply? Both were compromises to my honor. "Laora, I know of a kinsman whose honor is as great as mine. His name is Farzak, a great teacher and storyteller. I could think of no better father for your children than he, and he too wishes a family. He would be ideal as he is a kind and gentle soul and he knows our history better than any. He is a scholar and a bard of great renown. He could learn your people's history and teach it to us. With the learning comes wisdom and tolerance. Your marriage to him would go far to heal the gap between our people."

For long moments, she stood, her gray brow furrowed in thought. "Yes, that would be best for my people. But know this, Dorian Mytharia, I have lost my heart to you, and you will always be the one I long for. I will marry this Farzak if you spend one more evening with me."

The pain of my own past was reflected in her long regard, the memory of my askance for Jaguar's hand in marriage smote through my soul with her words. "I wish you had asked me some other thing. I love Harrakuli with all my soul, and am fain to do aught against her."

The agony of her gaze brought out all those feelings I had pushed aside so long ago. Bubbling to the surface, I remembered Jaguar's denial of the desire of my heart. There would not have been anything I would not have done had she asked it of me in return to spend the rest of her short life with her. That same desire was within Laora, and spoke to me deeply of her need. To satisfy the anguish of my soul, the need I had of Jaguar, I would give Laora her memories in this one tryst, and hope that Harrakuli might possibly forgive me.

"I will, but only because I know how it feels to be denied the desire of my heart. After this, you swear you will not hold any claim against me?" At her grim nod, I realized I had committed to another violation of my oaths, would I ever be a worthy kinsman?

The labyrinth of tunnels she led me through would have confused one of our scouts! Turning down an obscure path, we left the main funeral procession to the Mother's Heart, and after nearly a time cycle of convoluted travel, she stopped before a red granite wall. Fingers tracing a hidden rune, she spoke a word that sounded to me like the tongue of the ancients, but the pronunciation was wrong. Before I could figure out the meaning, a portion of the stone slid back and revealed a small round opening. On hands and knees I crawled through the dark entrance at her bidding, hoping there was nothing unpleasant awaiting me on the other side.

The chamber was a decent sized tube, the scoring of lava upon the walls testament to its origins. Regimented bunks lined the walls, and a dining area was laid out in the center. In one of the further chambers I could make out blankets, bandages, barrels and sacks of supplies and in another a surgery preparation chamber. Laora's people must have used the place on occasion to hide out, or were planning to in the future. But, before I could question her about the origins, she put her arms around me, kissing me passionately as her hands explored my contours.

The fierceness of her desire overwhelmed my curiosity and my caution. Her brazen sensuality intrigued me, invoking such deep memories that I had buried of Jaguar and her passion. It was as if she lived again and her hunger and my desire for her writhed within my arms like those days the priestess of pleasure was at my side. All the feelings, all the longings unfulfilled drained from me in the releases as each time we reveled in each other's presence. The pain, the long years of anguish dimmed and finally died as we had our last pleasure of one another, and for the first time since I left the surface I felt free of my obsession for Jaguar. Was this a part of the Maker's plan?

Her black hair mingled freely with the fiery red that covered my chest and shoulders, her gray skin a pale starkness against the coppery-bronze that she nuzzled against when she awoke. "By the Maker I wish this could last forever." Her breath stirred the curls, washing across my chest in a wave of warmth. Her gazez fastened upon mine, pleading for what she knew could not be.

"I must return to the side of my mate, Laora. This tryst was a gift of the Maker, a healing between our people and within my soul." Her puzzled stare bore deeply into me, but I could not, would not confess my past sins to her. "I have honored your request, please honor mine." Chewing her lip as if to keep in the emotions she wished to relay, she nodded her head slowly before rising to dress.

The last of the Kinsmen of Iron from the funeral procession raised a brow at our sudden appearance behind him, but said nothing. Following closely, we re-entered the great chamber of Zarakalduum leading up to the dark iron gates. The demonic guardians of the fortress sent a chill down my spine as I remembered how recently I had mirrored their form. Could my people forgive my actions? Tearing my eyes away from the hellish figures, my gaze met that of Harrakuli. Until that moment, I had felt no shame and no guilt, but as she sought my inner-most being, the crushing weight of what I had done smote my heart a heavy blow. She gave Laora a long and stern look of warning as she took my arm and led me to where our people were celebrating. Before we got to the bonfire, she took me aside.

"If I see her near you again, I will kill her." Helpless rage burned in her gaze before she turned from me. Pain leaked down her cheeks in crystal tears.

Warm metal met my fingers as they rested on her shoulder. A garment of vaarandril as fine as any armor covered her like silk, was a part of her as long as she wished it. "I do love you, Harrakuli. I would never leave you, for my heart would forbid it. It is not just my vow that keeps me at your side."

Light blue-gray lids closed, and a pained expression replaced her rage. "Sometimes I wish I had not lived as long. With so many years, there is not one motivation of mortals that I do not know or cannot see. Your deed is as plain to me as if you had proclaimed to the world your indiscretion." A shudder ran down her spine as if to throw off the rage and pain that threatened her. "But so too do I see how it has affected you. At last you are free from your past; I see it in your eyes. Now you will be able to give yourself to me wholly and without reservation, and that at least I can be grateful for." Her gaze snapped to mine as fires leapt within. "But mark my words, Dorian, I will not suffer any other!"

Our lips met as I pulled her to me. "You are right in that my pain has ended and my heart is now free to give. Our people are safe, and I can pledge you all that I am."

The fierceness turned to mischief remarkably quickly. "Oh really? Then after tonight's feast, you can show me this devotion?"

The schoolboy smile spread across my lips, but I couldn't help it. "Absolutely!"

Chapter 31

Krazakdain (War's End)

The celebration of victory raged on long after the magma stood cooling in the city of Zarakalduum. Shouts of joy rang in echoes through the tunnels, but not within my heart. Blood haunted my vision and again my hands struck down the kinswoman, murdered her for the pleasure of feasting on her soul. How could I eat, how could I celebrate the death and murder I had caused? My boots found the unspoiled streets of the city, assessing what had been saved before I found myself in the infirmary gazing upon the fruits of my labors. It was only fitting that I tried to help in some small way, and Waradain was only too glad to set me about the endless chores that needed to be done. The smell of herbs clung to me long after my arms were too tired to carry them any longer. My muscles ached from holding down the wounded as they screamed in torment of their injuries as the priests tried to treat them. Within the chamber, there was no celebration, no joy, only exhaustion, pain and the fear of death.

Why had I spent my time dallying with Laora when I should have been helping Waradain? The question haunted me as I watched them continue on, each of the priests ready to drop in their tracks. But they kept on, and worked at a fevered pitch until all of the patients had been treated. Wearily I slunk down on the stone outcrop beside the elder priest.

"Every general, every warlord or king should spend time helping the injured, Waradain. It is a perspective of the consequences of your actions that can only be shown in the pain of your people."

A grim nod accompanied a wan smile. "No greater truth has been spoken to me today." The darkness of the tunnels stretched out before us, swirling in layers of heat in eddies and flows. "What troubles you, Dorian?" The white mane of his hair was so much like Morakvaar's.

Was it that obvious? "I have a crisis of faith to confess." He waited patiently for me to continue as I tried to find the words to express the most heinous of crimes. "When the zardakkan took me, they chained me in a temple of Katzuk where I met the Destroyer himself."

A shudder traveled through the old priest as he stared at me. "You met Katzuk?"

The horror returned a hundredfold and I was suspended above the gray pool once more. "Yes. I was immersed in a pool of gray. The liquid seemed alive with the tormented spirits of the damned. I had no choice but to breathe, to take the vile fluid into my lungs, my throat. It changed me." Cold chills seized my spine and halted my words for a moment before I could continue. "While the fluid spread through my system, Katzuk told me his lies, whispered in my mind, rewrote my history, my memories. I became his creature of vengeance and destruction."

"The Demon!" The old priest whispered in awed fear as I turned away in shame.

"Yes, the demon. There is the blood of our people on my hands, Waradain. And worse, I have feasted upon the souls of our kin. How can I ever be forgiven?" The palms of my hands could not blot out the visions in my mind, nor the feelings of perverse pleasure as I consumed the souls of my kin.

"But the fact that you have returned to us, as you were, tells me that the Maker has forgiven you." May the Maker bless his clan forever.

"It is not Morakvaar's forgiveness that I fear, but that of our people. My crimes are great, and must be judged, but I do not know if I have the courage to face them. Three souls have I taken, three who will never see the Underhalls of the Maker. The blood of a kinswoman is on my hands, and that of seven kinsmen. Had I been able to, I would have slain even Harrakuli, but thank the Maker she was quick enough to escape me. And if those crimes were not bad enough, I ... had kinship with a tharilkanan kinswoman." Waradain regarded me with shock and his gaze burned into my guilt as I finished my confession. "All of the tharilkanan I have slain, and the worst of my guilt is in knowing that I did not have to submit to the Destroyer's lies. It was my own weakness that caused me to serve him."

A troubled frown deepened the lines on the elder's face. "This is grave indeed, Dorian. Our people's hearts are not likened to quick forgiveness. But the truth of the matter is that despite the lives you have taken, you have saved countless others. Your courage has brought an end to this battle and reunited clans that have warred for millennia on end. There is not a stronghold left for our enemies to hide, and they flee to the Rift in droves. You have made it possible for our descendants to live in peace until the end of time, and that is as great an accomplishment as any in all of our race's history. If it were my place to forgive you, I would. As Gorain reborn, our people owe you two great debts of gratitude. But that may not be enough for those families who grieve for their losses. All I can tell you is that you must allow them to judge for themselves."

The cold knot in my gut would not go away as a premonition of disgrace, a memory of what happened a lifetime ago haunted my mind. "Very well. Tomorrow I will face judgment by our people."

A heavy hand upon my shoulder prevented me from rising. "Dorian, before you resign yourself to death, I have news that will cheer you." How could he be so hopeful? "We treated some of the escaped slaves from Zarakalduum, and four of them are Soulsmiths!"

"Soulsmiths!?" The ironic chuckle escaped my lips. "At least there is hope for our people if not for me."

The old priest laughed as he led me to an enclosed area of the infirmary. Morina had been the closest I have ever been to meeting a Soulsmith in my life as Dorian. A chill of apprehension shuddered down my spine at the thought of what had been done to Gorain, but it was Morina's memory that burned brightly within. She was the daughter of a Soulsmith, a full blooded Kinswoman of Soul, but she and her mother had been taken when she was still a child.

They did not look much different than Morina had, slimmer of build and lighter of skin than a Kinsman of the Blood, and only a bit taller. The four of them stared hard at me as I entered, as if each of them saw me as something completely unexpected. Their gazes burned into my soul, laying it bare to the winds of the universe. It was as if I stood before them naked and unable to hide any part of what I was. Everything I had done in my life as Dorian was as exposed to them as if I they had been there with me. Every part of me that was Gorain was revealed to them in an instant. The itching feeling grew in me the urge to run, to hide, and to never seek out such violation again. But the faults revealed were my own, and something that no amount of running would ever hide.

The eldest among them, a silver-haired kinsman, cocked his head as if listening to an inaudible song. Without warning, his words formed in my mind. *'Gorain! It has been many generations since you came to our people. Again, we are in your debt!'*

The discomfort of their scrutiny vanished as if it had never been, and I found myself wondering why I had been apprehensive. "Well met! It is a joy to me that your people have not all been lost to us! When Balakarak fell, we feared that all had perished."

A warm smile touched the elder's lips. *'Our people have been separated, but not all destroyed. No amount of distance can hide the presence of our kin. Morakvaar has told us that you will find them for us and keep them safe.'*

Why could the Maker not confide such things to me? Between them and Harrakuli's vague references to Ungir, I felt as if everyone knew more about me than I did!

The elder laughed aloud, the first sound he had made and I belatedly remembered how well Soulsmiths read minds. "There is a relationship between you and Ungir, but you will have to discover that yourself."

"It grieves me to see that there are only four of you here. Will you be able to carry on? I mean..."

Again the elder laughed, and I could see the lines of laughter on his face that had been written over by sorrow and anguish became visible once more. "We will. Our training includes much about the secrets of life as well as the soul. We will breed true no matter whom we marry. As long as we live and our descendants are safe, our people will live." In a flash, he changed the subject, leaving me momentarily disoriented. "I have spoken with your daughter about her training already and have made arrangements to view the rest of your family."

"My daughter?" How come everyone knew things but me?

"Well... yes. Surely you realized her talents? She has used them enough on you, the mark is quite plain." No wonder she always seemed to know what I was thinking!

My ironic chuckle carried more of my sentiment than any words. What an unfair advantage! Why did I never guess? Morina was the daughter of a Soulsmith, but she had never exhibited much of the talent. I had not seriously considered for a moment that our children would display any inclination towards soulsmithing.

Again reading my thoughts, the elder smiled wearily. "The talent sometimes skips a generation if allowed to take its natural course. Your blood is strong, Gorain, and your line has been altered by our ancestors. Your heritage, along with Morina Tenedain's was enough to pass the talent to your descendants." The last words were an effort, and I realized how selfish I had been to keep them from their rest.

"Thank you for indulging me. I bid you well and hope that we may speak again later." The elder's tolerant smile turned to amusement as I bowed and left the room.

Dark circles framed the priest's eyes as he leaned on the cavern wall for support. "My friend, I must thank you for giving me some small hope in their presence."

His grip was firm enough though, as he clasped forearms. "I want to know what he said to you, but it can wait until I have rested."

The depression of my troubles weighed upon me as I considered the morrow. "What if our people demand my immediate exile? At least with Korina's new law I can no longer be executed, but what if they make me Tashor?"

"I will find a way to speak to you, brother. Good luck." He turned and limped slightly back to his quarters near the infirmary.

It was too easy to forget that his son had married my daughter. His reminder was intended to show his acceptance no matter the circumstance. All through the feast that night, I could only dwell on my impending trial of shame. Through all of the festivities only three mugs of ale passed my lips, and Harrakuli questioned why.

"I worry about the time I spent in another form." My explanation brought the light of understanding to her as she ushered me to the small chamber that had been set aside for our use.

The night was full of her passion, a renewal of our bond that allowed me to leave behind my troubles if only for a short while.

Murmurs ran through the gathering like wildfire as they surrounded the stone upon which I stood with my daughter. At the foot of the rock, Harrakuli silently sent encouragement as speculation ran rampant. There was still much work to be done in Zarakalduum and no reason for the gathering save some grave announcement, and rumors spread through the crowd even as apprehension burned through my soul. When the last of the stragglers arrived, I confessed the events that happened since I had been captured by the zardakkan.

For long moments silence reigned as they absorbed the shocking news, the brutal tale of murder and betrayal of their greatest hero. Disbelief was still plain on many of the faces. Helena's mother approached the stone, her face afire with anger.

"Helena was our only daughter in my mate's line for four generations! Our clan is devastated by her loss, and to know that she was murdered by a kinsman is beyond tolerance!" Each word smote like a hammer, driving me to my knees with the agony that shuddered through my soul. "You have taken the most valuable treasure from our house, murderer, thief! I demand adequate recompense for your crime! I demand the life of your child, your daughter in repayment for our loss!"

A gasp rippled through the crowd as the shock slammed through me like lightning. How could I give up my own daughter? Yet she had the right to demand not only adequate recompense, but also retribution. The life of their daughter had been viciously ended by my hand, and it was only fitting that a child of my blood replaced it.

"Know that I would have gladly given my life for your daughter had I control of myself, and if my life-force could be given to bring her back, I would gladly face my own destruction. But what you ask is a heavy toll indeed. I cannot deny the rightness of it, even though it is a cost to all of my clan and not just of me. You must realize that my daughter is not just a kinswoman, but has the gifts of a Soulsmith. She is a treasure beyond treasures, but I know you will care for her as your own." My breath gave out as the fist squeezed my lungs. Geria! How could I give her away? Halting, broken speech was all I had left. "When we return to Sorkarak, the arrangements will be made."

My lids closed to the pain, the vision of my youngest bright in my inner gaze.

"What of our families!?" Karador, father to one of those whose souls I had taken made his grief known.

Not daring to open my eyes to his accusation, I answered his demand. "All that is mine save my armor, weapons and some items I will need for my journey will be meted out between those families of those I have harmed and my children in equal portion. Though money and earthly goods will never replace those lives, it will ease the hardships of the survivors." It was all for nothing, the epiphany struck me only then.

Wealth and fame meant nothing, for they were transient in the universe. What was important was life itself, fleeting and fragile. For the first time in my life, I began to loathe the riches I had accumulated. Not one piece of gold could bring back the dead or save our people from the abyss that loomed before them. It meant nothing.

Karador nodded, the grief still plain in his gaze. "Though my son is lost to us for eternity, what you offer will help us rebuild his memory and provide for another. And though I say this with the wounded heart of a father, I see how you suffer." The pause brought my gaze to him, the depth of sorrow shared from a grieving father to a grieving husband. "I... do not begrudge you my son's life, Lord Dorian. For those lives you have saved and those you have allowed to be born into the future, I thank you. A new golden age will be seen in my lifetime, a reward greater than the many losses we have suffered. I also know that as long as you live, a part of my son lives in you." All around me were nods of agreement, and the mood of the gathering had turned from dark uncertainty to the light of hope. Had they forgiven me? My heart soared among the stalactites of the cavern. Though I could not share their future, I could share their hope.

The pallid features of my daughter told of her shock, but in the silence following Karador's proclamation, she turned to me with a half-smile. "If there are no more claims against you, I must agree with our people. Your deeds far outshine those few sins that were committed under the direction of the Destroyer. You had no choice in the matter, and the crimes against these families I attribute to Katzuk and not you. Any other kinsman would not have thrown off his influence and because of your strength, your courage, our homes shall be safe for generations to come. When we return to Sorkarak, we will end this. Driving the last of our enemies before us, we will seal the rift forever behind them." Her smile broadened as more nods of agreement were shared. "It has been your hand that has lead us to this victory, father, and your name will be honored as long as our people live."

A cheer rose through them like a storm, but inside I felt the weight of my actions. Would they be so forgiving if they knew of Laora? A queasy feeling roiled in my gut as I thought of what the soulsmith had told me, and I quickly forced the thought from my mind before Korina had the chance to read it. How had I ever thought I could keep a secret from her? The object of my angst must have also had the talent, for as I struggled to keep my thoughts from her, Laora came to my side. My kinsmen were about to disperse, but her presence brought their curiosity back to the fore. Maker please do not let her break her word!

"I have spoken to Lord Dorian at length, and he has shown me great wisdom. In order to unite our clans once more, there should be more than a spiritual union between us. Our elders have agreed that they would accept Farzak Soradain into our clan, should he so desire it. It is my intention to consider him as a hearth-mate." The jaw dropped on the storyteller's face.

"Me?" For a moment, I was uncertain if he were pleased or angered.

"You are the perfect choice, Farzak." He blinked several times as he simply stared at me. "It will go a long way towards healing the gap between our people. You can teach them our histories and learn theirs to teach our people." His brow drew down and he stood in silence for many long moments. Did I go too far?

After several minutes, he bowed to Laora. "I am honored, Lady, that your clan considers me worthy." His words were full of reluctance, but he knew what refusal meant.

There was a long moment of silence before murmurs spread through the crowd as they left. Laora's frown contained a deep sorrow as she watched me leave, a gaze that was not lost upon the storyteller that awaited her pleasure. My silent prayer to the maker wished them a long and fertile marriage and that Farzak would eventually replace her desire for me as Morina had eventually replaced my desire for Jaguar. Seeing her gaze, Harrakuli interposed herself between us and took my arm.

"Are you going to join the festivities tonight, Dorian?" Her hand was cool compared to mine as I pressed her fingers to my lips.

"I would not miss it for all the gold in Morakduum." Her brows drew down at my melancholy tone, but she led me to our tent anyway.

But, before we had the chance to enter, Waradain caught up with us. "Dorian, what did the soulsmiths say to you?" Harrakuli's impatience vanished in an instant as her wide gaze went from the old priest to me and back again.

"Soulsmiths?"

Looking her squarely, I tried to judge her reaction to what I had to say. "They told me I had a link to Ungir, but what it was, they would not reveal." She blinked several times, but other than that, there was no reaction. Disappointed, I turned my attention back to Waradain. "They also told me that my children had the talent to be trained as soulsmiths. So our people will be whole again. But what grieves me is that they spoke of the others, and that they were still alive and enslaved. Most of them in the worlds of men above."

"Then we must find and free them!" The old priest's vehemence amused me for a short time.

"Yes, I will. But I cannot risk the whole of our people on this quest. My sister also lies in captivity on the surface, and in my soul I know that I must go there to free her. It is the Maker's will that I do so, and once upon the surface, I will seek out the soulsmiths and the rest of our kinfolk who have been taken. The deeps will be sealed, though, so none of us can return without risking death for our race. It is therefore my intention to seek the fabled city of our ancestors, Dolamakduum." The shock on both faces forewarned me of the tirade.

"You would seek the fabled city? So many have perished in the attempt, Dorian! So many more have never been heard of again!" His voice trailed off as he realized I would never be returning anyway.

"I wish to see it, or die in the attempt. Our people need the help of the old gods if we are to survive. Our numbers are dwindling, our enemies are multiplying, and we are on the verge of extinction. I hope our elders can find an answer on their own, but if they cannot? Everything I have fought for would be in vain. Everything our kinfolk died for would come to nothing. I cannot let that happen if I have any means at my disposal to do otherwise." Waradain chuckled and shook hi21s head.

"Always in need of a crusade, eh Dorian?" The smile spread across my lips, he knew me too well. "What if the gods do not want to be found?"

"Well, they can kill me when I get there." The old priest joined my laughter, but Harrakuli cut through our mirth.

"They do want to be found, Dorian, but the quest is perilous. I have tried to return once. I never tried again. If there is some of Ungir in you, then perhaps it is time for us to return?"

Both of us stared with open mouths before I finally managed to make a sound. "Then you know where Dolamakduum is?" It was the difference between legend and history suddenly revealed.

Her laughter was bitter. "Yes, but not how to get there. The path is ever changing to keep the Destroyer and his minions from finding it while the gods sleep. The guardians of the gates spare no intruders." The finality in the last sentence spoke of personal tragedy that I could barely comprehend.

"Who or what are these guardians?"

A shudder ran down her spine. "I never saw them, only the carnage they left behind. I had left the camp for only a moment to see to my personal needs, but when I returned, all was silent, dead. The bodies of my kin, my children, filled the tunnels with the stench of their burning flesh. In the periphery of my vision I saw a retreating flash of flame, but as it sensed me, it began to draw near again. In the blink of an eye it disappeared, but I had no doubt it was stalking me. I ran, knowing the futility of dying beside my kin. I walked deeply into the stones, but heard the creature's rage tearing through the rock. I kept running, trying to get around it and to the sacred city until I was near exhaustion and collapsed in a small grotto. But the creature or creatures came swiftly behind me. I prayed to the Maker with the last breaths I had, and Morakvaar came to me. He told me to leave my dead kin in his care, and to return to our people, for it was not yet time to return to Dolamakduum." She fell silent, the pain deeply engrained upon her features, and I could not help but take her into my arms.

Waradain nodded and left us to our privacy.

Chapter 32

Forhun Morvaar (History's Circle)

Our warriors sang of old glory as we marched the long road back to Sorkarak. Miles of stalactites, grottos, hidden chambers, flowstones, rivers and pools of magma and of water passed by in a tapestry of dreams to my longing heart. Every detail wrote its song upon my soul, for I knew I would soon leave it forever. The vibrations of the Mother's Heart were like a mournful lullaby, singing a farewell in harmony with the ancient rhymes. The war was all but over, with only remnants of our enemies left to be swept away.

The river of warm bodies shining in my heat-sensitive vision parted for a good ten paces between where my kinsmen ended and the ranks of the Kinsmen of Iron began. But the songs on their lips were the same. It was at once, an encouraging and discouraging sight. What did the future hold? For me there was exile from my home, and the great task of freeing what was left of our people from slavery, but for them? At last it hit me with the warmth of the Mother's Blood. For them there was peace, the chance to save our race and to reunite with the Kinsmen of Iron, to forge a new world of harmony and laughter instead of war and death. Their future held hope.

Sensing the warmth within me, Harrakuli grasped my hand and I smiled. Behind us the Tashor kept pace, and I was glad to see they had survived the poisons of the zardakkan. Korina had agreed that they had fought bravely and that their clans would be exonerated of their crimes for their valor. All record of their treachery would be wiped away in celebration of the new era. Ahead of us the gates of Sorkarak were thrown open in the wonder of peace for the first time in eight thousand years.

A low chuckle caught Harrakuli's attention again and she followed my gaze to my daughter walking among the soulsmiths with Waradain at her side. She was so much like me, stubborn to the core and refusing to ride in the wagons despite her gravid state. But her beauty was surely that of her mother, and her talents brought sweet sorrow to my soul.

Oh Morina, why did the Maker take you from me! 'May you be safe and happy in his halls until I may join you.' My silent prayer echoed in every fiber of my being. 'Great Father, thank you for the time you gave us together, and the beautiful children you blessed us with.'

Truly there was no luckier kinsman than I. Not only had the Maker given Morina and me time together and a family, but he had also blessed my union with Harrakuli. Our child did not yet weigh heavily on her, but I could tell she had undergone subtle changes.

My daughter Geria was less than six months old and already I had fathered another child, scandalous to say the least! But Geria was not my child any longer, a thought that tore at my soul. Her golden hair pressed against my palm as I held her reminded me so much of her mother, and my heart ached in sorrow. The thought of denying clan and family to my mother Geria with her namesake smote into me and stole the high spirits that had so tentatively manifested. Would I always be a disappointment to my mother? Thank the Maker she at least had no idea about my activities prior to my return to Morakduum!

Darkness shrouded my tongue in silence as Harrakuli sensed my inner anguish through our soul-bond. Her gray fingers slipped under my arm, drawing me nearer and her silent companionship soothed the raw nerves of my shame. But that was soon laid aside as we passed through the gates of Sorkarak.

Our kinfolk lined the streets, what few of them there were made up for their numbers with a fanfare to rival the greatest reception of our ancient heroes. Their cheers echoed through the caverns, chasing the darkness from the shadows as well as my heart if only for a short time. Happy flushed faces excitedly rushed forward for a chance to shake hands with the triumphant warriors, to welcome us with open arms and weeping joyful eyes. But there were some who kept waiting long past the line of our kin, still hoping to welcome those who would never return. Their anxious faces searching longingly down the road and their gazes meeting only that of the tharilkanan. Hopes broken as the last of the stragglers entered the city, they made their mournful way to the palace where Korina waited to address them.

The heavy tomes that had become the Book of Ancestors were spread open before her as she began the unpleasant duty of calling out the names of the fallen. The war had been costly, catastrophically so. Of the fifty thousand that marched proudly from the gates of Morakduum, only twenty thousand still lived. It was hardly a great victory, but we had managed one where there was originally no hope. If it were not for the bolstering of our numbers from the refugees of Zarakalduum, there would not have been enough of our people left to man the fortress while the Starrift was sealed.

So few of my kin remained, and I became even more determined to free those whom had been stolen by the zarakanan and sold to the humans as slaves. But, did I have the right to seek the aid of a soulsmith? Admittedly having one along would make the search infinitely easier. My thoughts were whisked away with the furor of our people when they recognized me. Their last word had been that I had been taken by the zardakkan. Cries went out to hear my tale, and I wished to the Maker that I could have hid and kept silent. But eventually my sins would find me in my hiding place, and it would be better to face them and the consequences than run like a coward. With rapt attention my people listened, their faces turning from wondrous admiration to horrified disgust.

"As agreed by those whom I have wronged, I now make reparations." I lifted my daughter's tiny form from my mother who stood next to me in shocked silence.

My child's wisps of golden hair caught in my moustache as I kissed her for the last time. Deep green eyes stayed riveted on mine, though I could hardly see through the moisture that fogged my vision. My daughter, my flesh and blood, how could I have ever agreed to give her away? For a moment, I was tempted to refuse, tempted to take her and leave regardless of my oath, but I could not conscience adding even more to my Clan's dishonor. She cooed as I held her against me, feeling her warmth, her life. As a piece of Morina, I did not want to let her go. A blue-gray hand settled upon my shoulder and the understanding pain washed through me from the soul-bond I shared with the Orudin.

"You have to let her go, Dorian. It will be a better life for her." The whisper was barely audible to me, but it resounded through my head like a booming cymbal.

The world was distorted in whorls of misty gray as I nodded. "Sara, as I took your daughter's life, I now repay in kind." My arms froze. How could I give away my flesh and blood!?

Another force took hold of me; one I knew was not my own as it took my child and made her another's. The accusing eyes of my mother tore through me with her shock and anger before she turned her back on me. Her final judgment of her son plain to all present as I stood, my arms still half outstretched towards my daughter as if I expected at any moment to have her returned to me. The pain of losing my father echoed through the wounds in my heart and soul, but they were nothing to losing my mother and daughter in one day. Again it was as if another took control of me, for I no longer had a will of my own. Did Gorain's strength prevail?

"And, to those clans of the kinsmen I have slain, the wealth that lies in my personal vault shall be distributed. The arrangements will be made within the week. I know that riches will never replace those lives, but I pray their families will find what comfort they may by what I have offered." My lips fell silent, the will gone as my daughter continued where I had left off.

"Dorian Mytharia, it has been our highest law that one kinsman shall not slay another, even in retribution, a law you yourself impressed upon me to return to our people. It is with a heavy heart that I tell you our law requires your exile. But since this fate has already been laid upon you, it is no punishment for these crimes to our people. There is, however, one thing that will be done to show all the extent of your trespass. Your name shall be stricken from the Book of Ancestors, never to be recorded in our history. You shall be known only in this lifetime as the enemy of our people to be slain if you ever return." The blows of her words beat me to my knees, rending what little hope was left in my heart. "Though we are grateful for what you have done, your crimes far exceed our gratitude. Your name shall be forgotten."

A summary execution would have been a kinder fate, and I could but stare in horrified pain as her judgment was made. Those around me simply stared in shock, unbelieving that a daughter could be so harsh and cruel to a father. Shame and the agony of my soul drove me from the crowd, but instead of running I stood and nodded to Korina, the light of my heart and the death of it. In my dazed despair I wandered aimlessly from the courtyard. Her words continued in the distance, but my ears had not the heart to listen.

Many untold miles swept beneath my feet before I remembered to see my surroundings. Long hours my kin celebrated elsewhere before I found myself in the garden of the singing stones. The harmony of their song only served to show me the ugliness of my sins and the terrible judgment that had been levied for them. Could not my own daughter forgive me? My knees dug into the soil before the shrine of the Maker.

"Father, I have given my life, my very soul for my people! How could they so easily turn from me? How can I live when none remember my name? How can I make it to your halls with none to herald my way? Father, I am grateful that my kin will now live in peace, but to never have lived at all!? And my own daughter!? How could she be so cruel?" Her words in Zarakalduum echoed through my memory. How could she have betrayed those words so utterly?

A gnarled hand lifted my chin to gaze on a face both ancient and young. "Those closest to you have been hurt the most by your actions, my son, but you too judge too harshly. You should have listened to all that was said." With those words he vanished leaving me confused and in pain.

The feeling had long receded from my legs as I sought answers in the low songs of the Mother. But no enlightenment came in the dark caverns, only wisps of chill wind to stir the heat strata in a dance of multihued spectral currents. They writhed and pulsed to the rhythm that was the Mother's Heart and lifeblood, another beauty that I would sorely miss with a finality of a sentence that brooked no return.

"Gorain! What are you doing here? You should be at the celebration in your honor!" What was she babbling about? How could Harrakuli be so mistaken?

"In my honor... To commemorate my exile? The loss of my name? My unspeakable crimes against our people?" Impatiently Harrakuli sniffed and crossed her arms as her brows drew down in stormy disapproval.

"You should have stayed instead of wandering off!"

"What, did she go on to tell everyone of my sins? What I did on the surface? How soon I lay with you after Morina's death!? Why should I have stayed for that?" Stars swam in my eyes as I shook the ringing from my ears after her blow.

"You are a fool! Would you believe your own flesh and blood would treat you so?" It finally began to sink in that she was quite serious about the banquet in my honor.

"You mean they really are feasting in my name?" How could that be after such a sentence was passed upon me?

"Gorain, you idiot! Get up out of the dirt and come with me!" Dazed, I let her lead me back to the great hall of Sorkarak, to the High Table and sat as she pushed me down in a chair next to Korina.

Kinsmen and kinswomen brought me food and drink, bowing and gazing upon me in awe that I did not feel appropriate after the pronouncement of my crimes. Some came offering clan badges, begging me to accept the hospitality of their families, each with a reverential awe I was not worthy of. The name of Gorain was upon their lips as they spoke to me, deepening my confusion and the odd disjointed reality.

The feast was ended as more ale was spread among our kin for the revel when Farzak called for silence. His harp was brought to the center of the hall as he struck the chords. Every eye turned to him as every tongue stilled but his. The notes were familiar and I remembered the ballad he had begun to write about me, but each instance of my name was substituted with that of Gorain. After the third stanza, our folk joined in the refrain with reverent notes as I tried to make sense of what my ears and eyes were telling me. By the time Farzak reached the new verses of Zarakalduum and the return to Sorkarak, it dawned on me.

The name Dorian was forgotten, my crimes attributed to the name as if by purging me of it, I was somehow exonerated of them. In place of my name was the title of my ancestor, the mighty hero Gorain, and in their eyes, hearts and souls, I had become that hero. Gorain was the founder of Morkilduum, and now the founder of Morakduum. He saved our people from the first and now the second and more deadly zarak invasion. The legend was remade and reborn, the hope and the soul of our people.

Epilogue

It took us three months to scout all the side tunnels, close them and roust the straggling denizens through the Rift. Korina gave birth to a son, Morian, the fire of vaarandril that burns forever, and I felt the pride of knowing she named him in honor of my true name. Harrakuli began to show her pregnancy, giving me both hope and worry about what would become of us when we passed beyond the Rift.

Another two months and our people had finished the work, closing off the tunnels to King Saveyo's lands. Fortifications had been put up along the trade tunnel into the deep realms from the Starrift to be manned by a large garrison of our people.

Farzak had endeavored the whole time to make a complete copy of my book so that an accurate record of my history would be preserved despite the heresy within. He vowed that he would only allow his own descendants and mine to view the book in privacy. I allowed him that in gratitude for all that he had done. I was happy for him when he finally confessed to me that he was growing fond of Laora, and that he suspected she might already bear his child. I only hoped that he would forgive me when he came to that part of my book, the time when I first met her. I had kept the pages I had written of our second encounter. It would not do to hurt him after what he had done for me. I only hoped the child was truly his. I started a new book, to keep pace with my new life in exile, one where I could again be known as Dorian.

Those that were still Kinsmen of Shadow were released on the other side of the barrier in groups of a hundred every other day. They had been kept separated by these groups since their surrender, so had no idea what was happening to the others.

Some of them begged and pleaded to remain, but the time for acceptance had been before the battle, not after. A month after the last of the shadow dwarves passed beyond the Rift, I stood before the fortifications. My people lined the tunnel on both sides, in reverent salutation as I passed among them. I clasped forearms of those I had known, hugged those I loved, and finally faced my daughter.

Handing her the Reaver, I addressed the assembled kinsmen and kinswomen. "Keep this with you, for a piece of my soul will remain in it forever. As long as it is with our people, so shall I be with you. In the future, I will come back to claim it once more when our people have great need." It bothered me that I had to play the part of some legendary hero, and I looked forward to freedom from that yoke.

Korina took the axe from me gingerly, but this time there was no lightning. "Gorain, you will always be remembered by our people. We will keep the Reaver until your return."

In a moment of deja-vouez, I remembered my dream as I walked through the assembly. My people bowed as I strode past them and through the opening to the Rift. The five kinsmen of the Tashor followed tight on my heels, and the expressions on their faces were as if this was the greatest honor to accompany me into exile. I sighed as fifteen kinsmen and five kinswomen followed tight behind them. They had no family or clan left after the wars, a painful reminder of the cost, and preferred to follow me into the future than to try to take up where their families left off. More had wanted to come, but I had told them I would only accept those with no clan. Those twenty were all that I had allowed.

On the other side, I turned and watched my people seal the Starrift behind us. Morakvaar appeared beside me.

"And now the adventure begins." He grinned.

I turned to look at him. "I am sure you find this vastly amusing."

"Of course. Just remember, there are many of my children on the surface that need your help. Someone has to rescue them, and I can think of none better than you, Gorain."

"Ah, but from now on, I am Dorian, just Dorian. I do not want to hear the name Gorain again as long as I live."

Morakvaar smiled and chuckled. "As you will, Dorian, but mark my words, it is to your advantage that you know yourself. I will call you when I need you."

He disappeared as Harrakuli stepped out of the rock and her people finished the wards on the stone surface. They had done an excellent job, and if I had not just walked through the opening, I would have never known it was there. Harrakuli put her arms around my neck and looked into my eyes smiling.

"Where to now, Gorain, my love?"

I cursed Morakvaar for his sense of humor, but only passingly. "To the surface, there are those who need my help."

She kissed me, "well, lead on, Gorain the Mighty..."

I gave her a stern look, turned on my heels and stalked off as she giggled with laughter.

Author's Note:

Stay tuned, Dorian will return to right the wrongs of the surface world in his mighty quest to find Dolamakduum. In the next adventure, he rescues his kin from slavery on the surface. In this adventure, he meets Tam Farovain, later renamed Tam Morkilvaar (who has a novel series of his own in the works) who is the hero of a lost kingdom, he just doesn't know it yet. Together they vanquish the evil Duke Heinrick who has been taken over by a demon prince.

Following on the heels of that adventure, Dorian will help his friend Liathrain fulfill the quest of her goddess, saving the Staff of Illumia from the hands of evil clerics and freeing Illumia herself from enslavement by a dark god bent on the destruction of all.

In his final novel, Dorian continues his quest to find the sacred city and forge of the gods, Dolamakduum, but finds the city besieged by the forces of the dark god Katzuk. He frees the city and beats back the denizens of Katzuk and lives in peace for a time, but the call of the gods cannot be denied. In the final confrontation between his ancestor gods and Katzuk, Dorian saves Morakvaar, but in so doing loses his own life and possibly his soul.

Also forthcoming will be a series of novels based on Gorain's third incarnation, Valkardain Mytharia. Set approximately thirteen thousand years in the future of Dorian's final battle against the gods of evil. Because of a bargain of the gods, Gorain's soul is returned to his people in their darkest hours. The novels culminate in a final showdown between the rest of Morakvaar's race that had turned to evil, the final battle. Will Gorain's ascension be enough to stop them? Read the Valkardain novels to find out! Vorvirkrazan (Prelude to War), Verekan Krazan (The Human War), Krazan Voor (War of the Damned), Krazan Moord (War of the Gods).

www.ingramcontent.com/pod-product-compliance
Lightning Source LLC
Chambersburg PA
CBHW060417030726
47495CB00003B/624